The
King's
Mistress

or by telepho

The King's Mistress is Emma Campion's debut novel. She has read and researched medieval history for many years, having studied for a Ph.D in Medieval and Anglo-Saxon Literature. She also writes historical crime novels under the name of Candace Robb. She lives in Seattle.

The King's Mistress

EMMA CAMPION

arrow books

Published by Arrow Books 2010

2 4 6 8 10 9 7 5 3 1

Copyright © Emma Campion 2009

Emma Campion has asserted her right under the Copyright, Designs and Patents
Act 1988 to be identified as the author of this work

First published in Great Britain in 2009 by
Century
Random House, 20 Vauxhall Bridge Road
London SW1V 2SA

www.rbooks.co.uk

Addresses for companies within The Random House Group Limited can be found at:
www.randomhouse.co.uk/offices.htm

The Random House Group Limited Reg. No. 954009

A CIP catalogue record for this book
is available from the British Library

ISBN 9780099497936

The Random House Group Limited supports The Forest Stewardship
Council (FSC), the leading international forest certification organisation.
All our titles that are printed on Greenpeace approved FSC certified paper
carry the FSC logo. Our paper procurement policy can be found at
www.rbooks.co.uk/environment

Typeset by SX Composing DTP, Rayleigh, Essex
Printed and bound in Great Britain by
CPI Bookmarque Ltd, Croydon, CR0 4TD

For Alice

Acknowledgements

I organised my research materials and drafts of this book to refresh my memory before writing these acknowledgements, and what is usually a dreaded task turned into a heartwarming reminder of the generosity of many talented people.

So here's my gratitude list:

Patrick Walsh, my agent and good friend, who has believed in this project – indeed, kept nudging me on, from the beginning.

Kate Elton, my publisher, and Georgina Hawtrey-Woore, my editor, for their enthusiasm, encouragement, brilliant editing, and absolute support.

Joyce Gibb for being far more than a first reader.

James Bothwell, whose paper on Alice's properties set me on the right path, who permitted me to use his map of Alice's properties as the basis for the one in this book, and who encouraged me to contact Chris Given-Wilson.

Chris Given-Wilson for opening up his files containing years of research on Alice.

RaGena D'Aragon, who accompanied me to St Andrews to guide me through the complexities of the primary source files in Chris's collection in the brief time available and to provide translations, whose expertise on medieval women guided my reading on the subject, and whose feedback on my papers and ideas was invaluable.

Mark Ormrod, who shared with me his discovery of Alice's first marriage and has continued to share his ongoing research on Alice. This book would have been quite different without Mark's generosity.

Laura Hodges, who shared with me her expertise on 14th-century clothing and provided immensely helpful suggestions in the first draft stage.

Gretchen Mieszkowski, whose monograph on the reputation of Criseyde inspired my interpretation.

Anthony Goodman for sharing his research not only on Alice but also Joan of Kent, and for lively discussions of the period.

The White Hart Society (International Congress on Medieval

Studies, Western Michigan University) and the 14th Century Studies group (International Medieval Congress, University of Leeds) for providing me the opportunity to present papers regarding my ongoing research, which reaped a bounty of information and feedback.

The scholars on Chaucernet, so many of whom I count as friends – especially the Thursday Night Ladies.

Candace Robb for sharing her research with me.

Charles Robb for the beautiful maps.

And all the friends and family who have cheered me on.

For this bounty of generosity and camaraderie, I am grateful.

List of Historical Figures

Royal Family: (* mentioned but not appearing)

*Edward II
King of England, overthrown by Queen Isabella and her lover
Mortimer

Isabella of France
Edward II's queen

*Roger Mortimer
Isabella of France's lover

Edward III
King of England, son of Edward II and Isabella

Joan of Scotland
daughter of Edward II and Isabella

Philippa of Hainult
Edward III's queen

Edward of Woodstock
Prince of Wales and Aquitaine, eldest son of Edward III and
Philippa

Lionel of Antwerp
Earl of Ulster, then Duke of Clarence, 2nd son of Edward III
and Philippa

John of Gaunt
Earl of Richmond, then Duke of Lancaster, 3rd son of Edward
III and Philippa

Edmund of Langley
Earl of Cambridge, then Duke of York, 4th son of Edward III
and Philippa

Thomas of Woodstock
Earl of Buckingham, 5th son of Edward III and Philippa

Isabella of Woodstock
favourite daughter of Edward III and Philippa

*Mary and Margaret
younger daughters of Edward III and Philippa, died of plague

John de Southery
bastard son of Edward III and Alice Perrers

Edmund
Earl of Kent, half-brother of Edward II

Joan of Kent
Edmund's daughter, eventually wife of Prince Edward, eldest
son of Edward III and Philippa

*Richard
son of Prince Edward and Princess Joan, King Richard II

*Elizabeth de Burgh
Countess of Ulster (in her own right), 1st wife of Lionel of
Antwerp

Blanche of Lancaster
Duchess of Lancaster, 1st wife of John of Gaunt

Constance of Castile
Duchess of Lancaster, 2nd wife of John of Gaunt

Katherine Swynford, nee de Roët
Duchess of Lancaster, mistress, then 3rd wife of John of Gaunt

Other historical figures:
Alice's daughters Joan and Jane, and possibly Isabella and Joanna;
Robert Broun (though I have no proof of more than a business
relationship between him and Alice); Geoffrey, Phillippa, and

Thomas Chaucer; Francisco Flocet; Dom John Hanneye; Bishop Simon Langham; William Latimer; Robert Linton; Richard Lyons and Isabella Pledour; John Neville; Richard Northland (Jane's husband); Henry Lord Percy and Mary Percy; Janyn Perrers; John Perrers; John Salisbury; Nicholas Sardouche; Robert Skerne (Joan's husband); Richard Stury; William Wykeham; John and William Wyndsor

Glossary

churching	the public appearance of a woman at church to give thanks after childbirth
crespinette	an ornamental hairnet
dagged	garment edge cut in long pendant strips or other ornamental shapes
dam	mother
enfeoffed	put in possession of the fee-simple or fee-tail of lands; the land belongs to owner and heirs
enfeoffement to use	a legal device allowing a landholder more control over the disposition of his property on his death – if he died without a male heir it would not immediately fall into the hands of his lord through a wardship but instead might be willed to a favoured relative; it would also not be forfeit if the landholder were accused of a crime against the king
escarlatte	the finest wool, also called scarlet
fillet	a narrow band worn round the head either for ornament or to keep a headdress or veil in place
gris	the fine fur from the backs of squirrels
intaglio	the figure or design incised or engraved on a signet ring
lamia	a fabulous monster with the body of a woman that sucks the blood of humans
Lincoln green	a rich green wool made in Lincoln
maintenance	undue exercise of influence over legal processes involving one's retainers, usually through payment of fees, etc, to judges and juries; also the keeping of retainers, liveried men, usually armed
miniver	even finer than gris, fur made of squirrel

	stomachs only, white with a little gray surrounding it
obit	mass performed on behalf of the soul of the deceased on the anniversary of death, usually each year
pers	a fine blue cloth
plantagenet pattern	a pattern inspired by the common broom plant
purpura	a costly purple dye derived from the secretions of molluscs
robe	singular, connoting the entire ensemble
tabby weave	a simple weave of weft over warp which produces a smooth, though textured, finish

Feast Days:

Candlemas	2 February, the feast of the purification of the Virgin Mary
Lammas Day	1 August
Martinmas	11 November, the feast of St Martin
Michaelmas	29 September, the feast of St Michael
St George's Day	23 April

Alice's properties mentioned in *The King's Mistress*

❶ Ardington
❷ Crofton
❸ Fair Meadow
❹ Gaynes
❺ Radstone
❻ Southery
❼ Tibenham

Royal residences mentioned in *The King's Mistress*

1 Berkhamsted Castle
2 Castle Rising
3 Eltham
4 Havering
5 Hertford Castle
6 King's Langley
7 Queenborough Castle
8 Sheen
9 Windsor Castle

● Extent of properties
  managed or held by Alice

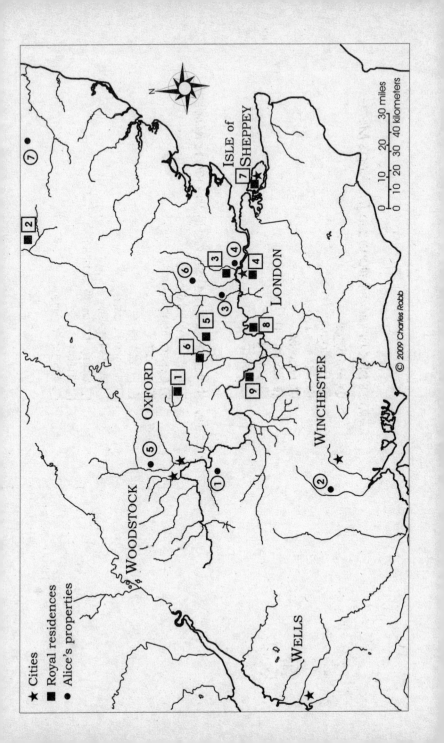

★ Cities
■ Royal residences
● Alice's properties

WOODSTOCK

OXFORD

WELLS

WINCHESTER

LONDON

ISLE of
SHEPPEY

N

© 2009 Charles Robb

0   10   20   30 miles
0 10 20 30
    40 kilometers

Book I

An Innocent Encounters the World

When had I a choice to be other than I was? Should I have been more selfish, more stubborn, more rebellious? Have I been too compliant, too quick to give the men in my life what they thought they wanted? Am I a fallen woman or an obedient handmaiden? As a female I was acceptable only as a virginal daughter, a wife, or a widow — unless, of course, I took vows. I have been all three, daughter, wife, widow, and one other — mistress.

My lover is now long dead, and I sense death drawing near for me. I write this for my children, praying that they might understand.

I began my life in a quite acceptable fashion, but the royal family laid such traps in my path that those who would throw the first stone are certain that I can never right myself even now. But when had I a choice to be other than I was? This is the argument of my life.

> *'Right as oure firste lettre is now an A,*
> *In beaute first so stood she, makeles.*
> *Hire goodly loking gladed al the prees.*
> *Nas nevere yet seyn thing to ben preysed derre,*
> *Nor under cloude blak so bright a sterre'*

— Geoffrey Chaucer, *Troilus and Criseyde*, I, ll. 171–175

London 1355

During the week, our parish church of St Antonin on Watling Street, east of St Paul's, hummed with chantry Masses. Ours had long been a parish of wealthy merchants who worshipped under the cloud of Christ's teaching that it was easier for a camel to go through the eye of a needle than for a rich man to gain the Kingdom of God, and so they bequeathed great sums for Masses to be said for their souls after death. The chantry priests of St Antonin's were kept busy with almost continuous Masses, for it was an old parish and had buried many wealthy men and their wives, anxious for redemption.

I loved to spend time in St Antonin's on ordinary days. The priests' murmured prayers embraced me, and the familiar paintings and statues of our Saviour, His Blessed Mother and the saints reminded me that, as long as I said my prayers and obeyed my elders, I need never fear the devil. To this day the scent of incense mixed with candle wax comforts me. To the community of saints in St Antonin's I confided all my hopes, fears, heartache and triumphs, and had no doubt that they guided and protected me. Other parishioners frequented the church during the quiet times, but like me they were intent on their own prayers and paid no heed to those kneeling nearby. It was the only place I had permission to go without a companion, a guardian, and I felt safe there.

On Sundays and important feast days the atmosphere of the little church lacked the comforting intimacy of the ordinary days, for then all parishioners except the bedridden attended Mass. The wealthy merchants flaunted their success by parading with their elegantly dressed families, while the gossips made note of any changes in the attendance or indeed the attendees – a swollen lip, a swollen belly hiding beneath an uncharacteristically voluminous skirt, an outrageously expensive new headdress – so that all observations might be argued over and settled after the service, and for days to come. On Sunday the church was too crowded, too filled with the scent of humanity (albeit wearing clothes sweetened by fragrant herbs and spices with which they had been stored), for me to recognise the incense and candle wax in the mix, but that is not to say I did not enjoy attending Mass on that day.

What made Sunday special was that we dressed up and attended as a family; my handsome father, my beautiful mother, my beloved siblings John, Will and Mary, and me in my best clothes. I felt as if we shone on Sundays, and I liked thinking of us with the beatific light of piety surrounding us, protected by God's love. I don't remember how I came to think of it thus, but it cheered me. I looked forward to Sundays in a different way from how I treasured the solace of the church during the rest of the week.

I must have long been aware that on Sundays St Antonin's was also a marriage market, but with that gift we have as children for ignoring what does not affect or fascinate us, I had paid no attention to that aspect of the day. Until it was my turn.

I begin my story with my first appearance as a vendible in that place that was my sanctuary during the week and my opportunity to bask in the light of my handsome family on Sundays and holy days. It was the autumn of my thirteenth year.

For years since that day on which I crossed over into adulthood, I climbed a precipice so steep and so treacherous that pausing to rest and perchance look down was to risk a panic that would send me tumbling into the abyss. I blinkered myself and mindlessly climbed higher and higher, far higher than I had ever desired, certain that I would at last reach a safe meadow in which to rest. But I found only one slippery ledge after another. This is the tale of that ascent, and my eventual painful fall.

*

It had come as no surprise to me that I was expected to wed at a suitable age. I have no memory of a time when I had not understood that as a girl my worth to the family was my marriageability, either to a mortal man or to Christ, and my parents had never spoken of the latter possibility, of my entering a nunnery. Father was a respected member of his guild, a trader in fine cloth and jewels and a partner in a shipping concern. My marriage should bring him even greater prosperity or status or, preferably, both.

I suited my parents' plans – pretty, well-formed, well-behaved, quick-witted but not openly opinionated. I was willing and eager to be betrothed, believing that my life would only then begin; and the outcome of the Sunday I am about to recount certainly shaped the rest of my life, for good or ill.

My mother had ordered a new gown and surcoat for me to be made from her latest cast-offs, a pretty azure gown and a Lincoln green surcoat. Unlike her usual instructions to make my gown shapeless, she had her maid fit this one to my blooming breasts and slender waist. To say that I had taken great delight in the maid's compliments would be a gross understatement. She quite turned my head, with the result that even when I wore my usual shapeless gown I began to take every opportunity to glance at myself in any reflecting surface, newly fascinated each time. I'd recently begun my monthly flux and my body was full of surprises for me.

That my moon cycle had begun had been fair warning to me that my parents would begin to discuss my betrothal to someone of use to the family. But I had not expected them to take action quite so soon. My brother John, two years older than me, had been told not even to think about marriage until he had finished his apprenticeship with one of Father's fellow mercers. When I pointed that out, Mother had explained to me in her usual chilly wise that I was now of an age to assume my role in the family, to link it with another successful merchant concern, and therefore she saw no reason to delay.

'The money we have spent for the grammar school you attend is better spent elsewhere. Your husband will not care whether you can understand his account books. Certainly, he will prefer that you do not. He will want you to see to the housekeeping, not meddle in his trade. I pray your father will observe that and will not insist that your little sister Mary go to school.'

Mother did not willingly waste anything, particularly affection, on me. That my clothes had always been cut from her cast-off garments was the custom, but that any attention I gleaned from her was purely accidental was surely not. She saved her affection for my brother John, the eldest, and those acquaintances she judged useful. I had tried hard to win her affection when I was younger, yearning to have her bright smile shine on me, wishing to be caught up in her silky, fragrant embrace. But, emulating the nobles, she preferred her eldest son, and indeed had declared her milk used up by nursing him; before my birth she engaged a wet nurse. My two younger siblings had in their turn been handed over to wet nurses, and when weaned we were all cared for by Nan, a servant who saw to our every need with affection and devotion – but she could not entirely make up for Mother's indifference. I tried to be more than a sister to young Will and Mary, not wanting them to feel so alone as I did, which was no hardship, for I loved them and enjoyed their companionship.

In truth, Mother was as dismissive of Will and Mary as she was of me, but not as cruel to them. She saved that particular talent of hers for me. I did not know why she favoured me with her venom, but I was ever her prey.

Father was my champion, and I thought that if I were wed to a man cut from the same cloth as he, I would be happy. It was true that he had insisted on my time at the grammar school, and what Mother did not know was that he had also taught me much about keeping accounts and negotiating a good price. With his encouragement I often hid behind the curtained doorway in our home's undercroft, where he stored his merchandise, and listened to his negotiations; afterwards he would explain his tactics. He seemed to enjoy my precocious suggestions.

'You are so quick, Alice. You have a keen eye. You will be an asset to your husband.'

I prayed that he was right in this and Mother wrong, for I considered housekeeping tedious in comparison with Father's negotiations. I enjoyed sharing this secret endeavour with him and told no one about it, not even Nan or my best friend Geoffrey Chaucer.

On that fateful Sunday, I sensed that the household woke holding its collective breath. Will sat still and spoke softly while Nan combed out the tangles in his curly blond hair, behaviour quite unusual for an eight-year-old boy. Mary visibly tried to mirror his behaviour. Father nervously whistled and twice asked Nan the whereabouts of his boots. John dressed early and paced in the hall. Nan's hands trembled as she dressed me with the help of another maid, who was also subdued. I suspected that they were praying that Mother would judge my new gown and surcoat satisfactory.

I hoped that once they had given their approval, my parents would at last reveal to me the name of the man they had in mind. Mother claimed that Father insisted on surprising all of us with his choice, so even she did not know the man's identity. I hardly believed her, for I was not aware of Father's ever excluding her from matters of such import. Yet there was something overly alert in her manner of late, as if she were watching out for something. For his part, Father had given me the smile meant to reassure me that all was well.

'Sweet Alice, do you not trust your father to choose a handsome, wealthy man who will be good to you?'

I spent every spare moment at St Antonin's praying for a blessing on my married life. It seemed a safe, polite prayer, and helped me set aside my feelings of frustration. It seemed a cruel secret to keep from me when it would affect the rest of my life.

And so, although I sat quite still while Nan brushed my hair that Sunday morning, my mind was aquiver with anxiety. I distracted myself by mentally wandering down a path lined with the young merchants I had seen in Father's company, choosing between them. I knew it was an exercise I might regret – Father would not content himself with the most handsome man with the sweetest temperament, for my marriage was an extension of his endeavours to establish his standing in the merchant community, an alliance of our successful house with another, preferably even grander, one. Nor could I hope for someone my own age.

I had once thought that my best friend Geoffrey might be the one, but his parents had recently sent him off to serve as a page in a noble household. Seeing my disappointment, Father had reminded me that though the Chaucers were sufficiently wealthy and respectable, before he might wed a young man must have a position or inheritance that could support a household, and few lads of thirteen had either. There was an older man, a widower, wealthy and exceedingly handsome, whom I had dreamed of wedding, but Master Janyn had not graced our hall in a long while. I imagined he was already wed.

I was distracted from my brooding when Nan slipped my new azure gown over my head. It was my first gown of escarlatte, the finest wool, dyed in indigo from India, and I loved how it felt against my skin as I swayed side to side.

'Do not move so,' cried Nan. 'I shall never be able to button your sleeves.'

She was not a young woman, and her fingers, stiff with age, fumbled at the small buttons and loops that had to be tugged together to fit in the snug manner that was stylish. I noticed how she winced as she pulled a button through the loop and wished I might help her, but it took two hands to achieve. My sister was too young to perform such a task, and it did not seem proper to ask one of my brothers or Father.

'Cook might help me with this,' I suggested. She sometimes assisted Mother's maid when both Nan and I were busy with something. 'Or Mother.'

Nan hissed and shook her head without looking up from her agony. 'Your mother is all atemper this morning and I'll not bother her or Cook. I was told to see to you and I mean to do so.'

At last she had me snugly buttoned, and helped me with the surcoat, and then the pretty silver circlet, this latter requiring much fussing on her part, its purpose being to hold my hair away from my face so that it would fall in cascades of golden-brown curls down my back. Stepping away, she motioned for me to turn around so she might check that all was buttoned, tucked and tidy. She clapped her hands as I moved about, but when I turned to face her again I saw that she was crying and my heart sank.

'Nan, what is wrong?'

'You will have a dozen marriage proposals by evening and be wed by Christmas,' she cried. 'And then I'll not see you again. You'll forget your old Nan.'

I hugged her so tightly she squealed and pulled away. 'I love you too much to forget you,' I said, and meant it with all my heart.

'You will undo all my work,' she cried, but I could see that she was well pleased.

Mary, a chubby five-year-old with sticky fingers and a runny nose, slipped into the curtained area to see what was taking so long. She let out a little gasp. 'Mama's gown! She will box your ears for wearing her gown!' She covered her open mouth with her grubby hands and giggled.

'Mother had this cut down for me,' I explained, but Mary shook her head.

'She will be so angry!' she giggled again.

'I just scrubbed and changed you,' Nan moaned. 'Alice, go out to the hall and wait. I will try again with this little one. I pray Will is still tidy.'

As I stepped into the hall my brother John sat up and began to say something, but abruptly stopped, blushed to the roots of his light brown hair, and dropped his gaze, swinging his head slightly as if looking for something on the floor.

'What is it?' I asked.

He looked up again, his eyes drawn to my now-flushed face, then my long neck, which was quite bare.

'I hardly know you, dressed so,' he mumbled.

'For pity's sake, Alice, do not bite your lip.' Father drew me aside. 'You have nothing to fret about. Indeed, this is your day to revel in your youth and beauty, eh?' He took one of my hands and bowed to it, kissed it, then stepped back to have a good look at me. 'God's blood,' he swore under his breath.

I was unsure how to read his expression. He did not smile, but neither did he frown.

'Do I look beautiful, Father?'

'You do indeed. Your mother will be proud of you today. We all will be.'

'Now will you tell me who will be watching me most closely as I pray today, Father? I know you have spoken to someone.'

He took off his hat and dabbed his forehead. He was sweating despite the chill in the hall – the fire had been allowed to die down as we prepared, and would only be stoked when we returned from Mass. 'You will see him soon enough, Alice, soon enough. Walk

9

meekly and smile sweetly to those who greet you. It will be all the better if there are suitors in reserve, eh?'

He raised his hand to pat my shoulder as was his wont, but suddenly corrected himself and dropped it. I realised that, like John, he found me changed and somehow untouchable. He looked almost feverish for a moment, his eyes too shiny, his colour high, and I recognised the look of covetousness. I had often seen him look so at Mother, and at particularly exquisite silks and furs. I felt hot and sick and wanted to flee.

But Mother had just entered the hall from the solar above. She paused at the door with such an air of grace and command that I felt as if I were my little sister, grimy and underfoot.

'Walk towards me,' she commanded.

I did so, shivering under her hard scrutiny.

'Turn around.'

Again I obeyed as if I were a doll she manipulated from afar.

'You look like a strumpet,' she said with a sigh. 'But we have no time to fuss. There is no remedy.'

'Margery, what are you saying? Alice looks lovely,' Father protested.

'You would think so,' Mother said with a withering look at him. 'But I will take cheer in the hope that she will lure in your chosen prey. Come John, Will. Where is Nan? Has she not finished dressing Mary?'

Mother did not look my way again. I stood in the hall, embarrassed and feeling discarded. It was Nan, dear Nan, who saved the day for me.

Placing Mary's dimpled hand in mine, she said, 'Tell your sister what you told me, Mary.'

As I looked into my little sister's wide eyes, I realised that I was seeing love, admiration, all that I had hoped to see in the eyes of my parents and John.

'You are so beautiful, Alice,' Mary declared. 'I want to look just like you when I grow up.'

Tempted to reach down and press the dear child to my heart, I forced myself to be satisfied with a peck on Mary's momentarily clean cheek and a press of her hand.

'Will you walk with me to church, my lady Mary?' I asked, and my heart melted at the delight in my sister's eyes.

'You are beautiful as a spring dawn,' Nan whispered. 'Your mother does not like to be outshone, while your father has realised his little daughter is about to leave his household. Do not judge them for their simple feelings, Alice.'

And so I relaxed, once more noticing how soft the escarlatte felt against my skin, how it draped with such a liquid weight and movement that I felt graceful.

I bent to Mary. 'Hold your head high, little sister. The Salisbury girls will turn all other heads this morning. You look so pretty in your gown.'

Holding my sister's hand steadied me throughout an increasingly terrifying ordeal.

Once the family was assembled in the hall I took my cloak from the peg on the wall, but Mother shook her head and handed me one of her own. It was grey, lined in *gris*: the fine grey fur made from the winter hides of squirrels – only the lovely backs. On her it was more of a short cape, but it reached below my knees and felt wonderfully soft and caressing.

'Take it off as you enter the nave,' she instructed. 'I do not want to have wasted the escarlatte by hiding the robe beneath a cloak. I purposed to show that your body is ready for bearing children.'

Her words embarrassed me, as if I were about to parade naked through the city. I must have had tears in my eyes because Father patted me on the shoulder – now sufficiently covered – and whispered that Mother had a headache and did not mean to be curt.

I nodded to Mary and grasped the hand that she offered me. 'Let us be gone!' I said with forced cheer.

It fooled Mary who giggled and hopped along beside me as I headed towards the door. Will suddenly charged ahead and opened it with a sweeping bow. Now I, too, giggled and was grateful for my younger siblings.

The autumn morning was damp with a river mist that would rise by midday but for the moment made me glad of the *gris* lining in the cloak. Such a damp, chilly morning usually inspired complaints on my part, but today it was comforting, as if I could be private a little longer. I tried to remind myself that I was not about to be wed, merely on display to potential suitors. It might be a year or more before I walked to the church porch to take a husband. But I could not shake the sense of stepping off the edge of the world known to me and into a void without boundary, without bottom. I shivered and pulled the cloak tighter round me with my free hand.

Mary still skipped along beside me. I pressed her hand, wondering how often I would see her once I was wed, how much of her life I would know. Heavy thoughts at thirteen.

At the church door Nan took the cloak from me and reached for Mary's hand, but I held firm. 'She will steady me, won't you, Mary?'

My sister tugged on my hand and nodded with such a gladsome smile that I took heart. The gloom of the morning had inspired dark thoughts. Now the beautiful nave, the incense, the familiar faces, would cheer me. I would feel like a princess in my escarlatte gown, my hair shining from Nan's vigorous brushing.

Stepping into the nave, I felt the reassurance of the familiar. I could not begin to count how many times I had stepped through these doors. The expanse of glass and stone above me seemed to lighten my step.

'Master Janyn Perrers! Good day to you,' Father exclaimed.

My heart danced. This was he about whom I had dreamed, he who at one time had been a frequent guest at our dinner table. He was as I had remembered: olive skin, dark eyes and lustrous, curly hair. A deep, resonant voice. The way his face lit up when he smiled. The grace with which he wore his elegant clothes. Next to Father, Master Janyn was my ideal man.

'Master John Salisbury. *Benedicite.*' Janyn Perrers bowed. 'And Dame Margery.' He bowed again, but I noticed that he did not look Mother in the eyes as he did Father. Now he looked my way. 'And is this Mistress Alice? Surely not. She cannot have grown so beautiful in the short time since I last saw her playing in your garden?' His eyes were so friendly that I could not help but smile.

I curtsied to him and was startled by his warm hand suddenly grasping mine.

Looking into my eyes as if I were the only person in the nave, he bowed over my hand, brushing it with his lips.

I felt myself blush to my fingertips. I could not seem to find my voice but stared at him as he bowed once more to my parents and moved away into the crowd.

'What is he doing here this morning?' Mother hissed at Father. Her head trembled on her delicate neck.

'He occasionally worships here, Margery, you know that.'

'Not for a long while.'

'That is true. But we spoke the other day and are once more at ease with one another.'

'God's blood, if you are planning what I think you are, I'll wring her neck before I let her marry him!'

Now I was horribly aware of eyes following us, but could not be certain whether I was the focus of interest or whether it was Mother. Her pale face was stained with unbecoming splotches of crimson and she held her head so rigid that her veil shivered like a delicate insect wing.

She would wring my neck before she would let me wed Janyn Perrers? That could not be what she meant. Surely.

After Mass, the Chaucers paused to greet our family and Geoffrey told me that he had not guessed I could be quite so beautiful as I was that morning. I tried to laugh at his confusing compliment, but managed only a weak smile.

'You look frightened,' he said. 'Are you?'

'The day is not unfolding as I'd dreamed it would,' I said, irritated to feel tears start.

'This will not do,' Geoffrey said with a most sympathetic look. 'Straighten up and meet the eyes of your fellow parishioners. You are worth all of them.'

'I wish you could hold my other hand,' I muttered.

He looked down at Mary, fidgeting now, swinging towards me and away and singing something under her breath, a million leagues away from us in some enchanted land.

'I would be better company, I suppose.' He laughed as his mother called him away. 'She is worried that we will defy them and pledge our troth. Shall we?'

With Mother's angry words still echoing in my head, stirring fear of what she might do, the thought of pledging myself to my good friend was like balm for my heart. Geoffrey was neither handsome nor elegant, but he was comfortingly consistent and I had never doubted his friendship. I cherished the thought for a moment despite my certainty that he spoke in jest. Indeed, his gaze was already on the others around us, and his mother had no difficulty moving him away. I could not run after him because other families with eligible young men were now approaching us, and Father proudly introduced each one in turn to me. Many of the young men I already knew, although they behaved towards me quite differently from the way they had in the past.

At some point in our lives we cross over from the carefree innocence of childhood to the weighty status of responsible adult. We are no longer greeted with vague looks and tolerant smiles but considered for our value to others and whether we are likely to be friend or foe. I remember almost every moment of that day on which I realised that what I had thought was a rehearsal for adulthood was in fact the deciding step – there was no going back.

By the time my family and I walked out into the churchyard the mist had been burned away by a warm midday sun the deep gold of autumn. The sudden brightness blinded me, and I stumbled on the shallow steps leading from the porch. I was caught up and set back on my feet by someone with strong arms, yet a gentle touch.

'God bless you,' I said, a bit breathlessly as I smoothed out my gown with one hand, shading my eyes with the other. I discovered my saviour was Janyn Perrers.

But I doubt he heard me for Mother had already pulled him to one side and was berating him in an angry whisper.

I did not rush to his defence, for fear of her reaction.

Father said something beneath his breath to Nan and she called to her four charges, hurrying us across the square to our house.

John heaved a loud sigh as we stepped into the hall. 'Mother will be testy for the remainder of the day.'

Will started towards the garden door, but Nan pulled him back, tidying his wild hair.

'Let us warm ourselves while we await your parents,' she said.

Mary fought back tears. 'Why is Mother so angry?'

I hugged her and promised it would prove to be nothing.

We were just huddling around the fire in the hall when Mother and Father entered, hissing at one another, faces flushed with emotion, gestures abrupt with anger. Inside the door Father grabbed Mother's elbow and roughly pulled her closer to have the last word. She snatched her arm from him, gathered her skirts, and rushed out of the door again. I could hear her stumble up the outer stairs to the solar. The boards creaked overhead.

With a tug at his clothes and a twist of his neck, as if to ease it, Father affected calm as he joined us.

'Your mother took offence at Master Janyn Perrers' behaviour. She did not realise he had saved you from a nasty tumble, Alice, and chided him for being so rude as to touch you, a young girl. It is most unfortunate for he is to dine with us today and your mother is now too shamed by her own discourtesy to join us. She believes we will all be more at ease with you presiding over the table as mistress of the house,' he said to me.

I could think of nothing to say but, 'Yes, Father,' though I felt uneasy about his lie.

It was a strange and most uncomfortable afternoon. In celebration of the lovely weather Cook and Nan had set up a trestle table by the door to a small courtyard in which, in one of her rare moments of happiness, Mother had planted herbs and flowers and Father had made a bench for her with a bower for climbing roses overhead. The flowers were all spent now, but as the sun warmed the plants their fragrances mingled with the delicious smells on the table. It would have been delightful – but as I looked out on her little garden, Mother loomed large in her absence. I did not feel in any wise prepared to play hostess in her place. I was not the only one discomfited. Father was too loud and jovial. Janyn's parents, Master John and Dame Tommasa Perrers, were plainly ill at ease.

But not Master Janyn. He was as charming as he had always been in our home.

Will and Mary had been bustled off to the kitchen with Nan, and a part of me yearned to be in there with them, at ease and at peace.

But Master Janyn made certain that I did not feel that way for long. While the other adults talked in stilted courtesy to each other, Master Janyn entertained John and me with stories of his travels to Lombardy, Naples, Calais, Bruges. I found myself doubting Mother's suspicion that he meant to wed me, for he knew so much of the world, was about twenty years my senior and so grand, he could not possibly want a child like me to be hostess in his home.

15

And yet . . . from time to time he would look at me with a curious expression, as if wondering about me, perhaps trying me out in different settings or different clothes. He inquired as to my preferences – colours, foods, even feast days – and listened with such concentration that he several times echoed my exact words to himself, as if determined to remember them. After an account of a journey or some other event he would glance at me, as if gauging whether or not it had been to my liking. He did not treat John in such wise. I believed it to be the behaviour of a man paying court.

I felt as if all that was familiar and reassuring had been packed in a cart that was pulling away too fast, much too fast, and I wanted to protest that I must have it all back at once, all in place, all as usual. But something prevented me and I realised that, before I could break free from the spell, the cart would be out of my reach. I wanted Mother at the table, laughing with the guests. I wanted to be able to slip away and play or to join Nan and the young ones in the kitchen. I wanted to be in my old shapeless gown and all but invisible. Despite liking Janyn, I yearned for my old familiar life. I bit my lip so hard fighting back tears that the next morning it was swollen and very sore.

At some point the dinner was over and I was at last at the door of the hall, bidding our guests farewell. Dame Tommasa touched my cheek and said that she hoped to see me again very soon. Master John was deep in discussion with Father about reports of a mutual friend's ship lost in the Channel. Master Janyn took both my hands in his and looked deep into my eyes. He was much taller than I was, but in that moment I felt our eyes were so close I might feel his lashes if he blinked. His skin was warm to the touch. He gave off a heat that was dry and somehow reassuring, and he smelled very pleasant. But he seemed too much a man, too knowing and strong, too able to bend me to his will. If we were to wed, my life would be swallowed up by his. Alice would be no more. I was dizzy with conflicting emotions and the turmoil made me mute. I wanted to tell him to go away and not return, and at the same time wanted him to lean closer and kiss me on the lips. As the thought occurred, I felt myself blush.

Janyn smiled, and for a moment looked quite mischievous, which suited his face. 'I believe you have stolen my heart,

Mistress Alice. I pray you, be gentle with it.' He kissed my hands, each in turn, and then bowed and let go of me.

I was terrified and thrilled. After the Perrers had departed Father asked me how I liked Master Janyn, and I burst into tears. I turned to him with my arms outstretched, hoping to be enfolded in his comforting embrace. But he stood with his hands at his sides, shaking his head at the ceiling.

'Ah, so he did not please you. Has she poisoned you against him? Did she say aught to you before he arrived?'

In spirit he was already up in the solar, continuing his argument with Mother. Again, fear crawled along my skin making me shiver with a sudden chill. I sensed a chess game all around me in which I was a pawn: unimportant, simple to move, easy to lose. I recoiled from the thought and assured myself that I was no such thing, that Father loved me, but that Mother had so embarrassed him and robbed him of his prize for the day's work, his daughter betrothed to a worthy suitor, that he could not turn his attention to me and see that I suffered as well.

'She said nothing to me after church,' I replied, and, whispering some excuse, fled to the kitchen seeking Nan. She saw my distress at once and pulled me to her, stroking my hair as she hummed and rocked me. She asked no questions, which was best, for my thoughts were so tangled I would have given her yet more worries. Already she seemed to have a new wrinkle between her grizzled brows.

I lay in bed that night comparing my previous night's fantasy about my morning at Mass with the actual experience, and thought with a sinking heart that I had just tasted the true flavour of adulthood. And found it sour where I had expected it to be sweet.

The household was subdued for days, Mother in her room, Father and my brother John avoiding any mention of Sunday's events, and on the next Sunday the Perrers family was not at St Antonin's. Again after Mass families with unmarried sons and a few widowers approached us for introductions. Father was friendly, Mother brusque, and they invited no guests to dinner that day. Mother joined us, occasionally glancing my way with a sneer, as if she needed but the sight of me to refresh her ill temper. Each time she did that, I felt myself shrink a little and the voices of the other members of the household grow softer, until I felt as if I were not actually in the room with them at all but watching them from afar, from behind some barrier that allowed me to see but imperfectly, hear but vaguely, while Mother stole hate-filled glances at my empty place at table.

Over the next few weeks she perfected this dismissal of me, working a powerful spell. I lost all appetite and kept to myself more and more.

Perhaps if Geoffrey had not been sent away he might have teased me out of my withdrawal from life, but with him gone there was no one save Nan who cared about my behaviour. Not even Father. In fact, several times I caught him regarding me with an annoyed frown, as if I had disappointed him. But no one spoke to me. I had no idea whether the Perrers family had found me lacking, whether I had neglected to do something they had expected of me. At no time did I feel welcome, much less encouraged, to ask what was wrong.

Sunday after Sunday no suitor was invited to dinner, and I began to think I had missed the moment at which a husband might be found for me. Christmas came, then Easter. Father made a few trips out of London, one to Castle Rising, the home of the former Queen, Isabella. I had never known him to be summoned by a member of the royal family before. In the past he would have invited me down to the undercroft after such an unusual journey to tell me all about the wonders he had seen, the interesting people, what an honour it was for our family, but this time I heard only what he recounted at the dinner table or in the evenings as the family sat around the fire in the hall. Indeed, he said little about that trip. In general he seemed increasingly uncomfortable, as if some great worry weighed him down, and I prayed that I had not unwittingly brought this on him.

My one consolation was St Antonin's: the familiar quiet in the church, its reassuring sameness, the certainty of Christ's teachings and the Blessed Mother's compassion. I prayed for guidance and, gradually, over the spring, an answer bloomed in my heart. After several failed attempts I gathered the courage to talk to Dom Paul, my parish priest, about how I might serve God. He listened to me with kind attention and suggested that I might embroider an altar cloth, or sew something for one of the statues, and of course be a good daughter and help out at home. I explained that I meant a stronger commitment, that I thought I would like to be a bride of Christ.

His heavy-lidded eyes opened just wide enough for him to abandon his habitual close-lidded listening expression and peer at me with a frown – all adults seemed to frown at me of late. 'You wish to take vows? Have you spoken of this to your family?'

'No. I am speaking to *you* about it.'

'You would need your parents' permission,' he said, and in his voice and his distracted eyes as he rose from the bench, I knew that he did not think they would grant this wish.

Dom Paul was conspicuously absent the next day, although I lingered long in the church.

On the following day Father asked me to join him in the undercroft after dinner, which he had not done since my mysterious transgression. He suggested that I change into my pretty azure gown and green surcoat. He would be entertaining some important customers and would like me to look my best. I felt as if someone had lit a candle inside me, the warmth and light filling me and inviting me back to life. I had been weeding the kitchen garden and was acutely aware of a sudden how soiled were my hands and even my face. I asked my little brother Will to look after Mary for a while so that Nan might help me clean myself and dress.

She shook her head over how loosely the azure gown now fitted me, and how pale I looked despite the sunny weather we had been enjoying.

'You are too much in church, child.'

'Or I have finally spent enough time there, Nan, for my prayers have been answered. Father has forgiven me.'

'For what?'

I shrugged. 'It no longer matters.'

By her muttering and jerky movements I understood that it still mattered to her, a great deal. She had been quietly fuming about my parents' treatment of me for a long while.

'Dame Margery is too selfish to love her children as a mother should,' Nan had told me. 'And Master John shirks his duty as a husband in permitting her vanity and selfishness to rage unchecked.'

'They are as God made them.' I had taken this as my set response to her frequent tirades about my inadequate parents.

'You are too ready to forgive them, Alice.'

'I foresee only more censure if I complain.'

'How can you say that when you see how your mother's behaviour, which includes a litany of complaints that grows ever longer, is met with such coddling and folk stumbling over themselves in their eagerness to please her?'

'She is very beautiful.'

'As are you, when you are in health. Folk believe what you make them think of you. If you cower and cringe, they believe they are right to condemn you.'

How I missed Geoffrey. We might have spent many jolly hours debating Nan's philosophy. I tried not to think about how things might have been had he not been sent away, but I did so yearn for a good laugh, for a friend who did not judge me and wanted to understand me.

So on that day I would not ask what had been set right, why Father had invited me to the undercroft after ignoring me for so long. Partly I feared that the invitation would be withdrawn, and I could not bear that after feeling so happy about the possibility of returning to our old comfortable ways.

It was cool in the undercroft, and I held my cupped hands close to an oil lamp as I waited for Father to finish instructing his clerk about how to display the cloth and ornaments he wished to show the customers. I had offered to arrange for wine and a little food for the guests, but the clerk had told me that he would see to that, as he always did.

Turning towards the displayed items, I studied them for a moment. 'The gold cloth glows against the blue,' I commented. 'Is it cloth of gold or just the colour of gold?' It shone so that I thought it possible it truly was gold wire.

'Merely a colour,' said Father. 'There is little call for such a costly fabric as cloth of gold among merchants. The nobles are more extravagant. Although for very special occasions, a merchant might request it. In small quantities!' He chuckled at that. He seemed uncommonly cheerful, and my heart fluttered to think it was from joy at our renewed camaraderie.

'I have missed our time together,' I blurted, then blushed,

having voiced the thought without intending to.

But Father smiled and patted my shoulder. 'I have missed talking to you as well. I was wrong to be ruled by your mother's temper.'

'Why was she so angry with me?'

'Your mother is difficult to fathom, Alice, and there are times, as now, when I think it best we do not attempt to understand her ill humour, for it might influence us.'

He had grown serious while delivering this little speech and sat for several moments afterwards with head bowed, seemingly studying his hands. I felt it to be a significant moment, that he had treated me as a mature woman for the first time. My heart swelled with quiet joy and I reached out for his hand.

But he jumped to his feet. 'They are here!' He ordered his clerk to welcome the guests. 'You will be surprised, I think,' Father said to me, his face bright with anticipation, 'and, I very much hope, delighted to see who is here.'

There were stacks of barrels between the doorway and the area in which Father showed his merchandise, so I recognised his voice before I saw him. My heartbeat quickened, and I had an urge to flee, though not to avoid him, but rather because I felt as if I were being swept up into a great wave that would carry me far from the familiar earth, an inexorable wave over which I had no control, and I was frightened and at the same time excited.

'Father, is it Master Janyn Perrers?'

My father's grin was so exaggerated, like a gargoyle's, that it, too, frightened me. 'So you remember his voice. That is a good sign, I think. *Are* you pleased?'

I crossed myself against evil or danger. 'I do not know what to think,' I said. This was no way to win Mother's affection, I thought.

But it was too late to say more. The small space was suddenly filled by Master Janyn and his father. I was glad of the shadows the men cast in the lamp-lit chamber because I could take advantage of them and feel less exposed, less readable. I did not want Master Janyn to see how I blushed beneath his direct gaze, nor how I, in turn, found it difficult to look away from him.

What a beautiful man he was: his colouring, his strong build, the grace of his movements, the deep resonance of his voice that made my bones hum, the spicy smell of him. He wore exquisite clothes – not just expensive and well-cut, but beautiful and seeming just right for him. His father was pale and ordinary in comparison, looking like all the other wealthy merchants, including Father. I thought it must be the Italian blood from his mother's family that made Janyn so beautiful.

In truth, I was his even before he asked for my hand.

Janyn's father, Master John, bowed to both of us and asked after my health.

Again I felt myself blush as I replied that I was in good health. His question embarrassed me. I assumed he had noticed how my clothes hung on my diminished frame. I wished I did not look so ill that it was the first thing on which he commented. It would not recommend me as a future wife to his son.

'I thank God that you have fully recovered,' he said. 'Dame Tommasa will also be gladdened by this news.'

I must have looked as confused as I felt, for Father coughed and shook his head at me, a sign for me to let it pass. He then drew both men over to the display of cloth.

I did not join them right away, trying to think why Master John thought that I had been ill if it were not for my present appearance – for he implied that his wife had also been worried for my health. I could find nothing that made more sense than that Father had lied to them about my health, and the only reason I could think he would do that was as an excuse for having avoided them and in such wise appeasing Mother, who so disliked Master Janyn.

Yet here they were today, in our undercroft, invited by Father. I wondered whether this meant that Mother had agreed to look on Master Janyn with charity. It was hardly something she would confide to me. My spirits lifted once more as I considered the possibility of being betrothed to Janyn Perrers. I would want for nothing, and have the most handsome, elegant husband. Noticing Father glancing my way, I joined him and his guests. They were discussing the cloth he had displayed, and some others that the clerk had fetched. One fabric looked as if it had been painted: gold stars and silver crescent moons against a dark colour, almost black.

I ran my hand over it to feel whether the gold and silver shapes stood out, but they seemed to be part of the fabric.

'Is this not a fantastical cloth?' Father said to me.

I nodded. No more fantastical than the thought of my being Janyn Perrers's wife, I thought.

'I do not know why I purchased it,' he said, 'for it is so strange. But I found it beautiful, and wilfully ignored my misgivings.'

Master John Perrers brushed beringed fingers across the fabric, then lifted it, feeling its weight. As he set it back down he said, 'It is very fine, John. My wife would tell me to buy it.'

Janyn chuckled, 'Yes, she would.'

Father shook his head. 'Where might she wear such cloth without censure from all in the parish?'

'Here in London she would wear it only in our home,' said Master John with a little shrug, tapping the cloth lightly with one finger. 'But in Lombardy she might wear a gown of such stuff at market . . . at feasts. Or line a cloak with it.'

I lifted a corner of the cloth and gently rubbed it between my fingers. It was silky and had a rich heft. I could imagine it as a surcoat over a dark or perhaps a gold gown. But such robes on a woman not of the court would be greeted with disdain by the other wives of the guild. 'Dame Tommasa must miss her homeland very much then,' I said. 'I should like to see a city where one could wear such a beautiful robe to market.'

Master John grinned broadly. 'Perhaps you *shall* see such a city, Mistress Alice. What do you think – shall I buy enough for the lining of a cloak? Or a gown?'

'Or a surcoat,' I said, feeling quite bold in revealing that I had considered what use I would make of such a beautiful cloth.

'Ah.' Master John nodded. 'With what colour gown beneath?'

I hesitated, looking to Father for permission to continue. He nodded his encouragement. Indeed, he appeared pleased with me.

'A rich gold?' I suggested. 'Or something even darker.'

'You have a talent for this,' said Master John. 'That is good. Very good.' He glanced at his son, who was watching me with his usual intensity.

'Which of these would you choose for my mother?' asked Master Janyn. He held up two gold cloths, one a much deeper shade than the other, almost a brown yet with a whisper of gold, the promise of light.

I pointed to that one. He turned to Father. 'Mistress Alice has inspired me to make a gift of her choices to my mother. Let us discuss the measures later.' Lifting another gold cloth, of a lighter shade, he asked me what I thought of it. 'Do feel it.'

It was not silk, but escarlatte, like the gown I wore, the costliest wool. The colour was beautiful.

'Escarlatte,' I said, very quietly, becoming too aware of his closeness, his intense gaze.

'The gold colour matches your eyes,' he said.

I looked up and my gaze was caught by his. I wondered at the power he had over me. I felt weak, as if all wit had flown from my head.

'Does it?' I whispered the question, not wishing to break the spell he cast over me by speaking too loudly.

'Perhaps it is time that we sat and discussed the true purpose of your visit,' said Father. 'Alice,' he took my arm, 'come sit beside me.' He gave me a little tug and at last I looked away from Janyn.

My heart raced as we took our seats. I hoped that we were to talk of marriage. I also dreaded it. To be so in thrall to anyone did not seem a good thing to me. And yet I felt a new sensation inside my skin, as if my body were awakening from a deep slumber. If this was love then I had never loved Geoffrey. I began to understand why love between a man and a woman worried priests so, for once felt, I thought it would take a deal of grace to vow never to experience it again. Any lingering thought of retiring to a nunnery fled.

'Alice, leave your dreaming and attend what I say,' said Father, a note of irritation in his voice, though he spoke softly.

Embarrassed as well as sorry to anger my father, I had to force myself to glance across the table and see how Master John Perrers took my vagueness. I was relieved to have my gaze met with a kind smile.

'Forgive me, Father,' I murmured. 'I beg your pardon, Master John, Master Janyn.' I looked only at the elder Perrers. I did not dare look at the younger.

'Daughter, Master Janyn Perrers has approached me about taking you to be his wife,' Father began, though it felt as if it were the end of his speech.

So here it was, the moment I'd dreamed of. Yet now that it was here I was frightened. I was not ready. Why was Mother not here? I did not dare ask, though the question burned in my throat.

'He is a good man with everything to recommend him, but a betrothal is not blessed by the Church unless both the man and woman agree to it. What say you, Alice? Would you be the wife of this man?'

Now that the moment had arrived, I felt ill prepared. Though they had made much of finding me a good husband, they had said little of what marriage entailed. Questions crowded my mind. *Might I have time to think about this, Father? Will loving someone in the way I believe I love him rob me of my soul? Has he said that he loves me? What happens between a man and a woman?*

'Daughter, I am owed an answer.' Father sounded angry, though he forced a smile, patting my hand. 'Were you not aware that Master Janyn was honouring you with his interest?'

I looked at each man in turn, trying not to be snared by Janyn's gaze. His eyes were opaque now, not drawing me in but observing. He did not seem overly concerned about the outcome. Master John looked puzzled. Father looked worried and irritated. I had no counsel, no confidant in that chamber. And it was clear that I was expected to choose now. I fell back on my obedience as a daughter.

'If you so wish it, I should be honoured to be Master Janyn's wife, Father,' I said.

I felt everyone at the table take a deep breath and the tension recede.

'God has blessed me this day,' said Janyn in a voice taut with emotion.

'Dame Tommasa will be so happy,' said Master John. 'May God grant the two of you a blessed and fruitful life together.'

'I pray that I please you in all ways,' I murmured.

Father smiled. I noticed a slight tremor in his hands as he raised his cup to toast the betrothal. Joy, relief, or sorrow at the prospect of losing me, I could not guess. This day I had learned that I did not know Father as I had thought I did. Or perhaps I had first learned it on that fateful Sunday months ago. I resolved that I would not allow his problems with Mother to dampen my joy. I was to be Alice *Perrers*, beloved of the beautiful man who sat across from me; *Dame* Alice, mistress of his household.

'Might I kiss my betrothed?' Janyn asked.

Oh, sweet heaven, I was not ready for that. Surely Father would reject such a request.

Master John Perrers clapped his hands together. 'But of course you may, eh, my friend?' He winked at Father.

I clutched Father's hand. He patted mine.

'A most appropriate seal,' he said.

Janyn was rising, his lithe body moving away from his side of the table. He held out one hand to me. A large, elegant hand. I rose, stumbling a little, and he gently held me steady as we moved towards one another. He was tall, so tall. I stood on tiptoe, he bowed his head and gathered me to him, lifting me off my feet. His warmth caressed me, and his lips – oh, dear God, what sin was in that kiss! Wine and figs, I tasted, and the heat of him. I rested my hands on his shoulders, savouring his warmth. When he set me gently on the floor again, I thought I would faint. I could not imagine ever moving of my own volition again. But I steadied myself and stood there and, hand in hand, we faced our fathers. Looking at mine, I had a moment of misgiving. He looked lost, frightened. Meeting my gaze, he quickly forced a smile. But I had seen, I had seen.

'May all joy be yours, dear Alice, dear Janyn,' he said.

'I pray God that I deserve such joy as I feel at this moment,' said Janyn. 'I pledge my troth to this most beautiful woman, Alice Salisbury.'

Father nodded to me. 'And you, Daughter, you must pledge as well.'

'I pledge my troth to Master Janyn Perrers,' I said, embarrassed by how breathless I sounded.

Janyn squeezed my hand. 'Not Master, sweet Alice. I am Janyn to you now.' He looked down on me with such love, I took courage from that look and could not think how I had been afraid.

'This is an excellent day's work,' said Master John.

Father clapped for his clerk to pour more wine, and we toasted the match once more.

'You must dine at our home soon. Within the week,' said Master John. 'My wife will wish to rejoice with you.'

When we were alone again, even the clerk having departed,

Father and I sat quietly, lost in our own thoughts. I bowed my head over my hands and inhaled the scent of my betrothed. Heaven must smell so.

At length Father chuckled and slapped his thigh. 'Well, Alice, I dare say that the prospect of being wed to a man like Janyn Perrers has put flight to your idea of entering a nunnery . . . taking vows!' He shook his head, enjoying the jape.

I thrust my hands into my lap and did not join in his laughter, shocked by the betrayal. 'Dom Paul told you of our talks?'

'He did, dear child, he did. And what of it? Do you not delight in the remedy?' His laughter had faded but still he grinned so broadly I felt a bit foolish to be so angry.

But angry I was. I had confided in the priest, and had expected my confidences to go no further than his ears, not to be repeated elsewhere, outside the quiet communion of our moments in church. If I could not trust my own parish priest, I could not think in whom I might trust.

I was discovering that my elders were universally unreliable. And I was betrothed to one. That gave me pause.

'But look now, Alice, we must proceed with care.'

I was pulled from my angry, anxious thoughts by Father's serious tone, such a dramatic shift from moments ago. He frowned down at the table, playing with his mazer of wine, pushing the heavy cup back and forth between his hands.

'Why, Father?'

'Your mother . . .'

'Yes. Mother. Why was she not here?' When he did not answer at once, I guessed. 'She does not know of this?'

He shook his head.

'She will not be happy about it.'

'No.'

'The Perrers are respected, wealthy – why would she disapprove?'

He sighed and wiped his brow. 'You are too young to understand.'

'Not so young as to miss her words in church the day I first wore this robe. She said she would strangle me before she'd see me wed Master Janyn. What enmity is there between them?'

He looked stunned for a moment, then angry. 'You heard that?'

27

'I did. She spoke it so that I would hear. Why would she threaten such violence, Father?'

'You never said a word.'

'Nor did you.' I held his gaze, imploring him to explain his silence, to apologise, to reassure me.

'Your mother says much that she does not mean, Alice.'

'What does she hold against Janyn? I deserve to know, Father.'

He opened his mouth as if to speak, then closed it and shook his head, dropping his gaze, as if in shame or confusion. 'You know that he is a widower. She did not like his wife. That is all.'

I did not believe him. 'Father, tell me what Mother dislikes about Janyn.'

'She dislikes nothing about him. I swear to you, Daughter. And that is all that I can say about the matter.'

'Why do you still push us together?'

'I will not have your mother ruin your happiness.'

'He is not the only marriageable man in London. Though I do like him above all other men, I should find happiness with another.' I did not believe that, but Father's lie frightened me. 'Someone who would not turn my own mother against me.' Not that I had ever enjoyed her favour. But the thought of her hating me was too awful. 'Let that be an end to it.'

Now Father looked me in the eye with a display of temper I had rarely witnessed in him. 'I will *not* bend to her will,' he shouted, bringing a fist down hard, shaking the lamp and the mazers.

'You cannot force me to go against my mother,' I said, quietly but firmly. I would not cower before his show of temper. This was far too important. It was my life.

'I can and I will, Daughter. You have pledged your troth to Janyn Perrers and you will wed him. I will hear no more argument.'

Never had my father spoken so to me. I was dumbstruck. I already felt depleted by the emotions I'd experienced while Janyn and his father were present; this took away what little spirit I'd had left. I waited in dread for what was to follow, feeling ever more frightened. I had a sinking sensation, as if I were about to drop through the floor and out of existence. In my place would be a doll who might look like me but would be merely an empty shell, moved about by cunning, conniving adults. I had ever taken care to hide my more passionate feelings, my rebellious thoughts, never dreaming that maturity would require I should stifle my spirit even further.

Father stood and paced out some of his temper, then returned to the table, fussing with his wide sleeves as he settled. More unusual behaviour.

'You will say nothing of this until I mention it with you present,' he said. 'I must decide how to announce your betrothal to your mother.'

'I ask you once more, Father. Why is she so against my marrying Janyn?'

He shook his head. 'I will not spoil your happiness with revelations about your mother's—' He shook his head again. 'She will not harm you, Alice.'

I had long ago decided that she had not meant she would in truth choke me or break my neck, but to hear Father say that she would not seemed to make it more possible that she would.

'If there is some ill she knows of Janyn, you must tell me.'

'It is not about him, child. I would not have blessed this union if I knew any ill of him.'

'You lied to the Perrers family, Father. You told them I'd been ailing.'

He forced a smile. 'You looked so happy while they were here, and now you are so full of questions.' He tried to look amused. 'Come now, a little lie. I had to keep them away while I considered how to proceed, but I needed to give them a reason for my delaying the betrothal that would not cause them to pause and reconsider the wisdom of the match.'

'So many lies, so much dissembling . . . it frightens me, Father. Why are you so desperate I should marry Janyn Perrers?'

'Desperate?' He shook his head. 'You are wrong in judging me so, Alice. Janyn will be good to you. He is a kind, gentle man, as is his father. You will thank me for insisting on this union.'

He did not hug me. He did not ask whether he had reassured me. He merely reiterated that I was to remain silent about this meeting until he had told Mother of the betrothal.

As I left the undercroft, surprised to feel the heat of the afternoon after its dim, chilly interior, I considered going to church to pray for guidance. But I was still too angry about Dom Paul's betrayal. Instead, I sought out Mary and took her for a long walk. Listening to her happy chatter was a soothing balm.

I slept little that night, lying awake for what seemed hours, keenly aware of how suddenly precious my siblings and Nan were to me, how I would miss them. Yet I thrilled at the mere thought of Janyn, of our kiss. When I finally slept, my dreams woke me with a yearning for him that I did not understand.

Needing the comfort of St Antonin's, I went to church early the next morning. When Dom Paul appeared in the nave, I asked him why he had spoken to my father about our talks. He said it was his duty, that a girl could not make such a decision without her parents' consent – primarily her father's.

Father's betrayal hurt and frightened me far more than did Dom Paul's. And I was angry as well, angry at both them and Mother. Had it not been for her hostility and my unease about Father's dishonesty, I believed I would feel nothing but joy at the prospect of wedding Janyn Perrers. Indeed, when I managed to forget about them, I tingled with delicious anticipation. But the tension between my parents tarnished that joy and dulled my excitement with an undertone of dread. I desperately wanted to believe that all might be well in the end, that Mother would see what a good man Janyn was and bless our union. What a young fool I was.

Father's and Dom Paul's betrayals weakened my trust in the adults all about me. I had believed they wanted only what was best for me. Now I felt terribly vulnerable and ignorant of the world.

Within a few days I received an invitation to dine at the home of John and Tommasa Perrers. The secrecy surrounding my betrothal had been so complete that sometimes I feared I'd merely dreamed the meeting in the undercroft. Father looked almost faint with relief that only he and I had been in the hall when the messenger arrived. He assured me that he was ready to tell Mother of my betrothal. I dreaded that moment, and yet I also yearned to have it behind me.

The next day Father presented Mother with a cloak of *pers* as blue as her eyes, lined with miniver, a cloak so warm and soft that she chirped with delight when she tried it on and said that now she could not wait for the first snow. The cloak fastened with a silver clasp made to look like delicate wings. I had never seen one so beautiful, and Mother only added to its beauty. My father watched her with a yearning that seemed almost sorrowful as she proceeded around the hall, spinning about every few steps to reveal the full cut and the pretty lining. She was sweet to all of us at the table that afternoon. Seeing Mary's and Will's joy in her mood, I lost what little appetite I'd had for I guessed that Father's announcement at the end of the meal would bring on a storm of epic proportions.

I had anticipated that he would call for a toast and announce my betrothal to the whole family at the end of the meal, so was disappointed when he rose from the table. Bowing to Mother, he held out his hand to her. 'My love, will you step out into the garden with me?'

She smiled at his grand gesture and rose, accepting his hand, and they swept out of the garden door.

Nan gathered the little ones and took them to the kitchen. The previous night, needing to tell someone before I burst, I had told her what had transpired in the undercroft and about the invitation to dine at the Perrers' home. She, too, expected a storm.

I had never seen her so angry as when I told her of my betrothal.

'What do you know about Janyn Perrers?' I had asked.

'It is not him, child. I am angry with the master for hiding this from the mistress. He forced you to act against your mother's wishes. That is not right. I cannot see how that can be right. God forgive me for saying so, but God forgive him for *doing* so.'

'Do you know why Mother is so against our betrothal?'

Nan's face had closed against me, as it often did when I wanted to know something she had been ordered not to discuss with us, her charges.

'I cannot say.'

'Do you think she will accept it now that Father is so determined to honour our troth?'

A subtle movement of her eyes suggested to me that Nan did not believe so.

'The master has put you in a position that no child should be made to take,' she said. That was all she would say.

I'd slept little after that. Nan's anger had frightened me and reinforced my own sense of his betrayal.

Now I paced the hall while listening to my brother John berating a servant for a petty mistake. On any other day I would try to mediate to keep the peace, but I had no heart for anything but holding my breath today.

When they entered the hall, Mother's face was as white as alabaster and Father's blotched with temper. As she fled past me to the door leading to the solar stairs, she glanced at me and I saw tears just starting to spill down her cheeks. She opened her eyes wide and appeared to be about to say something, then pressed a hand to her mouth and hurried out.

'I did not think her good spirits would last,' John said with a smirk.

Father turned on him. 'Be quiet, you young fool!'

Later that afternoon Father went out and returned a while later with Janyn, who presented me with a beautiful piece of escarlatte, a deep gold, he said, to match my eyes. I did not know whether it was the same one he had shown me in the undercroft. Our hands touched as I took the gift, and I felt a jolt as if I had been struck by lightning. A fleeting thought made me shiver: he might be a sorcerer, and that was what Mother despised. With good reason. But looking into his eyes, I decided that could not be, for I sensed no evil in him.

'You honour me with this gift,' I said, blushing as I bowed to him.

'As I am honoured to have you accept my love, Alice,' he said. Leaning close, he whispered, 'I have not forgotten our kiss.'

'Nor have I . . . Janyn,' I whispered, my heart pounding with his scent, his warmth, his nearness.

We stood for a moment, smiling into each other's eyes.

Nan, John and Mother were called to toast us. Mother obeyed, looking hideously white and without spirit. Nan cried. John beamed and seemed genuinely happy for me. Father found it difficult to sustain a cheerful mien, losing further light from his face with each glance at Mother.

And so was my betrothal made known.

Until that afternoon I had fought flutterings of joy in my heart when I thought of my betrothal to Janyn, wary of celebrating what might still be denied me. But from this point forward joy mounted in my heart. I was not unaware of the tension all about me, but I tried to disregard it. I returned to my frequent visits to St Antonin's, simply ignoring Dom Paul if he appeared. Our Lord, His mother and the saints were my comfort and my confidants. They alone knew how excited I was at the prospect of marrying Janyn. They alone also knew of my fear and sorrow at learning how false could be those who said they loved me.

> *'And I to ben youre — verray, humble, trewe,*
> *Secret, and in my paynes pacient,*
> *And evere mo desiren fresshly newe*
> *To serve, and ben ylike diligent,*
> *And with good herte al holly youre talent*
> *Receyven wel, how sore that me smerte;*
> *Lo, this mene I, myn owen swete herte.'*

— Geoffrey Chaucer, *Troilus and Criseyde*, III, ll.141–147

I had wickedly prayed that Mother would refuse to accept the Perrers' invitation to dine, but she was dressed in her finest gown and cloak and waiting in the hall for me when I emerged from Nan's ministrations. My green surcoat and azure gown, now so loose-fitting, did not feel very special compared with Mother's form-fitting gown. I wished there had been time to turn Janyn's gift into a new robe so that I might be elegant in something that had never been anyone else's, something beautiful and all mine, but of course that had not been possible in one day. Nan suggested that it would be most appropriate to wear it on the day I was wed. The thought of that day, and the puzzle of when it might be, how soon, had absorbed me for the rest of the time she helped me dress. Father had said nothing to me so far about when the wedding might take place. I would turn fourteen in September, and wondered whether he would consider that a suitable age.

Although I did not expect an answer, I asked Mother how old she had been when she wed Father.

'Too young,' she said. She seemed much subdued, speaking in a low voice, without apparent emotion. Although she had obviously taken great pains with her dressing, she was not pacing about with excitement as she usually did when about to dine at someone's home. For the first time in a long while she looked me in the eye. 'Do you think you are ready to be a wife, Alice?'

34

'How would I know, Mother?'

But she was looking past me, and I realised that Father had joined us.

'She is ready, Margery,' said Father.

Mother's expression was cold as she said, 'What would a man know of that?'

I was sorry he'd come at that moment. I'd hoped her question meant she was softening towards me, that she might advise me, be the mother I had prayed for as I knelt before the Lady altar in church. Perhaps it was not too late.

Moving closer to her, I touched her forearm. 'I pray you, Mother, advise me. Let us go out into the garden, where we might talk.' I felt a thrill of hope and tried to convey that to her with a tentative smile.

She looked on me with a confusing mixture of coldness and sorrow, as if the former were to protect herself from the latter. 'You do not know what you ask,' she said. 'You will be happier heeding your father's advice.' She brushed away my hand, still lightly resting on her arm, then gracefully moved away from me towards the door.

My breath caught in my throat as I watched her back, beautiful yet remote, almost colourless in its silvery silk. I felt foolish for having expected her to warm towards me. In truth, I was heartsick.

Father put a hand beneath my elbow and smiled encouragement as he led me to the door. 'Come! I cannot wait to see your eyes when you see how grand a home you shall have when you are wed, Alice.'

When you are wed. Those words thrilled me far more than the thought of having a grand home. I had been holding my breath. Now I felt a little dizzy as we stepped into the street. I had feared that Mother would advise me to wait a while, grow up a little more, and realised then that I did not want to wait. I wanted to be with Janyn. I understood at that moment that I feared what she might reveal. It *was* too late for us to talk.

I had seldom been in the homes of any but my own kin, and they were all much alike, suggesting prosperity without ostentation, their owners mindful of their good names, aspiring to hold civic offices such as guild master, bailiff, alderman, mayor. Even the Chaucer household was similar to ours. I had visited Nan's brother's home once, a hovel overrun by children and neglected by his ailing wife. I had not understood until then how fortunate I was. Compared with their level of comfort, I lived in luxury. I had come to believe that I was unusually privileged, that few enjoyed a better life than I did. I had no concept of the different approaches to living that might have prepared me for the home of John and Tommasa Perrers.

It was in a wealthier neighbourhood than ours, closer to London Bridge, the houses larger. Dame Tommasa welcomed us at the door, something Mother never did as she deemed it more seemly to have a servant show guests into the hall. With a cry of pleasure Dame Tommasa folded me to her bosom, then held me at arm's length and said, 'Welcome to our family, Alice. You will be as a daughter to me.' She kissed me on the forehead and then stepped aside to allow me to pass, the gesture stirring the sleeve of the overdress she wore. As it caught the light, I saw with delight the gold stars and silver moons.

As I stepped within I felt as if I were stepping into a dream. The colours dazzled my eyes as did the brightness of the hall, lit by so many lamps and wall sconces that it was almost like daylight. Tapestries and painted cloths festooned the walls; patterned and embroidered fabrics covered all the furnishings. My eyes were drawn from one beautiful item to another until I was dizzy. This house was more colourful than St Antonin's – I was amazed that a home could be so decorated, that I might abide in such beauty.

Master John, his kind eyes alight with welcome, took my hand. 'My dear Alice, you are a vision of beauty.'

I must have responded, but I cannot recall what I said for all my attention was on Janyn, who approached us with a warm smile. He wore a short, deep brunette jacket and dark gold leggings, darker than the cloth he had given me. He looked so handsome, I doubted he was truly my betrothed. I could not believe God would be so good to me.

'My beloved Alice,' he said, taking my hands and kissing each one, then looking deep into my eyes. I wished he would enfold me in his arms as his mother had. I loved the spicy, masculine scent of him and did not want to move away. But of course he continued on to greet my parents.

I was not so absorbed in Janyn that I forgot to watch how he and Mother greeted one another. My parents stood just inside the door, Father holding Mother's hand, his wide, beautifully draped sleeves revealing a slight tremor beneath. I guessed that he was tightly clutching her hand, or perhaps keeping his arm rigid in order to prevent her from making any ill-advised movement.

Janyn stopped a few strides from them, crossed his hands over his heart and bowed to Mother. 'Dame Margery,' he said. 'Welcome.'

She blushed, providing the hint of colour her pallor so desperately needed, and bowed her head. 'Master Janyn.'

She tried to meet his eyes but he prevented it, having already turned to greet Father. I had never seen my mother look so vulnerable, so uncertain.

Janyn reached out with both hands to Father and they clasped one another's forearms and gave little bows, then exchanged friendly greetings, appearing to be quite comfortable with one another.

Mother struck up a cordial conversation with Master John.

Before the round of greetings could lag, Dame Tommasa swept us all over to a table laden with food. It sat in front of double doors that stood open to a courtyard crossed and criss-crossed with beds brimming with plants. There were small arbours over which roses and flowering vines climbed and twisted. There were many varieties I did not recognise. As with the hall furnishings, the colours were so varied I felt dizzy looking at them, and yet they pleased and therefore I knew there was a pattern, a plan, behind them.

I sensed Janyn beside me. 'Shall we walk in the garden a moment?' he suggested.

'Oh, yes, please! But your mother—'

'The others will not begrudge us a moment of peace.' He offered his arm, and I put my hand on it. My heart pounding wildly, I stepped on to the gravel path with my betrothed.

'You must love this home,' I said, 'so full of light and colour. So beautiful.'

'I have happy memories of this house,' he said. 'And I still often dine here with my parents. But you must know that I no longer live here.'

I had forgotten, but I did not like to admit that, so I asked, 'Do you live nearby?'

'My house is farther down towards the river, between the grand Coldharbour and London Bridge.' A very fine location. 'Although the garden is plain compared to this one, I like to think that the house itself is quite beautiful and comfortable. I shall ask your father to bring you there, so that you might see it. After all, it will soon be your home as well.' He had led me to a far corner, to a bench beneath an apple tree heavy with fruit.

As I sat, I withdrew my hand to spread my skirts but also to hide the cold that I had felt seep into me, thinking of living in Janyn's home with him. One moment I wanted to cling to him, the next my stomach fluttered at the thought of leaving my family home and living with this man. I felt as if I had become part-stranger to myself. I took a deep breath and looked around, distracting myself by trying to name the flowers I knew.

Janyn had settled slightly sideways, so that he could face me. Now he interrupted my litany of flowers. 'I am as ill at ease as you are. Would it not be more pleasant if we had found one another by chance and begun to talk of what we like, what we dream about? It is difficult to feel comfortable when there are such expectations resting on us.'

I liked the way he had noticed my unease and did not pretend he had not. 'Yes. I feel as if the others are holding their breath and watching us while all the time pretending to ignore us.'

We both laughed then averted our eyes, as if we had become too familiar, too quickly.

'You do know that I am a widower, Alice?' he asked. 'That I was married before, and that my wife died?'

'Yes, I do.'

Daring to look at him, I found him watching me with furrowed brow, as if trying to understand what I felt. I wanted to reassure him, but I could not think what to say.

He took my hand, putting his other over it in a protective gesture. I felt comforted by his physical warmth, his compassion, and the strength I sensed in him.

'I begin life anew with you, Alice. Whatever you wish to change in our homes so that they are more to your taste and more comfortable for you, you must do. I want only your happiness.'

I knew nothing of how to choose furnishings for a home, even less how to make one look like this beautiful place in which he'd been raised. Nor had I ever planned a garden such as this. But I did not want to disappoint him by expressing my doubts.

'Did you say "homes"?' I asked. It was the first safe question that came to mind, and I did so want to keep him talking. I did not care to return to my parents, but at the same time I could not begin to explain my feelings to him when I hardly understood them myself. Practical matters seemed more solid ground. 'Do you have more than one?'

He grinned, his eyes lighting up. I did so like to make them do that. 'I do have more than one home. One in the city, one in the country, which is less than half a day's ride away. Do you like the country?'

'I do not recall ever having been beyond Smithfield. I have always lived in the city.' I studied a spider spinning a web on the corner of the arbour, not wishing to see Janyn begin to understand how young and dull I was.

'Then this shall be an adventure for you,' he said. 'Do you like riding? Have you a favourite place to ride?'

I wished he would stop asking so many questions. 'I have never ridden a horse, nor even a pony or an ass.' The spider was swinging out to catch a very small flying insect, but he missed.

'You shall have a gentle mare to begin, and you shall have lessons as soon as possible. Unless you do not wish to learn?'

I glanced up to see if he was serious. He certainly looked as if he was. 'I *do* want to learn to ride. Horses are so beautiful, so powerful. So tall! To lead them with my signals – I want to learn how. I want to feel the wind in my face. My brother John rode with Father on several journeys this past year. He looked so grand on horseback. He told me he felt free and powerful. He said that outside the city there were fields on every side, as far as he could see, and then dense woodland that could be dark as night in the middle of the day.'

Janyn was smiling, but not in such a way as to make me feel foolish to have prattled on. 'I thought you would like animals and the country,' he said. 'I look forward to riding out to the manor by your side, watching you see the land and the house for the first time.'

'I had not imagined we would live both in the city and the country,' I said, trying out the *we would live* to see how it sounded aloud. It sounded very fine. Indeed, marriage promised to be an adventure, more than I had ever hoped to experience, being a mere girl. I was framing a question about what other animals Janyn had when his father stepped into the courtyard.

'Janyn, Mistress Alice. Dame Tommasa understands how pleasant it is to sit and talk in the garden, but she has prepared a feast and will be disappointed if you do not join us at once.'

Master John's broad grin and wink underscored the humour and lightness of his message, and I felt an upwelling of gratitude that he was to be my father-in-law. I dearly loved my own father, but he had no such gift for cheery direction. Master John patted me on the back as Janyn and I proceeded with him to the laden table, and I felt truly part of the family.

I learned that day that, like many London families, they had continued the practice of mixing English and foreign blood and connections. Janyn had a younger brother who resided in a monastery in Lombardy, and a sister wed to a Lombard merchant – she lived in Milan. I was joining a larger family than I had thought, and wondered whether Janyn and I would ever travel to Lombardy to visit his siblings. Perhaps I would see the splendid market where Dame Tommasa might wear her fabulous surcoat of golden stars and silver moons.

The meal was as colourful as everything else in the Perrers household, and my appetite returned. Dame Tommasa saw to it that my wine was well watered. I was grateful to her, for with her help I enjoyed the occasion and did not make a fool of myself in any way. Mother picked at her food and said little, but Father was expansive, talking of a shipment of rare spices expected any day. Dame Tommasa asked me about myself in an easy way, already showing more warmth towards me and more interest than my own mother. Janyn discussed with her a mare for me – she knew of someone who wished to sell a horse that might do very well. My brother John teased me, certain that I would be fearful approaching a horse as tall as myself for the first time, and

Master John Perrers swore that I would prove my brother wrong.

The next morning I accompanied Janyn and my brother John to see the mare. Although I had no idea whether or not I would baulk at a horse, I had dreamed of riding through fantastic landscapes with Janyn, not so much *on* a horse as having *become* partly horse, strong and fast as the wind.

I was mortified when in reality I backed away from the enormous mare, despite finding her enchanting. She was no larger than any horse I had seen before, but I was expected to ride her, and that made quite a difference to my perception, I discovered. Janyn coaxed her to face me so that I might see how sweet she looked, how she responded to a gentle touch, and I opened my hand and held out to her the wrinkled apple I had brought. She seemed to lift it with her lips, and then she butted my hand as if to thank me. With Janyn guiding me, I stroked her face and then her neck, and suddenly I was being lifted up to sit sideways on her. It was only for a moment. Lifting me down again, Janyn let his lips brush my cheek and forehead. Oh, sweet Mary, Mother of God, was this how it felt to be beloved of God? I crossed myself, realising the blasphemy of that thought, and my brother laughed, thinking I protected myself against the mare.

It was the mare's owner who laughed at John's teasing. 'Not at all, young man. You saw how she sat so sturdily. Nay, it is love that has her blushing and praying!' He nodded at Janyn and me. 'May you be blessed with many children, and enjoy the begetting of them!' He showed his uneven teeth as he laughed with his whole face, his whole round body.

At first I was not certain whether or not to join in, but Janyn nodded to me as he laughingly thanked the man, and I echoed his words and cheer.

It was the beginning of a new, exciting life for me. But there were moments when I shrank from it, wishing I might return to being just a girl with no betrothed. Mother had said nothing to me after the dinner at the Perrers' home. Nothing. And when John and I spoke of the mare at dinner, she loudly embarked on a tale of her walk to the market that day, and what she planned to change in the garden. Father did not rebuke her. Nan was

41

white with indignation. I ached, deep inside, and imagined my icy hands shattering against the table as I pressed down on it in rising.

I had not been long with Janyn that day, though the short time together had been sweet, and it was several days more before I learned that the mare was now mine and my lessons would begin as soon as my parents might arrange to take me to the stables near Smithfield. Janyn would be away for a while on business. My heart sank at that news, but soared when Father announced at dinner the next day that the wedding was set for late-October.

Mother said – to him, not to me – 'Your mother has offered to help Alice prepare. To do this with as much ease as might be, she has suggested that Alice stay with her until the wedding. I told her that was quite suitable, do you not agree?'

I almost choked on the ale in my mouth, and looked to Father for an angry response.

But he nodded. 'I have already told Mother that I think it will work very well for all concerned if Alice lives with her until the wedding.' He spoke in an oddly soft voice and avoided looking my way.

Little Mary cried out, 'I want to go with her!'

'Grandmother should come here,' said Will, banging his fist on the table.

I would have laughed were I not in shock. Even John asked why Grandmother or I could not walk from one house to the other, we lived so close. Nan muttered something under her breath that I could not understand.

But Father said, 'It is already decided.' From the set of his jaw I read that to be the last word on the subject.

I had said nothing, and continued mute through the meal. I felt a numbing chill arising from my own mother, and a wall between my father and me. Father had always compensated for Mother's indifference towards me with affection and companionship. I had treasured my time with him, learning about his trade. Had been so grateful to him for insisting I attend school. But now, though I had done all he'd asked, my ally had joined my enemy. I knew no words to describe my sense of abandonment. The pain was deep and profound. I could not look him in the eyes. I doubt he noticed, for I could not imagine how he would have the gall to look into mine.

Afterwards I collapsed in Nan's embrace and wept until I felt too sick to do anything but curl up on my bed and try not to think. I was blessed with such exhaustion that I sank into sleep. In the morning I lay in bed wondering whether I had dreamed of my exile, but I had just pushed back the covers and touched my feet to the floorboards when Nan bustled in.

'I'm relieved to see you already rising,' she said. 'I've left Will and Mary in the hall while I help you gather your things. I dare not leave them long.'

'I'm to go at once? Before breaking my fast?' I cried, still too sleepy to check my despair.

Nan looked up from the chest she had opened. 'Oh, my sweet Alice. No, of course you are not being sent away without food. The master awaits you in the hall. He hopes to explain to you that you are not being punished, but that he thought you would enjoy spending some time with your grandmother, Dame Agnes. He says that his mother wished to do this for you, to have pretty gowns made for you and to provide a welcoming hall to which your betrothed might come to be with you.'

'Are you certain that you do not know why Mother hates Janyn so?' I asked her once more.

'To understand your mother . . .' Nan shook out my second best gown with more force than necessary '. . . I do not wish to try that. I imagine spiders in her mind.' Realising what she had said about her mistress, she crossed herself and told me to forget her comment. 'I am angry with her for frightening you and behaving as if she does not love you as she loves John, Will and Mary. But she is beset by devils, Alice. You are the victim, not the cause, of her poor mothering. How much happier you will be with Dame Agnes, eh?'

'But I won't have you and Mary and Will, or even John or Father there.'

That won me a sympathetic embrace and kiss.

'No, we cannot all go with you, my sweet.' The affection in her eyes calmed me a little.

'Will you visit?'

'I believe the master will visit you with your sister and brothers.'

'And you?'

She shrugged. 'It is his choice whether or not I accompany him. But you will see me, I promise, even if I come by myself.'

I gave her a grateful hug.

Although we had spent little time alone together, I loved being with Grandmother Agnes. She seemed genuinely to enjoy my presence, and always asked what I thought of the food, of her gown, of anything new in the hall. She was a handsome woman, tall and strong, and I admired the way she dominated any room she entered. Mother was beautiful in a soft, pretty way, and people always wanted to make her smile and fetch and carry for her; Grandmother Agnes needed to make more effort to look beautiful, which she did with her delight in beautiful things, and there was about her an authority and wisdom that inspired people to respect her and seek her advice. I thought I would rather be like my grandmother than my mother. I had thought about going to Grandmother Agnes for advice on my conflicted feelings about marriage. But she could also be unexpectedly critical, so I had hesitated. She always said she wanted only the best for me, but her sharp honesty could sting. Still, she was one of my favourite adults. And Grandfather Edmund as well, who was kind and gentle.

So it was not the prospect of biding with my Salisbury grandparents that pained me. I was disappointed that instead of leaving my home and my siblings on Janyn's arm I was to be sent off beforehand, as if Mother could not rid herself of me quickly enough. Father had said a few days earlier that he would miss the easy companionship we enjoyed, especially in the undercroft, looking at his wares, studying accounts, weighing strategies of sales or purchases. Now he, too, was pushing me out of the door. That hurt the most.

I did not believe at the time that anything I said would make any difference – for some reason Mother hated Janyn and the thought of my marrying into that family, and she was washing her hands of me. So be it. I resolved to make the best of it.

At last I joined Father and my siblings in the hall for bread, cheese, and thick ale. Mary began to cry the moment she saw me, and Will had little appetite. Only John expressed envy.

'The Perrers will give you all you desire,' he said. 'I must work for my keep.'

'I would not mind working,' I said. 'If you have no work, the day is too long.'

John laughed. 'You will soon be so busy at night, you will be sleeping all the day,' he said.

'John!' Father barked, his face flushed with irritation. 'I will not have you speaking so at my table.'

Though he dropped his head and muttered an apology to Father, me and Nan, John was smirking. I was sitting at just the right angle to see that. His comment had made me feel uncomfortably hot, and I hated the fact that he noticed my blush when he glanced my way and mimed a kiss.

But he was my brother, and I knew that this familiarity would fade once we were no longer together, day in and day out. I had learned this lesson two days ago. My best friend Geoffrey was home on a visit to his parents and we had been uncomfortable when we met, seeing each other so changed, not knowing what had happened in each other's life. He had looked so surprised by the news of my betrothal that I had found it difficult to decide what I might divulge about my feelings that would not embarrass him. It seemed easier to speak of the mare I would soon learn to ride.

The resulting meeting was so awkward and unsatisfying that I'd felt miserable afterwards. I saw that our friendship would die if I were not more forthright with Geoffrey. I had decided last night to ask my grandparents if he might visit me, and vowed I would confide in him then all I was feeling, and trust that he would try to understand. I needed his good humour and frank advice.

Too soon Father rose from the table and said that we must depart. Mary burst into tears again and I held her so tightly she squirmed a little, but when I began to release her she clung to me.

'Don't go!' she wailed.

I lifted her and sat back down on the bench, blotting her tears with the hem of my gown.

'I love you, Mary, and I wish you could come and stay with me. But you need Nan, and she cannot come too and abandon Will, don't you see? I would have been leaving in a few months, this is just a little sooner.' I was babbling, but she had stopped crying, her pretty face calming. When she began to hiccup, I managed to make her laugh about it. Will joined in our laughter. 'You see? Nothing has changed, we are all still as silly as ever!'

Mary clapped her hands with glee. I gently slid her off my lap and rose, brushing my skirt. Father nodded to me and we hurried out, a servant following with my belongings.

As we crossed the square, I asked if I might stop in the church to say a prayer to the Blessed Virgin.

Father sighed with impatience. 'I have customers to see today, Alice. We cannot linger. Perhaps my parents will accompany you to church later. St Antonin's is close enough to their home.' He reached for my hand.

I moved beyond his reach and stopped, forcing him to turn back to see what had happened.

'You are very eager to rid yourself of me,' I said. I had intended to hold my tongue, but his refusal to pause at the church was too much. 'I won Janyn, as you wished, and now I am so punished. Why?'

He glanced around to see who might overhear. Apparently he saw no one significant, because he did not chide me or say he could not answer that. 'I pray you, Daughter, believe me that I do not do this to punish you, but to give you more ease so that you might enjoy preparing for your wedding. I wish you joy, my child, and this seemed the best way to allow you that.'

'Because of Mother?'

Father lifted his open hands, palms up. He slumped a little, and his expression was a mixture of great weariness and sorrow. 'You have asked why she is so angry. She is angry with life, Alice, not you. She needs your prayers.'

I was young, I was in pain, I was frightened, and his answer sounded to me like dissimulation, not honesty. But I did not challenge him.

'Come,' I said, 'my grandparents await me.' I resumed walking, and Father fell in beside me. I could almost taste his defeat, and loathed him for it. I was raw with emotions I only vaguely understood.

Grandfather greeted us, and then sent me out to the garden to find Grandmother while he spoke to Father.

I found Dame Agnes, as she liked me to call her, kneeling in the kitchen garden separating bulbs. She enjoyed seeing to her own garden despite my grandfather chiding her for not ordering the servants to see to the dirty work.

'Hands that know the earth in all its moods know God's wisdom,' she liked to say, though she always wore costly gloves to protect her hands, and a coarse gown that she shed for her more elegant everyday attire before she crossed the threshold again, a wattle hut tucked behind a hedge reserved for this purpose.

'Talk to me while I finish my task,' she said. 'It will not take long. Then we shall begin to make our plans. But just talk about little things for now.'

I told her about my mare.

She sat back on her heels, clapping the dirt off her gloves and nodding with a satisfied look on her broad face.

'I told your father that Janyn Perrers would know how to treat you, and I am pleased to hear that I was right. You should have been riding long ago. Astride. It strengthens the legs and that will help you birth your babies without all the fuss your mother made about it.'

Horses and childbirth? Perhaps I was more ignorant than I had realised. I had seen animals birthing, and I knew the babies came out between the hind legs, so I understood how there might be a connection. But strength?

'Women sit in birthing chairs, don't they? Why need my legs be strong?'

Dame Agnes frowned at me for a moment, and then began to gather her gardening tools as she said, 'To carry the weight of the child, Alice. Now come, I would greet my son before he hurries away.'

Later that evening, when my grandmother came to see if I was comfortable in the pretty little solar room she'd had prepared for me, I was feeling wretched. I knew I was welcome and loved, indeed my grandparents behaved as if they could not believe their good fortune to have me all to themselves. Still, I missed Mary, Will, John and Nan, even Father. This pretty room felt unfamiliar; the pillows smelled of other people, not me. That I had several pillows to choose from, covered in soft, pretty linen, was something for which I knew that I should be grateful, and I was. But despite how comfortable the bed was, I felt far away from everything I knew.

'Might you stay awhile and talk, Dame Agnes?' I asked.

'On the morrow, child. You need your rest, and so do I. Tomorrow we shall look at cloth and decorations for your new gowns. Perhaps leather for shoes as well.'

'My friend Geoffrey Chaucer is home for a little while. Might he visit me here?'

'Of course, my love. Send him a message on the morrow. Invite his family to sup with us one day soon if you like.'

'Thank you, Dame Agnes.'

She smiled and kissed me on the forehead, tucking the covers up to my chin. 'Sleep well, my beauty.'

'May God bless you and keep you,' I whispered. I could not risk speaking more loudly because I was close to tears and it was clear that my grandmother did not want to be forced to linger at my bedside.

She gave me another hug. 'May He bless you and keep you as well, dear Alice.' As she straightened, she glanced around the little room. 'Just think how much grander your bedchamber will be when you are wed. Janyn Perrers will make a fine husband.' With a contented sigh she slipped out.

At least I was now with people who seemed genuinely happy for me and could begin to look forward with joy to my wedding day. Oh, but I was so lonely. For such a long time I'd slept with Nan, and then Nan and Mary. Now I was all alone in a bed that was hardly smaller than the one the three of us had shared. I flailed around for a while, finding it difficult to get comfortable. It was not that I was cold, I had all the covers I could want, but I felt exposed, unguarded. It occurred to me to hug a pillow. That helped, and I slept.

I woke to the sound of my grandmother singing in the next room. It was a hymn to the Virgin, I think, but what struck me was how happy she sounded early in the morning, and that I had known her for so long and had no idea she sang so beautifully. To wake in such an atmosphere cheered me, and the pain and loneliness of the past day receded.

Only now did I think about what she had planned for today – *we shall look at cloth and decorations for your new gowns*. It had not sunk in that I might have *new* gowns. My own gowns! While I lay there pondering this delightful prospect, a maidservant scratched on the tapestry covering the doorway.

'I've brought you some warm cider and a small loaf of bread to break your fast, Mistress Alice,' she called out.

I welcomed her in. 'But you need not have carried it up here,' I said. I had never been served food in bed unless I was quite ill.

She set the cup and loaf beside me, on a little stool, and then glanced around the room. 'Have you all you need, Mistress Alice? I shall fetch whatever you are lacking and bring it when I come to dress you in a little while.'

'I have no comb,' I said. I'd realised it last night; I had never needed my own.

Her sweet face lit up. 'I will return with one in a little while.' With a bob, she withdrew.

I pulled the stool over to the window and opened the shutters. The sun streamed in, and as I ate I watched a bird hop about on the neighbour's roof. I was happy, just simply happy.

In a while the maidservant returned with a comb, the frame of oak, the teeth of bone. It was plain, but the teeth were remarkably even and complete.

'Shall I comb your hair for you, Mistress Alice?'

Even if she had not sounded eager to do so I would have said yes, for I have always loved having my hair combed. She was gentle and thorough, complimenting me on the curl and thickness of my hair.

'And such pretty colours – gold, red and brown. It changes as you move.'

I asked her how long she had worked for my grandmother.

'I do not work for Dame Agnes, Mistress Alice. I work for Master Janyn Perrers. I have been here only a few days, to help prepare this room for you and to begin the needlework on your smocks.'

It had not occurred to me that she might be from outside the household. 'How long have you worked for Master Janyn?'

'It will be two years this Michaelmas, Mistress. I was a kitchen maid and he told me I could be a lady's maid if I kept myself clean and tidy, and if I learned to do fine needlework, paid heed to how fine folk dress and how they like to be served.'

I had turned to look up at her and caught a look of such gratitude on her sweet though plain face that I quickly averted my eyes before she noticed that I had intruded on her emotion. It had been a fine thing for Janyn to do, I thought.

'How old are you?'

'Seventeen, Mistress.'

Older than me, yet she was small and had no figure to speak of.

'How would you compare this household to that of Master Janyn?' I asked, eager to hear more of him.

'It is quiet here, and the mistress is so kind and patient,' she said. 'You are blessed with kind grandparents.'

'I am, I know. But tell me more. Master Janyn keeps a noisy household?'

'Busy. We are always rushing to prepare food and chambers and space in the hall. He has many guests – merchants and some-times even finer folk. And, of course, there is only Dame Gertrude who oversees us all.'

She had finished brushing my hair and now bent over my coffer of clothes, sorting through the shifts and gowns. In the bright morning light it all looked limp, wrinkled, and dingy, except for the azure gown and green surcoat.

'Finer folk?' I asked, not wanting to drop the promising thread of our conversation. She looked uncertain, but I could not tell whether it was about my clothes or the wisdom of answering my question. 'I'm soon to be mistress in his home,' I said. 'I should like to know all that I can so that I might be prepared.'

She turned to me with a broad smile. 'I know. You are to be the mistress of the house. And I'm to be your lady's maid, if you will have me.' She shook out my azure gown. 'Would you like to wear this today? Dame Agnes says you are shopping for cloth and other items for your new clothes after you see what she has already collected.'

I was not certain whether I should wear my only presentable gown for such activities. But Grandmother was not there to advise me. 'Yes . . . what is your name?'

'Gwen, Mistress Alice.'

'Yes, I will wear this.' I could change if Dame Agnes dis-approved. 'Now, who are these finer folk? Will I be entertaining nobles?'

Gwen looked worried. 'I was told never to gossip about those who came to the house.'

'Is it gossip to tell me? Is that not why you were sent here now to be my maid – to tell me about the household over which I'll soon be mistress? I'm choosing fabrics and decorations for my clothes today – I should know how grandly I will need to dress.' I almost took it back, I sounded so like my mother, assuming that Gwen was simpler than I was and using that to manipulate her.

But Gwen's face cleared and she leaned close to whisper, 'Once the King's mother, the old queen, dined in the hall.'

'The Queen Mother? Isabella of France?'

Gwen nodded, her eyes huge. 'Beautiful, she was, no matter how old she may be.'

'How did she come to dine with Master Janyn?'

'And his parents,' said Gwen. 'They all seemed old friends.'

My stomach fluttered. I had never been in the presence of royalty. Nor many nobles, for that matter. To be the mistress of a house that entertained Isabella of France, the King's mother – was this the source of Mother's anger? Was she jealous of the life I would have as Janyn's wife? I could imagine her delight in dining with the Queen Mother, a woman renowned for her beauty, and, I imagined, surrounded by important and elegant people and all that was luxurious and desirable.

'Was the Queen Mother gentle and kind?'

Gwen giggled. 'Oh no, Mistress. I would not say so. But she was once Queen and her father was King of France, so she need not please anyone but herself.'

And God, I thought. 'Does Master Janyn have other great folk as guests?'

'None so grand as she, Mistress Alice.'

I grew quiet as she finished dressing me. She took care to arrange my hair just as Nan had, catching it away from my face and letting it flow down my back. I felt a twinge of sadness, thinking of Nan, wondering what she and Mary and Will were doing.

I soon learned that I had been right to worry about coaxing information from Gwen.

I found Grandmother in her chamber surrounded by an assortment of cloth that would have seemed more appropriate in Father's undercroft. Her own gown that morning was a pale, patterned wool with pretty pearls swirled here and there on the bodice and the long fitted sleeves. It seemed very fine to wear on a day given to planning the clothing for her granddaughter's new life. Yet I had seldom seen her in anything as plain as my everyday gowns.

She noticed me looking at her gown and the surrounding finery and made a face, crinkling her nose and pursing her lips. 'Sinful, I know,' she said. 'I collect pieces that I like and save them until I find a use for them. I quiet my conscience with the thought of all this being given to the poor of the parish when I die.'

'We shall have elegant beggars on our streets then,' I said.

With a little yelp of surprise Grandmother dissolved into laughter, and I could not help but join her. We both laughed so hard we wiped tears from our eyes. It was a happy beginning, and I said a silent prayer of thanks for such a loving and good-tempered grandmother.

After we had looked at several pretty cloths in shades of gold and a brunette that was especially fine, which she thought suitable for everyday gowns, she showed me a most elegant brocade in a pale red.

'Perhaps it is too elegant for a merchant's wife,' she said. 'I have not found an occasion on which I thought this appropriate for myself, to be sure.'

I loved the pattern and the pretty colour, and it was so soft and smooth yet had substance. Dame Agnes held the cloth up to me and commented on how well I would look in the colour, how it brought out my sanguine complexion.

'The clothes cut down from your mother's were pretty, but your complexion is so different from Margery's that the colours suitable for her are not bold enough for you.'

I smiled and curtsied.

'Fit for a queen,' she murmured.

'Or for one dining with the King's mother?' I suggested.

She looked amused. 'I did not know you were such a dreamer, Alice. The Lady Isabella? Now when would you dine with her?'

'Gwen said . . .' I bit my lip. 'I must have misunderstood. Might something so fine be suitable for my marriage feast?'

But Grandmother was not so easily distracted. 'What else has Gwen said about Janyn's household?'

'I asked what it was like. She said they are always busy preparing for guests . . . merchants and even finer folk. I asked who she meant by finer folk. She was not gossiping, Dame Agnes. In faith, she said she was not to speak of the master's guests. But I insisted that she tell me about the household so that I might know how to prepare for my role as its mistress, how I might be expected to dress.'

Dame Agnes sighed as she nodded. 'It is true you must know what will be expected of you, Alice, but a maidservant must be discreet. You must be able to trust her not to speak out of place of anything that happens in your home. Janyn would not be pleased to hear that she had mentioned a guest about whom he has chosen to be secretive.'

'You did not know that the Queen Mother had been his guest?'

My grandmother shook her head, and I saw in her eyes an enigmatic expression, of concern bordering on fear.

'Have you met the Queen Mother?' I asked, hoping to glean more of her feelings.

'No. But when I was not long married, I was with my father when he spoke to our lady Queen Philippa. She is a blessing to this realm, a graceful, kind lady loved by all who meet her.' Her expression had sharpened. There was a glint in my grandmother's eyes then and an edge to her voice, even as she smiled and said such sweet things of the Queen. My puzzlement must have shown, because Grandmother shook her head. 'Such things were never said of the former Queen. You do know of her disgrace? That she made war against her husband, the holy, anointed King?'

'But the people supported her in setting her son – *the King's son* – on the throne.'

Grandmother pressed her lips together and shook her head. 'I'll say no more of her. It will be for your husband to tell you of her, as he knows her.'

I was intrigued, and not altogether pleasantly, but I deemed it best to return to the matter that most concerned me rather than aggravate Grandmother with more questions about the former queen, a woman of whom she clearly did not approve.

'I like Gwen, Dame Agnes. I do not wish to make trouble for her. If she is to be my maid, she should answer all my questions, should she not?' It was not so much that I could not bear anyone else to be my maid, but that her indiscretion was my fault, my doing.

'Calm yourself, Alice. I must consider this.' Dame Agnes stood for a long while gazing out of the window.

I wanted to ask her how well she knew Janyn, but I could not think how to ask it without sounding disrespectful. I wanted no strain between us. I needed Dame Agnes's love and trust.

I fingered the red brocade. 'It is so beautiful. Perhaps someday I shall have a red gown.'

Dame Agnes suddenly spun around, all smiles once more. 'And so you shall, my love. I have something quite wonderful to show you.' She held up a finger for me to wait and hurried out of the solar. As I waited for her I touched the cloth, imagining all the gowns it would make. In a little while Dame Agnes returned with Gwen, who carried a parcel wrapped in undyed cloth. Setting it on the small table at which we had been sitting, Gwen bobbed to both of us – I noticed that her eyes were swollen, as if she had been crying – and left the room. I was certain she had been scolded.

'Open it,' said Grandmother. 'It is a gift from your betrothed.'

'Another?' Upset about Gwen, I fumbled with the cord but finally loosened the knot and peeled back the wrapping. Within was a scarlet cloth dyed blood red, the colour much darker and more saturated than the pretty brocade. 'Oh, Dame Agnes, what a bold colour! Is this dyed in *graine*?' That was a costly dye derived from an insect.

'It is, Alice.'

I lifted a corner and touched it to my cheek. 'And such soft wool.'

'I confess, I could not resist peeking. He has an eye for colour, does he not?'

It was not as pretty as the brocade, but I could see that it would be more suitable for a merchant's wife, and much softer against my skin. 'Will this be a gown for me?'

'Who else? He said that it is a colour that most young women could not wear without looking as if they were dressed in their mothers' clothes, but that you already have the grace and bearing to wear it.' She draped the brocade over it. 'Perhaps we might make a headdress with this to wear beneath a thin veil.' She stood back and considered it, finally nodding.

'Is red not a colour for royalty?'

'There are those who say so. Do not wear it if the dowager Queen Isabella visits your hall, eh?' Grandmother must have sensed my uncertainty, for she added, 'Many women wear such colours, child, depending on the occasion or the guest list. You will see that your mother's taste is quite narrow. Permit yourself to explore all colours, textures, patterns, styles. Janyn will be able to guide you – with guests such as Gwen described, he must know how to comport himself and rule his household.'

Rule his household. That brought me back to the problem. 'Did you reprimand Gwen?'

'I did. I told her that I trusted she would not betray her master again, and she vowed she would not.'

'She will resent me now!'

'Her feelings are unimportant, Alice. A maidservant serves *you*. I did tell her that you did not mean to make trouble for her.'

I was about to say that I hoped Gwen would forgive me, but held my tongue as Grandmother's advice sank in.

'I will not promise that I'll say nothing to Janyn,' she said. 'I shall consider it a while longer. She is skilled in needlework, her stitches very fine. She would be difficult to replace. And your betrothed does wish for you to be well-dressed. But that he said nothing to me about hosting the King's dam suggests that Gwen was trusted to remain silent about it, and he should know of her indiscretion.'

I understood the seriousness of the situation, but my part in the matter was something I could not ignore. 'I will vouch for her. I shall be responsible for her conduct from this moment.'

'It is a noble offer, Alice, but one that you are too young and innocent to make with full knowledge of what it might mean to you.' Again I detected something like fear in my grandmother's voice. 'The royal family expect absolute loyalty from those they patronise, and if your betrothed believes Gwen is not to be trusted, you would find your support of her impossible to sustain. Still, I have not said for certain that I will speak with Janyn. And if I do, I would suggest that he speak to Gwen and then give her another chance to prove her obedience.'

'Thank you, Dame Agnes.'

'I've done nothing yet, and Janyn might believe it foolhardy to allow her another chance.' She set the red escarlatte and the pale red brocade aside and brought forward a Lincoln green silk patterned with gold stripes no wider than a strand of hair, holding it up to my face. 'Oh, that brightens your eyes. With pearls like these, perhaps?' She pointed to the lustrous ones on her own gown.

I liked the colour. It was deeper than the greens Mother wore. The silk rustled as I touched it, and I could imagine the shimmer the pearls would add to it. I still could not believe my own good fortune. I would be better dressed than my mother, and not because I wished it, but because my husband insisted.

'So Janyn cares how I dress because I reflect his prosperity and status?'

Grandmother looked at me with a bemused expression. 'Yes, but I believe it is also because he thinks you so beautiful, Alice.' She draped a lock of my hair over the green silk. 'You have won his heart, child. I have great hopes for your marriage. He will provide for, protect, and cherish you.'

Letting go of the silk, I sat down and took a deep breath. It seemed a good time to address my confused emotions about Janyn.

'What is amiss, child?'

'How should I feel about my betrothed, Dame Agnes? When Janyn is near, should I feel hot and as if I might faint?'

It was the first time I'd seen Grandmother blush. She averted her eyes. 'Such questions, Alice.'

'Why do I embarrass you? Did you never feel this way about Grandfather?'

Lifting the green silk, she stroked it with the back of her hand. 'So long ago.' She sighed and her face softened as she again brushed the silk, then held it to her cheek and closed her eyes. 'Oh, yes, Alice, I remember the sweetness. He was not so handsome as your Janyn, but he was tall and strong and had a wicked laugh and a devilish glint in his eyes, and I adored him.'

'Did you choose each other?'

Dame Agnes chuckled. 'Times have not changed so much as that. Of course we were not permitted to choose. But for us it did not matter, for we liked one another well enough from the start.' She set aside the green silk and lifted the red escarlatte. 'And it seems to me that it is much the same for you and Janyn.' Now she met my gaze. 'What you describe would be considered a sin by many, but I counted it a blessing that I felt so about your grandfather. Lovemaking can be a frightening thing for a woman who does not welcome her husband's touch.'

I could think of many men I would not wish to touch me, and shivered at the thought. I could not imagine ever shrinking from Janyn's touch. And yet I feared there was much I still did not understand.

'Is it . . . Does it hurt, Dame Agnes?'

She dropped the cloth and enfolded me in her arms, holding me close. 'The first time, yes, my child. I will not lie to you. But after that first time,' she stroked my hair, 'it is quite another thing altogether. And, in truth, I remember the pleasure of that first night far better than I do the pain.' She held me away from her and I was relieved to see that she was smiling. 'He has been wed before. He will know how to be gentle. Imagine the comfort of being enfolded in the warmth of your beloved's arms. Just the two of you.' She kissed my cheek.

But I was not entirely reassured. 'Is it like – I've seen the dogs . . .' My throat closed up and I could not go on, nor could I look my grandmother in the eye.

She took my hands. 'Yes and no, Alice. God raised us above the animals and gave us souls. When a man is cruel to a woman, he denies his God-given soul, becoming a lowly animal, a beast without a soul. When he is gentle and loving, it is not at all a beastly act. And I am certain that your Janyn will be gentle and loving with you. Oh, my poor child, your hands are so cold!' She rubbed them, then lifted my chin. 'Look at me, Alice.'

I reluctantly obeyed. It had taken all my courage to ask what I had so far.

'What frightens you?'

'Am I a beast without a soul to desire him as I do? To dream of him holding me?'

Tears welled in Dame Agnes's eyes and she slowly shook her head. 'Not at all, Alice. I still desire your grandfather and dream of him doing far more sinful things than simply holding me.'

'Truly?' My voice came out in a squeak.

'Truly. Now sit down and lower your head between your knees and take a deep breath before you faint.'

I did so, took a deep breath, and began to cough.

'Now another.'

Again I coughed. She rubbed my back in slow, calming circles.

'Your silly mother should have told you some of this. Well, we'll not mention her again.' She patted my back. 'I think you might lift your head now, but very slowly.'

When she could see that I was breathing more easily, she smiled. 'It is good to have that behind us. Now we can enjoy ourselves.'

For the rest of the morning we spoke of headdresses, veils, jewellery, gowns, cloaks and household furnishings, until I felt comfortable once more. In that space of time I learned much that I had not gleaned from either of my parents about the latest fashions. I felt as if Grandmother had opened a door on a new world of possibilities. As she was tidying me before we went down to the hall to dine with Grandfather, Dame Agnes tilted my chin again so that we were eye to eye. She was serious once more.

'What we discussed – your desire for Janyn and mine for Edmund – is never to be shared with anyone else. Promise me that you will keep this to yourself.'

Her hazel eyes were lit from behind by fire – apprehension, I guessed, from the pinching around her mouth and a certain breathlessness in her speech.

'I will keep it to myself, Dame Agnes. But why? You said it was natural.'

'There are those who would tuck such information away for a time when they could use it against us. A woman is to be virginal in public. Our virtue is our worth. Only our husbands may know of our passions.'

'And we of each other's.'

Grandmother smiled. 'Yes, my sweet.' She brushed my cheek and pressed her forehead against mine for a moment. 'Yes, my sweet Alice.'

By evening I was exhausted both in body and spirit. I retired early to my chamber and was tucked into bed, enjoying the sensation of floating between waking and sleeping when I became aware of my grandparents' voices. At first they were merely a hum in the background, a comforting reminder of their presence near me. But they gradually grew louder, until I could understand much of what they were saying.

'I intended to ask his leave to tell you, Agnes,' said Grandfather, his tone placating. I could imagine him with his hands lifted, palms out towards Grandmother, a sign that he wished to calm her.

'You have never kept anything from me.' The hurt in Grandmother's voice startled me. I could not remember having heard that in her voice before.

'We speak of the former Queen, Agnes. I did not think it prudent to mention her. I daresay she has spies everywhere.'

'What is he about, Edmund? Why would Janyn Perrers have aught to do with her?'

'Her indiscretions were many years ago, my love. She is an old woman. It seems a small miracle that she yet lives.'

'That was not my question.' Now Grandmother sounded irritated. 'What does she want from the Perrers family?'

'Or they from her?'

'No, no. She is the one in control, you can be sure of it.'

'I swear to you, I do not know. I have given it little thought. It is best we do not know.'

'But our Alice is joining that family, Edmund. Our sweet Alice. What does this mean for her?'

'That she shall not live a dull life,' said Grandfather with a chuckle.

'This is no laughing matter, Husband.'

I heard nothing for a moment and was about to rise and press my ear against the flimsy wall that separated us when I heard footsteps, one of them walking across the floorboards.

'After all, the girl has survived Margery's neglect and her unforgivable jealousy of late,' said Grandfather.

Jealousy? So I had guessed right. My mother resented my marrying into a family of such wealth and connections.

'Edmund! She is but a child.'

'She is strong and clever, Agnes. She will survive an encounter or two with the She-Wolf.'

I'd forgotten that the Queen Mother was sometimes called the She-Wolf for her audacity in declaring war against her husband and wresting his crown from him. Although her lover Roger Mortimer had been executed for his part in that, and for arranging the secret and most horrible execution of her husband, the former King, Isabella had merely been sequestered in the castle at Berkhamsted for a few years and then in Castle Rising, a comfortable place in which she was now free to entertain. And obviously she was free to travel to London and dine with my future husband.

My grandparents grew quiet, and I tried to drowse once more, but my mind was afire with what I'd overheard. They were uneasy about Janyn's acquaintance with the Dowager Queen, my grandmother going so far as to wonder whether my joining the Perrers family was still a wise choice. And my mother was jealous. I wondered how much she knew about Janyn's royal acquaintances.

When at last I fell asleep, I dreamed of a beautiful golden wolf devouring all the blossoms in Dame Tommasa's pretty garden, trampling the stalks and vines in her careless grazing. I stepped into the garden to call her away. Blood stained her muzzle and dripped from her lolling tongue, and in her eyes I saw that the destruction of the garden was a small thing compared to what she had devoured in the hall. She turned and trotted towards me. I could not move. I must have screamed in my sleep, for I woke enfolded in my grandmother's arms.

'Sweet Alice, you are safe. Whatever the dream, it cannot reach you here.'

I was alert enough to stop myself from describing it, fearful that Dame Agnes would realise I'd overheard; I valued the opportunity to hear what she and Grandfather were not telling me. As to the dream not reaching me in my waking world, I prayed that she was right.

In the next few days I was measured for boots by a boot maker who showed us leather in colours I could not believe were not painted, and so soft that I imagined it would feel as if I were barefoot when I wore my new boots and slippers. Dame Agnes, her own maid, and Gwen measured me over and over again, and

60

we all began to work on my gowns, using an alcove near my bedchamber in which shutters could be opened to welcome north and south light. It was a good time of year for such an endeavour, with the weather warm enough to allow us to sit by the open windows and the sun shining almost every day. While we worked, Dame Agnes talked about household routines, the duties of the lady of the household, and what clothing was appropriate for various social functions. She also bade me attend her when she was seeing to the household and the garden so that I might learn by assisting her. At first the complexity of the household and the authority with which Dame Agnes addressed the servants overwhelmed me. I could not imagine mastering such details or taking command in such wise. But with repetition the tasks grew familiar, and as I grew more confident I found my voice. Each day I felt a little less apprehensive about running Janyn's household.

Gwen had adopted what Dame Agnes referred to as a respectful silence, even when dressing me. At first I accepted it as the proper behaviour, but as it continued I detected a tension between us and felt more and more strongly that hers was a wounded silence. That would not do, not if she were to be my maid for many years to come. It was too uncomfortable. I feared that her resentment could bloom into something more hostile and that I would then be unable to trust her. I did not choose to live that way.

On the fourth morning since she had grown silent, I spoke.

'Gwen, I regret having put you in such a difficult position, wanting to please me and yet having been warned by Master Janyn to refrain from gossip about his guests. I apologise.'

I had not expected her to warm to me at once, but was surprised that her response was to stop combing my hair and to back away a few steps.

'Yes, Mistress,' she whispered.

'I've made you even less easy with me. What is it, Gwen? What is amiss?' I knew it was not the way I should address a servant, but I would not be waited on by a woman who nursed a grudge against me.

'I did not think you would tell Dame Agnes, Mistress.' Her eyes were lowered, hands hanging limply at her sides.

It was a hard lesson for me. I felt foolish and completely in the wrong. I did not like it at all. But I'd watched Gwen's needlework and was pleased with the way she dressed my hair and cared for my clothing and myself. To argue that I had mentioned the Queen Mother without intending to would perhaps make her even less confident of my discretion, so I accepted the blame.

'I am chastised, Gwen. In future I'll not repeat what we have discussed. But I expect you to be just as loyal to me. Do you accept that?' I turned to look at her, and felt quite bold and mature as I said, 'In faith, you must look me in the eye and tell me your decision. Either we trust one another or I find another lady's maid. You already know my preference. What say you?'

The eyes she lifted to mine were satisfyingly astonished.

'I—' She took a breath. 'I pledge my loyalty, Mistress Alice. I beg your forgiveness. I have been disrespectful in my behaviour. I am happy with you and Master Janyn. I pray you, believe me, I will be true in heart and speech.'

'I believe you. We'll say no more about it. Now come, Gwen, comb my hair.'

I was far more comfortable that day as we all sat with our needlework, and though she did not ask what had transpired, I could tell that Dame Agnes sensed the shift between us as well.

The following day our comfortable routine was happily interrupted when Geoffrey came to dine with us. I was so glad to see him. It had been a week since I had seen Nan or my brothers and sister, all of whom I sorely missed, and he was the next best thing – in some ways even better, because I could confide in him and ask his opinion, and I sorely needed a confidant.

While we dined Geoffrey entertained me and my grandparents with tales of his fellow pages and the embarrassing mistakes he was learning to avoid.

'I lacked education in the finer points of interpreting one's dress, you see. Suddenly I was expected to know a person's rank merely by looking at their clothing. I had thought to learn their faces, but there was no time for that.' He glanced at my new Lincoln green silk gown and said, 'For example, you are a propertied lady of the realm, or the daughter of a prosperous Italian or French merchant. But not a wife, for your hair is loose. Ah, you confuse me, my good friend, for I know you well enough to be sure I am wrong on all but your being a maiden.'

'Not at all,' Dame Agnes said, with a teasing light in her eyes, 'for she is the betrothed of a man who is Italian on his mother's side and trades extensively in Italy and France!'

Geoffrey bowed to her. 'You have my eternal gratitude, Dame Agnes. You have redeemed me.'

A lively argument ensued about whether or not he had been right from the start, and the meal continued with much merriment. Afterwards, my grandparents suggested that Geoffrey and I might enjoy some time without them and welcomed us to retire to the garden, where they might see but not hear us. I was most grateful. There was so much I wished to tell him.

But he was even more anxious to tell me something he had learned the previous evening.

'Your parents have been summoned to Castle Rising. Summoned by the Queen Mother, the Lady Isabella.'

I grew quite cold though the sun beat down on me.

'My parents at Castle Rising? Why? Where did you hear this?'

Geoffrey had been watching me as if curious how I would react. Now he slowly nodded. 'I thought you would be puzzled by this, as was I. Why? I do not know, nor did the man who told me of this. But he did say that your betrothed and his father are frequent guests of the Queen Mother, and that your own father has been there on another occasion – shortly before your betrothal.'

I had forgotten about that visit. 'Castle Rising? I had thought he meant the town.' Father had not specifically mentioned the Dowager Queen, though he had described the castle. I felt uneasy about saying more to Geoffrey, and just as uneasy about not doing so.

I began to understand how much Father might gain by my marriage to Janyn – the royal connections – and I did not know how I felt about that. But it was no wonder he had been willing to defy Mother. I pressed my icy hands to my hot cheeks, as if that might balance my humours and thus relieve my distress. Of course it did not work, and I noticed Geoffrey watching me with interest.

'Do you think this summons has something to do with Janyn?' I asked.

'There is gossip about his family, that they are retained by

Isabella. But that does not surprise me – she has done much to promote Lombard art in London, and Janyn's dam is a Lombard.'

'But I do not see how my family would be involved.'

'Nor do I, Alice.'

'Should I be worried?' I had always valued Geoffrey's opinion. He had seemed better able to comprehend the world at large than I was, and now he was part of a noble household, and well travelled.

He raised his eyebrows and shook his head. 'You now know as much as I do. I confess that I am disappointed you did not know this already, and more!' He chuckled, but in his eyes I saw concern.

'I have been cast out from my parents' house, am no longer privy to their comings and goings. But I begin to think that I have never been knowledgeable about their lives.'

'I did wonder why you are suddenly abiding here,' he said, 'for you'd said nothing when I last saw you.'

'I've been here a week. I wondered why Father had not visited when he said that he would. But now you tell me that he is in Norfolk.'

Geoffrey took my hands and squeezed them. 'I see that you are hurt, and I am sorry.'

'Bless you.'

I told him of my parents' apparent rift over my betrothal.

'So it is because of Dame Margery that you are here?'

'I believe so. Or because Father insisted on my betrothal to Janyn even against Mother's wishes. I don't know which one to blame.'

His eyes sought mine, for I'd looked away as I spoke of my pain. When I looked up again, he asked, 'Are you pleased by the prospect of being Janyn Perrers's wife?'

'For my part, oh, yes, Geoffrey. And yet I fear it as well. He is older, and knows so much more of the world. And I much fear that once I am wed, I'll not see any of my family.'

'As for the latter, that might be true no matter whom you wed. A woman joins her husband's family and is guarded by them against anything that might threaten her honour. But he seems a fascinating man to whom to be bound – handsome and so elegant that I would think him a noble. I see that your grandparents mean for you to dress as well as he does.'

I smoothed my silk sleeve. 'It is not all their choice. Janyn has made generous gifts and provided me with a maidservant who is accomplished in all the skills needed for a fashionable lady's maid.'

'Indeed. That gown becomes you. I think you will outshine your mother.'

I detected a slight barb but ignored it, refusing to let anything dampen my delight in my new clothes.

'I do not care whether I outshine her, but I am enjoying myself.' I twirled for him. 'You, too, are dressed in costly finery,' I noted, a bit out of breath and pleased by the admiration in his eyes.

His brown jacket was a fine, light wool, his boots were of beautiful red Cordoba leather and his cap was velvet with a pearl holding up the drape on one side. I had never seen him in such elegant dress. I did not think it livery.

I was satisfied by his slight blush.

'I thought jacket and hat were dark and simple enough that they would look modest. But I should know better than to think I could fool you! Yes, I am grand. I thought I might spend a little money to feel like a man of substance when I am about in the city.'

'I have learned even more about cloth, leather, and fashion this past week,' I said. 'I knew my grandmother loved to dress well, but her knowledge extends far beyond what I had imagined. It seems that I am to dress in escarlatte, silk, velvet and soft leathers, and be an ornament of my husband's household.'

'Criseyde's cloak,' Geoffrey said, looking bemused. His expressive eyes seemed to gaze at something vast and distant.

'Who?'

'A poem of Ancient Troy that we listened to night after night in the hall while a gentleman who fancies himself a bard was a guest in the household. My mistress particularly loved the part about Criseyde and her lovers. She is sent from Troy to the Greek camp, and dons a cloak redder than roses, whiter than lilies, and decorated with pictures of all the beasts and flowers on earth, fashioned from enchanted cloth and lined with the skin of a fabulous animal whose fur includes every colour God has ever created. The trimming comes from the hide of a beast caught in the River of Paradise. It is fastened by the two richest and most beautiful rubies that have ever been seen. Beneath it she wears a silk tunic, embroidered with gold and trimmed with ermine.'

The image captivated me. I could see an exquisite woman in fabulous dress illuminated by the campfire, dazzling the men who thought her a spectre.

Geoffrey bowed to me, his mood quieter now. 'I'll tease you no more.'

I did not understand why his mention of this Criseyde led him to a more serious mood.

'Are you finding time to compose ballads?'

'There is always idle time in which to compose in my head.'

'Are you composing one of Criseyde?'

'She deserves a better poet than me. Now tell me,' he said, laughing again and confusing me even more, 'has Janyn kissed you?'

The mere question made me blush with the memory of our kiss.

Geoffrey slapped his thigh. 'Ah! I see by your confusion that he has, and that it was much to your liking.' His eyes were very merry.

I laughed. 'Yes, he has kissed me, and yes, it was very much to my liking. And you? Have you met a suitable lady?'

'No. But parents are in no hurry to marry off their sons, just their daughters. In faith, I've seen few women younger than my mother.'

We shared companionable laughter, and I felt more at ease than I had in a long while.

'When do you wed?'

'Before Michaelmas.'

'So soon?' He looked disappointed. 'Then I shall not be there to witness it. I return to my new household in two days and shall not be in London until Christmas.'

'Oh, Geoffrey. I had so hoped you would be there.'

'Perhaps I can be second godfather to your first son, eh?'

'Children . . . I have not even thought about choosing god-parents.' Janyn would no doubt choose a man of some prestige for first godfather. 'I've been too occupied with preparing my clothing and household items. Yes, Geoffrey, I would like you to stand as godfather to our first son – or daughter.' I giggled about what came to mind. 'Dame Agnes says that riding will strengthen my legs for carrying the weight of children.'

Geoffrey smiled broadly and took my hands for a moment. 'I am happy for you, Alice.'

We resumed our stroll along the garden path.

'I feel most fortunate except for my warring parents and the She-Wolf casting a cloud over it all.'

'I am sorry about your parents. But perhaps you need not worry about the Queen Mother. The gossips love their clever names for those they fear. It makes them feel superior and less afraid. The King's mother is often at court now that so much time has passed since her treasonous and immoral behaviour. In the end, the people were glad of her rebellion. It was Mortimer's greed for power that soured them.'

'I overheard my grandparents speaking of her one night and they sounded uneasy about my marrying a man who communed with the Queen Mother. They must not have known about my parents being summoned to Castle Rising.'

'Perhaps, as Janyn's patron, Isabella wished to make certain that your mother will not cause trouble. I have observed that nobles often look on commoners as well-to-do servants. She may feel she owns him in some way.'

I paused and turned to him. 'Have you any advice for me, my worldly Geoffrey?'

He grew serious. 'I have seen good people seduced by wealth and finery to their ruin. Have a care, my friend.'

'Geoffrey, you make me shiver.'

He forced a laugh. 'You asked! But do not mind me. You know that I delight in hearing my own voice. You have ever been more practical and clear headed than me. You will fare well.'

It grew late, and my friend reluctantly departed. But he swore that he would not be a stranger, and I believed him. As I lay abed that night I tried to recall his description of the enchanted cloak. Fabulous beasts, every colour imaginable, great rubies . . .

In the morning, knowing that my parents were away, I coerced Dame Agnes into accompanying me to see Nan and the children. We sent a message that we would come the next day – I did not want Nan to feel that I was checking up on her with a surprise visit. I had made new hats for all three of my siblings with scraps of beautiful cloth. Gwen asked to accompany us so that the children might meet her.

'Then, when they visit, I'll not be a stranger to them.'

I was glad that I had made my peace with her.

I had not anticipated how odd it would feel to return home after little more than a week away. Nan greeted us at the door looking far more than a week older, and although I recognised the gown she wore it seemed more frayed and patched than before. The hall furnishings were unchanged, yet they seemed unbalanced, as if the room had grown and the furnishings had shrunk. Everything felt subtly unfamiliar, as if my spirit had been erased from this place.

After a tearful reunion with Nan, Will, and Mary – John would try to stop in later if his master could spare him from the shop – I asked about their activities since I'd left.

'Mother and Father are away,' Mary declared. 'Mother took all her prettiest gowns and her jewels.'

Nan put her fingers to her lips. 'Remember what I told you the other day, Mary. It is not wise to announce what treasures your parents carry on the road. Thieves have big ears.'

'But Alice is no thief!' Will said.

'What Nan means is that it is best to learn to say nothing of such things, because someday you might say it in the wrong company,' I explained.

I could tell by the expressions on their sweet faces that Will and Mary found that frustrating and wrong-headed, but they abandoned the topic and launched into questions about my life at Dame Agnes's home.

Later, when the children were absorbed in trying on their hats with Gwen's assistance and searching for a gift they had made for me, I asked Nan what she knew about my parents' journey.

When I'd arrived, my first impression of my beloved nurse was that she was weary and heavy of heart, and now her words confirmed that at least in part.

'A messenger came – well-dressed, thought highly of himself, insisted on waiting for the reply. Cook fed him while the master and mistress went above and spoke in hushed voices behind a closed door. I had handed them the note, but they had told me to leave the room while they spoke to the messenger, and then I was sent out with the children while they discussed it and, I presume, composed their response. As soon as the messenger departed I was ordered to look after the children while they prepared for a journey, and told that Cook and I would be seeing to them for a week or more. Such a fuss, Alice, I cannot imagine what it means. Your parents seemed excited and fearful at the same time. Cook says the messenger began to say something about a castle, but changed it to Norfolk. She said that he wore livery that had the royal fleur-de-lis on it, but she could make out no more. What do you suppose it means?'

I did not say that it all supported what Geoffrey had already told me. My experience with Gwen had taught me to pause and consider Nan's position in the household before I said anything. I thought it best not to tell her what I knew, for then she would be burdened by keeping a secret from her employers.

'I wish I knew what it meant, Nan. It sounds exciting. Mother must have been delighted to have an excuse to travel and be seen in her pretty clothes. Do you think Father has found another partner for a ship? He so wanted to buy another ship.'

As there was always much intrigue around large commercial investments, Nan seemed satisfied with that possibility.

'You are looking very fine, Alice. Dame Agnes is taking good care of you.'

'Every day I work on such fantastic gowns and headdresses, Nan. I never dreamed I would be so finely dressed. But it does not fill the loneliness I feel being apart from all of you.'

We held each other's hands and studied each other's face.

Nan broke the emotional silence. 'Try to be content in the home of your loving grandparents, Alice. I see how Dame Agnes and your maid treat you, I see calm and contentment in their faces, and I am no longer worried for you. In this house there are too many secrets. It is not a good place for you.'

'Poor Mary and Will,' I said. Mother's moods affected the entire household, but especially the young ones who invariably feared they were to blame. I had always felt so.

'You and John survived it, and so will they.'

'With you to shelter them. God blessed this house when he sent you here, Nan.'

I'd gone too far. She averted her face to hide her tears. But we were blessedly interrupted by Mary and Will, wearing their new hats. Mary carried a wooden bowl.

'For you, Alice!' she cried, handing it to me.

'From both of us,' said Will.

Smooth stones from the river were nestled in a lining of straw, looking for all the world like a tiny bird's nest brimming with eggs. I lifted a pretty speckled stone and found it warm and inviting to rub.

'They are beautiful,' I said, kneeling to hug each of them in turn. Nan caught the bowl before I spilled the contents. I thought it the most perfect gift.

Despite my initial feelings of strangeness, I enjoyed the day immensely and it was hard, very hard, to take my leave of them. I was almost out of the door when John rushed through it. My heart leaped with joy to see him, and to see how much he had wanted to catch me. We held each other tightly – it was the first time we had hugged one another in years.

He stepped back and looked at me, then pulled me out into the yard, away from the others. 'You've gained back your colour and some weight. I am more than glad to see you thriving, Alice. You are better off with Dame Agnes – I told Father that it would prove so.'

I looked at my brother and for the first time noticed how he had matured. There was little boyishness left in him, except perhaps for the lock of hair that kept falling down over his eyes – he hated wearing a hat – and his still slender body. He looked healthy yet anxious, a pinching around his mouth that I'd never seen before. I realised in that moment how much I loved him.

But then I recalled what he had just said. 'Father told you of his plans before I heard of them?'

'He told me to shut me up. I had asked him to do something about Mother's behaviour. You would have laughed – I told him that I would not stand for her treating you so.' He laughed at himself, a melancholy sound. 'As if I had it in my power to do anything to protect you.'

I was moved beyond words. 'She has been even more spiteful towards me of late than is her custom.'

He turned away with a great, shuddering sigh. 'Before my master silenced him, one of my fellow apprentices repeated rumours about our mother's jealousies, her nasty revenges. I believe she is jealous of you, and I did not want her to hurt you.'

Poor John, to discover his own mother the subject of gossip. 'What sort of revenges?' I asked.

'My master does not think all of them true. They were petty revenges – cruel rumours, betrayals of trust, no bodily harm. Very womanly.'

I shrugged off his last comment. I was too grateful for his affection and support to fault him.

'Bless you, John.'

'May God watch over you, Alice. Stay as far from Mother as you are able. I am glad you came today, when she is well away from here.'

'Please come to dine with us someday soon,' I said.

'An apprentice lives at the mercy of his master's whims, Alice. But I will try.' He took my hands. 'You did not ask whether I knew where our parents have gone. That means that you do.'

I shook my head. I did not care to speak a lie to my brother, who had been so good to me.

He looked disappointed, but not disbelieving. 'I am sorry. I had hoped you would know. The suddenness of their journey frightened Cook and Nan. I wondered who or what might inspire such haste.'

'In faith, I was so glad to hear they were away and I might see you and Mary and Will that, though I did wonder, I was too excited to care much.'

Dame Agnes came out to urge us to complete our farewells, for it grew late. Mary and Will ran out to embrace me and deliver wet kisses one more time, and John and I clasped hands as he promised to try to dine with us soon.

I cried myself to sleep that night. I did not understand how I could be both happy and sad about the way my life was changing. Nan used to say that God always mixed the bitter with the sweet so that we did not forget that every pleasure has its cost.

I-3

'And shortly, deere herte and al my knyght,
Beth glad, and draweth yow to lustinesse,
And I shal trewely, with al my myght,
Youre bittre tornen al into swetenesse.
If I be she that may yow do gladnesse,
For every wo ye shal recovere a blisse'

– Geoffrey Chaucer, *Troilus and Criseyde*, III, ll.176–181
(Criseyde to Troilus)

I woke with a clearer sense of what disturbed me so – I had not
been entirely honest with either Nan or John, and felt that Nan
had not been so with me. I felt horribly alone. It was not that I
thought them my enemies, but that none of us was absolutely
forthcoming with one another any more, and that frightened me.
It seemed that love was never so complete, so all-encompassing,
as I had believed it to be.

Noticing my sombre mood, Dame Agnes suggested I might
accompany Grandfather to their parish church for some quiet
prayer.

'I shall stay at home to complete your cloak and begin work
on the headdress for your red escarlatte gown. I think Gwen
should stay as well. But you are most welcome to go out with
your grandfather. You have worked hard of late and it will be
good for you to walk about.'

St Mary Aldermary was another parish church for wealthy
merchants, and as Grandfather and I stepped within, the
murmurs of the chantry priests sounded reassuringly familiar.

'I shall kneel in my usual spot, Alice. Come and fetch me
when you are finished with your devotions.' He had brought
with him a subtly embroidered cushion – I recognised
Dame Agnes's stitching – and was soon settled near the main
altar, his dark robes falling gracefully from his broad
shoulders. His head, warmly wrapped in a hood that draped

about his neck, bowed low over his folded hands.

I loved him so much in that moment. He had always been so kind to me, so comfortable a companion.

I went at once to the statue of the Blessed Virgin and knelt on the prie-dieu before it. Pouring out my fears and uncertainties to the gentle Mother of God calmed me.

On the walk back to the house, Grandfather talked of my own father's wedding.

'He could not believe that God had blessed him with such a beautiful wife,' said Grandfather. But there was no joy in his voice, and, glancing up, I saw that his high forehead was creased and his eyes sad.

'You need not hide his disappointment from me, Grandfather. I know that my mother has been difficult.'

He gave a startled smile and squeezed my hand. 'You are almost too good a listener. But that will serve you well.' The dark robes and deep red, draped hood made him look sombre, but his face was kind. 'Why do we force our daughters to wed so young? That was their problem, I believe. She had dreamed about a life with him that could never be, the sort of luxury and travelling that only nobles can afford, and even then the women seldom find exciting.' He squeezed my hand again. 'Forgive me, I pontificate.'

'So she would have been dissatisfied with anyone of her own station?' I asked.

'In truth, that is precisely the problem,' he said.

'Then her youth made no difference.'

He grunted and stopped near the gate to the house, considering, his ruddy face crinkling and wrinkling as he thought. I loved the way his entire body took part in everything he did, even prayer.

'You are quite right, granddaughter. Quite right.' His mobile face rearranged itself into a smile in which his pale eyes and white whiskers participated. 'You have released me from the burden of guilt I have borne for hastening your parents' betrothal and marriage. But you, Alice . . . you seem content to leave your family and embrace that of your betrothed.'

'I've been pushed from the nest, Grandfather.'

His smile grew uncertain. 'Of course. How thoughtless of me.'

'But I am well pleased with Janyn, and, for the moment, to be living with you and Dame Agnes.'

He beamed. 'It is delightful to have you in our home, Alice. And you have such a fine suitor. You shall have an exciting life with Janyn Perrers, I trow, if his gifts to you so far are any indication. And your grandmother told me that you know of his connection with the Dowager Queen Isabella.' He put a finger to his lips. 'A family secret.' Resuming his slow walk he added, 'I am much relieved by this talk. Bless you, child.'

We had reached the yard, and there, calmly eating an apple from Grandmother's hand, was my mare, accompanied by a man with the tanned leathery skin of one who spent little of his time inside.

'Ah!' Grandfather said with a very broad grin. 'This must be your fine steed and your riding instructor. Now we shall see who you will love best – your betrothed or your horse!'

He and Grandmother had odd ideas about horses and their significance, but I just giggled. I was very excited.

'There you are!' Grandmother waved us over. 'Alice, this is Master Thorne, your riding instructor, come to walk you about the yard so that you might become better acquainted with your mare while he judges how to begin your schooling.'

'Master Thorne,' I said, bobbing my head to him.

'Mistress.' He nodded to me, his dark eyes frankly assessing me. His face was as leathery as his leggings and short tunic.

'Is my dress inappropriate for walking about the yard?' I asked Dame Agnes.

She raised her eyebrows. 'Indeed it is. Gwen has your riding clothes prepared.'

'I pray you, Mistress Alice!' Gwen stood in the doorway beckoning me to follow her. She whisked me within to change into a gown less full, of a cloth easier to clean.

'You do not wish to smell of horse sweat at an elegant feast,' she said with a little laugh.

'Men often do,' I said, impatient to return to my mare.

Once I was back in the yard, Master Thorne brooked no delay. I was noting just how tall the mare was when I was ordered to step up on to a stool, and with Grandfather assisting me, I mounted. Sitting sideways on the platform felt awkward. I was glad of having changed – less skirt to manage. How far away the ground seemed, how close the sky.

'Her name is Maundy, but you might find a name that better suits the pair of you, Mistress,' said Master Thorne. He then made a little sound, and the mare began to walk, very slowly, very gently.

I was content. Better than content. I felt as if I were a part of the mare and she of me, and the grace with which we moved together filled me with a strange mixture of peace and delight.

Master Thorne looked at the mare's face, then mine, and nodded. 'God smiles on this match. It will bring me joy to school you, Mistress Alice.'

Too soon Master Thorne asked Grandfather to assist me in dismounting.

'I must take Maundy away to the stables, and you will come to me there on the morrow, in the early morning,' said Thorne. My grandparents boarded their horses a short walk away.

On impulse, I hugged the mare's head. She nuzzled my ear. 'The name does not suit her,' I said.

Master Thorne nodded. 'I thought you would dislike it. Choose another and we'll train her to it.'

'A good beginning,' said Grandfather as Master Thorne led the mare out of the yard.

'Have you any name in mind?' Dame Agnes asked as we returned to the hall.

'Serenity,' I said. 'That is what I feel in her presence.'

'It is an odd name for a beast,' Dame Agnes said with a chuckle, 'but it has a beautiful sound.'

The next few days flew by as I divided my time between riding lessons and putting the finishing touches to several gowns, surcoats and shifts.

'Why are we rushing with the clothing?' I asked one morning. 'There will be weeks of nothing to do before my wedding.'

Grandmother laughed. 'When Janyn returns, he means to escort you through your future homes so that you might tell him what you wish to change and how you wish to change it. You will be too busy for fine needlework. By then I expect you'll be asking us to work on cushions and hangings for the bedchambers and halls. We will also be planning the wedding feast.' Her colour was high and her eyes bright with visions of social delights.

I said little, choked by all that seemed to be spinning out of control around me. *What I wish to change in my future homes?* I crossed myself and silently prayed for calm as I left the hall with Grandfather.

On this day we were to meet Master Thorne at a park beyond the city walls. For the first time I was to ride Serenity with my riding master beside me on his own mount, rather than walking alongside holding my mare's rein. On any other day I would have been too enchanted by the new experience to think of anything else, but on that morning I was caught up in thoughts of the new responsibilities I would soon bear and the absurdity of anyone's expecting me to know what I wanted in my homes. Serenity grew restive under my vague commands, and Master Thorne told me to halt.

I dreaded what he would say, stiffening in response to his expected anger. But his eyes were kind, his attitude one of concern.

'You are elsewhere this morning, Mistress Alice. Serenity senses it and grows confused. I pray you, I do not mean to pry or be disrespectful, but if you are unwell it would be best for you to abandon the lesson for today.'

That was the last thing I wanted. I had hoped the lesson would distract me. 'I do not wish to abandon the lesson, Master Thorne. I shall work to calm myself and be attentive.'

His smile was kind, though it so webbed and tugged at his leathery skin that it looked painful. 'Do not doubt yourself, Mistress. A few days ago you had never ridden a horse, and now look at you. Serenity has not refused your mounting her, nor has she halted until you commanded her to do so. She is already sure of your mastery.'

His words, surprisingly perceptive, were the best that I could have heard. I nodded my thanks. 'I believe we can continue, Master Thorne.'

Indeed I was able to set aside my worries and be one with Serenity. Riding was not at all what I had imagined. I had not expected to feel such a bond with the horse, to be so aware of sitting on a living being. The power of Serenity moving beneath me, her response to my subtle movements – I became more aware of my own body by the way I was able to sense hers. In truth, it felt sinful.

That evening as Dame Agnes sat on the side of my bed wishing me sweet dreams, I confessed how I felt about riding.

'Oh, my sweet Alice,' she murmured, brushing my hair from my cheek and bending to kiss me, 'your feelings have been shared by many other young girls. Such feelings predict a happy marriage bed.' Her smile, meant to reassure me, embarrassed me instead.

'I am no wanton.'

'No, Alice, you are a woman. God does not condemn pleasure in the marriage bed, nor does he proscribe an innocent bond with your horse or a beloved pet, or deriving pleasure from appreciating the miracle of this form he gave you and how it supports you. You have not taken vows of chastity and self-denial, my dear. Too many wives send their husbands out to sin with other women by their own fear and ignorance about this. I told you – I predict happiness for you.'

I believed that she loved me and was encouraging me to allow my marriage to be fruitful and loving. But she also wanted to prevent anything that might create problems in the future. I saw that in her eyes, heard it in her voice.

'I pray for happiness, Dame Agnes,' I said, 'to follow your example in running a household with ease and grace, and to be a good wife to Janyn.' And to be blessed with joy in my partner, as she was with Grandfather. But I feared that such happiness was a rare gift.

My riding lessons proved to be the calm centre of my life, surpassing even the church in quieting my mind and heart. On one special day, the last chance for a longer expedition before Janyn's return, Master Thorne, Grandfather and I rode out farther into the countryside than I had ever been before. Serenity seemed to breathe more deeply as we left the city, and Grandfather broke into song.

But once the sounds of the city faded away, I grew uneasy. The blue dome of the sky was overpowering. I imagined it dropping down to cover the earth, crushing me. I felt light-headed. But as the woodland closed in around us, I felt safe once more. The birdsong, the cool, fresh breeze, the rich smell of earth and leaf and bark – I wondered what it would be like to sleep in such surroundings, without the tarry scent of ships and the smoke of household fires, without the raucous cries of the waterfowl and the shouts of street vendors, the clatter and squeal of cartwheels. I wondered whether Janyn's country house was in a woodland setting, and how soon I might see it.

I was exhausted by the time we returned, but happy as I was swept up into a round of baths and fittings and consultations about my various gowns. I fell asleep that night imagining a bedchamber with great doorways that might be left open to allow woodland breezes to pass through, and birds alighting on the tops of high-backed chairs.

Janyn returned to London half a week earlier than Dame Agnes had predicted, throwing her into a panic. She insisted that all my clothing be ready when he made his first appearance. She had invited him to dine the very day she learned of his presence in London, and he had accepted for the following afternoon.

When I entered the hall in my Lincoln green silk gown, I felt a stranger to myself. Over it I wore the gold surcoat and a jewelled girdle; my hair, curled and tumbling down my back, was held off my forehead by a narrow headdress sprinkled with pearls. I'd first worn the gown when Geoffrey had paid a visit, but the surcoat, the jewelled girdle and headdress were new, and Gwen declared that they entirely changed the effect of the gown. Peering into the mirror, seeing myself in bits and pieces, I saw what she meant. The gown was now merely a serene backdrop for the gold, pearls and jewels. Indeed, I felt bejewelled and untouchable. I imagined this must be how a queen would feel, distanced from her subjects by gold and gems. It was a heady feeling.

Janyn was splendid in a deep jewel-hued jacket, leggings and hat, the latter ornamented with peacock feathers. From his neck hung a heavy gold chain set with medallions of lapis lazuli. The sun had darkened his complexion. He looked glorious, as I imagined a lion might look. And as I approached I felt a sense of great power as his expression of impatience metamorphosed into a look of sheer delight, and then something darker, a hunger. As if he were a lion and meant to devour me. Yet I did not fear him. I felt I shone in his presence. I came alive.

'Sweet Mother in Heaven!' he said when I reached him. 'You are a vision, my beloved.' He took my hand and kissed it, lingering over it. The warmth of his breath robbed me of mine, but at the same time the warmth of his hand reassured me. He was real. Our betrothal was real. And he desired me.

'I have missed you, Janyn.'

Now he looked up, into my eyes, and held my gaze for a moment, as if assessing my regard. I was surprised by how familiar he felt to me.

'Master Thorne tells me that you ride as if you have been doing so all your life.'

'Master Thorne is most kind, but overstates my ability,' I said. 'I do enjoy riding, and Serenity is a most beloved companion.'

His high forehead creased in thought. 'You have named your mare Serenity? You are a delight.' His eyes lit up and his tanned face crinkled into a teasing grin. 'But you will not ride her for long. She is slow and wanting in refinement. I chose her only while you learned to ride.'

In that moment the spurious maturity the gorgeous clothing had loaned me deserted me, and I felt young and silly. I could not bear to think of parting with Serenity. I loved her. I felt foolish for not having understood that she was not a grand horse. I wanted to defend her, to insist on keeping her. I wanted to cry for the coming loss. I turned away from him and prayed I might regain my composure. I feared that if I were to follow my impulses, Janyn would realise just how young I was and withdraw his affections.

'Shall we be seated?' Dame Agnes said, motioning to Janyn to join Grandfather at the beautifully decorated table. With her hand beneath my elbow, she held me back. 'He meant no harm by his smile, Alice,' she whispered, 'and I am certain that he will allow you to keep the mare at your country house. Take a deep breath and be of good cheer. You look beautiful and he adores you.'

I had not thought about how difficult it would be to sustain the behaviour now expected of me. The realisation took my breath away. I could not suddenly wilt and beg to be excused from the company but must consider each word, remain alert and responsive even though I wanted to curl up in bed and pull the covers over my head. I wanted more time to become accustomed to such a change.

But there was no returning to my parents' house. They were finished with me. I was fulfilling my obligation as a daughter by wedding a man who would provide Father with additional valuable connections, such as the Dowager Queen. I reminded myself that I was most fortunate to find Janyn so much to my own taste.

I took the deep breath Grandmother prescribed and followed her to the table. With each step I tried to grow a little taller and more graceful, and although I was not smiling by the time I took my seat, I was composed.

Dame Agnes gave me a smile that expressed her relief I had not made a fuss.

'You have the strong colour of a man who has been at sea,' Grandfather said to Janyn.

The gorgeous feathers in his cap caught the light from the candles as he bowed his elegant head in response.

'The sun shone down on me as I crossed the Channel, it is true. Trade took me to France and Lombardy.'

'Do you often cross the Channel, Master Janyn, or do your factors do more of the travel for you?' asked Dame Agnes.

'As a widower I had little to hold me here, so I often made the journey. But now –.' he glanced at me '– I hope to make much greater use of my factors.'

I blushed. 'I am glad of that,' I murmured, managing a tremulous smile.

It seemed to please all at the table. Conversation continued along pleasant avenues with stories of his journey and Grandfather's anecdotes about my riding lessons. I noticed that Grandfather took care to compliment me with each story, as if Janyn needed to be reassured that I would make a suitable wife in all ways. I prayed that, though I had so much to learn, I might behave like a grown woman.

Janyn invited me and my grandparents to dine at his London home the following day.

'As we are to wed in less than a month, I am eager to show

Alice her new home so that she may advise me on what I must do to ensure her comfort. I would be delighted if you would escort her to our home tomorrow, Master Edmund, Dame Agnes, so that we might confer and then discuss our plans over supper.'

Our home. He took my hand and squeezed it while he said that, and when he was finished he kissed it and looked into my eyes with such an affectionate expression that my heart fluttered. Perhaps as husband and wife we might sustain a closeness that others could not. I prayed that my marriage might prove more like Dame Agnes and Master Edmund's than my parents'.

Grandfather regretted that he must attend a guild event on the morrow. 'But Dame Agnes and Alice are the ones you need there, and they will surely attend you.'

Janyn did not at any point mention my parents. Neither did my grandparents. That troubled me while we all sat in the hall, and it troubled me even more after he'd departed and I lay on my bed, resting a while before working on some needlework. I wondered why it bothered me so when my mother had turned against me and my father had been so eager to remove me from his home. Several weeks had passed without a visit from either of them.

My future home was much like Janyn's parents' house, the street façade matching that of its neighbours except that it was slightly larger, with more chimneys. And, like that of his parents, Janyn's hall door opened on to a fantastic world of colour and light. Breathless, I stood letting my eyes feast on the wall hangings, the cushions, the delicately painted wood and embroidered cloth, the statues, shelves and cabinets displaying pewter, wood and silver dishes, and Italian glass goblets, pitchers and flasks.

I could not imagine what I might add or change. A fit of shyness overtook me a few steps into the hall.

'Sweet Alice, this is to be your home,' said Janyn. 'I hoped you would be curious.'

I needed little more coaxing, for I did so wish to explore. I found the cushions wondrously thick and comfortable and the fabrics more than pleasing to the touch. The pewter was as fine as I'd seen in churches.

'That is York pewter,' said Janyn. 'The finest.'

'Everything is not only beautiful but well cared for,' I said. 'My compliments to the housekeeper. Will I meet her today?'

The question apparently reminded Janyn of something troubling. 'Gertrude is away at our country house today. And therein lies a tale. Cook encountered a problem earlier and became so intent on solving it that he is now very late in getting the food to table.'

Dame Agnes assured Janyn that she would find a way to save the day. Taking Gwen with her, she retired to the kitchen.

Janyn's air of unease dissolved as soon as they disappeared. I wondered whether he had arranged for just such a crisis so that we might be alone.

'At last,' he said with a conspiratorial grin. 'We will be more comfortable discussing the decorations for the bedchamber without an audience, do you not agree?'

I liked the fact that I had guessed correctly. He seemed more approachable now, less of a cipher. It was the sort of thing Geoffrey and I might plot.

'What I have seen so far is beautiful, Janyn. I cannot imagine what I might wish to change.'

'In truth, much of what you see displayed here in the hall is merchandise for sale. When we entertain, we are also allowing our guests to see what they might purchase to adorn their own homes.'

'Oh.' This was a shop then, like Father's undercroft.

'I've disappointed you. I pray you do not find that unseemly? I know that your father does not use his hall in such wise.'

'Well, it is not so very grand after all, and that is for the better. Using the house in this wise means it must be well cared for.'

'That is why we employ a housekeeper.'

Of course. But Dame Agnes had warned me to make it quite clear to the housekeeper from the beginning that *I* was in charge. I wearied of all the responsibility. I wanted to enjoy myself.

'When we return to the hall, you must point out to me what is yours.'

'Ours,' he said.

I smiled up at him and put my hand in the crook of his arm. 'I should like to see the bedchamber.'

As we climbed the outer staircase to the upper storey, Janyn said, 'Before returning to London I spent a day at Castle Rising, the home of Isabella, the Queen Mother. She is eager to meet you, Alice.'

I noticed a hint of concern in his voice. I had debated with myself whether or not to inform him that I already knew of his friendship with her, and had decided that I would act surprised, protecting my relationship with Gwen. I would have preferred to share everything with Janyn, to feel there was nothing I need keep from him, but I was aware how naïve I'd been to think that anyone shared their whole self with another, no matter how much they loved them. I took his slight unease as a sign that I had judged correctly and this relationship demanded discretion.

As we reached the upper landing, I turned to him. We were so close I could feel his warmth. Janyn reached out and touched my cheek with the back of his hand, a gentle, loving gesture that seemed effortless. I was learning that he was not a man who must needs struggle to express affection and I loved him all the more for that. I lightly pressed my face into his hand. Just a subtle gesture. I did not linger, stayed just long enough to sense that he'd felt my response. I was discovering I enjoyed the repartee of touch.

'The King's dam, Janyn? In truth? How come you to be acquainted with her?' I had no need to feign breathlessness, though it had little to do with Isabella.

'I know her by a long connection through my mother's family, who have negotiated Her Grace's purchases of fine artwork and jewellery from northern Italy. Her Grace has a keen appreciation for Italian design.'

'I can imagine Dame Tommasa in her beautiful new surcoat with the celestial bodies, bowing to the Dowager Queen. You were teasing me, saying that she might wear such elegant clothing in Italy. She might wear it to entertain the Queen Mother!'

I could see in his eyes that my excitement delighted him. But there was still a hint of something else as he said, 'No, I was not teasing. She might wear such a robe in Milan.' He smiled and pulled me close, but we were untimely interrupted by a servant opening the outside door to us. We exchanged rueful glances and then stepped into a passageway. It seemed like a screen passage, off which doors opened. I'd never seen one in an upper storey. This house was larger than I had guessed. The servant opened another door farther down the passage and stepped aside.

'Mistress, Master,' she said with a little bow and a gesture towards the room.

The bedchamber was at least twice the size of Dame Agnes's, and filled with light from several glazed windows on the south wall. Glazed windows in a bedchamber seemed to me an indulgence only the very wealthy might even consider. It was more simply furnished than the hall below, but everything in it was beautifully made and costly. I immediately moved about, touching surfaces, feeling fabrics.

When the servant had stepped back into the screen passage and closed the door behind her, Janyn spoke. 'You will never guess who I found to be Her Grace's guests.'

At last we came to the news Geoffrey had first brought me. I had wondered how long it would take for Janyn to confide in me. 'The King and Queen?' I played at guessing. Fortunately my glancing around the room made it easy for me to hide my face.

'Your parents.'

I was standing by the great bed, running my hands over the silken curtains. 'What wonder is this? Queen Isabella and my parents?' Now I turned, and my expression must have been sufficiently amazed. 'Janyn, you tease me.'

He broke into a glorious smile and laughed, a deep-throated sound. 'I speak the truth. Your father did think it a wonder when he was first invited. You see, I bring him opportunities by our marriage.'

'And great honour,' I said.

Janyn nodded. 'Honour and preference. Your family will want for nothing.'

I swept around, looking at the glorious furnishings, the spacious chamber. 'Nor shall I! Oh, Janyn, I am happy for all of us.' And I was, especially myself, Mary, Will and John.

Janyn sat down on the edge of the bed and took both my hands as I stood before him. 'But this connection is not to be discussed in public.' His voice was suddenly quiet and he studied my face until I looked him in the eye. He was now grimly serious, I saw.

'I shall obey you in this, of course, Janyn,' I said. 'But might I ask why it is to be a secret?'

'You know the Dowager Queen's history?'

I nodded.

'There are those who still see her as a traitor. Believe she wanted the throne for herself, not her son.'

'But that was long ago. And her son King Edward is so loved by his people.'

'It was, and he is. But there are those with long memories who hold their anger and resentment close to them, nursing their pain, eager to strike out.'

I did not want to know about these things. I wanted to explore what was to be my new home. I wanted to kiss Janyn. But he obviously wished to discuss this now. I was disappointed that this was why he'd brought me to the bedchamber.

'I understand, my love,' I said, working to keep the disappointment out of my voice. 'But how came my parents to Castle Rising?'

'By Her Grace's invitation. She wished to meet the parents of my betrothed.'

If he'd meant to cool my ardour he had succeeded. I remembered Geoffrey's suggestion that Isabella might feel she owned Janyn in some way. 'Why would she care about my parents? What could they possibly be to her?'

'Are you not pleased by this attention from the King's mother?'

'Of course I am,' I said quickly. 'It is beyond anything I ever dreamed.'

'It is an honour, and she is a noble and gracious woman. But I see that you are troubled, Alice. What is it?'

I had expected a simpler life than the one he was painting for me. This was overwhelming. I wanted to love my husband without worrying whether Isabella of France approved. And there was all the secrecy, his seriousness. Yet it *was* thrilling to be marrying a man who walked with royals; to imagine entertaining them, dining with them.

'I pray that my parents can be trusted to be silent.'

'Is that all?' Janyn looked relieved. 'Then I can assure you, be at ease, my love. Her Grace will have made it clear to them that they must be discreet if they wish to remain in her favour. You need not worry.'

'But surely in the very need for secrecy you have hinted at a certain danger to us all?' I did not intend to play the fool.

He nodded. 'I meant that you need not worry about your parents' discretion. Yes, the secrecy is for our own protection.'

'I am glad then you do not seek to protect me from the truth.'

Janyn crossed his hands over his heart. 'Never, my love.' Then he gestured towards the curtains, the other furnishings of the room, the great bed on which he sat. 'Does it please you?'

'I am delighted by all I have seen, Janyn. Glazing on the windows of our bedchamber? I would never have dared suggest it. And the silk hangings, the immense bed . . . I never thought to live in such comfort. It is as I've imagined palaces to be in Paris or Venice.'

'It is perhaps more in the fashion of wealthy merchants in those great cities. But my mother has always believed that God does not begrudge us comfort and beauty as long as we give Him thanks and make certain that all in our households share in these blessings.'

'I shall learn to be at ease with it all, then,' I said.

'You need to learn?'

'It does seem sinful.' I fought a smile.

'And yet bishops and popes live in far greater splendour.'

I laughed. 'Oh, Janyn, I have no experience of such exalted men of the Church, I spoke but in jest.' I moved away from him as I heard footsteps on the stairway.

Janyn reached for me and pulled me back. His smile was teasing, but in his eyes there was something more. Suddenly I feared him.

'Why do you move away from me when you hear a servant on the stairway?' he asked, his voice soft, coaxing. 'We are betrothed. We might do what we will in our bedchamber.' Slipping his arms around me, he pulled me so close that my chest was pressed against his.

'But, Janyn—'

He silenced me with a kiss. More than a kiss. His tongue pressed against my lips. I had begun to fight him, but thought suddenly what a fool I was being. This was, after all, what I wanted, and no one, not even God himself, would condemn me for giving in to Janyn, my legally betrothed. I melted into his arms. As I opened my lips to his he pressed me to him so tightly that I could feel his excitement.

I boldly touched him there. He moaned, and then released me from his embrace.

'My sweet Alice, I think we will be more than fond of this bed.' His eyes were strange, darker and softer than I'd seen them before. 'But let us save our passion for our wedding night.'

'Why? You said yourself that we might do what we will.'

'I promised your father, my vixen, that is why.'

I took a deep breath, feeling confused and a little angry. For reasons I did not understand at the time – what fourteen-year-old girl understands frustrated desire? – I wanted to punish him.

'Why is my mother so against our betrothal? What is between you?'

'Your mother?' Janyn frowned in apparent puzzlement, but as I watched he rose and stood at a little distance, his expression changing to one of discomfort. 'Let us not speak of your mother.'

'No one wishes to speak of my mother, and yet she is at the centre of everything that is happening to me. I am sent from my own home because of her response to our betrothal. Do you think this has been as nothing to me?'

'It is your parents who should explain.'

'And if they will not? It colours everything for me. I yearn to be happy, yet I fear that there is some hidden threat to our joy.'

Janyn took off his hat and raked a hand through his hair, a gesture of unease that I had never associated with him before. Perhaps my seeming unkindness was in truth a way to evoke a response from him.

'I had thought to speak of this after we were wed.' He sat back down on the bed, hands resting limp on his thighs, head lowered. 'I was selfish. Fearful lest you choose your mother over me.'

I thought I would be a great fool to do so, Mother never having expressed love for me. But I said nothing. I needed to hear what he had to say.

'Your mother is an unhappy woman, Alice, and she blames others, never herself, for that unhappiness. She expected your father to lift her out of her black moods and, when he did not, began to resent him. To tell him that another husband would have been able to save her.'

'Yes, she could speak in such wise to my father.' It saddened me to imagine it, knowing how much he loved her. 'And being the good man that he is, he would suffer it without complaint to others.'

'He is a good man and a kind friend,' said Janyn, 'but she does not see beyond her own hunger. She does not see that she has been blessed with a loving husband and a good life. Instead Dame Margery has poisoned her own happiness. She has taunted your father by favouring his friends in ways meant to embarrass him and inflict pain.'

'And you were one of those men?' I guessed it by the sting of his words, the pain in his voice.

'To my great regret, yes.'

'She is jealous of me? But that would mean she truly loved you . . .'

There was sadness in his face. 'Perhaps she told herself that she loved me, but she knows nothing of my heart or soul, Alice. I think it far more likely that she envies you the life she imagines you leading in my household. More exciting than hers, more gowns, more jewels . . .'

I could not argue with this depiction of my mother but sensed him holding his breath, hoping he'd said enough to satisfy me.

'That is why you avoided our home?'

He grasped my hand and pressed it to his cheek. 'Yes. Margery desired me, Alice, and she assumed that I desired her.'

'Did you ever love her, Janyn?'

To his credit and my immense relief he did not rush to respond, but looked inward, remembering. He slowly, sadly, shook his head.

'She is a beautiful woman, and she knows how to give a man her full attention so that his heart warms to her. I have no doubt that I made a fool of myself praising her when I first beheld her. But it took little time for me to understand that she has nothing to give – she sucks the life from all who love her, and hoards that love, giving nothing in return. I thank God that I was never such a fool as to fall in love with your mother.' He looked into my eyes. 'You need have nothing more to do with her, my love. No one would expect you to do so after her unnatural behaviour towards you.' He reached out and pulled me close, holding me in what felt to me like a fiercely protective embrace. 'I pray that you believe me.'

This explained all the secrets my parents had kept from me regarding our betrothal. 'Now that I know why they behaved so, I am no longer afraid.'

'Do you regret pledging yourself to me, Alice?'

'No. You need never doubt me.'

He held me close for a moment, and I felt his heart pounding. When he released me I stepped back and took a deep breath.

'This summons to Castle Rising, was it to appease my mother? To show her that she will share in some of my good fortune?'

Janyn seemed relieved by the shift to more recent events. 'I had confided in Her Grace my suspicion about why our betrothal was delayed, and it would be her way of seeking to help – by flattering Dame Margery with her attention.'

'That was kind of Her Grace.'

'She is a kind and loving woman. A great lady.'

'She must value your friendship.'

Janyn nodded. 'Even the powerful have need of trusted companions.'

He chose his words with great care when he spoke of Isabella of France, pausing longer before responding then than at any other time. My grandparents' apprehension about the connection had perhaps inspired me to observe these moments closely, but his hesitation seemed to me plain enough that I might have noted it anyway. 'Shall I meet her?' I asked.

'You shall, and very soon. She will be on progress to London shortly after we are wed. As she is most eager to meet you, she will pause for the night at our home north of the city. We shall, of course, be there to greet her.'

My heart fluttered. It did sound exciting. And perhaps, once I had met her, observed Janyn's behaviour with her, I might be reassured. I prayed it would be so.

'What of my grandparents? Will you tell them about my parents being guests at Castle Rising and your friendship with the Queen Mother? It will be difficult to say nothing, and surely Father will wish to speak of it with them.'

Again he hesitated. I feared that Janyn's friendship with the Dowager Queen was not merely a private matter but one of secrecy and loyalty, and that he meant to guard that secret with his life. In the next breath he assured me that he had intended all along to tell Dame Agnes that very day, while we dined. He said that Grandfather already knew, but had sworn to keep it a secret, even from his wife.

'There *is* danger, Alice.'

I crossed myself. Grandmother, too, would be sworn to secrecy, I thought.

It was precisely so. Dame Agnes bristled when Janyn spoke of the importance of secrecy, insulted that he would consider her so simple as not to understand.

'Befriending the She-Wolf,' she said, tutting her disapproval as we walked home afterwards. 'I question his judgment, Alice, and that of Dame Tommasa's kin. The Dowager Queen has been trouble since the day she landed on this island. He is your betrothed, and it is plain he loves you, so I shall say no more against him. But be careful around that woman, Alice. Have all your wits about you when in her presence.'

'Do you think I will be easily influenced by her?'

Dame Agnes glanced at me and her expression softened. 'No, not you, dear Alice. It is plain Janyn loves you. That is all that matters.'

Her reassurance was affectionately meant but sounded insincere. The rich food curdled in my stomach, and I went to bed with a terrible ache in my belly that night. But as my thoughts turned to Janyn himself, his kisses, his willingness to answer my questions about Mother, I felt better. I fell asleep imagining lying beside him in that great bed.

After the day at what would be my London home my heart seemed to be divided between fear of all the change I rushed towards and eager anticipation of my wedding day.

Shortly after dining at my future home in the city, Janyn, Gwen, Grandfather, and I rode out to the country house, Fair Meadow. The house nestled in a gentle valley, surrounded by woodland. The undercroft was built of stone, the upper storeys of wood. What it lacked in elegance it made up for in spaciousness and such pretty views I wished the window openings were larger. Janyn teased me when I said so, swearing that I hoped to freeze us in winter so that we would never step out of bed. His eyes caressed me and I laughed and kissed his hands. I was very happy.

My parents dined with me at the home of my grandparents several times. Mother was subdued, Father loquacious. Janyn was always otherwise engaged. Mother was once again speaking to me. She admired my gowns and asked about the horse and the house in the country, going out of her way to avoid Janyn's name. When Father spoke of the honour of being guests at Castle Rising, Mother said little but her eyes shone. I noticed that she had several new gowns as well, one of a silk that looked like the reflective surface of a lake, and guessed it to be costlier than anything she had ever owned. Clothing for her visit to Castle Rising? I did not believe they had been given enough time to make such preparations. Father must be bribing her to behave.

I saw Mother in a different light now, as my equal rather than my elder, as the competitor who had lost. But when my grandparents stole worried glances my way, I wondered whether I would someday regret my victory.

'Resoun wol nought that I speke of slep,
For it accordeth nought to my matere.
God woot, they took of that ful litel kep!
But lest this nyght, that was to hem so deere,
Ne sholde in veyn escape in no manere,
It was byset in joie and bisynesse
Of al that souneth into gentilesse.'

– Geoffrey Chaucer, *Troilus and Criseyde*, III, ll.1408–1414

For several days before my wedding Nan, Will and Mary stayed in my grandparents' home with me, sharing my little bed-chamber. It was a bitter-sweet time. Mary and I alternately giggled and wept, and Will tried to tell me in great detail all that had occurred in his life since I'd left home. Nan was close to tears at all times, but as she became better acquainted with Gwen she declared herself at ease about my well-being once I was wed.

'He must be a good man to have found such a worthy maid for you,' she said.

Father had accompanied Nan, Will and Mary to his parents' house and walked with me in the garden while they settled in. Just as with Mother, I now saw Father from a different perspective than I had before Janyn and I spoke of their unhappy marriage. He and I had little to say to each other, our old easy affection ruined by all that had transpired. The estrangement between us was a blot on an otherwise precious day, and I was relieved when he departed after the midday meal, grateful to be free to go riding with Master Thorne and Grandfather. The exercise and the company of Serenity and the two men whose quiet strength I'd grown to appreciate calmed and cheered me. This was now my life, and I was content. I thanked God, His mother and all the saints for my good fortune.

*

My wedding day dawned sunny and cooler than it had been so far that season, a blessing for all who would be wearing their most splendid robes, which were seldom their lightest. I had slept little and could not eat for the roiling of my stomach at the thought of lying with Janyn that night – so I would have been shivering with chills no matter what the weather.

Gwen, Nan, Dame Agnes and her maidservant Kate dressed me on my wedding day. The red escarlatte gown had been so well fitted that I could freely move about, dance a jig, reach and bend, despite the manner in which it hugged my body like a second skin. The colour brought a blush to my cheeks on a day when I might otherwise have lacked it. A surcoat made from Janyn's betrothal gift of dark gold escarlatte, which Gwen had lined in a matching silk, brought out the gold in my hair and the hazel of my eyes. On my head I wore a delicate circlet of gold and pearls, a gift from Dame Tommasa. My slippers were made of red satin and a leather that had been tanned to match the dark gold of my surcoat. I thought my garments fit for a queen.

'You are a vision of beauty,' said Dame Agnes, almost choking on the words as her eyes filled with tears.

Gwen held a small mirror so that I might see myself. I turned back and forth, twisting and bending, standing on tiptoes and crouching. I could see only tantalisingly small parts of the costume at one time.

'Would that we had a larger mirror!' I said.

'At night, the windows in your bridal chamber will reflect much more of you,' said Gwen.

'Sinful,' said Nan, shaking her head. 'But you should see how beautiful you look.' She smiled, and I noticed that her eyes were red. I'd not seen her crying. She must have made quite an effort to hide it from me.

'Do you think Janyn is as frightened as I am?' I wondered aloud.

'He has been married before,' Dame Agnes said. 'And even if this were his first marriage, a man does not leave his family, nor does his life change as much as a bride's. He will continue with the same work, live in the same house, and for the most part his life will change very little. For you, it will all be new.' She looked ready to burst into tears herself, and her voice shook.

'How sad,' I said. 'This day will not be nearly so exciting for him as it is for me.' I was desperate to lighten the mood. I did not want my own eyes swollen from crying when Janyn beheld me in these robes into which Gwen, my grandmother and her maid had put so much effort and love.

Dame Agnes laughed, her tears gone. 'Oh, I've no doubt he'll find the day exciting enough. He'll enjoy showing off his beautiful new wife to his friends, and all the while he'll be anticipating tonight.'

When someone knocked on the door, Kate went to see who it was while the other three hid me from sight with their bodies.

'Dame Margery,' the maid said, stepping to one side.

My stomach fluttered. I had wondered when Mother would appear, for I knew that no matter how she felt about this marriage she would not forgo an opportunity to be, if not the centre of attention, then very nearly so.

The others moved away, as if unveiling me. Mother stood in the doorway, uncertain of her welcome. In her finest silk gown and a crespinette sprinkled with pearls she looked as much a bride as I did, except that her fair hair did not fall free.

I stretched out my hands to her. 'Mother, I am glad you are here.'

As if distrusting my gesture, she tucked her arms behind her. Taking a few steps closer, her pretty pale grey slippers peeking from beneath her hem, she gave me a little bow, then turned to Dame Agnes and did the same.

'I shall leave you with your daughter while Kate dresses me,' said Dame Agnes. 'Would you like Gwen to leave as well?'

Mother shook her head. 'I should like her to stay as witness that I have come in peace.' Her voice held a sharp edge with which I was familiar. She felt ordered about, unappreciated, and experience taught me that she would soon lash out at someone in retaliation. Probably me, the person she apparently blamed at present for her unhappiness.

'Peace?' I softly repeated. 'We are not at war, Mother.'

'Your father thinks otherwise, Alice. Come now.' She moved over to the window, her rich silk gown rustling as she walked. 'There are things I must tell you.'

Dame Agnes bowed out of the room with her serving maid. Gwen busied herself with tidying the chamber.

Now Mother reached out to examine my surcoat, feeling the two layers, then lifting my skirts a little to see my shoes.

'You've done well for yourself, Alice. Such rich cloth, fine leather, silver and gold. And pearls in your hair.' She frowned as she touched her own fair hair coiled beneath the pearl-powdered crespinette. 'You have studied me.'

I'd had no part in choosing the pearls, but there seemed little point in correcting her. 'I do not think it unnatural for a daughter to emulate her mother,' I said, working hard to keep my voice soft, calm.

She waved away the comment. Her eyes bored into me, hard and cruel, as she said, 'I must tell you what to expect tonight.'

Had I not already been apprehensive about the bridal bed, her look and tone would have made me so. 'There is no need. Dame Agnes has told me all that I need to know.'

Mother raised an eyebrow. 'Has she? But she does not know your betrothed as I do.'

'What has that—' I realised what she was implying then and my hand flew towards her smiling face.

She caught it and laughed. 'Were you unaware that I knew Janyn? How could you think your parents would agree to your betrothal to someone they did not know?'

I thought for a moment that she had not meant to imply what I'd thought she had, that Janyn had wooed her and possibly even bedded her, but she glanced over at Gwen to see if she was listening and then I remembered her expressly wishing my maidservant to witness this conversation. She was teasing me while cleverly choosing her words so that to Gwen she would sound almost loving.

'Yet in thanks for his careful choice you made your father so unhappy. I do not understand such ingratitude. Your father returned the other day, so filled with remorse that it broke my heart.'

My mother was a skilled performer.

'You wish only to ruin my wedding day, Mother. I'll hear no more.'

'But you must! You must know what your father made Janyn

95

promise. There will be no lovemaking until you are sixteen. That is what I meant – Dame Agnes did not know of it, so she could hardly tell you.'

No lovemaking for two years? 'Then why are we to be wed now?'

Mother tilted her head and fussed with the front of my surcoat. 'Business, Alice. Your marriage is all about the guild and trade connections. But your father has ensured your protection – see how he loves you? If Janyn breaks his vow by bedding you tonight, he forfeits your dowry.'

I refused to address this attempt to twist my heart about Father. She had always resented our closeness. 'Janyn is so wealthy he does not need my dowry,' I retaliated.

'Do you then think yourself such a prize?'

I did not flinch from her cutting remark, though it did sting. But surely Janyn did have all the wealth he could want. I was confused. I had been apprehensive about lovemaking, but now that I might be forbidden it, I felt as if I'd lost something most precious to me. She had robbed me of my sense of excitement before the coming ceremony and feast. For the next two years I was to be married in name only. Because Janyn wanted my dowry and Father wished to protect me. Could that possibly be so? Janyn himself had said he'd promised Father to wait only until tonight.

'You've little to say for yourself today.' Mother used her veil to hide her malicious smile, but I saw it in her eyes.

'What is there for me to say?'

'Well, come then.' She held her hand out to me. 'Let us go down to the hall.'

I shook my head. 'I would be alone for a little while.'

Mother loudly sighed and reached for my hand. I pulled away from her.

'Leave me,' I said, with no shadow of respect in my voice, my eyes, my whole posture.

She laughed, but I knew by her blush that this response was not what she had expected. 'Come, Daughter. Be grateful. Your doting father means only to protect you. You are so young. If you were to conceive at once, you would suffer carrying a child.'

'Women my age bear children every day,' I said. 'Leave me,

Dame Margery.' I could not call her 'Mother'. 'I'll not walk out with you.'

Heaving another great sigh, she left the room. As soon as I heard her on the stairway, I turned to Gwen, who had finished tidying and resorted to rearranging items in order to look busy.

'Ask Dame Agnes to come to me here,' I said.

I sat down on the bed to wait, fighting tears.

Gwen returned. 'She has gone down to the hall, Mistress.'

'Fetch her.'

I hugged myself, chilled by Mother's final blow. I vowed that I would hear nothing more from her lips. Her mere presence distressed me.

When Grandmother sailed into the room, her green silk gown rippling behind her and her kindly face crinkled in concern, I fell into her embrace. I realised at that moment how much I would miss her constant comfort, the ease I had felt in her home.

She pressed me to her bosom, then released me and stepped back to get a look at me. 'What is amiss? Gwen looked so pale, I feared I would find you lying on the floor bleeding. God be praised, you look unharmed.' She stepped closer. 'It was Margery, I trow. What did she say to you?'

I told her, and although she expressed indignation that her son would demand such a thing, or that he would deem me so fragile, she admitted that she did not know for certain whether or not it was so.

'But, my sweet child, I cannot believe Janyn would agree to it. I have seen you together. And he is rich as Croesus.' She sank down on to a bench and fanned herself as she thought. 'But of course!' she suddenly said. 'Gwen, what are your orders regarding the bridal chamber?'

Gwen's face brightened. 'I am to prepare the bridal chamber this evening for all to toast you when you are abed. Together.' She looked at me, then Dame Agnes. 'Would Master Janyn observe this ritual if he had promised what Dame Margery suggested?'

'It is the custom, is it not?' I asked.

'Only a fool would challenge his vow in such wise,' said Grandmother. 'So be of good cheer, Alice!' She lifted my chin and with a linen cloth dabbed at my eyes.

I had not been aware that I'd been weeping. 'Do I look horrible now?'

Gwen lifted a mirror so that I might see I looked no worse than before.

'I am sorry that I doubted my son's complaints about Margery for so long,' said Dame Agnes. 'She is every bit the venomous lamia he described.'

The rest of the day was a blur but for brief encounters with Janyn, who watched me with such hunger and kissed me with such enthusiasm that I thought we would both go mad if Mother's story were true. For Dame Agnes's argument had not convinced me. Upon leaving the church, Janyn – my husband! – took my hand to escort me to the guild hall in which we would have the wedding feast, and I was seldom out of his reach for the rest of the day. I diligently avoided looking at Mother and must have met with success in shutting out her voice as well, for I remember nothing of her after she'd left my bedchamber in Grandmother's house. Father kissed me and held me close for a moment, saying that he prayed we would be happy and that life would treat me gently. I hesitated to ask him about the vow, knowing that if Mother had lied my question would widen the rift between them, but I could not help myself.

The hall was crowded and smoky, and Father's hat was at just the right angle to cast shadow over his face, so I could not be certain of his expression. But there was a sadness in his voice as he said he had considered asking it of Janyn. 'Perhaps I spoke of it to your mother.' He was not convincing. 'But, in the end, I decided against it.'

So Mother had concocted a hurtful lie. Father had corroborated this. The rift between us widened.

When the time came for Janyn and me to progress to our London home, half the inebriated crowd came along. I had drunk little, but as Gwen and Dame Agnes undressed me, they coaxed me to drink some brandywine.

'To calm your shivering,' said Grandmother.

In truth, I could not speak because my teeth chattered so. The brandywine was welcome. My night shift was too thin to provide any warmth, and though the bed was piled with wonderfully thick blankets, my feet felt as if they were encased in ice. I sat propped against an extravagant pile of cushions all covered in softest linen, embroidered with our initials, AS and JP.

Janyn arrived through a side door, wearing a shift shorter and of a more substantial linen than mine. As he sat on the bed and swung his legs up, I kept my eyes on the straight, silky black hair on his calves, the surprisingly graceful shape of his ankles and feet. He kissed me on the forehead and lifted the covers to slip his legs beneath. His warmth was so sweet and comforting, until the fuss at the main door of the room reminded me of what this was all about. As Grandmother opened the door to the celebrants, Janyn slipped an arm behind me, resting it on the pillows, his hand gently cupping my trembling shoulder.

'I love you with all my being, Alice,' he whispered. 'When they are gone we can talk into the night. I'll not force myself on you.'

It helped. I was able to turn to look at him, and we kissed for all the guests to see, a gentle kiss.

It was received with cheers, jeers, and the demand for a more passionate kiss.

We embraced, and now the kiss was hard and lingering, and I was no longer cold, no longer frightened.

I remember nothing of the toasts to our health and my fecundity. I was living for the moment we were alone.

And when at last our guests had departed and we were alone in our great bed, we turned to each other and embraced. There was no speech between us. I twined my legs around him as he cupped my breasts with his large, warm hands. When he penetrated me, I cried out in hunger and held him tightly, wanting to envelop him. His deep, surprised laughter, his groans and cries, his final, violent thrusts, were all beautiful to me, and I thanked God for such a gift as our love, our passion.

Later, the memory of the momentary pain surprised me, and the evidence of the blood stains. I wondered at the power of passion to numb all other senses.

We talked, drowsed, kissed and began all over again. In the morning Gwen and the chambermaid exchanged smiles over the bloody sheets and gently bathed me. I was pampered and petted for several days, napping in the afternoons, for our nights were far too active to be restful. I had never been happier. The only shadow on those days was the memory of Mother's malicious lie, and Father's cowardly refusal to condemn her for it. But she could hurt me no more.

As we settled into our domestic routine, my passion for Janyn was not the only attraction for me. He behaved towards me with a level of consideration I had never experienced. Father had told him how he had taught me his own trade practices and encouraged me to make suggestions; he said I'd become a valuable partner. Janyn was delighted. He sought out my opinion on all manner of issues: household purchases, social engagements, trade negotiations. Dame Gertrude, who had served him as housekeeper while he remained a widower, had been instructed to hand over the keys and all governance of the household to me at once. But as women do, we found a comfortable compromise, one that allowed me to learn all that she might teach me while testing my own abilities. I was still only fourteen, and everything was new to me.

I discovered that my strengths lay in ascertaining the quantities required and judging the qualities of goods and furnishings, while Gertrude was far better than I could yet be at supervising the servants. What was most difficult for me was accepting that I must defer in all considerations of diet to Angelo the cook. But so be it. I was busy enough, and had little knowledge of the Italian dishes Janyn loved and I was growing to like. I loved the heft of the keys hanging from my girdle; it was a relief to me that Gertrude seemed to have no misgivings about handing them over to me.

Though my days brimmed with new experiences, I missed Mary, Nan and Will, saving up stories and experiences to share with them. Two weeks after our wedding Janyn suggested we invite my family to dine with us. My Salisbury grandparents, Father, Nan and my siblings came; Mother claimed to be ill. Mary and Will were stiff with shyness at first, but Gwen soon engaged them in games of tag in the garden and around the hall, and thanks to her that day was filled with their laughter. Father seemed more comfortable with Janyn than he had been on our wedding day, which suggested to me that they had met since then over business. I caught him watching me several times with a bemused expression, as if surprised to see me in charge of my own home, affectionately teasing my husband, laughing with Nan over mistakes I'd made in my first attempts to perform tasks she'd always done for me. I thought perhaps he was surprised by how comfortable I was in my new life.

But he did not ask after my well-being or whether there was anything he might bring me from my former home. Nan asked such questions, not Father. Even so, the day was one I would cherish in my heart for a long while. By the time they departed, Mary and Will were comfortable with me and even with Janyn, John had obviously enjoyed the food and Janyn's friendliness, and Nan was overjoyed to see my happiness. Dame Agnes and Master Edmund lingered a while after the others departed, and I took Grandmother aside to ask her about the signs of being with child.

Her gaze went at once to my waist, slender as ever in my well-fitting gown, beneath a beautiful silver and enamel girdle from which hung the major household keys. I laughed as I ran a hand over my belly.

'I know that a fortnight is not long enough to tell,' I said, hugging my dear grandmother. 'I am not quite so ignorant, though very nearly.'

Grandmother relaxed, and told me about missed fluxes – she preferred to call them flowers, as her mother had done – and recurring nausea in the mornings. I did not look forward to the latter, for it was in the morning that I rode.

'I'll not be able to ride then?'

'You should not ride in early pregnancy, my sweet. Indeed, if it is possible you should not travel at all while carrying a child.'

I was reluctant to pray that I was not with child, but the thought of not accompanying Janyn to Fair Meadow cast a shadow over my heart.

'So it is good between the two of you?' Dame Agnes asked.

I smiled and nodded.

'God be praised.' In a softer voice, she asked, 'Did you learn whether your father asked Janyn to swear not to sleep with you for two years?'

'He did not, though he said he'd thought about it and might have said something of the sort to Mother.'

Dame Agnes gave me a long look. 'And do you believe she told you that out of love?'

I shook my head. 'I do not hold out such hope. I doubt I shall ever see her again in private. We shall pass as acquaintances in our circle, and avert our eyes or say a cordial, meaningless *Benedicite*.'

After my grandparents departed, Janyn asked whether there had been anything lacking in the day, anything I might have wished to have happened that had not.

'No, my love, nothing. All my loved ones were merry and well fed, and happy to see our contentment.'

He pulled me close and whispered, 'Little Will and Mary inspired me to wonder what it will be like when our little ones are dashing about the hall and gardens . . . squealing, shouting, laughing.'

'Do you dread it?'

'Dread it? I think it will be the most joyous place with such noise and activity.' He slipped his hand inside the low neck of my undergown and pressed my breast.

I bit his lip. 'Then let us go to bed, my lord, and make a baby for your pleasure.'

His voice suddenly husky, he ordered the servants to put the hall to rights and told Gwen to prepare me for bed, for I was uncommonly weary after the long day.

As the time grew near for our move to Fair Meadow I tried to learn more about Isabella of France, to prepare myself for meeting her, but Janyn said that he wished for her to tell me what she chose; that it would not be wise for me to wish to know more than that.

'But I want to please you, Janyn. Everything must be right.'

'It will, my love, it will.'

'There are things I should know,' I countered one evening, 'such as whether she travels with a lover, and if so whether he should be bedded near her?'

Janyn laughed. 'That is the sort of thing Her Grace would never hesitate to tell you.'

I had lately learned from Gertrude that the woodland beyond Fair Meadow was Epping Forest, and that Isabella would be hunting there the morning before she dined with us. Janyn would hunt with her. The housekeeper much admired the Dowager

Queen and her good health – she was said to be at least sixty years of age, yet still rode and hunted.

'You must study her preferences, Mistress, and follow her diet in all things. Then you shall enjoy a long and active life and retain your beauty.'

'Advise Angelo about the diet,' I said with a laugh. 'Hunting must add to her vigour, I imagine.'

Gertrude nodded. 'Pleasurable activity is reportedly a key to long life; toil, on the other hand, causes a depletion of healthy humours. But you need never worry about a life of toil!'

Still attempting to learn more of Isabella, I asked Janyn, 'Should we hire minstrels and musicians? If she hunts, she surely dances.'

'Indeed she does, and her own minstrels and musicians accompany her wherever she travels.'

I clapped my hands and hopped about in a merry jig.

'I am sure she will adore you, Alice, my love.'

'Might I join the hunt, Janyn?'

'When you have hunted with me a dozen times, then you shall hunt with the Dowager Queen. She has no patience at her age with those who fall behind.' He quickly added, 'She is like a woman half her years, and to slow her down is to cause great offence. Which reminds me . . . although I have promised not to separate you from your beloved Serenity, you do require a hunting horse. I must see to that while we are in the country.'

So I was to hunt. The anticipation of taking part in that pursuit kept me humming joyfully through all the preparations for our journey. Janyn's parents would accompany us, and for several days beforehand we stayed in their home while ours was being packed. The room in which we slept was separated from his parents' chamber by a mere wooden wall, little more than a screen. I was upset to see it, for it seemed a certainty that we would have no lovemaking while there, our passion being no quiet engagement.

'The room is not to your taste?' Janyn asked, seeing my face.

'Your parents will hear us,' I whispered, touching the flimsy wall.

He grabbed me up and tossed me on to the bed, then climbed on top of me and held his warm, strong hand over my mouth as he pulled up my skirts with the other hand. Suddenly he was inside me. I do not know how he managed all that with one hand, but he did. And we were not altogether silent. I mentioned this afterwards as we lay back on the bed, side by side, exhausted but satiated.

'Do you think they would not expect such noises from our bedchamber, Alice? My mother will make offerings of thanks in church, she so yearns for grandchildren near at hand to fuss over. My sister's children are so far away.'

We were a large and merry train of wagons and riders as we wove out of London and into the country on a grey but dry day. A storm had blown throughout the previous day, ripping many of the beautifully coloured autumn leaves from the trees, and the road was slippery with their sodden remains, but there was still enough colour remaining to be magical, and as the day warmed a mist hung over the valleys and woodland. Janyn and his parents had suggested we spend Christmas at Fair Meadow. We might invite my family. I thought Will and Mary would enjoy the countryside. We would see how we all felt about it after Her Grace's visit.

Arriving at Fair Meadow as the lady of the manor was a very different experience from my earlier visit. Now it was a homecoming, and the servants warmly welcomed me. I could not imagine being happier.

Janyn departed before dawn on the day he was to hunt with the former Queen. I rolled over to his side of the bed to enjoy what lingered of his warmth and his beloved scent, but as the sheets cooled I grew restive, my feet too cold despite the heavy bed-clothes, the curtains around the bed shielding me from draughts, and the brazier I could hear simmering out in the chamber, close enough to keep the chill from the bed. It would be mid afternoon before he returned with the Dowager Queen and her party, and the house was ready. We had worked hard for two days arranging all that we'd brought from London, planning the meals, the sleeping arrangements. In truth, Janyn, Dame Tommasa and Gertrude had had little need of me, but I had watched with care, asking questions and committing it all to memory for the next time. I meant to take my responsibilities seriously. Yesterday a company of the Dowager Queen's servants, including a lady-in-waiting and a priest, had arrived with many chests and some furniture.

I was confident that Gertrude was already up and discussing the day with Angelo, reviewing the plans with the rest of the household. Gwen would be there as my eyes and ears. So why should I not drift back into a calming and renewing sleep?

My feet being cold usually bespoke fear, and though I lay there trying to convince myself that I was not anxious about meeting the Queen Mother, I had been praying for days that I would please her, and in so doing please Janyn. Beyond that, I feared Isabella of France. It appeared most people walked softly in her presence.

The daughter of the King of France and the Queen of Navarre, she had been bred to be a queen. Her betrothal to the young Edward of Caernarvon had been urged by the Pope as the best hope for peace between England and France. Beautiful, educated and fabulously robed, according to my grandmother, she had arrived in England to discover that her handsome young husband had already lost his heart and pledged his undying devotion to his comrade-in-arms, Piers Gaveston. Not one to concede defeat easily, Isabella had worked to bring the barons around to support her against Gaveston, and devoted herself to the young King, her husband, making herself his indispensable partner.

Years after Gaveston's execution, another handsome knight, Hugh Despenser, usurped Isabella's role as Edward's partner. Despenser was not satisfied with fortune and favour like Gaveston, but thirsty for power and ruthless in taking it. Isabella sailed to France, arranged for her son, Edward's heir, to join her there, and allied herself with Roger Mortimer, an English baron whom Edward had exiled and robbed of land and title. She shared Mortimer's bed and with him planned and executed an invasion that led to Despenser's long, painful, and very public execution, and eventually the murder of King Edward, her husband and father of the present King Edward. Even in her waning years, Isabella was a powerful woman, entertaining the ruling families of Europe in her elegant palace at Castle Rising or one of the other royal residences.

I had not known a woman could hold so much power. And even if she had wielded it while queen, to have retained some of it after her own lover arranged for the murder of her husband, an anointed king, went against everything I'd ever been taught about the role of women, or our abilities. I imagined her having male genitals hidden beneath her elegant skirts and a demon for a familiar on her left shoulder. But everyone in the household spoke of her as beautiful, profoundly feminine, graceful and just, if not overly merciful.

Thinking of Isabella was not calming me. I rose and told Gwen I would go riding before I dressed for the Dowager Queen's arrival. I knew by the crease in her forehead that Gwen disapproved, but she did as I requested. Serenity was saddled and ready for me when I stepped out into the yard. Janyn's father stood beside his own horse.

'I welcome your company, Master John,' I said as I kissed him on the cheek, 'but a groom would have sufficed as my companion.'

'Not today, my dear daughter,' he said. His eyes were merry, and in them I read that he had leapt at this chance to escape the last-minute flurry of preparations.

The morning was beautiful, a beneficence of warmth – for late-October – and sunshine after a stormy night. My father-in-law was loquacious, recounting past feasts in the company of Isabella, the Queen Mother. He seemed in awe of the mere fact of her speaking to him, much less inviting him to Castle Rising and later visiting his own son's homes.

'Should I be jealous of her?' I asked.

Master John looked puzzled. 'For having been a queen?'

'No!' I laughed. 'That would be madness, for certain. Should I be jealous of her friendship with Janyn?' Whether it was more than friendship was the question in my heart.

It was my father-in-law's turn to laugh, and he did so, loud and long. 'You will soon understand why I laughed as I did,' he said when he had composed himself. 'You will see that she is far too regal ever to cast her eye on a man with no noble blood.'

'Roger Mortimer was not a king,' I said.

'No, but he had noble blood.'

I was yet innocent of the natural order that set merchants – no matter how wealthy, educated, splendidly garbed, pious and charitable, and regardless of how much the monarchs and barons needed their monetary assistance – far beneath those with royal blood running through their veins.

'Any woman would desire Janyn,' I said.

With those words I won an affectionate smile from my husband's father.

'I am overjoyed that you think so. But do you mean to convince her to steal your husband?'

'No!' I know that I blushed, realising how foolish I must sound. My fear was that I was too happy. I was not entirely certain whether it was God, Dame Fortune or the devil who worked in such wise, but I was apprehensive that one of them would look on my happiness and judge it too complete, demanding payment of a forfeit. Rob me of Janyn, of his love, of my health . . . I did not know what my debt would be, but I felt it was inevitable, as night follows day. I had done nothing to deserve such complete happiness.

'Why, then, does she favour him, Master John?'

'I wish you would call me "Father",' he said. 'As to your question, Janyn has found his mother's family most excellent partners in trade, and the Queen Mother is pleased to engage his services.'

'But not you, Father?' I saw no reason to deny his wish, feeling as I did that I had lost my birth father. 'You are not partners with Dame Tommasa's family?'

A happy wag of the head bespoke Master John's satisfaction in my form of address.

'I had my own thriving trade when we were wed, and Tommasa's brother was yet alive. Besides, I grow too old for such journeys.'

I had reassured myself that I had only to conceive a child to keep Janyn by my side indefinitely. For another child would soon follow, and another, and then he would give up the wanderlust. I asked Master John if Isabella would be offended by my keeping Janyn at home with children.

'Keep him at home?'

I did not like his bemused expression. 'He told my grand-parents that once he was wed he would depend more on his factors and travel much less.'

'I am sorry to distress you, sweet Alice, but I cannot imagine him ever doing so. Janyn could not prosper if he were to bide at home with you, and never travel. I am certain that he will now find his journeys far more onerous, but at the same time he will travel when and where he must, to bring bounty to his family.'

My disappointment rendered me unable to speak further. Here was the reckoning I'd known must come. I imagined pacing the floors in the dark of night, unable to sleep for fear that Janyn, from whom I'd heard not a word in months, had been set upon by thieves and left for dead on a treacherous mountain pass. More immediately unsettling was the part he had played in my disappointment. I worried what other untruths he had uttered to appease me . . .

'Alice?' Master John had dismounted and was standing beside me. 'Are you faint? Do you need help dismounting?'

'Father, forgive me. I was imagining how empty my home would be without my husband.'

We had returned to the yard. I did not remember entering the gate, so powerful were my fearful imaginings and unease about Janyn's dissimulation. Gwen and Dame Tommasa were soon beside me, hurrying me back to my chamber to bathe and dress so that I might be present in the hall the moment the herald announced the royal visitor approaching. Despite Dame Agnes's warning that I should not wear red when entertaining the Dowager Queen, my mother-in-law had insisted on it, brushing aside the well-meant advice with assurances that the Lady Isabella would approve of my wearing it. I was to wear my wedding garb, red and gold, but of course this time my hair was gathered up off my neck and partially covered by the beautiful red brocade headdress. I was now a married woman, welcoming a great lady and her company to my home – someone I had never met and already feared and distrusted.

Dame Tommasa kept up a flow of chatter as she assisted Gwen, determined to see me smile.

'It is proper that you are fearful lest anything should go amiss, Alice, but rest assured that you have the best help, and the household knows what is expected of them.'

'Not to mention the ten servants, a cook, and a lady of the chamber,' Gwen murmured, her eyes amused.

But I found it impossible to be light-hearted. 'What is expected of me, Dame Tommasa?'

She gave me a hug, a most comforting gesture, her ample bosom warm and fragrant, her heart beat slow and steady. I loved her very much, and it was not only because she was the mother of my beloved Janyn – she was warm-hearted, generous and beautiful. She made everything interesting and every day festive. I believed that she loved me as well.

When I withdrew from her embrace she fanned herself. Her brocade gown, though beautiful, was heavy for the warm autumn afternoon, and her face was damp. I was the opposite. Despite the fitted wool gown, the surcoat, the headdress, the woollen stockings, I was so cold, particularly my hands and feet, that my fingers and toes ached.

Gwen noticed my hands. 'Can you be so cold, Mistress? I will warm your wine over the brazier.' She took the cup from my hand.

Dame Tommasa took my hands in her warm ones and rubbed them as she said, 'What is expected of you? To make Her Grace welcome and comfortable, to shower her with praise and admiration, to be witty and pretty and gladden her heart – and make your husband the proudest man in the kingdom. She brings great honour on your house, and upon our family.'

'I am no wit,' I protested.

'All you need do is be yourself, speak as you always do.'

I could not imagine being comfortable enough to behave as usual in the presence of the woman called the She-Wolf of France. Janyn had bade me not to use that term for her with his parents or in front of the servants, for it was an insult and he did not want to risk anyone mentioning it in the hearing of any of her company. I reminded myself that she had been kind to my parents, and that Janyn and his parents, three people I had grown to love and respect, loved and respected her.

'I have never been in the presence of royalty, yet now I am about to welcome the mother of my King into my home and converse with her. I am frightened, Dame Tommasa.' There, I had said it, though it embarrassed me to admit my doubt. Although the priests urge humility, life seems to teach us that folk would rather not bear witness to any doubts we might harbour about ourselves, particularly when they depend on our performing as others have planned. The Perrers family had chosen me for this role, and I must play the part without hesitation. My mother-in-law's response increased my regret for having so spoken.

She shook her head at me and with a half-smile said, 'You *would* ride out this morning. Now you are weary and making much ado about nothing. Her Grace is your guest, Alice, and you shall be a most gracious hostess.' Giving my hands a final vigorous rub, she let them go, chucked me beneath the chin, and said, 'Now I must finish my own dressing.' With a last hug that seemed intended to shake me into my senses, she sailed out of the room in her gorgeous green brocade.

'Mistress?' Gwen looked at me with concern. 'You are ready. Would you like to see the chamber we have prepared for Her Grace, and how we have decorated the hall?'

I gathered myself and resolved to enjoy Her Grace's visit. We had done all we could do to prepare. A glance in the mirror reassured me that I looked sufficiently elegant. I nodded to Gwen. 'Of course! The chamber first, then the hall.'

We swept out of my bedchamber and descended to the lower level where a beautiful chamber that Janyn used for his meetings with merchants or his steward, when he wanted more privacy than the hall might afford, had been transformed into a bedchamber for the Dowager Queen. A large, grand bed had arrived two days earlier, together with chests bursting with wall hangings, bedclothes and cushions. I had at first been offended by the implication that we had nothing fine enough for Her Grace, but Janyn assured me that Isabella always provided her own bed and bedding if possible. It was the custom of nobles.

'But what could possibly be more beautiful than what we might provide?' I had asked.

Janyn's laughter left me feeling naïve. It was a jolly, full-throated sound, as if I had said something very funny. 'I forget that you have never seen a royal residence, my sweet, innocent Alice.' He looked at me, then hugged me to him. 'Forgive my laughter, my love. God knows I would not insult you. I delight in your innocence. I will be sorry when you have seen all that I have seen.'

'Will you take me to Italy?'

'Why would you ever wish to make such a journey? I must do so, but you are free from such onerous responsibility.'

'I think I should like to travel with you.'

'On this beautiful isle, yes, there is much to see. We shall take many journeys here.'

Janyn had led me to the bed then, and the conversation had been forgotten. For a time.

Now I looked at the gold and silver thread, the lapis lazuli pigments, and saw it was indeed true, we had nothing so fine. On the window ledges cushions of indigo embroidered in gold and silver thread welcomed one to sit and gaze out at the fields and woodland. Several maidservants sat sewing near the south window, and one was stirring something over the brazier. Lady Jane, Isabella's lady-in-waiting who had been sent ahead to ensure that all was ready for Her Grace, kept them well in hand. At dinner the previous evening she had been sweet company, making up for the priest who was a dour Frenchman, too rude and dismissive for my taste.

'I would choose reds and greens for those cushions,' I said, thinking aloud, but softly, 'and patterned cloth rather than embroidered, for comfort.'

'I agree, Mistress,' Gwen whispered. 'But they are very pretty. And so stuffed with down that Her Grace will sit high enough for her maid to comb her hair as she gazes without.'

I could imagine the comfort, the ease. 'I should like such cushions on my windows,' I said more loudly.

Gwen nodded. 'I shall begin as soon as your royal guest departs.'

So easy. I had just to say I wished it so. Life was sweet at that moment.

A great wooden bath stood in one corner, by the brazier, and an intricately carved wooden screen nearby, ready to shield Her Grace from draughts.

'All seems ready,' I said. 'Let us move on.'

Down in the hall there was little evidence of the frantic rushing about of the past few days except for the transformation of the great chamber. Unlike our home in London, the hall at Fair Meadow was not tiled but stone-flagged and softened with rushes, a true country house. Fresh rushes strewn with fragrant herbs sweetened the room, and a fire merrily burned in the fire circle. No dogs lounged about, and the great trestle table was set up, covered with a brightly painted cloth, and the benches piled with pretty cushions.

Gertrude appeared, dressed in what looked like a new if simple gown of dark wool, respectable and tidy. Trailing her came a serving boy carrying more cushions, so many that he looked ready to topple over with them. I wondered where she meant to put them, and then I saw – there were more benches ranged along the wall.

'How many will be in Her Grace's company?' I asked Gwen.

'Thirty at least,' she said, 'but that includes the twelve who arrived last night. She has been known to bring as many as fifty.'

'I should think she'd travel seldom if it requires such a party!'

Gertrude sent off the serving boy and joined us. 'Mistress, how beautiful you look today.' Her smile was sweet and she gave me a little bow.

'I am pleased with all you have done,' I said. And so grateful that she had experience of such events.

We all turned towards the yard as a horn sounded.

'That will be her herald,' said Gertrude. She gathered her skirts and hurried from the hall.

Once more my hands turned to ice. 'Where shall I stand?' I asked Gwen.

But it was Dame Tommasa who answered, sweeping into the hall bedecked in pearls. 'You shall stand at the hall door when all the party has dismounted, Alice. Until then, let us sit by the window and enjoy the breeze.' She guided me by my elbow to one side of the hall, beneath a long window, too far from the fire to my liking.

Gwen, blessed Gwen, was soon at my side with a cup of spiced wine, steam rising from it most promisingly.

'How you can be so cold on this mild day I cannot understand,' said my mother-in-law, fanning herself once more. Her silks rustled as she shifted in her seat to take a good look at me, her gaze lingering on my middle, which was mostly hidden by the warm mazer I clenched. 'Is it possible that you are with child?' she asked, her eyes widening with excitement.

I shook my head. 'I believe what is chilling me is my worry that I shall fail Janyn in some way, when I want so much to make him proud of me.'

Tommasa looked up into my eyes. 'Mayhap. But, in case, I do pray you will refrain from riding for a few days.'

What could I say? *I want to ride with Her Grace and my husband, damn you,* like a petulant child? I thought that I might lie about my flux if it should come to that. My mother had carried four healthy children to term and never ceased any activity until late in her pregnancies. Though my conscience reminded me that she did not ride.

I was saved from saying anything by the arrival of Lady Jane, lovely today in a dark silk gown.

'Oh, Dame Alice, what a vision you are!' she exclaimed as she joined us. She gracefully perched beside us and gazed at me, then the room. 'It is no wonder my lady loves this place. I have been walking in the gardens, and cannot remember so peaceful and lovely a morning.'

'Have you seen Dame Tommasa's garden in the city?' I asked. 'It is a wonder of peace and beauty in the middle of noisy, crowded London.'

'I should love to see it someday.'

'You would be most welcome,' said Dame Tommasa with a beatific smile. She had lowered her fan and now gave me a little bow in thanks.

My heart leaped at the sound of the hunting party's arrival, but when I began to rise Lady Jane stopped me, gently resting one hand on my shoulder.

'They will not dismount at once. I pray you, be at ease a while longer.'

Though I sat still, I was anything but at ease. When I was finally guided to the hall door my knees wanted to lock with every step and my hands ached most fiercely with cold fear. The yard, so peaceful when last I'd walked through it, was now roiling with people and beasts moving in all directions. And then I spied Janyn, resplendent in hunting green. He was speaking to a woman who must be Isabella of France, the quiet centre of the throng. She stood beside a black horse unlike any I had ever seen before, so sleek, so graceful, yet large, and with a hint of wildness in his eyes. I noticed that the men surrounding her were clad in leather tunics and leggings with her coat of arms on their tabards. Isabella was in widow's weeds of style and elegance. Over a black gown she wore a black leather surcoat, with matching long gloves and hat. I imagined that the leather had been chosen to protect her clothing from the horse's sweat. It created a dramatic contrast, the soot black against her pale hair and skin. She knew the effect she created, I was certain.

I wondered for whom she wore the weeds, for whom she mourned – her late husband or Roger Mortimer? Or if she simply mourned her own lost queenship?

As if she had sensed my regard she swept around to face me, looking right into my eyes. Though we were at least twenty strides apart, I felt that her gaze penetrated to my heart and she saw my fear. She gave me a cold smile, then turned back to Janyn. I felt breathless with awe. Could not believe that I was welcoming such an august person into my home.

Janyn had bowed to Isabella and moved to one side as she proceeded through the crowd, everyone allowing her to pass. Did they, too, watch her in awe beneath their lashes? I wondered. She glided as if her feet merely skimmed the ground. She looked neither to right nor left, but neither did she watch where she walked, which I certainly would have done in an unfamiliar yard, with horse and dog droppings likely to be all about. But her gaze was turned upwards, towards the lintel of our great door. What confidence she had that no one would allow her path to be befouled. As she grew close, she lowered her gaze to note our little gathering in the doorway – Dame Tommasa, Master John, and Lady Jane standing behind me.

Trembling with terror, I bowed low and managed to welcome her to Fair Meadow as my mother-in-law had rehearsed me. When she was within a few arms' lengths of me, I realised with surprise that Isabella was shorter than I was – from afar she had seemed to tower over the others. Her eyes were hazel, like mine, her expression one of impatience barely masked by a polite smile.

'The hunt was glorious and we are weary, Dame Alice.'

Only then did I notice the shadows beneath her eyes, how short was her breathing.

Lady Jane stepped forward, offering to lead her mistress directly to her chamber.

As they progressed through the hall the line of servants bowed, and then several scurried off to fetch the heated water for Her Grace's bath.

Now a wry-faced nobleman, dressed almost as elegantly as Isabella, stepped up to me.

Janyn introduced him as a count . . . I no longer remember of where or what his Christian name was. I do recall him bowing to me and declaring himself heartsick that his friend had found me before ever he had chance to woo me himself. I fear it turned my head a bit, and I floated away with him and his younger, English companion, Sir David, to sit with them while they enjoyed some wine and cold refreshment. Janyn went off to dress for the feast. Lady Jane had informed me that Sir David often acted as the Dowager Queen's courier between her and Janyn, and that I would see him often. The Count was a distant relation of Isabella's apparently, no one I need remember.

Sir David brought welcome news of my good friend Geoffrey.

'He is to join the household of Prince Lionel and his wife, the Countess of Ulster. Lionel is the King's second-born son, and the Countess of almost equally noble blood. It is quite an honour.'

I was happy for Geoffrey, and amused to hear that he already had a reputation for witty banter.

'Indeed he is very well liked,' said Sir David, 'and will continue to rise in the noble households. Since you are favoured by Her Grace, you will have opportunity to see your friend again, I should think.'

'I am grateful for such gladsome tidings,' I said. I had not thought to see much of Geoffrey now that our paths had so diverged.

The musicians had set up in a corner of the hall, and now began to play a merry tune. I felt as if I were dreaming: the hall so beautiful, the company so elegant – including myself – and the food and music promising a most delightful afternoon and evening.

My delight dimmed as soon as the Dowager Queen joined us in the hall. I could not imagine any queen more resplendent than

Isabella – I was certain that her daughter-in-law, the present Queen of England, must feel lacking beside her. I certainly did. I had previously felt guilty about the splendour of my robes, jewels, shoes, veils, but saw now they were modest indeed in comparison with royalty's – or at least with Isabella's. The jet and obsidian adorning her dark-silk velvet gown caught the light with such a shimmer it seemed as if they were alive, as if she had gathered thousands of butterflies and commanded them to flutter their wings above her as she moved. Her robe scintillated so that when she was in the room the eye was drawn continually to her. And she wore it with such ease and grace, absolutely accustomed to her own splendour.

I bowed to her, but it did not seem enough. I felt I should walk on my knees with my gaze on the ground when in her presence. It was even more humbling than I had imagined, to welcome her into my home. At first her demeanour towards me did nothing to alleviate my sense of being an awkward and unlovely duckling, presuming to greet a regal and most beautiful swan.

My Janyn, I was glad to see, did not seem to feel inferior in any wise, and I did think he looked as elegant as any in her company.

It was my first lesson in the importance of believing oneself elegant as well as dressing thus. I struggled to regain my self-assurance, praying for God's help, for I did not want to disappoint my husband.

To my great relief, Her Grace seemed to warm to me as the meal proceeded. Janyn had been speaking of how quickly I had learned to ride and teased me about my fondness for my slow-gaited mare, saying I had named her Serenity.

'But that is a very fitting name for a beloved mount,' Her Grace declared, and turned, tilting her head to one side, seeming truly to look at me for the first time. 'She blesses you with serenity?'

'She does, Your Grace.' I searched for something to add. 'The noise around me seems to recede when I ride her, and the air softens.'

She graced me with a breathtakingly beautiful smile. Her eyes lit up, her ivory skin gathered at her temples and a dimple appeared to the left of her wide mouth. How her King could ever have looked at another when she was near, I could not imagine.

'Your husband tells me that you wish to hunt? You shall join me when you have had some experience. I like a woman who feels at one with her horse. I should think you might also enjoy hunting with a hawk.'

Later I heard her comment to Janyn, 'It is a pity her parents have not had her riding and hawking, but they did seem to be of very simple stock. How fortunate that you plucked their swan from the nest before she sank to their level.'

Later, as she sat listening to the minstrels in the hall, Isabella fell asleep, her face slack, a thread of spittle slipping from one corner of her mouth. Both Janyn and his mother looked exceedingly uncomfortable – not disgusted, but fearful. I did not understand their distress. Isabella was an old woman who put on a good display of vigour but could not sustain it. I had found it comforting to see this human side of her. Their unease troubled me.

In bed that night Janyn was fulsome in his praise of both Isabella and myself, almost too much so, as though desperate to believe that all was well. But perhaps I was being too sensitive. He was wild in his lovemaking, which must be a good sign. I did not speak of my own anxieties and uncertainties. I ached with love for him, and when we made love I thought of nothing but pleasuring him as he pleasured me.

The next day Janyn and Dame Tommasa conferred with Her Grace in her chamber for several hours while I enjoyed a ride around the estate with Master John, the Count and Sir David. My riding clothes might not be as elegant as the Dowager Queen's, but when away from her I felt beautiful. Serenity's slow gait was no problem as Master John told us the history of the many fields and woods around us, the streams and the village. The Count offered stories of his own country estate in France, and Sir David had us all laughing over his account of his first attempts to sail a boat on the Severn.

At the feast afterwards I caught snippets of exchanges between Janyn and his father about a journey to Lombardy in late-winter. There was an air of tension to their conversation, I thought, though I prayed I was mistaken in this. The minstrels were singing, there were many conversations in progress, and it was possible I was mixing up the words of one group with another's.

Isabella had been with us several days before she turned her attention to me. After instructing me on a point of etiquette about how I addressed Gertrude, about which I was mortified despite having been warned she might say such things, she declared herself very glad that she had made certain our marriage would take place.

'I am as delighted with you as Janyn said I would be,' she said. 'The effort to guarantee your union was not wasted, I see.' She then leaned closer to say in a conspiratorial voice, 'I see by the way your husband looks on you that your bed sport is everything he had hoped.'

That he had spoken to her of his taste in lovemaking seemed to suggest a relationship inappropriate to his station – like her relationship with Roger Mortimer had been. I studied her, wondering with dismay whether this exquisite bird of paradise had been my husband's lover. How else would she understand his looks?

'Your Grace,' I said, 'I am the happiest of brides, and deeply honoured by your interest.' I managed to say it without choking on my sudden suspicion.

In bed that night, I was brimming with questions and close to tears. Janyn noticed at once.

'My sweet Alice, my love,' he murmured, stroking my hair. 'What troubles you?'

'What had Her Grace to do with our betrothal? How can she guess from your eyes that we enjoy our lovemaking?'

He said nothing for a while, lying back on the cushions and folding his arms behind his head. The soft black hair on his chest attracted my hand, but I resisted. I wanted an answer, and the moment I touched him I would doubtless lose my chance.

'She values my services, and knows that an unhappy man is a reckless man. Therefore she wanted me happily married once more, with a beloved wife and children to inspire caution in my travels. As for my eyes, I cannot say.' He chuckled at the ceiling. 'How strange that she spoke of that to you.'

He turned on his side, and gently pinched one of my nipples. I tried not to respond. His eyes caressed me as his hand idly skimmed my belly and slid between my legs. I squeezed them together.

'Were you lovers?' I asked.

He withdrew his hand and sat up, pulling me after him by the shoulders. He was smiling, a lazy, lustful smile.

'You are jealous? How delicious! But Isabella of France and Janyn Perrers, merchant? No, my beautiful Alice.' He cupped my breasts in his hands, kneading them.

I groaned, but managed to ask, 'Are you away to Lombardy?'

'Eventually, my love.'

He sat me on his lap and I could not help myself, but lifted up a little to sink him into me. Such was the pattern of our night-time discussions.

I did not see at the time how he used our lovemaking to silence my questions, subtly suggesting to me that in wanting to know more than the little he told me, I risked my own happiness. I was only fourteen and so much in love.

'But right as when the sonne shyneth brighte
In March, that chaungeth ofte tyme his face,
And that a cloude is put with wynd to flighte,
Which oversprat the sonne as for a space,
A cloudy thought gan thorugh hire soule pace,
That overspradde hire brighte thoughtes alle,
So that for feere almost she gan to falle.'

– Geoffrey Chaucer, *Troilus and Criseyde*, II, ll. 764–770

On the day the Dowager Queen was to depart, I awoke feeling ill. My first thought was that I had eaten some bad meat, and I feared our guests and other members of the household might be ill as well. But Gwen and Dame Tommasa assured me that no one else had fallen ill; some of them were green from too much wine the previous evening, but they were accustomed to such discomfort. By then I had guessed the true source of my illness, though I did not say it aloud. They ordered me to stay abed, kindly reassuring me that I would feel much better soon. I did.

Until, to my dismay, Her Grace came to me in my bedchamber to say farewell.

'Your hospitality is beyond reproach. And now you are with child! You will make your husband so happy.' She put a finger to her lips, her eyes teasing. 'I have said not a word to him, nor shall I. It is for you to tell him the good tidings.'

I was so overwhelmed by her presence that my first thought was relief that Gwen had combed out my hair and wrapped my shoulders in a fringed shawl of deep rose silk. It took me a moment to hear what the Dowager Queen had said.

'Oh, Your Grace, I cannot be with child,' I blurted out, hotly blushing as I realised how foolish I sounded. I hated the fact that she had guessed the news before I'd had a chance to tell Janyn.

Her laughter was high and sweet. 'And why not? I see how it

goes with you and Janyn, I do not believe that you "cannot be with child".'

'But I want to ride out with the hunt, Your Grace,' I cried. Sweet heaven, I sounded more childish by the moment. I realised then that I'd hidden the truth even from myself so that I would not slip up and tell Janyn while we had guests, while I still hoped to ride.

Isabella tilted back her head and laughed, a pretty, fluting sound. Her eyes were still teasing and friendly when she leaned towards me again. 'And that is the proof. You humours are awry! Do you not hear yourself? The greatest joy a young wife might have, conceiving a child, and you are petulant about not being permitted to ride out with the hunt!' She levelled her gaze on me, looking serious now. 'Do not let them deny you fresh air and exercise, sweet Alice. Walk. Walk as much as you desire, as much as you may. But riding?' She shook her head. 'You will not wish to endanger the child.' She stood up. 'And when you are delivered, you shall have a fine horse and learn to hunt. Do not doubt it.'

It is impossible for me to describe the joy with which Janyn received the news of my being with child.

His eyes, always so expressive, seemed to melt with love for me. He reached out for me, then seemed uncertain.

'I will not break under your touch, my love. In truth, I need you to hold me,' I said.

I slept in his arms that night, and it did not matter that when I woke I felt ill again. I felt cocooned in a nest of such love that I regretted nothing, not even the illness. Indeed, though I'd already felt as if nothing were denied me, it had been nothing in comparison with the way Janyn and his parents and all the household now indulged my every whim.

I had only two regrets: that I could no longer ride Serenity, and that we departed for London within a few days of Isabella's departure. Master John could stay away from his trade no longer and Dame Tommasa felt that she should accompany him, and yet she did not wish to leave me at Fair Meadow with only the servants and Janyn to help me adjust to my first pregnancy, a situation no one found acceptable.

Despite the regrets, I quickly cheered up, thinking of sharing my happy news with Nan, Mary, Will and John, and was eager to become familiar with All Saints, the parish church of my new home in London. Her Grace's chaplain had rebuffed my attempts to talk to him and I yearned for the sort of comfort I'd found all my life in St Antonin's. I was quite certain that a welcoming church would be a blessing to me as the child grew in my womb and Janyn resumed his travels. I returned to London in a cart well cushioned by bedding and covered in sail-cloth, and Serenity stayed behind in the country stables.

We resumed a comfortable rhythm of domestic routine, church, and entertaining. Janyn made no delay in introducing me to his circle. He had only one concern.

'Make no mention of the royal guest we entertained while at Fair Meadow,' he warned.

'But surely folk know that you trade in her name.'

'Of course. But it is never discussed. And as for her favour to me, it is unusually personal, Alice, and might therefore inspire jealousy or suspicion.'

'Suspicion of what, my love?'

'The royal family are ever in need of money to fill their coffers, and those merchants and bankers – especially the bankers – who make them loans are most favoured.'

'You have loaned money to Her Grace?'

'A little. But others would surmise that I had loaned her far more, and then, thinking I must have money to spare, would wish to borrow from me as well. And I have none to give!'

'You spend it all on me.'

He laughed. 'And it is well spent, my love.' He quickly grew serious again. 'Favour brings preference, and there are guild rules, though the royal family and the great barons are not bound by such constraints. So we do not speak of such things.'

'What of the servants? Surely some of them gossip, they are only human.'

'What matters is that *we* say nothing, my love, so there is nothing but the gossip of servants, which is hardly proof. Do you understand?'

'I shall not refer in public to Her Grace.'

He was well pleased. In truth, to say nothing of Her Grace's visit was so simple that I found it no burden; nevertheless, the thought of the rule chilled me. I worried that such a secret presaged more, and feared what might ensue. The not knowing cast a shadow over my happiness.

Despite my condition, I was soon busy with the household. I shopped, sewed, and even hired additional servants, being certain to consult Gertrude, Angelo and Gwen about my plan first. I enjoyed bargaining with merchants, choosing more materials to brighten up the house – Dame Tommasa had inspired me. In general, I found my duties immensely satisfying.

But my moods were increasingly mercurial, and I was glad of the daily round of prayers at my new parish church, especially once I had found a confessor who put me at ease. John de Hanneye was a young priest assisting the elderly pastor, in preparation for his first preferment to a parish of his own. He knew Janyn and liked the Perrers family, but that was not why I was drawn to him. From the first I felt a strong sense of connection to him, a familiarity I could not explain. Gwen liked him as well, and was good about wandering away to entertain herself while I spoke to him. I took the huge risk of telling him of my anxiety concerning Her Grace's influence over my marriage, upon Janyn and his mother, wholeheartedly believing that I could trust him. I prayed I was right in that, appreciating the way he listened but did not offer me empty reassurances. Instead he suggested we both pray that God should protect my family.

I met a great many of Janyn's guild fellows and their wives, and made some new friends. But one occasional dinner guest I disliked and distrusted from the start, a Fleming by the name of Richard Lyons. By his rough manner and the coarseness of his speech he was clearly of low birth, but Janyn's fellow merchants tolerated his unpleasantness because he was wealthy and very influential, particularly in the lucrative court circle. He leered when he first met me, with his bold gaze unclothing and ravishing me on the spot. I yearned to slap him.

But Janyn squeezed my hand and whispered, 'Pay him no heed. Speak to him as if he had all the courtesy of a knight in the Court of Love, Alice. I need him. He has an uncanny ability to be in the right place at the right time. He has ingratiated himself with much of the royal family and other noble houses by being the first to offer loans when they are embarrassed for coin.'

At that first dinner I was grateful to be seated far from Lyons. One of the other wives commented that I had now met the worst of the lot.

'Do you find him unpleasant?' I asked.

'I would put it more crudely,' she said. 'I feel I must scrub myself clean after being in his company.'

'It is his way, then, to look on a woman as if she were the roast on the board?' I asked.

Those seated around me laughed at my description.

'We are all loath to invite him into our homes,' said David, the husband of the woman who had spoken. 'But he has made judicious loans to the right people, and his favour opens doors.'

'Cecily finds him delightful,' said Martin, looking as if he might cast up his dinner.

David's wife, Ann, rolled her eyes at that. Martin's wife was a silly young woman and he was quite an old man. It was plain that Cecily yearned for younger blood.

I saw amongst this company how fortunate I was. My parents' unhappiness with one another seemed the rule rather than the exception, and there was much open flirting at guild functions. But there was also a great deal of laughter, the stories of journeys far and wide enthralled me, and there were few among Janyn's friends I actively disliked. The only two I remember displeasing me were Richard Lyons and Nicholas Sardouche, but we only rarely entertained Sardouche.

He was a member of Janyn's other set of friends, connections of which Father had apparently been unaware before our marriage. These were Lombard merchants – financiers and traders; although they were elegant, courteous, full of exciting tales, and all in all delightful companions, I considered them dangerous to know. My father usually referred to them, as most Londoners did, as the 'Society of Lucca'. Janyn was not considered a member of their group but he knew these men through Dame Tommasa's father and a cousin, Francisco Flocet, a dashing older man who had once served in the King's guard. Janyn explained to me that he associated with the 'society' because he traded in their territory, and therefore felt he needed to assure himself of their friendship.

The problem was that the London merchants considered them their rivals, and indeed the Lombards enjoyed advantages – such as lower taxes and other favours from the King, in exchange for loans – that the London merchants did not share. The Society of Lucca were also notorious smugglers, and it was understandable that merchants who passed up on potential sources of wealth, in order to obey the law of the land and the rules of their guilds, resented smugglers above all other folk. I feared that our association with them might jeopardise our reputation, but Janyn said much the same of them as he did of Richard Lyons: that he needed them. As was not the case with Lyons, however, he also enjoyed their company.

At Christmas we entertained Janyn's parents, but not mine. Father told me that our connection with the Lombard merchants was unacceptable to his guild of grocers. There was doubtless some truth to this. It was enough for me that he did not prevent Nan from bringing Will and Mary round for weekly afternoons of games and jollity, and nor did my brother John's master suggest he should not sup with us on Sundays.

It sounds as if I was often unhappy, but that is not so. Some shadows passed over my heart from time to time, but for the most part I still could not believe my good fortune in having a husband I loved and who loved me, in-laws who loved me as their own daughter, fascinating friends, a confessor who listened and gave me gentle counsel, and a baby in my womb. Besides all this love and good company, I lived in such comfort, a comfort that went far beyond necessity. The occasional fear or doubt seemed a small price to pay. I had only to think of Janyn and my heart would swell with love.

In late-winter came a blow for which I should have better prepared myself. Janyn announced that he would depart for Lombardy in a few weeks. We were lying in bed after very gentle lovemaking. I was secretly yearning for the old days, when our lovemaking was rough and wild. He lay beside me, his head propped on one hand. I loved the smell of him.

'Alice, I must leave in a fortnight for Lombardy. I wanted to tell you before you heard it from my parents or my factor.'

'No!' I reached for his thigh.

He pressed my hand. 'You knew that this day would come. I have never hidden it from you.'

'But it is not yet spring,' I moaned. 'Should you not wait until the spring?'

'What if I should be delayed and not return in time for the birth of our first child?' he asked, tenderly laying his warm hand on my swelling belly.

'Are you not risking not returning at all, by travelling in winter?'

He cupped my face in both hands and looked long into my eyes. My body responded with such desire for him I gasped. He kissed me and held me close.

'My love, I must go now. I have made the journey at this season before, and was home well before midsummer.' Which was when Dame Tommasa believed I would be brought to childbed. 'You must trust in God. Pray that He watches over me.'

'Is it the Dowager Queen who sends you and puts you at such risk?' I asked.

He lifted his head. 'In part. But we have agreed not to speak of her.'

'In the company of others. Surely we may discuss her here, in our bedchamber, with none to hear?'

'The less you know, the easier it will be for you to say nothing.'

As I moved to protest he silenced me with a kiss.

'You are not a fair player,' I pouted.

'What say you of this? To compensate for my silence on my travels for Her Grace, I shall discuss all my other business affairs with you and take your suggestions into consideration. I shall take care that you meet all with whom I trade, so that you may make informed decisions.' He cocked an eyebrow. 'Well?'

I may have been young and inexperienced, but I saw in his proposal a way to be part of his life, not just a pretty pet.

'Yes. It is a fair trade. But you forfeit all peace between us should you go back on it.' I knew just where to stroke his spine to make him shiver, and did so then.

Our new agreement did nothing to ease my fears about his

journey, but Janyn immediately began to fulfil his promise: introducing me to yet more men with whom he traded, showing me through the storerooms, explaining the value of the spices, jewels, cloth, statues, and sundry other merchandise. He even showed me the lists he kept of his contacts and what he judged to be their strongest points. There was little time to teach me more, but I took heart from his obvious approval of my questions and suggestions. I was grateful for his tutoring later. It was to prove an invaluable gift.

And then he was gone. He did not simply disappear from the house one day, no, he was not so cruel but most loving and considerate. His parents accompanied us to the staithe, and I was welcomed on board the vessel that would take him across the Channel. I had been aboard a few ships with my father, so this was not alien to me. But when I saw the cabin where Janyn would take shelter – for storms were common in the Channel in this season, with high seas, waves that crashed against the ship and washed across the decks – it looked so small, so fragile, bare and inhospitable, that the knot of fear in my stomach twisted tighter. Janyn held me and recounted pleasant memories of voyages aboard this ship and others like it until I could manage to breathe freely again.

His cousin Francisco, Janyn's companion on the journey, swore to me that he would bring him safely home. 'I have vowed before God and all the saints that I shall do this, dear Alice,' he said with his usual grandiosity.

I was grateful, remembering his background in the King's guard.

As word came that they were ready to depart, my beloved Janyn took my face between his large, warm hands, and we kissed as if our lives depended on it. Then he whispered, 'I will be at home when you are brought to bed with our child, Alice. Know that I will be there. Pray for me, and have faith in the power of your prayers. I shall pray as well, that you remain in good health and good cheer, and that our child is whole and hearty.'

I was weeping, as breeding women are wont to do, but managed to nod and rest my hands over his, looking into his eyes. 'You will be at home when I am brought to bed with our first born, Janyn. And we shall be whole and hearty and blessed.'

I was escorted from the ship and gathered up by Dame Tommasa and Master John, who had arranged for my favourite minstrels to perform in my hall that evening, continuing their lovely music and song until I was well asleep. I felt blessed, in the bosom of a loving family, curled around the child I believed would combine the best qualities of Janyn and myself.

Although part of me was often inattentive to my companions, I did not lie abed nursing darksome thoughts. Gertrude had suffered a fall and would be confined to a chair throughout the spring, so I was learning to deal directly with the lower servants. Janyn had instructed his factor to consult me on certain accounts, Dom Hanneye listened with calm and sympathetic attention to all my fears and hopes, and the wives of the guild included me in gatherings spent embroidering cushions for the benches in the guild hall and the church. I was particularly honoured to be asked to stand as second godmother to the infant daughters of several guild members, an important bonding practice among the families.

Members of the guild and many of the Company of Lucca kept me informed of news along the route Janyn was taking, even occasionally bringing word of him from conversations with merchants newly arrived from the continent who had encountered his party. Master John and Dame Tommasa dined with me almost every day, and Dame Agnes and Master Edmund often joined us as well. Nan continued to bring Will and Mary to spend the afternoon at least once a week.

My younger brother and sister were a particular joy to me. Their presence reminded me of my own childish innocence, the belief I held then that no matter how abrupt Father was with me, he did love me. Mary was now the recipient of clothing cut down from my old gowns and Mother's, and loved remembering who had worn the cloth and what they had done while wearing it. Her remarkable memory taught me that children hear and understand far more than adults think that they do. How strange that I had already lost sight of that. Will was clever with his hands, and was learning to carve – our cook, Angelo, was quite skilled in carving and enjoyed tutoring my little brother. Does this not sound like a happy household? It was. I had no complaint but that Janyn was not at home.

I enjoyed the embroidery I did with the other guild wives. I eagerly practised stitches, challenged myself with increasingly complex patterns, and bought fine silk thread, which I also used on my own clothing – Gwen and I, and often either Dame Tommasa or Dame Agnes, were busy with items for the baby as well as wider shifts and a few loose gowns for my swelling body.

Of course there were also arguments and sleepless nights – I was as emotional and impatient as any woman with child. But only a few arguments troubled me long after all else had been resolved or forgiven.

On a morning in early-spring Dame Agnes, Gwen and I were at our needlework in my bedchamber where the light was so lovely. I had been telling them of a dream I'd had in which Janyn's ship was attacked by pirates and he alone survived, sailing home by himself, weary and bedraggled, but laughing about it as if it had been a great adventure, nothing more.

'Happy dreams of your love, that is good. God is blessing you with reassurance,' said Dame Agnes. 'Is he travelling for the Dowager Queen?' She shook her head. 'I mistrust that woman's influence over your home. Your father put you in harm's way, insisting on this marriage.'

'She is the King's dam,' I said half-heartedly.

Grandmother dropped her work and pressed her fingertips to her temples. 'She committed a great sin, Alice. To take the life of an anointed King was worse than mere treason and murder. What sort of woman commits such a sin? Of what other horrors is she capable?'

Her comments brought to mind all my own unease about Isabella, though not from the same cause as Dame Agnes's. 'What would you have me do? Janyn is my husband. I respect and honour him, as is my duty. And I love him more than my own life.' I had begun to shake with emotion and put down my work. 'She is an old woman, more frail than she cares to admit.' I worried to remember suddenly how Janyn and his mother had blanched at the signs of Isabella's ageing. It had been plain to me that they feared her death, and it frightened me that this was so. 'She is a child of God as are we all, swept up in events I cannot even begin to understand. Therefore I do not judge her.' My mouth had gone so dry that my last words were barely whispered.

'Forgive me. I cannot help but worry. Your connection with her endangers your safety and your reputation. Others might not believe you are not directly involved in her affairs.'

Gwen had bent closer to her work, as if wishing to disappear.

'What do you hear?' I asked my grandmother.

'It is how little one hears of Janyn's trade that worries me. Is he part of the Society of Lucca?'

'No!'

'Thank God for that,' Grandmother said, smoothing out the cloth on her lap. 'So he *is* travelling for her?'

I abruptly rose to fetch a cup of wine, dropping my embroidery on the floor. Gwen had anticipated my need and handed a cup to me, then assisted me back to my seat and gathered my work up. But she did not hand it back to me.

'Perhaps you need a nap, mistress,' she prompted me.

'Janyn trades in Italy, Dame Agnes,' I resumed. 'It is what he did when Father chose him for me, and it is what he still does. We are making a family, and he must continue his trade.' I would not have believed I could sound so calm, so matter-of-fact, when I was trembling inside. There *was* something wrong. Janyn and his family were too secretive.

'Oh, Alice, I did not mean . . .' Dame Agnes reached out a hand.

Fearful lest I confide too much in Grandmother and endanger her, I begged a sudden weariness. 'Forgive me, Grandmother, but I must take some rest. Gwen will see you out.'

'I have upset you. I am such an old fool.'

'No, Dame Agnes, it is the baby,' I protested.

Her ruched hat trembling as she rose, Grandmother made a great business of gathering together her needles and threads. 'God go with you, my dearest Alice.'

When she was gone I sank down on to the bed and stared up at the canopy for a long, long while. I was shaken. I had over-reacted to Dame Agnes's question, I told myself.

Gwen returned and silently sat beside my bed, continuing her needlework. Later that day Dame Tommasa came. As we sat and talked she noticed my mood, and inquired if there was anything she might do to cheer me. When I said that I was merely tired she probed no more. I said nothing because there was nothing to say. She and Janyn had told me all they intended to.

In late-spring my love returned. He had written that he expected to sail up the Thames in early-June, but God blessed his travels and he arrived a week earlier than I'd had any hope of seeing him. Heavy with child as I was by then, I lacked all grace and feared that Janyn would greet me with cold indifference. But he did not do so. Although our kisses required some careful positioning, they were long and passionate. We agreed to disregard the suggestions that we sleep apart for my last month.

On the first evening we left the lamps burning longer than usual so that we might gaze on one another. He was stroking my stomach when the baby kicked. Startled, he withdrew his hand and stared as my belly moved, seemingly by itself. I reached for his hand and guided it back.

'Is it not a wonder?' I whispered. 'Our child is alive within me, kicking and stretching and letting me know that soon he will be bored and choose to come out into the light.'

Janyn's dark eyes were wide and moist as he moved his hands over my belly, seeking more contact with our child.

'A miracle. A blessed miracle,' he said. 'But is it not painful?'

I shook my head. 'The weight is painful, and the stretching of my hips, but from the moment our child moved, I have felt –' I searched for a word to describe the companionship '– I have felt a part of life, not simply an observer.'

'You are most precious, my love,' said Janyn. 'I pray that you may never suffer, that God will guide and protect you in all ways.'

When I woke in the night I was in Janyn's arms, safe and warm, and my heart swelled with love.

Sir David, who had been so charming when he was our guest at Fair Meadow in Isabella's company, arrived a few days after Janyn's return. I thought it a coincidence, but soon learned from his conversation that the Queen Mother had been even better informed than we had about the timing of my husband's return. As we dined, Sir David expressed his hope that my lying in would occur while he was yet in London, so that he might be the one to give Her Grace a first-hand account of her godchild.

'Godchild?' I looked at his smiling face, then at Janyn whose smile was more guarded. He watched me closely for my reaction.

'I did not know we were to be so honoured,' I said to Sir David, but I meant it for Janyn. He might have warned me. I did not welcome this news, and especially not coming from someone other than my husband. I imagined that Dame Agnes would be shattered by this. I had said nothing to Janyn about my grandmother's outburst; she had since apologised for voicing her feelings regarding Isabella in such a way that she had upset me. But what troubled me far more than my dread of breaking this news to her was a sense of being owned by the Dowager Queen, of being controlled by her in every aspect of my marriage, to some dangerous purpose. I felt suffocated by her patronage.

I fought to calm myself as the talk moved on to other matters, and after the meal Janyn and Sir David retired to the parlour used for such meetings. It was a fine afternoon, warm and sunny, and Dame Tommasa had sent word that she would meet me in the garden with a surprise. I took my needlework there, determined to set aside my fears for the sake of the child in my womb. I did manage to calm my agitation and fell asleep, leaning against a lattice with the sun warming my feet. Gwen woke me when my mother-in-law arrived.

'She has come with a cart filled with seedlings of your favourite plants from her garden,' Gwen said, gesturing behind her.

Dame Tommasa came bustling out into the courtyard garden followed by a cart pushed by a profusely sweating servant, an elderly man who looked as if this task would be the death of him. As so often at that time, I momentarily forgot my condition and lurched up, ready to run to his aid. The weight of the baby unbalanced me, and I would have fallen had Gwen not been right by my side. She steadied me and helped ease me back down. Dame Tommasa called for a servant to bring me some honey-water.

'The air is too dry out here,' she said. 'I should not have asked you to wait for me in the garden.'

'Be at ease, Mother,' I said. It was difficult to worry in her cheery presence. She nurtured me, behaving more like a parent to me than Margery ever had. 'I am happy to be out here in the sunshine. I was drowsing so comfortably. The birdsong and the drone of the bees put me to sleep. I woke confused, forgetting my condition!'

We laughed, amazed that I could possibly forget my size. For the rest of the afternoon I fell into the excitement of planning a garden. Though I could not work the soil, I enjoyed consulting Dame Tommasa on the placement of the plants and imagining how the garden would look the following summer. This garden was a testament of faith in the future, much like the child growing in my womb.

My delight in Dame Tommasa's description of how the garden would look the following year distracted me from Sir David's surprise comment until Gwen and my mother-in-law had helped me up to my chamber. Remembering, I told Dame Tommasa. Her eyes filled with tears.

'Such gladsome news! Son or daughter, they will be helped along in life by a connection to the royal family. I cannot wait to tell John.' But my perceptive mother-in-law noticed that I was not so sanguine. 'Are you not pleased?'

'I am aware of the great honour she does us,' I said, hanging my head more than was necessary for Gwen to comb out my hair.

'And so you should be, my child.'

I could not stay bent over for long. Straightening, I asked, 'But if her favour to us is to remain a secret, how do we explain such a godmother? And are we to name our child Isabella if it is a girl?'

Tommasa opened her mouth as if to respond then shut it, her large, beautiful eyes sweeping the room as if she might find inspiration in the fabrics or furnishings.

'That is a difficulty I had not considered,' she said, more in a murmur than to me, as if she were speaking to herself.

I refrained from voicing my deeper concern. She was subdued and distracted after that, and I was relieved when she departed. I was weary to the bone and fell asleep almost at once.

It was late when Janyn came to bed, waking me with the cough he had brought with him from his travels.

'Is Sir David gone?' I sleepily asked.

'Yes, he is biding with his wife's family nearby.'

'Did your meeting go well?'

'Yes. He is a most courteous and agreeable man. I stepped into the hall and saw Mother working in the garden. Are you pleased with all the plants she's begun for you?'

'You know that I am, and grateful for all that she is teaching me about their care.' I stuffed another pillow behind my head so that I might see him better as I asked, 'Why did you not tell me of Her Grace's offer to be godmother to our child?' I fought to keep my tone light.

'Because I did not know of it until Sir David mentioned it.'

'You did not say so.'

'I know. God help me, but I stumbled on my pride. I was disappointed that Sir David is so much more in her confidence than I am.'

'When do you imagine she intends to inform us?'

He placed his hand on my stomach. 'Soon, I trust, else she would be too late!' He laughed, but it was a hollow sound.

I made a fair attempt at companionable laughter, but the now-familiar fear almost choked me. In all other things Janyn was confident, assured, but regarding the Queen Mother he seemed to feel he walked on shifting sand, and that though he had so far managed to stay upright, he knew himself to be ever in danger of sinking.

'I told your mother that Isabella intended to stand as godmother.'

'Of course you did,' Janyn said. 'I would wonder had you not.' His confidence was shaken. I could hear how he forced his words, despite speaking in a low, affectionate tone.

'We wondered how we are to keep it secret.'

'I wonder as well, my love.'

'If we have a daughter, will she be named Isabella?'

'That would follow by custom, a child taking the first godparent's name, but Her Grace may choose, as many do, to suggest another name.'

I could not sustain my light tone. 'I am frightened, Janyn. She has such a hold over you. Over us.'

He paused for a moment, his hand on my stomach moving slightly, as if he'd begun to clench it and remembered he must not. When he spoke, he sounded weary. 'She was queen of this realm, Alice, and she is the mother of our King. We are her subjects, and if she singles us out for preference we are honoured, and bound to honour her in all ways.'

'You sound as if you are repeating something your mother told you many times.'

Janyn laughed and squeezed my hand. 'Already you know me so well.'

'You have in the past chafed at your responsibility to Isabella?'

'She did not favour Janet.' His first wife. 'She summoned me to Castle Rising a week after my wedding and made it clear that I was to come with my father and no one else. I wanted to refuse, but Janet and my parents convinced me that I was being childish. That I would harm our comfort, our future, by disobeying the Queen Mother.'

'You must have loved Janet very much.'

'I did.'

'Her death was painful to you?'

He took a deep breath. 'Let us not dwell on old sorrows. The baby will hear and have a bad night.' He kissed my hand.

Remembering that Janet had died giving birth to a stillborn child, a double tragedy, I understood why he would not wish to speak of it to me. Had she also been afraid?

I pushed that question away and took up a harmless topic. 'How old must a child be before he or she can ride?'

I was rewarded with a wide smile. 'Already planning!' Janyn turned down the lamp and snuggled up against my back, his hand on my belly, on our child. His warmth eased my backache and quieted the baby. We slept through the dawn. That was the blessing of being with child – until the last few weeks I slept well, no matter what the chaos in the rest of my life.

My grandparents supped with us in that time between Janyn's homecoming and my lying in, and I asked Dame Agnes to be with me when I gave birth.

'Me?'

'I would like someone from my family to be with me.'

'I should be honoured, sweet Alice. Of course.'

'Bless you, Dame Agnes,' said Janyn. 'You make us both very happy.'

It was less than a fortnight before my lying in that the Queen Mother finally sent a messenger stating her intention of standing godmother to our child. If it was a girl she would of course be first godmother, and our daughter would be named Isabella. When I broke the news to my grandmother she crossed herself, and there was fear in her eyes, but she held her tongue.

My sweet Isabella was born at the end of June after a long labour that I later learned frightened Janyn. Dame Agnes and Dame Tommasa were lovingly present throughout my ordeal, as well as my dear Nan and Felice, a midwife I liked very much.

My first daughter was rosy-cheeked and dark-haired, with wonderfully long fingers and toes and the appetite of a ploughman. From the moment I beheld her, and especially once she found my heavy breast and gave suck, I adored her. Of course I still loved Janyn above all men, but from the moment she was born Bella was the centre of my life. She was always 'Bella' to Janyn and me and all the family.

Dame Tommasa stood in for the Dowager Queen at Bella's baptism, with the wife of Janyn's guild master as second godmother, and Geoffrey Chaucer as godfather. My Salisbury grandparents were delighted with her, and Janyn's parents were almost giddy with love for her.

My parents attended the christening, I presume because it was quite a social affair, though of course I was still sequestered in my lying-in chamber. Mother did not bother to slip in to see me, though most of the other women attending did so. It was from them that I learned that she was with child herself, a startling piece of news considering my parents' coolness towards one another. I wondered whether Father had succeeded in winning her back by shunning me. The thought did not lessen my pain.

I wept as I nursed Bella that night. Of course my emotions were raw so soon after childbirth, but I believed that Mother's slight was intentional. Fortunately, this sorrow did not, could not, consume me, for something far stronger lifted me up – I loved motherhood. I refused a wet nurse because I wanted to enjoy everything about this time, and Janyn did not try to refuse me, for he, too, shared my absorption in Bella. He often sat with me as I nursed her, his face alight with love.

In July I wore a beautiful gown of red and gold patterned silk for my churching. The Perrers and my grandparents, my brothers and sister, Nan, and many friends attended the church ceremony in which I lit candles on the Lady altar in thanks for my safe delivery. It was an elegant, merry occasion, made more exciting by the fact it signalled my readiness to resume lovemaking. Janyn brooked no further delay.

A month later we were informed that Isabella the Queen Mother was on progress to London and would grace us with a two-day visit to Fair Meadow in a fortnight. She expected, of course, to meet her goddaughter and namesake. I told myself it was a great honour and averted my mind from the familiar worry. Distraction was easier. The household was thrown into a frenzy of activity, preparing for the move. There was much useless debate about the wisdom of our travelling in late-August, with the foetid summer air clinging to the valleys, but to me London was more foetid than anything in the countryside and I looked forward to the change.

Only then did I agree to engage a wet nurse, for I understood that when travelling and meeting my obligations as hostess to the Queen Mother and her entourage, I would find it difficult to nurse my dear Bella. I understood the need, but mourned the loss of our intimate connection. Janyn tried to cheer me by having Serenity brought to London for my eventual reintroduction to the saddle. I was eager to ride on horseback to Fair Meadow rather than travel in a bumpy cart, but wished I might bind Bella to me and carry her on Serenity also. My suggestion horrified my household and family.

'It seems that no one shares my confidence in my ability to control Serenity,' I complained to Janyn when he followed me as I retreated to our bedchamber in frustration.

He held me and stroked my hair. 'It is not you we doubt, but the wisdom of carrying a swaddled infant on a woman's saddle. Bella is safest in a cart with my mother and the nurses.'

'Then I shall ride in the cart as well.'

He surprised me by disagreeing. 'It is important that you begin to trust Bella to others, Alice. You must not neglect responsibilities by clinging to her, and you will disturb the household by refusing to follow custom.'

'Janyn! How can my devotion to Bella be wrong?'

'It is not, Alice, my sweet Alice. But as my wife you have responsibilities. I need you by my side, with the Queen Mother and whenever we entertain. There may come a time . . .' He stopped himself and looked away. 'I see you have begun packing.'

I reached up and took him by the shoulders to turn him back to me. He looked down with an apologetic smile.

'You were saying, there may come a time . . .'

'Alice, come.' He drew me over to a bench and sank down with a sigh, patting the space beside him. 'I am your elder by many years. One day, God willing not too soon, you will be fully in charge of our daughter and all our children, and will need to find your way without me. My wish is for you to learn my business and the customs of our circle so that you may move forward without fear. I do not mean to be harsh.' He put his arm around me.

I rested my head against him, feeling the pounding of his strong heart. I willed myself to believe there was nothing more to his comment than he'd said.

We rode side by side to Fair Meadow, and my precious Bella was none the worse for being hours without me. In fact, it was lovely to see her face light up as I approached her in the courtyard of our home, and hear her gurgling laughter as she pinched my nose.

Once there we had two days to prepare for the Queen Mother. Gwen and Dame Tommasa fussed over my gowns, making tucks – I seemed to have lost more weight in the past few days – and adding jewels. My hair was washed in a complicated mixture of oils and lotions, requiring me to sit outside in a wide-brimmed hat with a gap in the crown through which my hair was pulled to allow the sun to brighten it. At the same time my face was subjected to a disgusting paste that hardened painfully – it was to erase the freckles that I'd collected working in the garden the past fortnight.

'I am not wooing the Queen Mother,' I protested, but my tormentors did not even pause in their endeavours.

I complained to baby Bella and her wet nurse as they sat in the shade nearby.

'I can think of little more delightful than having such a fuss made over me,' said Mary, the nurse. 'Do you not feel like the Queen herself?'

Peering at her through the strands of hair that drooped from the hat, I burst out laughing. Soon she was laughing as well, and Bella gurgled and kicked.

That is how Janyn found us. He gamely teased me about my frightening appearance.

Our time at Fair Meadow was everything I'd hoped for. The long, late-summer days, the slow, languorous lovemaking, the hours spent admiring our daughter and planning for more children. How I loved Janyn and Bella, how happy we were. I see our country home as always in sunshine. I was determined that it be so.

But before we could relax together there we faced two days of entertaining the Queen Mother and her retinue. I did not sleep well the night before her arrival, dreading the subtle change in Janyn and his parents as they subjugated their own strong wills in deference to royalty. I had found the last visit difficult, and did not know how I would cope if she tried to interfere in unacceptable ways with her goddaughter's upbringing. I refrained from speaking to Janyn of my fear, however. In the matter of the Queen Mother we were wont to argue.

We received word in the late-afternoon that she would have in her company her grandson John of Gaunt, the King's third son. He would not stay the night, but after feasting move on to a royal lodge.

'Does she mean that as an insult?' I asked.

'Of course not,' Dame Tommasa quickly assured me. 'And it is a great honour to welcome the young Earl of Richmond.'

Later, before he fell asleep, Janyn told me how lovely my hair had looked in the firelight, touched with sun.

'Richmond will fall in love with you. He is but a few years older than you are, and very handsome. I think I shall be jealous.'

The difference in our ages seemed much on Janyn's mind of late. Instead of continuing the flirtatious banter, I said, 'I see no man but you in my dreams, Janyn, my love.'

I was rewarded with a long kiss that built in intensity until I was engulfed in heat and consuming desire, all thought of the approaching royal party crowded out of my head and heart.

A long while later, Janyn murmured, 'I adore you,' and rolled off me, falling asleep at once.

I curled up against him and fell easily asleep, but not for long. When I woke, in the dark, I tiptoed into the nursery and picked up Bella. While I held her, it mattered not what the Queen

Mother or her grandson thought of me. I was content. But soon she wanted to suck and I'd been warned that if I started nursing again I would leak into my elegant gowns. So I reluctantly handed her over to the wet nurse and returned to my bed. If Janyn had not turned over then and gathered me in his arms, covering me with kisses, I am certain that I would have wept until dawn. His caress reminded me that I was loved and cherished, and that I would surely have more children.

In the morning I made an effort to enjoy Gwen's fussing, and could see in the polished glass how the sunshine had brightened my brown hair, and how flawless my skin looked. I wore a gown of deep gold in a diamond pattern. Over it a red brocade surcoat, and a gossamer veil of pale, pale red, threaded with gold and pearls, that hung down from a gold and pearl fillet. A matching necklace dipped down between my breasts. I felt ready to welcome Isabella of France and the King's son.

Albeit as fabulously dressed in her elegant black with jet and obsidian as she had been on her last visit to Fair Meadow, Isabella seemed more subdued. Even with the assistance of her groom, she stumbled on dismounting and for a moment seemed shaky and confused. All the fear I'd tried to ignore returned to me. I crossed myself as the elegant Earl of Richmond and Sir David rushed to support her on either side. It was as if her years had suddenly caught up with her.

'*Deus juva me,*' Dame Tommasa murmured beside me. She had turned quite pale.

But the Queen Mother gently waved Sir David away and lightly rebalanced herself against her grandson's proffered hand. Although her steps were stiff rather than fluid as in the past, she did not falter as she approached us. Janyn ran forward to bow to her and welcome her to our home, and I followed close behind.

Her smile was radiant and her eyes clear as she regarded us with affection. After compliments all round we entered the hall, and when Isabella was handed her namesake, Janyn beaming beside her, Gaunt presented my daughter with a silk-clad cushion alive with embroidered unicorns and other fanciful, merry little creatures.

'And when she is ready, a pony shall be added to your stables for my namesake,' said Isabella, kissing my daughter's forehead.

Then Gaunt touched my arm and asked if I would return to the courtyard with him.

His eyes were blue-grey, with dark brown lashes and arched brows, his hair blond, jaw square and strong. He was a tall man, with wide shoulders. He was so handsome he seemed more a god than a man. I followed him out of the door – for how to refuse him? – with apprehension, wondering whether he was about to instruct me regarding his grandmother's condition.

Isabella's groom stood in the centre of the yard holding the reins of a magnificent mare, muscled and sleek, coat dark and glistening. She pawed the packed earth and shook her head with a throaty whinny as we approached.

'The Lady Isabella says she promised you a hunter,' said Gaunt, 'and she has kept her word.'

I stopped, staring at the beautiful creature now regarding me with cautious interest. 'Mine?' I asked in a choked whisper. I wondered how I could possibly control such a horse.

'Would you care to give Melisende an apple, Dame Alice?' the groom asked. He nodded to a young servant who stood at a little distance, and the lad ran to me and proffered several apples.

Of course I stepped forward, took one of the apples and held it behind me as I gently stroked the horse's side. Melisende nudged my shoulder, searching for the fruit. Her careful training was evident in the way she took the treat from my open hand.

'You have made the Lady Isabella very happy with a namesake, Dame Alice. I thank you.'

I said something sufficiently courteous and grateful, all the while wondering how these royals were schooled to express themselves so calmly and naturally while offering such obvious untruths. Once Isabella had decided to stand as godmother for our child, I'd had no choice in the matter.

My hunter was to be curried and rested, and as soon as time permitted I would have my first ride. I was eager to ride such a beautiful horse, yet felt disloyal towards Serenity and reluctant to be even more in Isabella's debt. I was also discomfited by the direction of the Earl's gaze – to the point at which my necklace disappeared between my breasts. However, I expressed my thanks to him as fulsomely as Janyn would wish me to.

The meal was lively with banter and descriptions of the latest tournaments and feasts at court. I learned that our King revelled in lavish and elaborate displays, particularly enjoying dressing up as legendary heroes. Isabella was proud of him, and Richmond seemed painfully aware of walking in a great man's shadow. I wondered how it would be to meet the King, and whether I ever might. I closely studied how Janyn and his parents interacted with the royals, in order to follow their example. They seemed at ease, except that they took care not to contradict or fail to respond to either the Dowager Queen or her grandson. Even Sir David seemed less at ease than my family did. I was proud of being a Perrers at that moment, and grateful for all that my marriage had brought me.

After the meal everyone dispersed to rest for a while. Gwen had piled the cushions on my bed so that I might recline without needing my hair redone. I had dozed just a little while when she woke me.

'The Queen Mother is asking for you. She says she has something to show you in the stables.'

But I had seen Melisende. Surely she knew I had seen the hunter. Gwen hurriedly dressed me in a riding outfit, and I found Isabella in the hall. She was dressed much as she had been when I'd first seen her, in her dark hunting garb, and seemed revived by her rest.

'At last,' she breathed as I appeared. 'Proceed!'

Out in the stables, my new hunter had been saddled, as had Isabella's beautiful horse, Janyn's, Master John's and Sir David's – the Earl of Richmond had already departed for the royal hunting lodge. We walked out of the stables, the grooms guiding the ladies' horses and the men walking their own, and moved towards the mews. The falconer appeared with a hooded merlin on his wrist, her tiny bells jingling as she fluttered a little. He carried a glove.

'In thanks for permitting me the great joy of standing as godmother to your daughter, and of giving her my name, I present to you this merlin,' said Isabella, her beautiful face lit with the pleasure of presenting a fabulous gift. 'May Dido hunt well for you.'

'My lady,' I said, trying not to gasp, 'you honour my family. May God watch over you and bless you in all ways.'

I was ready to babble more, but the falconer handed me the glove and requested that I slip it on. As soon as I did so, he secured the merlin's claws with the jesses on my glove and said, 'Once her hood is removed, do not blink or she might attack. If you hold her too far from you she will flap her wings as a sign to bring her in closer.' With that he disappeared, returning with the others' hunting birds as I wondered what on earth I might do to prevent myself from blinking.

As the merlin moved, her bells sounding so sweetly, I turned to her, this beautiful and powerful creature on my arm. Her tiny hood was fashioned from what looked like buttery soft leather tanned a pale gold, with a perky plume of red and gold feathers. With the bells and the fashionable hood she might have seemed a pampered pet – but her fierce beak and claws and powerful wings were a clear reminder of her true character. I loved her from that very first moment.

'My lady Dido,' I whispered, 'I am Alice, your companion in the hunt.'

Sir David, the only one close enough to overhear me, chuckled. 'Well done, Dame Alice. You hold her as if you'd had many such falcons, and you address her with the respect she deserves.'

His compliments helped me relax, though I still worried that my arm was not sufficiently strong for me to carry the merlin and ride on horseback, especially on an unfamiliar mount. But this last worry was banished. Once the others had their birds, the falconer returned and took mine from me.

'I'll hand her back when we've ridden into the fields.'

Janyn had joined me.

I was speechless with excitement and also fear, not so much of the horse and merlin but of making a fool of myself with so many firsts in such august company.

'Come.' He'd brought a mounting stool and held out a hand to me.

I accepted Janyn's help with immense gratitude. Soon I sat high up on my beautiful new hunter. My experience riding Melisende was quite different from that with Serenity. I did not feel that I could lose my heart to her for I feared her a little. But once she found her stride I softened towards her, and when I had taken her through her paces and confirmed that she was well trained, I did indeed lose my heart. She was still a challenge, and therefore a little frightening, but that seemed as it should be – she was a large, powerful animal, and I learned that her training was but a cloak that might be shed at any time. I wondered whether this was why powerful people so enjoyed hunting and hawking: the danger inherent in riding a powerful animal, handling a wild bird, letting loose the tracking dogs. Certainly Isabella glowed with life astride her hunter and Janyn moved as one with his powerful steed as we rode to the meadow in which we were to hawk.

After dismounting, with my merlin now on my glove, I followed the falconer's careful instructions and removed Dido's hood. Her eyes were wild and cunning, and for a moment I could not breathe, as if she had ordered me to stop all motion while she considered me. And consider me she did. God watched over me, though, for I did not blink during the long examination. When the Queen Mother called out that we were ready, I must have moved a little, holding Dido farther from me. She flapped her wings with annoyance, but calmed the moment I drew her closer.

'Forgive me,' I said to her. 'I am new to this.'

The falconer showed me how to loosen the jesses for the hunt. I had hardly completed the task when the merlin took off after a bird. I remember it as a crane, but the prey does not matter. What did was the beauty of my merlin's flight, her fierce attack, and, the best part of all, her return to my glove when I tapped it as the falconer had shown me, dangling a gobbet of meat from my gloved fingers as a lure.

Both Janyn and Isabella nodded their approval. That, too, warmed my heart.

We spent a quiet evening in the hall, everyone pleasantly tired, and withdrew early to bed. As it was warm, the glazed windows in the house stood open. In the quiet hours I was awakened by voices in the garden below. I thought I recognised them as Isabella's and Lady Jane's. I began to rise, but Janyn held me back.

'Her women will see to her, Alice. She is often restless at night. Let her be.' His tone was stern, though his voice was hoarse with sleep.

I lay back on the cushions, by now wide awake. 'Do you think that she knew her lover had ordered her husband murdered? Do you think that is why she wakes in the night?'

'We do not speak of that, my love.'

I raised myself up on one arm and touched his shoulder. 'But we are so bound to her. Is it not our nature to want to know the truth about someone we serve?'

'She is generous with our family, Alice. Why should we question her?'

'There must be a way to learn the truth without such directness. Without her even knowing. Surely you must have tried that. Are you so worried about losing her custom?'

Janyn sat up, brushing his hair from his forehead and rubbing his eyes. 'God's blood, Alice, leave that in the past. She is the daughter, sister, widow and mother of Kings, and we are but common folk. Though we might wish to know the truth about what happened to our former king, and though we might rightly feel it is in the interest of our own safety to know more clearly the woman who so favours us, we *must let it be.* It is too dangerous to challenge the King's family. There is far more at stake here than the loss of some trade.' He tousled my hair. 'I would have thought you would be happily dreaming of falcons and beautiful hunters.'

'I was.' I tried to calm myself, but it was no use. 'Why does she so favour us, Janyn? Godmother to our child . . . the bird . . . the horse . . . her assistance in convincing my parents to allow us to wed. What are we giving her in return? It must be more than your services as a trader.'

To my surprise, he began to laugh. 'I do not know how I thought to quiet you on this. For all the reasons I love you and value your counsel, I should have expected your impatience over a mystery.'

'You do know more than you've told me?'

He turned up the wick on the oil lamp, allowing more light. 'Is there any wine left in the mazer beside you?'

I lifted it from the shelf beside me and found that it was almost half-full. I passed it to Janyn with a fleeting wish that we were about to make love, not discuss the Queen Mother's past.

He seemed to be downing the rest of the wine.

'You'll be too drowsy to talk,' I teased.

He lowered the mazer, but did not hand it back.

'Our lady Queen Isabella led a successful revolt. She had gathered a formidable force, a huge force, and most of them were the King's subjects. When her own son seized her lover, the commander of her troops, she feared for others who might also be taken. Some of these men escaped to the continent. A few important ones settled near my mother's birthplace. Isabella writes to them, and they write to her. My mother's family are her couriers.'

'Including you?'

He nodded. 'At present Francisco and I are the most active from here.'

I crossed myself. 'But that was so long ago. Thirty years. How many are still alive? Why would they yet fear the King?'

'Many yet live. As to why they have not returned, I do not ask.' His voice had grown tense. 'I am merely a courier. And the Queen Mother is very grateful for our service, and especially our discretion. Now, let us sleep.' He lay down with a weary sigh, his back to me.

'Thank you for confiding in me, my love,' I whispered as I snuggled against his warm back.

But sleep would not come for me, my mind still grasping at questions. Isabella and Mortimer had been lovers for a long while – had they had any children? Had she truly loved him or had he merely been useful? I wondered whether she might have been relieved when Mortimer was taken; whether by then she had been ready to hand the throne over to her son.

And her men, her soldiers . . . they were right to fear the present King, for they had murdered his father and he had executed their commander. How long does rage over a beloved parent's death last? Had our King truly loved his father? Did he love his mother? She spoke of him with such pride. How had he forgiven her? Had he? Did he trust her?

If the soldiers stayed in Italy out of fear of the King's wrath, or of others who had supported Isabella's husband, Janyn and Francisco took a terrible risk in playing courier between those men and Isabella. No wonder we were so favoured, and so secretive. I shivered as I prayed that when she died we might be released from this burden and live peacefully.

The morning dawned sunny and warm. Despite my protests

that I was too tired, Janyn told Gwen to dress me for more hawking.

'More hawking? But you were to hunt.'

'We will not hunt this day. Her Grace is not so moved.'

Despite my protests, once I was on Melisende I woke up to the beauty of the morning, the freshness of the air, and was eager to ride out into the countryside. I did not yet feel as graceful on Melisende as I had felt on Serenity, and on that morning my merlin was less willing to return to my glove than she had been the day before, but I would not have wanted to be anywhere else but in the fields with two such powerful creatures and in such a lively company. Only the Queen Mother seemed subdued, hanging back from the rest of us, letting her falconer hold her bird most of the time. I tried not to stare at her, but I had noticed shadows beneath her eyes and lines about her mouth.

The remainder of the day proceeded in an orderly fashion. We'd returned from hawking, eaten a marvellous meal with Isabella's minstrels providing merry entertainment, and the Queen Mother had then retired, fatigued. I worried that her mood might signal dissatisfaction with me, but Lady Jane assured me that the Queen Mother was delighted with me and apologetic about being unwell.

She did rise early the following morning and asked to see her namesake once more. As she bent over my Bella, remarking on her beauty and gentle demeanour, I was a proud and happy mother. But as the Dowager Queen lingered, poised above my beloved baby, her gorgeous dark clothing glittering in the morning light, I had a passing moment of unease, seeing her dark, deathly appearance so close to the child's rosy face.

I was much relieved when her party rode away.

On our return to London, Janyn informed me that he had acquired property in Oxford in my name 'to provide you a comfortable income in rents should anything happen to my fortune'.

'Are you in danger, my love?' I could not think why else he would couch it in such words.

'Each day we wake to uncertainty, Alice. I can no more predict how long I shall live, or whether I shall remain in favour with the Queen Mother and my guild, than I can predict when you shall bear another child and what sex it will be.'

I watched my husband with new concern and listened intently to all he said, paying close attention to every nuance. It seemed the closer I attended him, the more cautious he became around me. I wish my fear had proved misplaced. But it was not.

An incident shortly afterward suggested what Janyn had to fear. I noted it because he suddenly stepped up his efforts to improve my education. I was to assist him in reviewing his business accounts, and a tutor appeared who was to improve my French and Latin, speaking, reading and writing.

'Have I displeased you?' I asked. Who would not?

Janyn assured me that he meant it as a gift that would support me through life, the most precious gift he could think to give.

It was as I sat with the tutor one morning in the hall that Dame Tommasa hurried in, her beautiful eyes wide with alarm and fear. She took Janyn by the arm and drew him off to a quiet room. In a little while my mother-in-law departed, without having said a word to me. Never before had she ignored me. Janyn looked grave as we supped, but said nothing. Even in bed that night, he would not say what had so upset his mother.

'It is worse for me not to know,' I said, kissing his neck and shoulders, 'for my imagination conjures terrifying things when I worry.'

'Later, my love. I would rather not talk of it until I know what truly happened.'

I had wild dreams that night – floods, imprisonments, fires, my sweet Bella burning with fever, Janyn injured by a runaway cart in a narrow street.

My younger brother and sister came with Nan the following morning, and at midday my brother John joined us for a festive meal. Janyn had left early on business. Now I learned that two of our acquaintances among the Lombard traders claimed they had been attacked by a group of mercers the previous day, and that accusations were flying between the Society of Lucca and members of the mercers' guild.

'Were they badly hurt?' I asked.

'Do you know them?' John asked, looking ill at ease.

'They have been guests in our home,' I said, 'though I do not know them well.'

'Dangerous friends,' he said.

'Are they?' Nan asked. 'I heard that the attack was unprovoked. Why would a group of mercers attack a group of merchants who had done nothing to them? The mercers broke the King's peace – does he not hold the Lombards in his protection?'

'The King's protection makes the Lombards bold. Many of them are smugglers on such a scale as a London merchant would never attempt,' said John.

I could not argue with that for it was true of some of them, and though I might correct John on the 'many', I chose not to, for I did not wish to silence him. I wondered whether the society was connected to Isabella's men who hid in Italy.

'The two Lombards have made loans to the King,' I said. 'They all have. That is why he protects them.'

'If they enjoy the King's favour, what could the London mercers hope to gain by allowing these attacks? That is what I wonder,' said Nan. 'Master John said that the guild has done nothing to punish the men accused.'

'They do not know who took part in the attack,' he said.

I could see by Nan's expression that she had heard otherwise. This was nothing I wished to know, balancing as I was on the fence between the factions. I was grateful that Janyn was not to join us for the meal, as diplomacy was not a skill my brother John had mastered. Once I sensed that I'd learned all I cared to know of their understanding of the incident, I turned the conversation to happier topics. We all fussed over baby Bella, admired the carving of a kitten that Will had made for her, and applauded Mary's performance of a lullaby, her voice sweet and her lute-playing remarkable. My younger siblings were maturing with such speed it took my breath away. So, too, would my sweet Bella.

After my family departed I was overwhelmed with a sense of divided loyalties. Janyn and Bella and all I held so dear were being threatened by an evil we could hardly escape, and it was possible my own family would find themselves on the other side of the argument. I went to church and confided in Dom Hanneye my fear that Janyn's sudden rush to educate me had something to do with the growing enmity between the London guilds and the

Lombards. He reassured me with the news that some mercers had gone to the Mayor in support of the victims.

'It is not as simple as the Londoners against the Lombards. I suggest that you cease to worry and accept your husband's gifts of knowledge and experience with love and gratitude. Seize the opportunity he is giving you. Few women – indeed, few men – are granted such riches. I do not mean to deny the enmity between foreigners and London merchants, Dame Alice, but your family is respected in this community, and your husband and his father are Londoners by birth and guildsmen – they are not the enemy.'

I was grateful for his advice. That evening Janyn told me of the attack and I was able to respond with a calm maturity that I could see relieved him. He told me little that I did not already know, but it was significant that he told me as soon as he felt he had all the facts. I took it as his being forthright with me. I was not yet at ease, but immensely comforted by his candour.

Shortly after my education had begun in earnest, my good friend Geoffrey Chaucer appeared. His mother was ill and he'd been given a fortnight's leave to visit his family. He had grown into his grand clothes, his bearing, speech and gestures more refined and confident than before.

'The Countess's household suits you, Geoffrey?' I asked, though I had no doubt the answer would be yes.

'It would suit me better if I were better suited for it,' he said, then burst out laughing as I applauded his wit.

Reversed sentiments were an old game with us, and his show of wit at once put me completely at ease. It was good to be with a friend who had known me for so long. I'd begun to feel that now I was Janyn's wife and Bella's mother, I had ceased to be merely Alice. As we talked, I felt that older part of me awaken.

Janyn welcomed Geoffrey and invited him to stay and sup with us. 'I must attend to some work, but I look forward to our later meeting,' he said, and tactfully disappeared.

'He is a handsome man,' said Geoffrey. 'Courteous, well-spoken, wealthy, successful . . . Has he a fault?'

'I'm searching for it, but I fear I search in all the wrong places, for I've yet to find one.' I blushed.

Geoffrey laughed. 'No doubt you have yet to find a fault in my godchild either.' He cocked his head and lifted a brow in query. 'The Earl of Richmond is very open about his grand-dam being your daughter's godmother.' He sighed and shook his head. 'My parents were wrong about your limited prospects, eh?'

I smiled but did not reply at once, adjusting to the news that our efforts to conceal the Queen Mother's favour towards our family had been undermined by Richmond.

'Are you not pleased that he does not seek to hide your favour?' Geoffrey asked.

'I am puzzled why the Earl would mention it to anyone. We are unimportant folk, so surely he was not bragging.'

'Perhaps he was. He is fond of his grandmother and fiercely defends her when the old rumours are repeated.'

'Is his brother Lionel also fond of her?' That was the brother Geoffrey would know best, being in his household.

'Less than John, more than Edward,' said Geoffrey. 'Perhaps she has grown more affectionate with each grandchild.'

'In truth, I am uneasy about even our slight intercourse with the royal family. I do not think a crown brings peace or contentment.'

'That is not their purpose.'

'Nor does the royal family seem warm and loving.'

'Because they all want the crown!'

We laughed.

The afternoon was over too soon, but I had memories of our happy conversation to review for days afterwards. Janyn had been delightful with Geoffrey's company and pronounced him ever welcome in our household.

'I am glad you have such a friend,' he said as we sat before the fire late in the evening. 'We see many people now but few we are likely to know throughout our lives. Most are pleasant company for the moment, or we are happy that our need to spend time with them will not be unpleasant, but we do not care for them at heart, nor they for us.'

'Are you often lonely?' I asked.

'When away from you and Bella, I am. I had not known what was missing from my life. Now I feel cold and bereft without my two loves nearby.'

We kissed – a gentle, affectionate kiss.

'Will you be travelling again soon?' I asked, suspecting that a separation was on his mind. I had learned to recognise his mood before he departed, whether on brief or long journeys. He would hesitate to tell me of them, knowing how I hated his absences, how I missed him.

'In a few days,' he said. When I exclaimed in distress, he added, 'Both of us. We are invited to a hunt at Hertford Castle, where the Queen Mother is in residence.'

'We? Invited to Lady Isabella's palace? To hunt?' With each question my voice rose in excitement. The truth was so much better than I had expected.

'Is that delight or dismay?'

I was to travel with my love! I threw my arms around Janyn and kissed him on the neck, on each cheek, and then on the mouth – a much longer kiss.

'Ah, delight,' he said, his eyes merry. 'You are so beautiful, my Alice. You bring me such joy.'

King Edward might attend the hunt as well. I might meet the King himself. Hunt with the King and his dam.

'Someday I shall look back on this time and wonder how I dared breathe the same air as such mighty folk,' I said to Janyn as we shared a cup of wine in our chamber. My anticipation was not without apprehension.

'The Queen Mother enjoys your company, my love, and the Earl of Richmond has praised you to others. I foresee a long relationship with the court circle.'

'I prefer our friends here in London, our guild circle,' I dared to say.

'The royal family care little for your preferences, my love, unless they happen to share them.'

'But al to litel, weylaway the whyle,
Lasteth swich joie, ythonked be Fortune,
That semeth trewest whan she wol bygyle
And kan to fooles so hire song entune
That she hem hent and blent, traitour comune!
And whan a wight is from hire whiel ythrowe,
Than laugheth she, and maketh him the mowe.'

– Geoffrey Chaucer, *Troilus and Criseyde*, IV, ll. 1-7

1357

Even so long after the event, I recall my excitement as we
departed for Hertford Castle. We had been married for a year –
a year filled with so many new experiences for me – but this visit
was my first to a royal household. I had asked to ride Serenity, but
Janyn said that it was an excellent time for me to become better
accustomed to my hunter. There was a cart in which I might rest
with Gwen from time to time.

The previous night my excitement had been dampened with
worry about how my sweet Bella would fare for just short of a
week without me. In truth, it was equally about how I might fare
without her. But once seated on Melisende in the brisk morning
air, Janyn riding beside me looking handsome and full of life, I
asked God to help me shrug off the futile worry. He answered my
prayers, for I was soon caught up in the bustle of the London
streets, absorbing it with eyes, ears, and nose. And then, as we
rode out of the city into the countryside, the sudden quiet oddly
startled me at first until my ears adjusted to the low hum of life
all around me.

I had never before made a journey of more than half a day. By
mid-afternoon I was grateful for the opportunity to rest in the
cart a while. We bided at the country home of a friend that night.
I was sore from the long ride, and grateful for Gwen's surprising
strength in kneading my aching body. Janyn expressed sympathy

and concern, urging me to alternate between riding short distances on horseback and spells in the cart for the remainder of the journey. But I resisted the easy way, hoping that after experience of a long ride, I would be more at ease.

'You would be more comfortable riding astride,' he suggested as an alternative to the combination of cart and horseback.

'I have heard it said that women who ride astride are more likely to have difficulties carrying children full-term. I do not want to risk our chance for more children, Janyn.'

'The Queen Mother believes the opposite is true, and so does Dame Agnes, I might remind you.'

I was hardly appeased by that, already chafing at the leash on which Isabella seemed to keep my family, particularly Janyn. Why should we consult her before making any decision? It sometimes seemed as if our marriage had become Isabella's accomplishment; that she felt, or rather Janyn felt, that she had the final say in any disagreement.

'I brought neither the saddle nor the clothes for it.'

'We brought your other saddle, and I am certain Gwen can adjust your skirts for you.'

'Janyn, I pray you, respect my decision in this.'

'But Lady Isabella, the Queen Mother . . .'

'I did not wed the Queen Mother!' I said, in a louder voice than I'd intended.

'Watch your tongue, Alice,' Janyn responded, and abruptly walked out of our chamber.

Gwen, apparently having passed him in the corridor, returned to massage my aching muscles a little more. She never commented on my relationship with my husband. Her discretion was impeccable.

He did not stay away long. Upon his return he apologised for his show of temper. I too apologised for the way in which I'd spoken. Neither of us wished to prolong our discord, a situation that was unusual in our marriage. It was our first argument of any substance or length. Although we kissed and made our peace with one another, it had exposed a significant undercurrent. I, for one, could not entirely put it behind me for it had been simmering for a long while. Yet having sensed Isabella's suffering at Fair Meadow, I did begin better to understand her. I had seen her vulnerability. I had no idea how much pain she had endured.

Later, as Janyn lay asleep beside me, I propped myself up on one elbow to study him in the soft lamplight, noticing his long dark lashes, his expressively arched brows – recently with a sprinkling of silver visible in them, the full, beautiful lips, softly curling hair. Beholding his beauty, I felt my heart swell with love and gratitude for the life that God had granted me with this man. The little day-to-day irritations so easily dulled my gratitude. I prayed I might become more aware of God's blessings, and ignore the minor penances. I pushed aside the nagging feeling that Isabella's influence was hardly small but truly a substantial penance, and a potential danger.

In the morning I chose to continue riding side-saddle, but promised Janyn that I would confer with Isabella and her physician while at Hertford. He seemed content with that. As we rode together through the beautiful morning, he pointed out the lands of our acquaintances and landmarks of amusing events in his travels. One piece of information was particularly interesting.

'To the west of us is Berkhamsted Castle, where the Queen Mother was confined after Sir Roger Mortimer's execution,' Janyn told me.

'How strange that she chooses to abide so close to a place that must harbour darksome memories for her,' I said, squinting in the direction in which he had pointed. 'But I see no castle.'

'No, it is not on our way.'

'Her heart must break to think of that time, losing two men she so loved.'

Janyn looked at me with curiosity. 'Has she spoken of this to you?'

'No, but I believe she is a loving woman of delicate sensibilities.'

'She was also a warrior and a queen,' said Janyn, 'and many find that difficult to accept in a woman.'

'Why should a queen not behave as a queen? She is the mother of her people. And a mother will fight for her children, boldly defend them with sword, if that is what is necessary. Should a queen be otherwise regarding her kingdom?'

'I shall never worry about my daughter as long as you are near,' said Janyn with an affectionate laugh. Then he spurred his horse forward to speak to the groom who was leading our small party.

I wondered whether he had allowed us a little conversation about Isabella's dark time in reparation for our argument of the previous evening. I chose to think so.

As we approached the grim outer walls of the castle, I wondered whether it would be possible to enjoy myself there. I had not wondered until that moment who else might be in residence, or visiting, in addition to the King. I was terrified enough to be meeting *him*, though of course I was equally thrilled. I wondered whether he would *look* like a king – more than a mere mortal man – wise, powerful. As we passed through the outer gate and rode into the bailey, I stared up at the elaborate façade of the keep, an elegant ashlar paint with soft red accents rendering it more inviting than the bare stone walls surrounding it. Stationed at regular intervals outside were elegantly dressed guardsmen. I was overwhelmed by a sense of my own insignificance, my common background. This was so obviously a royal residence, and I was but a merchant's wife. In my excitement I had not really considered that before.

As Janyn helped me from my horse I clung to him and whispered, 'What in heaven's name are we doing here? This is not our place. We are merchants, not courtiers.'

He kissed my cheek and gently stepped back from my clinging embrace.

'You are an invited guest, Alice. It may be a royal residence, but you are welcome here. Be at ease.' He lowered my travelling hood and kissed my forehead. 'You are weary from the journey, that is whence comes your distress.'

I shook with fear as we climbed the steps to the hall, my sudden painful awareness of the gulf between my status and that of the Dowager Queen adding a terrible weight to my body. A merchant was a merchant; noble blood was noble blood. I did not belong there.

I was awed by the size and magnificence of the palace's interior. We entered by a short corridor lined with beautiful hangings, gold and silver torches and lamps, then stepped into the echoing expanse of the great hall where we walked on tiles such as I had seen only in the grandest churches. Servants better dressed than most Londoners were stationed behind intricately carved screens or against the walls, as if guarding the immense chests and cupboards. They moved quietly, spoke softly.

On a dais at the far end sat two men deep in conversation. A servant led us very close to them. I tried not to look, but my eyes seemed to have a will of their own, and I found myself staring into very blue eyes, wide and penetrating. They belonged to a man with high, prominent cheekbones, a long, elegant nose, and although a trimmed white beard hid it, I detected a strong chin. His handsome, well-proportioned face was framed by white hair that was luxuriant, wavy, and adorned with a crown.

It was the King! Sweet heaven, he was everything I'd ever imagined a king would be. From broad, straight shoulders hung a most exquisite blue silk robe powdered with gold and silver fleur-de-lis. He seemed to consider me for a few instants and then, with a nod, he turned away. I tried to hide a gasp as I sucked in air, for I had held my breath while King Edward's gaze touched me. My steps faltered and Janyn put an arm around me.

'You are so weary, my love?'

With tender concern he assisted me as we followed the servant into another corridor, just as beautifully decorated as the entry, and were shown into the Queen Mother's parlour – a jewel of a room. The stone walls were three feet thick and therefore let in only muted light, but they were white-washed and decorated with painted flowers and hung with rich tapestries. Woven mats and cushions in brilliant colours softened the weighty furniture and the tiled floor.

Isabella the Queen Mother rose from a small day bed on which she had been lounging and greeted us warmly.

'You will rest awhile, and then meet our other guests at the feast in the hall. Tomorrow we rise early to hunt.'

I had managed to speak only a few words to her, dumbstruck by all the magnificence. We were shown to a small but luxuriously decorated chamber, tucked into a corner of the upper storey. Gwen undressed me and I fell at once into a deep sleep. When she woke me later, I was confused by my surroundings.

'Where is my baby? Where is Bella?' I cried.

Janyn and Gwen reassured me that all was well, and reminded me where I was. My confusion frightened me, but they both believed it was caused by the long journey, my first experience of travelling so far. I wanted to believe them, but just in case I had sensed that something was truly wrong with my daughter, asked if I might slip into the chapel to pray.

'First let Gwen dress you for the feast. Then I shall escort you to the chapel for a brief prayer. But we must not dally.' Janyn bowed to me and withdrew to a cushioned chair by the door.

Behind a tall carved screen that seemed to be writhing with fantastical winged creatures, Gwen had laid out a new gown of red silk shot with gold, with an undergown of silk in a blue as rich as lapis lazuli. My crespinette was gold. For the first anniversary of our marriage, Janyn had given me a ring of silver, gold and lapis. My shoes were a deep blue as well.

In the mirror I could see my dazzling self. I did so love to dress in exquisite clothes. Yet I stared back with frightened eyes. I did not belong in a royal household. I did not know how to behave.

But Janyn's expression when I stepped out from behind the screen reassured me. 'What a beauty you are, my Alice,' he murmured, kissing my hand, my wrist, my neck . . .

Gwen reminded us that we had little time to spare for our visit to the chapel. With a bow, Janyn escorted me from the chamber. We glided through corridors made quiet with wall hangings – I wondered how much of her fortune Isabella had spent on these trappings, for surely they had not been here when she arrived. They seemed to me to reflect a woman's taste, stories from myth and romance, no battle scenes or even religious motifs. It felt as if I were walking through a fabulous romance.

The chapel was a stark contrast, a painted Dance of Death appearing on one wall, the skeletal figure at its centre a terrifying reminder of our mortal existence. I crossed myself for protection. Yet the stained-glass casement behind the altar was quite peaceful, depicting the Blessed Mother and Christ child. I knelt at a prie-dieu before a statue of the Virgin Mary and bowed to my prayers. I prayed for my Bella, that she was safe and at ease with her nurse. I prayed for Janyn, that he would always enjoy God's protection in his travels. I prayed that I might be a good wife, all that Janyn wished me to be. I prayed that I might not embarrass or disappoint him here at the court of Isabella of

France, once Queen and now mother of the King. I prayed that the King himself might not judge me to be a common, inelegant woman, and then quickly took back that prayer, embarrassed by my pride.

While I had knelt there someone had joined us in the chapel. I had smelled a beautiful, sensual perfume from his clothing as he passed me, and then heard the sounds as he knelt near the altar. He had paused near me but I had not glanced up, feeling safe in Janyn's protection.

Janyn, who had knelt behind me, whispered then that we must go. As I rose, I turned towards the altar. It was King Edward who knelt there, head bowed and resting in his hands. I took Janyn's arm and let him rush me from the chapel, my heart pounding. I had prayed in the presence of the King! Was that why I had prayed that he would not look down on me?

'We were in good company,' Janyn commented as we checked the condition of each other's clothing. 'That was King Edward himself.'

'I know,' I said. 'His crown . . .'

We shared a nervous laugh and then continued to the great hall.

It was a grand company in which we dined that day, Isabella the Queen Mother, King Edward and his plump and vivacious Queen, Philippa – I liked her at once; John, Earl of Richmond, whom I'd already met; Lionel, Earl of Ulster, the king's second son, and his wife Elizabeth, Countess of Ulster; and several foreign noblemen whose names Janyn did not yet know. Arriving just before us was someone I had not expected to see in such august company: Richard Lyons.

'What is he doing here?' I asked Janyn.

'I should think he is ever welcome, considering the loans he has made to both the Queen Mother and the present Queen,' he said. 'They both spend far more than they can afford. That is his wife, seated at the far end of the second table, Isabella Pledour.'

She was not a pretty woman, heavy-set and sour of face, but tastefully and expensively gowned.

We, too, were seated at the second highest table with the less important folk, which was a great relief to me. Our fellows were a merchant and his wife from St Albans, two Grey Friars from

London, another merchant couple from London, and, much to my delight, my good friend Geoffrey.

'Alice! You look more beautiful each time I see you,' he exclaimed.

Relieved that I had someone to talk to, Janyn turned to the merchant from St Albans.

I was glad that Lyons was at the far end. Except for a few words overheard in lulls in the conversation, I barely noticed him though Geoffrey did find fault with the Fleming's bright hat and painful mispronunciations.

'Surely he might better learn the language in which he trades day-to-day,' he muttered. 'You see how even his wife winces when he speaks.'

'He is more fluent in French,' I said.

'But he lives in London, my friend, and please do not play the innocent with me. You despise him. I feel you bristle when he glances your way, or you his.'

'You know me far too well,' I said.

He shook his head. 'I know you not at all these days, Alice. A guest of Isabella of France, mother of her most beautiful goddaughter, passionately in love with your husband, a Lombard merchant, your home filled with luxurious items I shall never afford . . .'

'He is not a Lombard but a Londoner born, Geoffrey.'

'I did not intend it in the derogatory sense, my friend. His mother is Milanese, is she not?'

'Yes, and his father and his father before him and his father before *him* were all born in London, as was Janyn.'

Geoffrey smiled and bowed to me.

'You are different as well,' I said. 'Serving in the household of the King's second son, the Earl of Ulster. Supping with the Queen Mother and the King and Queen . . .' I smiled and bowed to him. 'We have both come far in a short while.'

Janyn suddenly leaned into our discussion. 'We must find a suitable wife for you, eh, Geoffrey?'

'Do you have a sister as handsome as your mother?' he asked, his eyes alight. 'I should like a pretty wife.'

'I've no unmarried sister, but cousins . . .' Janyn's eyebrows danced and his eyes twinkled.

I loved him so in that moment. I believed he had noticed the sudden tension between me and Geoffrey and had come to my aid, lightening the mood. It was a loving gesture.

Later, as I walked in the garden with two of the merchant wives and one of the Grey Friars, one of the women said, 'Is that not your husband speaking with the Queen, Dame Alice?'

It was. My heart burst with pride to see how comfortable Janyn looked in such company.

'Yes, it is Janyn. Is he not the most handsome man?'

The women, both older than I was, teased me about being so in love with my husband.

'God is smiling down upon you,' the friar said. 'May your union continue to be so blessed.'

We moved on to other matters – there was much gossip about King Jean of France being in London, held for ransom since his capture in battle in France. It was said that he felt honour-bound to live in exile himself rather than substitute one of his sons, and had proved to be a most gentle, courteous 'prisoner' – as a King, of course, he lived in great comfort.

'The folk of London so adore him, it is as if they would prefer *him* to be their King,' one of the women said with clear disapproval.

The other woman quite obviously loved collecting details of the elegant life the French King led, even in captivity. 'The Queen Mother has loaned him several of the romances she so enjoys,' she said. 'And the Queen herself has sent him household furnishings and rich foods. The King visits him. They play chess!'

I had heard much of this, of course, as many guild members were supplying King Jean's household, but I was ill at ease discussing it in the garden of a royal residence. It smacked of disapproval of the King's decision to ease King Jean's distress. Yet all spoke of the French monarch as a kind, pious man.

'I think it most Christian of the King to treat his peer with such respect and grace,' I said. 'And most courteous of Queen Philippa to ensure King Jean's comfort.'

My companions did not respond, but gazed seemingly aghast at something or someone behind me.

'I am indebted to you for your kind support, Dame Alice,' said a woman behind me.

I turned and beheld Queen Philippa. Though she was smiling at me, I dropped at once into the humblest bow I could manage with my sore legs, and stayed there until Janyn put a hand beneath my elbow and guided me upright.

'Your Grace,' I said for at least the second time. I could think of nothing else to say.

Janyn suggested that we walk, and the three of us, my husband, the Queen and I, drew away from the others.

'The Queen Mother speaks with such delight of her god-daughter,' said Philippa.

I was dumbfounded that she even knew of my sweet Bella. 'I pray each day that God shower the Queen Mother with blessings for her kindness to my family, Your Grace.'

'As I am certain she prays for you and your little family, Dame Alice. Your husband has been telling me of the garden you are creating at your home in London. I have heard that my husband's father found great satisfaction in digging in the earth, shifting soil. He said that it helped him find his feet and legs. Does it do so for you?'

It was such an unexpected topic that I hesitated, needing to think. I felt her eyes on me, deep green eyes that held both kindness and something much more calculating. I almost stammered some foolishness, but then remembered how proud I had been just moments ago of Janyn's ease with the Queen. I took a deep breath.

'When I've spent hours on my knees with my hands in the soil, I am reminded of the miracle of life, Your Grace, and I thank God for the gift of waking each new day. The King's father must have been a wise man.'

The green eyes clouded over for a moment. 'In some things he was said to be surpassingly wise.'

She studied the long, pointed toes of her embroidered shoes for a moment. When she raised her head, her mood had shifted and she beamed as if life delighted her again. I noticed that her skin was as translucent as the pearls on her headdress and collar. I'd thought her plain, though exquisitely dressed and elegant of manner, but saw now that she had an inner beauty that shone when she smiled.

'Your husband tells me that he consults you in financial

matters and that you have proven an excellent adviser. Do you enjoy such occupation?'

'I do, Your Grace, and am honoured that my husband finds my advice worth considering.'

'The King chides me about my lack of interest in such matters. I could use a woman near me who might engage me upon such issues, or at least suggest what I might say to the King to satisfy him.' She smiled at me, gave Janyn a teasing glance, and then turned the conversation to Milan and other favourite cities.

I was left to wonder over that last little exchange, but perked up once more when I was included in a brief discussion about children. Then the Queen nodded and left. Janyn complimented me on my conversation and courtesy.

We were soon interrupted by the merchant from St Albans, who wished a word with Janyn. I needed a respite from this heady company and sought out Gwen, wishing for her solid, familiar presence. As we were strolling past the chapel we came face to face with the King and dropped at once into deep bows.

'Do rise, my ladies. I do not care to be an object of worship in my mother's home, among her friends.' His blue eyes were teasing. 'Janyn Perrers's wife, I think?'

'Yes, Your Grace. Alice.'

'I am told you are a very clever young woman, with a mind for business. So I ask you, would I do better to invest in fine things to decorate my palaces or in spices?'

At that moment I wanted to be known for my beauty, not my cleverness in business. There was something in his voice, his eyes, the scent of him . . . I wanted him to look on me with desire. The thought made me blush. Only Janyn had ever had such an effect on me before.

'Your Grace,' I murmured, bowing my head for a moment to compose myself. 'I would advise you that spices would bring you more coin, but beautiful possessions would enrich your soul. It is similar to the choice between cloth of gold and escarlatte – the cloth of gold enhances your image as a mighty king, but chafes the skin. Whereas the escarlatte impresses only those who know its value and recognise the way it drapes, yet it is most pleasing on the skin . . .' I realised I was babbling. Even worse, that my mention of escarlatte on skin had invited him to look on me in a way that made me feel like his prey – a far from unpleasant sensation. 'Forgive me, Your Grace.'

'For what, Dame Alice? I see that you are clever indeed. And pretty enough.' He averted his eyes from my low-cut bodice and said in a hearty tone, 'Can you hunt? Can you ride? On the morrow we shall see if you possess all the graces, eh?' With a nod and a chuckle he continued into the chapel, his man hurrying afterwards, finding it difficult to match the King's long stride.

'Pretty enough,' I whispered.

'He is magnificent, just as they said,' Gwen murmured.

I had little to say for myself for the rest of the evening, stunned into silence by the encounter with King Edward. I had never experienced a presence such as his. While he spoke to me his blue eyes had held mine captive and his voice had resonated in my head, my heart, my belly, and down my bones to my extremities. I had no words for the sensation at the time; now I might call it enthralling. I felt as if I had actually been unfaithful to Janyn, and made it up to him with a show of passion that night, though I caught myself fantasising that it was the King who groaned with pleasure.

On the following morning I was uncomfortably aware of the King's eyes on me, but as soon as I accepted a merlin from the falconer, I focused only on her. She was not as large as my own, and of course she did not know me. Before I removed her hood, I spoke to her for a while so that she might hear that I meant her no harm. The falconer nodded his approval; King Edward did so as well. I willed myself to give her all my attention. Once she took flight it was no struggle to lose myself in her, to see nothing but her. We had some success, the merlin and I, that morning, and I was in high spirits as we returned to the castle.

Geoffrey had not participated in the hunt. As I took my seat beside him in the hall for the day's feast, he congratulated me on my prowess and on attracting the interest of the King. The news had obviously travelled before me.

I glanced at Janyn, fearing that he had heard, but he was engrossed in conversation with a friar. Turning back to Geoffrey, I found him grinning, but his eyes were more searching than amused.

'What think you of the most admirable of kings?' he asked.

'He is my monarch. I hold him in great respect, and pray that God blesses him and keeps him safe from all harm.'

Geoffrey waved all that aside. 'But as a man?'

I considered. If I refused to play his game, Geoffrey would guess that I was delighted by the King's attention. If I played the game, he would guess I simply enjoyed being admired. I did particularly enjoy the latter, having spent so much of my life in my mother's shadow.

'I have never felt such an imposing presence as his, nor have I ever seen such blue eyes. Why did you not hawk with us?'

He raised his brows in a show of surprise. 'Me? Have you seen me astride? I am the clumsiest of riders, and all birds dislike me on sight. I swear it is true! They chide and criticise me until I want to pluck them.' He laughed with me. 'You would have disclaimed me had you seen me among the others this morning. But animals have always found you calming and worthy of their trust. I am glad for you that the Queen Mother saw to it that you have a hunter and a merlin.'

I turned the conversation to questions about Geoffrey's travels with Lionel, Earl of Ulster.

Janyn eventually joined our conversation, and Geoffrey told him tales of how as a child I'd collected kittens that my mother refused to allow me to keep and then worked hard at finding them good homes, coaxing and cajoling neighbours to adopt the sweet creatures. Janyn enjoyed the tales.

The Queen Mother gave me a precious gift before we departed for home. I had boldly confided in her my misgivings regarding riding astride. She had said little, turning the conversation to Bella. But evidently she had heard me. She now suggested to Janyn that, while I was in my breeding years, I be free to choose whether I rode side-saddle or astride

'Surely it matters far more to Alice than it possibly could to you,' she said with an affectionate smile to my husband. 'If she worries that her riding will endanger her children, she will cease to enjoy one of the great pleasures in her life. I am certain you do not wish to cause that, my good and dear friend.'

What could he say?

'My daughter-in-law finds you most pleasant,' Isabella added, as if it were something she'd reminded herself to mention.

'The Queen is most kind.'

'My son admires the way you leave your body and soar with your hawk.'

I blushed under Isabella's keen regard.

'His Grace is most perceptive,' said Janyn.

We returned to London in a merry mood. I took pride in how happy I'd made Janyn, and in my courage in trusting Isabella to side with me on the question of saddles. It might seem a small victory, but to me it was comforting.

A few months later I found myself again with child, a cause of celebration for Janyn and me. My grandparents and the Perrers were overjoyed for us. I thought it would be a perfect time to encourage my siblings, Mary and Will, to participate more in Bella's life, assisting me with her care both before the new baby was born and afterwards. But Mother managed one more cruelty, forbidding Nan to bring Mary and Will to my home, and forbidding me to see them in their home either. Nan apologised for her, saying she had not been quite right in her mind since losing the child she herself had carried through the summer.

I went to Dame Agnes, hoping to learn how Mary and Will were faring.

'Dame Margery has no gift for mothering,' sighed Grandmother, 'and no room in her small heart to love anyone other than herself. I wish it were otherwise, for you children and for my son. He had hoped that another child might heal their marriage, more fool he! Why he thought she would change, I cannot understand. He never could accept her dislike of motherhood.' She embraced me. 'Do not worry about Mary and Will. They shall meet you here. Margery will not dare interfere in my household. Now let us speak no more of her. Bring my great-granddaughter next time you come, I pray you. She brightens my day.'

She asked about our time at Hertford Castle, making an effort I much appreciated to be curious and neutral about the Dowager Queen. I returned home in much better spirits.

It was a more difficult pregnancy than my last. When I grew restless with enforced rest, missing the release I found in riding,

Janyn encouraged me to apply myself to the studies he had set me. I did enjoy them, particularly languages and composition. I appreciated the way they brightened my thoughts and set me puzzling over realms far removed from my unhappy parents.

And there was always Bella, to amaze and delight me.

But clouds gathered on the horizon. In February we heard that the Queen Mother was very ill at Hertford. Dame Tommasa and I spent many hours praying for her. I was alarmed by my mother-in-law's obsessive piety. But it seemed our prayers were heard, for in a few weeks Isabella recovered and resumed her usual activities. But Janyn remained convinced that the Dowager Queen would be dead within the year, and the prospect seemed to suck the life from him. I could not understand it. Of course she had been most generous to us, and his journeys on her behalf had been most lucrative, but the accounts that I reviewed with him were all in excellent health, his trade encompassing much more than the affairs we conducted on her behalf. His reputation in London was growing, and his guild master referred to him as a future mayor. Yet Janyn grew fearful, overly protective, cautious to a degree that frightened me.

Often now he turned his back to me once we were abed, denying even this comfort to both of us.

'Do you no longer love me?' I finally summoned the courage to ask when he turned away once again.

He turned back. 'My sweet Alice, I love you more than words can say.' He pulled me close and held me for a moment. 'I pray you, forgive me if I have caused you pain. My mind and heart are overburdened. I am searching for a way to protect you and our daughter.'

'Protect us from what?'

'The uncertain future.'

'You and God will protect us, Janyn, my beloved.'

'You are so young and innocent, Alice. So loving and trusting.' He looked away as his voice filled with tears.

I sensed more and more that he was weaning me from him, from my need of him. I faltered in my resolve to be strong and to trust in God's guidance. I spent hours in church, praying and pouring out my heart to Dom Hanneye. Neither God nor my confessor offered any comfort beyond reminding me that Janyn loved me, and I loved him.

I felt almost relieved when Janyn departed in late-March on 'one last trip' to Milan for the Queen Mother, for then I might at least regain some calm.

'If anyone should enquire, I am in France,' he instructed me. 'You must not mention Milan or Lombardy.'

'Why must we lie about this journey?' I asked.

'For our safety.'

'Do your parents know where you will be?'

He nodded. There were shadows beneath his eyes and his breath smelled sour. He had not been eating well, but had been drinking far more than was his custom, late into the night.

In April there was much talk in the city of an extravagant St George's Day celebration at Windsor. It was said that our King and Queen, the Queen Mother, King Jean of France and his son Phillip were all in attendance, and that knights from all over Christendom were taking part in the tournament. I looked forward to reassuring Janyn on his return that all was well with Isabella.

It was at that time, on a day like any other, when a sudden pain brought me to my knees in the hall. Within moments I was kneeling in a pool of blood. I am told that my screams were so loud that neighbours came running with weapons drawn, certain that I was being attacked. Dame Tommasa and Gwen were at my side at once, but I wept for Janyn, I wanted only Janyn. Unfortunately he was at sea, headed for Milan, believing that when he returned I would be big and fat with child.

But it was not to be. And with the change in him, I feared it might be some time before I conceived again. I mourned that child as I had never mourned for anything in my life. I so wanted a sibling for my little Bella, a brother or sister she might love and with whom she would share secrets and treasures.

'You shall have many more children, Alice,' Tommasa assured me.

Felice the midwife agreed. 'What happened is as common as a cough in winter, and has no influence on your next pregnancy.'

Dame Agnes arrived with gifts of food, new bed curtains, a

tisane she said had helped her after she lost a child. She sat by me, talking of happy things or telling her paternoster beads. Yet I drew no comfort from her or anyone else for many a day. Janyn's drawing away from me, his dread of the future, and now this loss – it all seemed more than I could bear.

Until one morning I heard my sweet Bella weeping and telling her nurse that she had dreamed I had gone away with her father and left her all alone. My daughter's fear lifted me from my bed and into life once more. When I knelt to her where she sat in the hall, kicking her heels and refusing to be comforted by her nurse or her grandmother Dame Tommasa, her tears dried up and a smile lit her swollen face. She reached out for me and in a heartbeat I'd gathered her in my arms. She rested her hot little head on my chest and gave a great, trembling sigh. I had never held anything more precious.

For weeks I kept her near me, whether I was gardening, reviewing the accounts, studying, doing needlework.

I had hoped to find some calm in Janyn's absence, but my sense of underlying disquiet was hardly dispelled. Our acquaintances did not include me in festivities as often as they had the previous year, nor did they seem as friendly when I was among them. I noticed uneasy pauses in conversations when I approached, and I stood as godmother to none of the newborns – I thought this might have been because of my own loss, but would later learn that was in truth only a very small part of it.

The culmination of this dread took human shape one day in mid-May. I was at market with Gwen and a manservant when a stranger approached us, asking after Janyn. He was elegantly dressed and had a soldierly bearing. This was no merchant asking after a peer.

'I pray that his business in Lombardy is quickly resolved,' he said.

'You are mistaken, sir, for my husband is in Rouen,' I said.

He had the gall to finger my *gris*-lined cloak. 'Royal patronage brings many privileges. And dangers.'

'Unhand my mistress!' my manservant demanded in a loud voice.

'You are obviously a madman,' I hissed, and quickly took my leave, my companions staying close to me on either side. I do not know how I managed to reach home, my legs shook so.

Janyn's parents tried to hide their distress on hearing of the incident, but I judged it no coincidence that they suddenly decided we must attend to some improvements at Fair Meadow. When we departed for the country in late-May, I was glad to leave the city and the shadows that haunted me there. Once settled at Fair Meadow I took every opportunity to ride and hawk. Bella grew brown and chubby, more beautiful than ever.

But I had a recurring dream from which I woke with a frightening sense of foreboding that carried through the day. In the dream I stepped into a puddle on my way to the market and slipped into a dark, fathomless sea, sinking, sinking. I woke in a bed that looked like my bed, but when I rose the household staff and the family abiding in the home were all strangers – and they could not see me. I did everything I could think of to get their attention, but to them I was not there.

Janyn's return in late-June did little to reassure me, though I was relieved that he looked healthier than when he'd departed and had lost his haunted look. He'd not received the letter I'd written to him about losing the child until he was on his journey home, so that was a fresh grief. He held me close and murmured sweet and loving things. Yet I did not sense in him the same intense pain I still held within my heart. Perhaps it was different for a man, not being the one who bore the child. Yet, remembering his delight in Bella, I found myself worrying about the quiet resignation with which he accepted our loss. Though he seemed less haunted, he also seemed unable to settle to anything or to relax with Bella and me. He seemed impatient with the slow pace in the country and wondered aloud often whether he ought to return to London.

'But you have only just arrived, my love. I'd hoped we would enjoy riding, hawking, being together again. Perhaps planting a new seed.' I pressed my flat belly.

He kissed me absently. 'There is much to resolve, much to plan.' He still believed the Queen Mother would be dead before Christmas. He had seen Isabella at Leeds Castle, where she had been taken ill once more as she was resting before returning home from a pilgrimage to Canterbury. 'They say she is suffering from an unfortunate mistake in the strength of a medicine, but in truth I believe that medicines are failing her.'

'Your devotion to Isabella is proper and commendable, Janyn, and I am sorry that she is so ill, but we have so much to be grateful for beyond her patronage. Our daughter thrives, and with some pleasurable effort and God's grace, we shall have more children. Your guild master sees much success ahead for you. And we have our love, Janyn. Your sorrow over the Queen Mother will pass. Your life is ahead, not behind.'

'I should meet my guild master.'

His coolness stung me. 'Of course. But would you not like to rest here in the country for a while? You have been travelling since early-spring.'

'It is difficult to rest when there is so much to do . . .'

But there had always been much to do. I could not understand why he viewed it with such urgency now. Nor why he avoided speaking of our family and our future.

'How fared you in Milan, my love?'

'I cannot talk of it, Alice.'

'Can you at least tell me whether you accomplished what you had hoped?'

'For the most part, yes. But we must not speak of it. Mother told me of the man at the market. Tell me all you remember.'

Perhaps that was why he wished to head to London, to find out more about the stranger. Over and over, I told him all I could remember. I described the stranger each time for Janyn. Each time he would shake his head, say he knew no one who fitted that description, and commend me for remembering not to acknowledge that he had been in Milan.

'But the man knew. Or guessed. And he let me know that he guessed you were on royal business. What does that mean, Janyn?'

Each time we reached that question, he would assure me that it was nothing and walk away with a deep scowl.

He was home no more than a month when we received word that the Queen Mother and her daughter, Joan, Queen of Scotland, would be passing through on their way to Hertford Castle and we were to attend them at the royal hunting lodge in a few days.

'Why is she not staying here?' I asked Janyn.

'Her party is too large for this house.'

I dreaded it. 'Do we stay the night?'

'Of course.'

'Does she want us to bring her goddaughter?'

'No, my love, this is an official visit, not a social one.'

'I do not like the sound of that.'

'We are commanded to attend the Queen Mother, Alice. You know that we have no choice.'

The hunting lodge was a handsome stone and timber home, at least thrice the size of Fair Meadow, set in beautiful parkland groomed with care only to seem wild. Perhaps it would be pleasant to spend a few days in such a pretty place. For Janyn's sake as well as my own, I set my mind to enjoying myself.

But my calm was tested immediately upon our arrival when we found that we were to be escorted to Queen Philippa in the hall of the lodge. Apparently Isabella was exhausted by the journey and would see us in the morning, after she had rested.

I looked at Janyn. 'The Queen?' I mouthed, startled.

'I was not told that Queen Philippa would be here.'

Something in his posture said that although he'd not been told, he was not surprised. And that frightened me more than simply meeting the Queen unexpectedly.

Resplendent in green silk trimmed with gold and decorated with pearls and gold filigree buttons, Queen Philippa cut an imposing figure. Yet she greeted us with friendly words and a kind smile, asking about our ride, about baby Bella, and expressing her sympathy for my miscarriage. The Queen Mother must have told her about the latter, for I had not been with child when I had met the Queen at Hertford.

'I should like you to come to my chamber for a light meal at sunset,' Philippa said to me. 'Your husband will dine with the others. It will be pleasant to have a quiet meal with you and Joan.'

The Queen of Scotland, the Queen of England and me. 'Your Grace,' I managed to say as I bowed, though I was dumbstruck. A few years ago I'd been a child whose greatest thrill was to accompany Father to the market or spend time in his undercroft. Now I was to dine with two queens. I was terrified. As with my marriage, I felt other powers were at work here.

Servants showed us to a beautiful bedchamber. When Gwen

and Janyn's man Thomas had withdrawn, Janyn drew me into his arms.

'You make me so proud, Alice.'

I pulled away from him a little so that I might see his face as I asked, 'Why do I sense that you and Queen Philippa have some plan for me? A plan you've not mentioned as yet?'

In his slight pause and his frown I saw that I'd guessed correctly.

'You know that I've worried about your future, Alice. I am so much older than you . . .' He beamed at me as if just his smile should comfort me. And when I did not respond as hoped, he added, 'Let us see what the Queen has to say, eh?'

'Sometimes you speak as if you see Death standing at the door, beckoning you. Are you ill, Janyn?'

'I could hardly hide an illness from you.'

'You have been less amorous,' I thought aloud.

'Worries. I am in good health, my love. I shall prove that tonight, I swear.'

'Janyn, your evasions frighten me. I beg you, tell me what is wrong. Has someone threatened your life?'

For a fleeting moment I saw a flicker of fear in his eyes and a twitch at the corner of his mouth, as if cursing the possibility that I'd heard something he'd tried to keep from me, but he recovered admirably and laughed at the question.

'You are so impatient, my love. Rest now, so that you can enjoy your evening with the Queens of England and Scotland.'

'Rest, when I am about to dine with two queens?'

We laughed together and he drew me down on to the bed in a playful embrace. In a short while he had proven to me that he was in excellent health. We had not made love with such passion in a long time. The result was to calm my fear about the evening enough for me to manage to sleep for a while.

The bedchamber in which I dined with the two queens looked out over the park and had large windows that made it wonderfully airy and filled with the delicate scents of summer. A table had been placed near the window, and a brazier glowed nearby to ward off any chill as the sun set. Queen Joan was pretty in a brittle sort of way – she reminded me of my mother, which did not endear her to me. Her personality was likewise brittle. But she was courteous to me, and pleasant enough. We spoke of children, households, the price of silk and leather . . . the sorts of things women talk about when relaxing together. It was not until the food had been cleared that Philippa came to the point.

'The Queen Mother has spoken so often of you,' she said to me. 'She tells me that I would benefit by having you in my household.'

'Your household, Your Grace?'

'As a damsel of the chamber, assisting me in dressing, and, I hope, teaching me the value of money – your husband has spoken so highly of your understanding of his business.'

As she spoke I recalled our conversation in the garden of Hertford Castle, the puzzling comment about someone like me being useful to her. But dressing the Queen? On the one hand, it would be a great honour, but on the other, in my experience servants dressed adults, and I hardly found it an appealing prospect. 'Your Grace, I have never imagined such an honour.' But Janyn had, I was suddenly certain of that.

'In Hainault, my homeland, it was the custom for nobles and merchants to feast and celebrate together. We believed it important to understand one another. Edward and I wish to have a deeper connection with the merchant class of London. We need to understand how you view the world. Your husband agrees.'

With those words she erased any possible doubt about Janyn's collusion. 'Your Grace, I have a family, two houses, a daughter . . .' I began, grasping for a lifeline.

'You shall see them often, I promise you.' She rose and held out her hand for me to kiss. I did so.

'My husband is likewise delighted. I think we shall all benefit from this arrangement.' She nodded to a servant to show me out.

I managed to withdraw without mishap, though I found it difficult to breathe.

'Dame Alice, what is amiss?' Gwen said when I rushed into the bedchamber.

Janyn rose from a table near the fire, his head tilted in the way he had when he was trying to understand what he was seeing. 'You are unhappy, my love?'

'I am summoned to the royal court. To live at court. Away from you, away from Bella. I'm to be a servant to Her Grace. You knew! You knew and you did not warn me. How could you let me find out in such wise? Why are you doing this to me?' I fell on to the bed, face down, burying my face in my forearms and letting the tears come.

I felt Janyn sit down on the edge of the bed, but he did not touch me. In a little while, when I turned my head to one side to breathe, Gwen gently touched my shoulder and asked if she might help me disrobe.

I turned, sat up, and without speaking submitted to dear Gwen's ministrations. Only when she had withdrawn did I turn to Janyn again.

'Is this what you want for us?'

He looked weary, and as if he'd suddenly aged.

'If the world were a safer place, no.' He held up a hand to silence me when I began to speak. 'But this is a great honour, Alice. Your position will be much like your friend Geoffrey's, but even closer to the King and Queen. My love, it is a wonderful thing.'

'Why did you not prepare me for this? Discuss it?'

'Look at you now, Alice, how you resist this. Would you have come had you known?'

'Listen to yourself! You resorted to trickery. I have trusted you, Janyn. I have obeyed you in all things, and this is my reward? You deceive your wife?'

He raked his hands through his hair, his breath ragged. 'It is best this way, my love.'

'Best for you! So tell me now, did you ask the Queen Mother to arrange this?'

'I did.'

I turned away from him, my mind connecting all things mysterious in the past months. 'My tutor . . . all that was in preparation?'

'Yes.'

'Why, Janyn? Have you tired of me?'

'Oh, my love.' He pulled me into his arms. I felt his heart pounding. 'Oh, my love, I've done this for you. And for Bella.'

I tried to free myself but he held me tighter, then began covering me with kisses. He knew where to kiss me, he knew my vulnerable places and made it impossible for me to resist him. I was afire. I needed to satisfy the desire that overwhelmed me. Afterwards I was angry with myself for succumbing to my passion, for seeming to accept Janyn's betrayal. But perhaps there was hope. I prayed that I had conceived. Surely if I were with child, I might be passed over for the honour of dressing the Queen.

An early-morning hunt raised my spirits a little. The woodland was beautiful. But later, in our conversation with Isabella, the Queen Mother, I clearly saw that anything but gratitude for my position in her daughter-in-law's household would be met with regal anger.

Ever obedient, I held my tongue. I suffered in lonely, desperate silence. Most painful to me was Janyn's deception. I saw I was always to be at the mercy of others' decisions. How I would keep my faith, how I would nurture my own child when I felt so powerless, I could not see.

Some people dream of being at court, imagining a privileged life replete with luxury. I had never wished to be at court, and once I had wed and felt the insidious influence of the royal family, had prayed only to break away from them. I had felt overwhelmed at Hertford Castle, woefully unprepared for court life. I did not know the rules, had not the wit or grace to hold my ground amongst the nobly born. Janyn's attempts to educate me would make little difference, I was sure.

My courses came shortly after we returned from our visit to the Queens. I wept most bitterly and refused to rise from bed for a day, my hope for a reprieve from court dashed. Dame Agnes held me close, and when I babbled about why I was so desperate to conceive, murmured prayers. I went to Dom Hanneye and spoke to him from my heart. I told him everything, even my drowning dream. Afterwards, he sat quietly in prayer for a long while.

All the dreams of my life with Janyn – all were shattered by the prospect of long separations. I was too desperate to find my way to prayer.

I felt Dom Hanneye shift to look at me. 'My heart tells me that God's plan for you takes you to court,' he said in a soft, gentle voice.

He reached for my hand, enfolding my icy one in his warm clasp.

'We cannot always understand the path we walk, Alice. Can you imagine how bewildered the Blessed Virgin was when the Angel Gabriel announced that she was with child, a divine child? Or Saul, blinded by God on the road. Do you not think he felt as if he were drowning?'

I wanted to be comforted by his words, but a part of me believed that all around me had gone mad.

I sought out Geoffrey's advice. He listened to me with a grave expression.

'The only possibility that makes sense to me is that some danger to your family lies behind this, Alice. It is not necessarily a good thing to be close to Isabella of France, the Queen Mother. There is much blood in her past.'

'That warning was too late long before I wed Janyn.'

'I know.'

'In your experience, do couples at court see much of one another?'

'If they so desire, yes. The royal family would prefer fewer illicit liaisons at court – unless, of course, the affairs are their own.'

I crossed myself.

'I do understand your unhappiness, Alice. Janyn has chosen a perilous path. But perhaps the court is the only safe harbour for you.'

'And what of my daughter? Do you think I will be permitted to see Bella frequently?'

'That will be more difficult. I think you must resign yourself to seeing her only on occasion.'

My heart hurt. 'Why is obedience so painful?'

'If it were not, there would be no need to insist upon it.' And then Geoffrey did something unexpected. He took me in his arms and hugged me, then kissed my cheek. 'You have been sorely tested these past few years. Always know that you have a friend in me. If you send for me, I will come if I am able.'

'If you are able. That is the sad truth of our stations, is it not? We are servants, though all see us as blessed with great fortune.

We are bound body and soul to our lords or ladies. As is Janyn, and as indeed were his parents before him.'

I hugged Geoffrey back. 'I thank God for your friendship. May we both find a way to happiness despite our servitude.'

'Amen.' He kissed me once more on the cheek.

'I have more questions,' I said.

'More?' Geoffrey looked alarmed.

'I must be prepared.'

He fled after a while, claiming that my questions were draining all wit from him. I did not blame him. I knew so little of court, and from what he had told me there was so very much to know. I might have bled him all night.

I lay awake thinking about my drowning dream. It had been a premonition of my summons to court, I was sure of it. I fingered my paternoster beads, praying for courage.

Book II

The Queen's Handmaid

When had I a choice to be other than I was? The Queen Mother and Janyn had decided I was to be a lady of the court, and short of running away I must accept their plan. They said it was for my good, for my daughter's good.

But what of my heart? Janyn promised me that he would visit me often, and we would have time together in our homes with Bella when the Queen was nearby. My husband would visit – I wanted to live with him. I wanted to live with my daughter, to bring her up to be the woman I dreamed she could be.

I did not like the fact that this separation must have been planned long ago, that it had led Janyn to insist on hiring a wet nurse, that the Queen Mother's being my baby's god-mother had been the first step. I wondered why Janyn had pursued me, why he had wished to wed me at all. I hated the way such questions tainted my most precious memories.

Our happiness, though it had lasted for so short a time, could not be sustained because of the risks Janyn and his mother's family had taken in exchange for the patronage of Isabella of France. It seemed to me a terrible price. Though I yearned to follow him into the danger from which he protected me, I was once again called on to practise obedience. I was also counselled to be grateful for all that I had. Obedience and gratitude were difficult for me when my heart was breaking.

II-1

'How myghte it evere yred ben or ysonge,
The pleynte that she made in hire destresse?
I not; but, as for me, my litel tonge,
If I discryven wolde hire hevynesse,
It sholde make hire sorwe seme lesse
Than that it was, and childisshly deface
Hire heigh compleynte, and therefore ich it pace.'

– Geoffrey Chaucer, *Troilus and Criseyde*, IV, ll. 799-805

August 1358

Janyn and I were summoned to Hertford Castle in mid-August
that fateful summer. Between the time of our summons and our
departure I was haunted once more by my nightmare of the
golden wolf. As in the original dream, she devoured the blossoms
in Tommasa's garden, crushing the delicate plants in her heedless
grazing. In the hall all my family lay broken, drained. Their blood
stained the wolf's muzzle and dripped from her lolling tongue.
Though the horror of it weighed my every step, I kept the dream
to myself. Janyn had not trusted me with the truth, and I would
not give him cause to doubt my courage. Even so, I rode towards
Hertford with such dread that he and Gwen both feared I was ill.
I felt as if I were riding into the wolf's maw. A royal residence
could soon cease to be a marvel and become a prison, be it ever
so richly appointed.

On our arrival the Queen Mother sent word that she wished to
see me alone. Something in his face told me that Janyn had
expected this request. I followed the page with feet of lead.

As I entered Isabella's bedchamber I could see at once how ill
she was, how close to death. Her eyes had withdrawn into her
skull; her once erect spine had crumbled. She sat propped up by
a mound of cushions and her hand trembled as she extended it
for me to kiss. All the fragrant oils burning in the room could not
mask the stink of the sickroom. She patted the space beside her.

'I've little breath. Sit up here near me, Alice.'

When I was seated beside her she ordered her servants to leave us alone. When they hesitated, Isabella brusquely waved them out.

'But what if you need assistance, Your Grace?' I was not comfortable being responsible for such a great lady.

'Then you shall call for them. I should like for just a moment to be free to talk to a friend without being overheard.' She settled her sunken eyes on me. 'I know that you are not happy about being summoned to court, to Philippa's household.' She spoke slowly, summoning up breath with painful effort.

'It is an honour I did not desire,' I admitted, having no reason to demur if she'd already guessed.

'I have arranged this for your safety, and your daughter's. Especially for hers.'

I crossed myself for protection from evil, from the terrible golden wolf that haunted my sleep. 'What danger threatens us?'

'I will not tell you all, for they would only rip it from you when I am gone.'

'They? Who, Your Grace?'

She held up a hand for me to be patient as she caught her breath.

This was the moment I had both yearned for and dreaded. I was about to learn the truth from the Queen Mother herself. I was torn between consideration for her and my own need for information. Fearing that I might silence her by my insistence I said, 'My lady, perhaps later—'

She waved me to silence. I pressed my hands together and fiercely prayed for her and for my family. I needed her alive, understanding now Tommasa's panic at signs of Isabella's decline. When I heard the Queen Mother's breathing grow less laboured, I opened my eyes. She nodded.

'Janyn's grandparents saved someone most precious to me, at great risk to themselves. The family continues to serve me, still at great risk. I vowed to save you and my goddaughter. For your husband, who loves you as his life.'

The words twisted my heart. 'What of Janyn? Is he in danger?'

'Every moment.' She reached towards my hands. I pried mine apart and proffered one. She took it in hers. 'Do not doubt his love.' She was so weak, her hands dry and cold.

Though I shook with emotion and was desperate to hear all she knew, I forced myself to be patient. 'Your Grace,' I managed to say.

'You must take care and be guided by others.' She pressed my hand. 'Pray for my soul, Alice. Do not curse me.'

I could not promise that. I kissed her hand, though through my anguish and fear another, stronger emotion was rising. Anger. Anger about all the planning, the secret arrangements made behind my back.

'I must rest,' said Isabella. 'Call my servants. Go to Janyn.'

I was unsteady on my feet when I rose from the bed, but I reached the corridor and summoned Isabella's attendants before stumbling into Janyn's embrace. I was relieved to find him waiting there, desperately in need of his strength. He led me out into a quiet part of the gardens and we walked for a while, arm-in-arm, not speaking, just being together.

When I trusted myself to speak sensibly, I asked, 'Who is the beloved that your family protects?'

'Did she not tell you that I am sworn to secrecy?'

'She did. And that if I knew "they would only rip it from" me when she is dead. But who are *they*? Why would they believe that I know nothing? This is not a joust with polite rules, Janyn, this is my life, our marriage, our family.' I gasped, so angry now that I found it difficult to breathe. Who was it he visited so regularly? Not soldiers, as he had told me, but someone 'precious' to Isabella. I turned away from him. He could not comfort me, for it was he, his family, that had brought me to this moment of understanding that all I loved teetered on the edge of disaster.

Janyn drew me to him. 'You will be protected in the Queen's household.'

I stiffly endured his embrace, refusing to yield. 'What of our daughter? What of *you*?'

He released me. 'The plan had been that our Bella was to stay here, with her godmother.'

My anger softened at the distraught note in Janyn's voice, seeing how he clenched his hands. All of this was the planning he had talked of since the Queen Mother's illness in January.

Perhaps Bella might be safe in the bosom of the Salisbury family. 'What of her own great-grandmother, Dame Agnes?'

Janyn took my hands. 'Look at me, Alice.' When I met his gaze, I saw a plea in his eyes. 'For the sake of our daughter, we must keep her apart from my family, and from yours.'

'I would not think of allowing her to be brought up by my parents. I—'

'Listen to me, Alice. Look at me.' I had glanced away. 'There may come a time when I will ask you to do something,' he began. When he was certain he had my attention, he added: 'It will, I think, be the hardest thing you have ever had to do. You must walk away from me and both our families.'

'Walk away from all I hold dear? I will not desert my daughter!'

He shook his head. 'The King and Queen have promised to find a way for you to be with Bella. Eventually. Another foster home will be found – but eventually she will be placed with you in the royal household.'

My heart lunged towards that shaft of hope. 'God be thanked! But walk away from you? Why, Janyn?'

'Isabella has told you why. Now, listen. If someone gives you these beads,' he held out his favourite rosewood paternoster beads to me, 'you will know that it is time for you to walk away. That is your signal.'

'Janyn! Walk away from you? I cannot. I could never do so.'

'I love you more than my own life, Alice, and I mean for you and Bella to have long, wonderful lives. My family foolishly agreed to something long ago that brought them wealth, but at what cost they had not then fathomed. How terrible it would be . . . how it might destroy our family. I do not want you to suffer for it.'

'But without you I will suffer, Janyn.'

'Then think of our Bella.'

'What could be so dangerous, my love?'

'Knowledge, Alice. I'll say no more. Never doubt that I love you and Bella. I have been so happy with you.'

Trembling with anger and frustration, I backed away from him, shaking my head. 'How could you do this to us? What possessed you to pursue marriage when you knew what lay ahead? What right had you to bring this curse down upon me and our innocent child?'

'Hush, hush, Alice, my love.' Janyn reached out to me. 'I prayed the Queen Mother would live a long life. She appeared hale and hearty.'

I was torn between running from him and seeking comfort in his arms. While I hesitated the tears came and he gathered me to him, holding me close as I wept. We clung to each other so hard that the next morning I saw the bruises on both our arms. I prayed to God, His mother, and all the saints to take this burden from us. To bring a miracle to save us.

Within days of our meeting, Isabella, the Queen Mother, insisted on a large dose of the physick she had been taking and died in peace. When a messenger arrived from Hertford with the news, Janyn and Tommasa, who was dining with us, both looked as if the messenger had brought word of their own imminent deaths. Pale and wooden, they received the news with a terrible quiet, so unlike them that the servants looked as frightened as I felt.

When I was summoned to Windsor Castle shortly after Isabella's death, I thought my heart would shatter with the pain of leaving Bella and Janyn. But when I saw how my emotions affected them, I forced a brave countenance. I would find a way to reunite my family. Until then, I would see this as an adventure. I would make Janyn and Bella proud of me.

I had thought Hertford splendid, but it was modest in comparison to the royal couple's grand palace. I was overwhelmed by its vastness, bewildered by the opulence, and spellbound by the magnificence of colour and light within. My resolve weakened in the face of such a foreign domicile. In our first days at court, Gwen and I were often lost in the maze of corridors and buildings. When the Queen realised why I was often late to the sewing room or to attend her in her chamber she assigned a young page to me, Martin, who had been at court long enough to know every nook and cranny. Every night I cried myself to sleep.

Through that first autumn and winter, I lived only infrequently at court, for in the brief time between my meeting with Queen Philippa at the lodge and my joining her household she had fallen from her horse while hunting with the King. She suffered grievous pain in her lower back and hips that kept her to her bed, unable to participate in state occasions, requiring fewer attendants. I watched the other ladies as we sewed or tidied the Queen's chamber, listened to the gossip, and tried to learn as much as I could as quickly as I might, so that I would not embarrass myself or Janyn. But my heart was so heavy I felt slow and stupid.

At home I tried to treasure each moment with Bella and Janyn, but the precariousness of our situation haunted me and confused the household. Our housekeeper Gertrude and a new nursemaid helped Janyn with Bella when I was called to court, with Dame Tommasa in attendance as much as possible, and they were loath to change their routine when I was in residence. My sweet Bella, in her second year, was happily adaptable. I was not so fortunate. I hovered about her to such an extent that she grew querulous under my regard.

Things were little better with Janyn. Since Isabella's death he seemed far away. I persisted in wooing him, desperate to have another child, holding firm to the belief that if I were to conceive, I would be released from the Queen's household and all would be well in my little family.

In my desperation I consulted a Dominican friar, Dom Clovis, whose name was passed on in whispers among the women of the Queen's household. I asked him to concoct a love potion for Janyn and me. Clovis created a charm of holy words and fragrant oil, but it did not ease our estrangement. On the contrary, when Janyn questioned me about the oil, he was outraged.

'You accused me of being irresponsible in wedding you, in having a child when I knew the danger we faced if the Dowager Queen were to die . . . and now you try love spells to conceive another baby? Are you living in a dream?' He had taken hold of my shoulders as I tried to hide the flask of oil. Now he shook me.

'Would you kill me? Would that make it easier for you?'

We turned from each other, shocked by the anger between us.

We grew more and more distant, feeling most comfortable when discussing accounts. I could see that he was ever more anxious, yet I could not reach him.

My duties at court became more regular in April, when Queen Philippa insisted on taking an active part in the annual celebration marking the Feast of St George at Windsor, with the gathering for jousts and tournaments of the members of the Order of the Garter. The Order had been founded ten years earlier by King Edward after the glorious victory at Crécy. Twenty-six knights companions pledged loyalty to Edward and to one another. They met for a grand celebration each year on St George's Day, the twenty-third of April, at Windsor, where the King was building a new hall for them.

For such festivities all the members of both the King's and Queen's households visible to the guests were dressed to complement the main theme of the event, which for the Garter meant accents of azure, blue and gold. It seemed frivolous to me to spend so much time and money on special robes, but then I resented everything about court and was in a particularly darksome mood. My darling Bella had just been sent to live in the household of Queen Joan of Scotland at Hertford Castle.

Queen Philippa had informed me of this arrangement one morning as I worked beside her in the sewing room.

'Scotland?' I groaned. 'So far!'

'Joan is unlikely to return to Scotland with her husband,' the Queen said, quietly, for my ears only.

I forced myself likewise to speak softly, though I was screaming inside.

'Why must she be taken from her home?'

'You know why, Alice. For her own protection.'

My heart was in my stomach, but I tried to reason with her. It was better than facing my fear, the question, *Why now?*

'Your Grace, if it please you, why might Bella not bide with me, here at court?' Of Philippa's eight living children, her youngest son Thomas was but three years old, not much older than my Bella. Her two youngest daughters, Margaret and Mary, twelve and fourteen, were often in residence, and even Isabella, the eldest, at twenty-six the subject of much gossip for not yet being wed, was a frequent resident. The Queen loved her children, and I had hoped she would understand my yearning to have my daughter with me.

But she was adamant. 'I require your full attention when you are in residence, Alice. You would weary yourself between your daughter and your other duties and be of no use to me. I expect you to use your leisure in healthy activities that replenish you.'

She seemed blind to my agony, my fear, and my loneliness.

My duties hardly depleted me. There were two levels of well-born women in the Queen's household. Those of us who were of birth status above serving women but yet not of noble birth were her dressers and fetchers, and those of noble birth were her companions and sometimes messengers. Throughout the day I was one of several responsible for assembling the Queen's robe for her various activities – gowns, headdresses, jewels, shoes, cloaks, cleaning and mending as needed, as well as spending time most days doing the decorative stitching on new garments. I was also in attendance when the Queen consulted the sempsters, designing her own gowns and the accompanying livery for her household for feasts and state occasions. And in general we attended the Queen: serving her refreshments, accompanying her to chapel, walking with her when she had the strength, sometimes reading to her when she was unwell. The duties were not arduous, nor were they nearly as challenging as running a household. I was bored, which added to my misery.

I had been permitted to bring Melisende with me to court, and escaped to the stables to be with her as often as possible. If a groom could not be spared to accompany me on a ride, I groomed Melisende and dreamed of a time when she might once again reside in my own stables. But I felt that life receding farther and farther into the past.

Overwhelmed by the strangeness of court, confused by its rituals and unsure what was expected of me, I made mistakes, overreached myself.

I forgot myself one day when Queen Philippa asked my opinion about the cloth spread out before her on the great bed in her chamber. Cloth of gold, richly dyed wools and silks, intricately patterned . . . though it was a more costly collection than ever I had seen in one place, I felt comforted by the familiarity of it all. I knew cloth. I asked what sorts of garments she was planning, for what occasions, and then made suggestions.

Too late I noticed the tell-tale sounds that indicated the noblewomen were taken aback by my audacity.

The Queen heard them as well and, turning to them, declared, 'Listen to Mistress Alice and learn, all of you. She is all that I had hoped she would be.'

From that moment they were my sworn enemies.

They would sit to one side of the airy sewing chamber, idly plucking at their needlework while gossiping, their elegant head-dresses trembling as they leaned closer first to one companion, then the other. Across the tiled floor we lesser women eagerly applied ourselves, delighted to handle the exquisite cloth, the silken thread, even the gold or silver wire that cut our fingers receiving our admiration. We would comment on the quality, and I would get carried away, expounding on the virtues of the various cloths on which we worked, their weaves, dyes, finishes.

'The pattern in this tabby weave is clever, is it not? Every third strand picked out, then every sixth, every ninth, and back to third,' I might note with enthusiasm.

'It is all of a colour. You will ruin your eyes with such counting,' Lady Ann would say with a lazy laugh. The other headdresses shivered in glee.

Admiring a satin border we were sewing on to a patterned silk bodice, I might exclaim, 'Look how the indigo draws out the blue cast to the red in the patterned silk.' I could not help myself.

'Such an eye for colour, Mistress Alice,' Lady Eleanor would say. 'How clever of you. Is that how the mercers coax their fellows' wives into debt, by such subtle description?'

I had not realised that the high-born proudly feigned ignorance of such details.

'And what might this blue be called, Alice? Is it costly? Or might a fisherman's wife afford it?' Lady Mary would ask.

Their amused glances at one another as they goaded me on to reveal the depths of my commoner's mercantile knowledge eventually silenced me.

Among my peers I was considered arrogant. Among the noblewomen I was considered an inferior, a commoner who did not know my place, and I was treated as a servant when not in the presence of the Queen. I kept a modest demeanour at all times, praying that in time I might win acceptance.

For the nonce I was bereft of all comfort, for I was not free to be with my extended family, either my siblings or my grandparents, or, most painfully, Bella, my precious child. She would receive an august upbringing, far removed from me. I was wretched, terrified that my own daughter would forget me. When I thought of her cheerful wave as she'd departed with Queen Joan's party my heart twisted in my breast, a pain that left me breathless.

Although Philippa's stated purpose in adding me to her household – to be reminded of the practical considerations in which a woman of the merchant class had been trained – had been doomed from the beginning by her own extravagance, she continued to consult me. She spoke of the merchant class as practical, prudent folk, when in truth it was the wealthier members of that class for whom she yearned, those who had feasted and jousted with her family in Hainault. And so, instead of learning from me how to make practical choices, she taught me instead how to let go of my inhibitions and indulge my desires, my natural delight in all fine things. In my dress I spent lavishly on gowns of silk, escarlatte, and even one of silk-velvet, enjoying the way the soft fabrics caressed my skin, and shoes and boots of softest leather that seemed to lighten my every step.

Janyn encouraged such spending, considering it a sign that I was embracing my new life, and, in truth, it was worth seeing the light in his eyes as I twirled about showing off my latest gowns. He would lift me up by the waist and dance me round the hall, and I would forget all my misgivings about my current situation for the joy of that moment with my beloved. But it was no substitute for his daily company, the intimacy of living with him.

On the occasion of Bella's third birthday in June, Janyn, Bella, Dame Tommasa, Master John and I spent a wonderful month at Fair Meadow as a family. Bella grew very close to her father during that time. Janyn presented her with a pony and taught her to ride. I rode with her as well, but she much preferred preening in the admiration of her handsome, adoring father. The weather was glorious, and everyone seemed determined to be out of doors, riding, walking, gardening. At night, much to my surprise and joy, Janyn and I rekindled our love with renewed passion. It was a happy time, giving me new hope, and returning to the Queen's household in July was one of the most difficult things I have ever done.

After the happy month with my family loneliness plagued me more than ever, and, though I knew it for a sin, I found myself unable to conquer my self-pity. My increasingly infrequent and brief visits to Janyn and Bella only increased my pain. I was heart-broken and lonely.

Even my familiar confessor had been taken from me, Dom Hanneye having been sent to Oxford. In truth, I had seen little of him once I joined Queen Philippa's household, for on those fortnights that Janyn and I spent in London, I was loath to spend too much time outside my home, away from my husband and all that was so increasingly precious to me. My new confessor, Dom Creswell, a man of the court, urged me to seek out the blessings in each moment. He was kind in his counsel, seeing my unhappiness and expressing sympathy while gently suggesting that, as I had no choice in the matter, I could either be miserable lamenting what could not be or learn contentment with what was. I did recognise the wisdom of his advice. Dame Tommasa had urged me to do the same when I had wept in her loving embrace earlier in the year.

I could not deny that I was surrounded by beauty and had only to ask for most of my material wishes to be fulfilled. Music filled my days, as well as poetry, ballads, tales of far-off lands. There was much dancing and I enjoyed learning new steps, delighting in the heady feeling of being swept along by the music and my fellow dancers. There were weeks of feasting, with guests from royal houses and legendary bloodlines, and hunting, hawking, riding, watching jousts and tourneys. In the quiet in between we embroidered with precious threads on the most beautiful cloth, and prayed in exquisitely fitted chapels, the servants ever ready with mantles and lap rugs to warm us if we felt chilled.

Still my heart cried out for my sweet homes with Janyn and Bella, and despite our happy coupling in June, he and I had as yet begun no new life. It seemed that God had other plans for me.

In September Janyn departed on a journey to Milan. It was to be a brief one, and he promised to send word of his progress by merchants passing him on their return to London. But when November arrived and I had not heard from him, I was terrified for him and all the family, including Bella and myself. Despite his weaning me from him, I had not thought that this time Janyn would not return.

I sought leave to go into London to visit Dame Tommasa and

Master John, taking the opportunity before the Queen's household left Sheen, so near to the city, to hear some news of Janyn. I caught the Queen in a distracted moment. She agreed as long as household guards escorted Gwen and me. Surely by now someone journeying from Lombardy might have returned to London and reported seeing Janyn.

My page Martin accompanied us to the city, and two guards followed us at a discreet distance. As I approached the Perrers' house I grew horribly anxious, my mind spinning out tales of terror. I paused in St Mary Aldermary to compose myself. The church was blessedly quiet as I knelt before the Lady altar. Gwen covered me with a warm mantle and withdrew to join Martin on a bench well behind me and away from the draughts. I knelt there for a long while, praying that I would hear good news, any news, of Janyn, praying for my daughter, for my husband, and for all our family.

My heart finally steadied, I felt I might continue to the house. As I prepared to rise, I noticed a drably dressed woman with a baby in her arms standing to one side of the Lady altar, quite close to me. As I rose I must have jostled her, for she dropped her prayer beads. Seeing it would be most awkward for her to bend down with her burden to retrieve them, I reached down. My hand froze midway. God help me, they were Janyn's rosewood beads, the ones that were to signal my walking away from him and our families! I felt dizzy as I grasped them and straightened up. I must be mistaken. I had convinced myself that disaster was at hand, and thus I had seen what I dreaded seeing. I held the beads out to her in my shaking hand.

'You dropped your beads.'

'You are most kind, Dame Alice,' said the woman as she reached out, palm forward, to refuse them, 'but you must keep them. Know by this from whom my message comes. He and his mother have safely crossed the Channel. They will not return. He commends you to the protection of the household in which you serve, and prays that you forgive and forget. As you vowed.'

'Forgive and forget?' I repeated, staring down at the beads in my hand. 'How did you come to have these?'

When I looked up for her response she was gone, and now Martin, standing beside me, was asking if the woman had harmed me. I shook my head and pressed the beads to my nose, inhaling, hoping to catch Janyn's scent. But they were merely rosewood beads, though these mere beads held such a horrible weight I could not bear to have them in my possession. I stepped up to the statue of the Blessed Mother and wound the beads round her wrist until they blended with the other offerings that adorned her.

'Holy Mary, Mother of God, watch over my beloved.' I looked round for someone from the church who might know the woman who had brought me the beads, but Gwen, Martin and I were the only people in sight. 'Is it not unusual to have a church in the middle of the city all to ourselves?' I said, more to myself than my companions.

'Do you know her?' asked Martin.

I felt as if I were trapped in a nightmare. It would not have surprised me had my companions not seen the woman or the beads.

Martin repeated his question. 'I am responsible for your welfare, Mistress Alice. Why did she give you the beads? Do you know her?'

'She was a stranger to me. I had not noticed that I had dropped the beads. I'd forgotten I had them in my hands.' I needed time to think, to comprehend what had just transpired. I did not want Martin and the guards to insist on my returning to the palace without seeing Master John. 'Let us continue to the Perrers' home.'

I hurried now, anxious to learn what Master John knew, frantic for his reassurance. I did not want to believe the beads signalled my separation from Janyn. But the moment I stepped through the hall door I sensed an absence, a void in the spirit of this place, and knew that something terrible had happened. The servant who showed us in excused himself at once, which was not his custom. He was wont to ask after Bella and beg to hear what wonders I'd seen at court since we last spoke. As I waited I noticed clutter and dust, and the absence of some of the most colourful cloths that Tommasa used to cover tables and benches. The servant returned in silence, and still in silence led me to where my father-in-law sat in a small screened-off part of the hall in which he worked on his business records.

Master John rose from his chair with effort, moving as if his joints were stiff. He had a dazed look in his eyes.

'What has happened, Father?' I asked as we embraced. He smelled sour as if he'd already had much to drink though it was not yet midday.

'She is gone . . . my Tommasa. First my son, now my wife. God in Heaven, what am I to do? How am I to live?'

He held me so tightly I could feel each of his fingertips through several layers of cloth. This was Master John, always a source of strength and wisdom in my life. To find him like this was a moment from my darkest dreams.

'Father, what do you mean?'

He let go of me and stumbled back. His servant, who had quietly waited behind me, helped his master into his chair and then, after bowing to me, his face solemn, moved out of sight behind the screens. Master John covered his face with his hands and shook his head.

I crouched in front of him. 'You are frightening me. I pray you, tell me what you mean. What has happened here?'

With a moan he uncovered his face and looked at me.

'The message came. After all these years, I did not believe it ever would. But it came. "Flee". And Tommasa said that she must leave at once. Without me. She said that Janyn must have received such a message earlier, or had known it was coming. She thanked God that the Queen Mother had found protection for you and our granddaughter.'

'Flee . . . without you? And Janyn too had received such a message?'

Master John nodded once and took a great, shuddering breath.

Things like this did not happen to my people. We were mere merchants, so ordinary as to be invisible. God-fearing, worthy members of trade guilds. But even as I thought that, I remembered we were no longer ordinary, for we had been cursed by our connection to Isabella of France.

'Did Dame Tommasa not question the message at all?' I asked. 'At least her heart must have protested? It cannot have been easy for her to leave you.'

'She behaved as if she had no doubt it was what she must do.' He searched my face as if hoping I might know more. 'So many years ago she had warned me, but I had not believed it.'

'Who brought the message?'

He shook his head. 'A servant, hooded. I would not recognise him if he were to reappear. Tommasa said that she did not know him, but she knew that he was the one she'd been expecting.'

'How?'

'She said only that she knew.'

'And you asked no questions? Demanded no further explanation than that? She is your wife, Master John. Did you give her permission?'

He flinched as if I had hit him. I was only trying to make sense of what he was telling me.

'I had agreed when we wed. I had foolishly believed the day would never come . . .'

I told him what had happened in the church, describing the woman who had handed me Janyn's beads in as much detail as I could. 'Does she sound familiar?' I asked him.

Master John's eyes filled with tears at the mention of his son's rosewood beads, but he said the woman did not sound familiar.

I told him the significance of her giving me the beads.

'Then you had been warned, as I had.'

'Why did you not send word to me, Father?'

He just shook his head.

'Can you suggest how I might find the woman? Perhaps if I learned how she had known I would be there . . .'

'Let him go, Alice,' Master John told me. 'He is gone. They are gone.'

'Do you not wonder?'

'Of course I do. But it does no good.'

'*Where* have they gone?'

'Home. To Milan. Or wherever her family might find them safe haven. *If* they make it to safety. They will not return, Alice. To return would be to die.'

I stared up at him, momentarily robbed of the ability to speak. *They will not return. To return would be to die.* I had lived with the possibility that Janyn might not return from a journey someday, dying from illness or a wound, but I had never thought he might be forced to choose between returning to me and remaining hidden but alive.

Yet it was what the Queen Mother had warned me of. For their loyalty to her, Janyn and Tommasa and all her family were in danger once Isabella was dead and the protection with which she had surrounded them had eroded. Like Master John, I had not wanted to believe it. Not wanted to . . . but the seed of understanding had been there, pushing against my efforts to bury it.

I forced out the question, 'Neither Janyn nor Tommasa will return?'

Master John shook his head. 'Tommasa said we should consider ourselves widow and widower, you and I.' He broke down in sobs.

'Widow?' I whispered, horrified by the word.

I rose and moved behind him, absently rubbing his shoulders, his neck, needing to touch another human, to give or be given comfort. I stood at the edge of understanding, terrified to step over, resisting making it real.

'Have you heard anything of Janyn since September?' I asked.

Master John crossed himself. 'Not a word, not a sign. May God protect them – ' his voice broke and he struggled to regain his composure '– and keep them in His loving care.'

I crossed myself and murmured, 'Amen,' and then regretted saying it, for it seemed like acquiescence. 'But I do not understand how you could let her go.' *How could he leave me?*

'I keep my word,' said Master John. 'When we wed, I promised Tommasa that I would honour such a pronouncement if it ever came.'

So Janyn and Tommasa were gone. All warmth had been taken from me.

'What will you do?' I asked him.

'Live as a widower. Thank God for my other son, safely in the Church, and my daughter living in Lombardy. You must forget us, Alice. Find a new life for yourself at court. The son and daughter of our benefactress owe you and your daughter better lives, the best that can be arranged for you.'

Arranged. It had all been arranged with great care: Tommasa's other children out of harm's way, and Janyn's wife and child in the care of the royal family. Were their hearts not breaking to be forced to desert their families?

Arranged. I'd had enough of other people's arrangements. They'd pushed me into Janyn's arms where I had found such joy as seems rarely to be found, and now I was in more pain than if I had yet awaited a husband or a daughter. For a moment I wished I'd never married Janyn. But at once my having thought that frightened me, as if I might have wished him away for good. In truth, I could not regret the joy I'd had with him and Bella. Might yet have, please God. Would have – at least with Bella. I would not succumb to grief. I would ensure that my daughter had a good life.

'Who did they protect for the Dowager Queen, Father?'

He shook his head. 'I never knew.' He had risen and stood now, idly shuffling the parchments and tallies on the table before him as if the movement calmed him. Perhaps it did calm him, touching familiar items. 'There was a rumour I heard years ago. Folk whispered of a man our King Edward met on a journey to Rome. He was called William of Wales, and it was said he claimed to be our King's father, the old King Edward, the Lady Isabella's husband whom we all believed had been murdered.'

I crossed myself. 'What did our King do? Did he have him executed?'

'No. That was the part of the story that gave me pause. The King invited this man to accompany him the rest of the way.'

'So it was his father?'

John shrugged. 'I know not. I could never coax Tommasa into commenting on it. It was as if she feared to say too much.' He shoved aside a parchment and stood there watching as it skittered across the table and dropped to the tiles below.

Someone most precious to me. The husband Isabella had so wronged by her liaison with Roger Mortimer, the husband she had forced to abdicate? Might he have once again become 'most precious' to her? I could not judge, for I'd come to see the royal family and their baronial retainers as so separate from the people among whom I'd grown up that they were a distinctly different breed, as alien from us as birds from dogs. The royal family lived as if they were already figures in legend. Nothing was too costly, nothing beyond their reach. How the royal family felt about one another, I could not begin to guess.

Master John advised me to find a new life among these legends. He said they owed me this in exchange for Isabella's curse on my husband. I did not deny that. But I could not imagine any lasting joy coming of such a life. My father-in-law's simple solution – to consider ourselves widower and widow – ignored our deep, agonising pain. I did not believe he could so easily shrug off his yearning for what had been, for the love and companionship he'd shared with Tommasa and his son, and I most certainly did not want to shrug off my past. I wanted Janyn and Bella safely with me in our home in London or at Fair Meadow. I wanted what had been.

'Will you stay here?' I asked. 'In this house that echoes with their voices, their footsteps?'

Master John raked his hands through his thinning hair and looked around, as if seeing the past in every object surrounding him. 'How could I leave the memories? This was the setting for all my happiness.'

'What of my homes?' I wondered aloud. 'Am I entitled to them?' I felt petty for asking, and yet I needed something to grasp, something familiar.

'I – I will find out about your London home and send you word. Fair Meadow was a gift from the Queen Mother. Perhaps you might more easily enquire about that property at court.'

To speak of my homes as properties took the heart out of me. 'I cannot believe all this. It is a nightmare. Father, I pray you, tell me it is a nightmare? Shake me awake.'

His eyes filled with tears and he bowed his head, I thought in prayer, but when he straightened his expression was that of someone who had made a decision and wanted no argument. His eyes, though still swimming with tears, had hardened, his jaw set. 'My dear Alice, you must let go of your old life, let go of the dreams you and Janyn shared. My son arranged for your financial security. I will honour all his arrangements.' His tone was curt and impatient, as if I had outworn my welcome. 'Embrace the opportunity to begin anew at court. It is such a gift the Queen has offered you. You should be grateful for such a life.'

I realised he wanted me gone.

'May God go with you, Master John.' I rose to leave, stumbling. Martin and Gwen steadied me.

'God go with you, dear Alice.' Master John made no effort to mask his relief.

*

Gwen held my arm all the way to the barge that awaited us on the Thames, but she did not ask what had happened until we were alone that evening.

'How did the woman in St Mary's come to have Master Janyn's paternoster beads?' she asked then.

I recounted our brief conversation. It was difficult to speak the words. I did not tell her that Janyn had foretold this day. 'I wish I knew more.'

My dear Gwen, more a companion and guardian than a servant to me, draped a warm mantle round my shoulders and poured more wine into my cup. I was grateful for her thoughtful ministrations.

I agonised over whether to confide in Queen Philippa regarding the incident with the beads and Master John's terrible news, and decided it was best that I do so. I thought – indeed, hoped – that she had permitted my visit because she had known what I would learn, and might now tell me more.

That evening, as I accompanied Her Grace to the hall, I recounted my afternoon. Her steps slowed as I spoke, and the distress on her face alarmed me.

'Your Grace?'

'We have a spy in the household, Alice. A spy! How else would that woman know you would be in the city today? You shall make no more trips to London. No more.'

'But what of Janyn, Your Grace? What of my husband's disappearance?'

She shook her head. 'That cursed woman,' she murmured, looking at her beringed hands, not at me. 'You heard Master Perrers, Alice. You are safe here, you and your daughter are well provided for. All will be well. I shall make it up to you.' Resuming her walk, she waved away my attempts to speak further.

I moved through my days in a fog of pain and self-recrimination. I desperately wanted to reverse time, to return to the life Janyn, Bella and I had shared – a time so brief I feared I might someday soon believe it had been but a dream. In a way it had been just that. Even in the time we had been a family Janyn had foreseen our separation; what had seemed permanent to me had never been so to him. I tortured myself with the thought that he might have refused to leave me behind had he loved me more, had I been a better wife, had I done something more to please him. In faith, I still prayed that God would show me what I must do to deserve my happiness, to bring Janyn and Bella back to me.

I must, meanwhile, do all I could to protect Bella and provide for her future. I had only myself to rely on now. I was ever more grateful for the friendship of Queen Philippa, for she tried to cheer me by including me in all the evening entertainments, and kept me close to her in the sewing chamber, protected from the quivering headdresses. I expressed my gratitude by making more effort to fit into her household, performing my duties with humility but enthusiasm, deferring to the high-born in all things.

'I have asked the King to include you with those of my women who ride out in his company from time to time, hunting and hawking,' she announced one evening.

The forests surrounding the palace of Woodstock made it a favourite for large hunting parties.

'Your Grace, I am most grateful.' I could not believe my good fortune in being so favoured. I was determined to prove worthy.

I kept my distance from the King, having rarely spoken to him since I had first met him at Hertford Castle. In truth, I was in awe of all the company.

One morning King Jean of France rode out with us. I was startled when he complimented me on a Lincoln green riding hat with a dove feather that Dame Agnes had made for me. But he soon put me at ease, and we talked of the skill necessary in choosing the appropriate cloth for an article of dress.

King Edward joined us. 'Mistress Alice is too modest to tell you of her own skill. Though she has been at court but two years, she has become indispensable to the Queen in all matters of her wardrobe. The Queen relies on her advice.' He smiled on me. 'Her father saw her gift and trained her well.'

I blushed under the appraising and approving regard of the two Kings. That King Edward was aware of how long I had been at court and knew of my duties in his wife's household surprised and pleased me. But they called too much attention to me. Lady Eleanor in particular watched as closely as did the hawk on her arm.

King Edward coaxed me out of myself, instructing me on the handling of the hawks, discussing aspects of horsemanship. My delight in both grew as I gained confidence, and the release these activities provided from my constantly guarded behaviour elsewhere perhaps made me reckless. I ached for the fresh air and the sense of freedom, and though I followed all the correct forms of conduct, I revelled in my hawk's predatory magnificence and in my bond with such a wild and cunning creature, and exalted in the power and grace of Melisende as we rode. When I applauded my hawk's attack and kill, the King would join in. When I rode hard, I would find him pacing me, and when he caught my eye I felt the kinship we shared in the power of our mounts. He encouraged the side of me that I otherwise subdued, and I was grateful.

Perhaps I was too grateful. One morning I could not hide the ravages of the tears I'd shed because of a dream in which I'd become a woodbine to search for Janyn. In the dream I willed the vine I'd become to extend from east to west, with tendrils spreading out north to south, growing as my tears watered my roots. The King noted the pretty way my hair escaped my red hat, and said that the blush of colour in my face all but erased the signs of my sorrow. I found myself describing the dream to him.

He declared himself shot through the heart by the stead-fastness it revealed. 'I have never encountered such loyal devotion. How did your husband inspire such loving loyalty in you, Dame Alice? I must know how I might do so.' His deep voice caressed me, his eyes drew me in, as if he sincerely wished to know.

I wished I had held my tongue, or better yet avoided the hunt that morning. I had allowed myself to fall under his spell again, as I had at Hertford.

Christmas 1360
The Christmas court was at Woodstock that year, with most of King Edward and Queen Philippa's sons and daughters and their families in attendance, as well as King Jean of France. There were so many guests that most of the servants slept in hastily constructed 'houses' hardly worthy of that name, and some, mostly guards and retainers, in campaign tents. Fortunate in Queen Philippa's affection, I was one of the half-dozen women sharing her bedchamber in the palace. This was much pleasanter

than my usual arrangement in a dormitory with the other ladies. For this crowded Yuletide my living quarter was peaceful on the surface, and for that I was grateful. Janyn had now been gone for almost four months and with all my worry and reliving of all he had said and done my temper was too easily tripped.

On Christmas Day King Edward entered the chamber of his wife the Queen to escort her to Mass before the festivities in the hall, and I almost cried out as I recognised the design on his gorgeous coat. Embroidered in gold and silk thread were two woodbines twisting and twining across the black satin, and in gold thread was written the motto, 'Seeking like the woodbine'.

It was usually the King who designed the themes for tournaments, jousts and feasts, for he enjoyed devising ones based on moral mottos or tales of Arthur, the long-ago King of England. So it was not uncommon for him to wear a coat bearing a motto. But this one he had taken from me.

Discovering me watching him, he mouthed, 'Your inspiration,' as he glanced down at his coat.

I prayed that the little wine I'd drunk had fevered my mind, but it seemed clear that the woodbine coat was a warning his kindness to me was no longer innocent in intention. I prayed that I flattered myself, that he meant the design to do no more than symbolise his famously happy marriage with Philippa which had been blessed by many children, and perhaps to honour my faithfulness to my husband.

I had never sought the King's attention. I was too vulnerable. I must not jeopardise my place at court, or Bella's in the household of the King's sister, by seeming anything but obedient and grateful to the Queen. I had a great affection for her. I did not intend to wound her by flirting with her husband.

In truth, I had little stomach for flirtation that Christmastide for my heart was heavy with memories of my few Christmases with Janyn. Perhaps if I had found a friend in whom to confide my conflicting feelings I might have found some relief, some release, but my grief had little outlet. If there was any benefit in my beloved Bella's absence, Queen Joan having chosen to avoid the festivities in her mourning for her failed marriage, it was that my daughter was spared my feeble attempts at explaining her father's absence. Were I not so desperate to hold her, my baby, my own,

I would have thanked God for sparing me the task of trying to cheer Bella while my heart was breaking.

Even my old friend Geoffrey was no substitute for a sister or a grandmother to whom I might pour out my heart. He danced away from deep feelings.

As he sat beside me on Christmas Day, enjoying the grand feast, my good friend sought to amuse me – and therefore eliminate the threat of my confiding too much to him – with the highlights of an old book that was popular at court, a cleric's explanation of the art of courtly love. It was clever and worldly, not to my taste, but in gratitude for Geoffrey's friendship I feigned interest, seeing that he found it immensely witty.

'No one can love unless he is impelled by the persuasion of love.' Geoffrey paused, cocking his head, a silly grin on his face, as if to say, *Dare to refute that.*

It did make me chuckle. 'That would seem obvious.'

'Every lover regularly turns pale in the presence of his beloved.'

Now I laughed out loud. 'That is silly, Geoffrey. Of course we know that they often turn quite a deep red.'

He bowed in acquiescence. 'The essence of the art, according to this cleric, is the love-yearning for someone other than your husband or wife, the never quite attainable.'

That one disturbed me. 'Why do they all wish to live in dreams, Geoffrey, or as players in elaborate pageants? Have none of them experienced the joy of a simple love? Of a marriage between a man and woman who love and honour each other?' *Why does the King toy with me?* He could not be sincere in his flirtation, for I was so far beneath him. He stirred in me feelings he did not mean to satisfy. Nor did I wish him to.

'Was yours a simple love, Alice, your love for Janyn?'

'But he is my husband.' I fought tears.

Sobering, Geoffrey caught my hands and pressed them as he apologised. 'My tongue too often wags before my wit awakens. Forgive me, my dearest friend. I meant only to cheer you, and look what I have done instead.'

His eyes were so kind and blessedly familiar. Geoffrey, too, had been lost to me for a time, a prisoner in France, quickly ransomed and just as quickly sent off to carry messages from his lord, the

King's son Lionel, to his household while he was fighting and then working on the treaty in Calais.

'Do not blame yourself. I am not angry with you. In faith, I am deeply grateful, selfishly so, that you are here with me now.' I stopped at that, not wishing to embarrass him with my need.

'I wanted only to make you laugh, to suggest to you a way to find some joy, an innocent liaison.'

I knew that he had been carried away by his own thoughtless wit. 'I am quick to bleed these days, Geoffrey, but you are the best physick for me this court holds and I'll not deprive myself of your company by nursing some imagined wound.'

He kissed my hand.

I smiled and simpered. 'Perhaps I should make this playful love to you.'

'Me?' He shook his head so hard he almost lost his bright red cap. 'I am unworthy. What of the King?' His eyes teased me. 'The woodbine – is it not the flower you have been sewing into everything you own? How comes he to embrace it in his new motto? Did you speak to him of your dream?'

I meant to deny it, but he saw the truth in my face.

'Alice!' He looked confused. 'Has he made love to you? Have you ridden out alone?'

'No! He is kind to me, knowing my sorrow.'

'Is that all it is? Think again, my friend. You would not be his first conquest since the Queen. You know that.'

I did not want to think about it. I had been haunted of late by the story of Criseyde and Troilus, the tale that Geoffrey had first told me, one I'd heard often since at court.

When Troy was besieged by the Greeks the Trojan seer Calchas fled to the enemy camp, leaving his daughter Criseyde in Troy. Troilus, who was the son of the King of Troy, fell in love with her and she with him. But when a Trojan warrior was captured by the Greeks, Criseyde was offered in exchange for him. She vowed to Troilus that she would return, but once she was in the Greek camp King Diomedes desired her and told her to forget Troilus and pledge her troth to him. She acceded to his demand. Troilus, learning of her betrayal, went into battle, fighting with such abandon he was eventually killed. Criseyde was blamed and accused of luring him, of pledging her troth and then abandoning him, breaking his heart and his will to live.

Each time I heard it I dreamed of the horror of being Criseyde, of being blamed for her obedience. She had been traded to the enemy and desired by a king whose affections she had not sought. She had obeyed, and for this and her beauty was condemned. I had caught the judgment in the eyes of the courtiers in the King's party as he spoke to me, and I understood full well how she'd felt.

I took Geoffrey's hand and looked into his eyes, willing him to be serious for a moment, for he was wont to skitter off into humour at the slightest discomfort. 'Do you remember the tale you once told me of Criseyde and the magnificent cloak and silken gown she wore when leaving Troy and Troilus?'

He looked confused. 'What has that to do with your woodbine?'

'As you told the tale, Criseyde was damned for dressing so richly – as if her purpose were to catch a lover. Yet she was being *sent* from Troy into the camp of Troy's enemies, *traded* for a captured warrior. She did not choose to go – at least, that is not how you told the tale. I very much doubt she had much choice about how she dressed for the mission either. Yet *she* was damned, not those who sent her. *She* was blamed for betraying Troilus. But had she any choice? When Diomedes, a king, told her to forget Troilus, was that not a command?'

Geoffrey shook his head, frowning. 'I still do not understand, Alice. What am I to see?'

'The King, all unknown to me, copied my emblem, and you are thinking that I lured him, are you not?'

'Am I?' He seemed to be asking the question of himself.

'Do you see what I mean about Criseyde?' I asked it without censure, just a simple question.

My old friend, in his fashionable red and black clothes, holding the mazer of fine wine we shared, surrounded by fair folk eating, drinking, laughing, gossiping, sat utterly still, digesting my words. I felt oddly light, as if my ability to make him see that Criseyde was wrongly accused would change my own fate. I was desperate to make him see, as if once *he* understood, it was possible *all* would. At last he nodded.

'Yes, I see that if it were a story about someone you know it would be a gross injustice to blame her. But it is poetry, Alice, an example of the inconstant woman. A symbol, you see.'

My heart sank. 'No, Geoffrey, it is not that innocent. She was not inconstant by choice, and I cannot believe you are blind to that. People hear such judgement in tales, and judge the folk they know likewise. I innocently tell the King of my dream, he uses my emblem, and suddenly I am a wanton woman, a siren, luring him to sin.'

'Oh. Yes. Yes, I do see.'

He looked so crestfallen I almost consoled him, but caught myself before being so foolish.

'I am judged, Geoffrey.'

'You are. That is true. And I dare guess that little of it is spoken in your presence. You've no idea what the courtiers say about you.'

'I wanted only to be a quiet cog in the wheel of the household, calling no attention to myself. But any little joy I take is noted. I see the censure in their eyes. What can I do? What might Criseyde have done?'

'You cannot confront the King about his indiscreet use of your emblem.'

'Of course not. But, Geoffrey, do you say they know? Tell me what you have heard.'

'Already they believe you seek his eye, Alice. They notice every look between the two of you, every new piece of clothing you wear, whether you are wearing the same colours as the King.'

The same colours? 'I have never sought to match him. I do not seek to catch his eye.' Such talk frightened me. 'How can I protect myself against illusions? Lies?'

'You cannot, Alice. The court is a dangerous place for anyone who inspires envy.'

The daughter of a merchant a target for envy? They were all mad. 'Do you think they know about the woodbine?'

'I've no doubt they know whence came the woodbine theme.'

I must stop riding out in the King's company. 'I am so ignorant of court. My dear Geoffrey, you must be my ears in future. Will you promise to tell me what they say?'

Poor Geoffrey. His discomfiture was writ plain on his expressive face.

'I promise, as long as you do not punish me for my obser-vations. Remember that I merely repeat to you what I have heard and that I am not one of the gossips.'

'You have only to remind me of that and I will recall the dogs I have unleashed on you,' I said.

Geoffrey smiled and kissed my hand, then grew serious. 'Have you any news of Janyn?'

I shook my head. I dared not speak of him in public, though we were speaking so low and the music, song, and conversations all around were so loud as to drown us out. The danger to my family was not worth even the consolation of sharing my story to receive Geoffrey's sympathy. I would tell him all if a better opportunity arose.

Geoffrey was telling me of his adventures across the Channel when I noticed a quiet falling around us. I'd been clutching our shared mazer of red wine and now I glanced down, fearing I'd spilled it on the indigo gown that had been my last gift from Janyn, but saw no stain. Glancing up, I beheld King Edward standing across the table from me, his expression merry. I stopped breathing. He bowed to me and held out his beringed hand.

'Dance with me, Mistress Alice!'

'Sweet Mary in Heaven,' Geoffrey breathed.

'Your Grace,' I murmured, rising, and at once a page was behind me to help me climb over the bench and move round to the King. I do not know how I managed on my trembling legs. I told myself it meant nothing, he pitied me for the loss of my husband and no doubt felt he owed me some cheer since it was his mother who had brought this trouble on my family. But the woodbine design taunted me.

When King Edward took my hand I felt pierced by heat. I am quite sure I made some sound, some exclamation, but he was waving the musicians to lift the tempo and we were off, hand in hand, rushing to join the other dancers. From that moment the alchemy of the King's touch, of his presence, of his vigour, worked on me, caught me up in his mood. The King, despite his nearly five decades, was agile and light on his feet. I'd never danced with a more skilful and graceful partner.

'Do you like my emblem for this feast?' he shouted, sweeping his free hand across his gorgeous tunic. 'You are my inspiration!' His grin teased, but his eyes lingered on my low-cut bodice with a hungry intensity.

'A simple plant, Your Grace, but you have worked a wondrous alchemy. Gold and silver!'

As we moved close his deep blue eyes met mine, and again I felt his extraordinary power of attraction. I was a young, giddy girl again, wanting nothing so much as to be desired.

I danced as if I had not a care in the world, and laughed and responded to his compliments with an ease that I would not have believed possible. In faith, he had enchanted me. Some might say bewitched me. Most would say that I had bewitched him. The music was all my body needed to cue me to the movements of the dance, but the King's presence added a lightness that I had not felt since last I'd danced with Janyn. We were part of a pattern of swirling colours and our jewels caught the torchlight and added to the enchantment.

After the dance the King bowed to me and the page escorted me back to my place beside Geoffrey. When I'd caught my breath I glanced round to see all eyes turned towards me as people murmured to their companions.

'I am ruined,' I said, dismayed by my own behaviour as I woke from the King's spell. I was a moth to the flame of his presence, despite all that I had said to Geoffrey. What I honestly felt was disappointment that the magical, exhilarating moment was over.

Geoffrey, of course, heard only my words, not my scandalous thought. He took my hands in his. 'No, Alice. It was but a dance. The King has done far more with many women who hold their heads high here at court. It was plain you were surprised. Indeed, at first your terror was visible, and I saw in his eyes how you pleased him later by falling under his spell.'

Falling under his spell? I had. Oh, God forgive me, I had. But reason reasserted itself.

'The women of whom you speak are of noble blood, Geoffrey. I will be condemned for overstepping my position in the chain of being.'

'Yet you did enjoy the dance,' he said, handing me back the mazer we shared.

'I did. Oh, yes, Geoffrey, I did. Of that I am guilty.'

We shared a frightened, slightly giddy, laugh.

And therein lay my weakness. For I knew in my heart that not only would I not dare defy the King if he invited me to dance again, I would not wish to. It was one thing to hunt in a crowd with the King, occasionally garnering brief conversation with him; it was quite another to touch him, to match steps with him, to share the exhilaration of a dance.

The King danced with all the young, pretty women at court, especially this Yuletide when he was celebrating peace with France, I told myself. And resented the thought. I wanted to be singled out by King Edward. He had reawakened something in me that I had not felt since the happy times with Janyn – a delight in my power as a woman. I understood the danger – I was so lonely, so hungry for affection. Once before I had been a moth to a bright flame. To Janyn's. He had brought me to court, set me down close to an even brighter flame. I wondered whether he'd been at all aware of the danger in which he had placed me. But then, had he ever fully considered the risk to me when he wed me? I crossed myself, frightened by my own disloyal thoughts.

After the feast I dreaded Queen Philippa's reaction. Could she see how her husband stirred me? How much I enjoyed his touch . . . arousing him? I had not dared glance towards the high table to see how she received my dance with the King. But I could not avoid her, for that very evening it was my turn to bring to her in her bedchamber the almond milk she enjoyed as she rested after her feet, hands and shoulders had been rubbed with warm, fragrant oils. The task involved warming the milk on the brazier in her chamber, and while I stood there the Queen would review with me the events of the day, asking for my impressions. I had come to look forward to these evenings. But not that night.

Reclining against an array of cushions covered in bright silks, her large, wrinkled body draped in a loose gold silk robe, a colour unbecoming to her but which she loved, the Queen appeared to be in a merry mood. She was sharing a laugh with Lady Neville. While I held the cup over the brazier, stirring it, they traded some amusing gossip, and then Lady Neville departed.

'You danced prettily with His Grace,' said the Queen as I set the mazer of warm almond milk next to her. As she shifted in the loose robe, the fragrant oils on her skin perfumed the air around her.

'You are kind, Your Grace. And so is His Grace. I was deeply honoured by his benevolent courtesy.'

'Benevolent courtesy?' The Queen smiled to herself. I was terrified that she had *seen, understood.*

'He told me of your dream of the woodbine and what it meant to you.' Her smile had faded and she grew thoughtful. 'He thought it charming, such a testament of loving loyalty. Thought me cruel to complain of your refusal to accept what is. But it is best you do. You must forget your old life, Alice. The old Queen left that in tatters with her death, as she did so many other lives. I do not like to speak ill of the dead, but you are my responsibility now and in need of guidance.'

'Your Grace, I—'

'I am not finished. Isabella of France controlled us all. She delayed my crowning for so long I began to think I'd never be Queen as long as she lived. She rose up against the man who was not only her husband but a divinely anointed king, not merely forcing his abdication but attempting to put her lover in his place. My sweet Edward had to take command so young, so very young. Because of her.' She spoke in a quiet, pensive tone, not so much angry as resolute.

'Forgive me, Your Grace,' I murmured, feeling disgraced and hating her for treating me like a child.

'But be of good cheer. My husband the King and I are allowing you a new life, eh, my pet? I've taken care that here at court your past remains unclear and that Janyn Perrers is not known to have a part in it. Of course, there are those in London who know you are his widow, but their memories will fade. A minor noble, Sir Robert Perrers, has agreed to pretend you are his daughter.'

Janyn Perrers is not known to have a part in it. Those words clutched at my heart. 'Your Grace, I am not a widow.'

'Do you prefer to be an abandoned wife?'

'Nor am I an orphan, Your Grace. I do not need a pretend father. I am a Salisbury.'

'Do not contradict me. I know what is best for you.'

If the Queen's intent was to be cruel, she was succeeding, and

I understood how easily she might sever my ties with Mary, Will and John. Yet her expression, her tone of voice, the soft hand she pressed to my cheek, were affectionate. I believed she was sincerely concerned for my welfare. But she was a queen, and before that the daughter of a count, and her view of life was worlds apart from mine.

'At least as an abandoned wife I might hope to see Janyn again,' I said.

The Queen gave a silken shrug and patted the bed beside her. It took me back to my last meeting with the Dowager Queen Isabella, when she bade me sit close to her on her bed while she told me of the danger to my family once she was dead. What was it Philippa had said? Isabella had left my old life in tatters. It was true that all my pain stemmed from whatever it was that Janyn and his mother's family had done for her.

When I sat beside her, Philippa took my hands in hers and looked long into my eyes, unblinking, as if testing me.

'You are a strong-willed young woman, Alice, with a backbone that others will not easily bend. I like that in a woman of my household, for you reside in a court ripe with temptations certain to overwhelm the weak. Be true to me and my Edward and we will prove faithful and generous.'

I waited for more, but she was apparently awaiting my response. Her swollen hands pressed mine. Her steady gaze unsettled me. I sensed that she meant to communicate to me something of great significance that I was still unable to grasp.

'I do not understand, Your Grace. Have I done aught to make you doubt my loyalty? If so, I pray you forgive me, for it was done unwittingly.'

Philippa reached out and again touched my cheek. 'I forget you were not brought up to this. For now, try to be happy, Alice. Forget the past, revel in the honour and delight of being at court. You are young, beautiful, and will conquer many hearts. But remember that your first loyalty is to the King and me. That is all I meant. If there comes a choice between us and another, remember who protects you.' She patted my hand. 'And now you may retire. I am ready for sleep. Tomorrow you shall meet another who has lost her husband. My sweet Joan of Kent. I raised her, you know, after her father's horrible death at the order of my mother-in-law's lover. Do you know the tale of Joan's marriage? The scandal?'

'I do. She was secretly wed to Sir Thomas Holland, he went off to seek his fortune, and she was so young – eleven? – that she did not dare contradict her guardian when he betrothed her to his son and heir, Montague.'

The Queen made a sound between a chuckle and a snort. 'Is that how the London merchants perceived it? In truth, Holland was not the match we wished for her, and when her guardians noticed her sulking about and ascertained for whom she yearned, they consulted me and her mother as to what was to be done. We all agreed that she must wed William Montague at once. But Holland was shrewd . . . we'd no idea how shrewd. Seven years he waited, until he had the fame and the wealth to go to the Pope. Seven years Joan lived as Montague's wife . . . only to be handed back to Holland. Scandal! The Pope did it to annoy us, we are well aware. I would have sworn that Joan's heart was with Montague, but she seemed far happier with Holland.'

Fortunate woman, I thought.

'Alas,' Philippa sighed, 'Holland died a few days ago. If love could have kept him alive, he would yet live by Joan's power. They tell me that she is in deep, grievous mourning. I believe now that her heart was his from the moment she saw him in her guardian's household. You will have something in common, both having lost a great love.'

At least she understood that Janyn was that. 'Yes, Your Grace.' I had not lost him, not as Joan had lost Holland. Yet I saw that it was no use arguing with the Queen. She intended to consider me a widow.

'Were you and your Janyn a love match? Did you go against your parents?'

'No, Your Grace, though I loved him with all my heart.'

'Good, good. I count on you to be obedient.'

I left her chamber that evening in much confusion. I had spoken of my love of Janyn in the past. I realised then I had given up all hope of ever seeing him again. But I must not give up trying to learn the truth. I must do everything in my power to find my husband. If someday I learned I might have done something to reunite my family, I would never forgive myself.

*

Shortly after the Christmas court, in a time of quiet weather, I asked leave to see Bella.

Still abed midday, resting from the festivities, Philippa said, 'It was a pity our sister Joan did not attend the court and afford you the comfort of your dear daughter. I have little need of you until next Sunday. I shall arrange it.'

'Your Grace, I am most grateful. I have not seen my Bella since early-summer.'

She touched my hand and looked me long in the eyes. 'You mourn your husband and your separation from your child. I am not blind to your grief, dear Alice.'

On the way I asked to stop for a brief rest at an abbey in which the Dominican friar, Dom Clovis, who had made me the potion for Janyn, was rumoured to be biding. I slipped away from my escort and managed a brief interview with the friar, asking his help in divining my husband's location and condition – I was formulating a plan to engage one of the more daring Lombard merchants to take me to him. But Clovis said that this was beyond his abilities. I knelt to him, kissing his hands, pleading with him to help me.

'Dame Alice, in your imagination you have endowed me with gifts I have not. Nor would I wish to possess them. My skill lies in discerning the imbalance in humours and prescribing time-honoured means of rebalancing them. To find your husband requires a spy, not a healer. Someone who might go in search of Master Janyn.'

I hated the friar for denying me, though I knew in my heart that he was being honest with me, not avoiding a task he might perform but chose not to.

My party continued on to Hertford Castle. My precious Bella had grown so in the half year since I had seen her that I was all the more aware of being robbed of her childhood.

'Where is Father?' Bella demanded. She looked more and more like Janyn, in colouring and in her dark, luxuriant mane of curly hair. 'Why has he not brought my pony?'

I held her tight and confessed that I did not know where her father was, but promised her I was searching for him. She pushed away from me, looking over my shoulder, seeking him. I felt as I had done when forced to wean her, a terrible sense of separation, as if part of me were no longer there. I feared she might grow to hate me, to see me as I saw my own mother. I needed to know the truth about Janyn, not only for me but for her.

'For of hire lif she was ful sore in drede,
As she that nyste what was best to rede;
For bothe a widewe was she and allone
Of any frend to whom she dorste hir mone.'

— Geoffrey Chaucer, *Troilus and Criseyde*, I, ll. 95–98

1361

It was a winter of burials for the royal couple, and as I witnessed their grief I understood that even they were not immune from suffering. The death of Joan of Kent's husband, Sir Thomas Holland, had been a painful blow to the King, for he had been one of his trusted commanders. This death was followed swiftly by those of two more of the King's trusted counsellors. And then came the cruellest blow of all: the death of Henry of Grosmont, Duke of Lancaster and father of Blanche, wife of the King's third son, John of Gaunt. Both Queen Philippa and King Edward, and indeed most of the barons, had considered the Duke the foremost commander of the realm, and he had been a close friend to the royal couple. His Requiem Mass was attended by all the noble families, but though it was a magnificent spectacle it was yet solemn. The King himself had contributed expensive brocade cloth for the vestments and livery, some of it from Lucca, including gold brocade for the pall. Some murmured that the brocade cloth from Lucca might be infected with the pestilence, for the sickness was rumoured to have returned, moving west and north from the Mediterranean as it had before.

I had been but a child of seven or eight when the pestilence first raged across Christendom. Father later told me stories of the time: how we had fled to his sister's home in Smithfield to distance ourselves from the river, rumoured to be carrying the deadly miasma, only to discover that she and both her children had succumbed. In the Queen's sewing chamber we were all one in our fear, speaking in hushed voices of nightmares in which we relived our horror at the pustules, the stench, the corpses piled in the streets. For once I was welcomed and included, part of the life we all feared might be foreshortened.

Several weeks after rumours of pestilence reached the palace, Queen Philippa sent for me after morning Mass. Although she was sitting in the spacious room known as the Queen's hall, Philippa sat alone by the fire, none of her ladies in attendance. Blanche of Lancaster sat apart from her near the high casements, petting a small dog and gazing out at a sudden snow shower. A few serving maids were tidying on the far side of the room. The Queen nodded to me the moment I entered the room, patting the space beside her on a wide cushioned bench. Our privacy and the indication that I was to sit so close warned me that she was about to tell me something she did not want others to hear.

I took a deep breath and pulled myself up as straight and tall as possible so that I did not seem so small and alone as I felt while crossing the echoing room and taking a seat beside the Queen who held my life in her hands.

Her eyes were sad, her voice soft, and I prayed that she had not received bad news of my Bella, for it was said that children were particularly vulnerable to the pestilence in this visitation.

'Queen Joan reports that your daughter Isabella already speaks so well that people guess her to be at least five, and they ask why she is so small, whether she has sufficient food. Is that not delightful? She is so bright, Alice, so very bright.'

To hear of my daughter's progress in such wise, second-hand, when I was prevented from seeing her as much as I yearned to, shattered my carefully sustained composure. I could not stop my tears from flowing.

The Queen sighed. 'Alice, I meant to cheer you. I shall tell you no more news of your daughter if it upsets you so.'

Blinded by my tears, I heard rather than saw the Queen's irritation, her impatience, and forced myself to speak though my throat was tight with grief.

'Your Grace, I am most grateful. My seeming ingratitude is no more than a mother's natural sense of our separation.'

I felt a cloth being stuffed into my hand.

'Dry your eyes, Alice, and look at me.'

I obeyed as best I could. With the fragrant piece of linen, I blotted my tears so that I could meet the Queen's gaze.

'I had feared that word of your daughter's progress would be lost on you if I told it to you after I gave you more difficult news – I will not draw it out, for I can see that you guess I chose a private moment in which to convey it to you.'

I crossed myself and prayed for strength.

'We have received a message from Master John Perrers.' The Queen placed a plump, beringed hand on my forearm and fixed me with such a solemn look that her sad eyes pierced my heart. 'You must be strong, Alice.'

'I pray you, Your Grace, what ill has befallen Master John?' But I doubted it was sorrow for my father-in-law that had so softened her demeanour.

'Both his wife and son, your husband, have been felled by pestilence in Milan.'

'No,' I gasped. 'No!'

Blanche of Lancaster rose and brought her stool closer. I guessed that their partnership had been rehearsed and this had been her cue to join us. Her silks rustled, and yet she thought it necessary to cough as if to warn us of her presence. I said something in that space, but my sense was that the heavens and the earth halted in all sound and movement for a long moment.

'Dame Alice, I too grieve,' said the Lady Blanche. 'I have lost my father.'

'But how can they both –' I said. 'They were both healthy, grown . . . children and the ill . . .' I stopped, hearing how I babbled. But then I must have spoken of my nightmares and how I had feared for Janyn and Tommasa.

'You sensed their deaths?' Lady Blanche asked in a breathy voice, as if aghast.

'No. I did not mean . . .'

'This dream,' said the Queen, 'was it the result of seeing Friar Clovis?'

I had looked away, but with her question the Queen drew me back. Her mouth was pinched. She no longer looked sympathetic.

'Friar Clovis? Your Grace, I did not speak of him.'

'You know that you are not to leave the palace without an escort,' said Philippa. 'You remember how you were followed in London.'

'I was being escorted to Hertford, Your Grace. We rested at the abbey . . .' I stopped myself. She knew that. 'No, my nightmares and fears had nothing to do with the friar. I had asked him to help me find Janyn.' I had thought myself so clever – and had underestimated the determination of the Queen. My own naïveté frightened me. I felt suffocated, surrounded and overwhelmed. My heart faltered, my courage seemed a paltry, limp affair.

This recognition of my weakness allowed the dread news that had been hovering on the threshold of my consciousness to breach my shield, obliterating all other thought. My beloved and his mother were dead. It was difficult for me to breathe. A darkness closed in on me from either side as the Queen's round face swirled about in the gathering darkness.

I dreamed I woke in a large chamber densely inhabited by secrets. Up in the ceiling high above me secrets prowled in the corners, flickered in the shadows, fluttered just beyond my sight, and the subtle draught from the pulsing wings of the livelier ones stirred the tiny hairs on my forearm. I sensed secrets murmuring just beyond my hearing. The winged ones teased, as if half-hoping to be heard. The murmuring and shadowy ones were dark, heavy, frightening. Many of these, garbed in gorgeous widow's weeds, were the former Queen's secrets. Many were those of the present King and Queen, crowned and gloriously robed. Some were from the wider court, and even clerics kept drably robed secrets in this room. Secrets no one must admit to knowing. Inconvenient secrets. Dangerous secrets, delivering death to the over-curious. I tried to shrink into the bed, drop down between the feathers and slip out below and escape. I did not know how I had come to be in such a frightening room. I had no need for secrets, no desire for them . . .

When I woke from the dream it haunted me, seeming more real than my usual dreams. Nan once told me that dreams we remembered as we awoke, as vividly as if they were memories of real events, were significant dreams, sent to warn us. I lay in the dark, thinking of rooms like the one in my dream. Church naves and chapels with gargoyles, carved heads, ornamental bosses, statues – they were what came to mind. I remembered the woman in the church who had dropped Janyn's paternoster beads, and how I had wound them round the Blessed Mother's arm. Secrets – certainly it was secrets that had robbed me of my joy.

Too soon I remembered the terrible interview in the Queen's parlour. That was why my belly felt weighted down with cold, cold stones and I was pinned so hard to the mattress that I could not spread my ribs to breathe. I could not even gasp for air. I would trade my soul for Janyn's warm body beside me, for the gift of his presence. But I had accepted I might not see him again. Now the nightmare of Isabella's curse continued. I believed Janyn and Tommasa were dead, but not that they had died of the pestilence. They had gone into hiding, they had been in danger. This explanation was meant to silence me, to kill the need for further questions.

Gwen bent over me, my dear Gwen, offering me a sip of brandywine. Somehow she lifted me up in her arm despite the weights that had pressed me to the bed.

'Drink, Dame Alice. Slowly. Slowly.'

I sipped.

'Queen Philippa and the Duchess Blanche have sent messengers every hour to enquire after you. I – oh, Dame Alice, I am so sorry!' Gwen's eyes were swollen and red from weeping.

Secrets. Master John had spoken of a tale that could mean Isabella's Edward, the present King's father, had survived his imprisonment in Berkeley Castle and escaped, been hidden in Lombardy. Lombardy. Milan. Tommasa's family. Secrets. Favours. Someone dear who was protected. Had Janyn and Tommasa known of this, it might not have been enough for them simply to disappear. Perhaps they had to die. Or at least the King and Queen must believe them to be dead. Secrets. Secrets choked the life from all who fell into the web of the court. The secrets of the royal family had choked my marriage. Choked my heart. My thoughts tumbled and turned on themselves until I wished for unconsciousness.

All my life I had obeyed those who cared not a whit for my welfare, for my happiness, who loved me not at all. I had loved passionately . . . my siblings, my father, so many others. I had given Janyn and our daughter Bella everything I had to give, and had hoped only for more of my sweet, simple life, a few more children and a gradual ageing with my beloved husband, nothing grander. Now I had nothing.

Except Bella. I would not abandon Bella. I had been abandoned by everyone I had loved, and I would never do that to my daughter. I knew that I must gather my strength. I took a good, long drink of the brandywine. And another.

Gradually over the next few days the frightening dreams abated, but my waking thoughts were still haunted. I almost regretted having been moved to a corner of the bedchamber that could be screened off for privacy, near a wide window so that the fresh country air might cheer me, for the privilege isolated me with my darksome thoughts.

I felt adrift at court, as if the solid ground of my life had been pulled away and I hung suspended above a vast emptiness by strings held by the Queen and King. Yet I depended on their protection.

As I grew stronger I remembered the solemn Requiem for the old Duke of Lancaster and felt humbled. I was not alone in my suffering. I lifted my chin to receive the gentle breeze from the unshuttered window. I wanted occupation, distraction.

To my immense relief visitors began to appear – first the Queen, then some of the ladies who had snubbed me but now found me a fascinatingly tragic figure – they had been told that a man I'd hoped to wed had died of the pestilence. Best of all was Geoffrey's arrival. The others had been curious to see how I behaved, how my grief had changed me, and were intent on convincing me that my life lay ahead of me, bright as ever. In Geoffrey's eyes I saw my sorrow mirrored. So far only he and Gwen seemed to comprehend the enormity of my loss, perhaps because they alone knew that my existence at court was far from what I had ever desired.

'I pray that you will find joy again,' said Geoffrey. 'And until then, that your love for Bella will sustain you. I do not want to lose you, my oldest and dearest friend.'

He was holding my hand, sitting close to the bed in which I reclined against a small mountain of pillows that Gwen had collected for my comfort.

'I miss him so, Geoffrey. I had held out hope.'

I could see on my friend's expressive face how he struggled to find some reassurance for me, but he was not one to lie in order to cheer up a friend. At last he raised his cup and toasted me – 'To your courage' – and drank.

Courage. I wondered how far that would support me, whether it could suspend me above the void.

'To your rebirth as a lady of the court.'

I felt forlorn after he departed and regretted having wasted so much of his visit in tears. His friendship was precious to me. Bella was precious to me. And Gwen. And Dame Agnes and Master Edmund. My sister and my brothers. There were still many people holding me to this life. The realisation heartened me.

I thought about Geoffrey's second toast, 'To your rebirth . . .' Perhaps in passing through the agony of losing Janyn I *had* undergone a rebirth. I recalled sermons describing how sacred such an experience was, and that the reborn had been divinely blessed for a purpose. What, then, might be my purpose? I wondered. Perhaps that was my way forward, to accept that I had been reborn and must now discover the reason. Once the idea took root, I felt an unfamiliar calm.

When at last I was strong enough to kneel in prayer in the chapel, my prayer had changed from begging that things were not as they seemed, to that I might retreat from here in time, that my pain might pass. Now I prayed, 'Holy Mary, Mother of God, I kneel before you humbled and ask for guidance. How may I best serve you?' I bowed my head, let go of all thought, all worry, and opened myself to divine grace. Gradually, over the days I was filled with a sense of peace and imagined the Blessed Virgin's translucent hand resting on my head. I believed that I would be guided by grace.

When Gwen came to tell me the Queen was asking for me, having heard that I was walking about, I was ready to re-enter life. I felt as if I should be in widow's weeds, but the Queen had made it clear that I was not to do so.

'I honour your mourning, Alice, but we want others to forget you were ever wed. They were told you lost a *potential* husband. We want no enquiries into the cause of your late husband's long absence, do we?'

It was clearly a statement couched as a question, and I meekly agreed. For a time I would wear only my simplest gowns. I prayed that if Janyn looked down from Heaven he would understand.

When I returned to the Queen's chambers her ladies smiled at me and expressed their joy at my recovery. I had never been welcomed by them with such apparently sincere friendliness.

Philippa stood in the midst of benches draped with cloth, ribbon, strings of buttons, impatiently poking at the various gorgeous piles with her cane and muttering imprecations. Her demeanour softened as she noticed me.

'Come, Alice, tell me if any of this is worth my bother,' lightly patting my arm as I joined her. 'In the morning we have a theme to devise and costumes to design and must begin preparations for the move to Windsor for the Feast of St George. The King wishes it to be the most splendid feast and tournament, to ease the hearts of the mourners and the fears of all about the pestilence.'

As we sorted through the samples, discarding some, putting others aside for further consideration, I relaxed and grew absorbed in the familiar process.

At last, fatigued, the Queen sought her bed for a rest before we supped in the hall. 'Praise God that you are returned,' she said, kissing me on the cheek as I handed her the cane.

Windsor was beautiful that April, and the festivities defiantly grand and celebratory against the undercurrent of fear the pestilence wrought. Those who were yet in mourning for the great knights who had died the past year wore gorgeous garments of scarlet and black, while the rest of the Garter Knights wore the blue and gold of the Order.

The Queen had much need of me, changing her exquisite attire many times each day. We worked with splendid silks and velvets, many with intricate patterns including garters and fleur-de-lis. I exhausted my diplomatic skills in guiding the Queen's choice of patterned cloth. Her plump and increasingly uneven figure required strategic use of draping, layers, and avoidance of many patterns that emphasised her shape, particularly in the more fitted gowns.

At all times six women were kept busy snipping pearls and jewels and exquisite buttons of gold, silver, pewter, some with pearls and precious gems, from one piece of clothing and sewing them on others, and as ever some of the patterns we had envisioned looked wrong when executed, so work must be unpicked and redone. We also discovered that the hems of several of the Queen's new gowns were quite long, pooling about her feet as she stood, which was the fashion, but in her condition I thought ill-advised. I insisted that they be re-hemmed, for the Queen was too unsteady on her feet to be trusted not to trip. I enjoyed the responsibility of ensuring that our beloved Philippa looked every inch a Queen.

When not engaged in dressing Her Grace, I did have opportunities to see Geoffrey, which did my heart good. Knowing me as well as he did, he could tease me out of my deepest despair, though he swore he was losing sleep over his failure to coax a laugh from me. He was not the only man trying to cheer me.

Richard Lyons, one of the executors appointed by my husband, offered to secure Janyn's home in London until such time as I might afford to buy the lease from him.

'I thought you might prefer to keep it, with the courtyard garden you designed. And Bella will like to see it.'

I was encountering a side of him I had not witnessed before, a gentler side.

The one person who might most successfully have enticed me back to life, God help me, had notably kept his distance since the news of Janyn and Tommasa's deaths: King Edward. The deaths of his own comrades-in-arms and the approaching pestilence were the Queen's explanations for his frequent absences from court and lack of sporting activity when present, but I saw him walking with an assortment of beautiful young noblewomen and suspected I had simply been discarded. I told myself I was relieved, that his flirtation had always been a misbegotten game, but my heart did not agree.

There was, however, someone who seemed ready to take the King's place in flirtation, Sir William Wyndsor, a man of some reputation in the military, handsome and slightly arrogant. He made it difficult for me to ignore him, the way he devoured me with his wide hazel eyes and paid me compliments whenever we met, which was far more often than mere chance could explain. During the festivities at Windsor he invited me to dance several times.

'Mistress Alice, you are a feast for the eyes. How is it that we have not met before?'

'I trow it is because you have been occupied with making a

reputation on the battlefield, Sir William, and I have been safely occupied in the Queen's household.'

Such was the depth of our conversations, but I thought it admirable that we managed to say as much as we did while dancing. I particularly enjoyed dancing with him when the King was present.

'It is rumoured he will be the Earl of Ulster's captain in Ireland,' Geoffrey told me after one of my dances with Sir William. 'He's already valued by the King, and if he survives Ireland and keeps Lionel alive, may rise at court. In time you might come to think of him as a worthy spouse and father for Bella. You could do far worse than wed William Wyndsor.'

I met his comment with a confusion I tried to hide by protesting, 'I am in mourning, Geoffrey, despite my lack of widow's weeds.'

'Forgive me, I merely point out a potential escape from court.'

He might be that. 'Do you think so, Geoffrey?' I shook my head, filled with remorse for even considering the possibility. 'I am not ready for any of this. I am consumed with guilt for enjoying Wyndsor's attention so soon.'

Geoffrey squeezed my hand. 'Dare to be happy, my friend. At least dream of it.'

How could I not, with the beauty and wit all round me? Life at court did much to raise my spirits, yet I had only to hear someone speak of a child to be overcome with yearning for Bella.

After the Feast of St George the King was off to the Isle of Sheppey to consult the masons and clerks of works on the Palace of Queenborough he was building there for Queen Philippa. To her deep regret the extravagances of the feast had so seriously exhausted her that Philippa cancelled her plans to accompany him to the site. She agreed with her physician that the long journey from Windsor to northern Kent was too much for her. But that did not mean she was willing to forgo having a voice in the palace's design, and so was inspired to send me along in the King's party, a woman whose taste she counted on. I was to travel with the King. My heart pounded at the news. I was to be one of several ladies from the Queen's household in the party, but the Queen singled me out, consulting with me at length regarding the details to which I should give my utmost attention.

'Where is your excited smile, Alice? You are to design a palace for your Queen. Create beauty. I am honouring you, entrusting you with something very dear to me.'

I was, in truth, overwhelmed by the great honour and trust she was bestowing on me. But equally I was frightened.

I forced a smile. The Queen was impatient with any lack of confidence. 'Your Grace, I was caught up in the litany of all we have discussed, committing it to memory. I pray you will forgive me.'

I must have divined the right excuse. She smiled. 'You are forgiven.'

'I confess, I was also thinking how much more delightful it would be were we there together.'

She pressed my hands, satisfied, and was soon on to other topics: the sad state of her health, the ravishments of so many pregnancies, and since her accident the lack of activity that seemed to be leading her into a downward spiral. This talk eventually wearied her, and she, apologetically and I think with sincere regret, sent me off to prepare for the journey.

Gwen was anticipating the journey with high excitement and packing with an enthusiasm I'd rarely witnessed in her. She took pains to learn as much as she could about the island and the route we would be travelling, ensuring that I would have enough warm clothing.

'It is said to be damp, with thick morning mists,' she explained.

'Well, it *is* an island,' I noted.

I could see by the set of her shoulders as she resumed her work that my indifference disappointed her.

'I am excited, Gwen, but I am also keenly aware of my duty to Her Grace. I fear I shall crowd out her instructions with details about the journey.'

But it was plain that Gwen worried about me. I did as well. I prayed that I remained steady, that I would not make a fool of myself with the King and ruin Bella's future. I tried to appear more enthused. When I could not avoid it, I pretended to listen to the chatter about the expedition.

'You are so quiet, Mistress Alice,' one of the Queen's ladies remarked the day before the journey.

Of course I was. I had heard nothing of their conversation.

'I have never taken part in such a journey,' I said, 'so thought it best to listen and learn.'

Who could find fault with that?

On the evening before our departure Queen Philippa summoned me to her chamber rather late. Gwen at once began to fret that the entire expedition had been cancelled or postponed, and I found myself also praying that we were still to go. For all my dread of disappointing the Queen, I did look forward to the journey and prayed I might return with my spirit refreshed.

Rising with haste, I succumbed to Gwen's efforts to erase the signs that I'd already been drifting off to sleep and hurried along the corridor. I slowed down as I saw several of the King's pages standing just outside the door. I did not wish to interrupt a conjugal visit. But a servant knocked twice on the door when he saw me and stepped within to announce my arrival. I heard the Queen call out for him to show me in, and the door was opened wide. Inside I found a cosy domestic scene, the King and Queen sitting at a table by a brazier, their postures relaxed. Queen Philippa waved me to the vacant chair between them.

'I daresay you were abed, catching all the sleep you might before the journey,' said the Queen. She was looking better than she had in days, her colour soft, her eyes clear. Even her voice held more life. 'But Edward was delayed by every courtier not accompanying him to Sheppey, asking for last-minute advice, orders, favours, were you not, Husband?'

King Edward patted his wife's plump hands, folded loosely on the table before her, but he looked me in the eyes. 'Forgive me for the late hour. As you say, my love, the night before a journey the court realises that they have left everything too long and try to right that before they sleep.' He clapped his hands and a servant brought us all jewelled mazers filled with wine. Raising his cup, the King said, 'Let us discuss what we must before this fine claret calls us to rest.'

I rejoiced that we were still to depart on the morrow. But to sit between my King and Queen awed me. Fortunately the wine was delicately mulled and heated just sufficiently to soothe. The Queen launched into a list of considerations essential for a beautiful, inviting palace, particularly considering that Sheppey was marshy.

'Alice, when you walk the land with the masons and the clerk of works, I bid you breathe in and pay heed to the dampness. Notice your feet as well. Steer the men away from the worst spots. Keep them on the highest ground.'

'My love,' the King interrupted, 'the location of the palace is already set. It will replace the old castle.'

'I remember it as an abysmally damp, dreary place, yet I have other memories of beautiful spots in the grounds. You know better than to question my memory for such things, Husband.'

The King's laughter brightened the room. I felt it warm my blood. But my heart ached to recognise in both their faces the deep, abiding love I myself had enjoyed with Janyn.

Philippa had continued with her description of a pretty walled rose garden for strolling and sitting in on warm days – 'even by the sea there are certain to be warm, sunny afternoons' – and a suite of rooms specifically for her and her ladies that should include a hall large enough for music and dancing: 'For though I no longer dance I delight in watching others.'

That provoked a hearty laugh from Edward. His was a deep, full-bodied laugh, a kingly laugh indeed.

'My love, I am ever wary of planning aught with you if I have any thought to the health of our coffers! What begins as a simple castle for occasional, brief visits, grows to be a magnificent edifice before it is even begun.'

Philippa shrugged in a manner that must have been pretty when she was younger, her smile bright and her chuckle light.

'Then do not ask, my love, and you will happily achieve a plain, uninviting, damp and cheerless castle safe from thieves for no one will dare leave furnishings there to moulder.'

They shared laughter. I downed the remainder of my claret and wished for more. In a moment a servant had stepped forward to refill my mazer.

Philippa tapped the table by my hands.

'Too much wine will make tomorrow's journey more tiring.'

'But the excitement, my love. Mistress Alice may need the wine to sleep.'

They looked at me expectantly.

I forced a little laugh, a pathetic sound. 'You are both right. I shall drink just a little more, though it is a pity to waste it.'

'Wine is never wasted,' said Philippa. 'The servants drain the cups before they wash them. You make friends of them by always leaving a little in your cup.'

The King yawned, the Queen patted her mouth to stifle a yawn, and after a few more rather aimless comments the King proposed we all hie to our beds. I stumbled back to my room, a little drunk and missing Janyn so badly I cried myself to sleep.

Though it was spring the air was damp and chill on the Isle of Sheppey. We arrived late in the afternoon, the chatter of our company overwhelmed by the warring clamour of wind, waves, and sea fowl. The land was so flat and low-lying that it seemed the breaking waves would wash over us. Though I had lived all my life in London, in the flat land by the Thames, I had been surrounded by buildings. I had never seen earth and sea and sky joined so.

I slept in the small convent, in a room crammed with cots for the Queen's ladies. We were none of us comfortable or happy, but my bad temper threatened to pull me down into darkness, my lethargy preventing me from being Philippa's representative. On that first night I slipped out of my room and sought the chapel. Though cold, the sacred space was blessedly peaceful. I knelt before the altar and prayed for release from my mourning, for the wisdom to provide a good life for my daughter, and for the grace to fulfil my duty to the Queen. I was discovered just before dawn and shooed back to the crowded bedchamber. I was grateful to be outdoors again after Mass and a simple meal of bread and thin ale.

One of the convent servants led me to where the King and several other men walked near the old castle. In the flatness of the marshy island the men looked like giants, and the King the tallest of them all. He moved with head held high, back straight but not stiff. Indeed, he was the very model of grace in motion.

'Your Grace,' I cried out, my only hope to be heard over the wind that rushed past my ears and snapped my clothing. I bowed to him.

Much to my confusion, the King reached out a gloved hand to

me. As I moved to kiss his ring he withdrew his hand, crouched down and proceeded to draw me up by my elbows. With his height, he soon lifted me too high for my feet to gain purchase on the rock. Our eyes were almost level, and the look in his surprised me. I felt that he truly saw me, acknowledged me as Alice Perrers, neither a nameless servant nor one of the many ladies of his wife's household. For the first time in a long while, I felt seen. For so long I had felt that no one saw me, saw *Alice*. I remembered how before my marriage I had feared that I would lose myself in my love for Janyn.

'The wind is so strong you looked as if you might take flight, Mistress Alice,' the King bellowed with hearty cheer, though the expression in his eyes was quieter, gentle. 'My wife would never forgive me if I lost you to the wind and the waves.' He set me down, holding me until I was safely balanced. 'Come now. Walk with me and tell me what you think my Philippa would be saying.' He took my hand firmly in his. 'I shall be your anchor.'

Though his familiar behaviour confused me so that I feared I might dissolve into giggles, my good memory served me well, and the kindness I had seen in his eyes put me at ease. I was able to repeat the Queen's priorities, shake my head when the ground oozed beneath our feet, and nod when we were at a higher elevation and the marshy island swept away from us like a sea of green and brown. But all the time my mind was feverishly arguing against the flutter of hope he had lit within me, that I might not lose myself entirely at court, that I might prove to be of some worth, and that even without Janyn I might find joy in life.

Suddenly the King stopped. We had outpaced the others and were quite alone with the seagulls and the wind.

'This gloom is unacceptable, Mistress Alice. I will see your smile before the day is out.'

'Your Grace,' I said, bowing to him, which was awkward on the rocks. I would have sworn that I had been smiling. I kept my eyes downcast.

Gloved and beringed fingers reached out and lifted my chin. The King's blue eyes bored into me, and again they were kind and caring.

'Sweet Alice, you have much to grieve for, I know, and this

subterfuge of not calling you "Dame" and forbidding you to wear a widow's weeds must seem harsh. But you have all your life yet to live, and I wish to provide you with the opportunity to live it fully, with grace and joy, free from worry. I owe you this, for it was my mother's work that deprived you of husband and mother-in-law. I promise you that as soon as I am certain your connection with that business is forgotten I shall have your daughter brought to court.'

'My lord!' I could say no more, for emotion choked me. His kindness overwhelmed me.

He smiled. 'I remember a time when I suffered as you do. You are too young to know how dark the court was when I took the throne from Roger Mortimer. I might have spent years doing penance, filled with remorse and grief. But that was not what my people needed. A wise man advised me to take my joy in the role that God had given me. Now I advise you to do likewise.'

'It is difficult to forget, my lord.'

'You never forget.' He tilted his head, studying me. 'You are a most beautiful young woman, Mistress Alice. You will find joy with another man.'

I was grateful to be spared the need to respond, for I could not find my voice. He thought me beautiful and had promised to bring Bella to court.

'Your Grace,' I managed to say, as the others caught up with us and whisked us back to the house in which the King and his knights were lodged, where we sat down to a modest meal.

I found it easier to stay in my bed that night, listening to the other women whisper and snore.

In the morning Gwen woke me while most of them were yet abed.

'The King summons you for some hawking!' Her eyes were bright with hope that such an invitation would cheer me.

I rewarded her with the smile of happy anticipation I did not try to hide.

Outside, the air was chill with the morning mist that swirled in strange colours, lit by the dawn.

'It will be warm today,' Gwen said.

'Later, but not now,' I said, disappointed. A hawk would not fly in this. But out of the mist came the King and a servant on horses, leading two others. They carried no hawks.

We rode out on to the beach, then sat our horses, as close together as possible, gazing out on the swirling mist.

'Yesterday I said that I understand your grief, your pain,' said the King. 'I want to tell you a tale of a young man, younger than you, who discovered that the happy dream of his childhood was just that, a dream.' He told me of the moment when he understood that his parents, the King and Queen of England, were at war with one another. His mother, my old acquaintance the Dowager Queen Isabella, had sailed to France, her home, where her brother was king. She was furious with the way her husband favoured the brutal, conniving, greedy baron Hugh Despenser over her. She tricked her husband into sending his son, the Edward who now told me this tale, as his representative at her brother's wedding, for she knew that the King himself did not intend to attend for fear that his barons might rise in revolt against him while he was absent from his kingdom. And then she kept her son in France despite increasingly angry letters from her husband, demanding the return of the prince. 'And so I was forced to choose between them,' Edward said to me now.

'How cruel of them.' I thoughtlessly reached out to touch his arm in sympathy and then quickly retrieved it, embarrassed by my presumption in almost touching the King so. 'And did you choose?' I asked a little breathlessly.

'I told myself that I was not choosing, that I was refusing to choose. But in my dreams I knew that I had chosen my mother. I had chosen treason. I had chosen the path that led to my father's violent death, the sacrilegious murder of a divinely anointed King. And I knew that I had done so because I feared my mother and her French support more than I feared my father, and that I hated Hugh Despenser more than I hated Roger Mortimer, my mother's lover.'

'Those were dark times.'

'They were.'

'Dame Tommasa, my husband's mother, told me that your mother endured much, and that she had suffered.'

'She did. And in her pain, took a terrible revenge. She never found joy again. Indeed, I could not imagine that I would ever do so again. But I did. I have found joy and purpose.' He reached for my hand, and held my eyes with his startlingly blue gaze. 'And so shall you, Mistress Alice, I am certain of it.' He smiled. 'I insist upon it!'

'I am grateful for your kindness, Your Grace,' I said, aware of the warmth coming through his glove, aware of his eyes on me. 'But I confess that I do not trust to hope for another chance at the joy I had with my husband, our little family. I cannot think that God blesses anyone with such joy a second time.'

'My mother cruelly used your husband's family. You have suffered for that. But I pray that you find joy again.'

'May God bless you, Your Grace.' We sat quietly for a moment, our hands joined in the space between our mounts. 'I pray that you do not take this question ill, Your Grace, but it would help me if I knew. Who was it that my husband's family protected for Lady Isabella, the Queen Mother?'

He looked away from me, and I guessed that he did not wish me to see his true feelings about my question. I began to understand he was not skilled at hiding his feelings. 'Not now. But I shall tell you someday, I promise. When we are sure of one another.' He moved in the saddle. 'Come. Let us ride a little.'

The fog had begun to thin and the sea stretched out before us, glimmering in the sun, shimmering as the tide rocked it.

The King's falconer rode up to say that a little farther inland we might now hunt. He had the falcons there. The King was very pleased. I did my best to appear cheered by his kindness. I was grateful, I truly was. We hawked, and afterwards the ladies and knights joined us for a long, wine-soaked feast, and then the company walked about the old, tattered castle and talked of how beautiful it would be very soon.

My time alone with the King had been noticed. In the evening the ladies with whom I shared a bed allowed me some more room than they had on other nights and refrained from sending me off on errands. But they were no more friendly. I guided my thoughts back to those moments I'd shared with the King on the beach, remembering the eerie beauty of that multi-coloured mist. Nothing I had seen since Dame Tommasa's home had so stirred me. The court's extravagance was gorgeous, breath-taking, but did not move me, stir me, spark my heart as that place did in its many moods.

I shall tell you someday, I promise. When we are sure of one another. And he would bring my Bella to court. The King had promised me. It was a beginning, something to cling to, and I hugged those promises to my heart as I fell asleep.

In the night I woke, thinking someone had whispered in my ear. But my companions were all asleep, Gwen lying curled up on her pallet at the foot of the bed, and there was no one moving about. I lay back, feeling a calm and peace I had not felt in a long while, and remembered the King's promises. Smiling, I closed my eyes, and the sounds of the sea and the wind crept in to fill the room. Remembering how beautiful it had been in early-morning, I wondered what it would be like now, when all were abed and the light was the silver of moon and starlight. I thought it a good way to celebrate my rekindled hope, to walk to the sea. Indeed, I felt too agitated to lie still.

Not wishing to awaken anyone by fumbling for shoes or a cloak, I stole out of the convent as I was, in a shift, my hair loose. It was a calm night, with bright stars overhead, and I walked out on to the hard, wet sand, letting the salt air play in my hair and tease the loose skirt of my gown, the wide sleeves. I felt light, as if I might easily take flight. I felt life rushing up from my feet, as if I were rekindled. I felt free.

When the chill salt water reached out to embrace my feet I hesitated, but I had come that far, I refused to turn back or hesitate. Its movement was so gentle, welcoming. The soughing of the sea and the wind in my ears closed me off from the rest of the world. It was an intimacy with the earth that I'd glimpsed when riding. The water felt sensual, daring, as it crept up my calves. The wind teased my nipples to hardness, tickling them by fluttering the soft linen of my shift over them. Part of me noticed that I was cold, very cold, but as I moved out farther it felt more like excitement than cold that had me shivering. I was up to my waist. I felt the sand sifting between my toes, moulding itself to the curves and gaps, and found it a pleasant sensation, reminding me of moulding myself to Janyn's body at night. It would be so easy to lie down in the water and let it take me where it would, to fantastic isles. The sea and the wind welcomed me.

I was startled by a tug on my arm from behind. Then someone grabbed it.

'Stop! You are hurting me,' I cried.

The grip was so tight, I cursed and tried to pull away. But I found it difficult to move in the water. I screamed as I was grabbed by the waist and dragged out of the sea, then roughly wrapped in something that smelled of wood fire and horses. I was confined in it. Unable to move my arms and gasping for breath, I was hoisted up and carried like a sack of wool. When I was unwrapped, I hissed that they had almost killed me. But they were all too busy talking among themselves, the servants and a glowering prioress. No one asked me what I had been doing. They wanted only to force brandywine down my throat and leave me to the infirmarian.

Dame Edburga, a sweet, elderly nun, tended me. With warm blankets and hot stones, she lulled me into a sound sleep for hours. When I woke she was praying by my side. She looked at me with a sorrowful expression.

'Why did you wish to end your life?'

'End my life?' I thought about that last moment, the temptation to let the water take me. But it had been a fleeting thought and had held no flavour of death. 'I had no intention of doing so.' Though I understood how it might be otherwise interpreted.

'I know about your losses, Dame Alice. His Grace told me how recently you were widowed. And your husband's mother dying as well, a woman you loved. But that is no reason to wish for death.'

'His Grace told you?' I prayed that his taking such a personal interest in me was a good sign.

She nodded.

'But I did not wish for death. The sea was so beautiful tonight . . . I had never before stepped into it. The sand oozing between my toes . . . I had never felt that before.'

She shifted on her stool, looking into my eyes. 'You were not attempting to drown?'

'No.' I thought of the anger of the 'rescuers' who had carried me in and tried to force down more brandywine. Their behaviour made more sense now – they had thought they were subduing a woman intent on killing herself. 'God help me, they all believe I meant to drown! Even the King must think so. I am mortified that I caused such worry.'

The nun rose. 'His Grace must be told that you were merely foolish, beguiled by the sea.' She hurried out.

I prayed. Had I realised what everyone thought I had been attempting, I might have corrected them before the thought solidified into certainty. One of the horrors of living at court was the speed with which one person's interpretation of an event overwhelmed all other interpretations, to become the truth of it. It was always the most exciting or most damaging version. Now I would be watched, prevented from being alone, questioned about every frown, every tear.

And indeed, when I joined the company in the yard to prepare for the journey home, the King turned to me, hands on hips and puzzlement in his eyes.

'Dame Edburga says that you were beguiled by the sea but meant no harm to yourself. Is this true?'

Breathless with fear, I dropped to my knees before him and asked his forgiveness for causing a stir in the night. He commanded me to rise.

I did so. 'Your Grace, I meant no harm to myself. The sea made me restless, and as I walked into it the water wrapped round my legs, so soothing, and the sand moved beneath my bare feet as if it were a living thing. I felt alive. I did not go out there to die, but to find the joy you spoke of.'

The company had grown very quiet and looked away or at their feet, none of them meeting my searching gaze. A nun sighed and shook her head with disapproval, another crossed herself. I looked back at King Edward and found him watching me, and I was grateful to see that he smiled.

'Your Grace, I have taken your counsel to heart. I pray that you believe me.'

His smile was not the broad, regal smile he used to draw his subjects to him, but bemused, as if I had somehow surprised him.

'I do believe you, Mistress Alice. The sea is a temptress, a dangerous one who often lures us with her gentle face. I believe that you did not understand the danger you courted. I shall make a point of explaining such dangers to you in future – before you risk your life again.' He gave me a little bow, then motioned to the groom who stood by my horse to help me mount.

We spent a day in Canterbury, where I prayed to St Thomas Becket to help me carry myself in such wise that the King would honour his promises. I meant to hold him to them. I understood that I must be mindful of my behaviour, grow out of my childish thoughtlessness. And I must accept that I could not reclaim the past.

'He say his lady somtyme, and also
She with hym spak, whan that she dorst or leste;
And by hire bothe avys, as was the beste,
Apoynteden full warly in this nede,
So as they durste, how they wolde procede.'

– Geoffrey Chaucer, *Troilus and Criseyde*, III, ll. 451-455

1361

I vowed to heed the King's kind advice and find contentment in my life, ease my terrible grip on past happiness. More easily vowed than carried out, but I was determined to try. To shelter my child from harm, I must retain the protection of the royal couple.

The pestilence undermined King Edward's efforts to reassure his people. Law courts were closed, reopened, closed. By midsummer we were sequestered at Sheen, though the officers of the household were considering the wisdom of fleeing farther into the countryside. Lionel, Earl of Ulster, had lingered at Sheen after his sister Mary's wedding, and with him of course his household, so I had the pleasure of Geoffrey's company at many meals. It was a mixed pleasure, for he was honouring his promise to be my ears among the courtiers, and from him I learned that I was rumoured to be sharing the King's bed. I was not surprised by such a rumour – since Sheppey the other women had treated me with icy caution – though the fact that I shared a bed with at least one other woman every evening, in a room assigned to six of us, should have proven it false. Perhaps because I was the only one of the six who slept in that chamber every night, I was the only one who knew I was the one true celibate among them. But though I was not surprised, I was frightened. I could not think what would happen were the King to learn of the rumour, or even worse the Queen, my mistress. Would they understand that I had no power to silence the gossips? Would they believe I had said nothing to provoke such talk?

I prayed for guidance as to how I might clear my name, having no one to whom I might turn for advice. I could hardly ask the Queen how to cope with such a rumour. My confessor Dom Creswell knew nothing about women and precious little about the human heart. I had never felt so alone. Even when my mother had shunned me and I'd yet to be welcomed into Janyn's family, I'd had Nan and Dame Agnes. I hoped that perhaps enough time had passed since the death of the Dowager Queen that I might be permitted to see my grandmother, and one morning broached the subject.

But the Queen pursed her lips and shook her head at me as if I were a frustrating child, wilfully stupid. 'Even if I thought that you might slip away to see one of your Salisbury kin without endangering them, I would not allow you to risk going into the hot, pestilence-ridden city. No, I do not give you leave.' She fanned herself with a vigour that heated rather than cooled her. In the humid warmth of high summer she shed layers and replaced them with dry ones numerous times each day and well into the evening. The laundresses grumbled.

The Queen's affection for me had soured since hearing about my night-time walk on the sands of Sheppey. Although she still asked my advice on clothing, furnishings, and how her hair was dressed, she made it plain that in all other things my opinion was suspect. I had proved silly and reckless.

I had explained the allure of the sea and reminded her I had not drowned. I assured her that I had learned from my foolish mistake. But she would have none of it. She even forbade me to visit Bella until such time as she might be assured of my maturity.

'How, then, might I prove it, Your Grace?'

'It is not for you to prove, Alice, but for me to observe in your demeanour. We have sworn to protect you, and we will.'

I felt I was a prisoner. I mourned for Bella, so near yet so inaccessible. I told myself my confinement to court was for my own safety, and Bella's, but that did little to cheer me. I had few companions. There were two young sisters living in the household, the orphaned daughters of a lesser knight who had been the Queen's countryman, with whom I enjoyed spending time, although they were only girls. They had a more easy grace than the other children being fostered by the Queen. At all times there were ten or so young souls in the household, some to be companions to the royal children, others orphans who had touched the Queen's heart. The two girls from Hainault were Katherine and Philippa de Roet, charming and curious and hungry for learning, bitter-sweet reminders of my dear sister Mary.

My other occasional companion was Maud, one of the Queen's ladies, who treated me kindly and sometimes invited me to walk in the gardens with her, where she would talk of her lost marital joy; her husband, a knight, had suffered a head wound in battle that had rendered him so helpless he was now cared for in an abbey in the West Country. She knew me as 'Mistress' Alice and was unaware that I had been wed. While she relived happier memories, describing her courtship, her wedding, her hope for many children, I visited my own. She thought me an excellent listener. I enjoyed her company, and did learn from her something of the happenings outside court, for she often spent time with her married sister who lived in the countryside near Canterbury. I enjoyed hearing of crops, fairs and markets, and domestic concerns. Life at court still seemed a world of its own, having no relation to my old, ordinary life.

It was from Maud that I began to appreciate how fortunate I was to be in the safety of the Queen's household. Because of the closing of the law courts, women suddenly widowed had no recourse if their liege lord arranged a marriage for them to his own advantage or decided that their property was best protected by his taking it over and seizing the income.

That did not seem to be the King's intent for me. No one had prevented Richard Lyons from protecting my London home on my behalf. For that I was deeply grateful. It allowed me to dream of someday living there with Bella, and riding out to Fair Meadow in the heat of summer. Fair Meadow had been the Dowager Queen's gift to Janyn, and the King had seen no reason to take it from me. One of his stewards held it in trust for me, until such time as I might be able to care for it once more. I felt God watched over me, providing me with those two homes, and was grateful. I felt ashamed when I remembered my pettiness about how unattractive Lyons was, for he had proved to be a good and loyal friend. Though as the summer progressed and pestilence spread in the city he stayed away, in June he had made a habit of bringing me bouquets of flowers from my London garden. I felt that I had grievously misjudged him.

William Wyndsor had returned to court, paying more attention to me than he had in spring, even inviting me hawking in a party that included Geoffrey and my friend Maud, who both teased me afterwards about William's inability to keep his eyes on his hawk rather than on me. It was silly and pleasant. William was dark like Janyn, but with fair skin and hazel eyes. He reawakened my passionate nature with his intense gaze. I was sinfully aroused by the way he undressed me with his eyes, something I despised in other men. He was my favourite dance partner despite the way he rendered me breathless and too weak in the knees to dance the next set.

He was not my only dance partner. The rumour of the loss of my betrothed tantalised many courtiers. John of Gaunt often danced with me, as did his elder brother, Prince Edward.

But Gaunt also happened upon me in the gardens, far more often than seemed likely to be the workings of chance. 'Do you not find it significant how often we seek out the same walk, Mistress Alice?' he teased me once. He was one of the handsomest men I had ever seen, but he was not only already married, he was as out of my reach as the King himself. I was disturbed by his attentions. In truth, his words often stung, suggesting that his game was not altogether friendly. Once, when I nervously prattled about the various flowers along the path on which we walked, he interrupted me.

'Ah! So you are schooled in the mysteries of gardens as well as costly cloths and clever tailoring, Mistress Alice. You are no common merchant's daughter.'

I did not know what to make of him.

It was his father who yet enthralled me. But since Sheppey I had not spoken to the King, nor had I been in his presence except in crowds. I no longer caught him watching me, and though I prayed for the wisdom to be grateful, I was not. When I saw him walking with a woman other than the Queen, my heart tightened with jealousy.

Despite my mourning Janyn, I could not ignore the way my

body was reawakening, how it yearned again for the love of a man. Perhaps that is why I was not altogether displeased by Maud's news that William Wyndsor had enquired of her whether I was betrothed. She was thrilled for me.

'I cannot think of a more handsome man . . . except perhaps John of Gaunt, and as he is already taken, wed to the second most beautiful woman in the land, Wyndsor is the handsomest *eligible* man,' she said. 'Would you have Wyndsor if he asked your father for your hand?'

Sir William's effect on me suggested we would be well matched in bed – faith, I spent a great deal of time at night imagining it. And for me to wed a knight would improve Bella's prospects. But I did not know what was possible; whether the Queen would permit me to wed and abandon court, leave her protection. I wondered whether she would send a suitor to my real father or the Hertfordshire knight Sir Richard Perrers who had agreed to pretend I was his child. And what of that? Did Sir William believe me to be a knight's daughter? Such deception sat ill with me. Perhaps the King and Queen had another suitor in mind for me, a thought that could not but make me anxious. And over all these complexities hung my own contradictory feelings about marrying again so soon after losing Janyn.

To distract Maud from more questioning, I tried to engage her in considering other eligible men. But she kept shifting the conversation back to William. I learned that his father and grandfather had been loyal supporters of Thomas, Earl of Lancaster, who had opposed King Edward II before Isabella and Roger Mortimer had formed their rebellion, and that their families had suffered for it. His was another family that had risked everything by supporting someone who challenged the King, as Janyn's mother's family had done also. Perhaps it was not so unusual. Perhaps William and I might be kindred spirits in our unease at court.

Whether I was falling in love with him I was not sure, but I did enjoy his company and how alive I felt under the warmth of his attention.

The gift of such attention lay in opening my heart and mind to the pleasures all about me – my beautiful clothes, the wondrous palaces in which I lived, my Melisende, the music in the hall and the dancing that sent me to bed happily exhausted. In the garden I drank in the beauty all around me as I walked. I particularly enjoyed walking with young Philippa and Katherine, naming the plants for them, encouraging them to try to remember the garden in their home in Hainault. They remembered little, for they had been so very young when brought to England, but they surprised themselves with random memories and seemed truly happy when they did so. The Queen remarked on my revived spirits and included me once more in her daily gatherings.

Geoffrey, too, noticed my improved mood and accused me of being in love with William. I laughed so much as I denied it that he smugly declared he was right. I refused either to worry or feel guilty about my heart's awakening.

In August dire news of more deaths from the pestilence was tempered by the exciting rumour that Prince Edward had secretly wed his cousin, the Countess Joan, widow of Thomas Holland. Being in such close contact with the Queen I almost immediately saw that it must be true for the Queen's fury was impossible for her to hide from us. Her whole body reeked of rage.

'That whore,' was how Joan, once so dear to her, came to be known in Philippa's chamber. It seemed that Joan's having been raised at court deepened the offence for she 'should know better'. The King's representatives had been involved in negotiations all year for a marriage between the prince and Margaret of Flanders, the young, wealthy and beautiful only child of the Count of Flanders and his wife, the widow of the Duke of Burgundy. The betrothal would have bound the Flemings to the English at a crucial time for such a liaison. But we were soon informed that a messenger had gone to the Pope to annul Joan and Edward's clandestine vows and to grant the dispensations necessary for the cousins to wed formally. As the deed had been done, the King would see it through. Planning began for an autumn wedding.

'Such an extravagance. The bribes to the Pope! The festivities! And she brings no alliance with another royal house,' the Queen muttered. 'That whore.'

I had conflicting loyalties. The Queen had encouraged Joan and me to be friends, thinking that as we had both been recently widowed, we might find comfort and healing in consoling one another. But Joan had good reason to avoid anyone who had been a friend to the late Dowager Queen, her father having been executed by Isabella's lover, and at first had shunned me. However, as she came to know my story, how Father had set me against Mother in order to be joined with the Perrers family in marriage, and how Janyn had abandoned me with a young daughter, she befriended me, and eventually told me all about her scandalous past. She had grown to trust me enough to confide that while wed to William Montague she had taken care not to become pregnant, though they had lived as husband and wife for seven years.

'You know how to avoid conception?' I asked, having heard of such things, but never having known anyone who had actually gone to such lengths.

Joan had become serious, glancing round to make sure no one could hear us. Seeing that we were quite alone, she said, 'If you ever have need of such protection, come to me. You must drink some of an herbal mixture before and some after the act.' She had patted my cheek then. 'You have had enough heartache from dumb obedience. Now you shall take control of your life.'

I thanked her for her advice, though I did not consider it possible for me to follow it.

She was truly a most beautiful woman and revelled in life, dressing and moving to show off her sensual body, plunging wholeheartedly into the activity of the moment as if tomorrow might never come. This passionate, whole-hearted approach to life excited those about her, lifting spirits and creating possibilities where none had appeared to be before. She spoke her mind and made no effort to be nice as a general principle – one earned her friendship.

'We women are treated with less courtesy than men treat their horses, dogs or hawks,' Joan told me. 'God granted us souls, like men, and minds with which to reason our way to grace, yet we are expected neither to think for ourselves, nor to mind being unappreciated and neglected. They think of us as domestic beasts and find us annoying if we behave otherwise . . . if we question their commands or doubt their wisdom. We are to be obedient unto death, and to bear many sons. And, of course, priests and monks fear us because they desire us and have little control over their own appetites; so they blame us and call us sinful, for they cannot admit to their weakness. I do not understand why God does not better support us.'

I did not disagree with her, although I had considered my own anger at such things sinful and would never have expressed it aloud. I had begun to feel crippled by the obedience expected of me. She opened my eyes to the possibility of trusting in my own wisdom, something the Dowager Queen Isabella had spoken of also; but Isabella had, I believed, gone against both God's and nature's laws in destroying her husband and King. Joan's way of honouring her own wisdom was far more palatable to me.

I had not known that even as she had spoken to me with such anger about men, she had been falling in love with Prince Edward. When I later discovered it, I watched her with keen interest, trying to learn how she both loved a man and honoured herself.

I prayed for the wisdom to know when to be a Joan and when to be meek. I felt that in my life so far I had been more the latter – oh, yes, I had expressed my passion to Janyn and Geoffrey and others very close to me, yet I obeyed. I obeyed. And it had earned me only heartache. But I also appreciated that there must be something in me that drew people to me, for in so many ways I was blessed. I felt more accepted among the Queen's ladies of late, and my old friend Geoffrey was loyal, Richard Lyons was proving a careful guardian of my finances, Dom Hanneye wrote often with prayers and guidance.

I do not believe I would have had the courage to do what I did next had Countess Joan's fiery words not fanned a flame within me.

On a stormy August afternoon a page announced to me that Geoffrey waited to speak to me just outside the chapel, in the little porch. I thanked him and took my leave of the women with whom I'd been sewing, already praying for strength to bear whatever it was he had come to tell me. For by his choice of a meeting place where we would not be overheard – the storm would keep strollers away – I knew it must be terrible news.

His leggings were saggy with rain, and though he wore a short garment fashionably padded around the chest there was yet a caved in quality to his torso that spoke of sorrow. He stood with chin up, apparently studying the carved figures decorating the arched doorway. As I moved closer I saw that it was not just his leggings that were limp and dirty, but that his formerly bright red and sharp black gown needed to be dried and brushed.

'You've travelled far?'

Now he lowered his head to look at me and I saw the unease in his expressive eyes. 'Not so far. To London and back. But I was there a few days.'

'Geoffrey – you have been to the city? Risked the pestilence?'

'I was worried about my family.'

'Who is dead?' I asked, a question uppermost in everyone's mind when someone arrived from London.

He crossed himself. 'I am sorry to tell you, Alice, but your mother, your brother Will, and Master John Perrers have all been taken by the sickness.'

'So many!' I gasped. I would have fallen to my knees if Geoffrey had not caught my elbows and drawn me to him.

I remember the sound of rain thundering on the roof of the porch overhead and how cold my feet were from the splashing of the rain on the stone threshold. I had one of those odd practical thoughts that intrude on one in times of sudden, awful news – when I returned to the hall my tears would look like rain and no one would comment.

'I am so sorry, Alice, so very sorry. I wanted you to know as soon as I heard.'

'How long ago?'

'Will died yesterday, your mother and Master John a few days ago.'

'No one told me.'

'In the Queen's household? I am not surprised. They would not want you rushing off to London. My master will be displeased with me. Indeed, the Queen would be angry to know you were even seeing someone who has been in the city.' As he spoke the last he began to pull away, as if fearing he might pass the pestilence to me by his embrace.

But I held him tight. I needed to feel his arms around me.

'I will go to Father,' I declared into his shoulder. This loss would be a terrible blow to him. I worried even more for Mary.

He patted my back. 'He has your sister to comfort him.'

'But who comforts her?'

'You cannot go without the Queen's permission, and you know that she will not grant it.'

I heard him as if through a thick cloth. My head pounded, I gasped for breath, and then the sobs rose up and overwhelmed me. Geoffrey held me all the while, though the wind picked up and the small roof above us gave us little protection. When I stopped weeping, he drew me into the chapel and took off his shoes, draining the water from them.

I did not care about my own wet clothes but knelt to pray for the souls departed, and for the survivors – my brother John, my sister Mary, and Father. I do not know when Geoffrey knelt beside me, or when Gwen arrived to cover me with a mantle and kneel at my other side. But they were both there when at last I lifted my head. Gwen wanted to hurry me back to my chamber to change into dry clothes, but I waved her off.

'Geoffrey, you must tell me all that you know. We can go to the hall and sit near the fire.'

'No, I must away to my chamber to change. If anyone sees me looking like this, they will guess I've been to the city and I'll be sent away. In truth, I do not wish to return to London at present.'

'You will not take me?'

He looked at me, as horrified as if I had asked him to swallow a live rat.

'Alice, you cannot mean to go to the city? What if the Queen were to learn you had been there? She would send you away. And then where would you go?'

Surely she would understand my need. This was my family. 'What of you? You risked it.'

'And I've brought you news of your family so you need not go. Besides, there is still danger for you there.'

'I sometimes wonder whether that danger has been overstated.'

Geoffrey's expression was carefully veiled, but I could see that he no longer doubted it.

'There is some rumour you would keep from me?' I asked.

I watched the skirmish on his expressive face, heart versus head. Heart won.

'Master John Perrers dined with guild members the day of his death, and he had seemed quite well then, showing no signs of illness.'

My breath stuck in my throat. Another victim of Isabella's cursed secret? 'So he was murdered?'

'That is the suggestion.'

I crossed myself with a trembling hand. 'What was the condition of his body?'

Geoffrey shook his head. 'I do not know. The dead are buried so quickly.'

'Are Mother and Will already buried?'

'Your mother is for certain, and I have little doubt that Will is as well by now.'

'Master John . . . you think it was the trouble with Isabella of France?'

'Or that he had other dangerous connections. A friend told me he had seemed frightened of late. Went abroad only with two large men protecting him.'

I crossed myself. 'Where are they now?'

'His servants have not seen them since they found their master's body in his parlour.'

So much loss. My heart was heavy with grief. 'May God grant him peace,' I whispered.

'So, you see, you should not go to your father.' Geoffrey squirmed in his wet clothes. 'Nor would you wish to. They say he is a changed man . . . sullen, suspicious, unkempt.'

I felt my childhood, my entire past, being ripped away from me where I stood. 'Is he ill?'

'No. But like so many, he cannot cope with the cruelty of so much death.'

'Poor Mary! If Father is so changed, what must it be like for her?'

'She has Nan, does she not?'

She did, I supposed, though even that I could not know for certain. 'I pray Dame Agnes takes an interest in Mary.' My grandmother might see it as her duty, but I had learned enough of her ways to fear she might also be too busy, trying to keep herself and my grandfather safe. I yearned to go to Mary, my sweet, precious sister, left all alone.

In the hall during the evening meal I found myself wondering what Joan would do in my place. But she would never be in my place. No one would forbid her to go to a member of her family who was in need. I was poor company to those seated near me.

When I rose from the table William Wyndsor approached me, enquiring about my pale face and sorrowful air. Even in my grief I noticed how elegant he looked in Lincoln green and gold, a soft felt hat of deepest gold tilted to one side to show off the curl of his dark hair. The colours called attention to his large hazel eyes, which now regarded me with affection and concern. I wished I might pour out my heart to him. Thought I might at least tell him enough so that he would not feel as if I were shunning him.

'In faith, I am in mourning, Sir William, for my mother and a brother.'

'I knew that I read great sorrow in your eyes and manner, my dear Mistress Alice. May God grant them peace.' He bowed his head and crossed himself, and then he took me by the hand and drew me away from the crowd, into a quiet corner of the hall. 'Did they die of the pestilence?' he asked in a low voice.

I hesitated to acknowledge the horrible truth, as if it might somehow not be fact as long as I did not voice it. But I needed to admit the truth, to accept it. 'Yes, the pestilence took them.' My heart clenched.

His sympathetic expression threatened my composure.

'Are they far away?' he asked.

Remembering that to the court I was known as Sir Robert Perrers's daughter, I did not know how to answer that.

He leaned closer. 'Dame Alice—'

I looked up at his use of 'Dame'.

He nodded. 'I know that you are the daughter of John Salisbury of the London guild of grocers, that you are widowed with a young daughter.'

'How?'

'I am John of Gaunt's man. And your friend.'

My heart softened. God had been watching over me and, seeing my need, had put Wyndsor in my path. 'Then you know that they are in London.'

'Will you go to be with your family?'

'No, I cannot.'

'But surely you must wish to see them?'

It was too much. The tears came and I sobbed, 'Yes, I wish to see them, but the Queen forbids it.'

'Indeed?' His tone turned angry. It was enough to distract me from my self-pity. 'The King would have us behave as if there is no danger, but the Queen forbids her own household to enter the city?' William had grown quite loud.

I'd heard of his famous temper, but this was the first time I had witnessed it. I did not wish to call attention to myself. 'Might we walk out into the air? My head is aching.'

We escaped to the castle yard, where the heavy damp heat combined with the smoke from many torches caused my head to pound even more. I led us around strolling couples, clusters of men crouched over games or drunkenly insulting one another, past the armed guards positioned at regular intervals, to a walk that led to a walled garden, the torchlight from the castle yard and light spilling out from the hall allowing me to find the way. William kept a hand beneath my elbow and steadied me when I stumbled.

Within the little garden I chose a bench near the entrance, as far as possible from a couple farther along the path who were locked in an embrace. The air was fresher now that we were away from the hall and yard, and I breathed more easily.

'When did you learn of your loss?' William asked, taking my hand and gently stroking it.

'Earlier today, after the midday meal,' I said. 'Queen Philippa is most kind to me. But she fears the pestilence, and with good cause.'

William studied me for a long while as I sat mute in my grief. The damp air was not as refreshing as I had hoped, and I realised that my gown might be taking on moisture from the bench. As I rose to feel behind me, William startled me by grabbing my hand and pulling me into his arms. For a moment he simply held me. I wanted to melt into the comfort of his strength, the reassuring sound of his heartbeat. He bent to kiss my forehead. I pushed out of his embrace.

'I was not asking for sympathy,' I said, shaking out the skirt of my gown.

He raised his hands, palms towards me. 'I beg your forgiveness if I have transgressed, Mistress – Dame Alice. But I cannot help but feel sorrow for your pain. I love you. You cannot be unaware of my feelings. And in loving you, I am sad for you in your mourning.'

'Love? We'd not spoken of love.' I backed away. I could not trust myself, my judgement, when my mind was so dull with sorrow. But despite his charm, his declaration of love disturbed me. It was too soon.

'Forgive me. I do not mean to take advantage of your need.' He took a few steps away, then turned back with an air of decision. 'You must see your family in London.'

If only it were so simple, to know what I must do and to take care of it myself. 'The Queen will not have it.'

'I will take you there.'

My heart leaped, but reason quickly intervened. 'I cannot let you risk the Queen's anger for my sake.'

'It is what you need, and I offer it to you.'

He was a knight. The Queen might see her way to forgive me for going with someone who could protect me. The Countess Joan seemed to whisper in my ear, *Take his offer*. I did so, and despite my misgivings about his sincerity, did not ask what William sought to gain by risking this.

Early the following morning we slipped out of the palace, Gwen and William's servant Alan accompanying us. A groom waited for us with three horses – William had not been certain that Gwen could ride, so she climbed up behind Alan – and we made our way downriver to the barge awaiting us. I was impressed by William's having planned the journey in so little time. I could see by Gwen's expression that she was touched by all that he was risking for me, and the care he'd taken to see to our comfort. I was grateful that he left me to my own anxious thoughts as we travelled downriver.

How strange it was to return to my childhood surroundings after all this time. I remember it seemed both wonderfully familiar and disturbingly changed. Of course, it was I who had changed. Having lived in palaces for several years, the courtyard of my old home looked cramped, the hall dim and shabby. But it was all precious still to me.

Nan burst into tears on seeing me, and my sister Mary, now a beautiful young woman, did likewise. I laughed and cried as I held them both in tight embraces. Father stood at a slight distance, aged beyond his years, stooped with grief, his eyes dull. I went to him and hugged him, but he merely patted my back once, as if acknowledging my presence and my effort but having nothing to give me in return.

'Margery could not hold on, she would not wait for me. Your mother would not wait for me.'

Seeing him so shattered, I could no longer be angry with him for pushing me at Janyn when he knew it would alienate Mother. I saw him for the weak man he always was.

'I am sorry I was not here to help in their illnesses, Father.'

'She would not have you in the house, Alice. I wanted to send for you, but she would not have you here.'

Mary put her arm round me and led me away. 'He does not mean to hurt you,' she whispered.

'How is John?'

'He is well. You'll remember that he has a kind master with a big family? I do believe that he will wed one of his master's daughters when his apprenticeship is over. Her name is Agnes, like Grandmother, and she is a gladsome woman who sees to it that he is well cared for.' Mary's eyes were bright with affection.

How happy I was to be with my sister. My heart was a little lighter for being in her dear presence.

'How have you managed since Janyn's death?' she asked. 'I wished I could come to you then, to comfort you.'

'Bless you, Mary.' I kept my voice low, not wishing to share such feelings with William. Gwen had disappeared with Alan, into the kitchen, but William had remained in the hall. He stood gazing out of the partly open doors into the garden beyond, pretty even in the rain. 'I have managed as well as any grieving widow manages. Mornings are the worst, when I wake and gradually remember why I am sleeping with other women. Janyn and I were together only four years and yet it feels as if we always shared a bed. I do not understand how my heart works. It has its own sense of time.'

Mary pressed my hand. 'He is handsome, your friend,' she said, glancing over at William.

'This is not Janyn,' my father suddenly said. He must have been watching her.

'No, Father, Janyn is no longer with us. This is my friend, Sir William Wyndsor. It is thanks to him that I am here today. He arranged for the barge and escorted me here.'

'Who told you of Mother's death?' he asked, ignoring William.

'Geoffrey told me about Mother and Will yesterday.'

In his diminished state, I did not think Father a suitable guardian for Mary. Nor could I bear to think what it must be like for her, living in that house of mourning, a place haunted by such recent suffering. Conceiving of a scheme to rescue her, I took Mary aside and asked her how she liked her grandmother, Dame Agnes. When she said she liked her very much, I decided on my plan. I would take her and Nan to Dame Agnes and ask her to take them in.

Dame Agnes had aged also, but with grace, and though she seemed uncertain about how she should respond on recognising me, soon folded me in her arms and wept with joy.

'You look healthy and so beautiful, my Alice. I have worried about you, suffering so much loss away from your family.'

'I have missed you and worried about you as well . . . all of you,' I told her. When I felt I'd answered enough questions to content her for a while, I made my proposal.

She nodded. 'I have myself considered such an arrangement. I did not like what I saw there.' She looked over my shoulder at Mary. 'What think you of your sister's idea?'

Mary looked to me for a sign of how to respond.

'I was very happy living here,' I said. 'I think you could be happy too.'

Mary's smile was shy. 'Then I would like it.'

Dame Agnes clapped her hands. 'It is settled! And dear Nan shall be both your lady's maid, Mary, and a help to me in managing the household.'

I saw in Mary's and Nan's eyes their release from fear, and I hugged Dame Agnes with all my strength.

'And you, Alice,' she said, holding me at arm's length and looking deep into my eyes, 'what of you? Will we see more of you?'

I explained that the Queen still believed it to be dangerous to visit the city, with the pestilence about.

Agnes nodded and hugged me. 'Then I hope when it passes we

might see you more often. Perhaps if you remarried?' She nodded towards William, who had quietly settled on a bench near the fire, his long legs extended to the dry warmth. A servant had brought him ale and bread and cheese, and he'd contented himself with that while we talked. 'He is handsome. You called him "sir". He is well-born?'

'I am most grateful to Sir William for risking the Queen's ire to bring me here today, but we are merely friends.'

'It is a good beginning.' Agnes and Mary exchanged glances.

William had not noticed my regarding him, but he did look up as Dame Agnes approached him, her hands outstretched. His guarded expression undercut the generosity of his gesture in bringing me here, to come among the family the Queen forbade me to see. I could not help but wonder again at his motive.

He rose to take Dame Agnes's hands.

'God bless you for what you've done for my Alice,' she said, 'and for all of us.'

'My heart was heavy to see her grief yesterday and to learn that she had been forbidden to come to her family, Dame Agnes. I feel blessed to have witnessed this reunion.' He bowed his head to her and the smile on his face when he looked up again lit the hall.

A knock on the door prevented further conversation.

A servant introduced a page from the King's household. He bowed to Dame Agnes, and then the rest of us, and informed us that the King had sent an escort for my safe return to Windsor. The King! I felt weak in the knees, terrified what this might mean. We had not only been discovered, but the King himself had commanded our return. I glanced at William, who simply nodded to me, his expression blank. That did nothing to alleviate my panic.

Dame Agnes questioned me with her eyes, but aloud she offered the King's men some ale in the kitchen while I bade farewell to my sister. William followed the page to see to the men.

'He is very handsome,' said Mary again.

'A bit like Janyn?' asked Dame Agnes, seemingly to herself.

They were babbling, pretending nothing out of the ordinary had happened.

I hugged Mary. 'Be happy, my dear sister.'

My mind was racing, wondering what it meant that King Edward himself had sent an escort. At least I had done some good. I had no doubt that Mary would be in loving, competent hands in my grandmother's house. She was so pretty and good-natured, my grandmother would soon be fussing over her as she had me.

Nan held me tight, weeping for the joy of being reunited and the pain of its being for so brief a time.

'I shall try to return,' I said, my attention already elsewhere. I feared what the Queen's ire might mean for Bella, and cursed myself for taking the risk. Yet I had helped my family, and prayed that would earn me some grace in God's accounting.

In parting from Dame Agnes, I saw that she was moved as well. She stroked my cheek. 'You look so well, so beautiful. Master John Perrers explained nothing to us. It was your friend Geoffrey Chaucer who finally told me why you never came to us.'

I could not imagine what explanation he had made, for he knew how dangerous the truth would be to them. 'What did he tell you?'

'How your mother's venom had frightened you away,' Agnes said, nodding as if to reassure me that she understood. 'She was a madwoman.'

I was thankful for Geoffrey's clever explanation.

William and I had little chance to talk as we hurried through the noisome streets to the barge. Once we were on the river, I asked him what he'd learned from the men in the kitchen. 'Am I to be punished? Sent away?'

'His Grace is not angry with you but with the Queen, Alice.' William watched my reaction.

'What do you mean?'

'What I said. He heard Queen Philippa ranting about your having gone to your family, how you could not be permitted to return when you would bring the pestilence with you, on and on, and silenced her with some quiet comment. The page says that you are never to be denied the protection of the Queen's household.' He took my hands, still searching my face. 'Am I in competition with the King in loving you?'

'No.' That he should even think so troubled me. 'I am grateful for his protection, but I should think his anger with the Queen is over something else, and I was – most fortunately for me – a convenient argument.' I touched William's hand. 'I cannot remember a more loving gift from a friend than that which you've given me today, William. I pray that someday I am able to give you something as precious in return. Bless you for the peace of mind you have brought me.'

He took my hand and kissed it, then pulled me into his arms and kissed me on the mouth. It was like kissing Janyn all over again, sending heat through my body and leaving me breathless afterwards. William had felt my response. He smiled with satisfaction.

'You shall be my wife, Alice. I swear.'

It was a most unexpected declaration and too much to contemplate with all the emotions roiling inside me from seeing my family again. I chose my words in response with care, for I was grateful to William. 'As to that, I cannot say. But I pray that God grants you happiness.'

I was sorry that his only response to this was a brooding silence for the duration of the journey. Having no pleasant distraction, I gave myself over to my fear of facing the Queen and King.

When we arrived at the Windsor dock I was escorted to King Edward's private parlour. William insisted on accompanying me, and I appreciated the gesture. Despite what he'd heard from the page, I knew how quickly the King and Queen could change their minds.

Regal in red and gold, his intense blue eyes touching briefly on William and holding steady on me, the King thanked my escort for keeping me safe and sent him off. Then, with what seemed sincere concern, King Edward invited me to sit with him, share some wine and a light meal, and tell him all that had transpired. He commended me for taking Mary from that unhappy household and asked if there was anything he might do to ease my mind further about my family.

'Your Grace, I would see my beloved daughter.'

'And why not? Queen Joan is not so far away.'

My heart sang. 'And as soon as you judge it safe, Your Grace, I would visit my sister Mary more often. She will soon be old enough to wed and I treasure these last years of her girlhood.'

Placing a beringed hand on each of my shoulders, he vowed to arrange for me to see my sister as soon as he deemed it safe.

'For I would not knowingly help you walk into danger, but neither do I wish to prolong the lack of a sister's companionship. And I have not forgotten my promise that your daughter will one day abide with you. But why did you not come to me with your fears for your family, Mistress Alice?'

'I did not think it appropriate, Your Grace. I am answerable to Her Grace, Queen Philippa.'

'Remember Sheppey, Mistress Alice. I swore there you would be happy.' He kissed me on either cheek. I was glad he still held my shoulders, for I fear I might have dropped to my knees had I not been so supported.

A page escorted me back to my chamber, a courtesy for which I was grateful. With all that had happened since I had departed early that morning – the reunion with my family, William Wyndsor's declaration of love and vow to marry me as well as my own complicated feelings about him, and the kindness of the King – I was dizzy with emotion, and might easily have lost my way. I was not familiar with the part of the castle housing the King's chambers, so the route back to my own room was not known to me.

Gwen met me at the door with a fierce hug and then pulled me into the room and shut the door, leaning against it. I saw by her ravaged face and by the twisted cloth in her hand that she had been weeping and worrying all the while.

'Forgive me, Mistress Alice, but I must know – are we to be punished for disobeying Her Grace?'

'As I told you on the barge, the King defended our action. In truth, he understands.' But I was still unsure how the Queen might treat me. She had her own subtle methods of punishment. 'Have we been summoned?'

'You are to make her almond milk this evening.'

A private conversation. I dreaded it.

'And you are to bathe, and all the clothing we wore is to be burned so that we might not bring the pestilence into her rooms. I have already bathed and changed.'

After the evening meal I followed Her Grace to her chamber with trepidation. But she expressed only pleasure that I was able to give comfort to my family, and then said no more about the incident. I had expected at least to sense in her some irritation with me, even if she did not speak of it, but I detected no such animosity in her behaviour. I found that most strange considering how adamant she had been that I not go into the city to see my family. Even if the King had convinced her of my need to do so this one time, I would have thought to encounter some resentment. But she treated me as if I had not in any wise displeased her. I expressed deep remorse for disobeying her; she said she understood, and spoke merely of her own grief at the loss of so many friends and relations.

That night I cried for my losses and those of the Queen, and relived precious moments with my sweet brother Will, his life so brief.

As if to compensate for such heartbreak, I also dreamed of William Wyndsor, of lying with him, exploring his naked body. The memory of the dream excited and confused me – confused me because I could imagine lying with him and delighted in that imagining, but in the light of day could not see him as Bella's foster father. Something about him did not feel trustworthy enough to share with him my precious daughter. Or perhaps I was still too bedazzled by the King's kindness.

To my amazement, from that time King Edward began once more to make note of me, often pausing to speak to me after morning Mass. He chose mundane topics, such as the weather or the music in the hall the previous night. I responded with modest gratitude, eyes always cast down, desperate not to reveal my adoration. I did not need to look at him to feel his eyes upon me. All my senses seemed tuned to him. His attention was like manna to me in my loneliness. I prayed to have the sense not to make too much of it.

In late-summer Philippa took to her bed for days after the pestilence took her two youngest daughters, Margaret and Mary. It was a terrible blow to her, to have her young chicks, both recently married and launched into their new lives, cut down within a month of one another. The Queen was inconsolable. She had never been close to her one surviving daughter, Isabella, the King's favourite. Margaret and Mary had been the Queen's heart's delight.

On the second morning on which I attended Mass without her, King Edward paused in the corridor as had become his habit, but instead of a brief exchange of pleasantries he invited me to go hawking. Our party included only the falconer, two grooms, and the pair of us.

'I did not think either of us would wish for the noise of a crowd,' the King said.

I was glad that I had recently taken in the waist on my Lincoln green riding robe as was now the fashion and replaced the old feathers in my hat with new, brighter ones. The King and I spoke little, attending to our hawks and horses, allowing the woodland and the soaring birds to soothe our spirits. I was aware of him watching me as I talked to my merlin, but did not turn his way. Apart from my attraction to him, I felt a bond of quite another sort between us when we rode through the woodland, into the wind, free to shout, to laugh with abandon, to wonder at the perfection of beauty, grace, and unbridled power exhibited by our birds. Away from court we were at ease together without speech, alike in our appreciation of God's magnificent creation. At peace.

The King invited me again the following day, and the day after that, and on the fourth morning, after our hunt, we talked a little of our recent sorrows. I was glad if I might help the King in his grief as he had helped me. We stood side by side in the middle of a pretty meadow. The falconer had retrieved our birds and departed. Only the grooms were with us, and they were off to one side, holding our horses at the edge of the wood.

'In a year I have lost so many men who fought beside me, on whom I depended and trusted without question to defend my Kingdom. They were brothers in arms and brothers in my heart – my dearest friends. And now I've lost two of my precious daughters, so dear to me, both of them so young.'

King Edward's eyes stayed fixed on the trees, as if he could not trust himself to look at another human soul while he voiced his loss.

Without thinking, I took one of his great hands and squeezed it. I do not know what inspired such audacity. He looked down at me in surprise, then gave me the saddest smile I had ever seen.

'I cannot speak my heart to many people, Mistress Alice. Even my Queen reminds me that I am King and must not show any weakness.'

'No one will know, Your Grace,' I promised. 'In faith, I do not understand how anyone would think ill of you for grieving for your daughters.'

'A commander may grieve for his men-at-arms. No one else.'

I knew I would be greatly honoured to count as his friend, but that I must not touch him again. To do so was to fly too close to the flame. I fought for composure.

'I do not understand how God means us to live our lives,' I said. 'We both strive to be good, to fulfil our duties. I do not understand His purpose in testing us with so much loss.'

The King drew me to him then and kissed me on the lips, a peck, no more, then kissed my forehead, and held me close for a moment. I heard his great heart thundering, and reached up one hand to touch his pale hair. Then he lifted my chin and thanked me for my friendship.

When he released me, I feared my legs would collapse beneath me.

'Your Grace, I am your good and faithful friend.' I bowed to him even though he was not looking my way, relieved to hear none of my terror reflected in my voice.

He nodded, still not looking at me. I wondered what he was thinking.

'Our horses wait,' he said, striding away.

I followed him, my heart swelling with joy. He had kissed me, he had held me. My good sense quickly intervened, shouting warnings. I should not have touched him, for I doubted he would have kissed me, be it ever so chastely, had I not taken his hand. I could not believe I'd actually had the gall to touch his hair! I'd made a fool of myself. Would be sent from court. Sent from him. I could not bear that. I prayed for a sign from God as to what I should do, how I might avoid further temptation. It was a sin, coveting another's spouse. I could not betray his wife, my Queen and mistress. Yet I could not stop thinking of how it felt to be in his arms, to feel his lips on my skin. Every part of me had been intensely aware of him, intensely aroused.

He did not attend Mass the next morning. I told myself it was for the best. Indeed, it was my salvation. I obviously needed a mate, a husband. William Wyndsor would do nicely. He would save me from my dangerous, foolish obsession with the King. That evening I looked for William in the hall. I had not seen him since our journey to London, and feared that the only likely reason he might be avoiding me was that he knew of my mornings with the King. I remembered his suspicion when the King's men arrived at Dame Agnes's house. Eventually I learned from one of his friends that William had been sent north to the border near Scotland. He had received his orders the day after our excursion. It was an honourable posting, but unexpected. I expressed disappointment for having had no opportunity to bid him good fortune.

God help me, as I walked out of the hall, I almost danced with relief.

II-4

'Allas, of me, unto the worldes ende,
Shal neyther ben ywriten nor ysonge
No good word, for thise bokes wol me shende.
O, rolled shal I ben on many a tongue!
Thorughout the world my belle shal be ronge!
And wommen moost wol haten me of alle.
Allas, that swich a cas me sholde falle!'

– Geoffrey Chaucer, *Troilus and Criseyde*, V,
ll. 1058–1064

Autumn 1361

I had little time to brood over my feelings for the King. The Queen devoted most of her waking hours and mine to planning the official wedding of Prince Edward and Countess Joan. She was determined to make the best of the situation, setting aside her disappointment in the match. As for all such festivities, the entire household would receive special garments for the event so that all contributed to the theme. Green and white were the Prince's colours, so although the wedding would take place in October, rather than echoing the autumn bounty and colourful decay all around, the chosen colours suggested the freshness and promise of spring.

I needed all my wits to adjust and readjust to the Queen's imperious demands and shifting moods. On the one hand she was happy to see her son and foster-daughter so happy; on the other she was furious that they had been meeting at the home of Joan's late husband's sister, a woman who had recently made a scandalous marriage herself. Queen Philippa always enjoyed an excuse to plan an extravagant feast, but resented the fact that here would be no political gain; this was a marriage that would afford the family no new strategic alliances. Whether joy or resentment would dominate at any moment proved to be impossible for me to predict. I attended her every gesture or change of tone, trying to respond in the way that seemed safest at that moment. Every night I fell into bed exhausted, despairing of ever having a life of my own. The Queen's temperament at this time made life with Mother seem serene. But there were moments too in which Philippa expressed her appreciation – and that made up for much. She could be generous with gifts and praise.

In late-September the royal family accompanied the coffins of Mary and Margaret to the abbey at Abington, and the Queen chose me as one of her companions for the journey. Although folk came out to honour the solemn royal procession as we rode through villages, their demeanour was solemn and often frightened – plague corpses, no matter how royal, were to be feared. But of course the villagers were filled with awe to see their King and Queen, and it was in their eyes as they considered me too, wondering who I might be in my fur-lined cloak and beautiful leather boots, riding a magnificent horse. For the first time I appreciated how those outside the court perceived my place in the Queen's household. Mine was an honoured position, and I was fortunate beyond imagining.

In faith, I did not know how to resolve my warring feelings. Just as the Queen's moods flickered between light and dark, so now did mine. One moment I was mortified by my own self-pity, the next felt fully justified in grieving for my old, purposeful life. I had enjoyed running a household, entertaining Janyn's guild members and trade associates, bringing up my daughter. I still felt adrift at court. But I saw the faces of those villagers again when I tried to sleep, and they watched me as I lifted the Queen's delicately embroidered night shift from the trunk and walked across stone floors strewn with sweet-smelling flowers and fresh rushes. I lived amidst beauty and abundance, in comfort and safety. Those lined and weathered faces taught me humility and gratitude.

I had sent a message to Dom Hanneye by a clerk in our party who was continuing on to Oxford. I hoped that my beloved confessor, whom I saw only occasionally when he accompanied his Bishop to London, might find some way to come to me in Abington. To my immense relief he arrived the day before we were to begin our return journey, and the Queen gave me leave to spend some time with him.

With each new loss in my life Dom Hanneye grew dearer to me, for he had known all those for whom I grieved. At first we gave ourselves over to reminiscing about my mother and my brother Will, about Master John and Dame Tommasa, mostly about Janyn. We wept and embraced. Only when the dead had been lovingly honoured did I ask the question that weighed on my conscience.

'Do you think God and the Blessed Mother look down on me in disgust as the most ungrateful woman on earth?'

It eased my heart to have Dom Hanneye assure me that anyone in my situation would grieve.

'I watched you with Her Grace in the chapel. You saw to her every need and treated her with respect and love. You fulfil your duties with compassion and grace, Dame Alice. I find no fault in you.'

He suggested what he had before: that I seek the path of acceptance, look for contentment in simple joys and offer my suffering to God.

'Much as monks and nuns do throughout their daily tasks,' he said. 'But in much more comfort.' His teasing smile eased the sting. 'You have not asked how I was able to come so quickly.'

It was true. I had not. 'A life in elegant surroundings has blunted my sense of wonder. When every day I am surprised by something, it becomes unremarkable.'

We shared a laugh over that. Now that I looked closely at my friend, I saw that he had lost weight; his once round and childlike face seemed drawn as if he did not sleep well.

'I am grateful that you came. Your reassurance comforts me as no one else's. How *did* you receive permission and hie down here in such haste?'

I still expected a simple explanation. But as he paused and appeared to be collecting his thoughts, I understood he had a tale to tell.

'The brief answer is that I had requested permission several days before I received your message.'

'But how did you know I would be of the company?'

He shrugged. 'I might have guessed, but that was not necessary. Richard Lyons had come to Oxford, arriving a few days before your party reached Abington. It was from him that I heard you were to be travelling in the funeral procession.' He looked concerned as I shifted on my seat, murmuring Lyons's name. 'I know that you have not always liked him, but he has proved to be a good friend.'

'Yes, he has proved most generous. But what did he want of you?'

'It was I who had enquired of him whether you might be ready to purchase another property very near your present one in Oxford. I thought it a good opportunity. He insisted on coming to Oxford to see it. I do believe he wanted to ascertain my competence in the matter.' He bowed his head for a moment, folding his hands one way, then another.

Dom Hanneye had been caring for my property in Oxford, a responsibility he had executed with efficiency and honesty. I was very grateful, and concerned that others would respect him as my representative. 'I pray he did not insult you,' I said, seeing his discomfort.

'It was clear he thought a priest could hardly have a head for trade.' He shrugged.

'Then he does not know you.'

Dom Hanneye laughed. 'He does now.'

'Good. I would like to see the property,' I said.

'You would?' Dom Hanneye looked surprised. 'Do you wish to be a part of the decision?'

'I do. I wish to make the decisions on my own investments.' I was far more at ease with business than with anything else in my current situation, more clear-headed about money than I ever seemed to be about men. 'The rents will bring an income to support Bella and me, and add to the dowry Janyn established for her.' It was the one area in which I had some semblance of choice, some power over my life. 'I shall ask the Queen if I might return to Oxford with you for a day or so.'

'Richard Lyons would escort you back to London, I am certain.'

'That would suit me.'

Unfortunately, it did not suit the Queen.

'No, I cannot spare you, Alice. You know how much we have yet to do before the wedding. No, you shall return with me.'

I understood her concern about the approaching event, but could not believe that all would collapse if I were delayed by a day. Perhaps it was selfish of me to wish to go to Oxford, but the prospect had lifted me from my dullness of the past weeks. I tried to explain this to her, but she was adamant.

Help came from an unexpected quarter. The Queen sent her ladies away in the late-afternoon so that she might rest for the journey. Maud and I sought the quiet peace of the garden. We were walking there, talking little as we simply enjoyed the late-September sunshine and the lovely warmth that took away the chill of death, when the King's page appeared.

Had it been the Queen's page I would have resented the summons. But the King's . . . My heart pounded as I followed him to the chapel, where he opened the door and bowed me through. King Edward sat on a bench just within, leaning his back against the wall, his legs stretched out before him, a study in ease. I do not believe I had ever seen him so. For a moment he was merely a man, not a King, albeit a large, physically imposing man. Rather than feeling awe, I felt only pleasure to see him and be seen by him.

'Come, Mistress Alice. Sit with me and tell me about this property in Oxford.' His tone was friendly, pleasant.

I took a deep breath and tried to calm myself as I sat beside him.

'Philippa tells me that your former confessor came from Oxford to discuss your investing in a property, and that you wish to see it for yourself. You are interested in owning land?'

'Yes, Your Grace. My late husband purchased a tenement in my name so that I might have revenue from rent if . . .' I was uncertain how to continue, whether it would insult him. 'If I should find myself in need.' I almost whispered the last part as I kept my eyes lowered.

'Commendable. But he should have known we would not abandon you.'

'Your Grace.' I bobbed my head in a sign of respect, while thinking that he was as blind to his own inconstant behaviour as was his Queen and his mother before that.

'My mother, the Lady Isabella, spoke of your cleverness. That your husband consulted you regarding his business.'

He shifted a little, the motion perfuming the air around me with his scent of spice and leather. I found it intoxicating.

'He did. And before him my father likewise. Father would have me sit with him in the undercroft while he explained the accounts books, and often permitted me to listen to trade discussions.' I stopped myself, realising I had said more than required. His alchemy was working on me as it did with everyone, drawing me out, and I felt myself trying to please him. And more. It seemed I could not be in his presence and not want more. A kiss, a touch.

'I see that your skill in hawking and grace in dancing are but hints of your talents, Mistress Alice. Beauty and a mind for trade . . . hunting and dancing . . . what else should I know of you?'

I felt myself blushing under his regard and was glad that the light was dim and we were side by side, so that he could see little of me.

'Your Grace, I do not know what else I might tell you. I am little but what others wish me to be.' I regretted my words as soon as I'd uttered them.

The King drew in his legs and shifted on the bench so that he was facing me. He took my right hand, turned it over, looked at my palm and with one beringed finger traced the line that ran from between my thumb and forefinger to my wrist.

'So easily I touch you,' he murmured as he did so, 'so recklessly I summon you, then tease you and take your hand. How thoughtlessly I pluck your strings, as if you are but a lute.'

The intimacy of his touch and his voice, the suggestion of playing me like a lute excited me far too much for safety.

He let go of my hand, touched my chin, gently, oh, so gently, while looking into my eyes. I had not intended to look up, but could not prevent myself.

'Forgive me if I have made you feel so used, Alice.'

I did not trust myself to speak, my flesh burned at his mere touch.

'Do you forgive me?' he whispered.

'Your Grace,' was all I managed.

'Edward. My name is Edward.' He spoke in an intimate whisper.

I shook my head, an embarrassingly jerky motion.

He straightened up, the mood between us suddenly changed, the tension discharged. 'You must of course return to Oxford with Dom Hanneye. But we depart tomorrow. Had you any plan for an escort back to London?'

I could not so easily switch my attention. How did he? Was I just a game to him? 'Richard Lyons is returning to London in a few days, Your Grace,' I said, hating how breathless I sounded.

He tilted his head as if considering, then nodded. 'He is a trustworthy man. I shall send him a message that his life will be forfeit if anything happens to you.' He took my hand and kissed it, looking me in the eyes while still holding it. 'That is no jest.'

I shivered and withdrew my hand. 'I am grateful for your permission, Your Grace.'

'Edward.' He smiled.

'Edward,' I whispered, and fled the chapel before I did something foolish like kiss him in gratitude. For I understood, at least on my part, that no kiss between us could ever be innocent.

Once again, as when the King had sent an escort for William and me from London, the Queen expressed no irritation about my plan to leave her company briefly.

'I am trusting you to return a mere day behind us,' she said. 'A day and a half at the most.' And then she smiled and sent me off to assist with the packing.

Dom Hanneye and I made the trip to Oxford without mishap, and in the late-afternoon joined Richard Lyons to tour both the property I already owned, which I'd never seen, and the one on the same street that I might purchase. The houses and out-buildings were leased out to craftsmen and students at the university, a mixture that commended them to me for I would not be dependent on one class of people for tenants. The buildings were in satisfactory condition, certainly nothing grand.

'You will continue to oversee both of them for me?' I asked the priest.

'As long as I am here in the city, I am pleased to be of service to you, Dame Alice.'

I noticed that he called me 'Mistress' only when others might overhear. This secret sign of respect deeply moved me.

We supped with Richard Lyons that evening, in a private room at an inn near the convent where Gwen and I would lodge for the night. We discussed the properties at length, and agreed that

Dom Hanneye should arrange the purchase. Both men treated my comments and concerns with respect. It was with a renewed sense of confidence in my own knowledge and skill in trade that I lay down to rest in a small but comfortable bed, my faithful servant and friend Gwen by my side.

I was jolted awake by a sound, and then the horror of an oily rag being pressed to my face. I could not catch my breath, I was so terrified. I opened my mouth, gasping for air so that I might scream. Before I managed a sound, my assailant shoved the rag into my mouth. He did so with such force I felt a jolt of pain in my right jaw. Panicked and gagging, I kicked at him, thrashed my arms and clawed at whatever I could reach, but another came to his aid and they quickly tied my ankles, tossed me on to my stomach, wrenched my arms behind my back and bound my hands. Suddenly all was darkness as a smelly cloth became my shroud. Gwen whimpered somewhere nearby. I made a muffled complaint when I was heaved over a man's shoulder and carried away like a trussed lamb. It was, I think, a doorway unskilfully manoeuvred that hit my head. I felt a sharp pain, and then nothing for a long while.

When I came round I found myself lying against soft cushions, much softer than those on which I'd fallen asleep. I moved my foot and pain ran up my leg. My head pounded above my right ear.

'Where am I?' My voice was weak and my jaw hurt so that I mumbled the words. But someone heard.

'She wakes.' It was a woman's voice. 'I'll tend to her now.'

'Let me see to her, I beg you. My mistress will be afraid with a stranger after what she has suffered.'

My heart leaped. Gwen was here! She was alive. Her beloved face appeared over me.

'What happened? Who . . .?'

'Mistress Alice, you are safe. Richard Lyons has proved a good friend, and the King is sending an escort for us.' She lifted my head and helped me drink something that tasted of honey but warmed me like brandywine. 'Are you in much pain?'

I wondered the same about her – her left wrist was bandaged and one eye was swollen and bruised. I gingerly touched the right side of my head. My hair was undressed but there was no bandage. I felt a tender lump.

'You have a bruise, but there was no blood.'

Only then did I notice that both my wrists were lightly bandaged.

'The ropes were old, rough, and bound too tightly,' said Gwen. The strength and steadiness of her voice reassured me that we were safe more than any number of words could have done.

A stranger had joined us, hovering behind Gwen. She was a tall woman with dark, expressive eyes. At the moment she seemed eager to observe me. Her hair was tucked into a crisp white scarf, her clothing simple, but she was not a nun.

Gwen noticed me looking behind her and turned.

'This is Dame Juliana, a healer. Dom Hanneye sent for her. She has been very kind.'

'God bless you,' I said. So few words, but they caused a sharp pain in my jaw. I covered it with my cool hand, which felt most welcome.

Juliana nodded to me. 'You will quickly heal, God be praised,' she said. 'Did they injure your jaw?'

I nodded.

'They shoved a stinking rag into your mouth.' Juliana's frown was so fierce it might have been comical in any other circumstance. 'I am glad they are dead.'

Dead? I looked up at Gwen, knowing she would read the question in my eyes.

'Master Richard's men, Dom Hanneye and a bailiff caught two men carrying us from the convent and set upon them. Several more rushed out from the darkness,' she explained. 'It was a frightening battle, made all the worse because you lay so still beside me, Mistress Alice, and I could not lean down to hear if your heart was beating.'

'You?' I asked.

'I have sores where they bound me, nothing more. I was more fortunate than you.'

I was glad. 'The others?'

'Master Richard has a deep wound on his left upper arm and Dom Hanneye a broken nose. Four of the men who tried to take us are dead. The fifth is being questioned.'

I embarrassed myself by bursting into tears, and once begun could not stop. My heart had been breaking for a long while over the deaths of so many who were dear to me, and this last terrifying night had been the final blow. The two women fussed over me for a while, and then all grew quiet except for my sobs. Finally spent, I slept. I woke a few times to darkness, the curtains closed round my bed, Gwen sleeping beside me.

In the morning Richard Lyons and Dom Hanneye came to see for themselves how I was recovering. Dom Hanneye approached first, blessing me and assuring me that although his nose and eyes made him look as if he were in great pain, he felt better with each day.

'I believe I shall have a more interesting face, more trustworthy in its imperfection, when I have completely healed.' Though his smile was oddly contorted by the swelling, he did seem to be himself.

'God is merciful,' I said. I, too, was feeling better and found it easier to talk than I had the previous day.

Hanneye withdrew to a seat and at once bowed his head in prayer.

With his good arm, Richard Lyons pulled up a chair beside my bed. His injured arm was bound close to his side.

'Mistress Alice,' he said, bobbing his head, 'God has answered our prayers.'

'How is your arm?' I asked.

'It will mend. Are you in much pain?'

'Better today. Who were they?'

'I do not know. I have been told only that the King commends us for saving your life and that of your maidservant, and that the men clearly intended to kill you. Other than that, the King's man says that his information is for your ears only.'

His manner was much humbler than usual, and I sensed a mixture of weariness and unease in it. I did not understand how the King had already heard of this.

'The King's man? But the company left Abington for London only yesterday.'

'Several days ago, Mistress Alice. You were set upon three nights ago.'

Three nights. 'I slept so long?' That I had lost so much time was not at all reassuring. I crossed myself.

'You slept a day, and they say you then woke for a little while, and afterwards slept another day. In that time a messenger reached the King and returned with Richard Stury, his most trusted esquire, and a small retinue. Stury will come to speak to you later.'

I crossed myself at this news and prayed for God to watch over me. Stury was an esquire of the King's chamber who had risen from the position of valet by his unflinching loyalty to his master, his cunning, and the fact that his grandfather had been in the diplomatic service of the King's father. Courtiers were uneasy when Stury was about, for he was rumoured to spy for the King as his grandfather had done for the previous King Edward. If the King had sent a man such as Stury, he must believe this attack had something to do with his mother's secret, the business that had already robbed me of so much. Would I ever be free from Isabella's curse? I imagined I would have been questioned by my abductors and then, when they were satisfied that I knew nothing, I would have been murdered, as had Master John, Janyn and Tommasa. I had never believed their deaths were natural.

'You've nothing to fear now, Mistress Alice,' said Richard. 'You are well protected. We shall return to Windsor Castle with a strong escort.'

I might have believed I had nothing to fear had it been my person someone wanted. A man thinking to violate me would now know that I had powerful protectors. But Isabella's secret, whatever it was, seemed to have a power of its own, and I could no longer doubt the danger it had brought me to. I was a prisoner in the Queen's household. No matter that my prisons were royal palaces, they still enclosed me.

Richard waited for my response. I felt humbled by the danger in which he had placed himself on my account.

'Tell me what happened,' I said. 'Who raised the hue and cry? How did you know to come?'

Gwen interrupted, bringing a physick she insisted I drink at once. It was unpleasantly thick and slimy, and tasted of rotten greenery and damp earth. I tried to hand back the cup after a little sip, but she shook her head and would not take it from me.

'Dame Juliana says that a head wound such as yours that cannot be bled must be fumigated with a strong physick. This will restore your strength and your memory. Do you not think that worth a brief bad taste?'

I drank, though it was the most disgusting liquid I had ever forced down my throat. Gwen rewarded me afterwards with spiced wine, which did wash down most of the aftertaste.

Richard had waited quietly throughout the interruption.

'In answer to your question, we had planned all along to guard the convent. But alas, we gathered too late. They must have already been within the walls when you arrived. The moment they appeared in the yard, we fell on them.'

'Did you recognise any of them?'

'No.'

'What caused you to plan a guard?' Again, this evidence of his courage on my behalf overwhelmed me.

He shrugged with his good shoulder. 'Your husband's disappearance, his mother's soon after, and the mystery surrounding his father's death. Plus the fact of your being taken into the Queen's household while your daughter is fostered in the home of the Queen of Scotland – it is plain to me that you married into a family singled out in some way, most likely their loyal service to the Lady Isabella.' He waved his good hand at me and shook his head as if I'd begun to tell him, though I'd not opened my mouth. 'I confess, I do not care to know more for fear my own life might be forfeit. But for these reasons, Dom Hanneye and I believed we must protect you.'

He sat back in his chair and picked up the cup of wine beside him, gazing down into it.

I was grateful for his courtesy, for the chance it gave me to rein in my emotions. Richard was rightly fearful of sharing our secret.

'I pray you do not suffer for coming to my aid.'

The blush that spread even to his ears suggested a vulnerable side to him that I had not seen before.

'I thank God I had the foresight to be there, and to include the bailiff in our plans.'

My vision blurred then and Richard's voice seemed to come from far away. When next I woke a stranger sat beside me. For a moment I thought he had been conjured from the unholy slime I had obediently drunk. Dark brown hair and eyes, dark cloak, a dull green jacket, brown leggings and boots.

'Mistress Alice,' he said, bowing his head. 'I am Richard Stury, King's esquire.'

Only then did I recognise him. How strange that seemed to me. I feared the physick had worsened my condition, not improved it.

'Yes, I have seen you at court, Master Stury.'

For a moment I thought we were alone in the room and was about to ask that Gwen be permitted to return, but she came forward just then, proffering a cup I was loath to accept until she assured me it was merely watered wine, not a physick. She quickly withdrew to a seat near the door.

'Your lady's maid has your complete trust?' asked Stury.

'Yes.'

I sipped the wine as he explained how he came to be there, most of which I had already learned from Richard Lyons. While he spoke I studied him. He might have been a clerk with his tall, skinny body and pinched features. His mouth seemed to hold a perpetual grimace, and though I would have guessed him to be no more than ten years my senior, he already had deep creases between his brows – indeed, they remained knitted together even when he uttered a pleasantry or paused to think. He held his hands on his lap as if he were forcing them still.

'I am most grateful for the King's concern,' I said. 'Knowing you to be one of his most trusted esquires.'

He inclined his head in acknowledgement of the compliment. 'His Grace had no doubt that the attackers knew of your late husband's service to his mother, the Lady Isabella. That is why I am here – I am one of only a few in the household who have been entrusted with the knowledge of your family's connection to the former Queen.'

'Do you know the men who attacked me?'

'I have known of them, though I met them only as corpses.'

'I thought one was yet alive.'

'He died this morning.' In his dark eyes there was not a flicker of emotion.

I crossed myself and said a prayer.

'I would not pray too fervently for his soul, Mistress Alice. It will do little good. He meant to interrogate and then defile you before he murdered you, I have no doubt.'

I pressed my hand to my throat, shuddering at the realisation of what might have happened. 'For whom did they work, Master Stury?'

'You do not need to know that.'

'Are you mad? How am I to defend myself if I know not my enemies?'

'The King protects you, Mistress Alice.'

'It was not the King who saved my life and that of my maid.'

'You need fear nothing.'

'Why? Are you taking the lives of all my would-be questioners as they become known to you, before they have a chance to attack me?'

Stury rose. 'We shall escort you to Windsor in the morning. I pray you, rest before the journey.'

And so I learned the extent of the prison I inhabited. I feared I might now never again be free to move about outside court. And I began to wonder . . . was I protected or was I the lure? Why did that question suddenly occur to me? I prayed for courage. I prayed for my daughter's safety.

On the journey I felt a heaviness, as if I were returning in disgrace. If I could not be trusted with the names of my enemies, what was my true worth? I won a small victory, though, convincing the men I would be more at ease on horseback rather than being bruised afresh occupying the cart. The weather had turned colder and a drizzle kept us all hooded and quiet, so my brooding silence went unnoticed.

Richard Lyons was subdued in Stury's company. He had greeted me in the morning, then left me to make my farewells to Dom Hanneye, who had hoped to return with us to attend the Prince's wedding but had received the disappointing news that his Bishop wished him to remain in Oxford.

'Are you being punished for defending me?' I asked, gently touching the discoloured flesh between his brows.

'To my surprise, I am being promoted to a more significant

benefice here in Oxford, on the understanding I will not talk of the recent incident.' He bowed to me.

'I am happy for you, though this promotion be a form of bondage.'

He shrugged. 'I willingly took a vow of obedience. Never hesitate to summon me if you are in need, Dame Alice.'

I thought of our silken bonds all the way to Windsor Castle. Dom Hanneye's promotion in exchange for his silence: an imprisonment of the mind, a restraint on speech if not on thought. The protective custody in which I travelled. And, once back in the Queen's household, my restriction to the more than comfortable palace where all my physical needs were cared for with the best of everything, yet still I was caged. All those I loved were unreachable, untouchable.

Weary and disheartened, with a pounding head and throbbing bruises, on my arrival in the inner bailey of the castle I wanted nothing but to go to bed. Gwen and I walked slowly, arm-in-arm. My head, ankles and lower back complained but I was glad to be moving on my own account. In the Queen's hall we were met by a servant who led us past the Queen's Chamber, and far past the one I shared with the other waiting women, to an unfamiliar room that was pretty and private, and just before the doorway to the King's part of the palace.

'Master Adam, His Grace's surgeon, has been informed that you have arrived. He asks that you send a servant to fetch him when you have taken some refreshment and have rested.'

He was gone. A moment later a maidservant arrived with wine, cold meats and bread. 'Do you require anything else, Mistress Alice?'

When she departed, Gwen and I stood for a moment in the warmth of the brazier, gazing around at the pretty wall hangings depicting young men and women hawking, the large bed hung with gold and green curtains, and my best shift laid out ready. A washing basin stood beside a simmering kettle.

'Is this to be your chamber now?' Gwen wondered aloud.

'Surely not. Perhaps we were shown here for the surgeon's ease – so that we might be alone, and in a chamber near the King's household.' But I did wonder whether it signalled I was thought to be in danger, even in the palace, and so I was kept close to His

Grace's guards. I pushed aside my fear, too weary at the moment to consider it.

'The King's own surgeon!' Gwen breathed, and I read in her eyes a fear that perhaps I'd been more seriously injured than Dame Juliana had confided to her.

'Do not worry, Gwen. Look how well I rode, and walked all this way.' I considered the room, remembering how difficult it had been to share with the other women after having enjoyed my own beautiful bedchambers as Janyn's wife – usually with the man I loved. 'Oh, Gwen, what a gift to have a night in such a beautiful chamber, without the others. We must put all other thoughts from our minds and enjoy this!'

She smiled and clapped her hands.

By the next day Master Adam had pronounced me fit enough to go about my usual activities as long as I had a long rest in the afternoon. That evening Her Grace requested that I prepare her almond milk. While I sat with her a servant showed me the progress made on the beautiful clothing for the wedding festivities. A most enjoyable pastime.

'You shall have new gowns as well,' said Queen Philippa. 'Indeed, I have decided that after my eldest son and his new wife are thoroughly wed and have departed to Berkhamsted, you and I shall amuse ourselves by fitting you out with an entirely new set of clothes.' Her smile was enigmatic.

I had brought with me from my married life what I considered to be a gorgeous collection of gowns, capes, headdresses, shoes, jewellery, and other accoutrements suitable for a wealthy merchant's wife, and had added to them in my time at court. 'Your Grace, are my gowns displeasing to you?'

'They were suitable, Alice, but now you are a woman of the court.' She seemed about to say more, then waved me away. 'To bed with you. I shall need you tomorrow, so you must rest.'

'Your Grace, I called for a servant to move my belongings back to my usual bedchamber and he said that I am to remain in the private one. I think there is some confusion.'

'There is no confusion. Now off to bed!' She shooed me out of the room.

After my nap the following afternoon I felt much revived. I asked Gwen to help me go through my gowns and give me her opinion on their suitability for court. I could see her puzzlement, and recounted the Queen's comment.

'This chamber, the King's surgeon, the clothing . . .' She shook her head. 'It is as if your ordeal has caused the King and Queen to examine their parts in unravelling your family and they are trying to make amends.'

Our shared ordeal seemed to have removed any last constraint between mistress and maid. I squeezed her hand.

'You are one of my greatest blessings, Gwen,' I told her.

Her eyes filled with tears and her smile was uneven. 'God graced me when I joined your household, mistress.'

After a thorough study of my gowns we conceded that a few had been redone too many times – buttons, pearls and ribbons removed and replaced so often that the cloth was unevenly worn and holes and pulls remained, despite Gwen's best efforts. At last we stood thoughtfully regarding the pile of clothing on the bed.

'Well, what else?' I asked.

Gwen wrinkled her nose. 'Some of the fur is too long dead.'

This simple comment inspired laughter.

Later, when we hastened down to the Queen's hall, certain that I had been missed, we discovered Richard Stury pacing near the Countess Joan who was playing dice with my friend Maud.

The Countess, with a private smile, said, 'Would he not make a most fitting executioner, Alice?'

I pretended to consider him beneath my lashes, then shook my head. 'His arms are too thin, like a spindle. Who would fear him?'

We were laughing when the cause of our merriment approached me.

'Mistress Alice, you are to sup with His Grace the King this evening. I shall come to your chamber to escort you an hour earlier. Before the other guests arrive, he would speak with you about your recent ordeal in Oxford.' He bowed to me and withdrew.

Joan raised her eyebrows, a gleam in her eyes. 'It seems you are deriving good fortune from bad. A meal in the King's chamber! I wonder who else will be there?' She kicked the fur-trimmed hem of her gown as she turned towards me.

I recalled Gwen's comment about my own furs and smiled.

Maud studied me hard, her expression finally easing into a

smile. 'It is good to see you looking cheerful. Much better than I had expected, in fact. I trow you are sleeping more soundly without Jane and Agnes snoring in your ears.'

I was not at all surprised that the news of my new sleeping arrangements had been quickly passed around the Queen's household. 'I am.' I took a seat beside her.

'You must take this opportunity to ask His Grace to return William to court,' Maud said.

'A lover?' asked Joan. She did so delight in anything to do with mating.

'No, not a lover, but a good friend,' I said.

Maud wrinkled her nose and gave a little laugh as she shook her head, signalling that I was not being honest. It seemed to me a betrayal of my confidence. I had not seen this side of her before and was hurt and disappointed. I had thought her a friend, but a friend would not have spoken of William when I had not.

'Do you speak of William Wyndsor?' asked Joan.

'Yes, she does,' said Maud. I tried to nudge her foot beneath the table, wanting to silence her, but she prattled on. 'And he has declared his intention to wed her!'

I was taken aback by that. I had known he'd asked her of my availability, but not that he had spoken thus. And I had certainly not confided in Maud about his vowing to wed me.

Now Joan was very interested, leaning forward to whisper, 'Did you speak of your intention to wed him, Alice?'

I shook my head. 'No. We are not betrothed, I assure you.'

'Alas that it is Wyndsor.' A sympathetic frown creased her pretty forehead. 'For the King has need of him in Ireland, ensuring that Lionel succeeds in convincing the Irish to behave themselves. Wyndsor is part of the company sailing over to prepare the way for the Earl and his household.' Joan watched me closely as she spoke. 'Are you certain you did not respond in kind? You might be legally betrothed.'

'I did not.'

'Of course you might wed him and remain in Her Grace's household as long as you were not with child,' said Joan. 'It is only those who work the land who are always at home. Even merchants spend much of their time travelling to markets.'

I assured her that I had not thought about wedding Sir William. She watched me with an enigmatic expression.

'Have you dined with His Grace before?' Maud asked in the long pause that had followed my denial.

I shook my head.

'But you've often gone hawking with him alone, have you not?' Maud's look, her tone, were challenging.

'In the past, but not for a long while.' I excused myself and took my leave.

As I passed Joan, she touched my arm and said softly, for my ears only, 'I am your friend. Come to me if you are confused.'

I left the hall in a whirl of emotions. Once outside I could not think where I might find ease. I had thought Maud my friend, my only one in the Queen's household. But now it seemed she favoured me only for what gossip she might glean from me, and I was sorely disappointed. I should have seen the shape of her discourse before this: the searching questions, how she shared just enough to engage me. On a happier note, I was grateful for Countess Joan's kindness. The news of William's departure for Ireland relieved me too. Indeed, it was his good fortune that we were separated, for since my abduction in Oxford I had become keenly aware of the danger I might bring to anyone attached to me. It had been good of Countess Joan to tell me about him, and very kind of her to offer friendship, even if I could not imagine why she encouraged me to seek her out if I were confused. How could she be my friend, a woman about to wed the future King? Within days she would be *Princess* Joan. Once again I would be alone.

'Dame Alice?' Gwen stood behind me, holding a light mantle. 'Would you walk in the gardens?'

'I wish Geoffrey were here. Or my sister Mary.' I held out my hand. 'Walk with me, Gwen. Be my friend.'

We walked and walked while I related the conversation.

'I am sorry that Maud has proved false,' said Gwen. 'But how kind of the Countess.'

'I want to think it kind, but do not dare to count on her. She is soon to be a princess, Gwen. Why should she befriend me?'

'Is it not possible that some at court are sincere?'

All too soon it was time to dress for the evening. I chose my prettiest gown: a red fitted bodice and sleeves with a swirling pattern and a skirt the colour of dark berries. The buttons on the bodice and sleeves were silver. Gwen dressed my hair in soft loops round my ears, gathered in a silver crespinette and held by a silver fillet.

At the door to the King's parlour, Stury held out his arm to stop Gwen.

'You will wait with me out here,' he said. 'I shall send for some food and wine, and a brazier to warm you.'

Gwen fussed a moment longer with my dress. 'Perhaps I should not have accompanied you. Perhaps it is not appropriate.'

I squeezed her hand, and then nodded to the page that I was ready to be announced.

Splendid in a short green jacket embroidered in silver thread in a plantagenet pattern, the King strode across the room to me and embraced me, kissing me on the forehead.

As ever, his ready intimacy flustered me. Surely he must perceive how I felt about him, how he affected me.

'My sweet Alice. God be praised.' He held me at arm's length. 'I heard that it was a terrible ordeal. But you look well. More than well. You are quite beautiful this evening.'

'Your Grace, I am honoured to be invited to sup with you.' I did not dare look into his eyes but stared instead at his long-toed shoes.

He put his hands on my shoulders – no gloves this time – and I felt the heat of them, and of his gaze.

'You shall not be harmed again, Alice. I swear to you. My mother's curse on your life ends now.'

He pulled me closer, and bent his head to kiss my forehead again, then, lifting my chin, kissed me on the mouth. Gently. Oh so gently. But his hands slid behind my shoulder blades and caressed me in a way that was anything but chaste.

'My lord,' I whispered when he released me. I still had not dared look into his face. My head was spinning with desire, fear, sadness. 'Your Grace, what are you about?' It sounded too harsh. How dare I question the King? 'If it please Your Grace, I am confused.'

'Look at me, Alice.' His voice was gentle. 'Look at me.'

At last I did raise my eyes to his and saw great tenderness

there, and something else, a yearning. His gaze held me, and I knew great danger. I felt how easily I might lose my self and my soul, how willingly I might succumb to his desire.

'You know what I am about. What we are about. It began with the hawking. We are kindred souls, Alice.'

We were, we were – but I felt myself shaking my head. 'You are my King.' If he had been any other man, I would not be so frightened. Would not mind how his touch aroused me.

'But in my private hours I am a man like any other. You shall come to see that.'

'Your Grace,' I murmured, too confused and frightened to say more. I did not want to be one of his quickly discarded mistresses. He said we were kindred souls – but for how long? Until he discovered a woman who shared some of his other interests . . . music, perhaps, a singer with a voice matched perfectly to his? And then what would happen to me? Surely Queen Philippa knew of his liaisons. What would happen to Bella if I fell from grace?

Yet I could not help but thrill to what he was suggesting.

'When we are alone, I would have you call me Edward.'

I merely nodded, not trusting my voice. If he were not King . . .

He drew me to him once more and kissed me on both cheeks. His hands on my shoulders were gentle but proprietary, his eyes dark with desire. 'Alice, do not fear me.' Finally he kissed my hands, then stepped away. 'Now, before the others arrive, you must tell me all that you recall of that night.'

How easily he moved into normal conversation. My mind and heart could not perform these lightning shifts. Stupidly, I stared at his boots and worked to calm my thoughts.

'They will soon arrive, Alice.' He forced his voice to stay calm, but I sensed his impatience.

'I recall very little.' I told him then all I remembered. 'My maid-servant was awake during the attack and might tell you much more. She awaits me in the ante-chamber, with Master Stury.'

'Summon her.'

Gwen seemed far more composed than I felt as she described the attack and counter-attack. Edward asked some questions which she answered. When he was satisfied he thanked her for her account and for her loyalty to me, and then gave her leave to depart.

I was daring to look at him more closely than before. I saw the way he'd given Gwen his complete attention. I also noticed fine lines around his eyes and deeper ones beside his mouth. Signs of age. The Queen had recently spoken of his being in his fiftieth year. He might be my father, yet he was nothing like. So alive, so exciting.

'Master Stury told me little. Who were those men, Your G—'

He shook his head, mouthing his name.

'Edward,' I said, though it almost caught in my throat. I feared I might have crossed a boundary I was not yet ready to leave behind. I feared my own desire for his touch.

He smiled at my use of his name, but then grew serious. 'As was your late husband's practice, I would tell you as little as necessary. To protect you.' He tilted his head and regarded me with a look that seemed to say he expected me to be satisfied with such an answer.

Despite my fear, I trusted him. I never doubted his sincerity. But if we were indeed friends, well, then he should know me in all my stubbornness. 'As I argued with Janyn and with the Lady Isabella, those who would harm my family have no reason to believe I know nothing. They will come after me again to find out what they want to know. As they did in Oxford.'

Edward bowed his head, his hands clasped behind him. I held my breath, waiting for the revelation that would explain my torment of the past years. I feared it would be something far too trivial to have cost so many lives; feared it would be so significant that I would be forced to endure a lifetime of pain.

'In good time, Alice.'

I opened my mouth to protest. He put a finger to my lips.

'I will tell you this. Your husband's family was beset on either side: by those who expected them to sell what they knew, and by those who wanted to force them to tell what they knew. Members of my family and powerful barons are on both sides, as well as wealthy merchants who hope to make powerful alliances. But now that they all know without a doubt you are under my protection, they will desist.'

'Is that why my attackers had to die?'

It was a suffocating sensation, having those remarkable blue eyes fixed on me with such intensity. When he suddenly broke the spell and shook his head, I almost lost my balance.

'Surely you would not expect me to allow them to go free? What punishment would you have preferred? That they die slowly in a dungeon, deprived of food and water, of sunlight and the Sacraments? Was death then too easy?'

'No!' I made the Sign of the Cross, banishing the horrors he had described. 'But I would have preferred to talk to them first, to question them about my husband and his parents.'

'That is not your part to play, Alice.'

His air of finality infuriated me. 'What of my daughter? What if someone were to take Bella to force my hand? How am I to live with such a fear, Edward?'

'You have nothing to fear, sweet Alice. My sister fully understands the danger to your daughter.' He drew me to him. 'I told you, they shall not harm you or your daughter. Those who dared harm you died in the attempt, the survivor executed. That should serve to warn those who would try such a thing again.'

This time I did not respond, but merely endured his embrace. I did not understand how I could both thrill to his nearness and chafe under his control. When he released me, I asked if I might withdraw to my chamber.

'No, Alice.' He did not say this in anger, but his expression was serious and his tone firm. 'I want my household to know you better.'

But what of his Queen? To introduce me to his household . . . I was to have no privacy, no choice. Once so presented, I was forever branded.

Yet, in truth, I was already believed to have taken the King as my lover, ever since Sheppey. Had already been tried and found guilty.

I concentrated on breathing through my panic. I told myself that this was what my heart had inwardly desired, that I might find a way to gratitude and even joy in it.

Prince Edward and his bride, Princess Joan, shone in green and white robes heavy with precious gems and pearls at their wedding feast, and all their households wore the same colours, including Joan's sons by Thomas Holland. The couple looked so happy –

Prince Edward even managed to dance with grace. It was a bitter-sweet day for me, evoking memories of my own joyous wedding, yet I was happy for Joan. And very happy for myself, for Edward had fulfilled his promise that Bella would attend in his sister Joan's company. I had not seen my daughter for months.

The King ignored me during the festivities, not once to my knowledge looking my way. To see him in such an official role, the white-haired King glorious in robes emblazoned with his heraldic devices, conferring his blessing on his heir, I wondered how I had ever thought he might desire me. Surely it had all been but a dream.

My delight rested solely in my Bella's presence, her eagerness to see me, the sweetness of her embrace. Geoffrey declared her the most beautiful creature in the great hall, and she giggled and twirled and curtsied with delight at his compliments. We shared but a few days of sweetness, all too few, and then she was swept away once more to Hertford.

So began a time in which Edward and I played an increasingly strange game of cat and mouse. I was included in his morning hawking parties and in informal dinners in his chamber with members of his household. But he did not kiss me, did not touch me. I was intoxicated by his presence and terrified of the enormity of what seemed to lie ahead.

In between these engagements, Queen Philippa insisted on participating in the planning of my new clothes, observing my fittings, inspecting the work before it was finished. I argued against all but a few of the silks and velvets, but my resistance was often overruled by the Queen. She favoured all shades of red from rose to purple for me, as well as deep golds and indigo, adamantly refusing any suggestion of mourning or widow's weeds. Indigo was always combined with a brighter colour. My confessions and prayers were filled with my guilty delight in these sensuous fabrics and splendid colours. Dom Creswell seemed amused by my urge for restraint. I did not dare confess to the true sins in my heart, my betrayal of the Queen in every smile I gave Edward.

He and I were never alone during this time. He was always courteous and complimentary, but no more. Though on one occasion he revealed that he paid close attention to my appearance – or perhaps Philippa had commented on the need for extra fittings, which irked her. He sent Master Adam to enquire as to the cause of the shadows beneath my eyes and my dwindling weight.

For the first time in my life I was sleeping so lightly that the slightest sound woke me, and upon waking was beset with the fear that strangers were in my chamber. Of course, it was the memory of the attempted abduction in Oxford that haunted me, for though the men were dead I yet feared that, as it had happened once, it could happen again. Master Adam suggested a sleeping draught.

'Then I should be truly helpless.'

'You are safe, Mistress Alice. You are in the King's protection.' Looking down his great hawk-like nose at me, he clearly thought I was a fool for doubting my safety.

'I was in the King's protection when I was attacked, Master Adam.'

He snorted. I did not take the draught.

Queen Philippa too noted my weight loss and that I looked as if I were not sleeping. She listened to my explanation with sympathy. She shared with me her own reason for melancholy: that she had so much pain in her pelvis she would never bear another child, and that she and the King now lived as brother and sister, not husband and wife. Then she declared that she would find something to cheer me. To cheer us both.

I had heard previous speculation from the women waiting on Her Grace that her riding accident had ruined her for sexual pleasure, and that shortly afterwards her courses had stopped. However, I had never heard her speak of this herself. I felt honoured by her confidence, sad for her, and unsettled by a sense that she was absolving me from guilt. The new gowns, this confidence . . . I became increasingly convinced that I was being prepared to become Edward's mistress, a realisation both thrilling and terrifying.

As we prepared for the Christmas court, the Queen's inspiration to cheer us both was that we should dazzle the court with light, drawing it to us wherever we walked. She grew quite merry as we discussed, planned and chose bright, shiny fabrics and jewels. She hugged me often. Gradually my sleep improved.

I do not think it was so much because of the work, though I enjoyed it, but because of the Queen's relaxed affection. I felt more a part of her life than I had done before, part of her extended family. That went farther in reassuring me of my safety than anything else.

But there was still danger of a different sort. Not Isabella's curse but Edward's desire, and mine. One morning in November I entered my chamber to find a length of the most beautiful, soft, richly dyed crimson cloth – escarlatte, the Queen of wools – on my bed, with a note from Edward, sealed with a signet I came to know well.

'What better colour for hawking? E.'

The King was a canny hunter.

So was I.

At the Christmas court the Queen wore gowns with so many jewels and pearls to catch the light that she did indeed seem to dazzle. So, too, did I. Geoffrey told me of the continuous murmurings among the knights about the Queen's intentions for me, for surely my new clothes were meant to exhibit me in the best light to promising suitors. Once he dared to ask whether I was being displayed to the King, for of course he had heard the gossip about how I was now included in the intimate circle who enjoyed dinners and hawking with Edward.

His words verified my fear that all at court saw the royal couple's design for me. Of course they would note that Philippa dressed me as a younger version of herself. Of course all knew that I attended Edward's dinners, and that we hunted and hawked, sometimes without companions. I assured Geoffrey that Edward and I were never alone of late, but felt like Criseyde, being dressed to impress the King. And who was my Troilus? Janyn? Would he look down on me from Heaven and think me a faithless wife? What I was being drawn into was sin, no matter how sincere my love for Edward, for he could never wed me.

If Philippa's purpose was that her husband should notice me, she was successful in her unholy goal. He seemed most drawn to my low-cut bodices, and made no attempt to hide the hunger in his eyes when they dwelt on me. Indeed, he often caught my attention, and then held my gaze for a moment before looking down again at my breasts. He knew what he was about. Had he been bold enough to lift my skirts, he would have found me most ready to yield, God help me.

Janyn was gone. I believed that now. And I had been too happily wed and too long abandoned. My body yearned for a man's attention, and that man was my King.

So on the fateful early-spring day when I arrived at the mews and discovered only Edward there, I knew where our morning's sport would lead, and, God forgive me, I was more than ready, I was eager.

On that morning I wore red beneath a short, Lincoln green cloak lined in *gris*, but my red skirt was prominent, and my red hat. Blood red, cut from the escarlatte Edward had given me. He wore a jacket and leggings of the deep purple called *purpura*. He wore it well. We shone like jewels as we rode through the woods to the marsh. It was early-April. We were enjoying our last days at Sheen before leaving for the St George's Day festivities at Windsor. An early-morning mist swirled along the ground, helping me imagine I was riding into a dream, a space outside time.

We hunted with falcons that morning. Mine, when I stroked him, looked sharply into my eyes for a heartbeat then turned to gaze away, ready for the hunt. As always, looking into his eyes, sensing his wildness and the potential damage he could wreak with beak and claws, I thrilled to the bond between us: two predators, who might so easily kill each other, joining to hunt. We could not speak to one another, could not make a pact, and yet we trusted, we touched, we thrilled to the power we shared.

The falconer and a boy had gone ahead to choose the best area of the marsh while another boy and the dogs waited with us. The two returned with news of herons and ducks very near. We were cautious in our approach, the need for silence adding to the excitement. My falcon saw the birds before I did, suddenly leaning away from me. I felt his tension. The dogs flushed out a heron. I held my breath, my heart pounding, as I released my falcon. I watched him climb, then dive. The heron rose, so awkward until airborne, then so graceful. I almost regretted the skill of my bird as he swooped and struck. The falconer sent the best swimmer to pluck up the catch. My falcon returned to my glove, his feathers quivering, blood on his claws and beak. I murmured my admiration.

Edward's bird was now aloft, diving down towards a duck, and quickly afterwards his took a heron as mine went for another duck. We laughed and congratulated one another with our eyes. Edward had once told me that the lack of human voices during the hunt brought him a strange peace – strange to find peace in the midst of the brutality of sudden death. But I had understood . . . the cries of the birds, the rush of wings, the panting of the falconer's dogs, the sudden baying.

The falconer and his boys were busy with the prey as Edward now moved close to me, his eyes shining. He looked glorious in the *purpura*, his long white hair wild beneath his hat, his face ruddy with the early-morning chill and the riding, his blue eyes piercingly beautiful and intensely focused, his posture straight and soldierly. He leaned towards me and wiped my cheek. Matted feathers dropped on to my lap.

'Blooded,' he said as he put a proprietary hand on my thigh. And looked me in the eyes as if in challenge.

I laughed, feeling reckless and alive.

'Your wildness draws me, Alice. You know that. When you are one with your hawk, your horse, at ease in the woodland – that is when I most desire you.'

Though my gut clenched in fear I slowly smiled, for I could not deny to myself that I liked the way he touched me. I liked it very much. We played a dangerous game and one that I would not have chosen had I any say, not because it would be distasteful – I found Edward desirable in every way – but because he could never be my lawful husband. But I was thrilled to have caught the heart of the King – or, at least, his eye and desire.

Seeing so clearly now that I had no choice, that he had chosen, I thought I might at least play with all my heart, as I rode, as I hawked. I prayed that I might also keep my wits about me. We had been approaching this moment for a long while, but in my wildest imaginings the Alice whom the King undressed and caressed was older, wiser, more experienced. I was but myself, uncertain and overwhelmed by the power this man, this king, wielded against mightier folk than I would ever be. In my daydreams I *chose* to lie with him. But I understood, I felt in his touch, his eyes, that the choice was really his, and I saw that he had been luring me for a long while, subtly, patiently, oh, so skilfully.

If there was a way to refuse a King, I had not learned it. Nor would I.

After the hunt Edward simply said we would retire to his chambers. As we rode back to the palace he entertained me with his wit and snatches of song – he had a rich, deep voice. In his chamber he offered me brandywine. It seemed a heady drink for mid-morning, and too heating, for though it had been cold on the marsh I felt a sheen of sweat beneath my gown and knew my face was flushed with my body's own heat. But a few sips helped calm my trembling – until he took me in his arms and kissed me with a rough passion that left me weak with fear and desire, in such a powerful and confusing mix that I pushed out of his embrace and turned away from him.

What am I doing? I asked myself in something like panic. The enormity of what this meant, to lie with my mistress's husband, my *Queen's* husband, stopped me.

The King had removed his jacket. The linen shirt beneath it exposed white hair on his chest mixed with dark blond. With his long pale hair and beard, he caught the light from the fire and seemed more than human. He reached for my hand.

'I am frightened, Edward.'

He put his hands on my shoulders and gave me a gentle shake. 'Look into my eyes and say that you do not want me to make love to you.'

I looked into his eyes and felt myself drifting down into their depths. I felt welcome, warm. I leaned closer to him despite my fear.

He stroked my throat as he would his hawk. 'Alice,' he whispered. He dropped his hands and took a step backward. 'The motto I first used for a great tournament was, "It is what it is". I accepted what God brought my way. I vowed to face without faltering all that He presented to me and to find the best way to conquer it. You would be wise to resolve to do as I did. You are a young, beautiful, desirable, wise widow who has caught the heart of her King. Take him and keep him well, Alice. Welcome him into your heart and body, and he will care for you with such devotion and passion you will never regret it. He promises.'

'My lord, my body and my heart are willing. Do not doubt it. But I am bound in duty to the Queen. How can I betray her in such wise? For this seems the very worst betrayal.'

He bowed his head, his long, pale hair falling forward a little. I almost reached out to touch the silken, silvery strands.

'My beloved Philippa is consumed by pain. To lie with her would cause her such torment that it would be a grievous sin on my part. She knows that I am yet a man, Alice. My Queen is no fool.'

He reached for my hands, brought them to his chest so that I might feel the pounding of his heart.

His words had reminded me of Philippa's veiled blessing on our union. I had been readied for this without anyone asking whether or not it pleased me. I was yet a pawn. But looking at the King, seeing his desire, I sensed I yet held some power.

It gave me the courage to say what was in my own heart. 'I have a memory of love that is not yet in the past for me, Edward. Can you tell me that you know for certain Janyn is dead? And will you promise me that my daughter Bella will be brought into the court where I may raise her?'

He closed his eyes and made an odd sound.

'Can you also promise that you will not discard me in a few weeks?'

He pulled me close, his hands moving down to the small of my back. 'You would bargain with me, Alice? Like a merchant's wife?'

'I *am* a merchant's wife, Edward.'

He pushed me away so suddenly I lost my balance and stumbled into a chair. 'You are a merchant's *widow*, Alice,' he said, his voice rough with frustration. I had never seen him look so angry, his blue eyes pale in his flushed face, his long white hair wild. He frightened me. 'Janyn Perrers is dead. You were right to doubt that he died of the pestilence . . . he died by a murderer's hands, strangled and then stabbed through the heart.' He spat the words out as if to stab me in turn.

Though I feared him, the manner in which he was telling me what I had begged to hear infuriated me. I rose up and slapped my King's cheek. I slapped it as hard as I could. He grabbed my fist then scooped me up and carried me through the curtains to his bedchamber, throwing me down on the bed and roughly reaching beneath my skirts. I grabbed his hand. His eyes burned into me.

'My lord!' I cried.

The fire left his face. He let go of me and crossed himself.

'If you want me, take me as a lover. Naked, both of us. As equals in lovemaking.'

For a long while we stared at one another, gradually calming.

At last he said, 'As equals in love.' He smiled and rose to remove his shirt and leggings. His great, strong body was not so beautiful as Janyn's. Scars tugged at his skin, and it sagged a little with age. And yet I wanted him.

I slipped off the bed and undressed, pushing away his hands when he would hurry me, smiling and shaking my head.

At last he lifted me up and I wrapped my legs around him. He entered me easily and cried out as I moved around him. Too soon he came, too soon.

Afterwards he lifted me on top of him and gathered my breasts between his palms, sucking and tugging at my nipples with his teeth until I ached so with desire that I cried out. Only then did he enter me once more and possess me.

He had promised nothing but that I would be grateful. But once I had tasted his body I could not turn away from him.

II-5

> *'Hire armes smale, hire streghte bak and softe,*
> *Hire sydes longe, flesshly, smothe, and white*
> *He gan to stroke, and good thrift bad ful ofte*
> *Hire snowissh throte, hire brestes rounde and lite.*
> *Thus in this hevene he gan hym to delite . . .'*
>
> – Geoffrey Chaucer, *Troilus and Criseyde*, III, ll. 1247–1251

1362

After our first lovemaking, both of us riding the powerful waves of passion, anger and release, I woke to myself. The image of what Edward had told me of Janyn's death overwhelmed me and I turned away from him, sick with grief.

'What is it, sweet Alice? Did I hurt you?' He stroked my hair.

His tender concern melted the ice around my heart and my tears began to flow. *Janyn, Janyn, my first love, my husband. Murdered. His beautiful body bereft of breath and then torn open.* I did not know how I could ever bear the pain of imagining the agony of his last moments.

'Is it what I told you of your husband?'

I cried out, and Edward held me.

'There is no shame in grief for a beloved,' he said.

I slept, waking to find those incredibly blue eyes watching me.

'Alice,' he whispered, stroking my breasts, my thighs. I moved beneath his touch, and he eased himself on to me. We made slow, gentle love. I found comfort in it.

'I swear that I will not abandon you,' he said afterwards. We lay side by side, holding hands in quiet contentment. 'And when I deem it time, Bella will be with you.'

In mid-afternoon, Gwen was summoned to dress me so that I might move through the palace to my chamber without causing more gossip than had already been stirred up by my relationship with the King. Gwen's hands trembled as she helped me with my shift, whispering of her worry, her fear. With gentle care she undid my headdress and wrapped it so that it draped about my face and neck, hiding evidence of the King's beard on my tender flesh.

Once back in my chamber, Gwen's voice broke as she asked, 'What will the Queen do to you?'

'I do not know, but I believed His Grace when he said that he would take care of me.' I took off my headdress and sank down on a bench by the little window. There I sat for a long while, a cup of wine in hand, staring out at the birds chasing one another. Somehow the violent details of Janyn's death had renewed my mourning, as if I had held on to a belief until then that he would miraculously reappear. I envied the birds. It was mating season, after all, and I was a hen. I wondered what they did when they lost a partner. Birds had no souls. They did not pray over their choices. But it was said that swans mated for life. I wondered what a widowed swan did. Once the cygnets were flown, did she live out her days in mournful solitude? I imagined that most female birds with young would welcome a male to help them protect the nest. But would they welcome the attention of a King who had his own nest to tend? Would they have a choice? Had I simply been foolish to think that, like the swan, I had mated with Janyn for life? It had always been likely that I would outlive him, for he'd been twenty years my senior. I had not wanted to think beyond my happiness with him.

When I noticed that as Gwen moved about the room she was casting worried glances at me, I thought it best to share with her the shocking news.

'His Grace told me that Janyn was murdered – strangled and stabbed through the heart. I do not know how I shall ever have the courage to tell Bella how her father died. Or if it would be best to let her continue to believe he died of the pestilence.'

I wept then. Gwen joined me on the bench, praying and weeping with me, as if she, too, had held back the full force of her grief until now. We prayed for Janyn's soul, and then we shared memories, talking of his many virtues and graces.

When I rose from our private requiem it was as if my heart had opened and I was able both to mourn Janyn and rejoice in the promise of Bella's return. I hesitated to rejoice in the King's affection. Though I believed he would honour his promise not to abandon me, that promise could be fulfilled in ways other than by keeping me as his mistress, such as seeing that I remained comfortable in the Queen's household or finding a man who would wed me despite the gossip. I was honoured and a little giddy to have caught the passion of my King. Yet I had been at court long enough to know that the moment courtiers had begun gossiping about Edward and me, I had become a target of their sharp and cruel wits, and it was yet possible Edward would find it necessary to abandon me. I tried not to imagine more lovemaking, but of course that was exactly where my thoughts wandered, and my body responded as if he were indeed touching me. I felt like a wilting flower that had been watered. God had created my body to receive a lover, to rejoice in union. When Janyn had first entered me I had known completion, known a profound pleasure, and had not been ashamed. Neither was I ashamed now. Edward completed me. I felt a part of life once more.

Late in the afternoon the Queen sent for me to join her and several other women working on an embroidered altar cloth. Gwen's eyes were like those of a cornered puppy as she arranged my hair and headdress to cover the marks on my neck. I was frightened as well. I did not know what to expect. My own red eyes stared back at me from the mirror. Grief was not so easily disguised.

The Queen greeted me with affection. She did not enquire about the signs of tears. I wondered if perhaps she had already spoken to the King and knew that the cause was my widowhood, one of the topics we did not discuss before the other women.

But the others were sympathetic, asking if I was unwell or if I'd received unhappy news. We all feared the return of the pestilence with the spring weather.

'I had a bad dream,' I said. 'Do you ever have a dream that frightens you so much that in the dream you try to wake yourself up, only to move to another dream?'

'Oh, yes, I do!' said Lady Eleanor.

'Is that not very strange and frightening, to think you are awake and then see something you've been told can only be found in dreams?' said young Philippa de Roet. She and her sister Katherine were beginning to join the women for needlework and such. They had both proved skilful, particularly Pippa as she was called.

The Queen smiled to herself as she bent over her needlework.

I attended her that evening. She did not mention Edward, but she did know that I had been told how Janyn died.

'May he rest in the peace of salvation,' she said, kissing me on the forehead. 'Queen Joan will of course say nothing of this to young Bella. She will learn of it from you in good time.'

That Bella would be told the truth of her father's death by anyone but me had never entered my mind.

'You will wish to arrange for Masses for Janyn's one year obit here at the chapel.'

I felt as if I were outside my body, observing the two of us discussing Masses for my husband's soul. It seemed impossible that it was only a year since he had disappeared. So much had happened, I felt I had changed utterly.

I wondered whether Philippa had just received word of how Janyn had died or whether she had been biding her time until someone slipped and told me.

'What of Dame Tommasa, his mother?' I asked. 'Do you know how she died, Your Grace?'

Fussing with her cushions, a signal to me that I was not seeing to her comfort, she said, 'I know no more than you do, Alice. Let us talk no more of death. We have festivities to plan – St George's Day is not so far away.'

I bent to adjust the pillows. Her behaviour left me unsettled, uncertain whether or not she knew what had happened between me and her husband. Her husband . . . *Jesu*! I trembled as I sat beside the Queen, pretending to look at fabrics and jewels.

As we looked at a red cloth woven in a small, vine-like pattern, she said, quite casually, 'You were a vision of ripe womanhood in that red escarlatte riding gown, Alice. We must dress you in red more often. And pearls. Though low-born, you are a beauty, and precious to us.' She squeezed my hand, but did not look up from the fabric.

She had seen me at some point with Edward. *We must dress you . . . Ripe . . . precious to us.* I could not believe she meant to reassure me that I was doing what she wished, but could not think how else to interpret her words.

On the following night, shortly after I'd retired to my chamber, the King's page appeared to summon me to Edward. Fortunately I had not yet disrobed.

Gwen was beside herself – how was I to get my rest, how would she prepare me for bed? How indeed. All this was outside any sort of life for which I had been readied. Though excited, I was filled with unease. Was I now his plaything, to be at his beck and call, with no life of my own? He had encouraged me to spread my wings, but I feared that his own shackles might destroy all he claimed to love in me. Then I must go to him willingly, hungrily.

Servants were arranging cots for the sergeants-at-arms who slept in the outer chamber. They glanced my way and quickly averted their eyes. When I was shown into the King's chamber, he was already in a simple robe and barefoot. He crossed the room to me, picked me up and carried me to the bed. He lay there beside me and guided my hand to his groin, showing me how his body anticipated the pleasure to come. He asked me to undress. Slowly. Near the fire, so that I was not in shadow. When I was naked, Edward came to me and lifted me up. I wrapped my legs round him, and he slid into me so easily we both laughed. Wicked, wanton laughs.

'We are birds of prey, Alice my love, with no thought of spiritual life. There is only the flesh. Our flesh. Our hunger.'

In the morning, Gwen woke me. The King had already risen. On his pillow was a large pearl, and a note: *'The first of many. E.'*

In a few days the court removed to Windsor to prepare for the St George's Day festivities. With so many expected, I once more shared a chamber with Maud and other higher born ladies whose husbands could not be present. On those nights I was called away, I would return in the early-morning to dress for Mass and then perhaps hawking. None of the ladies, not even Maud, asked where I had spent the night. Not for a moment did I doubt they knew. That they were so cautious in their looks and speech emphasised for me the rank of my lover. When away from Edward I was beset by doubts and fears, not at all easy in my mind. But my heart was constant, and I felt a bond between us that was strong and true. I would strive to keep it so.

Edward and I had resumed hawking together at Windsor, in company. I was included in his private dinners with members of his household and old friends. I found it exciting to catch him watching me then. Our secret. Our sin.

When Joan arrived with Prince Edward, she summoned me to walk with her in the gardens. She looked more beautiful than ever, her face radiant, her clothes subtly revealing that she was with child.

She saw that I'd noticed and her face opened up into a most beatific smile as she touched her stomach. 'With God's grace, I may be carrying a future King.'

She kissed me on both cheeks then stood back to study me: my face, my pretty new gown. She startled me by pressing my belly. 'You are not with child, are you? But then, I think it might be too soon to know.'

'You have heard about the King and me?' She had not been at court since Christmas. But even before she responded, I thought how foolish I was to think she might not know.

'That the King has taken you for his mistress? Oh, yes, I do. The two Edwards send messengers back and forth with news of the realm and their daily activities.' She affectionately kissed my cheek. 'My Edward's father is like a child boasting about you, Alice. Be glad. Let your heart rejoice.' Then she grew serious. 'I must speak to my maid, have her give your Gwen the recipe for a physick you must take before you go to him, and one you must take if, despite this precaution, you quicken. You do not want a royal bastard.'

It frightened me that messengers carried news of our liaison. I had hoped that as long as we said nothing, it would remain merely a rumour. I had begged Edward to speak of us to no one. I must have made a face, which Joan misread.

She shook her head at me. 'You cannot afford to be foolish. Even with my royal blood, though I have never denied my fleshly desires, I've heeded the dangers and done all that I could to protect myself. I would be sorry to see you suffer.'

In truth, my heart and my head were at war over the issue. I feared such precautions would take the passion out of our lovemaking and might sicken me. And yet I did not wish any child of mine to be a bastard.

Joan patted her belly again. 'Of course you are but nineteen and dream of more children. I assure you, such physics will not ruin you for a future husband. I have taken them, and had no difficulty conceiving.'

I thanked her for the advice, and guided our talk to the roster of guests arriving for the festivities.

The conversation left me keenly aware of how vulnerable my position was. We had talked for a long while, and in all that time Joan had not asked how I felt about being chosen by the King. I had sensed that she could not conceive of my being anything but grateful, and that she would not welcome any expression of doubt. I wished I might go to my sister, to Nan, to Dame Agnes. But I would only frighten them if I described my situation. Plainly I had no choice. I was *his* choice, and he was King. To them he was more than human, and they would hardly dare advise me.

Such was the flaw, the imperfection in our union, that undermined our love: the power he held over me.

How strange then that it was Edward who reassured me on this point. One night after our lovemaking he noticed my tears and asked if I was thinking of Janyn again. I thought to lie and say yes, that it was grief that filled my heart. While I was still weighing this, he asked another question.

'How can I comfort you?'

I believed that only the truth might serve me. 'I am frightened. I fear what will happen to me when you discard me.'

He drew me to him and kissed my forehead. 'Alice, my sweet Alice, why are you so certain I'll prove faithless?'

'It is said that you have discarded women after a fortnight, again and again. I cannot think why I might be different.'

'And you believed the gossip?'

His sad tone gave me pause. I had not thought to question the rumours. I propped myself up on one elbow so that I might look him in the eyes. 'Is it not true?'

I found it endearing how the skin crinkled around his eyes when he smiled, as he did now, an affectionate smile, a reassuring smile.

'I have strayed from my Queen before, but seldom. Though I have often enjoyed the companionship of pretty young women, most of them have been disappointed by how chastely we dined and talked. The few to whom I have made love still enjoy my protection and discretion.' He dabbed at my tears with the counterpane, then kissed my lips. 'You will be ever near me, my comfort and my delight,' he declared.

'And when you tire of me?'

'I shall never tire of you.'

I wanted so to believe that. 'But what if you do?'

'Then I shall find you a husband. Someone worthy of you. But I do not like to think of that.'

His voice had sharpened and it was that change in tone rather than all his reassurances which made me believe him, or at least accept that he believed he would not tire of me.

'I shall owe you much if that day ever comes, for I feel as if you have returned my youth and vigour to me, Alice. But I would owe you for more than that. I fear I have not been so discreet about our liaison as I have been with other lovers. In truth, I do not wish to be. I confess, I have boasted to my close friends how you have renewed me.'

I felt sick to my stomach. 'And are the pearls part of your pennace?'

For each night or day we lay together, Edward gave me one large pearl or several small ones.

'No, the pearls are not signs of penance,' said Edward. 'I have told you what I wish.' He wished me to wear them on my gowns, my headdresses, my slippers or in my hair, so that whenever he saw me he would know that I cherished him. 'They are not so much gifts for you as for me. And so you must tell me what I might give you for you – what is your heart's desire?'

'My heart's desire?' I could not think what to ask for.

'Search your heart, my sweet Alice.'

What I truly wanted was to be with Bella and to give her brothers and sisters, legitimate children fathered by a man who was free to wed me. But even as I formed this wish I felt torn, being otherwise so happy with Edward. How could I not cherish his love? What things might I ask for beyond the beautiful clothes and jewels, the hawks and horses, the fabulous surroundings? I owned Fair Meadow, and Richard Lyons held the house in London for me, and though I could not use either home until such time as Edward felt it was safe for me to do so, I felt reassured by knowing I might return to them someday. The tenements in Oxford provided the income to maintain my homes. Beyond that, in order to ensure that Bella had the opportunities that Janyn and I had wanted for her, I needed to build on the foundation he had left me using the training he had given me.

I thought about his emphasis on the acquisition of land. He had believed that though a man acquired gold, jewels, silks and spices, if he did not own land, if he had no rents, he was merely a merchant. Land brought respect and a voice in civic matters. He had told me that my father's one flaw was his neglect of this part of his potential. If a man did not step into the civic arena, he was irresponsible. Selfish. Although as a woman I had no place in civic affairs, extensive landholdings would provide me with a status that would attract eligible suitors for my daughter. It was essential I achieve a status in my own right that might overshadow any taint from my liaison with the King.

'Property,' I said when I was next with Edward. 'I wish for more land and city rents in my name. For myself and Bella.' Inwardly I cringed at how acquisitive I sounded, but reminded myself of the loss of reputation I suffered from this liaison.

We were lying in Edward's great bed, wrapped in delicately scented silk bedclothes, with a casement wide open to invite within the soothing sound of a spring rain. Now he propped himself up on some pillows and looked down at me. I lay flat, stretching my limbs. He ran his hand from the middle of my breastbone to the soft hair between my legs, then idly stroked my nearest thigh. 'I am glad you have given this some thought. You are so young. You will live on long after I am dead, and I want to leave you with a comfortable income, worthy of a King's mistress. I would grant you a life of ease. I had not thought of property, but it does seem precisely what you need. As I recall, that is why you had left our party for Oxford – to view a tenement near one you already owned. Did you take it?'

'I did. It was so close to the other that Dom Hanneye can easily manage both, and the first has profited me well.'

'You speak of such things with confidence. I recall your pride in speaking of how much you had learned about trade from your husband and father. What else did you learn from your late husband?'

Even at such a moment, secure in Edward's love, I held my breath in anticipation of the pain inherent in conjuring up that happy time, receding now so quickly into long ago. 'Before our betrothal I had never ridden a horse or held a hawk.'

'Such an innocent!'

'Nor had I been outside London.'

'He opened up the world to you.'

Memories of those joyous days overwhelmed me for a moment. How sweet they had been.

Edward took my hand and kissed it. 'You loved him very much.'

'With all my heart and soul,' I whispered.

'I pray that you can forgive me for the manner in which I told you of his murder.'

I took a deep breath to steady my voice. 'It is the absence of him that tightens my throat, the thought of him suffering, not how it was told me.'

We talked into the night then of how my life had changed with my betrothal to Janyn. It was an evening that brought Edward and me closer as friends, sharing food and wine, laughing, even teasing one another, and for me it was a turning point, lending me more assurance. I felt it was extra security for me to be Edward's companion, someone with whom he enjoyed being, both in and out of bed. I believed he might be more faithful to a friend than to a lover.

'I shall include you more often in my dinners with merchants,' he said. 'It will be most helpful to me to hear your impressions.'

I began to see how I might fit into his world, and that was a comfort to me. But I also regularly drank the bitter mixture Gwen had learned to prepare.

I did not see Edward every day, managing to find a balance, a way to live what seemed a double life, between the public and the very private. I noticed others again, paying attention to my friends Geoffrey, Richard, the de Roet sisters, as well as the other women of the Queen's chamber and my mistress herself.

Sadly, it was becoming increasingly plain to all at court that

Her Grace was ailing. As far as I knew she had never been a beauty, always slightly plumper than the ideal, with an awkwardness of movement and a voice that creaked and cracked from chronic coughs and catarrhs. But with clever face paint and skilfully designed gowns and veils she had always looked pleasant, indeed often radiant, and never less than regal. Alas, it grew much more difficult to mask the broken veins on her face and her crooked posture. She now quite visibly limped. She was forty-seven years old, two years Edward's junior, but looked a decade older.

She did not allow herself to be deluded by the reassuring platitudes and denials voiced by many of her ladies, instead talking openly of her ageing. In fact, she had recently commissioned her tomb. I was not privy to its design, for she considered my gifts to lie with clothing and the furnishings of a chamber; another of the ladies was her choice on evenings when she wished to discuss the tomb. But she often spoke to me of her wish to be beautifully gowned and bejewelled to await Edward, who would lie beside her. I cannot count how many times she changed her mind about how she wished to be dressed for her burial. I could appreciate the difficulty of choosing between all her beautiful robes and jewels, but I did not like thinking about Edward joining her.

'You think me mad to worry about my appearance after death?' she asked me one evening.

'You are and always shall be Queen of England, Your Grace, and therefore must look like a queen even in death. Your people would wish it. They will need to see you so.'

My answer pleased her.

This talk of death reminded me of my own uncertain future. I had been naïve, enjoying the dream too much, basking in Edward's attention and love. I must never forget that this joy would not last forever. I was a commoner. Once she was gone, would Edward take another wife, and would she willingly share him with me? I was troubled as well by the spectre Philippa had raised of Edward's own eventual death.

Despite her failing health, Queen Philippa insisted on attending all the Garter festivities over the days around the Feast of St George, even those requiring her to walk a distance on uneven ground, to stand still for long periods of time or sit on uncomfortable seats for most of the day and well into the evening. Her face would be pale as alabaster when we helped her to bed, and she would cry out or moan most piteously as she sought a comfortable position. Her physician mixed potent drinks to ease her pain and induce a healing sleep. He urged her to have a day of rest. But each morning she would insist that the sleep had worked its miracle. Of course it had not.

Along with all the Queen's other ladies I was fully occupied assisting her through that busy time and heard of the arrivals of only those especially favoured by my companions and the Queen. And so I was taken by surprise when I glanced up from the dais in the great hall where I was arranging cushions on the Queen's chair, in preparation for her imminent arrival at a feast, and beheld William Wyndsor striding towards me through the crowd of servants. He hesitated as he reached me. Though he was smiling there was a guarded quality to his eyes. He took my hands.

'You are more beautiful than ever, Alice.' He tried to pull me close to him.

I had thought little of him – was it possible he still thought of me as a future wife?

I took a step back and tried to withdraw my hands, but he held fast and stared at me with a boldness I did not like.

'I thought you were in Ireland,' I said.

'Soon. You must say that you will be my wife now, Alice. I love you more than ever. Let us wait no longer.'

'That is impossible, William.'

He put his hands on my shoulders and searched my face, his frown deepening. 'You've been promised to someone else?'

'You do not know?' Was it possible that a man supposedly in love with me would not have enquired, would not have heard about Edward and me? I drew him away from the servants setting out the wine cups so that we might not be overheard. 'The King has taken me as his mistress.' I thought the clean thrust of the truth would, in the end, afford the cleanest break.

He stood there for one of the longest moments of my life. Then a sound began in his throat, like the low growl of a wild animal, and gradually rose in pitch.

'He has no right!'

'Hush, William, I beg you.' Some of the servants were watching us with interest. 'Of course he has the right. He is the King. And I love him.'

An unwise comment. He lifted his arm to strike me, but caught himself and rushed away, pushing servants out of his path as he went. As I watched him kick over a small table and storm out of sight, I felt a deep sense of dread.

My unease lasted through the evening. I did not see William. Heard nothing of him. That night, as I lay watching Edward sleep I wondered whether I had been a fool to send William away. A husband might take me from court, give me a life no one would censure. William had done me a great favour by taking me to my family during the pestilence, at considerable risk to himself. But even as I thought these things, I knew in my heart that such a refuge was not for me. I loved Edward. I could not abandon him.

Over the next few days I searched the crowds for sight of William, remembering his anger, dreading his next actions. For such emotion seldom gave way to peaceful resignation. He'd asked me nothing about my wishes, feeling only the blow to his own self-importance and storming out. I alternated between understanding how he felt and anger – as well as dreading how he might give vent to that anger. For three days I fretted.

As the Knights of the Garter arrived, the castle grew so crowded that I and the ladies with whom I shared a chamber were moved into the Queen's chamber to free our room for a knight, his lady, and their servants. There would be no slipping away from here to sleep with the King. I surrendered myself to the full-time task of seeing to the Queen's comfort, grateful to have little time to think, for the grandeur of the nobles crowding the castle humbled me – in faith, I cringed to think of my presumption in believing the King could love me when he could choose among myriad noblewomen who'd suit him as I never could. But he did profess to love me.

In the intimate setting of the bedchamber or on the marshes with our hawks and dogs, Edward and I were a man and woman who enjoyed being together, mutually satisfying our appetites and sharing stories. But the grand processions, the tournaments and jousts, the splendour and the sense of ancient rituals and noble blood surrounding the Feast of St George and the Holy Order of the Garter, all this overwhelmed me with Edward's status as a divinely anointed King. I felt small, common, naïve, alone.

He seemed beyond human as he rode at the head of the twenty-six Garter Knights. All were dressed in the indigo and gold ceremonial robes of the Order of the Garter but his cloak was the most magnificent, lined in ermine, his white hair flowing beneath his crown. They rode in solemn ceremony around the jousting field as family, fellow knights, archbishops, bishops, retainers, clerks and servants cheered. The Queen proudly stood in the centre of the stands wearing a matching robe of indigo and gold, an honorary lady of the Order of the Garter. Her surviving daughter, Isabella, and her sons' wives encircled her, and the wives of the Garter Knights stood behind the royal family. I was one of half a dozen of Philippa's ladies waiting beside the stands, ready to come to her aid with cushions, lap robes and refreshments. The sound of the horns sent shivers down my spine, as did the answering cheers. I was thrilled to witness such magnificence, but felt no part of it. It was impossible I could ever share the King's public life, that I would ever stand openly as part of the royal family rather than a lady-in-waiting to his Queen. But in truth, imagining myself on Edward's arm at such an official event sent a chill through me. I had not the blood or breeding to stand so.

Philippa and her daughters, by blood and marriage, impressed me as much as the knights on their high-stepping steeds. They looked so tall, so regal from head to toe. Just this morning sweet Blanche had received devastating news of her dear sister Maud's death. Philippa, Joan, Isabella, and Elizabeth, Countess of Ulster, had gathered round the stricken lady to comfort her, sharing tears and memories. And then, almost as one, had resolved to say nothing of the tragedy until the close of the Garter festivities.

'Then we shall announce the sad news so that all may pray for Maud's soul's salvation and mourn her.' Queen Philippa promised Requiem Masses throughout the realm.

Blanche agreed, ever anxious to bring ease to those around her, particularly her mother-in-law, and understanding her role. Now as I stood gazing up at her in the stands, I saw how pinched and pale she was, listless in her gestures, and how often she sank down on to her seat even though all the others stood blocking her view of her husband and his fellow Knights of the Garter on the field. My heart went out to her. I was not the only one who suffered in the strictures of court life. But the royal family knew well how to hide their pain.

Later that day I enjoyed an hour with Geoffrey, who had arrived the previous day in the company of the Countess of Ulster.

'You shall be in Ireland soon,' I said, thinking of William, 'with your lord.'

'Perhaps not. I think it more likely I shall remain here, with those who oversee Lionel's estates.' He laughed at my expressions of sympathy. 'In truth, I am relieved. I am good friends with several of the King's knights-of-the-chamber, and have hopes of joining His Grace's household as an esquire.' He peered at me closely and added, 'I hear say you might also exert some influence with the King? Is it true, Alice? Are you his mistress of the hawks and the bedchamber?'

I bowed my head.

He put his hands on my shoulders and bent closer to see my expression. 'You are not happy?'

Unable to escape his curious eyes, I lifted my head. He made a sympathetic sound and caught one of the tears rolling down my cheeks. I felt too keenly the gulf between Edward and me.

'I am both happy and miserable, Geoffrey. The King professes to love me, yet I have lost my beloved husband, my daughter is being raised far from me, and now I have lost my honour to a man of whom I could never be worthy.'

'I grieve for Janyn, and your loss of all his loving family and your beautiful daughter. But the King must consider you worthy, my friend, for he chose you above all other women at court.'

'I have no station, Geoffrey. I do not belong here. At any moment I might be cast out, and then who would take me in?'

'In faith, Alice, you can expect no less than the King's protection, his patronage. They have protected you from the Perrers' fate, have they not?'

'Yes, but I have transgressed.'

'Are you still thinking of Criseyde?'

'Yes. More than ever.' I lifted a sleeve to show him – silk with pearls stitched to form a vine. Edward's pearls. 'My magnificent robes.'

'Hardly magical. But I do see, I do. Is William Wyndsor your Troilus?'

'No, no . . . only my beloved Janyn. His memory.' I sobbed the last words, and to my surprise and comfort Geoffrey held me, silent for once. At least *he* still counted me a friend, and I loved him for it.

On the fourth day William approached as I walked in the garden with the de Roet sisters.

'Might we speak alone?'

I could not decipher his tone.

The girls urged me to listen to my handsome knight.

I noticed how travel-worn William looked as we searched for a quiet place in which to talk. We found a seat in a hedge that hid us from view. He studied my face as if learning my features by heart.

'You departed in such a temper,' I said. 'You left court?'

He grunted. 'Riding until I could ride no longer. Drinking until I could drink no more. Cursing the King. Cursing myself for waiting until we had known one another longer. Did you not understand that we pledged our troth, Alice? That you are my wife?'

'That is not true. I promised you nothing.'

His jaw muscles revealed how he worked to control his emotion. 'Do you not love me then, Alice?' His handsome face was clouded by indignation.

His pride was hurt. *His* pride. So far he'd not asked how *I* felt, whether *I* suffered. He wanted only to know whether he had my love. 'You've not asked how I feel about my new circumstances.'

His hands tightened around mine. 'Do you love him?'

'I've already said that I do, though I did not wish for this . . . to be neither free nor honestly wed.' I regretted those last words. As soon as I'd spoken them I felt that I had betrayed Edward. 'But I do love him, William, beyond all other men.'

His face twisted with pain and he bowed his head for a moment, fighting for composure. Tension charged the air between us.

I tried to think of a way to end our confrontation but suddenly he straightened, his expression carefully neutral.

'He will tire of you. We've but to wait.'

I might have laughed at his inept wooing were I not still aware of the tension with which he held himself. That is what the gallant William had resolved during his riding and drinking: that the King would tire of me! He expected me to be grateful that he meant to wait for me, but I would have expected more from a man who claimed he wished only to wed me. He spoke of love, but did not think to console or reassure me.

'Do not wait for me, William. I release you from that vow. My destiny is in the King's hands.'

'I will have you, Alice. You are my wife.'

He moved towards me as if to kiss me, but footsteps approaching halted him.

'I am *not* your wife, William,' I said as quietly as my frustration permitted.

'I shall tell the King that we are betrothed, and that I will be waiting for you,' he insisted.

'You must do nothing of the sort, William.' He could not be such an innocent as to think that such a declaration would find favour with Edward. What was his game? Edward had said that if he tired of me, he would find me a husband. But I doubted he would share me with another before that. Nor would I want him to. 'His Grace says he will not tire of me. He would not receive your words with pleasure . . . your implication that he will not be steadfast.'

Shaking his head, William chuckled in the cold way of someone who believes he has caught another out. 'He is an old man desperate to grasp at youth, Alice. The first time he fails to complete the act, he will discard you to soothe his pride. But I'll say nothing. You must get a message to me at once when that day comes. You shall always know where I am.'

'Do not wait for me, William. Marry another.' And God help her!

We parted then. Pippa and Katherine asked so many questions I laughingly told them they made me dizzy, but in truth I was irritated by the exchange with William. He was an arrogant bully. I yearned for a husband – but the man I yearned for was not

William but rather the impossible: for Edward, free and asking me to wed him. Though I danced with William several times over the next few days – to refuse might have invited curiosity – we had little chance to talk and my feelings about him remained uneasy.

Edward, my home, my anchor, was soon of more concern to me than William. I began to notice much talk among the royal family of the King's decision to give his elder sons parts of his kingdom to govern. The women believed it to be a sign that, just as Philippa's mind was focused on her imminent death, so was Edward's, though he showed no outward sign of illness.

'Father is old,' said his daughter Isabella one evening. 'As with our mother, so with him. They are preparing to pass on.'

The Queen had retired for the evening and the women of her family, as well as many of those of us who waited on them, had lingered in the Queen's great chamber, exhausted yet wakeful.

Princess Joan glanced at me with a teasing look and did not join in with the desultory comments about how seldom Edward had danced or how he'd required rest after participating in the tournament. I was deeply troubled by such talk. I had been so occupied with my duties for the Queen and dread of William's possible retaliation that I had not noticed my love's condition.

When the others rose to retire for the evening, Joan stayed behind and motioned for me to do likewise. She wore a gold fillet and crespinette over her pale hair, and gold thread shimmered throughout her gown of yellow and indigo, catching what little light there was in the room. In truth, she glittered. I could not take my eyes from her, for to do so was to plunge into darkness. I wondered whether that was why moths flew into flames.

'Isabella and Elizabeth seem to be unaware that the King lies with you,' she said, laughing. 'If they knew, surely one of them would have said something, or at least glanced your way.'

'What of Blanche?'

Joan rose and warmed her hands over the brazier. 'Blanche knows, I am certain, but does not care to think about it.'

'My lady, why are you telling me this?'

'For friendship's sake, and do call me Joan when we are alone, Alice. We are friends, are we not?'

'I am honoured to call you friend. And Joan.'

'Good! It is not true, is it, that the King looks towards his death?'

'I have heard no such talk from him. I am puzzled why they choose to see a natural progression as a final act.' I tried to speak with confidence, but something in my expression or posture betrayed my fear.

'You must practise hiding your feelings, Alice. The knives at court are sharp and seldom sheathed. Have a care.'

'I am out of my depth, Joan.'

She poured us both some wine and sat down close to me, giving me a little hug. 'I am fond of you, Alice, and so I wish to give you the advice that you need, not having had the advantage of being brought up in the court. The King has been indiscreet about you. How Isabella and Elizabeth have not heard of your relationship I cannot imagine, but I think soon most of them will know. And then they will envy you. Envy is an ugly emotion. It inspires cruelty. Meanness.'

I crossed myself. 'Sometimes I am so frightened, I cannot bear it.'

'And often you are delighted to bask in the glow of his love, are you not?'

I nodded, reluctantly. It was true.

'He is a wonderful man, beloved of his people – including most of the court. So is the Queen. If aught goes wrong, you are one of the people who will be blamed. Because you have no connections. Because he loves you. And the King is impetuous. I do not say you are the only one they will blame. They will call down one of his sons as well – not my Edward, for he is a hero and the future King.'

'What then must I do?'

'Revel in your love, but keep your eyes open. At all times remember who you are, where you are, who he is. Find and nurture a few trustworthy friends. But do not blindly trust them. Nor should you blindly trust the King. He is a man, as William Wyndsor is a man. Your William is angry. I noticed that. He may yet be your salvation if aught goes wrong, but if you wed him, try to keep some of your property secret. Just in case.'

God forbid. I did not like her referring to *my* William, but Dame Agnes had often chided me for arguing with someone who was offering useful advice, so I did not contradict her.

'Is this how you live?' I asked.

She sipped her wine, staring out into the dark room. 'Yes. I have always followed the love in my heart, but with my eyes wide open. My father, Edmund, was executed for his loyalty to his half brother, my Edward's grandfather. Executed by the lover of Isabella, my husband's grandmother. As a child I heard many refer to my father's shortcomings, especially his loyalty, as if he had been at fault and deserved to die. Most people live according to fear, not love. My father was fearless in his love for his brother. He was also a loving father, always had time for me. He remembered everything I told him.' She was close to tears.

'You are safe now, as Princess.'

She shook her head. 'No, Alice, I am not. My dear Edward is a child in some things and has a temper like your William. Like the King.'

'He is not *my* William. I have made that clear to him.'

Joan shrugged.

'You have given me much to think about,' I said.

'Good. It is offered in love.' She hugged me, and then swept from the room with a rustle of silk.

I remained in the chamber, staring at the brazier, thinking about all that Joan had said. The details were new, but not the warning. I had been naïve in praying that I might trust Edward – or anyone – completely.

Gwen found me still sitting there and urged me to retire for the night. 'What happened, Mistress? You look so sad.'

I was not surprised that I looked sad. I told her nothing had happened, I'd just been enjoying the solitude. I did not know how to express what I felt. That I was the only person in the world on whom I dared depend filled me with sorrow and not a little fear. The love of a man or a family was sweet, but unreliable. During the Garter festivities I had clearly seen and understood the gulf between me and Edward, a gulf I could not possibly cross. As Queen Philippa used me to understand the merchant class, so Edward apparently found excitement, or perhaps comfort, in lying with a woman quite unlike himself and his peers. We were all needy. We clung to those who helped us feel loved or supported. Someone we found reassuring. But, in the end, we were truly alone.

In the days that followed I took every opportunity I could to spend time in the chapel, and when that was not possible, I kept my paternoster beads in hand as I walked or waited. I found that meditating on the life of the Blessed Virgin Mary comforted and inspired me as I went about my chores. Although Mary had been given no choice in becoming the Mother of God, she had accepted her role with grace in every meaning of the word. I prayed for her help in lifting my self-pity and in gathering grace. I prayed to her for patience and for wisdom. Of course, I did not see my situation as similar to hers; being chosen by the King to be his mistress was in no way equivalent to being chosen by God to bear his son. But Mary's surrender to her fate was an example I found consoling and inspiring. Surely if I prayed, made confession and sought to walk a path of virtue in all things *but* my being the King's partner in sin, I might find redemption.

By the time the guests departed and we began preparations for our remove to Eltham where the royal households could rest after the celebrations, I was resolved to follow Joan's guidance. I would be twenty that September, a mature age. I had been a mother for almost five years, a wife for almost six, two changes that had taken me from girlhood to womanhood. I had lived at court for over three years. Yet something innocent in me had remained – or, more accurately, I had clung to a naïveté I now understood I must shed, for my sake and for Bella's. It was time for me to win my daughter back to me.

> *'Tho gan she wondren moore than biforn*
> *A thousand fold, and down hire eyghen caste;*
> *For nevere, sith the tyme that she was born,*
> *To knowe thyng desired she so faste . . .'*

> – Geoffrey Chaucer, *Troilus and Criseyde*, II, ll. 141–44

On the day after we arrived at Eltham an Italian priest, Dom Francisco, arrived. Philippa had us dress her to receive him despite her obvious exhaustion from the journey and extreme pain – she was so unbalanced in her gait that we all feared she had exacerbated her old injury, for nothing now seemed to ease her discomfort and she struggled to straighten up. I shortened her hem in front and we moved her headdress a little farther back on her head to mask how far forward she pitched as she walked. Her dignity and gentle behaviour while suffering such pain were an inspiration.

She and Edward were sequestered with Dom Francisco for the best part of the day, and afterwards they assembled all the household who might be spared from their work to join them in prayer in the King's chapel. It seemed to be a Requiem Mass for a man of the Church, but we were not told who. Edward knelt with head bowed, often covering his eyes with one hand. Philippa was her usual subdued, pious self at her devotions; she did not seem personally moved by the proceedings. Whoever had died, it was Edward who was in deep mourning. The priest alluded to the deceased being of royal blood. It caused quite a stir in both households, but that was nothing compared with my own churning thoughts. For, of course, I wondered whether it was Isabella's precious one who had died, the one for whom so many Perrers had died, someone in Italy, the person whom Edward had once invited to join his travelling party, the one rumoured to have been his deposed father. If this were so, I might now at last be free to leave court.

Now that I no longer wished to leave court, to leave Edward.

I wished I might comfort him. I had never seen Edward in such distress. I was also desperate to ask him whether he might now reveal the great secret that had destroyed my wedded happiness. It would not bring back Janyn, but at least I might understand why he had died. As Edward passed me leaving the chapel, he noticed the swirl of seed pearls on my sleeve and lifted his head to give me a wan smile. I pressed my hands to my heart, and he did as well, though by then he was past me.

I was not summoned that evening, either by the King or the Queen. Perhaps I was mistaken, perhaps the news had nothing to do with my family. But Philippa and Edward must have known that I would wonder. Surely they might have afforded me the comfort of some word, some explanation. I slept badly, my dreams fevered and incomprehensible. I woke several times in the night with my heart thundering. At last I gave up the attempt to sleep and knelt beside the bed, trying to pray. But my mind only conjured nightmarish images of Janyn's bleeding body, his agony, his death.

In the morning I saw the King's favoured chamber knights and servants in the yard, sumpters loading their pack-horses, and several wagons already loaded. As we dressed Philippa she informed us that Edward was leaving for one of his hunting lodges. My fingers were clumsy over her buttons as tears welled in my eyes. I had hoped he might send for me, to allow me to console him and perhaps tell me who had died; his departure without a word cut me to the quick. I feared he was taking this opportunity to discard me. I had just resolved to work hard to keep Edward's love, and he had shut me out.

'He requires rest and prayer,' said Philippa. 'As do we all.'

I require answers! I silently screamed. *For pity's sake, let me know all so that I might put this agony of wondering behind me.* But I said nothing, for I saw by the swelling of her face that the Queen had taken extra physick during the night. Whatever she had heard had weakened her. Even so, she insisted on dressing and attending Mass. After the midday meal, a simple affair with the King gone, Philippa told me to attend her as she went to speak once more with the Italian priest.

Perhaps at last I was to learn something. My legs shook so

that I was grateful that two servants were assisting the Queen in her halting progress to her parlour. I tried to distract myself from anxious fantasies by observing how her pale grey silk gown fitted her – badly. In less than a month she had lost weight and height. Yesterday's alteration in the hem of the gown had simply made it safer for her to walk. Truly opening my eyes to her decline filled me with yet another anxiety – my uncertainty as to what would happen to me upon her death. I might be cast adrift without a guiding star.

The priest was already in the parlour, rising and bowing his respect as Philippa entered. He was slender and graceful, with pale eyes that looked almost milky in contrast to his dark brows and olive skin.

Philippa dismissed the servants who had assisted her. As soon as she introduced me to Dom Francisco, he turned those eerie eyes on me with a discomfiting intensity.

'Dame Alicia.' He honoured me with a slight inclination of his head. 'His Grace the King has instructed me to tell you of my mission, particularly the history of the man whose death is the occasion of my journey.'

The Queen nodded her approval and settled back, a cup of wine in hand, as if for a long story.

I sat and shivered.

The queer story of a William of Wales being brought to King Edward twenty-four years earlier was now fleshed out. He had been the guardian of a child brought to an abbey outside Milan as an infant. A child who was to be hidden and protected: the son of Queen Isabella and her lover Roger Mortimer.

The precious one had been a child, not the deposed King! The illegitimate son of the Queen and her lover. The Perrers had protected their knowledge of this child.

After Mortimer's capture and execution, Isabella had been kept in seclusion through her lying in and churching. This was no mere bastard, but the son of a former queen who could be used by barons or foreign powers to challenge the reigning King – or whom *she* might use. She had taken up arms against her husband; it was not inconceivable she would do so against her son for executing her lover, and threaten to replace him on the throne with her son by Roger Mortimer.

Tommasa's family arranged the baby's journey to Italy, and my mother-in-law was his wet nurse for the journey. Thereafter her family were couriers of messages and gifts between mother and son, and eventually my Janyn had become the primary courier.

'But my father-in-law swore he did not know whom they protected.' I had not intended to speak.

Dom Francisco did not seem surprised by my outburst. 'That is true. Master John had been told, and apparently chose to believe, his wife's journey concerned a family emergency.' Their daughter, whom Tommasa had still been nursing, made the journey as well.

'You see the terrible secret they guarded,' Philippa said to me, her eyes surprisingly entreating. 'Lady Isabella rewarded them with property, coin and patronage, grateful for their loving care and silence.'

I doubted that Isabella had willingly given up her child. She had not been a woman to relinquish control of anything important to her. But both the priest and Philippa insisted that Isabella had never considered keeping the child in England. Perhaps it was one of the many things I would never truly understand regarding the royal family, that ready acceptance of their children being reared in the homes of others. I wondered whether they had any conception of how difficult I found my separation from Bella.

'Do you know what happened to my husband and his parents?' I asked when the priest seemed finished with his story. My voice was a mere whisper as I found it difficult to breathe. I feared to hear repeated what Edward had told me, but I also feared to learn that he had lied.

Dom Francisco's pale eyes seemed to be on me, but when Philippa subtly shook her head the priest shrugged and brought up his hands in apology. 'I know only the part of the story that involves the abbey. I am sorry.'

I did not believe him, but if the Queen did not wish me to know more than that, I would waste my time and try her patience by asking any more.

'And now this child of Isabella's is dead, the secret is no longer dangerous,' I observed. *Too late. Five years too late.* I felt ill.

'Of course, you understand that you must never speak of this,' said Philippa. 'Except, perhaps someday, when she is old enough, you might explain to your daughter what a precious secret her father and his family guarded. But you will speak of this with no one else. One never knows how unscrupulous people might seek to use such information.'

'I am ever your servant, Your Grace.' I almost choked on the words.

The priest rose. 'My mission is now complete. *Benedicite,* Your Grace. May God watch over you and all your family and household.' He blessed her, and then me. A servant showed him out.

The Queen had not stirred. Servants entered and set out more wine and some fruit, cheese and bread. I rose and stood for a while looking out of the small window, forcing myself to remain silent, to wait for the Queen to speak. I prayed she would express remorse on the part of Isabella and Edward. My thoughts were wild, frantic. I wished I might rush to the stables. I yearned to ride hard, the wind in my hair, to scream my frustrated anger where it would harm no one. I might ride forever, a ride with no destination, for no one would be waiting for me at the end, no one expected me. No one. A sob escaped.

'Do not think that I am unaware of the pain this meeting has resurrected in you, Alice.' The Queen's voice pulled me back into the blue and gold parlour.

Slowly, focusing on recapturing my breath, I returned to my seat, accepting with gratitude a cup of wine offered by the servant. I took a long drink, trying to steady myself.

Philippa motioned for the servant to leave.

'Your plight touched me from the moment Lady Isabella asked me to bring you into my household. I blame her for your unhappiness. I harboured much anger towards her also for the pain she brought to my husband and his family, and your situation gave me a cause to champion. But after hours of prayer and reflection, I had to acknowledge my own role too in this sad history. It was Edward and I who insisted the child be smuggled out of the country and hidden. We made the arrangements for it. And then, until he was brought to us on our journey to Rome, I forgot about him. Poor child . . . abandoned to utter strangers.

317

'My heart misgave me when I met him. I had just been delivered of my son Lionel. In that difficult time when I missed carrying my child within, easily brought to tears by anything, but particularly the thought of handing over my baby to a wet nurse . . . seeing Isabella's son at that moment, a boy of seven, a sweet, timid little boy, I silently prayed forgiveness for my cruelty towards him and his mother. He spoke a little French, but mostly Italian, so I did not understand much of what he said, and he did not understand my speech at all. He was a handsome child. He looked more like Isabella than any of her other children. I never spoke to her of the visit.'

Philippa bowed her head.

I had initially hung mine and only half-listened, but as the Queen went on I found myself staring at her. She deserved contempt surely for such treatment of a child? But Isabella had done worse . . . much worse. My anger towards Philippa did not last. She was too ill, and in many ways too admirable for me to hate. Yet as I absorbed this sorry tale of adults fearing the power of a former queen's bastard son, and in their fear using my husband's family as their shields, I found little pity in my heart.

'How did Janyn and Tommasa die? Were they murdered when they would not betray their oath of secrecy?'

'Yes. Tommasa was forced to watch her son tortured and finally murdered. Her captors did not know of her weak heart. Their efforts to force her to speak killed her. Mercifully, I think.'

I pressed my stomach, though it was my chest that felt as if it were being crushed.

'I see in your eyes why my husband did not wish to be the one to tell you this,' said Philippa. 'You condemn us.'

I managed to halt an inner vision of Janyn's torture and Tommasa's torment long enough to speak. 'I am no saint, Your Grace. I have lost so much. And why? Because the most powerful family in the kingdom feared a baby boy. A saint might see God's plan in this, but I cannot. My dear husband tortured. My gentle mother-in-law forced to watch. Would that Isabella's bastard had died years ago!'

I drank the rest of the wine and rose to pour more. Despite my anger, I served Philippa as well, with wine and food. It helped me to move, to keep my hands busy. Though she was Queen and might consider that I was merely doing my duty, she thanked me, the expression on her face vulnerable and fond. Something in this exchange pulled me back from the brink of dangerous recklessness, and I remembered the deference due to the woman before me. No matter how responsible she was for my loss, I was her servant, I depended on her for almost everything, and she had been generous to me. And I was always uncomfortably aware of how, in the eyes of most people, I would be seen as the usurper of her marriage.

'Your Grace, I pray you, forgive my outburst. You have been good to me and my daughter. I am in your debt.'

Her eyes held mine as she said, 'You may have lost much, but consider what you have gained.' She lifted her fingertips to her forehead in a gesture that signalled a headache, but instead of pleading illness, said, 'Still, you deserve an apology. I pray that someday you may forgive us.'

I dropped to my knees before her. She placed her hand on my head.

'Let there be peace between us.' She urged me to take some refreshment. 'I have a little more to say. Then you are free until morning.' Her speech was halting. She needed to pause frequently for breath. Her physical collapse was making everything difficult for her, even breathing.

'Your Grace,' I whispered, rising. I had no appetite, but busied myself quartering a blanched winter apple.

We sat in silence for a while, both of us pretending to eat but merely moving the food about in our bowls. The sound of Philippa's laboured breathing inspired in me both shame and relief – shame for supplanting her in the marriage bed, and relief to realise she could no longer find pleasure in lying with Edward. I found myself praying that the latter cancelled out the former for her. But what if he no longer wanted me? What if, now that I might walk freely, the secret of the precious one no longer a threat to be used against the King, he felt relieved of his duty towards me? I'd be free, but heartbroken.

After a time, Philippa set aside her pretence of eating. 'You have proved a skilful and clever sempster, concealing the collapse of my body and shielding me from humiliation. And you have proved a trustworthy and steadfast companion in a confusing and often difficult arrangement. Many might have proved otherwise. As a token of my gratitude, I would relieve you of unnecessary discomfort by speaking from my heart.'

I found myself shivering as I listened to her halting speech. I could not imagine how she might relieve me of unnecessary discomfort. And what was the necessary discomfort? She had paused to sip some wine.

'Your Grace, you must not tire yourself.'

She shook her head. 'I will not do more than I wish to, Alice.'

Though I knew I'd had sufficient wine, I poured a little more to keep myself busy.

'The love of husband and wife changes over time,' Philippa resumed, 'of necessity. You did not have sufficient time with Janyn to experience this.' Her smile was sad and kindly. 'The year before you were wed, I was delivered of my last child, Thomas. I prayed that he was my last. Thought I might go mad if I found myself again with child. So many months of discomfort, before and after. I selfishly prayed that God would stop my courses so that I might live out the rest of my days in a little more comfort.' She crossed herself. 'My womb could not complete the next child conceived, and I lost it. Then I fell. That part of my marriage was over. God often works in unsatisfying ways.' A bitter laugh, then: 'You are taking nothing away from me, Alice. He loves me in all the ways still possible.'

She leaned her head back against the chair for a moment, her eyes closed. 'To love a King, Alice, is to dance a dizzying dance. Spinning towards him . . . spinning away.' After a deep sigh, she said in a strained voice, 'Now you must call the servants to assist me to my bedchamber, and you may take your ease until morning.'

'Your Grace, thank you for allowing me to speak with Dom Francisco, and—'

'Go now, Alice. We have said enough.'

As ever when I did not know what to do with my racing mind and tumultuous emotions, I changed into riding clothes. Knowing me as she did, Gwen insisted on accompanying me. We spent most of what was left of the day riding. As I rode I opened my heart and soul to the emotions boiling in my stomach, permitting myself to feel my sorrow, the terror of Janyn's and Tommasa's last hours, and the fury that built within as I imagined all of this. I was furious with Isabella's and Edward's use of my family, furious with Edward for not having the courage to be there when I learned the truth, furious about his heartless retreat. Though Melisende was accustomed to carrying me as I wept or cried out to the wind, that day my emotions were wild enough to make her shy a few times, bringing me back to my senses. I would slow, compose myself, and reassure her. In such wise we rode through many cycles of both fury and calm that day.

When the groom insisted that my horse must rest we turned back towards the stables. Gwen and I walked then, through the gardens to the river, and at last I confided in my long-suffering friend. I told her what I had learned of Isabella's bastard, and what the Queen had told me of the murder of my husband and his mother's death shortly afterwards. I felt the need to speak of it all just once, and knew that I could trust Gwen to remain silent. I had spent my anger for the moment. What I experienced as I spoke was a desperate yearning for a different truth, a different outcome. Had Isabella's bastard died earlier, my life might have been so sweet. But that child had grown to manhood, and my husband's family had suffered because of him. And now so did I and my precious Bella.

Though I was grateful for Edward's past love and generosity, it carried a taint that would ever be present.

I also told Gwen of Philippa's acceptance of my liaison with her husband.

'At least now you know that Her Grace does not intend to throw you out,' said Gwen.

'But I do not know Edward's heart.' I had thought I did, and then he'd left without a word. A dizzying dance, Philippa had said.

'Would she have spoken of your liaison if he'd meant to abandon you?' Gwen asked.

'No, I think not. Bless you, Gwen.'

When my body was exhausted but my mind still churned, I retired to the Queen's chapel to pray. I prayed for Janyn, Tommasa and Master John, I prayed for Bella and myself, I prayed for the grace to find peace with what could not be undone, I prayed for the balance necessary to hold steady in my dance with Edward. Afterwards Gwen brought me a little food from the kitchen, which we shared in the garden. I managed to sleep that night, my body and mind too depleted to do aught else.

On the following day I received a summons to Hertford Castle to spend a few days with my daughter. When I asked permission of Queen Philippa, she was bemused that I had not guessed at once she had been the one to suggest it.

'With Isabella's bastard dead, you are safe to visit your daughter. There is no longer any secret to protect. We have ensured the news has reached the right ears.'

In my rush of joy I could think of nothing more eloquent to say than, 'God bless you, Your Grace.'

She seemed to take pleasure in giving me even more good news: Fair Meadow was being readied for me and any members of my birth family I cared to invite. It would take a month or so to prepare, and she and Joan had thought it a good idea for Bella and me to have a little time together at once. She would spare me for a few months in the summer.

When I returned to my chamber to prepare, Gwen and I hugged each other and cried.

'I am free, Gwen! Free to be with Bella, free to be with my family without putting them in danger. I will think only of that now, of this modicum of freedom.' Not of my fear that Edward would forsake me.

Indeed, my heart was overflowing with joyful anticipation of seeing my precious daughter as we chose clothes for the journey. I fretted about not having time to make a pretty gown for her. Gwen calmly suggested that we take one of my old gowns and that the three of us might turn it into something for Bella while we were together. I said many prayers of thanks that night, quite a few of them for Gwen.

I remember nothing of the river journey except that the countryside seemed to me more beautiful than it had ever been, and it made me cry.

Bella was at an age in which even a few weeks could work great changes. As I approached the castle I feared I might not recognise her. But stepping into the garden where the children were at play, I knew her at once, for her curly dark hair and large eyes were those of her grandmother, Dame Tommasa. She was tall for her age, slender and graceful. She would be five years old in a matter of weeks, yet she seemed more mature to me, more reserved than Mary, Will or I had been at that age.

Her wide brow crinkled in confusion when I rushed to her and crouched down.

'Dame Alice,' she said, with a little curtsey.

I nodded, my heart too full to speak.

She touched the pearls on my sleeves. 'Nurse says we can be together again, and I can call you Mother.'

'That is so, sweet Bella.'

Something shifted in her face and I realised she fought back tears. 'My father called me Bella.'

'He did, my love, and so did I. Do I.'

'Her Grace told me that he is dead. And both my grand-mothers.'

The fear in her eyes told me more of the climate in this household than I would surely learn if I asked.

'Many more of your kin are alive and will be so very happy to see you this summer. Do you remember the pretty house where your father and I taught you to ride a pony?'

It took little time to win her over. Our days together were delightful. We made a pretty gown and headdress, we planned parties and long rides in the country, and when it was time for me to depart, Bella clung to me and I to her. I swore that she would not return to Joan's household, though I did not say so to Bella. First I would ensure it was possible.

All of this did not bring Janyn back, but I felt as if I might find some happiness if I could be with Bella and my family now and then. I had lost so much: years of my precious daughter's life, years of joy with her father, years of my siblings' lives. I prayed that Edward might hold and cherish me for many years to come, for I needed his love now, more than ever, as I closed the door on the past and my former dreams.

Book III

The King's Mistress

I had been holding my breath for four years, half-believing Janyn would reappear, fearing how Queen Philippa felt about my love for her husband. I had found life at court overwhelming — so grand, so impenetrable. I'd followed a steady course by narrowing my attention to caring for the Queen's wardrobe, being the best companion to her that I might be, and, of late, in loving my King.

I had begun to understand Edward's delight in costume, in ceremony, in riding, hunting, hawking, dancing, luxurious furnishings, and lovemaking. The pleasure that rose from within when his body was fully aware of being alive, when his senses were aroused and delighted, these sensations of the flesh anchored him amidst the enormity of his role. I was now part of that anchor, and I had thought that he, in turn, might anchor me.

But I learned that he was my siren. Philippa had said that to love a king was to be caught up in a dance, towards him and away from him. I was to learn that dance all too well — in one movement being pulled towards him in heady surrender, the next being sent spinning away in sad solitude. I would know moments of exquisite joy and tenderness, feeling that we shared one body, one heart, and I would know desolate stretches of loneliness, emptiness, as he became a figure out of legend, unreachable, untouchable, unfathomable. I must find my own balance in the momentum of that dizzying shift.

When had I a choice to be other than I was?

' *"Allas," quod she, "what wordes may ye brynge?*
What wol my deere herte seyn to me,
Which that I drede nevere mo to see?
Wol he han pleynte or teris er I wend?
I have ynough, if he therafter sende!" '

– spoken by Criseyde, *Troilus and Criseyde*,
Geoffrey Chaucer, IV, ll. 857–61

1362

One of the first times I remember Father inviting me down to his undercroft was to meet a merchant from Ormuz who specialised in pearls. He had brought with him a small drill used to pierce them, promising to show Father how it was done, and he thought it something I would never forget. At first it was the merchant who fascinated me, so tanned by the sun that his skin looked like well-worn leather with wrinkles fanning from the corners of his dark eyes into the folds of his white and silver turban. He had the whitest teeth I had ever seen, and showed them a lot as he grinned at me. His hands were of two shades, dark leather on top and what I thought of as 'skin colour' beneath. He wore many beautiful rings. When he moved he perfumed the air with anise and cinnamon and sandalwood. I wondered what it would be like to live in a land where all men smelled so sweet and dressed so richly.

When he picked up a pretty, not quite perfectly round pearl that shifted colour as he moved it under the lamplight, I asked him what he had done to the little holes. For everyone knew that all pearls had little holes so that they could breathe underwater. At first his dark eyes grew wide – so wide that I could see that the whites of his eyes matched the brilliance of his teeth.

'So that the pearls might breathe?' he repeated, eyes widening even more. Then his entire face creased and he threw back his head to laugh, a deep-throated, anise-scented laugh.

And his turban did not fall off.

'Alice, who told you such a tale of pearls?' Father asked, clearly embarrassed.

'I thought that it must be so.'

The merchant – I do not recall his name – asked me if I had ever seen an oyster. He drew a misshapen grey shell from his pack. Cupping his dark, beringed hands around it, he told me to examine it closely. Bringing his hands nearer to the lamp, he opened them, the shell falling open as well, and in each palm appeared a vessel lined with pearl, as if many pearls had melted and flowed over its rough surface, blanketing it with beauty.

I timidly touched a fingertip to it, expecting it to be frozen like ice around a branch. But it was merely cool. And solid.

'It is called mother-of-pearl,' said Father.

The merchant told me that the oyster produced fluid to line its shell. 'For comfort!' he said. 'Is that not a miracle?' And when a grain of sand or some other rough particle flowed inside the oyster would cover it as well with the pearly fluid, until it was so smooth it was no longer a source of irritation. 'It is a gem to us, but a featherbed to the oyster. Or perhaps a featherbed covered in silk.'

'Is this not clever?' Father asked me. 'And now he will show us how he pierces this pearl.'

The merchant brought out a very slender steel drill, driven by a lead wheel and belt, and held the pearl to it. It was simple to see how it worked, though I cringed to watch such a beautiful thing pierced, expecting disaster. But there was only a little dust. He widened the hole using wire and a little sand, and then slipped the pearl on to a silken string.

'God bless the oyster,' I said. I do not remember saying that, but Father told the story over and over again. He said that neither he nor the merchant had the heart to complete my education by reminding me that the oyster would have been eaten.

Edward clapped his hands at this story of how I learned the true nature of a pearl. We were sitting in a pretty meadow, our horses tethered nearby, and he had just given me a most exquisite comb for my hair, bone overlaid with mother-of-pearl and several discs of lapis arrayed along it, as if drops of a beautiful blue liquid had splashed across it. He had asked me to remove my headdress and, after showing the comb to me and watching me with pleasure as I ran my fingers over the beautiful pearl and lapis, had tucked it in my hair. It was such an intimate, tender gesture after my suffering so much fear that he had abandoned me, I felt my heart might burst.

We had been together at the hunting lodge for several days, and on each day he had given me pearls or items decorated with them. I had not lost my wits, I was well aware I was being bought, yet this was Edward's way and came from his heart. I chose to be grateful for such loving generosity. I understood that his leaving me at Eltham had been a foretaste of how our life would be. Of the dance.

'You are the pearl in my life, Alice, my comfort, my solace, a creature of beauty and light.'

In his remarkable blue eyes I saw only love when he spoke those words. I fell into his arms, holding him as tight as I might.

'I have dishonoured you with my heedless talk,' he had said before making love to me on the first night at the lodge. 'As your lover I should protect you, cherish you, uphold your honour. In this I have failed you when I owe you so much. You have restored me.'

I had asked if we might talk at once of Dom Francisco's revelations regarding the great secret Janyn's family had protected. I did not wish to waste our precious days together cautiously circling the issue. Edward was blessedly willing to oblige me. It was a difficult conversation, but I had prayed over it, and felt God's guidance in my impulse to be honest with Edward, to reveal to him the pain and confusion in my heart. He expressed remorse for all that I had lost for the sake of protecting his kingship, but assured me that hiding the child had been the only solution, both for himself and the boy. A child of such lineage would never have been safe unless hidden as a peasant or in a closed community such as an abbey – a foreign abbey.

'Even so, your mother might have given up any contact with her child and spared my family the dangerous journeys,' I said.

He nodded. 'That was her choice. In all such things my mother thought of herself first, and only very much later, when she could no longer avoid it, acknowledged that others had been affected. She never asked forgiveness or expressed remorse.'

'What was done then cannot be undone. For Bella and I to flourish, I must seek the light, not fester in darkness.' The relief in Edward's eyes, the subtle relaxing of his body, was my reward for absolving him. I entertained him then with a description of my happy reunion with my daughter, and expressed my joy in the prospect of being with her, my sister and grandparents at Fair Meadow in summer.

He listened quietly, contentedly, and then talked to me of his own children. His worry that his daughter Isabella would never wed. His plans for his three eldest sons, giving them pieces of his kingdom to keep them busy and content.

'Though I fear my Philippa means to leave this life soon, I have no such intention. Edward is distracted by Joan at the moment, but will soon grow impatient for my crown. He is for the Aquitaine. Lionel to Ireland goes.' He believed they would find their new responsibilities challenging. John would soon be invested as Duke of Lancaster; he would be an important power in the North. 'I shall then have more time to rest. I grow old, Alice. Though not yet ready to die, I should like some time to be quiet, to be with you, to talk of the small, everyday things.'

I, too, wished for more time with Edward. Away from court, alone with him, and no longer afraid of betraying Philippa, I had fallen deeply in love with him. As I opened my heart to him, he responded by confiding in me and becoming more curious about my dreams, my preferences. We had begun as lovers and now added friendship.

We spent most of our time in the bedchamber he had ordered the servants to decorate for me. It was filled with silk-covered cushions in jewelled colours, the bed was hung with indigo curtains embroidered with silver thread, the ceiling had been painted like the night sky, with a gorgeous silvery moon, and the walls hung with tapestries depicting the Goddess Diana hunting with a bow. We spent many happy hours in that room, making love, talking, playing chess, spinning out dreams of our life together.

When we were not in my chamber, we were riding out in the countryside. On one particularly warm evening, I sighed as we returned to the lodge. 'It seems a pity to go within.' While I bathed away the dust of the long ride, Edward ordered a tent erected on the lawns. What a wonder it was for me, who had grown up in the city, to sleep outside that night and wake to the birdsong and the dewy morning chill. I did not want that interlude with him to end.

But of course it did. One morning I woke to the sounds of the household preparing to move. Edward had already told me that he would not intrude on my time with my family at Fair Meadow. We would be together again in late-summer. In truth, I was glad I would have my family to myself, for they would not be at ease in his presence and we had so many years to make up for; but I would sorely miss Edward and the life we were creating together. I looked round my beautiful chamber – already every item evoked a happy memory.

As Gwen packed for me, Edward took me out into the garden, and there he presented me with a signet ring. The intaglio was an amethyst with the Virgin and child cut into it, symbolising me and my daughter, and in the surrounding gold were the initials A and E intertwined.

He put it on my finger, and kissed my hand. His eyes held mine as he said, 'Within is a charm to keep you safe. Write to me if you have need. All my people will know that a letter with this seal comes straight to me.' His seal, a crown twined with woodbine and our initials, would be for his messages to me.

'I should write if I am in trouble?' I asked. 'Not simply to remind you of me?'

'My love, I need no reminding. I think of you with every breath.' He kissed my hands. 'Write only if you have need of me or require counsel. I am determined that we shall not feed the gossips. I trust you to know when you need to write. And I shall reply as quickly as I may.'

The ring, the arrangements, all this felt more substantial, more secure, than what had gone before. I was content.

My grandparents, Dame Agnes and Master Edmund, had arranged for household servants and ensured that my home was readied for occupancy. Fair Meadow. As we approached the manor, memories of Janyn filled my mind. I had expected my former joy would haunt me on my return. But when it over-whelmed me as I rode through a village that had always served as my landmark for being almost home, I discovered that I was not as well prepared as I had hoped. My grief was an ache deep within despite my love for Edward and my renewed joy in life.

That ache would always be there; it was part of me. My heart could hold both joy and grief.

The air was sweet and sighed across the peaceful fields of Fair Meadow. As I dismounted in the courtyard, Bella rushed out of the door and I crouched down just in time to catch her in my open arms. Already she smelled of sun and earth, herbs and flowers and horses. I was strengthened in my resolve to win her away from the emotionally barren household of Queen Joan. Here she could be a proper child. She would know love, and she would love. We would be a full and happy household – my grandparents, Mary, Nan, Bella and me.

Hands that know the earth in all its moods know God's wisdom. Grandmother's wisdom was healing to me now. With my beloved Bella and Mary, I planted flowers, especially roses that Grandfather had brought from Dame Tommasa's courtyard. When the house had been vacant after Master John's death, my grandfather had slipped into the courtyard and taken clippings from various shrubs.

'I saved them for your homecoming, Alice.' Grandfather stood over them with an air of uncertainty. He had led me away from the dinner table to show me. They were arranged in little pots along the windowsill of my bedchamber.

I had seen this gentle side of my grandfather only when he rode with me before my marriage. Now, moved beyond words, I put my arms around him and kissed him on the cheek, then rested my head on his shoulder. 'It is the best gift, Grandfather.'

He patted my back and said nothing. Further words were not necessary.

Bella slept with Gwen and me, and we were seldom apart. She had been timid after her first exuberant greeting. Hanging back, wary, uncertain of her place. On our first night together I woke in the darkness and found my child sitting up, biting her nails and breathing in frightened little gasps. I did not ask why but simply gathered her in my arms and softly sang to her. Slowly her little body relaxed and soon she slept in my embrace. In the morning I said nothing of it. I asked if she would like to help me plant the roses. Working side by side in the gardens nurtured my daughter and me as much as it did the flowers and herbs we so happily tended.

It warmed my heart to see my sister Mary grown so beautiful and strong. She sometimes spoke of Father, remarried now and busy with an infant and a wife who was too pious to accept an invitation to visit his harlot daughter. Mary tried to soften all that she said of him, but it proved difficult.

'Let him be,' I finally told her. 'I have fond memories of him from before my betrothal. The years since have not robbed me of those early recollections.'

Mary's memories of Father were not so fond, and Mother had ever been distant. Will had been her best friend after I left, and his death had set her adrift. Nan had of course been ever present, ever loving. But the greatest blessing in Mary's young life had been Dame Agnes. With her, at last, Mary felt loved and protected.

Grandmother held herself slightly aloof from me. I sensed it the moment I embraced her. But she behaved with affection, and we worked in the garden side by side as well as measuring Bella for some new gowns. Together we chose pretty silks and wools for her out of chests of cloth that had been sent by Richard Lyons, merchandise he had saved from the Perrers household and my old home with Janyn.

It was an ill-timed comment on my part that at last revealed what Grandmother strove to conceal. Several of Janyn's former trading associates had appeared on our doorstep, saying that they were passing by and wished to pay their respects. On each occasion the talk eventually came round to their having heard of my 'favour' in the royal household, and the fact that they hoped I might now support their petitions or recommend their wares and services to the royal purveyors. I endeavoured to be gracious in my assurances that I had no such influence in the household, but that in the unlikely event that someone should ask for a recommendation, I would of course put forward my late husband's partners and guild members.

'They all know!' I cried one evening. 'I've been such a fool to think my relationship with the King was known only at court. Who will ever believe that I was sent there, that I did not seek the King's favour?'

'What also did you think when you took up your adulterous liaison with him – and you a lady of the Queen's household?' Dame Agnes asked. Her tone was carefully lacking in condemnation but her words stung nevertheless. She did not look at me.

I thanked God only Mary and Grandmother were present. I shook with emotion – she had voiced my shame. I replied as calmly as I could manage, 'I am sorry you disapprove of me. For my part, I had hoped that you would understand how little choice I had in this. I beg you, never speak of my relationship with the King to Bella or even allow her to overhear such talk.'

I told myself that she would not judge me so harshly had she known the whole story of my need for the royal couple's protection. Nor did she know of the Queen's complicity. But I wondered if that would have mattered to her. As she had judged the Dowager Queen, so she judged me.

'You cannot protect Bella from the gossip,' she said, her eyes cold.

'Are you warning me that I cannot trust you?' I demanded.

We both stared at one other aghast, witnessing the pent-up pain between us. I saw in her eyes the horror I felt in my heart.

Mary stepped between us. 'Stop this! We are together again at last, something we have all prayed for. Do not ruin it with angry words. You love each other. Alice had no choice in any of this. I beg you, both of you, remember your love for each other.' She had caught the right hand of each of us and now brought them together.

Dame Agnes's mouth trembled. She was close to tears as she said, 'Oh, Alice, I have been so frightened. You cannot imagine. With Janyn's disappearance, then Dame Tommasa's . . . The rumours of Master John's murder.'

So Geoffrey had not been the only one to hear of that, how healthy Master John had been shortly before his sudden mortal illness. I let go of her hand and put my arms round her. 'I know, I know.'

'Do you love him? Is he good to you?'

'Yes. I do love the King, and he is very good to me. I did not realise you had been forced to hear of this in public, to feel shame for our family, Dame Agnes. I am sorry.'

We sank down on our knees and prayed for our family. Mary joined us there. We came to a kind of peace.

I used my signet to write to Edward, asking if Bella might now live with Dame Agnes or some other suitable merchant family in London. He wrote back giving me permission to allow her to remain with my grandmother until we might discuss it further in person.

Bella, Mary and my grandparents rejoiced when I told them that, for the time being, Bella would abide with her family. It made my departure for court easier for them, though not so much for me, for I would have her by my side. But the Queen had summoned me, and I must obey. It was not only with Edward that I was set spinning in the dance.

Life back at court settled into a surprisingly domestic and ordinary routine for the most part. I attended the Queen before great feasts and celebrations, assisting her with dressing in a manner that would help enhance her dignity and station and mask her infirmity. When she could spare me, I alternated between happy, restorative weeks with Bella and Mary at Fair Meadow and enchanted weeks with Edward wherever he was abiding. Queen Philippa seldom ventured from Windsor. Travel had become far too painful for her. Edward bided at Windsor only for important occasions or feast days.

In November he celebrated his personal jubilee, his fiftieth birthday, investing Lionel as Duke of Clarence, John of Gaunt as Duke of Lancaster, and Edmund as Earl of Cambridge. With Prince Edward having already done homage for the Duchy of Aquitaine in summer and preparing to move his household, including Princess Joan, to France in late-spring, he was content to sit back and let his younger brothers revel in their own honours. As I looked round at the barons and their ladies from the vantage point of Queen Philippa's entourage, I saw that many whispered among themselves about King Edward's intention of preparing his sons to rule after him. Much was made of the wisdom of Prince Edward's yoking the Aquitaine with England in his future rule. The honours of the brothers so displayed during the jubilee festivities inspired in the people joyous hope in a glorious, strong future for the kingdom. Only I did not like to think of that future.

Philippa worried that more than a few in the crowd prayed for Edward the father's swift departure to make way for the glorious Edward the son.

'I wish my son Edward was already across the Channel,' she said, 'else his pride might become so exaggerated by the roars of the common folk that he will be in danger of stumbling over it.' She addressed the top of my head as I made some last-minute tucks in her gown. 'Would that Lionel were the eldest. He is so much easier in himself.'

Though she had a deep affection for all her children, Lionel was her favourite of those surviving. She believed Edward to be too ambitious and too quick with his temper. 'All refer to him as the noblest of knights, but should not a great warrior take pride in self-control?' John was too fond of bedding every woman who appealed to him. Isabella, the eldest daughter, worried Philippa with her continual rejections of suitors. 'If she were so inclined, I would think she intended to withdraw to a nunnery and take vows. But Isabella is as committed to the pleasures of the flesh as is her brother John.'

I saw that Philippa's children were her anchor, as Bella was mine. My daughter was blossoming under the love of her great-grandparents and her aunt as well as my own on my frequent visits. At court the sudden death of Queen Joan of Scotland shortly after Edward's jubilee reassured me that Bella would not be called back to her household. The rumour was that she had died of a broken heart. I might have felt guilty about my own relief if Edward had truly mourned his sister, but her death had merely dampened his good mood. He was frustrated by his brother-in-law King David's quick betrothal to his mistress. How I envied that woman!

'Joan and I were never affectionate, Alice. She had a sharp tongue and a critical eye that spoke even more sharply than her tongue. I do not wonder that David never complained of her refusal to live with him. But her death is the end of my careful plan. Now David of Scotland will have a child with his new wife, and all my hopes of uniting our kingdoms through a child of Joan and David are dashed.'

Our conversations were thus personal, practical, like the conversations of most married couples. My earlier efforts to learn about the war with France and other matters of the realm stood me in good stead as Edward confided in me now. I was honoured to have his trust. He sought my advice in his financial concerns, and in his dealings with merchants and financiers. I sought his regarding my hawks, hounds and horses, for I saw how he enjoyed teaching me about such things.

I hesitated to consult with him about more serious matters such as the appropriate etiquette regarding my ambiguous position in his household. Such questions stoked his temper. He insisted that I was the mistress of his household away from Windsor and all his servants should defer to me. There could be no argument. I knew full well it was not that simple. Though most of the nobles treated me with respect, many of the servants found subtle ways to insult me. I still found the machinations of court confusing and suspected I always would, for I was kept at one remove as an unofficial, politely overlooked, member of the King's household, and little more than a servant in the Queen's.

Edward's most helpful and insistent advice to me concerned the importance of developing strong friendships at court.

'You cannot thrive without allies among my courtiers, Alice. Find a few men powerful enough to come to your aid should you have need of them.'

To aid me and, as I saw with Philippa, to keep me informed about the King. I realised this was how Jean Froissart, a fawning Fleming, had bought his way into the household in the past year. He had presented Philippa with a history of her husband's earlier victories, and she saw his future usefulness. He had now become a fixture at court, Philippa's eyes and ears, though in private she complained of his overweening pride.

I was grateful that Geoffrey and I were much together of late, as he had been left in England to serve as a clerk overseeing the Duke of Clarence's properties near London, and was also working increasingly in the Duke of Lancaster's household, as Gaunt administered his now extensive properties. Geoffrey was always a reliable source of news.

My other good friend at court was William Wykeham, a cleric who had so impressed Edward in matters of building and the organisation of large projects that he was being given more and more responsibility. Geoffrey admired him as well, which further recommended him to me. I had spoken to Wykeham on several occasions and discovered we shared common interests in decoration and the art of balance and proportion. He had taught me that what I had thought purely a visual art was grounded in mathematics. He seemed to enjoy providing me with examples that proved his point.

Now that I had possession of my homes, I took an active interest in managing them – indeed, I took my responsibility as a landholder very seriously, finding in it the ballast I needed. It gave me a sense of purpose. Wykeham proved most helpful in advising me about the improvements I wished to make on the house and barns at Fair Meadow, to the extent that he even rode out there with me on several occasions to advise me. I enjoyed his company. He would apologise for his extended discourses on various aspects of construction and repair, and then laugh with delight when I plied him with further questions.

'But I applaud your eager curiosity, Mistress Alice. Too few landholders take such an interest.'

On one of our excursions he had witnessed my difficulties with Peter, the steward at Fair Meadow who had been chosen by Grandfather. Peter would shake his head at me, arguing that he had 'never known it to be done that way, mistress' when I suggested an improvement, and continue to plod along in the old way.

'His duties have moved beyond his depth of competence, Mistress Alice,' Wykeham said. 'I have had reason of late to employ a man, formerly a steward on Queen Joan's estates, who is wasted on my small projects. He would be excellent for your purposes, one who would blossom as your properties expand.' He knew of my resolve to provide for my daughter and myself through incomes from rents and crops, and of my interest in new methods of husbandry. I had recently acquired another small manor north of London.

'I agree with you about Peter's limitations, Master William, but as he is a worthy man, a good, honest worker, I must needs find a steward who would put him at his ease in a secondary position. It takes a diplomatic character to achieve that, and it must be handled well by the new steward as well as myself.'

'Robert Broun is such a man,' said Wykeham. 'But do not take my word for it. I shall bring him along on my next visit, and you may decide for yourself.'

They arrived at Fair Meadow on a sunny late-summer day that had begun quite chilly but was warming under the cloudless sky. Peter and I had been arguing about my adding a second groom to the staff. I had noticed a boy hanging around the stables when he was not needed in the kitchen for weeks. Seeing how well the animals responded to him, I told the groom to train him when the lad was finished with his other chores. Soon he proved himself indispensable. But Peter complained that there was not enough work for two grooms, and that he did not have the time to see to the training of the lad.

Wykeham rode up as I was pacing the yard, pondering how to deal with Peter. The stranger with him sat at ease on his horse, obviously enjoying the conversation and the journey. He was fair-haired and tanned, a man who had spent most of the summer out of doors. When Wykeham introduced him, Robert Broun's ready smile and specific compliments on what he had seen of the manor so far won my approval. I thought to test him out right away, explaining the disagreement over the groom.

'No doubt he is a one manor man,' said Robert. 'As you've recently added a second manor, he is resisting out of fear that he cannot cope with the added responsibility.'

I offered Robert the position of steward over all my properties if he managed to make such an arrangement enticing to Peter. Within hours the usually morose Peter was showing him around the property with a beaming, relaxed countenance. I was indeed indebted to Wykeham.

One courtier I counted no ally continued to pursue me from afar, by way of infrequent letters. I scraped the parchments, once read, and used them for accounts. I did not trust William Wyndsor.

I returned to court to find Edward ailing with gout. His physician Master Adam had consulted several colleagues before making his recommendations. Edward was advised to ride, hunt, walk more, and drink and eat less. The physicians assured him that gout was nothing his subjects need be concerned about, being a disease responsive to the prescribed changes in diet and activity. But Edward took it as a portent of old age, and was of two minds about what he must do. When determined to lighten his girth and live a long and active life he would keep me close to him, showering me with gowns and jewels, and making love to me as if to prove he could still do it. In truth, there were times when he could not, and those times seemed to be when he had imbibed more than usual. I swore to him that I was content simply to be with him, that my love for him was not dependent on bed sport. But after those embarrassments he would fear that he had offended God with his adulterous liaison with me and neglect of his wife, and would send me away. He would then hie to Windsor to spend time with Philippa.

I was frightened by Edward's pain, physical and spiritual. I tried not to feel wounded by his inconstancy, but to understand it.

I threw myself into managing my properties, the one area in which I had some control and skill, and making a home for Bella. With some thought to enrolling her in a small grammar school in our parish in London, where she would become acquainted with other merchant families, I began to ready Janyn's, now my, house in London for longer occupancy. While the school was close enough to my grandparents' home for Bella to attend from there, I took this as a welcome excuse to fuss over the home I so loved in the city.

But no matter how hard I worked, I could not completely forget my anxiety; for I saw Edward's absences as portents of his abandoning me for good.

When the Queen summoned me to work on her gowns for the Christmas court, she noticed my troubled state and gently counselled me to bide my time.

'It is a bit of temper at his own ageing body, Alice, nothing more. Be patient.'

Patience. Obedience. I tried to calm my mind with prayer and work, and when away from court spent as much time as possible with my family. Bella eased my heart. Dame Agnes and I grew close again, and my sister Mary and brother John became my favourite companions.

Winter 1363

In early-winter Father surprised us all by announcing his intention to betroth Mary to a member of his guild who had lost his wife the previous year and had three small children in need of a mother. I hated the thought of losing my sister's companionship. Mary, sweet, obedient Mary, was quite obviously unhappy, and yet assumed she must comply. She had met Thomas Lovekin on several occasions and considered him a doddering old man. His children were ten, eleven, and twelve, not so needy as Father claimed.

'But what recourse have I? Had you any choice, Alice?'

Avoiding that painful topic, I reminded her that the Church insisted on both parties freely agreeing to pledge their troth. 'Remember that when you are introduced to him after Sunday Mass. Say nothing implying agreement until you know that you might find him acceptable.'

Memories of my own presentation at Mass assailed me as Agnes, Gwen and I worked on Mary's new robe for her appearance. It was a joy to work on clothes for her. With her pale red hair, she looked best in Mother's old favourite colours, light blues and greens. We chose a tabby-woven plaid cloth in shades of green for the overdress, and a fancifully dagged short cape in pale blue to match her eyes. With these she wore a Lincoln green headdress adorned with a spray of seed pearls and silver embroidery. The embroidery looked so beautiful that we added an echo of it to the cape. She was a vision of beauty in that gown. But so young! Younger than I had been when presented at Sunday Mass.

God was watching over Mary. This Thomas turned out to be the nephew of the one she remembered, in his early-thirties only and quite pleasant and presentable. His children were two, four and five. Mary's heart went out to them. In a few weeks she was betrothed, the wedding to take place after I returned from Windsor and the annual Garter festivities in early-May.

God watched over me as well. As Edward's gouty discomfort lessened, he welcomed me back into his heart and bed with all the warmth that had been lacking during that dark autumn and winter. *Deus gratias.*

A year went by most peacefully but for an unwelcome change in Edward's attitude towards my financial independence. Suddenly he sought to control my business activities in subtle ways. One evening during one of my sojourns at Eltham he sent for me after I had retired for the night. I found him pacing in agitation – hardly in an amorous mood.

'I understand that Richard Lyons continues his interest in your business,' he began, holding up his hand to forestall my response. 'His role as executor of your late husband's estate has surely long been resolved.'

'Yes, but I have retained him as my adviser. I do not understand why you have taken an interest in this, my love. And why address it now? Did Richard offend you today?' He had been among the guests at dinner.

'I take an interest in all that concerns you. I know he also tried to interfere when John Mereworth enfeoffed his manor of West Peckham to you and Dom Hanneye.'

It had been an honour I had insisted on accepting, the trust of the knight. Mereworth was an honourable man and had offered a substantial fee essentially for little more than my signature and that of Dom Hanneye. I had been flattered by his choosing me.

'Richard dislikes Sir John, but I prevailed, my love.' It seemed a trivial concern, but the time of night suggested that Edward did not consider it such and that worried me.

'Lyons has petitioned the Pope to annul his marriage. A dishonourable act. I do not like you associating with him.'

Perhaps Edward was not aware of the absurdity of his judging Richard when he was unfaithful to his own marriage contract, but I was. 'He has been a good friend and I rely on his advice. We might not always agree, but I learn from our arguments.'

Edward remained adamant. I said no more, hoping that it would be forgotten.

A few days later, having returned to London, I was mortified to learn from Grandfather that Edward had issued an official order that Richard Lyons should keep the peace with me, and not interfere with my going where I wished on the King's business and on my own. Despite my sincere efforts to impress on Edward what a friend I considered Richard, I felt responsible for this very public embarrassment. I resented Edward's interference in the part of my life over which I felt I had some control.

I expected to be shunned by all of London for the incident, which would surely inhibit my ability to trade. But I'd underestimated the cachet of my position as the King's mistress and business partner. The guildsmen, merchants and lesser knights came courting me in even greater numbers for my business connection with the King. The only one avoiding me was Richard.

As time passed and I did not cross paths with him, I attended Mass in his parish, wishing to make peace. I approached him after the service. He was alone. His expression was guarded, of course.

I simply said, 'Richard, I did not know that His Grace meant to issue that proclamation. I knew that he wished me to be free to act on my own account, but I did not know what he had in mind regarding you. I have always spoken of you to him as a trusted friend.'

To my relief Richard's expression warmed as I spoke. He reached out, took my hands, and squeezed them. 'I am glad to hear that. I could not think how I had offended you and why you had not come to me to discuss it.'

I noticed many glancing our way, the wealthier merchants and their spouses, obviously expecting fireworks. They were disappointed.

'I would have come to you had I anticipated the King's action. You have been a good friend to me and my family over the years, Richard.'

'I admit that at first I was outraged. It was no small thing to have King Edward attack my honour. But when my temper cooled, I realised that I had perhaps overstepped my position on a few occasions. Thank you for coming to me, Alice. Let us begin anew as friends.'

He invited me to attend a dinner for some visiting merchants in a few days, and I quite happily accepted.

I enjoyed being in London after my sister's marriage. Thomas welcomed me into their home, and I rejoiced to watch her blossom in her love of her husband and step-children, and to witness the excitement with which they all anticipated her first lying in. On a rare sunny morning in January she was delivered of a daughter – fair of face and of the gentlest disposition.

Only after Mary's churching did I permit myself to look inward at a truth I'd avoided. My courses had not come in two months and my nipples were suddenly so tender that I gently distracted Edward when he would suck on them to arouse me. Though I had refused to think about it while Mary needed me, I had been haunted by memories of feeling thus about Janyn's attentions when I'd carried Bella. I was not ill in the mornings this time, but was quite certain I was with child. The King's child.

I was terrified, and in my terror hesitated to tell Edward. I did not know how he might take the news. Feared that he might send me away. At court the accepted practice was to arrange for a hasty marriage for an unmarried woman of good family suddenly with child by a noble, so that their bastards could plausibly be considered legitimate – by all but the new husbands, who would have been financially encouraged to ease the conscience of the true father. I feared that Edward would so dispose of me.

Joan had warned me not to conceive.

Gwen's tender ministrations suggested she had guessed and was only awaiting my confidence to express her concern. I realised that I was intensifying my fear by keeping it to myself. It was time to tell Edward. I wrote to him requesting a meeting. Before the evening meal I spent a while at the parish church, praying for the strength I so needed to protect my child – my children.

That evening I told Dame Agnes and Gwen and watched fear colour their response. Grandmother held her neck, as if imagining a hanging. Gwen gave a little cry and clenched her hands tight until her knuckle bones were visible through the taut skin. Though she had seemed to suspect my condition, to have her suspicion confirmed was clearly a shock.

'But the pessary,' she whispered, 'and the physicks . . . They protected the Princess. I prepared them just as I was taught.'

I reached over to press Gwen's hand, reassuring her. 'You are not at fault. They protected me for a long while. God must have a purpose in suddenly rendering them ineffective.' I fought to retain my composure though inwardly I was as frightened as she.

Grandmother asked, 'What will you do?'

'I have sent a message to His Grace requesting a meeting.' *And I am praying, praying.*

'He won't come here?' Gwen exclaimed, glancing around as if seeing a hovel.

'I doubt that he would, Gwen, but if he should, I would be proud to welcome him into my fine home.'

I spent the next few days endlessly pacing and praying. I was terrified.

Then Richard Stury appeared at my door like a harbinger of doom, glowering in his dark robes. Edward summoned me to Eltham. Stury would escort me. We would depart the following day. And then Stury was gone again, striding through the drifting snow. I was grateful to have so much to do to prepare for my departure that I could not waste time on further worry. Bella must be bundled up and delivered to her grandparents' house, my steward Robert Broun must be told of any business I had not had time to complete, Gwen must pack for us, the servants must be informed. I must go to Mary at her home and find an opportunity when her children were distracted to tell her my news, and that I would be away. I must rest a little.

But it was difficult to rest after my conversation with Mary.

'How will you explain a brother or sister to Bella?' she asked.

I did not know. That was another worry I was glad to have little time to fret about. But Mary wanted me to devise an explanation then and there.

'I cannot think of that now, Mary. I have all that I can possibly cope with preparing to tell His Grace. And Her Grace. What I might say to Bella I shall decide anon.' Bella might have more than a puzzling sibling to cope with if things did not go well with Edward and Philippa.

I was certain that this would end my role in the Queen's household. How could it not? And then what would become of Bella and me?

'You are wealthy, Alice,' Mary reminded me with a little laugh.

'But I am a woman alone.'

She hugged me. 'Forgive me. I see that you are frightened. I pray the King is worthy of your love and loyalty.'

*

Though I'd dressed warmly for the journey in a squirrel-lined cloak, I thought I would freeze to death on the barge. Gwen covered me with a fur mantle and still I shivered. It was not merely the weather, of course. It was fear that chilled me to the bone. Edward and I had never discussed the possibility of a child. I did not know how much men knew about preventing conception, but thought they must be blissfully, wilfully naïve else they would take more responsibility in sowing their seed. I had wept last night, remembering how different it had been when I knew that I was carrying Bella. Janyn's joy had buoyed me through all the long days when I ached and sickened. It had been a gladsome time, and after her birth I had yearned for another child. Now I dreaded what I might be commanded to do.

Snow softened the woodland and parks around Eltham. It was a beautiful palace, and I had experienced much joy there. But now I approached it as a place of judgment, the place in which I would learn my punishment. Richard Stury had not helped with his stern silence. As if he knew. But, of course, he could not.

Gwen and I were escorted to my usual chamber, already made comfortable with a glowing brazier, heavy tapestries to block out draughts, heated stones ready to wrap and place beneath our feet as we sat to drink hot spiced wine, eat fresh bread still warm from the oven and a stew that was fragrant and hot. It was a moment in which I gave thanks for being the mistress of a King. I took care over the amount of wine I consumed, needing my wits about me when summoned to Edward.

The summons came just as I was casting longing looks at the bed piled high with blankets and fur-lined counterpanes, yearning for a midday nap, a few moments of unconsciousness. I was grateful my escort was a page, not Stury. A moment of grace. I had chosen one of Edward's favourite gowns, red brocade over an azure blue silk undergown, and the braids of hair wound over my ears were held in place by a gold netting thick with seed pearls. I wore a pearl ring, earrings, and the largest of the pearls he had given me hung from a gold chain around my neck.

Edward had been out riding. His face was red from the cold and his eyes shining and clear. I could smell the fresh air on him as he crossed the room to me and lifted me up by the waist.

'My beloved Alice. Each time I see you, I think you more

beautiful than you were before. How is this possible?' He kissed me and set me back on my feet. 'I have ached for you for days. Tonight you shall stay with me.'

He was my love, my dearest Edward, and he loved me. How could I doubt that he would want our child? That he would love our child? But he was King, and I was not his Queen. Our child would be a bastard.

I forced gaiety. 'And you look hale and hardy, my lord. You've been riding in the snow. I can smell the fresh, crisp air on your hair and your clothes.' I lifted one of his hands and sniffed. 'And your skin.' I kissed his palm.

He lifted the palm to my cheek and bent to lift me, enfolding me in his embrace, warming me with a passionate kiss. He set me down with a laugh.

'You see my hunger! Come, let us catch our breath.'

I felt hope kindled in my loins, cradling our child.

We settled by the fire. A servant poured wine, then withdrew. Edward's long white hair glowed brightly in the lamplight and firelight, but now his eyes were cautious.

'So, my beloved, what is so urgent you must see me betimes?'

I took a deep breath. I had decided to speak plainly, quickly, not create additional suspense.

'Edward, I am with child.'

He made an odd sound, a little groan or sigh, so soft and fleeting that I was not even certain I'd heard it.

'How long?'

'A few months.'

A long pause while he stared at the fire. I had to remind myself to breathe.

'Mine?'

The question startled me. 'There is no doubt, Edward. My body belongs to you alone.'

He reached out and took my hand for a moment, squeezing it, studying my face. His expression was one of sad affection. My heart raced.

'Who knows?'

'My maid, my sister, my grandmother.'

He nodded. 'I must think, Alice. I will send for you.'

All warmth left me. I rose and withdrew from his chamber,

amazed that my legs supported me. Gwen took one look at me and then undressed me and tucked me into bed with heated stones. I did not protest. If Edward sent for me in a little while, she would simply dress me again. Now I permitted myself a large cup of spiced wine and, against all hope, fell into a deep sleep.

I dreamed I was adrift on a raft in the middle of a gently flowing river, naked, hugely pregnant, and all along the riverbank archers aimed at me, shooting tiny darts that stung and stuck, but did not draw blood. With each dart the child in my womb grew heavier, duller. I wanted to roll over and off the raft. I imagined how soothing the water would feel. But to move would be to sink those darts into my skin, and I did not know what harm that would do.

'Dame Alice, you are dreaming!' Gwen leaned over me. She held one of my hands to her heart. 'Quickly, you must rise and dress. You are summoned.'

'Is it morning?'

'Just after vespers. You have slept only a little while.'

'I am grateful to be awakened from that horrible dream.'

Edward stood looking out of a casement window when I was shown into the room, hands on hips, legs spread wide. A kingly stance.

'Your Grace,' I said, kneeling to him.

He turned round. 'Your Grace? You are carrying my child, wonder of wonders, and you call me "Your Grace"?' He crouched down to me, not an easy movement for him, and took my hands. 'Rise, my beauty. I have a gift for you.'

He presented me with a ruby brooch and ring, large stones resembling hearts surrounded with pearls, set in delicately filigreed silver leaves trailing tendrils. Ruby hearts caught in woodbine. I wept as he pinned the brooch to my gown and slipped the ring on my finger.

'They are so beautiful, Edward. Hearts and woodbine.'

'Yes – the blood of both of us will nurture this child, Alice. We are now bound as father and mother. Is that not the greatest of miracles?'

'Then you are glad of the child quickening in me?' I asked, searching his face. I saw only joy there, and love.

'Glad? I rejoice, Alice. Our love has been blessed. God has

granted us grace. I am young again. Potent. How could I be anything but glad? I have felt of late your hesitation before lovemaking. I am relieved to know the cause.'

So I had worried him. Perhaps that explained his behaviour towards Richard Lyons.

We made slow, beautiful love that evening. Later, when I woke to find him stroking my belly and watching me, I sat up, wanting to talk. First he insisted on wrapping me in furs and showing me the snow without, falling softly on the woodland.

'Do you not love the silence of snow in the country?' he said. 'Our child will spend all his or her childhood in the countryside. The city is no place for children.'

I loved him so much at that moment I thought my heart might burst.

'I did not see the countryside until I was betrothed.'

I turned to him and we were soon back in bed making love.

It was morning before I could finally ask him the question uppermost in my mind. 'What of Her Grace? When she knows, and how can she not know, she will hardly wish me to remain in her household.'

Edward surprised me by smiling and shaking his head. He was wrapped in a mantle of miniver, his flowing white hair and beard wild, his piercing blue eyes pale in his weather-roughened face. He looked as I imagined warlords of old, never happier than when riding to the hunt – or to war. He often spoke of past battles with a catch in his throat and fire in his eyes. He'd gained weight in the past year, an embarrassment to his pride – his favourite girdle had been lengthened by his tailor months earlier, a necessity that still chafed – but he was still a handsome and imposing figure. When he smiled and shook his head at me, I felt very young and not entirely comfortable about his bare foot exploring between my thighs as we sat in bed together.

'You are an innocent in matters of our kind, Alice. Do you think that Philippa never sought another man for satisfaction? Or that she does not know of us?'

'But I cannot think that any wife would wish to see another woman carrying her husband's child.'

'That much is true. Until you are churched, it is best that you stay away from court.'

Now that I was there, he wished for me to stay a while. With the heavy snowfall making riding treacherous, I was forbidden by Master Adam to ride with Edward. But my love ordered some garden paths cleared so that we might walk out together in the fresh air.

A few days later I heard that he was to entertain some courtiers and merchants at an elegant feast, and sent a page to the King, asking permission to dine in my chamber. I feared that someone might guess my condition and I was not ready for that.

One of Edward's physicians, John Glaston, appeared at my door. Of course Gwen showed him in. He was a pleasant man, kind and reassuring, but as I was not feeling ill, I was not happy to see him.

'Master Glaston, I fear you have been sent in error.' I did not wish to complicate the matter by attempting to lie.

'His Grace wished me to enquire after your health. Are you ill? In any discomfort?' He glanced round the chamber, moving closer to the brazier apparently to see that it was sufficiently stoked.

'I am quite well. My only discomfort is in your being called away from your duties merely to hear me say that.'

He considered the window, then turned to me. 'I am at your service, Mistress Alice.' He gave me a courteous bow. 'His Grace has told me how it fares with you, and has asked that I attend to any discomfort that requires a healer until a midwife is summoned.'

'His Grace is most kind. I am quite well. But I shall not hesitate to send for you if I have need of your services.'

He bowed again and departed with quiet dignity, his dark gown whispering softly in the draught from the open door.

Moments later a page arrived to inform me that I would be expected at dinner.

Thus ensued a most uncomfortable evening. Simon Langham, Bishop of Ely and Edward's new Lord Chancellor, was so attentive that I was certain he already knew of my condition. Fortunately, since his ascent to the post he had proved a good friend to me. He was a delightful man, a brilliant scholar, and at previous leisurely dinners in Edward's chambers we had found a bond in our love of poetry, music and hawking. I had dreaded our first encounter since breaking the news of the child I would bear, expecting that he would be offended by my presence, but it seemed his affection for Edward outweighed all else. He remained as courteous and kind as he had been from the start.

Also in attendance was a couple I knew only slightly, Sir Anthony de Lucy and his wife, who were also oddly attentive.

I half-expected Edward to say something indiscreet, but to my great relief he did not. I had gradually learned to enjoy these small gatherings, watching the King at ease among friends. But that evening I was painfully aware that I had no right by birth, marriage, or official position to be here among them. I withdrew as soon as I might with grace.

Hours later, already abed, I was awakened by a summons to the King's chamber. A servant took my hand to steady me as we stepped between sleeping men in the ante-chamber. Even the guards seemed subdued.

Edward apologised for waking me. He knew me so well he could tell that was so. He himself was already in a simple robe and barefoot, a sign that he had prepared for bed before deciding to send for me. He wrapped me in furs and drew me over to the fire, where he proffered me a jewelled mazer of spiced wine.

He settled in a cushioned chair so close to mine that our knees touched. Leaning towards me, his eyes loving and yet searching, he said, 'Now tell me, what was amiss that you wished to dine alone?'

Despite the furs I was shivering. 'I am with child, my love, your child, yet I am not your wife. I feared their censure and your unease.'

'Alice, my love, you must not be ashamed.' He gave a great sigh and pulled me on to his lap. 'You are precious to me. Both of you,' he whispered into my hair.

I held his great lion head in my hands and kissed him on the mouth. 'You are precious to us.'

He put his hands over mine. 'You are cold.' He reached for the furs and draped them round my shoulders again. 'Perhaps Dom Hanneye will attend you as your confessor when you are in retreat for your lying in. Would you like that?'

My heart warmed to Edward's loving care. 'I should like that very much. But what is this about retreat? I thought to be in London.'

He shook his head. 'No, Alice. I've told Simon Langham to look for an appropriate country house in which you shall retire away from court and any who might wish you harm or hope to gain my favour by seeking yours. You need your rest.'

'Wish me harm?' I had feared the Queen's reaction, but no other's.

'Do not worry. You are under my protection. Come.' He led me back to the seat and settled himself opposite me once more. He took my hands. 'As for seeking my favour through you, Mereworth was only the beginning of what you may further encounter. He sought to honour you by trusting you to enfeoff his manor. Others will do so as well. Charge them a good fee!' Edward's face crinkled in an affectionate smile.

I felt small, ignorant, and frightened. It seemed I had under-estimated the significance of bearing the King's child. 'Might my grandmother be with me for the birth?'

'Whoever you wish . . . within reason, of course. When Simon has found the house – somewhere in the fens, we thought, near Ely, where as Bishop he has influence – then we shall know how large a party you might accommodate. Be at ease, my love. You are my treasure. I shall take good care of you.'

In the end, we spent the night together. But although he warmed my body, my heart was chilled by my new under-standing. To bear the offspring of a King was no small, private matter. I feared for my child. Isabella had gone to great lengths to guard her bastard. People had died protecting the mere knowledge of his existence. I pressed the softness that protected the life we had begun. I remembered how vulnerable I had felt when great with Bella, my clumsiness, my sudden exhaustion. I was glad that Simon Langham was preparing a sanctuary for me – for us.

> *'Ago was every sorwe and every feere;*
> *And bothe, ywys, they hadde, and so they wende,*
> *As muche joie as herte may comprende.'*

> – Geoffrey Chaucer, *Troilus and Criseyde*, III, ll. 1685–87

Summer 1364

Bella, old Nan, Dom Hanneye and, of course, Gwen were with me in Southery from the beginning, and Mary would join us in September, in time for my lying in. Dame Agnes had wished to come but Grandfather had suffered a fall earlier in the year and his back was not healing. He might not walk again. Clearly her place was with him. She had suggested that Bella remain with her to attend school, but I treasured, indeed hoarded, my time with my daughter, and arranged for Dom Hanneye to tutor her while we were in the fens. I had met the midwife recommended by Bishop Langham and was very happy with her.

My old nurse Nan seemed reinvigorated by the responsibility of taking Dame Agnes's place in overseeing the household while I was unwell. As I was now twenty-two; by my reckoning she was sixty, Edward's senior by ten years. Yet she rose with the dawn every morning to make certain that the servants stoked the fires and that the cook had something warm and nourishing to coax my appetite and Bella's. Gwen had not come to know her well until our time at Southery; now she observed Nan's shrewd handling of the servants with admiration.

'Nothing is too small for her attention and the servants have learned that. They are so well behaved, I would swear they are not the same staff as when we arrived.'

The house had a solar above the hall, but as it was accessed by a steep and narrow set of ladder-like steps, I proposed that Gwen and I should share a part of the hall around which a local carpenter would design and install screens. The carpenter proved gifted and enthusiastic, creating an intricately carved set of screens depicting the seasons and wildfowl of the fens in a band across the tops. Our private chamber still left ample space for activities and meals in the hall. Bella and Nan slept in one part of the solar and Dom Hanneye in the other, with my steward, Robert Broun, when he was at the manor.

Robert had become a welcome constant in my life, both steward and friend. He proved himself trustworthy over and over again. He was not much older than I was, but seemed more mature and steadier than most men his age. His smile lit up a decidedly handsome face: blond, blue-eyed, fair. He carried himself with quiet ease and confidence, spoke with authority on shepherding resources, and loved the countryside. He was wonderful with Bella, often inviting her to accompany him on his rides about the estates. He spent most of his time on my other properties: seeing to projects, supervising servants, returning once a month to report to me. Dom Hanneye and Richard Lyons also grew to respect his opinions and often invited him to accompany them to properties on which we were considering transactions. I wanted to ensure that Bella and the child I carried would want for nothing. I would not simply depend on Edward to see to our child's future, remembering Princess Joan's warning that I would rue the day if I did so. I took her advice to heart, for I understood that she had thought long on the vagaries of love.

In the beginning I did not like the fen country. The manor house stood on a low hill, and although the immediate area was above the level of the sea, within a fairly brief walk I could reach the water meadows, vast stretches of whispering reeds and grasses hidden between the villages and manors that stood on higher ground. I found the flatness of the fens strangely threatening, as if I were too exposed. It was all too insubstantial – I could not trust the earth when it would so suddenly give way to marsh. There was a shimmering quality to the light, and water fowl dominated the sky with their wide-winged flight and their lonely calls. I remembered, too, the lure of the water at Sheppey, when I'd walked out on to the night sands and beyond.

I had become accustomed to riding out – or walking in my present condition – with only Gwen for company at Fair Meadow, and often when at Eltham or one of Edward's hunting lodges. At Southery I did not dare ride out or walk far without a guide. At first I chose to stay within the grounds.

But I grew restless. On my short walks I began to collect bits of shrubs and old nests, and with the odds and ends in the sewing baskets we had brought to Southery I fashioned fantastical costumes for Bella, particularly elaborate headdresses such as Edward and Philippa favoured for court festivities – birds rising from great nests, ships at full sail. At first, Gwen and Bella helped with the needlework, but gradually they began to question the value of the time so spent.

'Shall I see to the mending and to letting out your gowns for the babe, Mistress?' Gwen asked.

I agreed, though I thought it a great pity to lose her talented help.

'What is it for, Mother?' Bella asked. 'I am not invited to the court. I would rather help Gwen.'

I did not acknowledge the confusion in my daughter's eyes until one evening when she baulked at a large headdress depicting a pageant wagon on top of which a jester stood on his hands.

'It is horrid and heavy and hot and I will not wear it!' It was the first time she had ever shouted in my presence. Her face flushed with temper and her eyes wild, she raced so heedlessly up the ladder-like stairs that I feared she would fall. She flung the head-dress out of the solar window. Rushing back down to the hall, she threw herself into old Nan's arms and clung to her, refusing to speak to me.

I clumsily went to her, pressing my hand to her back. 'Forgive me, my love. I did not mean to frighten you.' She was hot to the touch, and I nodded in answer to old Nan's wordless advice for me to leave Bella alone for now.

'Dame Alice—'

I saw the concern in Dom Hanneye's eyes and fled out into the garden. But once out there I did not know where to go, what might help dissolve the knot of anguish in my belly and my throat.

'Bella is unharmed.' Dom Hanneye had followed me. He placed a calming hand on my shoulder. 'Come, let us walk.'

I nodded, unable to speak, uncertain what I would say if I could. I suddenly saw as if I had stepped outside myself how mad my behaviour must have seemed. When at last I found my voice, I said, 'It is little different from my reckless behaviour on the Isle of Sheppey, walking out into the water, is it?'

'It is not at all like that.' Dom Hanneye took my hand and paused until I looked him in the eyes. 'You are with child, in an unfamiliar place that you find threatening. You wish to make reparation to your daughter for all the time you've lived apart, but for all that, you are currently denying yourself the activities that have always been your succour and escape.'

I could not help but laugh at myself through tears of embarrassment.

'I recommend that you resume your long walks. The groom grew up near here and knows every twist and turn of the land. Take Gwen and walk with the lad. That is my advice.'

'And Bella?'

'She will be so relieved not only to escape punishment but also to escape the horrid costumes that she will count this as a delightful victory.'

Once again I took comfort in my walks, and Bella often accompanied me. Dom Hanneye had been right, she had the blessed resilience of any child. She loved the gardens, riding lessons, and the knowledge that we would have a long stretch of uninterrupted time together. I enjoyed listening to her work with her tutor – Dom Hanneye was proving quite able in the role. In observing her with others, I grew to know my child better than I had since she was an infant, and cherished this chance of a new beginning. As to her reaction to the news of my carrying the King's child, she seemed to see nothing wrong in it. That both delighted and worried me. But Dom Hanneye assured me that she was a devout and moral child, simply confident that her mother was a good woman.

Was I a good woman? Dom Hanneye said that God knew I held myself as betrothed to the King, and therefore our union was blessed. God understood that what separated us was man-made and therefore not His law. I knew that my confessor was grasping at slippery arguments here to reassure me and keep me from despair. As Edward's wife was yet alive, his argument did not hold. And yet I have always suspected that God is more understanding than most priests would have us believe – it is their way of frightening us into submission. My chief consolation was that Mary, Mother of God, must have known confusion, for she had neither invited the Angel Gabriel nor the virgin birth. Surely she'd had doubts and misgivings and could empathise with me.

On the long summer days with little to do I had a chance to look back on my life in the royal household, and came to see that the vague sadness I carried in my heart was not only grief for Janyn and his family and my brother Will, but also for the rift that I feared might grow between Queen Philippa and me because of the child I carried. To my eyes, my bearing Edward's child increased our intimacy and the bond between us to a higher level, one that Philippa had not suggested in our little talk at Eltham. I had come to love her, to look forward to the long hours we spent discussing fabrics, jewels, ribbons, leathers, buttons, veils, feathers. We would giggle like girls, daring one another to new heights of extravagance, would gasp at our own daring, and when she was being fitted we made a great show of tilting our heads together to appraise the sempsters' results. I believed she tried to compensate with such little kindnesses for my chilly reception from her other women.

All in all I was most fortunate in my mistress. Philippa was generous, warm, discerning, and valued peace in the household, often reminding us to pause and consider the damage we might do before repeating gossip. She would call on someone to read to us or sing when we found it difficult to stay away from the latest topic of scandal or worry. She also enjoyed hearing about others, especially their extraordinary behaviour, but wanted to know first that it was true and that the speaker was not exaggerating. I had learned to hold my tongue unless I had witnessed the behaviour for myself and would have felt at ease if the person discussed had walked into the room as I spoke. Queen Philippa was a wise and pious woman, worthy of all the love her people held for her.

I would be twenty-three years of age in September, when my child was due, and yet I felt far less responsible for the course of my life than I had imagined I would at that age. It was as if I'd tumbled back into late childhood when I'd first gone to court. When I carried Bella, I'd admitted to Dame Tommasa that what most frightened me was that I felt too young and inexperienced to be a good mother. She had assured me that as my child matured within, so would I mature, and when my child was ready, so would I be. *That is how we become wise, by living each day attending to the lessons God puts in our path.* How I missed Dame Tommasa's calm presence. Once again I was caught up in the fear that I did not have the wisdom to raise the child in my womb, this time because it was a child of royal blood, or half-royal blood. Dom Hanneye's attempt to reassure me only raised further worries. He'd said that if the child were a boy, I would have little to do with his upbringing, and if the child were a girl, I might bring her up as I wished. That the King would hardly care about another girl. Either way, it sounded as if this child would bring me sorrow.

In early-summer I was invited to Bishop Langham's residence near Ely – Edward would be there for a fortnight. He saw this as a lovers' tryst and insisted that we share a bedchamber.

Mostly he and I walked and talked and slept tangled in each other's arms. As we shared the large chamber with sergeants at arms and servants, who slept in an ante-room created by wooden screens, we did not indulge in lively lovemaking, although we managed a few stolen afternoons. The mere fact of my conceiving a child by him had cheered Edward and invigorated him.

On our last day together I dared to speak of my fears for the future.

'I do not wonder at your concern, sweet Alice. While the child is yet an infant, you will not be so much with the Queen,' he told me. 'You shall have a wet nurse, and any servants you require. When you are with the Queen, you must have someone to care for the children in a home in Windsor. When you are with me at Sheen, Eltham, Havering or beyond, likewise Bella and our child shall be near at hand so that you might see them often. Is that to your liking? You've only to ask for what you desire, Alice.'

That you might be my husband, I thought. 'Yes, my love.' I rushed to cover my imagined complaint with the more practical, realistic plans he'd come to expect. 'I should like to make some extensive repairs to my house in London, and perhaps use some of the street property for shops and tenements to lease. To provide more for Bella's dowry.'

He squeezed my hand. 'That's my Alice.'

The trouble was, I did not like all that he perceived in *his* Alice; I did not like the role of spy among my peers. He would name some merchants he wished me to approach when I returned to London, and asked about others with whom I'd dined in London or elsewhere since we had last had such an opportunity to talk. I took care to tell him all I knew of the former, all I had discerned about the latter, but I felt unclean. I prayed for God's guidance in learning to accept my situation. Edward had his reasons, and he was my lord as well as my lover. I must never forget that.

I was glad to return to Southery and retreat into my pleasant cocoon. I did not mind that I was missing the grand celebration of Edward's eldest daughter's marriage. The stubborn Isabella, who had refused all eligible suitors for years, had at last accepted a man who was to her liking and suitable for a Princess, Enguerrand de Coucy. I remembered him as a charming man, always elegantly robed and grandly capped – he favoured hats with large feathers that tickled people as he moved through a crowd. Of course, the Queen's household must indulge in some exotic and feathery headgear and colourful, glittering robes for the nuptials, and I had some passing regrets about missing the fun of planning it. But I welcomed the peace.

When Mary arrived in September for my lying in, she was bursting with the news that Geoffrey was betrothed to a young lady who had been brought up in the Queen's household, the daughter of a Flemish knight.

'How grand! Are you not happy for him, Alice?'

'Philippa de Roet?'

Mary looked disappointed. 'You already knew.'

'No. But she is the only unwed young lady of Flemish descent in the Queen's household at present.'

'So what do you think? Is she beautiful?'

'She is lovely. High-spirited.' Not at all the sort I would have thought to Geoffrey's taste.

'They are whispering that the betrothal has already been consummated, and that she is with child.'

I prayed that it was Geoffrey's, not the bastard of the Duke of

Lancaster. There had previously been rumours of a liaison between Pippa, as she was known, and Lancaster. The news stirred up too many emotions in me, too mixed, and I asked Mary if we might speak of something else while I thought on this.

I prayed that Geoffrey would love Pippa, delight in her high spirits and beauty. Of course, her connections and noble birth were just what his parents had always wished for him.

'A son.' Tears filled Edward's blue eyes.

Tears. I had not expected them from him. He already had five living sons.

'Since I sent Edward, Lionel, John and Edmund out into the world, I have keenly felt their absence. Thomas is eager to follow after them and I cannot hold him back much longer. Now I need not despair, for I have a new son to teach.'

'He will be fair like you,' I said. I could see it already in the newborn. Bella had looked darker, furrier. Just as beautiful, but different. 'Your joy is like a blessed balm to me.'

Edward had arrived but two days after our son's birth. He descended upon me in my little bower like a god of old, large and bellowing and overwhelming. And then, with the utmost gentleness, he lifted our child in his large hands and whispered, 'You are a miracle, my son.'

I wept and laughed at the same time.

But it was plain that I would not long enjoy my son's company. His godfathers were to be the Duke of Lancaster and John Neville, so his name would be John after the Duke. I was disappointed that Edward had ignored my suggestion that my brother John be our son's second godfather. My brother was a fine young man whose company I greatly enjoyed. He had matured into a steady, generous man, and I wished I might so have honoured him. But Neville was a northern baron key to border defences and I understood why Edward wished to honour him. I did have my way with his godmother, my sister Mary. But I knew that it was merely a courtesy. Our son would be fostered in a home appropriate to a king's son, and neither Mary nor I would exert much influence on his life. And yet, how could I regret that his father loved him so?

*

I was summoned to the Christmas court at Kenilworth, the palace of the Duke and Duchess of Lancaster. Queen Philippa wished to make the journey for once. Whenever my lady Blanche used to speak of Kenilworth, her voice rang with happy memories and her eyes shone. Had it not meant leaving John with the wet nurse, I would have been excited about being included.

I also wished I might stay with Dame Agnes, to comfort her, for Grandfather had died shortly after John's birth. But as it turned out she would find some consolation in the presence of her grandchildren. Though Edward had disappointed me by forgetting his promise to house John and Bella close to me, I was relieved that they did not need to make such a journey in winter, and I was happy for Grandmother, for she would find some joy with them in the household. It would soften her grief. I escorted them from Southery to London before continuing on to Windsor and then Kenilworth.

Geoffrey and Pippa were in London, staying with his parents. I paid them a visit before I left for Windsor. The Chaucer home had always been one of my favourite places, pretty and warm and always slightly crowded at meals – Geoffrey's parents both enjoyed a hall filled with people who loved to talk, eat, and drink – his father was a wine merchant, after all. I looked forward to seeing them and divining how my friend fared.

'How goes your little one?' Geoffrey asked.

'John is not so even-tempered as Bella was, but he has captured my heart. And Bella's. She is a loving sister.'

'I've heard that the King is most pleased with you. It was clever of you to bear him a son.'

'Clever? Is that your word or the gossips'?'

'The gossips', of course. Do you think me such a fool as to believe you could arrange the sex of your child? I presume you are going to the Christmas court?'

'I am.'

'Then I feel it my duty as your good friend to warn you to be wary of those who compliment you and seek your advice or support. They see you as their way to the King. He has not kept his promise to you to be more discreet about your relationship and your son.' Geoffrey looked most uncomfortable to be telling me this.

I gave him an affectionate hug. 'Be at ease, my friend. I already know.'

'It is not merely your son. The wording of Richard Lyons's public humiliation was such that all now see you as a business partner to the royal family.'

'I thank you for the warning.' If one could be thankful for troubling news. But I *had* asked him to be my ears.

'How goes it with you and Lyons?' Geoffrey asked.

'He knows that it was not my doing, that I still value his friendship. Indeed, I have retained him as an adviser.' As Pippa had joined us, I said, 'But let us speak of happier tidings. How do you fare with the child?'

She touched her belly and made a face both happy and rueful. 'I did not expect to feel so crowded already!'

'That is nothing compared to how you will soon feel.'

We shared some laughter.

I regretted that I could not stay longer in London, and it was with a heavy heart that I departed for Windsor. Grandfather's death, the eventual departure of my baby John, all this besides the usual pain of leaving Bella and now John as well, was difficult for me. Being a mother was such a troubling mixture of joy in my children and pain in the impermanence of our lives together. I wanted to crawl back into the womb of Southery, the gentle summer spent wrapped in dreams of my child.

But once I saw the work that awaited me on the Queen's gowns and hats for the Christmas celebrations, I had little time to ponder my own problems. I more than made up for missing the fuss of her daughter's wedding. Philippa's hunched and twisted frame was now impossible to disguise, and Edward's choice of a falconry theme had resulted in gowns layered with feathers that quivered with her intermittent tremors and emphasised her short and wide physique. She looked like a frightened chick, not a Queen. I spoke privately with Edward – *'You are tall and long of limb, your posture still wonderfully straight, but Her Grace . . .'* – and received his permission to render Philippa's emblems of falconry in embroidery and gemstones in colours that imitated those of the raptors' feathers. The drape of her garments was also increasingly important, and the sempsters had cut everything too straight. I was grateful to be useful, and also mindful to focus on enhancing the Queen's dignity rather than indulging myself in flights of fancy as I had with Bella at Southery.

In truth, perhaps because I was so grateful to be welcomed back without question after John's birth, I was becoming protective of Philippa. I worried that the journey to Warwickshire might prove too much for her. I wished I might put Her Grace on my lap and hold her in the jostling cart, but one does not suggest such an arrangement to a queen, nor would she have accepted it. She offered up her pain in expiation for the sins of loved ones who had died. By the time we reached our first night's resting place her face was pinched and her breathing shallow. I believe carts are often more uncomfortable than horseback, though of course riding was out of the question for the Queen. By the time we arrived at the beautiful Palace of Kenilworth, Her Grace was in such distress that it was several days before she appeared in public, and even then she was brought to the great hall in a litter and stayed only a short while. My fussing with the drape of her garments proved unnecessary.

The Palace of Kenilworth outshone any of the grand royal homes save Windsor for the grace of its design and the richness of its furnishings. And the light! The amount afforded by the long window embrasures in the great hall, even in the depth of winter, astounded me by day. At night it seemed a multitude of torches, candles and lamps pushed back the darkness. The colourful clothes and jewels of the courtiers were dazzling in the brightness, creating a swirling forest of enchantment.

The Queen's inactivity allowed me more freedom to move about the festivities and enjoy myself than I had anticipated. I hoped to call little attention to myself but to have dressed simply would have done so, and in such surroundings I could not help but take pleasure in being beautifully adorned, part of the gorgeous throng. My own falconry motif was a feathery headdress which I'd sprinkled with pearls, and a trim of feathers on the dagged edge of a short Lincoln green cape I wore over either a deep gold or pale green and gold brocade gown. Red did not appeal to me that winter. Along the spines of the feathers we had attached small pearls, and I'd sprinkled pearls all over the bodices of my gowns.

Our hosts, the Duke and Duchess of Lancaster, had greeted me with warmth and presented me with gifts for John and Bella. I had not expected to be welcomed for my own sake, but to be an inconspicuous part of the Queen's train. My lady Blanche was most kind, sharing her most recent experiences of childbearing and asking after my comfort. Never once did she allude to my child being the King's. My lord John, on the other hand, teased me about being related in some vague degree to the royal family and assured me that young John would be knighted in due course. I was flustered by the attention, feeling out of my depth, and greeted the assumption that my son would be brought up as a noble with ambivalence. I knew that I should be happy for my son, but with every honour afforded him by the Plantagenets, Edward's family, I felt more threatened; that he was one step closer to a foster home where I would never see him. He would be trained and educated to rise far above me.

Yet as I looked round the hall at the sumptuous dress, the proudly scarred men who had fought in France and elsewhere for their King, the elegant women who bore their children and held the families together when their husbands were away, and most of all John's half-brothers and -sisters and his father the King, I wondered how I could ever justify keeping him from this destiny to which he had been born, even had I such power. My son was a Plantagenet, though Edward had chosen to have him known as John de Southery. I set my mind to be happy for him.

Geoffrey had been right – as John's mother I no longer had the invisibility I'd enjoyed at such feasts in the past. I was cajoled into dancing when I preferred to sit in the shadows and observe; I was invited to walk out in the air with ladies who had ignored me before. But I was not free to be with Edward, and my heart sank each time I caught sight of him dancing with a beautiful young woman who glowed in the splendour of his smile.

Perhaps it was fortunate that so many courtiers suddenly sought my advice and partnership in business deals, shipping, land appropriations. It was clear that they thought to ingratiate themselves with Edward by approaching me with 'opportunities', though I found many of their proposals shockingly wrong-headed. No matter, for the distraction permitted me to move through the festivities with grace and prevented such a build up of jealousy as to ruin my next interlude with Edward. I had been taken aback by my possessiveness regarding him; bearing his child had changed our relationship in unexpected ways.

I need not have worried. Edward seemed to have had a satisfying time with his barons and family, and our lovemaking towards the end of our sojourn at Kenilworth was more passionate and vigorous than it had been since before I conceived John. Indeed, I worried lest I'd conceive again too soon, and resumed my old precautions. All in all, I felt more alive and more appreciated than I had in a long while.

Over the course of the next year, as my son John grew fat and mischievous, I found myself surrounded by courtly suitors – suing for money, not love. Sir Anthony de Lucy, for example, wished to offer me the use of and income from his manor of Radstone for life in exchange for a sum that would outfit his kinsman to make his mark in battle on the continent. Such deals would have been abhorrent to my father, who looked for solid value in ships and merchandise, but the Queen herself recommended that I judiciously choose a few such offers.

'In such wise you create a bond with courtiers who might prove of use to you at some future date. It is how it is done.'

Of all the people who suddenly befriended me, the most surprising was Richard Stury, Edward's grim retainer. At first I felt his compliments and small kindnesses, such as a seat closer to a brazier at feasts and information as to the arrivals of friends, were simply by order of his master. But one afternoon he asked if he might discuss a matter of some delicacy with me. I had grown accustomed to his new attempts at smiles, but the deference he showed me in seeing to my comfort and the true delicacy of the situation he revealed to me – a family disagreement over a trust – bespoke a fresh attitude towards me. He was asking for my advice, and I took care over my opinion. He queried me on several points, and then expressed his gratitude.

'I see why His Grace trusts you to go about his business,' he said. 'You can see the straight path through what appear to be twisting and devious laws and customs, and you have a clear head about you. I am most grateful for your counsel.'

'And I am grateful to you for all that you do for me.'

I felt as I had as Janyn's wife and Father's daughter when they conferred with me concerning their trade. It was a heady feeling.

But I learned to be wary of such feelings, particularly when with Edward. He was too quick to act on comments I had meant merely as idle conversation, often in unexpected and unwanted ways. A case in point: I was deeply moved by Geoffrey's grief on his father's death. As soon as I mentioned my friend's mourning to Edward, he decided then and there to offer Geoffrey a commission by which to test whether he would be a useful addition to his household. It had not been my intention to ask Edward to retain him. I was often uneasy with the King's quick generosity, for I was quite sure the courtiers interpreted it all as stemming from my greed.

I worried that this was Edward's way of compensating me for our less frequent lovemaking. He was affectionate and tender towards me but often was not well enough to make love to me. His embarrassment was an uninvited, unwanted interloper that made us both uneasy, unnatural, with one another. I did not seem able to reassure him that his inability to make love did not spoil my time with him. As usual, when Edward was ailing he showered me with even more gifts than usual, not only the ubiquitous pearls.

He presented me with a life grant of two tuns of Gascon wine for service to Queen Philippa, a most gracious gift. This was a gift that would appear in the household records. He said he wished to document my devoted service to Her Grace.

He presented me with a magnificent brown and white palfrey named Nightingale. 'It has long been my wish that you ride with no reminder of my mother's shadow on your heart,' he said with such caring in his eyes that I was choked with emotion.

I'd had no idea that he remembered whence came my beloved Melisende. In truth, I had loved her too well to hold her origins against her, but it was time to allow her to run free in the fields.

On another occasion he presented me with several falcons and a falconer for Fair Meadow.

'Or Radstone,' he said with a slight, smug smile.

I could hide nothing from him. This was a new game in our relationship that I found discomfiting.

'You know of Sir Anthony's offer?' I forced myself to say it with indifference.

'You are padding your nest well, Alice. Ardington – that is

another property at which you might abide from time to time.'

'Do you have people watching what I do when not in your company? Do you not trust me? I know that I am offered these properties only for your sake, though I tell myself I am the protectress of widows and orphans.'

He chucked me under the chin as if I were an infant. 'To demonstrate my love for you, I have recommended your friend Geoffrey Chaucer for a mission that I would not usually entrust to someone untried in my household. But in truth, you are not the only one with high regard for him. Both Lionel and John have been most satisfied with his service.'

As Edward described to me the mission on which he was sending Geoffrey, my heart sank. He was entrusted with bringing back from Navarre English soldiers who had hired out to the wrong side in a dispute between the rightful King of Castile and his half-brother. It was a delicate and dangerous mission.

I felt sorry for Pippa.

Despite my lingering unease about the subtle changes in Edward's behaviour, for a time my life fell into a comfortable rhythm. In most ways he and I grew closer as we watched our son develop – John often accompanied me on visits to his father. Bella often came as well, for John was most docile in her company.

My role in Philippa's household had also blossomed into affectionate friendship. We still enjoyed working together on her clothes for the great festivities, so accustomed by now to one another's preferences and dislikes that we needed little discussion, simply reached for the items that would best suit both of us and smiled in agreement. It had become our custom to design a beautiful litter that complemented her robes, and as her physical stature diminished we added more gold, more sparkling gems, anything that would catch the light and pick her out as a glowing presence in a crowded hall. Her appetite for beauty never diminished.

Nor did Edward's appetite for extravagance. Fortunately he was ageing with far more grace than his wife. His height rendered his spreading waistline insignificant, and glorious robes of cloth of gold and bright, intricate embroidery, cloaks with ermine or miniver linings, and hats sporting ships at full sail or life-sized hawks, all simply added to his regal image. With his flowing white hair, white beard and sharp blue eyes, his was a long-legged form that strode, never merely walked, into a hall.

But the heady days of our love were past. Perhaps Janyn and I would have grown to be more friends than lovers, given time, though I doubt it would have worried me, for we would have been legally bound. I could not help but worry that Edward's eye would stray, hoping that someone new might revive his flagging passion.

In the autumn of my John's second year I saw William Wyndsor for the first time in four years or more. He was soon to take up new positions as Constable of Carlisle Castle and Sheriff of Cumberland, and while still in the south of England came to me at Fair Meadow. He was as handsome as ever and made a point of being charming, but I trusted him no more than before. Since his letters to me went unanswered, I did not understand why he still pursued me.

He was biding near the manor, not with me, but even so I made certain that Robert Broun remained on the estate while William was in the area, and included him in the company whenever William supped with us. To be fair, he treated me with respect and made himself useful, offering counsel regarding a border issue with a neighbour and advising me on several projects. Following his advice, I was able to resolve the long-simmering unpleasantness with my neighbour, and for that I was grateful. He was also kind to Bella – when he noticed her. It was plain he'd had little experience with children and often launched into inappropriately bawdy or violent tales in her presence.

But every time he looked at me in that way of his, I grew uneasy. It stirred a hunger that had been slumbering, though not for William. Edward's decline in health and passion had emphasised the difference in our ages, making it far more of a problem than it had ever been before, and though I assured him I did not need constant lovemaking I still had a healthy appetite. And I did sometimes fear that his lack of interest was partially my fault, that I had grown too familiar. I yearned for the old days, and worried about the future. He was everything to me, but I might yet lose him to a younger woman, and most certainly would eventually lose him to a mistress against whom I had no chance – mortality. I found myself resenting William for stirring these feelings in me.

He had been in the area for a week when I received the Queen's summons to Windsor to prepare for the Feast of St George. It was a week earlier than I'd expected, but Her Grace often stirred herself up to a pitch that required action long before it was necessary. I chose to tell William when we rode out in the afternoon. It was a chilly late-March day. The spring thaw had begun, rendering the countryside muddy and unpleasantly damp, but I did not permit such conditions to trap me indoors. Bella had declined the invitation to come with us, so for once William and I were by ourselves. I was glad that she had stayed behind when suddenly the clouds burst open, drenching us as we rode hard looking for shelter. We found an abandoned shed, and with our horses tethered in one half of the low-slung interior, William and I took seats on what had probably been a sleeping platform to wait out the storm.

He opened his cloak and draped it over us both, drawing me close. 'I will warm you.'

I was grateful for the gesture, and despite the alarms in my head did not move away.

He turned my head towards him. 'I love you more than ever, Alice.'

'That is foolish talk, William. You do not know me.'

'That can be remedied.'

I did not like his smile. 'I must depart in the morning. I am summoned to Windsor betimes.'

He pulled me closer, kissing my forehead, trying to reach my lips. I began to push him away.

'Come north with me. Let us live openly as husband and wife.'

'William, I am not your wife, nor will I ever be.'

He held me firmly against him and kissed me hard enough that his tongue found entry as I gasped and pushed him away.

He laughed. 'How do I compare to that wizened, scarred, dithering old man you sleep with? You are young and beautiful, Alice. You deserve pleasure.' He lunged at me, pressing me to the platform and fumbling with the bodice of my gown.

I managed to kick him and roll away. 'What has possessed you?'

But he was suddenly alert, listening. He held up his hand to quiet me. I heard it as well – a horseman.

A man shouted our names. It was Robert Broun, coming into sight as he spoke. And, right behind him, Richard Stury. My heart pounded.

Stury bowed to us both from horseback. 'When I arrived, your steward was about to come in search of you with a dry cloak, Mistress Alice.' He turned to William. 'The Duke of Lancaster would meet with you before you ride north. I am to escort you to him. He is near. If we leave as soon as you've gathered your belongings, we will reach there before nightfall.' He did not look either of us in the eye.

Nor did Robert. When we arrived at the manor house, Gwen took one look at me and hurried me to my room.

'Nothing happened, Gwen,' I said when we were quite alone.

She looked me up and down. 'Your buttons . . . your hat and hair.' She shook her head.

'I know. I fear that Edward, were he to hear of this, might not believe my protests of innocence.' I fought tears of rage. 'That man is poison to me! His impudence could ruin me, destroy what is left of my family and my honour.' I sank down on the bed. 'I pray that Richard Stury is discreet. It is no accident we've both been summoned this day. How did they know?'

'Are you thinking Sir William intended to be caught?'

We looked at each other askance.

I felt as if a noose had tightened round my neck. When we returned to the hall, Stury and William were gone and Robert had disappeared. I cried myself to sleep that night. Wept for the memory of my early days with Edward that William's passion had stirred. I cursed him.

But I also feared what he was about, praying that I was wrong in suspecting that there was a connection between William's dogged persistence and his being Lancaster's man. If his pursuit had been encouraged by the Duke, this day might have far more dangerous repercussions for my family than a simple case of a man who could not accept rejection in love.

*

Back at court neither Philippa nor Edward mentioned the incident with William, and once I heard he had taken up his duties in the north, I thought little about him. I devoted myself to Edward, Philippa, and my children. Young John was a charming and mischievous child and Bella was proving something of a scholar. Both of them loved working with my hawks and riding. In Philippa's household I had learned to ignore the subtle inquiries and insults from her other ladies. I should say that I outwardly ignored them, but inwardly I learned that there were few women at court I could count as true friends. Princess Joan and Queen Philippa seemed the only ones I might trust. Edward and I grew ever closer, despite the waning of our lovemaking. At last he appeared to understand that I loved being with him, no matter what we were doing.

But this mostly quiet interlude could not last, and the ensuing few years proved to be a most difficult time for the King, a period of great loss and of grieving. My role was to be his shelter from the storm.

On fair days I would wake him at dawn for hawking or riding – hot spiced wine or a thick ale at the ready, to tempt him from bed. In his fur-lined robe, fur-lined boots and hat, he would soon warm with the walk to the stables or rookery. Our horses and birds were our most trusted friends. We both felt free when riding, our laughter ringing out as we shouted challenges to one another. With our falcons on our arms we enjoyed companionable silences, heads moving in unison to watch our soaring birds, the bells on their jesses a comfortably familiar music. Afterwards we often slept a while or lingered over a light meal, reminiscing about past adventures. These were our happiest times.

Edward often asked to hear of my day-to-day activities when away from him, imagining another life through hearing of my property management, the children, the comings and goings of London merchants – a life free from the cares of ruling a realm. I understood that he cherished me in part because I brought him news from elsewhere, a life he could never experience.

We slept together more regularly than when our love had been more passionate. Even on the nights when he did not wish to make love to me, he insisted that I lie with him, naked and perfumed.

'I need you more than ever, my love. I need to wake to your scent, to feel your warmth beside me.'

His need both reassured and worried me. And as trouble darkened his mood, I had the old sense of silken bonds tightening about me.

The first family disaster involved Prince Edward, who made an ill-advised promise to support Pedro of Castile in his battle against his half-brother Enrique of Trastamara for the crown of Castile. Although Prince Edward won the Battle of Najera, the men of Aquitaine who had fought for him could not be paid, for it turned out that Pedro could not hope to raise the sum he owed. Worse, illness swept through the camp, and many died; Prince Edward contracted the illness, and while still very ill was carried by litter in the company of his surviving troops back over the Pyrenees.

The effect that this had on my Edward frightened me. He was furious with the Prince, but also in anguish over reports of his heir's weakened condition and the growing threat from France. Queen Philippa's usual calming influence did little to soothe him.

I tried to understand the situation. 'How does this increase the threat from France?' I asked one evening, when instead of eating his supper he was pacing the chamber bemoaning the situation.

'The Prince has bled his subjects in the Aquitaine to pay for this war, but the expected replenishment from Pedro is not forthcoming. Now King Charles can bribe them to his service, leaving my ailing son, Joan, and their young sons betrayed and defenceless. I cannot leave them there . . . and yet to call them home will be to give up the Aquitaine, and thus my foothold in France. My son has ruined me! He chose to play the hero when as a ruler he should have been prudent and wise.'

Duke John returned with descriptions of his brother's frailty that sent me to the chapel to pray for Prince Edward, Joan and their sons, Edward and Richard.

My elderly, ailing love began to talk of leading an army into France to reclaim the Aquitaine. I prayed that something might happen to distract him. I listened, I comforted, I prayed. Perhaps I was too successful as his confidante and shield for Edward insisted on my presence more than seemed wise to me, demanding that I be present at official meetings with his barons or when he presided in the courts. I felt I did not belong in such places. Indeed, Geoffrey reported that I was ever more on the gossips' tongues, not only at court but elsewhere.

For a little while Edward's spirits were revived by the prospect of the coming marriage of his son Lionel, now Duke of Clarence, to Violante Visconti, the fabulously wealthy and reportedly beautiful daughter of Galeazzo Visconti, Lord of Pavia. They were to be wed in Milan.

But within a year Edward was in mourning for both Blanche of Lancaster, his beloved daughter-in-law, and his son Lionel, both of them succumbing to illnesses in their prime.

'Are we cursed?' Edward would often rise with that question on his lips in the middle of the night. I would comfort him, pouring him wine, rubbing his temples. Sometimes we made love. Sometimes he found comfort in just holding me.

Once, in one of his darkest moments, he asked me how William made love to me. Asked it bitterly, as if he had been suffering while imagining it.

'He has never made love to me, Edward. I would not have him.'

'Not that day in the storm?'

My breath caught in my throat. 'No. He had caressed me and expressed his desire, but I refused him. That is what happened.'

It was the only time Edward had mentioned that day, and it chilled me. Not that he had heard of the incident, but that he had nursed the knowledge deep within where it had festered until it burst from him in a moment of great pain.

'Who told you about that day?' I asked. 'Richard Stury? Or William's lord, your son John?'

Edward would not say. He took me roughly that night, as if seeking vengeance by forcing his seed into me. It was not an act of love. I could not sleep afterwards, sick with the bestiality of the act. When Edward woke from a slumber later in the night, he said, 'John told me. He warned me to keep William away from you. And I will, Alice, I will. He shall not have you.'

'You do not need to be rough to claim me, my lord.'

'My love, forgive me.' He reached for me, but I moved away. 'I love you beyond all reason, Alice,' he said. 'I was jealous. Jealous and afraid that you yearned for a younger man. My love, let me make this up to you. I swear to you that I will never touch you in such wise again. Only lovingly. Only lovingly.'

I curled up in his arms and wept bounteous tears – for my shame, for my fear, for the twilight days of our love, for the sad truths revealed in his apology.

A few months later I knew I was again with child. I prayed for a daughter. John was now three, and Edward often talked of placing him in one of the Percy households. I prayed for a daughter who might not be taken away from me.

But even with the joy of being with child, I was frightened. As his sorrows pulled Edward down into grief he grew less decisive, more open to the influence of others. Many openly resented me. Geoffrey told me of rumours that I influenced the King in judgements about my friends; that I dipped into his coffers to buy and lease my property. Until now I had been confident that if Edward tired of me, I could retreat to my properties and my children without much ado. But now I saw how vulnerable I was, realising that my enemies might hate me enough to wish to ruin me rather than allow me simply to disappear. I had no power, not even a man to stand behind me if Edward should send me away, or, even worse, when he died. And my fear of John of Gaunt grew – I could not fathom what game he played, pushing William Wyndsor at me, then telling Edward. Was he trying to undermine his father's faith in me? I would fight him.

I loved Edward, wanted no one else, but I needed a champion. And having loved such men as Janyn and Edward, I could not imagine marrying someone simply for security, not after having tasted the exquisite joy of love.

William Wykeham continued to be one of my most trusted friends. He had risen from the post of Edward's secretary to being Bishop of Winchester and Lord Chancellor of England. I believed he was the person Edward most trusted and so sought his advice in all matters regarding the King, barring those too intimate to discuss. He agreed that I must protect my wealth in preparation for the day when either the King died or I lost favour.

'Never believe that you stand on solid ground at court, Alice. We are all at the edge of quicksand.'

Even he, exalted to the position of Lord Chancellor, knew that his fortune could change at any moment, upon the King's whim.

He believed that it was in my son John's best interest that he be fostered by the Percys. They were the most powerful family in the north of England, crucial to Edward for their protection of the northern marches, particularly against the Scots. John would enjoy the added protection of a bond with such a powerful clan.

'And for your daughter Isabella, a minor knight for a husband or a respectable nunnery. Either should be possible.'

But what of a bastard daughter of the King or a second son? I did not tell Wykeham of the life quickening within me as we spoke.

Fear became my constant companion as I suffered a difficult pregnancy. Queen Philippa lay ill at Windsor and I prayed night and day that she would recover. I yearned to go to her, to cheer her with pretty baubles and shimmering cloth, to coax her back to health. But I was in my seventh month and would not flaunt my swelling womb in front of her – nor could I comfortably or safely travel. Edward did not ease my mind, threatening to take ship to Bordeaux and personally lead an army against King Charles of France.

I could not sleep for worry that the ageing couple who held my life in their hands were slipping away from me. I obsessed over my fate if Edward should die in Gascony, or if Philippa should die and Edward remarry. Now it was I being comforted by the King, who knew only that I was beset by nightmares.

But even with his loving concern, I lost the child. A little son, stillborn a month before his time. Edward and I were both diminished in spirit by the loss. He held me and comforted me. He sent for my sister and my children. In this he knew me well, for all three served to remind me that I had much for which to be grateful.

'We shall have other children, my love,' Edward whispered to me in the dark of the night.

He spoke no more of a French campaign.

One warm but overcast day in July, Edward, Mary and I were in the stables watching the antics of Bella and John with a litter of puppies. Mary and Edward hoped that it would cheer me. But though I loved my children, I saw in the puppies the promise of new life that I had been denied. It is a most terrible pain, losing a child one has grown to cherish in the womb.

Shouts in the yard drew our attention. Edward groaned as a messenger in the Queen's livery approached, breathless and sweaty.

Despite his obvious exhaustion, the man dropped to one knee to deliver his message.

'Your Grace, you are summoned to Windsor with all haste.' Queen Philippa lay mortally ill, and the physicians believed she had little time remaining.

Edward had clutched my hand as he listened to the messenger. Richard Stury, who had come rushing out of the palace upon the messenger's arrival, offered to assist him into the house and then make the preparations. I perforce accompanied them. Edward's ashen face and hollow eyes frightened me almost as much as the vice-like grip that locked me to his side. I had never seen him so. I saw in this terror of his wife's imminent death that he loved her as deeply and completely as I had loved Janyn.

'My love, I shall come with you,' I proclaimed.

He shook his head. 'No. You are still unwell, Alice. I would not have you risk a journey so soon. You will be everything to me when Philippa . . .' He let go my hand and took me into his arms. 'I must know that you are here waiting for me, safe and well.'

It was true that I ailed in heart and body and soul, but I regretted that I could not be with the Queen in her last days. I mourned for her almost as deeply as for my child. I had learned much about dignity and graciousness in her service. She had also instilled in me self-respect for my own talents. And I had loved her. As soon as Edward departed for Windsor, I withdrew to Fair Meadow and gave myself up to prayer for Philippa, that her passing might be peaceful and her eternal salvation be assured. She had been in pain for so many years, I imagined she was ready to die but for her concern for her husband and her children. Bella joined me in prayer. Although she had never met the Queen, she had heard so much about her most of her young life that she felt a connection.

As Edward later told me, when he arrived Philippa was anxious that he grant her three requests – that he pay all her debts, which were considerable; that he fulfil all her bequests and gifts to churches and all who had been in her service; and that he be buried beside her at Westminster, that he let no one coerce him into a burial elsewhere. He wept and promised her all that she asked.

He and his son Thomas of Woodstock were with her when she drew her last breath on the fifteenth of August, the Feast of the Annunciation, in the forty-second year of Edward's reign.

Requiescat in pace, noble and beloved Queen.

The Queen's death frightened me. She had given her blessing to my liaison with her husband. If the King were now urged to remarry, I could not hope for such a sanguine arrangement with a new bride.

I wept for Edward, I wept for the realm in losing such a gracious queen, I wept for myself and the uncertainty I now faced. *Deus juva me.*

III-3

I could not imagine Windsor Castle without Queen Philippa's throaty laughter, her exclamations of delight when sorting through cloth and decorations for her gowns, her almost childlike eagerness as the time approached for a long-planned celebration. I could not imagine the Garter ceremony without her. Indeed, I could not envision how the court would function without Philippa ordering it. Princess Joan was still in the Aquitaine, Duchess Blanche was dead. Princess Isabella had returned to court after her husband de Coucy returned to France, in essence deserting her, but I could not imagine her presiding over the court. She cared only for her own pleasures, and her household was like a tumble of ravenous and frightened dogs caged together, clawing and snapping at one another.

But more than all this, I feared that a part of Edward might have died with Philippa, and that he was now frighteningly vulnerable. I vowed to protect him, to envelop him in my protective love.

When he had realised that he would be at Windsor for a while, Edward had freed me to go to one of my homes as soon as I felt well enough. On my journey to Fair Meadow I witnessed how Queen Philippa's death had cast a pall over the entire kingdom. Even in the countryside I encountered tradesmen, the local parson, neighbours, my own tenants and servants, all mourning as if the Queen had been their dearest friend.

In London, on my occasional trip there to tend to business, I found the sense of loss so palpable it was almost unbearable. In the churches the priests prayed for the King and all his family, enumerating the losses they had suffered in three years, the death of the Queen being the culmination of a long, sorrowful time. I had not thought the common people knew of Prince Edward's illness, but they did, and all feared what would transpire on the death of the King. It seemed that the Queen's death had reminded the people of Edward's own mortality. They wondered how the Prince could rule if he did not recover his full strength, but worried that if he died the kingdom would be ruled by a boy younger than the King had been when he ascended to the throne. Had Prince Edward no male heir, the Duke of Lancaster might have ruled. People were uncertain how they felt about him, but at least he was hale and hearty and mature. But Edward and Joan had two sons who stood before the adult Lancaster in the succession, two children.

Geoffrey reported speculation about the King remarrying – his grandfather *had* married a second time. I tried not to think about it; arguing with myself that my beloved was too old, that he had sufficient sons. But in the dark hours I lay in bed feverishly planning what I must do to prepare myself for being abandoned, because simply to feel the pain of a possible parting was unbearable.

On a blue and gold day in early-autumn, as Bella and I were exploring the gardens at our manor of Ardington, enjoying the warm afternoon and visions of the beautiful garden we were planning, we heard several horsemen approaching the house. I expected no one, and except for Dom Hanneye and my steward, no one knew I was here in Berkshire. No one *I* had told.

Anxious to see who had arrived, Bella rushed ahead. I watched her long-legged run, graceful and swift, her skirts held daringly high, and felt such a glow of joy. Her beauty mirrored her gentle, loving nature. She was beloved by all, servants, friends, family. Edward said that Bella was the perfect name for her, for she was in all ways beautiful. I could not believe she was twelve years old. It seemed just yesterday that I had first held her in my arms and counted her fingers and toes.

She had reached the servant hastening to fetch me, then raced back to announce, 'It is the Lord Chancellor himself, Mother!

Himself!' Her dark eyes were wide in her flushed face. She did not ask, but I knew the question in her mind. Trouble? Another death?

I grabbed her hand and hurried back to the house with her.

William Wykeham stood quite still in the middle of the modest hall, his dark, serviceable travelling jacket, hose and riding boots neither obviously those of a Bishop nor a Chancellor, but rich and well made; part of his heavy gold chain of office escaped from between his buttons beneath the dagged shoulder cape. He'd developed a more elegant style of late, a charming hint of the pride he felt in attaining such high offices in both the clerical and the secular worlds.

'*Benedicite*, Dame Alice, Mistress Isabella. I regret intruding on your peaceful afternoon.' His smile was warm, genuine, and somewhat eased my worry about the cause of his visit.

Bella bowed to him. '*Benedicite*, my lord Bishop,' she whispered.

I echoed her and added, 'Welcome to Ardington. Would you care for some refreshment?'

'You are most kind. Wine is sufficient. I cannot linger.' His smile had faded.

Bella slipped away to summon a servant.

He eased himself down on a chair by a small table and proceeded to remove his gloves with meditative slowness, as if using the time in which to compose his thoughts. When he had at last set them on the table beside him, he took off his wide-brimmed hat and pushed back his hood, mopping his brow. But he did not remove the shoulder cape, indicating a brief visit indeed. I had seldom seen him look so ill at ease.

'You come on official business, then?' I asked. 'Something that you find unpleasant?'

When he met my questioning gaze, he looked apologetic. 'I am here to summon you to King's Langley. His Grace the King needs you.'

'Now?' I had not expected to be summoned until after the Queen's burial, which had been delayed until after Christmastide. 'Surely not. It is not appropriate for his mistress to come to him in his mourning.'

I could see by the conflict in his eyes that Wykeham agreed, but he said, 'And yet it is just so. He is the King and he summons you.' He paused to accept the mazer of wine proffered by a servant. 'The Duke of Lancaster has also urged me to ensure that you are by the King's side. He wrote that His Grace is best with a woman's gentle guidance, and that at present you are that woman, Dame Alice. The King is at ease in your company.' He paused to take a long drink.

I watched a bee explore the rim of my own cup, then fly away. I wished I might fly away as well. I had begun to look forward to a quiet autumn working on my properties, enjoying my children, caring for my ageing grandmother. Yet of course I missed Edward. 'Someone from the royal family might be more appropriate.'

'With the Princess Joan in Gascony and Princess Isabella sulking I know not where, you do seem the obvious choice. You will remind him of happy days.' His eyes implored me.

'Of course, I am my King's to command.' I touched my heart and gave Wykeham a little bow. 'Shall I – may I bring the children?'

'His Grace suggested that you might later. For the moment, he wants only you.' He set the mazer aside with a look of regret and rose with a sigh. Only then did I see how exhausted he was. 'Richard Stury will come to escort you in two days. Where will you be?'

My possessions were scattered about. 'Fair Meadow. My gowns are there. You might rest here awhile, my lord.'

He picked up his gloves. 'God bless you, I would if I were at liberty to do so. But I have others to see before nightfall.'

'How goes His Grace? What might I expect?'

'Much hawking, much riding, much drinking and gambling. As if he intends to outpace the sorrow that chases him. I pray that you help him embrace his grief.'

Wykeham kissed my hand, blessed me, and was gone before I could ask how he proposed I do so. I was familiar with the mood he described in the King, and though I had usually been successful at dispelling it for a time, in the present circumstance I suspected that only exhaustion, a complete collapse, would end it.

Bella reappeared before I'd had time to consider how to tell her that I would be leaving again in a few days.

'Will you be going to the King?' she asked.

She took my breath away, this beautiful child, so canny, so quick, so accustomed to her mother being summoned by the royal family.

I bent down – when had she grown so tall I did not need to crouch? – and hugged her. 'Yes, my beautiful Bella. I shall send for you as soon as His Grace permits.'

'Sometimes I wish he would find a queen he liked as much as you,' Bella whispered in my ear. 'Then I could have you all to myself.'

'Oh, Bella, has he not been good to us?'

'Not when he separates us.'

I could not explain to her my need to be with him. I was torn.

As I stood in the hall at King's Langley, slaking my thirst with a mazer of watered wine before continuing up to my chamber to bathe away the dust of the road, I marvelled at how long I had been with Edward. So long that I was at ease with ordering his household. I told a servant to remove the pack of hunting dogs snarling over a bone to the kennels.

'But His Grace brought them in, Mistress Alice,' said the young man.

They reminded me of the growing factions at court, snarling over favours, choice posts, hoping to procure as much as possible while Edward yet lived, worried about what changes Prince Edward might bring.

'Where is His Grace at present?' I asked.

'In the bathhouse.'

He would be washing for me. Forgetting for a moment that lovemaking was not necessarily his intent, I smiled at the thought of him in the bath and was tempted to join him there. But I remembered myself and, determined to attempt propriety during this time of mourning so that no one might find cause to separate us, I chose to wash in the privacy of my chamber as I had planned.

'Have the grooms remove the dogs, and replace the rushes they fouled.'

I waited until the servant bowed and moved off before I climbed to the solar. There I allowed Gwen to undress me, wipe away the dust of travel with damp cloths, and soothe me with fragrant oils. Then I slept for a while.

When I woke, Edward, in a thin linen night shift, nothing more, lay beside me, just watching me.

'I thought you would never wake,' he whispered. He knelt and peeled back the covers, then entered me with such ease that I must have been dreaming of just this moment. 'Would that my whole body might follow my cock and rest in your womb for all the remaining days and nights of this life,' he moaned with pleasure.

I felt the rush of his seed flooding me, and my body pulsed with such desire that I arched into him and cried out, and we collapsed together. Unlike our customary pattern – he would fall asleep and I would lie beside him, listening to his steady breathing – I slept as well, a deep, comforting sleep. When I woke I turned to him and caressed him until he was aroused, and then, though he was only half-awake, I mounted him and took him inside me so deep that my bones touched his. We were one, a swaying, breathing, pulsing being, needing no other, nothing more. I massaged his ribs and he moaned as all tension left him. Afterwards, I washed him with a cloth soaked in lavender water, and then he washed me.

'I understand, my love,' I said as he washed my thighs, 'I understand. We anchor each other with our bodies, with our passion. No matter what happens once we leave this chamber, we know that we can return to this union, this comfort, this tenderness and delight.' He was no longer my siren, but now my anchor. He steadied me amidst the storms of court, our very human love, our fond familiarity. I caressed his arms and back as he bent over me, my beloved.

He laughed. 'I cannot so soon, my love. I am depleted.' But with his oiled fingers he pleasured me. When I would touch him, he said, 'Do nothing. Let me do it all. Let me just enjoy you.'

We drowsed side by side until dawn.

When his manservant knocked, Edward sighed. 'I must attend a Mass in memory of Philippa.' He shook his head in wonder. 'I thought that a part of me had died with her, but I feel whole again.' He kissed my forehead, my breasts. 'My love for you never diminished my love for Philippa, my Queen. She was my succour and my salvation. She taught me how to win the hearts of all my subjects, from the common folk to the barons and archbishops.

She bore me magnificent sons and gentle daughters, and I loved her with all my heart and soul. Now you are all to me, Alice.'

'And you to me, Edward.' I was in no wise jealous of his declaration of love for his Queen. I could never take her place; no one could. I was content to have his love now.

My sense of profound union with Edward, of being his solace and retreat as he was mine, was something that I clung to in the months and years ahead, when it seemed that all the kingdom condemned our love, refusing to accept it as that. I wished I might somehow prove to them our sincerity, but how one 'proves' such a thing I did not know. Most of the time I believed that God had granted me the understanding of my own purpose, and was comforted.

I was certain that I'd conceived that night, and I was glad. I pushed away Gwen's concerns, her insistence that I drink a herbal potion to stop whatever might have begun. If God had seen fit to allow me to conceive from that night of love and union, I felt only joy and gratitude that soon I might again have the intensely private and miraculous sensation of a child blooming within my womb.

My intuition proved to be right. Happiness brightened my world. I was grateful for the comfort I derived from the beauty surrounding me and the solace of the chapels wherever I abided with Edward, and rejoiced in his delight that we were to have another child.

The most difficult time was Christmastide. John, Duke of Lancaster, joined us at King's Langley, as well as Edmund and Thomas, Edward's youngest sons. I felt a fraud, a usurper, while present at the table in the hall or in Edward's parlour. I had seldom been with the two youngest sons while Philippa lived. John welcomed me, but Edmund and Thomas were offended by my presence and made no attempt to hide their feelings. Thomas had seen little of me with Edward. Until his mother's death he had known me only as one of her ladies, though he had surely heard gossip about Edward and me. At sixteen, he was less in control of his emotions than his older brother, so his was the most hurtful voice and behaviour. Even worse for me, Bella and my own son John had not been invited and so spent the Christmas season with Dame Agnes, a failing Nan, and their nurse, Betys.

I was rescued from this unpleasant atmosphere by the burial of Queen Philippa. Her entombment had been delayed until the abbey was ready and Advent and Christmastide had passed. When the funeral procession accompanying her coffin to Westminster departed from King's Langley, I was permitted to retire to London. Richard Stury and a new man in Edward's entourage, William Latimer, escorted me.

My John, now five years old, greeted me with such tearful joy that my own emotion rendered me speechless. Hugs and kisses sufficed. Bella waited her turn with good grace, then flung herself into my welcoming arms.

That night, as Nan, Grandmother, Gwen and I shared some spiced wine in my chamber before we all retired, I learned that Henry, Lord Percy had visited with several kinswomen, assessing in which household John might best be fostered. Edward had not told me of the visit, and my first reaction was of fury.

'How dare they come here without my leave? He is my son!' I had known, of course, that John would likely be fostered by the Percys. But to frighten him with the possibility that they would take him while I was away was unforgivable. I could not sit still but started to pace angrily, holding my stomach.

'Have a care,' Gwen said, draping a soft wool mantle over my shoulders.

'I did not think they would take him from us so soon.' Dame Agnes dabbed her eyes. Since Grandfather's death my little family had become her succour and delight, the beneficiaries of all her needlework and worry.

'I would have warned you had I known it was imminent. And I would have found a way to prepare John.' It was made worse by the fact that I did not care for Henry, Lord Percy, nor trust him. He seemed to me a man out to advance his own family no matter who fell before his ruthless advance. Such blatant disregard for both John's feelings and mine was proof of it. But Edward did trust Percy.

'Your life is not yours to order, is it, Alice?' asked Nan. Sweet, elderly, frail she might be, but she still saw what was right in front of her more clearly than anyone else I knew.

'What woman's life is?' asked Dame Agnes.

'But I trow it is worse for the mistress of a King,' said Nan. 'Is that not so, Alice?'

Her words conjured up memories of my resentment when I'd first gone to court; how I had felt I was treated as a child.

'It is true. I command servants, live in most beautiful houses, own and manage property, and have the love of the King – it would seem that I have everything. But the price I pay is that my own life is not mine to order. The King commands and I obey.'

'Women rarely have a say in their sons' occupations,' Dame Agnes soothed me, 'and many of the wealthier merchant families send their boys away to be fostered in homes with good connections. I did not expect we might be left to raise little John de Southery in London, sending him to a grammar school in the parish as we do Bella. But I hated to see how frightened the children were by proud Lord Percy and his haughty women.'

After a fitful night's sleep, I asked Bella about the incident.

'They frightened John: picking him up, asking him if he would like to live with them. And they talked about his appearance, his speech, how he carries himself, as if they did not think he could understand. He thought they meant to steal him. He still cries out in the night if he cannot see me or Betys.'

I could not imagine that Edward would have agreed to such treatment of our son. I poured out my anger and frustration to him in a letter, certain he would agree, and sealed it with my signet. I'd sent a messenger with it to him at Westminster before doubt overtook me, doubt that I had a right to demand anything for my son. Then I prayed that I might put the matter out of my mind and enjoy being reunited with my children. This required the co-operation of Nan and Dame Agnes, who were loath to silence their irritation, but both of them remembered that a woman in my condition was easier to live with if she had her way.

One of my new pleasures was to lie down in the afternoons with my son. It began one afternoon when I realised his outbursts of anger resulted from tiredness – just like Bella's when she had been too stubborn to rest as a young child. When I stretched out on my bed I invited John to join me. Curled up against me, his head on my stomach, he fell asleep at once. With his calming warmth beside me I was able to set aside my fears for a while, and eventually I slept as well. On the following day he expected we would do the same after the midday meal, and I was delighted to comply. Again he slept, again I fell asleep as well. And so it became our routine.

As I lay on the bed with my beloved son, I would think back on my time in the Queen's household. I devised a game of re-experiencing the splendour of the court, the extravagant feasts and displays, particularly Edward's and Philippa's dazzling costumes. One afternoon I fell asleep while conjuring in my mind the feast at which Edward had worn a hat from which a falcon was taking flight. In my dream, he caught my eye from across the hall and began to walk towards me, the crowd making way. I, too, wore a hat from which a falcon was poised for flight. I held out my arms to him, welcoming him, and he mirrored my gesture. Suddenly our falcons took flight together. As all the hall gazed up at the birds in wonder, the sumptuous robes Edward and I wore vanished and in our nakedness we came together, coupling on a cushion of air, our bodies so unified in breath and heartbeat that we became one, a gorgeous phoenix, and flew from the court, alighting in a great rose bower furnished with a down-filled bed where we lay in sexual union and harmony of hearts and minds, soothed by the scent of hundreds of roses and the warmth of the sun.

'Why are you weeping?'

I woke to my son's anxious query. He was sitting up, watching me sleep.

I wiped my eyes. 'They are happy tears, my love. I was think-ing about a beautiful bird, a phoenix.' And I told him the tale of how the bird rises from its own ashes.

A week after I had written to Edward condemning the behaviour of Henry Percy and his family, a messenger from the King informed us that on the following day John, Bella and I would be escorted to the White Tower in the city. King Edward wished to show the children the exotic animals housed there, gifts he had received from far and wide: tigers, lions, monkeys, and more. I was delighted for the children, and I was excited as well. Later that day, however, I fell prey to worry about Edward's respond-ing in such an impersonal manner. Rather than being angry with the Percys, might he be angry with me? But I was determined not to allow my gratitude for the day's pleasure or my own worry soften my stance on the Percy family's high-handed behaviour, particularly their scheming to meet John when I was not there.

The White Tower was a tall stone keep surrounded by smaller timber buildings, set in gardens along the River Thames. The high, well-fortified walls encircling the entire area prevented any enjoyment of the riverside views, except from some of the upper storeys or the top of the wall, but it was lovely within.

'Did they build this so the animals could not escape?' John asked as we entered the inner ward from the gatehouse.

'No, John, this was built long ago to protect the royal family in time of war. The animals came later.'

Just then he caught sight of his father and began to jump up and down, waving his little arms. Edward had been frowning at his companion, his son Thomas of Woodstock, but as he noticed us, and his youngest child's antics, his face relaxed into an expression of such fatherly love that my anger eased a little. Thomas too came to greet us and then took his leave, behaving with far more courtesy than at our Christmas meeting.

How I loved Edward as we exchanged greetings now, his eyes warm and welcoming. John clamoured to be noticed. When he raised his arms in the hope of being lifted up by his father the King, instead a hand was proffered.

'Come, my son. You are beyond the age to be carried. We shall walk together.' Edward held out his other hand. 'And, my dear Mistress Bella, please walk with us. Let us confer with the keeper of the royal menagerie!' He winked at me and proceeded towards the area whence came animal sounds that made me ill at ease.

I followed with the nurse, Betys, who was dumbstruck by the grandeur of the place.

Edward delighted, as ever, in the children's excitement. He was charming to Bella and John, and both were fascinated by the creatures on display, though John chose not to reach into the cage to touch the male lion's mane when the keeper offered him the chance. Bella did stroke it and declared it rough and filthy. Edward roared with delight.

'You speak your mind, just like your mother. You shall lead the young men a merry dance, sweet Bella!'

I was grateful that he treated her with such affection. In awe of him, she treasured such moments more than all his lavish gifts. I understood, remembering the day on Sheppey when he had made me feel 'seen'.

While the children and their nurse talked to the keeper, Edward led me to a bench where we might rest and talk.

'You are beautiful today as always, my love,' he said. 'Are you well? This is not too tiring for you? You are pale.' He touched my cheek.

'I am comfortable,' I assured him. Then repeated to him the tale of young John's night-time fears since the ill-advised visit by Henry, Lord Percy and company.

'I apologise for their behaviour, Alice. I thought it would be easier for you if they met our son when you were not present. I am well aware of your reluctance to let him go. I am sorry for that. I love both of you – you know that.'

To say I was disappointed that it had been Edward's idea for them to visit when I was absent would be an understatement. 'Have you no heart, Edward? Henry Percy *frightened* our son. Does that not anger you?'

Edward chuckled. 'He is a loud lout! But what is done is done, and he is impressed with the way you have raised John so far.' He kissed my hand.

I was too angry to be charmed. 'So even after this breach of courtesy, John will be fostered by a Percy? You might have your choice of noble families.'

'He will go with Percy, Alice. John may be a bastard but he is my son and shall be raised as such, knowing his duties to me and the realm, able to move with ease among kings, emperors, archbishops, barons, popes . . . and Percys.' He marked my lack of amusement at his wordplay. 'You shall not stand in his way, and that is an end to the discussion.' He startled me with the coolness of his tone, the sudden abandoning of my hand.

We said no more, but sat observing the children. I was relieved that Edward did not invite us to linger once John grew weary and fretful.

Of course, I had always been aware of two Edwards, one who was King and treated me as his subject, and one who was my lover, who needed me, cherished and protected me. Sometimes this duality so frightened me that I would seek reassurance by cuddling up to him. It often worked, inspiring him to remember his other self and soften. But this was hardly the place to behave so, and I found myself wishing only to flee his presence.

Indeed, for the first time in a long while, I looked forward to being away from Edward. Afterwards I wrote a loving, gently apologetic letter, explaining that I had only wished to protect our son. I promised to argue no more against his being fostered by Henry, Lord Percy. Edward expressed his satisfaction at this, sending pearls and a miniver-lined cloak to reward me for my obedience, and agreeing that I might spend the remainder of the winter at Fair Meadow, awaiting the birth of our child.

By Candlemas I was settled at my beloved manor. Sacrilegious as it may sound, I felt as if God had held off the winter snows until I was safely installed, then covered the world in snow for several months, to shelter me there. John and Bella were with me, as well as Dame Agnes, Nan and Gwen, and my household servants, including Betys and Robert. Edward had also agreed that I might choose my own midwife, and I had immediately requested Felice who had presided over Bella's birth. She would bide with us closer to the time. Content, I allowed myself to become lost in the dream of this happy little household remaining undisturbed for a long, long while.

Robert and I grew close that winter and spring. He had recently lost his wife of a few years, and welcomed the opportunity to be away from his home near London where every room evoked memories of her suffering. She had fallen down the stairs in early pregnancy, losing the child and eventually her own life. For months she had lain in bed, barely able to move, speaking little, her mother looking after her. We talked of our lost spouses, and gradually he seemed to have said all that he wished to say of this and turned the talk to the coming child, to Bella and John, and to the work ahead on my properties and on his – he had begun to acquire his own modest estate. I felt I could say anything to him. The children thought of him as their uncle. I thought of him as an uncomplicated friend in whose company I could be at ease. It was a happy time.

While the snows lasted, the dreamy state of my comfortable little household did too. Even well into the thaw we received neither guests nor messengers. But early in April, towards the end of the Lenten season, a letter arrived from Edward announcing that an escort would arrive for our son John at the royal hunting lodge near Fair Meadow on the eve of Lammas Day. My son would be gone from me in less than four months.

Another blow came shortly after Easter, in late-April, when Nan took to her bed, refused food or drink, and within a few days simply stopped breathing. There was not a soul in the household who did not mourn the loss of her sweet presence.

Bella was the first to notice that she had stopped breathing: pressing her ear to the shrunken bosom, then lifting Nan's hand and finding it cold and lifeless. Her cry had brought me rushing to her side. After the burial, my daughter seemed to spend her days in prayer, her lips moving ceaselessly as she performed all her chores. This stopped only when she was busy with her lessons. I worried about her. Though I had always found comfort in prayer myself, and especially when I was with child kept my beads going whenever I had an idle moment, I found Bella's piety extreme.

But it drew me back into the habit of daily prayer, first for dear Nan's soul, later for myself and my family and all in my household. I found myself including Robert in my prayers more and more, appreciating the security he provided us with. And always Bella was with me in the chapel, rapt in worship.

It should have come as no surprise to me when on her thirteenth birthday in late-June she expressed her wish to take vows. But her announcement, coming just over a month before young John was to leave the household, gripped my heart with a terrible sense of loss.

'Is it a vocation, my love, or something else?' I asked. A mother always worries about such surprises. Bella was such a beautiful girl. It seemed a sacrilege to close her up among brittle old women who had never known life or grieving widows seeking safe havens. I had forgotten my own brief desire to devote my life to God. I was concerned that Bella as yet had only a vague sense of what she would be renouncing, and of the tedium of such a life if her vocation turned out to be simply an idea with no substance.

She lowered her head and looked up at me with a frown as Janyn had when I did not respond as he'd hoped. 'Is it so difficult to believe of me?' she asked.

I wished I were not so large and clumsy with child and could gather her up in my arms. 'No, Bella, that is not why I ask. I merely—' I stopped myself. I did not want to speak my fear: that my unholy alliance with the King had frightened or shamed her. 'I shall honour your wish, if that is truly your desire.'

Within days of Bella's birthday, I gave birth to another daughter, Joan. A daughter . . . It was no real surprise to me that Edward took a week to come and see his child this time. What need had he of an illegitimate daughter? He came for the day and then departed, leaving gifts of precious gems, silver and gold for Joan, and pearls for me. Beautiful things, of course, but I wanted him. I wanted him to hold me, to hold his infant daughter. Affairs of state called him away, he said. I was uneasy that my silence during the months at Fair Meadow had cooled his ardour. My time away from court had been peaceful and had allowed me the opportunity to become reacquainted with myself. In truth, as our separation lengthened – unlike my last lying in, Edward had neither sent for me nor visited, though he had written to me – I had felt more and more at ease in a respite I'd not enjoyed in the twelve years that the court had been my home. The peace of Fair Meadow had suggested another sort of life, one I found appealing. But I had not intended to push Edward away. I fought back my hurt at his lack of interest in Joan and rejoiced at her birth. She was mine, all mine. There was no danger of her being fostered. I told myself I had misread Edward, reminding myself that he had arranged for a 'suitable' wet nurse for Joan so that I might return to court betimes.

My infant daughter was flaxen-haired and blue-eyed like her father, and I adored her. She also reminded me of her first godmother, Princess Joan. With John's birth, Joan had decided I was not one to take her advice on preventing conception and had embraced the inevitable, demanding to be godmother to our first daughter. Of all the Plantagenet family, she was the most accepting of me, embracing me as a woman who completed her father-in-law's life in a way that was good and necessary for the realm, and as a friend whose company she enjoyed. I was in her debt. Her friendship meant more to me than I could ever express, and she was always in my prayers.

The infant Joan became the centre of our little world at Fair Meadow. Bella enjoyed helping Betys, me and the wet nurse, Ann. On the warm afternoons all the women would sit out in the garden and share in caring for Joan. Robert teased us that the child would grow up believing she had many mothers.

And then, abruptly, the interlude was over. Edward summoned me to Sheen a week before John was to depart for his fosterage. Bella and Joan were to bide in a house near the palace, and John would be with us for a few days before his departure. I felt an immense relief that Edward still wanted me, and yet a part of me found it difficult to leave Fair Meadow. I had for the first time been able to imagine without terror a life away from Edward.

This quiet time at my manor had inspired a yearning in me for a more ordered existence. Even for a husband. Knowing that could never be Edward, I had fallen to fantasising about life with someone like Robert, a man of the land with no ties to court, imagining his smiling face greeting me each morning or looking down at me as I nursed our child. I did wonder whether, with a more ordinary family life, Bella might still have felt called to the Church or not.

Nevertheless, I had been summoned, and as Gwen and I sorted through my gowns and began to redo them, I gradually set aside my daydreams. I was not yet ready for that life, not so long as Edward wanted me. But still I felt an unfamiliar lethargy as we worked on the silk, velvet and escarlatte gowns. Once I had seen my time with Edward as an enchantment, all passion and beauty, but now it was often frightening, and of late he had ceased to anchor me.

I was not comfortable travelling on horseback a little over three weeks after giving birth, but fortunately most of the journey to Sheen was by river barge. I worked with the grooms to assemble a sturdy side-saddle platform with enough cushions to ease the journey to the waiting barge, and we travelled at a slow pace through the countryside. Still confused by Edward's inconsistent behaviour towards me, I did not wish to appear weak by travelling by litter on any part of the journey.

My parting from my son was far more debilitating than the journey. I had dismissed Edward's suggestion that John should depart for the Lammas Fair believing he would be coming straight home afterwards. I insisted he be prepared. Of course, it was more difficult for me – those trusting eyes growing wide with apprehension and then filling with tears; the inevitable temper tantrum. I might have been spared that, but still I refused to lie to my child. I felt part of myself being torn away as I finally lost sight of him, riding off with Lord Henry's party.

But I had little time to despair. On my arrival at Sheen I discovered a crisis blooming. The situation in the Aquitaine had deteriorated as Edward had predicted, and Prince Edward and his family were to return to England in the autumn. My Edward was moving forward with a plan to lead a military expedition into France, formulating his request to Parliament for more taxes to finance the effort. The barons and archbishops warned of resistance. Landowners had not yet recovered from the devastation of the recurring pestilence, and the Crown's repeated demands for more funds for war were deeply resented. Edward needed a splendid victory to inspire confidence that the money would be well spent, yet he first needed money in order to gather the troops to win such a victory. I understood the financial conundrum, but my main concern was for Edward himself.

I did not know how many were aware that the King had suffered from vague maladies all winter and spring, rallying for Easter and the Feast of St George then collapsing for weeks afterwards. Parliament would surely be even more reluctant to grant his request for fresh taxation if they knew of his fluctuating health. I had certainly not known the extent of it. Had not understood what strength of will it had required for him to make the journey to Fair Meadow after Joan's birth. I was thankful that I had not confronted him with all my simmering resentments and doubts then. He did, in truth, need me. And he was not in any condition to lead an army into battle.

Loving him as I did, I devoted myself to him. I took it as my role to see that he ate well and drank more moderately than was his wont, and drew him out for walks, rides and hawking as often as possible. Although he chafed at the extent to which I watered his wine, in general he seemed comforted and restored by my ministrations and encouragement. In fact, those close to him expressed relief at the improvement in his health and manner;

some even had the grace to thank me for my part in the transformation.

Geoffrey congratulated me on staying so long away from court that the gossips had forgotten me. 'Though they are abuzz with your son's being a bridge between the Percy family and the King, they do not mention you by name, merely that the King's bastard, John de Southery, is to be fostered by Henry, Lord Percy. The King has succeeded in impressing all with his ability still to sire sons. One would think that he had managed not only to supply the seed but also given birth to the boy! You are absolved from all connection.' When I said nothing, he noticed my distress. Grabbing my hands, he kissed each in turn and apologised. 'I meant only to cheer you. I've lost the knack, I see. But are you not relieved to be forgotten?'

'By the crowd, not by my son.'

'Surely you do not believe that will ever happen?'

I did.

On days when my patience wore thin, I would chafe at the way Edward took all credit for our son and remained indifferent to Joan and Bella. We argued about my misgivings concerning Bella's vocation. Edward impatiently ordered me to cease my fretting and settle on a nunnery suitable for her. But in truth even John, had he not been safely far away, would have felt Edward's indifference, for he was impatient with anything that robbed him of my full attention. My life away from his presence concerned him not a whit.

Or perhaps not entirely. He had saddled me with a troublesome wardship that he hoped would eventually provide security for our son. Edward had encouraged the Under-Chamberlain of his household to sign over to me the wardship of the late Joan de Orby's daughter Mary and her estate; Joan had been the stepmother of Henry, Lord Percy. Wardships were by tradition and law sources of revenue for the King, for while the heir was in their minority, the income from the lands came to the King as well as the fees for eventual permission to marry and any other financial dealings regarding a match, save for the dowry. It was a desirable wardship, and Edward believed that the heiress, young Mary Percy, might be a match for our son John.

I was uneasy, wishing to confer with Robert about the

feasibility of adding such a large estate to his responsibilities. Buxhill, the Under-Chamberlain, had warned me that the estate was poorly managed. I also worried how the court – and even the public – would interpret this boon. And though I called it a boon, it was in fact a business transaction that would cost me a considerable amount if the land had indeed been indifferently managed. But Edward grew impatient with what he called my 'dithering' and insisted that I accept it without caveats. How easily he spent my money! When I told Robert about it, he assured me that we were quite capable of taking on such a challenge and managed to calm me.

Perhaps sensing that he had pushed too hard, Edward sweetened the burden with the dower estates and some other de Orby holdings shortly after I arrived at Sheen: 'In honour of the birth of our daughter Joan.'

For her sake I was moved by this gesture, but this huge addition to my holdings would be expensive to set right.

Our relationship was becoming confusing, my role in it more and more complex. Until I returned to Edward after Joan's birth, we had been lovers and companions in activities we both enjoyed – riding, hawking, hunting, lovemaking, dancing, music, chess. Our time together had been a refuge for both of us. Now Edward clung to me in the privacy of his chambers, and in public I was increasingly placed in the role of gatekeeper. I did not want to be both nurse and gatekeeper, for I did not feel competent to be so, but his two eldest sons encouraged this new role. I had not been brought up to be a courtier; all that I knew I'd learned by trial and error, which worked for me, but with the King – an error on his behalf was of much greater magnitude. Despite my diligent study there was still much I did not understand, much I did not know. I did know that I accompanied him to meetings in which I overheard much to which I should not have been privy. I shrank under the disapproving, indeed disbelieving, stares of others, often the only woman in the chamber.

In a strange way, playing nurse and protector to the King made me feel more his concubine than ever before. My presence was too public now. It felt far more presumptuous, and I was certain it put me in much greater jeopardy. Geoffrey had congratulated me on having been forgotten; it did not last long.

In late-summer, only a month after I had returned to Edward, we were once again in mourning. Young Edward, the eldest son and heir of Prince Edward and Princess Joan, had died in Gascony. I grieved for Joan; with the Prince's ill health, I doubted she would have more children. Their younger son Richard, a child of four, was now second in line to the throne after his father. It seemed cruel that this should happen just as they were preparing to return to England.

In the twelve years that I had been in the royal household Edward had lost so many loved ones – family, friends of his youth, his most trusted commanders; but the death of his grandson, the shining boy previously second in line to the throne, was the last straw that sank his confidence in what the future might hold for his kingdom. Prince Edward's long illness and erratic behaviour as Lord of the Aquitaine had, I was certain, contributed to my love's anguish. Of course Edward realised, just as I did, that Joan and Edward were unlikely to produce another heir. Young Richard must duly return to the safety of the royal court.

I sent a messenger to William Wykeham, asking if he might set aside his duties to come to Edward. He was most often at court as the King's Chancellor and close adviser, but he was also Bishop of Winchester, a pious and inspiring cleric, and in this time of grieving it was his spiritual gifts I prayed would lift the weight of worry from Edward's shoulders and give him succour. Wykeham hastened to King's Langley and stayed for a fortnight, sitting with Edward long into the night, listening, praying, consoling.

I took the opportunity to confess to Wykeham my own unease about my increasingly public role in Edward's affairs.

'What matters is that, through you, His Grace finds comfort and ease, which affords him the strength to rule his realm,' Wykeham counselled me. 'I know that it is not easy for you, but God will reward you for your devotion to the King. I cannot believe He would forsake you.'

'You once advised me to remember the uncertainty of my position . . . how all at court walk on shifting sand.'

'That has not changed. But I need not remind you of it. Indeed,

I commend you on your diligence in seeing to your future financial security and that of your daughters.' There was something in his eyes and in the tension with which he held himself that told me he was not saying all he thought.

'Is there anything else on which you might counsel me, my lord?'

'No. Be at peace.'

His counsel did ease me. No matter what my doubts, my duty was clear. Edward, too, seemed restored by Wykeham's visit.

All my children, including John, gathered round me at the Christmas court. Edward showered them with gifts and attention, and I felt truly blessed. It comforted me to see that John was thriving with the Percys, though I was also pleased that he still enjoyed my fussing over him. I treasured that yuletide.

While Parliament sat that winter, I insisted that I stay in my London home rather than with Edward at Westminster. To finance his battle over the Aquitaine he needed the support of the commons, the very folk most likely to stand in judgement over our liaison. It was better we should remain apart while living in their midst.

'Let them see me going about my business in London, worshipping in my parish church,' I urged him, and he eventually, albeit reluctantly, agreed.

Grandmother and my sister Mary fussed over Joan and comforted me over Bella's ever strengthening resolve to take vows. While at Sheen, Wykeham had suggested several nunneries, the two closest being St Helen's Priory and Barking Abbey.

'Barking is for the high-born,' I demurred.

'Your daughter is the goddaughter of a former Queen, Dame Alice, and her half-brother and -sister have the King for their sire. With a generous dowry, which you have already said you will provide, she would be welcome there.'

He had written Bella a letter of introduction. One dreary January day she and I rode out to the abbey, accompanied by Robert. The beauty of the church and grounds, coupled with the serenity of the abbess and the novices Bella and I met, calmed me, but what convinced me that this was the right place for Bella was her response to the abbey. She glowed with joy there and respectfully asked such pertinent questions that I understood then how much thought she had devoted to this decision. Perhaps my daughter was wiser than I.

The abbess, plainly delighted by and impressed with my daughter, suggested that she bide with them for a year while considering whether this course seemed right for her. Bella wished very much to do so. The abbess assured me that Dame Agnes and I might visit her a few times during that year.

My heart was heavy on the ride back to London without my daughter. Robert attempted to distract me with details of his autumn visits of inspection to my properties. I felt fortunate to have a steward who was also my good friend, and thanked God for other friends and family that evening at my parish church.

As ever, my peace was short-lived. Richard Lyons, Geoffrey and Pippa dined with me a few days later, all abuzz about the clemency shown to the murderer of Nicholas Sardouche, a Lombard merchant Janyn had known long ago. I had not heard of the incident which had happened in Cheapside, shortly before Christmas. Sardouche argued with a mercer who owed him over £100 sterling. The mercer, joined by two other mercers who claimed not to know him, beat Sardouche to death.

'London mercers against Lombard merchants – it is an old story,' said Richard. 'Even my fellow Flemings take precautions when travelling in the city at night. The London guilds claim the King unjustly favours the foreigners.'

'All three were set free without punishment,' said Geoffrey.

'How can the court be so blind?' I asked.

'You have been too long in the King's company, my friend,' said Geoffrey. 'You forget the angry undercurrents in the marketplace.'

'It seems to me they have taken that anger to Parliament,' said Pippa. 'They say the commons have turned on the King.'

News from Parliament had trickled through the city. I knew that the people were excited about it, seeing it as a triumph for the commons, who insisted on an upheaval in Edward's council in exchange for their agreement to new taxation. The commons blamed the clerical councillors for the failed war effort in France, particularly Wykeham and the Treasurer, Thomas Brantingham, Bishop of Ely, and insisted they be replaced by laymen. Edward had bowed to their demands. By the time I was reunited with him, I was agitated beyond wisdom.

'You asked William Wykeham to step down? But, Edward, he is your good friend and trusted adviser. He came to you so recently, guiding you through your mourning. You have sung his praises as Chancellor to me. I cannot understand why you succumbed to the rabble's demand.'

'Alice, my love, I hardly expect you to understand how a King must rule. Wykeham is still Bishop of Winchester, and he is still my wise counsellor. I spoke to him in private. He agreed to this for the sake of the kingdom. As did Brantingham.'

Edward's words were brave and matter-of-fact, but the vein throbbing in his temple and his clammy skin bore witness to his secret disappointment and anger – a frustrated anger. I feared, as had Lancaster when he had sent for me after Philippa's death, that the King's age rendered him increasingly vulnerable. He needed one of his eldest sons by his side. Edmund and Thomas were too untried to advise him.

'Promise me that you will indeed abide by Wykeham's counsel?' I implored. I was frightened for Edward. I did not understand this new power of the commons – for power they must have, to have coerced him into parting with Wykeham.

He lifted my chin and kissed me. 'I have already said I shall. Do not fret, Alice.'

But I did, even more so as further changes came in swift order. Edward made William Latimer his Chamberlain and John Neville of Raby, our son's second godfather, his steward. I was not concerned by Neville's appointment, but could not fathom what Edward saw in Latimer. I knew him a little through Richard Lyons and his time at court, and thought him an opportunist more suited to affairs of customs and the mint than the King's household. He could not possibly have been Edward's own choice. My beloved seemed no longer to be in control.

I was relieved to hear that Prince Edward and Princess Joan had landed and were expected at court at any time. I had forgotten for the moment why they had left Bordeaux and prayed they would know how to set things right. But I had my doubts when I beheld them. At the sight of his eldest son, being carried into the hall on a litter, Edward sought my hand and clutched it so tightly that tears sprang to my eyes. Princess Joan walked beside her ailing husband's litter, regal and elegant even after the long journey. As soon as she had instructed the litter bearers in the manner in which to proceed, she hurried forward to bow in obeisance to Edward. I nudged him to lift his eyes from his shattered son and attend to Joan.

When she straightened and allowed a servant to remove her mantle, the toll of the years in Bordeaux was revealed. Her beautiful face was fraught with lines of weariness and sorrow, her once lithe body plump now. Even so, she outshone anyone in the hall, and her kind eyes and bright smile lit me within as she greeted me with sincere warmth. An ally had returned.

Later, after a brief rest, the Prince managed to walk from his chamber to that of the King for the welcoming dinner. He leaned on both Joan's arm and that of a page, but made an effort to straighten up and give his father a slight bow before taking his seat at the table. The talk was of Channel crossings and the funeral arrangements for young Edward, which had been left for John to carry out in the Cathedral of St André in Bordeaux. Lancaster was still in France.

Edward wept in my arms that night. 'He was the bravest of us all, my glorious son and heir! Now he is a swollen, misshapen creature, crippled by humiliation.'

Early the following morning Princess Joan knelt beside me in the chapel as Mass began. It was comforting to have her there, exuding a perfume both flowery and spicy, softly whispering prayers as she fingered her ivory and jet paternoster beads. The King was sitting up above in his private area, warmly wrapped. He had slept little.

After the service Joan asked if she might accompany me to my chamber.

'It has been so long since we talked. I want to hear about my namesake Joan, and how John likes the Percy household. And beautiful Bella – is it true that she is at Barking?'

When I expressed my sorrow over the death of her son, she squeezed my hand. 'Let us not speak of my troubles, not this morning, Alice. I must find a way back to joy.'

In my chamber I drew out my latest treasure, a long mirror

that Edward had recently given me. Gwen had quickly become adept at holding it so that if I turned a little this way and that, for the first time in my life I could see almost my entire self.

I too had added some weight of late. Not so much as Joan, but enough to require alterations in most of my gowns. I stood before the mirror and growled at my own reflection.

Joan laughed. 'You are so lovely, Alice, and so young! Revel in your time, my friend.' She stepped forward. 'Now hold it up for me, Gwen, I pray you.'

Joan was beautiful this morning, her gown in several shades of green, a fleur-de-lis pattern on the skirt, the sleeves and bodice solids in varying shades, all decorated with pearls and silver filigree buttons. It was cleverly fitted to accentuate her breasts and disguise her thickened waist.

'The needlework is excellent, the body shockingly aged,' she said with an exaggerated frown. 'This is no avenue to joy!' Her silks whispered as she moved to the window. Picking up one of the many cushions, she admired its embroidery and the silk weave that shimmered in the light. 'This is exquisite, Alice!' She settled down on the window seat and patted the cushions beside her. 'Now come, tell me about your darlings.'

We talked for an hour or more. I had not laughed so much in a long while. She described magnificent feasts and tournaments, ridiculous lords and ladies, gorgeous gardens and water courses. By the time she left, I felt I knew something of Bordeaux and why she loved it so. Except for the toll it had taken on her family.

To my immense discomfort, Prince Edward summoned me to his chamber later in the morning, to glean what he could regarding his father's health and state of mind. It seemed father and son were mutually dismayed by the changes time had wrought in each other.

'My lord, with all respect, it would seem best you should ask such questions of His Grace, your father, and his physicians. I am neither qualified nor at liberty to discuss His Grace's health.'

'Who better?' Prince Edward barked, with a loud, brittle laugh. 'I wager you are more familiar with his body and his moods than any other in the kingdom! He has planted two children in your womb . . . or is it three?'

I blushed to realise how much the sons must talk of me. Of us. I wished Princess Joan had remained present.

'Can he still perform, eh?'

Can you? I wanted to say. But bit my tongue.

My silence seemed to rebuke him. He shaped his bloated face into an expression of tender concern. 'Forgive me. Discomfort makes me cruel. I pray you, hold it not against me. For, you see, I need you. I pray you, be at ease. I count on you to be my ally.'

He told me of his long illness, and with bitterness described the gradually escalating disrespect he had suffered from the Gascon lords. In his version it was not his own poor judgement and quick temper that had led to his abandonment by the Gascons, but rather their arrogant dismissal of his authority because of his infirmity – a lord who could not sit a horse on campaign need not be obeyed.

'This must not happen here. My father the King must not appear weak. The barons must never sense that they might gain ascendancy over him.'

His swollen face burned with outrage, yet his voice was but a whisper.

'My lord, I have seen no evidence of such dishonour or disloyalty.'

'What of this Parliament. How dare they question the King's authority to raise taxes in order to defend their pathetic lives.' Heightened emotion set off a coughing fit. A servant hurried forward with a warm drink to soothe him.

'My lord, I have no knowledge of the workings of Parliament. Perhaps the Bishop of Winchester might better inform you.'

'Wykeham?' He growled the name. 'His incompetence has brought us to this crisis! Do not speak of Wykeham in my presence.'

Then more fool you, I thought. 'What would you have me do, my lord?'

'Stay by the King's side as much as you are able. Review his dress. Recommend that he retire and see no one when he is unwell.'

'My lord, you describe an invalid. His Grace is by no means that. He rides, he hawks, he presides over meetings with his council.'

'Which brings me back to my earlier question – is he still active in bed?'

I had never been fond of the Prince, but liked him even less at that moment. Fortunately, his physician had just entered the room.

'Your physician awaits you, my lord. May God go with you.' I bowed to Prince Edward and withdrew.

It was one thing to obey the King, but the thought of being the pawn of his sons I could not bear. After I'd worked off my fury on a long ride, I felt ill and took to my bed for the rest of the day. It was not as pleasant as it might have been to burrow down beneath the bedclothes and doze, for my mind was troubled. I could brush aside the Prince's bawdiness and bitterness, but not his concern that Edward should appear hale and hearty at all times to the courtiers and the public. Had he not seemed so to his son? As the day wore on I grew more fearful that Edward was in a decline I had failed to see. I felt the deep sand shifting beneath me. I wanted to be his lover, not his keeper. Had that blinded me to the extent of the changes in him?

Yet I knew that I must manage to be gracious to the Prince. I could not risk offending him. I must do as he asked, though I felt he saw me as little more than a servant.

But taking on ever more responsibility for Edward's welfare might prove difficult for the next nine months or so. Gwen groaned when I became ill two mornings in a row.

'At least you will cease growling at the mirror,' she said. 'You know now why your waist is widening. You were wrong about your flux being delayed because the commons' behaviour upset you so.'

Weeks later, when I was certain enough to tell Edward the news, he bragged to his son that he had once more sired a child.

Prince Edward winked at me.

Princess Joan suddenly suggested that we leave the men to talk. She walked with me to my chamber, sitting on my bed and inviting me to join her.

'My husband is angry at the world these days, sweet Alice. I pray you, pay him no heed. His purpose was not to insult you.' She leaned close and smoothed my hair from my forehead, kissing me on the cheek. She smelled of lavender and sandalwood. 'You have made the King so happy. He is giddy with pride and reassured of his manhood.'

'Do you find him very changed?'

She sat back and tilted her head to study me, no longer smiling. 'Are you worried about him?'

'Your husband is.' I told her of Prince Edward's suggestions.

Joan took a deep breath. 'The King grows old, Alice. He does look much older than when I last saw him, but I expected as much. He has lost Philippa, Lionel, Mary and Margaret, Blanche – the list is endless, is it not? And the Aquitaine.' She glanced away for a moment, as if composing herself.

'Then I should heed your husband's advice?'

She shook herself as if emerging from a dream and smiled on me. 'Continue as you have been, Alice. I have heard of no one showing disrespect to the King.'

This time Edward insisted I remain by his side until a month before I expected to be lying in, and I did not argue. It was as if Prince Edward had lifted a veil from my eyes. I grew more aware of the King's lapses. One morning in late-summer he woke to no feeling in his right arm. I massaged it and made him perform simple movements until we were both reassured that, whatever had happened, it had passed. But often afterwards I would notice that arm hanging limply and would touch it to remind him that it was there.

'You must make an effort to use it more, my love, else it will wither.' One of his physicians had so advised us. He thought it was the result of an old wound that had been exacerbated while the King was hawking.

'Mother the child in your womb, not me,' Edward would growl.

When it was time for my lying in I moved only so far as a pretty house on the river at Windsor. Grandmother did not bide with me for that birth. Even such a brief trip was too much for her to contemplate. But Felice the midwife was with me, and Gwen, Mary and Joan.

In November I gave birth to my beautiful Jane. Little Joan was excited to have a companion. Edward was disappointed.

'You do favour the female sex, my love. Perhaps we should

consult an alchemist about turning females into males in the womb.'

'You have been too much in the company of your son the Prince,' I said. 'Your witticisms lack humour and grace.'

Edward glared at me and departed, but within hours he returned, assuring me that he had been teasing. He showered me with pearls, rubies and diamonds, and insisted I be with him at King's Langley for the Christmas court. John and his new Duchess were to be there.

Edward's rejection of Jane both chilled and offended me. Even the arrival of my dear Robert bearing gifts for Jane and me could not entirely warm me. But my steward's gentle presence was, as ever, a great comfort.

'In al this world ther nys so cruel herte
That hire hadde herd compleynen in hire sorwe
That nolde han wepen for hire peynes smerte,
So tendrely she weep, bothe eve and morwe.
Hire nedede no teris for to borwe!
And this was yet the werste of al hire peyne:
Ther was no wight to whom she dorste hire pleyne.'

– Geoffrey Chaucer, *Troilus and Criseyde*, V, ll. 722–728

Christmas 1371

At the Christmas court Edward and I dazzled the guests in gowns of cloth of gold and headdresses with ships at full sail, the rigging ropes fashioned out of the same gold wire that was used as the weft thread in the cloth of my long surcoat and his robes. The headdresses symbolised Edward's intention to sail to France in summer to win back the Aquitaine. We wore emeralds and diamonds set in gold. The warp of our cloth was green, and the livery of his household was green cloth with gold embroidery. Prince Edward and Princess Joan wore similar robes and headdresses, and many courtiers wore headdresses in maritime and martial themes. The effect was breathtaking. Edward and his daughter-in-law Joan both saw the gold and green as the sun on the stormy waters of the channel; it pleased them to imagine how the assembly might look from the ceiling of the hall: a fleet setting sail across a sun-dazzled sea.

When Edward had first proposed the maritime theme I'd tried one last time to dissuade him from the mission that had inspired it. King Charles of France was proving a clever strategist, unexpectedly effective in wooing back the lords of the Aquitaine. Many believed it was already too late for Edward or anyone else to influence events there. All this celebration of his intention to fight for the Aquitaine would only make it more difficult for him to change his mind. But Edward would not bend.

Abandoning that issue, I broached another, more personal, objection that weighed on my mind as we sat beside each other at a feast celebrating the tenth anniversary of Joan and Edward's marriage. I kept my voice as low as possible.

'I pray you, permit me to wear something more modest, Edward. I am not part of the royal family nor am I of noble blood. I should be less prominent, only a pleasing background complement to your magnificence.' I smiled and nodded at the servant offering to refill the jewelled mazer we shared. Beyond him I was keenly aware of the whispers of disapproval circulating regarding my presence on the dais, so publicly beside the King.

'You are the mother of my youngest son and daughters,' Edward said, not as quietly as I might wish. But courtiers were accustomed to a courteous pretence of not overhearing the King's private discourse. 'Philippa and I would sit for hours imagining the effect of various designs, delighting in conjuring such grand displays to celebrate the glory of our realm. I miss sharing such joy with her, and had hoped you would take her place by my side in such undertakings.'

'If it brings you joy, my love, I would as lief oblige. But you know that many will take offence.'

'I am the King. They expect magnificence from me. The court dare not criticise my mistress.'

'You would not betimes have believed the commons would coerce you into asking Wykeham to step down as Chancellor.' Edward's refusal to see how much control he had lost frustrated me. I feared it would prove our downfall. And indeed, in hindsight, this was perhaps our first grievous error.

In early-February, the City of London and all the court welcomed Duke John's new bride, the Duchess Constance. She was dark, angular, not unattractive yet not pretty. There was a stiffness in her movements and her character did not generally please, her dark eyes always full of censure.

When I was introduced to her she did not even glance my way but changed the subject of conversation and wandered away. I was shaken by her hostility, unexpressed though it was.

Princess Joan assured me that all around me were feeling the sting of her Spanish arrogance likewise.

'You do not need her approval. Duke John is your friend, as is the Prince,' said Joan. 'You know that, do you not? They are well aware of their indebtedness to you for your care of their father.'

I winced.

'Are you so young and inexperienced you do not yet see how loving the King is tantamount to caring for him? You see how my own beloved now needs me more as mother than as lover.'

'I know all this, Joan. That does not mean I am easy in my mind about my own competence.'

She patted my arm and remarked that the King was gazing our way, apparently requiring me by his side. 'You look more of a queen than Philippa ever did,' she said as I began to walk away.

That chilled me. I prayed that no one else thought so. Joan looked like a queen and it was most appropriate for her. She would make a magnificent queen in due course. I prayed that her husband recovered enough to rule wisely and without the bitterness that had darkened his character of late.

I wondered what would become of me when that time came.

In late-winter, only months before Edward planned to embark for France with the Prince and a large fleet, he had several memory lapses so alarming that I begged him to consult his physicians. He resisted my entreaties at first, though I knew he was as frightened as I was.

The first event I had initially taken as a slight to our youngest daughter Jane. She was in my chamber with me. When Edward arrived, he seemed taken aback to see her.

'Whose child is this?'

'Whose? Edward, this is Jane, our daughter.'

He gave me a sharp look, as if I had dared to insult him. 'Do not dissemble, Alice. We have a son and . . .' He hesitated, his mind quite visibly confused or blank. 'Have we a daughter as well? Yes, I believe – but older than this poppet. Who is she?'

I handed Jane to the nurse and gestured to her to withdraw. Edward, seemingly dressed for hawking, now sat down beside me and began to talk of his plan for new baths at Eltham, a project that had been completed several years earlier. I did not correct him, listening and nodding as appropriate. Suddenly he slapped his thigh, rose and exclaimed, 'Why are we speaking of this? We have enjoyed those baths for a year or more.' He glanced around the chamber. 'Was Jane here?' He rubbed his temples, then seemed to notice his clothing. 'I meant to hawk.'

What I had feared might be a prelude to accusing me of being unfaithful or a cruel way of ignoring his daughter was in fact far worse. As he left the room I followed, pretending to have some small item to discuss as I escorted him safely to the stables. He seemed more his usual self now, puzzled by Jane's nurse whisking her away before he'd had a chance to greet her. Yet there was a wildness in his eyes that worried me.

'I should like to ride out with you, my lord,' I said, trying to sound light and ready for an adventure.

'I need no nursemaid,' he growled and waved me off.

Though I regretted having irritated him, I had learned something that might prove helpful to know – he realised that something was wrong and was uneasy, perhaps even frightened. I prayed that would make him more approachable if I suggested he speak to his physicians.

Similar incidents occurred a few days later and a few weeks after that. Fortunately, Duke John witnessed the third occasion and supported my encouragement that the King's physicians should be told of events, in the detail only I could provide.

Edward's shoulders seemed to sag as he listened to our advice and studied our expressions. But I had guessed correctly; he was quite aware that something was wrong, and grudgingly agreed to do as we requested. Old age, too much wine, insufficient activity, too little sleep, too much sleep, too much food, too little of the food that would balance his humours . . . in the next several days Edward was subjected to so much conflicting advice that he threatened to exile all three physicians, but in the end he chose to heed the advice of the one skilled in soothing his headaches, reasoning that memory resided in the head. His was the diet appropriate for the King's unbalanced humours, with more activity and less wine.

I prayed he was right, but feared that soon Edward must accept a quieter existence, perhaps allowing his sons to participate more fully in governing – as he had planned, but not fully implemented. He clung yet to governing his own isle. I urged him to look to his sons rather than Latimer and Neville and several other courtiers and financiers, including Richard Lyons, who crowded around him. Edward found it amusing that I cautioned him against men with whom I myself chose to do business.

I did not in fact do business with all of them, but that was not the point. I did not argue but focused on my purpose. 'They are suitable for commerce, my love, not for ruling a kingdom.'

When he laughingly disregarded my opinion, I felt I had lost my voice. Long ago I had worried that, in loving a man, I might lose myself. But this was worse. Nothing I said seemed to count any more. I was chided for voicing an opinion even slightly contrary to his.

Duke John and Prince Edward instructed me to stay by the King's side when neither of them was present, guiding him if his memory should fail, making excuses if he needed a respite from courtiers other than his most trusted men.

'They will resent me. What if the courtiers and barons turn against me?'

'Have faith in us, Dame Alice,' said Prince Edward. He had been kind to me of late and far more courteous, at Joan's prompting, I imagined, although it might have been the result of a sudden improvement in his health. 'John and I will shield you from harm,' he assured me.

Of course they would say so. They would say anything to coerce me into staying. But the truth was, I had no choice. Once again I was powerless.

My life was by no means completely bleak at that time. No matter the troubles and disagreements Edward and I might have by day, our evenings were loving and affectionate, sometimes still passionate, and we often rode or hawked in the early-morning. Despite his wrinkles and complaints in his joints, Edward always dressed to look his best, and still looked grand and at home on his horse. We played more chess than in the past, and often of an afternoon I would read to him – letters, documents, but mostly sermons and poetry – or we would sit arm-in-arm, listening to a minstrel or watching a tumbler.

When I could, I went for more challenging rides to supplement the easy ones with Edward. A groom would accompany me, or a guest who shared my love of setting off without a goal, wishing simply to experience the joy of being one with a magnificent animal, challenging my body, drinking in the air. The activity helped me forget for a little while my fears for my beloved, and for my own future.

William Wyndsor's name had been on all tongues at the Christmas court. There was controversy surrounding his execution of his duties as Edward's Governor in Ireland. He had stubbornly enforced an unpopular statute requiring the English landlords to provide for the defence of their Irish properties under pain of forfeiture to the Crown, thus angering the Mortimers, John Hastings, the Earl of Pembroke, the Despensers, and other powerful families. Edward did indeed take many of the lands into custody, which to my mind indicated complicity, for he needed the income to fund the force he was gathering to attack France. But he eventually bowed to the growing clamour among the baronial families, summoning Wyndsor to Westminster to answer to their accusations.

It was Geoffrey who informed me of much of this. Edward and I did not speak of William.

'He is expected to return in spring,' my friend told me. 'It is good that you did not heed my advice to wed him. He seems to be a man destined to make enemies.'

I had been too confident that William would remain in Ireland, for no one else wanted the post. They wanted the glory and plunder promised from a French expedition.

'*Deus juva me*,' I whispered, crossing myself. 'I pray that something happens to cancel this summons.'

'Why? Surely he has forgotten you.'

'No, he has not, and it is partly my fault, my insistence on repaying what I felt was a debt I did not wish to owe.'

'To repay a debt is a worthy deed,' Geoffrey said, 'but I am amazed that you would have risked owing Wyndsor aught.'

'He solved a dispute with a neighbour that had long weighed on my mind. Months later he wrote from Ireland seeking my assistance in selling some land he held near Winchester, needing the money. Owing him a favour, I obliged. His letters since have grown more and more importunate. I have ignored them. But coming here . . . I do not trust him. I fear what rumours he might spread.'

Geoffrey shook his head. 'The gossips have more interesting rumours to digest. They are saying that His Grace has given you the late Queen's jewels.'

I instinctively touched the jewels on my sleeve, rubies surrounded by pearls. 'These were not Her Grace's.'

'The gossips say you wore familiar pieces at the Christmas court.'

I felt myself tempted to lie. I had never questioned the source of the jewels Edward gave me. Of late he had given me fewer pearls and more precious stones, which he urged me to wear. I usually ignored him. I feared reprisals if I outshone my betters, and told him so. But at Christmas he had insisted that I would ruin his design with my modesty.

'His Grace did insist I wear some of the late Queen's jewels then,' I conceded. 'But I knew they were never mine to keep. What else do they say of me?'

'That you control access to the King, and that his household is now filled with your friends.'

'Geoffrey! That is not true.' Perhaps the first was, to an extent, but not the second. Those perceived as my friends were the very men I had warned Edward against. 'They visit us here because we engage in trade together.'

Geoffrey held up a hand. 'I know that, and most other folk do as well. But they prefer to chatter about such nonsense rather than delve more deeply – where they might discover the uneasy fact that His Grace is not the man he once was, and neither is his heir. Prince Edward's son Richard is likely to be the next King, but he is so young – too young – and too much like the late Queen Mother Isabella for their tastes.'

I worried for Joan. I, too, had heard this said about her youngest son. 'Poor child, already criticised for a likeness over which he has no control.'

The shadow of Edward's sortie into France loomed over the household all spring, for essentially all the household officers, pages, grooms – all its males – were to embark with the King and the Prince. Two men in ill health confronting a wily fox on his own terrain – I feared for our two Edwards. I planned to retire to one of my manors in the countryside with my daughters and

Grandmother, if I could persuade Dame Agnes to make the journey. She had been frail and confused on my most recent visits, but I wondered how much of that was worsened by her withdrawal from society. She rarely left the house now, doing so only to cross the square to the church. I also had some hope that John would join us for a while; Henry, Lord Percy was considering my request to have my son with me for a few months.

All my bustling about in preparation could not drown out more fearful thoughts. Despite knowing how much it meant to Edward, I prayed that something benign might prevent his proceeding. He counted on a victory over Charles to take away his aches and pains, rejuvenate him, right all the wrongs of recent years. But neither victory nor defeat could change the truth that he was an ageing King with a troublingly broken heir. I feared how he would cope with disillusionment after victory even more than I feared how he would meet with defeat.

It had been months since he had been able to make love to me, though we continued to pleasure one another in other satisfying ways. I tried to convince him that we were as passionate and loving as ever. But I knew he felt diminished. One evening he urged me to seek out love potions or spells that might make it possible for him to make love to me again. My arguments that he *was* making love to me in all the ways that mattered only angered him.

'I fear such people as those who dabble in love potions and spells, Edward, my love. What if someone should find out and condemn us?'

'I am the King, Alice. Who would dare condemn me?'

Some questions were better left unanswered, but in my heart I doubted he was as safe as he thought.

In late-July I gathered my daughters and Dame Agnes, to whom the warm days of summer had been kind, and we began our travels with the short journey to Barking Abbey, to spend a day with our beloved Bella, now a novice. I had seen her earlier in the season, on her birthday, and rejoiced to witness her contentment. As I had hoped, Dame Agnes was comforted by seeing this as well.

We then continued on to the Manor of Tibenham in Norfolk. It was part of the de Orby wardship in which I had invested a great deal of money and Robert's time, hoping to return it to productivity. Henry, Lord Percy had suggested that his half-sister Mary, my ward and heiress to the manor, might accompany John and revisit the home in which she had spent her earliest summers. She was a few years his junior, and as Edward still considered her a possible wife for our son I agreed, thinking it worth observing them together. The manor was very near the sea. I did not like to journey so far with my frail grandmother and little Jane, who was still very young, but in the end Joan's excitement about seeing her brother won me over.

It proved to be a beautiful house, and Dame Agnes enjoyed sitting in the garden there, feeling the cool salt breeze beneath the hot sun in the late afternoon. I missed the bright mornings at Fair Meadow or Ardington, though. So near the coast, the mornings were often dull with fog.

I was soon distracted by a visitor I'd not anticipated. One misty morning as I stood in the hall looking out on what seemed to be a solid wall of grey just beyond the porch, two figures on horseback emerged from the fog. My first thought was fear that something had gone wrong in Sandwich. In June Lord Pembroke's fleet of ships sailing to La Rochelle in Gascony, carrying a small fortune to pay for the military support of Gascon lords and their men, was utterly destroyed by a Spanish fleet. After the initial hysteria, the silence into which the palace sank was more terrifying than all the cries and moans and shouted accusations that had greeted this news. I and many attached to Edward's household had invested heavily in the war as a show of confidence. We were stunned by our loss. Plans for embarking from Sandwich had resumed with a sense of desperate urgency. Both Princess Joan and Prince Edward had impressed upon me how devastating was the loss of our fleet and wealth; how essential it was to retaliate. They had asked me to go to Richard Lyons to ask for more financial support, which I had done, with much misgiving. The King, my beloved, was not strong enough for such a venture, either in body or spirit.

Now I crossed myself and said a prayer that these visitors did not presage ill news. As the men drew closer, a different dread now manifested itself – the taller rider on the fine horse was William Wyndsor.

'What is he doing here?' Grandmother hissed behind me.

I had not noticed her there. 'I do not know. I pray it is not bad news about the sailing.' I turned to her, looking into her gauzy eyes. 'But how can you recognise him from here?'

'I smell him . . . the rat who tore our family apart. Friend to the She-devil!'

She thought it was Janyn. 'It is not my husband, he is dead, Grandmother. It is Sir William Wyndsor.'

She looked confused.

'From afar his dark hair and his height could fool me as well,' I said. 'Shall we welcome him?'

I sent a servant to fetch a groom who then invited William and his companion within. I reached the screens shielding the hall from draughts just as William stepped through them, shaking out his damp cloak.

'God's blood, you are as beautiful as ever, Alice!'

'Is there some trouble?'

'No. I come merely to thank you for your assistance.'

'As I wrote at the time, there was no need to thank me.'

Courtesy required I should invite him into the hall. I sent his page to the kitchen for some food and ale.

Grandmother greeted William with cautious courtesy. Mary Percy, John and Joan looked up from their play to study him as only children can, openly staring, taking no care to hide their disinterest when he did no tricks.

But William strode over to them and crouched down. 'I am William Wyndsor, recently come from Ireland. Whom am I addressing?'

'Mary,' she said with a lisp and a finger up her nose.

'Joan.'

'John Southery,' my son said, scrambling to stand and give William a stout bow.

William expressed delight upon meeting them, then noticed Jane in her nurse's arms as he rose. 'And this lovely child?'

'Jane.'

'These are all yours?'

How little he knew of my life. 'Not Mary. I am her guardian, though she does not usually reside with me. John is being fostered by her half-brother, Henry Percy.'

William lifted a brow. 'The three others are the King's children?'

'Of course.' I felt myself blush though I knew his question was most likely innocent, not a suggestion that I had more lovers.

'They all favour him. But where is Bella?'

'She is now a novice at Barking Abbey. Her choice.'

'Such a beautiful child.'

'Yes, she is. Now come, William.' I led him out into the brightening yard, then turned to him and demanded, 'How did you know where to find me?'

'Does it matter?'

'Yes, William, I believe it may.'

'I asked. Discreetly. I have but a few days, Alice, then I must return to Westminster. I had to see you.'

'It is most courteous of you. And now, your deed done, you are welcome to refresh yourself before continuing on your journey.'

'You would send me away so soon?'

'Yes. Rest here in the garden. A servant will bring you some food and ale.'

'Will you sit with me a while?'

'I cannot. I must see to the children.' I hurried back inside the house.

Robert came to me in a little while to say that William and his servant had departed.

'Had His Grace sent him? Is there news?' he asked.

'He said nothing of Sandwich. Had come all this way, in fact, to thank me for arranging the sale of that manor – the one you took care of for me. But how he knew where to find me, and to come so far . . . I do not like it.'

Robert took my hands. 'If he returns, I shall deal with him.'

I pressed his hands. 'He is not your burden, my friend.'

'Nor should he be yours.'

I drew strength from Robert's concern. But I was still worried. Edward must not hear of William's visit, innocent though it was. In his frail state his reactions were unpredictable, often rash. I asked Robert to listen for gossip among the tenants. Days later, when he had heard nothing, I finally began to hope that nothing would come of William's unwelcome appearance.

'Your new tenants have benefited from your improvements, Alice,' Robert assured me. 'Even had they noticed anything awry, I doubt they would speak ill of you.'

Unfortunately, I soon learned that Henry, Lord Percy knew of William's visit. Not wishing to call more attention to the incident, I did not investigate whether John and Mary had spoken of it as children might, or whether it had been Henry Percy himself who had told William where I would be. I would not have considered the latter but that I knew how ambitious Percy was, and could well imagine his tucking this knowledge of William's interest in me away as possibly useful in future. I could not judge whether my concern for Edward's failing health and his reckless intent to lead an army had rendered me so worried about my own future that I suspected enemies where there were none, or whether I was right to sense ranks closing in round me. For the rest of our sojourn in Norfolk I walked about in a fog of fear and anxiety that dimmed the joy of having my children and Dame Agnes with me in such a beautiful setting.

I did not see William again until I returned to Westminster, which was much sooner than I had expected.

In late-summer the weather turned foul. The King, the Prince, the barons and all their men, ships and stores, were still waiting in Sandwich for the winds and storms to abate so they might cross the Channel to France when word came that the English-held town of La Rochelle had fallen to Charles's troops. The weather had defeated the two Edwards, father and son. In mid-October the expedition force was disbanded, having achieved nothing, gone nowhere, at great cost. It was a financial disaster, for wars were funded on the understanding that ransoms and plunder would refill the coffers. There was no hope of that this bleak autumn. Worse, the great Kingdom of Aquitaine was all but lost – little now remained in English hands but for some strips of land along the coast. Edward's dream of being King of both France and England was dead.

I thanked God that he was back in Windsor, but he returned aged and dispirited, craving escape in lovemaking, hunting, hawking, dancing, yet bereft of the will even to rise from his bed. In truth, he suffered from such debilitating despair that I agreed with Prince Edward that we must protect the King from public view on his worst days.

The desperate financial situation required Wykeham's calm wisdom and Brantingham's practical caution. But Prince Edward denied them both access to his father, saying the two Bishops had had their chance to advise the King and failed. All of us at court who had the wherewithal once again bought some of the loans, to provide the Crown with immediate cash.

I do not know whether a younger King and a healthier Prince might have made the journey to France that late-summer. On some days Edward was certain he had failed his people; if he felt that the Prince might better lead the people, he would have stood aside. But the horror of it was that the heir too had failed his people. On other days Edward railed against the winds and tides, the inefficiency of his captains, his son's plodding progress to Sandwich.

He began to slip back into the past, talking obsessively about the half-brother he had met in Italy, the bastard son of his mother and Roger Mortimer. He spoke of how he regretted never having made the effort to meet him again after that one encounter when the boy was about eight.

'My half-brother . . . What sort of man did he become? Was he bitter? Content?'

He also thought much about the rumour that his father had escaped from Berkeley Castle and secretly retreated from the world, living out the rest of his days in peace in a monastery. 'Would that I might do so! An old King is no good for the realm.'

Gradually a darksome aspect crept into this plan; he began to forget more and more often that his father had actually died at Berkeley, and that his retirement had been only a rumour. He reassured himself that he would be following his father's 'wisdom' in knowing when a monarch should abdicate with grace. I would try to distract him by drawing him out for a brief ride or, if he were not so inclined, at least to the mews to see the hawks. I hoped that being out in the countryside and moving freely would bring him back to the present. I remembered with what anxiety Tommasa and Janyn had witnessed the Dowager Queen's decline, and how right they had been to fear it. I prayed theirs would not be my fate.

As Edward's health continued to deteriorate through the winter, it was increasingly difficult to conceal his spells of illness. A moment I had long dreaded occurred during a feast at Windsor. Edward was seated on the dais in full view when he suddenly slumped in his chair. Princess Joan and I quickly shielded him, pretending to be discussing something about the jewels in his crown. Just as suddenly he opened his eyes, straightened, and commanded us to stop fussing over him. More often he would briefly lose the use of an arm or leg. I grew adept at staying close to him and masking how much I was aiding him in sitting up straight or holding his arm naturally.

I resented the ease with which Joan and the Prince would withdraw to their palace in Kennington for a rest, John would disappear to Katherine or Constance, and I would be left in charge of Edward, night and day. Of course he was surrounded by his household administrators, knights and servants, but they all looked to me for direction when the King confused them.

When Dame Agnes was on her deathbed, I left John Neville in charge of the King, with two of Edward's physicians seeing to matters of a more personal nature, and worried about him constantly during the weeks I sat with my dear grandmother. In faith, while I watched at her bedside, I imagined sitting so at Edward's deathbed. At thirty-one years of age, all my thoughts had turned toward the deaths of my elders.

I grew restive. To counteract it I rode as much as possible and sought the comfort of hawking in season. When I freed my hawks from their jesses, I would tell them to soar and imagine taking their place, flying free, enjoying the exuberant rush up, up into the air before returning to my master's glove.

On the rare occasions that I was freed from my duties at court, I would gather my daughters from the home of my sister Mary, send for Robert if he were not too far afield, and we would enjoy a respite in London or at Fair Meadow. But these interludes were brief and seldom.

My time with Edward was now bitter-sweet, his physical and mental decline reminding me that my days with him were numbered. My heart ached when I thought back on my life with him. In losing Edward, I would lose not only a lover and a lord but a confidant, a keeper of my secrets. I stood on the precipice of change. I expected nothing from Edward's family once he was gone, except the status he had sworn to give our son John – knighthood in the year of Edward's jubilee, the great celebration of his fifty years of rule. He had obtained promises from both Prince Edward and Duke John that they would carry out the knighting if he were to die before that date. As for our daughters, Edward felt certain that the estate I had acquired would provide excellent dowries for Joan and Jane, sufficient for them to wed minor knights or wealthy merchants.

'Why do you love our daughters less than John?' I asked him.

'How can you so accuse me, Alice? I greet them with as much affection as I do John. And I believe I have given them far more gifts than I've given him.'

'But he will be a knight, respected and honoured as your son. They will enjoy no such status. Could you not recognise them as yours, Edward? Give them the benefit of noble standing?'

'Were you happy as the wife of Janyn Perrers?'

'You know that I was.'

'Why should they not be happy in similar marriages?'

'Because they know they are daughters of the King. Your blood runs in their veins, Edward. They will have your pride.'

On this matter he would not bend. And, God help me, I could not forgive his slight to his daughters.

And yet I loved him still, though it was not as before. I felt a tenderness for him, an affection, as I imagine one does in the latter years of a long marriage. His white hair was thinning, his flesh hung slack on his still straight but often aching frame. His joints swelled with long sitting. He drooled in his sleep. Yet when he rose and was dressed in his kingly robes, he was still an impressive figure of a man, and most days his mind was clear and cunning, his wisdom deep, his love for me constant.

In the forty-sixth year of Edward's reign, when Philippa was almost four years dead, my love presented me with diamonds, rubies and emeralds that had belonged to her. Some were in settings I well remembered – a circlet with fleur-de-lis set with diamonds and rubies, a gold ring in which was set a large emerald flanked by insets of lapis lazuli, a girdle of interlocking gold and silver sprinkled with diamonds, to name my favourites. Others were loose stones to add to all the pearls he had given me – and still did. I remembered Geoffrey's warning about the gossip surrounding my wearing the less identifiable jewels at a Christmas court. How I could wear these new gifts I did not know. Edward was oblivious to the danger of such an action. It was madness.

One October morning at Havering, as I returned from a solitary ride, I encountered William Wyndsor in the hall, his shoulders hunched defiantly, his visage turned in on itself in anger. He was coming from the direction of Edward's chambers. Such was his self-absorption he did not notice me until I stepped in front of him and said his name, loud and sharp. Only then did he pause and look up.

Though I would have preferred to have avoided him, I could not, and therefore I put on my cordial court façade. 'William, what is amiss?'

He growled, shook his head and pushed past me, but had taken only a few steps when he turned back. 'You've done enough. Leave me be!' he said in the impatient tone he used with mis-behaving dogs – and he was not fond of dogs.

Having been blamed for what I did not know, I followed him. Once out in the yard, I grabbed his shoulder and demanded, 'If I'm to be blamed, have the courtesy to tell me what I've done.'

'His Grace has dropped the charges against me and is sending me back to Ireland.'

I almost laughed at his snarling delivery of such good news. 'I should think that is what you wanted.'

'I return as King's Lieutenant, not Governor.'

I looked into his beautiful eyes and saw there a spoiled, greedy boy. 'Titles mean little, William. You have been cleared of charges and shall resume your post. You should be celebrating, not berating me.'

With a look that chilled me, he removed my hand from his shoulder and walked away. I cannot say I was disappointed to see him go, but I was puzzled. And I felt subtly threatened, though I could think of no cause for this. I realised he had not explained what he thought I had to do with such news.

That evening Edward told me of his decision about William. He had been in a charming, amorous mood all afternoon. We had taken a long walk in the gardens, lingered over a delicious meal, rested together – he insisted that I join him – and since waking had sipped watered wine and reminisced about our years together. As he told me about William he seemed oddly gleeful, as if he were congratulating himself for besting someone. William, I supposed. Though I did not like to discuss him with Edward, I could not help myself.

'Forgive me, my love, but I do not understand your mood,' I said. 'You are happy you did not need to punish one of your trusted administrators, yet seem to feel you tricked him.'

Edward laughed, a deep, satisfied laugh. 'He claims you are his betrothed – that you've been betrothed for years. I wished him all happiness after I'm dead. For now you are mine, and he shall remain far from you.'

I thought I might choke, it was suddenly so difficult to breathe. I felt more than betrayed by William, I felt defiled.

Still smiling, Edward reached for my hands, looking me in the eyes. 'Alice, I love you too much to share you with another man.' He kissed both my hands. When he looked up once more he had ceased smiling. 'I am protecting you from a man who does not deserve you. He is cunning and greedy, and angry with the world for its imagined slights.'

'Edward, my love.' I had found my breath. 'I agree with all you say about him. I saw through his shallow charm long ago, and I never swore to wed him. I sent him away. I love you. Only you.'

'I do not blame you for seeking pleasure with a younger man.' He held up a hand to stop me from protesting. 'I have known that you have been with another when you are away from me.'

I cringed under this blow. He had said on several occasions that his indifference toward the future of our daughters was inspired by doubt that they were indeed his children. I had sworn every oath I could think of that his doubts were utterly unfounded, that it was impossible they were not his. Indeed, Joan, with her flaxen hair and deep blue eyes, looked so like Edward that he often swore it must only be Jane about whom he was unsure. Jane favoured me, her bone structure softer than his, her hair a little darker, her eyes grey-green. These doubts only assailed him on the days when he woke confused. On his more coherent days he sometimes declared he would acknowledge Joan and Jane.

'Wyndsor is my son John's creature, Alice.' He chuckled and kissed my hands once more. 'I have urged him to marry Wyndsor off to a dark beauty from Constance's household and send him to Castile in some dangerous post, but he makes excuses, pretends to have forgotten. Beware, my love.'

Of all the accusations and slights I had endured, this was the most bitter. I had been impeccably faithful to Edward and he did not believe it.

'I told you how he pestered me. Why would I have told you had I anything to hide? I have lain with no man but you since Janyn. Did he say we had lain together?'

'He did not need to.'

I was furious to find myself both insulted and unheard by this man who had won my heart by making me feel both seen and heard.

In spring of the forty-seventh year of Edward's reign he named a ship after me, *La Alice*. It was a beautiful ship, and I was touched by the joy it gave him to blindfold me and lead me along the dock. He had greeted me that morning with an air of happy antici-pation, and the wondrous vessel before me certainly exceeded all my expectations. But it was far too public an honour, the sort of extravagant gesture that could only do me harm.

When I next saw the Duke of Lancaster, he said, 'Give thanks for your moments with my father, Alice, but remember that he is old, he is failing, and when he is gone you shall need another protector, whether a ship rides at anchor on the Thames bearing your name or no.'

'I live with a keen awareness of the precipice just beyond my sight, my lord. I am most grateful to have your friendship.' I believed it imperative to pretend I still considered him my friend, concealing the fact that I had become ever more wary of him.

The Duke looked pleased. 'I am glad of that.'

This encounter chilled me. Why he had felt the need to warn me, I did not know. There were few at court I felt I could always count on. Indeed, at that moment I could think of but one –

Princess Joan. I still had Wykeham's friendship but his influence was now limited. Despite Edward's advice I had failed to make any deep friendships at court; those I had were all shallow, based on business not trust.

I walked the palace corridors with eyes cast down, avoiding the cool looks, the knowing grins, Lancaster's words echoing in my head.

In spring of the following year, Edward planned what would prove to be his last great tournament, an event that was to bring home to me how justified was my deepening sense of dread. To be staged at Smithfield in early-May, the event would extend over seven days, with jousting, tourneying, and feasting in celebration of the glory of Edward's realm and reign. True to his lifelong delight in devising elaborate themes for such festivities, Edward chose to be the Sun King, and I, his lady of the lists, was to appear as the Lady of the Sun. All such tournaments began with processions through the city, and I was accustomed to playing some role in these, but this time he meant for me to lead the ladies of the court, riding in a golden chariot. I imagined Lancaster, indeed all of the courtiers, watching me with scorn.

'As my Lady of the Sun you shall be as regal and fiercely beautiful as that magnificent bird, Alice.' Edward sat with head flung back, watching a falcon in flight.

'Edward, no, it is impossible that I should play such a role. Let Princess Joan be your lady in this.'

I had drawn him out to watch the falconer training new hawks, hoping to distract him as I argued against his scheme. We sat on a bench beneath a pretty arbour, the sun warming us.

'You are my Queen in spirit if not in title, Alice, and I will have it so.' His voice was low, his tone conversational, his eyes fixed on the birds.

'I am not your Queen, Edward, but a merchant's daughter. I was raised to know my place.'

He reached for my hand and squeezed it. 'Your place is beside me, my love.'

I did not need more enemies. I slipped my hand from his grasp and knelt before him. 'Edward, look at me for a moment.'

He squinted down at me, his once wondrously blue eyes clouded with age now. 'You are so beautiful . . .'

'Edward, I pray you, listen to me. You must understand that you endanger me by insisting on my being the Lady of the Sun.'

'You shall not deny me this pleasure, Alice.' He was no longer smiling.

'Princess Joan—'

'No. My son is too ill to take part. His wife would not wish to call attention to his absence by appearing on my arm.' The peacock feathers in Edward's hat shivered as his head began to shake, his temper rising. 'You must trust me. You must be there.'

His health was too fragile to risk an angry outburst. I retreated at once. 'My love, my love, please be calm. We shall discuss this later.' I rose to sit beside him once more, kissing his hand, his cheek.

Each time I tried to dissuade him, he frightened me with his temper. In the end, I accepted defeat and buried my fears, doing all that I could to ensure that the tournament would be a success.

It was at such times that I most missed Queen Philippa: her enthusiastic encouragement of us throughout the weeks of work, her almost childlike delight in our progress and astonishment at the results. She had lifted our hearts and rendered it all innocent fun. I still took immense pleasure in the sumptuous cloth and feathers, buttons and jewels gathered for the costumes, the silver and gold wire, the cloth of gold and silver, but I had no one with whom to share my delight. Princess Joan and Edward's daughter Isabella were vaguely interested, but the sempsters and servants working with me were for the most part quietly intent on their assignments, and I did not have the Queen's talent for lightening their spirits.

It was Edward who finally engaged their enthusiasm. He took it upon himself to appear in the sewing chamber at the end of each day, to examine our progress. The women would sit with eyes meekly cast down, listening while I pointed out the fine details of their work. He would lavish praise on it and urge me on to more splendid designs, more gold, more silver . . . more, more, more.

'We are proclaiming the glory of England,' he would declare to the room at large. 'I would dazzle my people.'

On the morrow the women would crowd round me, eager to see what I had added to the design, that they might better honour their beloved King. He was still the King of their hearts. I could not help but be caught up in their excitement.

When all was ready I stood in awe of the robes, the sheer spectacle in which I was to be one of the central figures. My gown, like Edward's, was cloth of gold. The background, or warp threads, were red silk and the foreground, or weft threads, were the most delicate gold wire. Red was for the rubies associated with the sun. Once cut and fitted, our gowns were embroidered with gold thread, sunbursts surrounding balas rubies and diamonds, which were also emblematic of the sun. Even my mantle was of cloth of gold, caught in back to free my shoulders and reveal the lining, the reverse of the gown, gold background with red foreground. From my neck to the low-cut top of my bodice, I wore gold tissue so fine as to be almost invisible, sprinkled with large rubies and diamonds set in gold sunbursts, as if even my flesh were transformed. For once I might feel like his Queen as I stood by his side.

On the morning of the procession my heart beat so fast I felt faint, all my earlier misgivings returned. It did not help that the elaborate headdress, of gold tissue built up to create a sunburst around my head, had to be firmly fastened to my hair, which was coiled beneath, to prevent it from taking flight. I felt the restraint whenever I made a sudden movement. Gwen needed six assistants to dress me. My hair, skin, everything, was covered in gold cloth. Finally the women stood back from me, their eyes wide. The sempsters, standing by to make last-minute repairs, applauded.

When Gwen held the long mirror up to me, I did not recognise myself. It was how I imagined the pagan goddesses to look.

Striding into the room, deriving renewed vigour from his own glorious costume, Edward spread his arms wide and proclaimed me to be every inch the Sun Queen.

'You are magnificent, Alice, my beloved!'

'As are you, my King,' I said, gliding towards him to take his proffered hand. Though my headdress was light enough, my robe was not. But I did not complain. I would not ruin Edward's day.

The ladies of the court simpered over my costume as we moved into formation for the procession, but their eyes were cold. They were to walk behind me, all in silver cloth with simple silver veils held with silver fillets, leading horses on which rode their lords, also dressed in silver. Their only jewels were pearls. Cool moonlight trailing my blazing glory.

Our procession would move through the London neighbourhood of Cheapside, not so far from where I had grown up. My golden self and the wake of silvery courtiers followed a goodly distance behind Edward, who had wished for a pure white stallion but had been persuaded to ride in a gold chariot as well, so that he might save his strength for the ceremonial ride on horseback to begin the tournament. Cheering throngs greeted their King, but as he passed and all eyes turned towards my advancing chariot the cheers faded. I shall never forget their eyes, first startled, then dazed, then shocked and quickly outraged as murmurs of protest gave way to jeers.

'Whore!' they called me. 'Harlot!'

Though the sun beat down warmly, I was chilled to the bone. These Londoners did not see me as a symbol of England's glory but as the usurper of their beloved Queen Philippa. I made manifest their suspicions that the monies for the war had been spent on the court's excess, an aged king's obsession with his young, greedy, common mistress. Though I was hot with shame, I held myself straight and proud and told myself that any one of them would have done just as I had if the King had chosen them. Just as the sempsters had leaped at the chance to please him. But I knew I did not belong in that chariot.

During the entire week of festivities, I felt the threat to me whenever I passed crowds of commoners. No one touched me, there was no need. I shrank from the hatred in their eyes.

'I pray that you will look back on these glorious days with joy, Alice, and remember our love,' Edward said as we watched a joust.

I squeezed his hand and smiled my warmest, happiest smile, for I had not seen him in such a gladsome mood in many a day. I could not bring myself to point out to him the chilly and blatantly condemning looks we received, the resentment on the faces of far too many of the lords and ladies in my train, and the loathing on the faces of the people of London, my people. That Edward did not comprehend he had raised me too high in naming me lady of the lists was evidence of his failing mind, his increasingly frequent inability to distinguish between what he might dream about and what was acceptable behaviour in a King – or in a King's mistress or 'concubine', as Geoffrey reported the multitude calling me, though I had heard 'harlot' and 'whore'.

I feared for Edward that he could not see the dangerous mood of the crowd regarding his extravagance. He had thought to fool them with the appearance of being yet the Sun King, the glorious warrior, the young and vital monarch; he had thought to fool his people with my appearing as his young and vital Queen. The illusion had failed as I had dreaded it would.

Princess Joan had once said that I looked like a queen; but I looked like a usurper queen. The people had loved Queen Philippa. Geoffrey had warned me that folk were appalled when I wore her jewels. But this . . . this went far beyond it in hubris. I remembered his warning to me of long ago about those who fell prey to their own weakness for finery and flattery.

Yet when had I the choice to be other than I was?

The event being too much for him, Edward retired to bed for several days afterwards. I thought to go to my home in London for a while, but Geoffrey warned me to avoid the city for now. All there claimed that I had insisted on parading myself as Edward's Queen. No champion defended me, for who but the King could do that? And he was incapacitated, beyond caring about the mood of the crowd.

In the end I remained by his side at his insistence. I felt myself to be a leper at court: all eyes watching me, judging me, all avoiding contact with me. Joan agreed that it had been a dangerous choice to make me lady of the lists and parade me in a robe so much more magnificent than those of my betters, though she had not attempted to convince Edward of his folly beforehand. I wondered now whether she merely pretended to be my friend.

In late-summer a party of louts descended on my Manor of Finningley in Nottinghamshire, stealing some cattle, mutilating or driving off the rest – the stampede destroying crops – and holding my servants and tenants hostage in the house until they swore an oath to leave my service. The violence of the attack shook me. I thought that if I did not respond with force they would feel free to repeat the action. In truth, I wanted vengeance. But Wykeham advised me to investigate the disturbance in a quiet manner, not to call too much attention to it. I sent Robert and Richard Lyons to look into the matter and assess the damage.

Edward's spells were coming upon him more frequently, and he had developed painful boils that we at first feared were marks of pestilence. But his physicians were confident they were the product of his diet and his often agitated spirits. That they remained by his side and cared for him reassured me more than their words had done. The King asked often for Bella, and with the permission of her abbess she came to help me in the long vigils in his chamber. Edward derived great comfort from her presence, as did I.

As he succumbed to the toll of his years and his maladies, I felt increasingly helpless to draw him back to the present, to clarity. My paternoster beads and my sewing kept my hands busy when I was with him, and when I was away from him I knelt in the chapel or rode until exhausted, my tears a sacrificial offering to the wind, as if I believed the air so mingled with my essence might enter Edward and revive him. I wanted him back with me. I wanted our lives to be as they had been.

I wondered whether he had felt this with Philippa, missing the woman who had been his succour and anchor, unable to be still with his grief. I wondered whether I had been his equivalent of his horse, his beads and sewing, a distraction from his grief.

My sweet daughter Bella was my succour and delight in those dark days. When Edward slept, she and I would sit in my chamber and talk of him. Bella wished to know all about our years together, about the joys we had shared. She asked, as well, about her father. I had always hesitated to tell her the story of his family's loyalty to the Dowager Queen and the tragedy it had wrought. Had feared that she would hate Edward for his mother's part in it and blame me for staying with him. Now it seemed the right time to tell her everything, to explain to her how Janyn had lost his life, and how I had come to reside in the Queen's household. I spun out the story over the course of several evenings. Her behaviour towards me subtly changed during those days. She was watchful, curious, and in the end sympathetic.

When I had completed the tale, Bella reached over to me, putting one hand to either side of my face, and held me gently, looking deep into my eyes. After a while, she kissed my forehead. It felt like both a blessing and an absolution.

'I almost said that I did not know how unhappy you were, but that is not true. I have always sensed an unspeakable sorrow beneath your gaiety,' she said. 'Why did you never tell me this?'

'I did not wish you to grow up beneath a cloud,' I said. 'When I saw how frightened you were in Queen Joan's household, I was determined never to send you back and to do all that I could to give you the joy Janyn and I meant you to have.'

Bella bowed her head for a moment, the veil hiding her face from me. I feared she was weeping and my old guilt was rekindled. Though I'd had no choice, I had felt then I should have insisted on seeing her more often. But when my daughter looked up, she had regained her equanimity.

'In truth, I have some happy memories of my life there. Few include Queen Joan – not because she was unpleasant or frightening to me but simply because she had little to do with her wards. The household servants saw to us, and most of them were kind. No harm was done by my being there, except that I missed you and Father.'

Later, as we lay side by side in my great bed, she said, 'It was always painful to be parted from you. I feared you would disappear as Father and Grandmother Tommasa had.'

'Was I then wrong not to tell you?'

She rolled over on her side and kissed my cheek. 'It was probably best that you waited until the King was so ill, since now I cannot find it in my heart to condemn him.'

I found the courage then to explore my fears about her vocation. She was now Dame Isabella; had taken her vows at fifteen. 'Did you choose to take religious vows because of my liaison with Edward?' I asked.

'No, Mother, I have told you over and over again – I was called. And have no regrets.'

My daughter had grown up to be not only wise, pious and beautiful, but compassionate too. I was grateful for it and terribly proud of her.

'What will you do when His Grace is gone?' she asked.

'I do not like to think of it, Bella. For a while I will allow myself to grieve – for Janyn and for Edward.'

My daughter nestled closer and put a protective arm round me. 'May God grant you peace after all this.'

I prayed for the same, but did not dare to hope too much.

I believe Bella spoke to the King's physicians, for without my saying anything about being exhausted or heavy of heart they came to me as a group to suggest that I spend some time away from Edward's sickbed. I resisted the idea at first, but Bella convinced me that I would return to him with a lighter heart, which might do him good as well.

After a few days of rest at my home in London, I invited Robert and Richard to discuss the repairs to Finningley and the reparation to be paid to those who had been injured or imprisoned by the attackers. Robert spoke with confidence about setting all to rights, but his expression was guarded. When he was finished, he and Richard exchanged a look. Richard nodded and sat forward, taking his turn to speak.

'A number of those who worked at Finningley wish to leave your service,' he said. 'Some out of fear of further reprisals and some because they have come to believe the lies their attackers have spread about you.'

I had imagined the former but not the latter, having prided myself on being a caring and responsive landlord.

'What sorts of lies? You can tell me, Richard. I am not so fragile, and should know what people say of me.'

Robert interrupted. 'Alice, perhaps—'

I shook my head at him. 'Go on, Richard.'

It was a long and varied list. I had put a spell on the King and replaced his counsellors with my business partners and lovers. I'd prevented his wise counsellors from seeing him. Had weakened his manhood with fornication. I was blamed for high prices, the loss of the Aquitaine, even the debilitating illness of Prince Edward.

'Dear God in Heaven, they believe me to be a sorceress!'

Richard took my hands and waited until I looked into his eyes. 'You will survive all this, my friend. We will make certain of it.'

I could not see how, but was moved by their loyalty and love.

I thanked them and withdrew to my room, where I knelt and prayed that Edward might return to health long enough for me somehow to redeem myself in the eyes of the people. Foolish prayers.

One evening in London, after the children were abed, Robert found me silently weeping by the dying fire in the hall. He joined me on the bench and put his arm around me. I leaned against his shoulder and took deep, shuddering breaths. With his free hand he stroked my hair, and whether he spoke the words or I just divined them from his heartbeat, I heard his gentle reassurance that all would be well, that Edward could not have found a more loving companion for his last years, that I was yet young and would find love again. I felt my body and my mind released from grief for a while.

When I was breathing with ease, Robert drew his arm away and rose. 'Come,' he said, 'Gwen waits for you above.' He held out his hand.

I rose into his embrace.

'God was looking to my welfare when he sent you into my life, Robert,' I whispered. 'You are my solace and my anchor.' Edward had once been my anchor but those days were long gone. I remained tethered to him by the ropes of memory and the demands of his sons. But it was Robert I longed to be with now. From depending on him, trusting him, I had grown to love him.

'I will ever be here, to comfort and steady you,' he promised.

III-5

*'My lords, we have declared to you and to the whole council of
Parliament various trespasses and extortions committed by
various people, and we have had no remedy; nor is there anyone
about the King who wishes to tell him the truth, or to counsel
him loyally and profitably, but always they scoff, and mock,
and work for their own profit; so we say to you, that we shall
say nothing further until all those who are about the King, who
are false men and evil counsellors, are removed and ousted
from the King's presence; and until our lord the King appoints
as new members of his council men who will not shirk from
telling the truth, and who will carry out reforms'*

– Peter de la Mare speaking for the commons, Good Parliament,
1376 (trans. Chris Given-Wilson)

Throughout Edward's illnesses I remained by his side, sometimes
sending for Joan and Jane, finding comfort in the company of my
young daughters. It lifted my spirits to see the palaces in which
we lived through the curious eyes of my children, to hear their
laughter and shouts of delight echoing down the corridors or
wafting in through windows. My sweet ones were affectionate
towards me but wary of their father, who as often as not thought
they were someone else's little girls.

But Edward never forgot that John was our son. When we had
seen him at the Smithfield tournament, John had been warmly
affectionate towards his father. Our son had spoken politely to me,
but had shown no great affection and seemed eager only to leave
my presence. Of course, he would be most impressed and proud of
his father, the King of England, and it was seemly that a boy be
closer to his father than his mother, but I had hoped he would
remember how he had loved to rest with me and listen to the
stories I wove for him on those lazy afternoons. Since he had
joined the Percy household I had seen him only on state occasions
or at Christmas, and gradually he had grown distant from me.

Though friends assured me that it was the way with young boys, I feared the Percy clan were poisoning him against me but prayed I was wrong. He was growing into a handsome boy, looking very like his father. Edward had proudly taken him round to his uncles, aunts and cousins, declaring him, 'Undeniably a Plantagenet, eh?'

Geoffrey empathised with me, but gently reminded me that it was no small honour that the King was so proud of our son. 'And have I heard correctly that John is to be betrothed to Mary Percy?'

'It is true.' That had, of course, long been in Edward's mind. But as I now confided to Geoffrey, I had been surprised that Henry Percy had so readily agreed to the betrothal.

'You do not look pleased?'

'I would have been a fool to reject the proposal, for the marriage will elevate my son more than I had hoped possible. Yet I do not care for Mary. At the moment she is a wilful, spiteful and unimaginative child. I pray she will grow out of her spiritual ugliness.'

'She is still so young. Surely you might influence her, having her in your household?'

'I can only pray.' They were both still young . . . too young to bind them so.

I also disliked the fact that Henry Percy was one of John, Duke of Lancaster's staunchest supporters. I increasingly felt as though all my life was being arranged by Lancaster towards some unknown purpose. I remembered his warning about my needing protection when Edward died, and Edward's warning that William Wyndsor was John's man. I imagined that my son's marrying a Percy might be part of such a scheme, but did not trust Henry Percy and his clan. What sort of protection would the marriage provide? And for whom?

The Duke continued to promise that he and his brother Prince Edward would ensure that my children and I would be safe from any harm, and that after his father's death I would be free to withdraw to my estates and live in peace and comfort. It was the frequent repetition of that promise that worried me. And how everyone who crossed my path was now so tightly bound to Lancaster.

*

In May of the forty-ninth year of Edward's reign he had once again to approach Parliament requesting a tax to raise funds for war. Not only did he need to repay loans made towards his failed attempt at crossing to France and to rebuild the fleet lost at La Rochelle, he had also inexplicably begun to believe once again that the Crown of France was within his grasp and dreamed of yet another mission across the Channel.

In the weeks leading up to the audience with Parliament he was in much better health, the boils having finally diminished and his episodes of confusion and weakness having eased. We retired to King's Langley in late-April for a brief respite after the Feast of St George and before the ordeal with Parliament. Edward was riding again, and hawking, though wisely declined invitations to hunt – too vigorous an activity at his age. Even with this display of caution I could not rest easy, too aware that his confusion and weakness could return at any moment. His love was both a blessing and a curse for I lived only for him, to keep him content and calm.

My suggestion that while Parliament sat I should go to Gaynes, my manor near Havering, disturbed him. He did not want me away from him so long.

'I need you, Alice. You complete me.'

We held each other. I, too, felt that we moved as one while we were together; I had worked hard to learn to anticipate his needs. That he believed it was the natural outgrowth of our love for one another had been a boon, allowing his sons' scheme to work. The seriousness of his condition was hidden from his subjects. But I craved some peace, some freedom.

I backed out of Edward's embrace for a moment, stroking his gaunt cheek with the back of my hand, kissing his forehead. 'How long could Parliament sit, my love? No more than a month, surely. It would not be so long a separation.'

That night we slept naked together, each affectionately exploring the other's familiar, beloved body. I massaged oils into his joints, his groin. He explored me with his tongue and fingers until I cried out in a bitter-sweet release. How different was that night from those of our earlier years together. In truth, this felt more like love in some ways than our lust ever had, for we each sought only to please the other, not ourselves.

In the end he agreed to my plan, and though he did not explain why he had decided I was right, his exhortations for me to hie straight to Gaynes convinced me that he, too, had heard the rumours of expected trouble and thought them plausible.

This anxious time would only grow worse. Richard Lyons sought me out after a meeting with Edward to warn me that one of the most powerful barons of the moment, the Earl of Pembroke, was fomenting anger in the commons against what he called the 'court party', those of us who had shielded Edward from gossip during his episodes of weakness. Of course, by design few knew why we had shielded the King. Here was the public censure I had long feared. It was of no comfort to me that even Lancaster was suspected of supporting the 'court party'.

The beauty of the spring garden at King's Langley dimmed for me. 'I will bide at Gaynes while Parliament sits. It will be good to be free from court.' I tried to sound resolved. 'Perhaps Henry Percy might allow my son to be my guest for a time.'

'Do not count on it. I do not know which barons agree with Pembroke. Or with Mortimer, Earl of March.'

I had my own reason to dread any mention of the Mortimer family. Though Edward had never chosen to tell me *who* had shadowed Janyn and Tommasa for the secret they kept for the Dowager Queen, I had always suspected the obvious – the Mortimers, who would have been thus exalted to the Crown family. They were powerful, as William Wyndsor had learned in Ireland, but not as powerful as they would have been in possession of the bastard son of Roger Mortimer and Queen Isabella. Yet as far as I knew, Richard had no knowledge of this, so I wondered – and worried – at his mentioning Mortimer.

'Why should I worry about the Earl of March?' I asked. 'He was brought up by Wykeham. He is hardly my enemy.'

'He is no longer under the Bishop's guidance, Alice. You know that they are furious with Wyndsor over his heavy-handed governing in Ireland. The Earl of March and his friends, who might have been your allies against the commons, will not be looking kindly on you.' Richard had never before mentioned William to me. Now he regarded me with interest, apparently curious to see how I would respond.

'Why should they connect me with William?'

'Is it not true that you are to wed him upon the King's death?'

A cold hand clutched at my heart. 'No!' I cried out, as if to ward off a curse.

'Ah. I did wonder at that.'

'Who said this?'

'Wyndsor. When we met to sign a business agreement. He was insufferably smug.'

'I shall never wed him. Never!'

'You know that Wyndsor will be returning soon, do you not? Nicholas Dagworth is to preside over his investigation.'

'Dagworth? But he is William's sworn enemy. His Grace knows that.' I had cause to condemn William, but yet believed he had been loyally trying to enforce the law in Ireland in order to assist Edward with his war chest.

With a shrug, Richard said, 'That is what I have heard.'

My constant Robert headed our small company departing King's Langley for Gaynes at Upminster in early-May. Anticipating my needs as he so often did, he had already fetched Joan and Jane from Mary's home in London. They lent a gladsome mood to our journey down the Thames that spring afternoon. My son John had arrived by early-evening. He was to stay for a fortnight; Henry Percy had not forsaken me. I felt blessed and comforted by my children, Gwen, and Robert.

I had come to prefer Gaynes even over Fair Meadow. It was a pretty house, with windows that caught all the best light of the day and views of rolling woodland and meadows. I prayed that violence never shattered the calm there as it had in Finningley. Even my son John fell under its peaceful spell, reverting to his old loving and giving self, a delight to his little sisters and a great comfort to me. I still treasure as one of my life's most precious moments the afternoon when he asked if he might rest with me as we had in years past.

Yet however much comfort I found in my children and Gaynes, during that sojourn I often sank into anxiety, sorrow and fear. From the beginning, that Parliament was out for blood – that of William Latimer, John Neville and Richard Stury as the courtiers, and Richard Lyons as the financier who had advised them in what the commons saw as their fraudulent use of power to fill their personal coffers.

Apparently Pembroke's man, Peter de la Mare, stepped forward to lead the commons, and managed to press forward with their complaints. Though Prince Edward, adamantly opposed conceding any ground to the commons and had been present for the start of proceedings, he was so ill that he withdrew immediately after that.

I feared that public condemnation of me would surely follow. I was terrified by the prospect, knowing nothing of how Parliament worked. It had never seemed important to me before. How I wished I had feigned illness and not displayed myself as the Lady of the Sun! I might lose everything now. I might lose my daughters' dowries . . .

Blame hung in the air. Even working in the gardens at Gaynes, I would interpret birdsong as chiding. Riding out with Robert or my children, I would hear a litany of my sins in my mount's hoof-beats. No matter how my family and friends tried to distract me with pleasant activities, I felt as if I were continually examining my conscience in preparation for the Sacrament of Confession, and was increasingly terrified to take my turn before my confessor.

While I watched Joan and Jane play in the garden, I would read missives from Geoffrey and my brother John. Joan's amusingly imperious voice instructing Jane in the ever-shifting rules of her games, would suddenly in my mind announce more frightening news.

The commons claimed that the 'court circle's' loans were grossly criminal, defrauding the Crown of huge sums owed it; that, in short, we had profited from Edward's financial problems. They claimed that in his dotage he had been led into error by us, and that we controlled him – conveniently forgetting the strong arms and close involvement of Prince Edward and the Duke of Lancaster.

The accusations against Richard Lyons worried me for both our sakes. It was true that he had benefited from Edward's financial difficulties, but it had been his cleverness in investing that had first attracted the King's notice and inspired him to use Richard as an unofficial member of his council. It was Richard who had taught not only me but all the courtiers now accused how to buy Edward's letters of debt for a low fee and then bargain with the holders of the loans for a lower payment. The debtors had grown less sanguine about their settlements over time. Peter de la Mare was giving voice to their grievances. Even worse, Richard was a foreigner, a Fleming, of low birth and a bastard – it angered Londoners in particular that such a man was so trusted by the King that he had been made Warden of the Royal Mint and held high civil office in their city.

Richard and I had been raised up higher than our backgrounds would commonly allow, intruders in a class to which we did not belong, fraudulently enjoying the King's favour. I remembered the angry and disbelieving looks as I'd progressed through Cheape in cloth of gold. God's blood, what had Edward been thinking? The commons hated both Richard and me.

I learned much of which I had previously been unaware, and knew that it would be impossible now to convince anyone I had not been part of the more outrageous profiteering, for I was not without blame. I had accepted Edward's largesse and used it to buy what I'd thought would bring me security.

My brother John risked a visit to Gaynes. We sat on the window seat in my bedchamber while we talked.

'The commons have found fault with Richard Stury's stature at court. They condemn him for the wardships, lands, offices and marriages with which the King has rewarded him, though they do not suggest what might be done to remedy the matter.'

'Even Stury?' I wondered aloud. 'There are few the King trusts more than him. He has proved his loyalty and worth for eleven years or more.'

The commons judged Edward's benevolence and gratitude for service as weakness on his part. They had apparently forgotten that all property in a kingdom is in the King's gift, that all rulers use such gifts to reward loyalty – or so Edward had told me. I saw now that I had condemned myself in others' eyes by accepting presents given in love.

I drew out a casket of my most treasured gifts from Edward, primarily pearls, including the comb set with lapis that he had tucked into my hair so many years before, but also the ruby ring and brooch he had given me the night I told him I carried his first child.

'Would you take this casket and keep it for me, John? These are most precious to me.' I would not give him all; if they came for my jewels, they would find only the costliest ones and search no further.

It was uncanny how like Father my brother looked at that moment: the crease between his eyes, the set of his jaw. But his shoulders did not cave in as Father's had in a crisis. My brother lifted the small casket. 'I am glad to be of service to you, Alice. You have only to ask.'

By late-May orders had been given for the seizure of Richard Lyons' goods and those of other merchants implicated. Richard had reportedly offered a gift to the Prince in exchange for his protection, but had been refused. Prince Edward had also reprimanded Stury for softening his daily accounts to the King of the parliamentary proceedings. I was certain that Stury had meant only to protect the King, but the Prince was in too much discomfort and his temper too short for him to hold his tongue long enough to consider how Parliament would interpret his anger. All walls had ears, it seemed. We must watch our every word.

Everything happened so quickly, I felt unable to catch my breath. It was as if the poison that had collected for years in people's hearts and minds burst out all at once. I had just heard of the confiscation of Richard's goods when I received the terrible news that Prince Edward was grievously ill. His physicians believed he would die within days. The Prince had summoned me, intending me to swear once more that I would shield his father when he suffered his spells from the eyes of those who would ridicule him and call for his abdication. My brother advised me to stay away, but I meant to go. John did not, could not, understand my role at court.

While I was arranging for a barge I learned that John Neville was no long Steward of the King's household. Even a member of a powerful family could fall, it seemed. Robert and Gwen urged me to change my mind about going to Westminster. The fear in their faces mirrored my own. But I still held out the hope that my heeding the Prince's summons would inspire him to continue to support me.

'But if he is dying?' Robert asked. 'How then can he help you?'

I had never heard such fear in his voice. My own hands were clammy with dread.

'Robert, I must try. For Joan and Jane.' Bella's dowry was safe at Barking. 'For His Grace.'

'You do not need him. Any of them. I will take care of you and your daughters, Alice, I promise you.'

I took that promise into my heart, but could not yet clearly hear and accept it. I felt tied to Edward and his family despite a sense of impending betrayal.

I arrived under cover of darkness on the eve of Trinity Sunday, the feast that Prince Edward held most dear. I was shown to the King's chamber and was greatly grieved to find him looking so lost. I held him in my arms throughout the night and sang his favourite songs as he wept for his son. I knew then that Robert had been right, death was in the palace.

The Prince died the following day, past remembering that he had summoned me. I felt cold and numb. But when Edward returned from the death chamber of his heir, looking near death himself, pale and hollow-cheeked, I knew that God had meant for me to be here, caring for him.

'My heir now is but a child, Alice. Young Richard stood there, so slight, his eyes too large for his sweet face. The barons will devour him.'

'My love, my love, you have many happy years ahead of you before young Richard takes your place.'

Edward grasped his velvet hat and slid it down the side of his head, then let it drop to the floor, as if the effort of lifting it off and placing it on the table before him were far too much for him. His white hair now hung straggly and thin, the bald spot more visible than usual with his scalp red from the exertion of his walk.

'Let me undress you and cool you with cloths dipped in scented water.'

He sighed and lifted his arms from his sides to allow me to remove his robes.

As I washed his body and then rubbed it with soothing oils, Edward muttered about Parliament and how they had robbed him of Neville. His body felt different, diminished somehow, as if some of his spirit had departed with his son's death. I tried to guide his thoughts to plans for a summer interlude at King's

Langley or Havering. But he kept drifting back to Parliament's outrageous, insulting behaviour. Later he grew agitated once more about the danger of having so young an heir.

'I thank God that no one knew of my half-brother – a Mortimer on the throne? Never!'

'My love, you have sufficient legitimate sons. No one would have thought to place your bastard brother on the throne.' Indeed, from what I had managed to learn, few had ever known of the child. 'You must never speak of him. Never. Lest you slip and mention him when others could be listening.' They might think him mad.

'Do you doubt me, Alice?' Edward, suddenly lucid, glared at me.

'Never, my love.' I knew my role. I must focus on his state of mind, not let him see that I knew he was frail and frightened.

Princess Joan took some refreshment with us in Edward's chambers that evening, mostly wine. Newly widowed, she looked almost as pathetic as her father-in-law and my heart ached for her. She had been so in love, had shared such dreams with the Prince. She would have been Queen of England. But she had despaired of that dream in Bordeaux, having guessed even then that her husband would die before his father.

'It is a curse to outlive two beloved husbands,' she sighed into her mazer, then tilted her head back and emptied it. A servant stepped forward to fill it once more.

'You will be sick from so much wine on this warm night,' I cautioned.

'I shall find no comfort this night, Alice, with or without the drink. It is no matter.' She shook her head, the jewels in her crespinette glittering in the candlelight. Her golden hair was dull with streaks of white. This small sign of neglect told me more than words of her suffering of late. She must have known her husband's death was near, to have neglected the regimen of lotions and sunlight that kept her hair golden. Suddenly she planted her elbow on the table and shook a finger at me, peering at me rather unsteadily. 'You, my friend, should not be here. They plan to banish you from His Grace's presence.'

Edward grabbed my hand. 'No! I am the King. My beloved stays with me.'

Joan shook her head. 'They intend to sweep all your council into the Thames, Your Grace, though they would prefer to take them down the Thames to the sea and sink them with stones! Alice is too clever for a woman. They do not like the thought of a cunning, beautiful woman whispering in your ear.'

The following morning, Edward ordered Richard Stury to escort me back to Gaynes.

'I shall come to Havering as soon as I may,' Edward promised me. 'Stay there no matter what you hear, my love. They shall not deprive me of your comfort in my grief.'

His timing flawless, Lancaster met me on the steps as Richard Stury escorted me to the barge. I shivered, wondering what his purpose had been in intercepting me. I did see on his handsome face, so like the King's, the marks of grief.

'My lord Duke, I grieve with you on the loss of your dear brother the Prince,' I said.

'It is a terrible blow to all the family and the realm.'

'May God grant him peace,' I murmured.

We both bowed.

'Are you travelling as well?' I asked.

'No. I came to warn you that you may hear reports I have expressed what would seem like censure of you. It might be necessary for me to seem to agree with the commons, in order to calm them. If anyone questions you, do not fear the truth. Do not attempt to hide anything. Lies and evasions will only complicate the matter. I promise you that you shall not be touched, and that any separation from my father will be brief. I know that he needs you now more than ever.'

His cold eyes offered me no comfort, none of the reassurance that his words would seem to imply.

'Your Grace.' I bowed to him and continued down the steps, accepting Stury's hand to steady me. His grip was strong and reassuring. I was surprised to look into his eyes and find understanding there.

As we moved downriver Lancaster's words haunted me – *any separation from my father will be brief.* Was I then to be thrown to the lions and rescued just in time? My future, it seemed, was now in the hands of the Duke, a man I did not trust. Cold comfort indeed.

Once back at Gaynes, I discovered my daughters distraught over the abrupt departure of their brother. Percy had sent an escort to retrieve John in this uncertain climate. I did not blame him. Indeed, I feared staying at Gaynes. My accusers might think it too near Havering, making it easy for me to slip over to Edward under cover of darkness.

Soon after Richard Lyons's goods were confiscated, he himself was arrested and sent to the Tower, as were others. Surely I was next.

I did not know what to do. Lancaster's proposal might be my best recourse: to bow my head in shame before the public, and trust he would uphold his side of the bargain and see to me and the girls on Edward's death. Robert would have me, but though I wanted nothing so much as that, I feared he could not protect me. That I would bring him down with me.

Nor did I have the heart to leave Edward now, so soon after he'd lost his once-glorious heir. Besides, if I did, I feared that in one of his fits of Plantagenet temper he would take our children from me. Definitely John, possibly even Joan and Jane. Though he might not acknowledge them as his daughters, he did love them.

The commons would come after me, for Lancaster said he could not afford to stand by me. I knew why he would betray me: the mighty Duke of Lancaster and would-be King of Castile was cowed by the commons and their disapproval of his love for his mistress, Katherine de Roet Swynford. They cursed him for the good health they would rather he'd bequeathed to his well-loved brother Prince Edward, now dead.

As I sat with Gwen over my needlework I imagined being rowed downriver from Westminster to the Tower of London and led to a cell, trembling so violently with fear that it took a guard on either side of me to move me forward. I doubted I would be much comfort to Edward after suffering such terror.

Not long after the death of his father, the young Prince Richard was presented to Parliament. They requested he immediately be given the principality of Wales, which had been his father's. The King agreed, and then retired to Eltham. I understood why he did not keep his promise to come to me, but I grieved.

The Parliament dragged on to the tenth of July, on which day representatives took barges to Eltham to take their leave of the King. Stury, still adamantly devoted to Edward, came by barge to Gaynes to bring me word of the accusations made against me. Edward had sent him, wanting me to know and be prepared. *Do not let them see you weak.*

Stury had aged since spring, his grim visage worn by the events of the past months. I received him in the small parlour from which Robert and I conducted business, a sparsely furnished room – table, several chairs, a brazier, a cupboard for the accounts – but with a south-facing window that allowed the gift of daylight.

'Dame Alice, I find no joy in bringing you these tidings.'

'First tell me, how fares His Grace?'

Stury dropped his gaze to his long-fingered hands, and shook his head. 'I fear for him. His Grace needs you beside him.'

I caught my breath and took out my paternoster beads, something to hold on to. 'Tell me my fate, Master Stury.'

I was accused of using my unnatural influence over the King to protect my friends and household, and to interfere in the courts in the interests of my retainers.

'But I merely attended His Grace at the courts, and I have no retainers.' I had never even considered maintaining household guards. 'I must protest.'

'You are neither summoned nor permitted in any way to speak in your defence. Truth is not what they seek, Dame Alice, but someone to blame for all the ills of the realm.'

I crossed myself. Stury did as well. He was being deferential and kind, for which I was most grateful. And yet it frightened me all the more that he should pity me, the stoic Stury.

I was warned that if I were to be found practising any form of protection of my 'people', such as interfering in the courts or bribing officials, my property would all be forfeit. What most frightened me was the vagueness of the terms of forfeit – for it was not clear who was to judge whether any act of mine might be construed as interference, nor whom they accused me of protecting. It seemed to me a gift to my enemies, an accusation they might pull out of the air to condemn me at any time.

Despite my years of loyalty and devotion, I was condemned

for my efforts to secure a good future for my children. Abandoned by those who had sworn to protect me. How had it come to this? What a fool I had been to ignore my doubts about the sincerity of Prince Edward and Duke John. What a fool I had been to follow my heart rather than my head.

My most immediate agony was that I had been officially banished from Edward's side, as Joan and Lancaster had warned. I had been right in guessing that he had chosen to retire to Eltham rather than Havering so that he might avoid endangering me. Stury warned me to stay well away from the King for the nonce.

'You will be sent for when sufficient protections are in place.'

So Lancaster had promised. I prayed he would keep his word, but did not know how I could trust I would be allowed back. Lancaster was so changed from the handsome, courteous young man I had met with his grandmother so long ago, who had presented me with Melisende.

When Stury departed I sat staring out of the window, seeing nothing, blind with shock. I feared for my daughters if I were imprisoned. They needed their mother. Robert and Gwen found me there, steadied me and insisted that I eat and drink and then walk out into the air, assuring me that they would see to the safety of Joan and Jane.

I could not think what best to do. Robert had some property to which we might retreat, but I feared he might be one I was accused of 'maintaining'. I urged him to go about his duties quietly, and to retreat to his own property at the first sign of trouble. My brother John suggested I hide in the open, where no one would think to see me, in London, at his house. But I feared for his family and Mary's if I were noticed. And what would happen to me then? What of my precious daughters? The spectre of the Tower loomed large in my nightmares.

Help came from an unexpected quarter. Robert Linton, a knight in Edward's household who had always been kind to me, offered me sanctuary at an estate deep in the West Country, where my daughters and I might await rescue.

'They have no cause to connect us, Mistress Alice. They will not look for you there.'

'You and yours shall be forever in my prayers, Sir Robert,'

I vowed. His kindness and courage gave me hope in that dark time.

It was a long journey by barge and along rutted country tracks with carts and children, all the while watching over my shoulder for my enemies. But once we arrived without mishap I gave myself over to the beauty of Somerset, devoting myself to my girls, and deeply grateful for the respite. On the feast of the Virgin Mary's Assumption to Heaven I attended Mass in Wells Cathedral with Geoffrey, who had come to visit. My one other guest was William Wykeham, riding from Winchester in mid-September to celebrate my thirty-fourth birthday with me. He encouraged me to count my many blessings, though he did not in any way pretend I had nothing to fear.

'The King loves you as his life, Alice. If he is able, he will summon you and protect you.'

If he is able. So Edward, too, was caught in the frightening gyre.

I heeded Wykeham's advice, using my paternoster beads to count my blessings over and over, interspersed with frightened prayers for the safety of my family and friends, for Edward's health, for Robert, and for myself.

On an ordinary autumn afternoon, as Gwen and I were absorbed in undoing my daughter Joan's latest attempt at embroidery, laughing at the remarkable knots she had achieved – taking care that Joan could not hear our laughter, for she was quite proud to be trusted with a needle – we were surprised by a servant announcing a visitor.

'It is Sir Robert, Mistress Alice, Sir Robert Linton.'

I travelled from hilarity to terror in a heartbeat, grateful that I was seated or I might have lost my balance. Our benefactor had been careful to stay away. I could only think he had come to warn me of my imminent arrest. I crossed myself and dared not look at Gwen, for I knew she must be equally frightened.

At first I did not believe the sincerity of the smile with which Sir Robert greeted me as I joined him in the hall. It took a cup of brandywine to calm me enough that I might absorb his news.

Lancaster had found a way to reverse Parliament's judgements on his father's proven friends. On the twenty-fifth of January the kingdom would celebrate Edward's royal jubilee, his fifty years on the throne. In honour of the occasion the King would offer a general pardon, a gesture with a long tradition. Considering the enormous number included in the pardon – two thousand four hundred people – the list was already being put before Parliament.

'Apparently a "general" pardon is not what I had thought. Not all crimes are pardoned, not all forfeits reversed, hence the list,' said Sir Robert. 'Your name is prominently featured, however, for the Duke says His Grace needs you beside him. As soon as may be.'

I could not believe my good fortune. My prayers had been answered. I was free to join Edward – in fact, Lancaster was searching for me. To that end, and to avoid his discovery of my retreat, Sir Robert had come to escort me to Gaynes.

Gwen lost no time in making the preparations. I would leave Joan and Jane at Gaynes in the care of Mary, and join Edward at Havering.

When I was reunited with my sister we held each other tightly and wept. She had been widowed while I had been in hiding in the West, her husband having succumbed to a summer fever. She and her children had moved to Gaynes to recuperate in the countryside.

'I was frightened for you,' she told me.

'Hush now, Mary, all will be well.' I forced myself to say the words I needed to believe.

My dear Robert was also there to welcome me. He brought me news of my properties. I had feared more uprisings as at Finningley, but all had been quiet. I was so happy to see him that I forgot decorum and fell into his arms, rejoicing in his warmth and strength. We were a loud and merry group at dinner, and for that one night at Gaynes I could almost pretend that all was well.

It was at best a bitter-sweet time for me. My daughters remember it as a happy period, having seen their brother in early-summer, spent months in the beautiful West Country exploring a huge, unfamiliar house and wild gardens, and then enjoying autumn at Gaynes in the company of their cousins. They were far too young to understand the crisis we faced.

As soon as all were settled at Gaynes, Gwen and I departed for Havering. It was no wonder the Duke had sent for me. I found my

Edward heartbreakingly diminished. He had suffered one of his worst spells the previous month and was lethargic and inconsistent in his memory. His balance was so poor that he could not ride. Nor could he hawk, for he was convinced that the birds had decided in a Parliament that he deserved death, and meant to attack him. This last, more than anything else, convinced me that I must remain by his side as much as possible, for he had never before suffered such a severe delusion.

In more lucid moments Edward was obsessed with ensuring a comfortable future for me and our eleven-year-old son. He was stubbornly determined to push forward with John's marriage to Mary Percy and his knighting at the Feast of St George in April, alongside Prince Richard. I was moved by his ambitions for our son, but expected him to meet with resistance. Once again, Henry Percy surprised me by agreeing that the marriage should be formally celebrated in January. Nor, to my knowledge, did anyone object to John's being knighted. He was, after all, the King's son.

For my future comfort Edward urged me to transfer some of my jewels to a trustworthy friend so that they would be safe in case his enemies tried to attack him through me again. He did not know of the cache of jewels I had already entrusted to my brother, nor need he. Edward had been most generous. This scheme made it clear that at least in his mind the pardon was no guarantee of my safety. I could not decide to whom to entrust my remaining jewels. Geoffrey? Robert? Perhaps Princess Joan?

While I was deliberating, I sent for them and was informed that the Duke of Lancaster had already arranged a custodian for them. This was delivered to me as reassuring news: that he had been so moved by his concern for my daughters as to ensure the security of my jewels. I could only pray I was wrong about him.

Edward's moods left me spinning and confused. As he often woke in the night in an agitated state, I fell into a dangerous state of exhaustion. My only restful nights were on those occasions that his physicians gave him a strong sleeping draft and suggested that I sleep in my own chamber. I would do so with gratitude.

I was increasingly anxious about Lancaster's manoeuvres regarding the jewels and everything else he seemed to control.

Shortly after Martinmas I was privy to what was apparently an ongoing argument with his father about investigating William Wyndsor's deeds in Ireland.

'I understand you have not yet issued the order for Nicholas Dagworth to represent you at the Irish council. Why do you hesitate, Father?'

'Dagworth?' Edward shook his head. 'My mind misgives. Surely he is not the only possibility. I prefer to send someone known to take no side in this issue.'

Lancaster made no attempt to conceal his irritation with his father. 'Wyndsor is my man. Do you accuse me of acting against my own man? If Dagworth says that the charges are without weight, all will believe him and the matter will be settled for good.'

'And if he finds the charges just? No.' Edward swept out his arm, upsetting a flagon of wine. As I reached out to catch it, he growled at Lancaster, 'You are wrong in this. It is not reasonable that any man's enemy should be his judge. Dagworth shall not go.'

Though I rejoiced to hear Edward so lucid, I shivered for the cold glare with which his decision was received.

After a subdued Christmas at Havering, which included only Edward's children and their families and some of his most trusted friends, Henry Percy and his family arrived with John and Mary. For an eleven year old our son was tall and strong, excelling in martial arts and a particularly gifted horseman. I saw in him what a beautiful young man his father must have been. Yet there was a sulky aspect to his looks, too, like his uncle and godfather the Duke. I hoped it resulted simply from impatience regarding negotiations for the coming marriage ceremony. He was as immature as most boys of his age, and lacked any interest in such events.

'Do you not like Mary?' I asked when he had complained of the uncomfortable robes he must wear.

'No. Nor she me. She says I smell of horses.'

'You do not like her because she insults you?'

'Is it an insult if it is true? Of *course* I smell of horses. She is proud and dull, and that is also the truth.'

I could not help but laugh. I hoped this outspokenness was a sign of John's resilience, for as the bastard son of an aged King, he would need it. I had no power over his future. Could be of little help to him. I prayed he would not forsake me.

On the day they took their vows, Mary looked lovely and John remarkably elegant. My sister, brother, and John's wife Ann all attended, thrilled to be part of such an intimate celebration in Westminster Abbey. The ceremony was brief, with Bishop Houghton of St David's, now also Lord Chancellor, officiating. Houghton, a kind, gentle man, had agreed to keep the ceremony short to prevent the guests from seeing too much of the King, for Edward was again having difficulty with his right arm and was in one of his more forgetful phases.

Within a few days all the guests had departed, Mary and John returning to their interrupted lives. We had agreed they were too young to consummate the union as yet. They would set up a household together in four years. Until then Mary would remain in my household. Edward had wished them to bide at Havering for a while, but his physicians, Lancaster and Houghton had all convinced him that was ill advised.

He was also disappointed on being advised not to appear at the opening of Parliament. He had looked forward to declaring that two thousand, four hundred pardons were to be given – an extraordinary number. But his family and physicians prevailed, impressing upon him the disruptive effect one of his spells might have on the glorious proceedings.

Bishop Houghton went on to Westminster without Edward. His opening sermon incorporated the charge to Parliament, in which he made use of the first public acknowledgement of the King's illness while assuring them that Edward was almost recovered and would soon return to public life. He urged them to support the general pardon as a token of reconciliation.

As if Houghton's words had worked a miracle, Edward's mind cleared within days. He began walking round and round the hall to strengthen his legs, and in early-February proceeded downriver by barge to Sheen. He wore a magnificent red cloak embroidered with his arms and tiny fleur-de-lis. It was lined in ermine as was his red escarlatte hat and the purple wool robe beneath. I was determined he should not take a chill. He looked in every aspect a King. As the barge passed Westminster, the parliamentarians assembled on the riverbank to cheer him. I was riding in an enclosed area of the barge, carefully hidden from the crowd but able to see Edward. I rejoiced to see him straighten in his seat and acknowledge the cheers with a regal wave. For a moment I allowed myself to dream that all might yet be well.

Indeed, our time at Sheen leading up to our remove to Windsor for the Feast of St George was a peaceful, happy period, but for news that I tried to keep from Edward. A mob had attacked Lancaster's Palace of the Savoy, damaging the outbuildings and the gate and gaining access to the hall before being stopped by armed retainers. The Duke had escaped over the Thames to Kennington, seeking to shelter behind Princess Joan's popularity there as the widow of the beloved Prince Edward and mother of Prince Richard. She had calmed the crowds.

It was Geoffrey who explained to me why Lancaster was so distrusted, even despised, by the common folk. 'He undid all that the commons felt they had achieved in the last Parliament. There is also a rumour that he is behind the omission of the Bishop of Winchester from the general pardon.' Though Parliament found fault with him as Chancellor, Wykeham was beloved as bishop.

That was a topic of interest to me as well, our good friend being so unfairly singled out. I had been shocked to hear he was the one victim of the Parliament of the previous year who had not been pardoned.

When I'd asked Edward why he had not pardoned Wykeham, he had said, 'He sided with those who attacked the honour of my trusted Chamberlain William Latimer.'

'He spoke the truth about him,' I had said. But I did not remind Edward that Latimer was no longer Chamberlain. I was learning that it only angered him when I pointed out such confusions, and I did so only when it was crucial.

'We shall speak of it no more,' he said. I saw by the set of his jaw that he meant it.

'Is the rumour true?' I asked Geoffrey later. 'The decision was Lancaster's?'

He nodded. 'He loathes Wykeham. Blames him for all the losses in France. The commons also resent Lancaster's support of Henry Percy using his influence in the governing of the City.'

'What else should I know of the Duke?'

'I believe you know the rest. I do not know what to think of him these days.'

Nor did I, but I very much feared him.

Edward often drew me out of my darksome thoughts, rejoicing in his regained strength. Though we no longer rose at dawn to ride out into the countryside as we had done in the past, we did take short rides together and walked in the garden. In the evenings we played chess or listened to music and song. But I could not ignore the milkiness of his once piercingly blue eyes, how easily he tired.

One morning, as we walked beneath a rose arbour, Edward paused and took both my hands. The sun shone on his pure white hair and for a moment he was the man I had first glimpsed in the great hall of his mother's castle.

'You have given me such joy in my old age, Alice, my love.'

'You have given me equal joy, Edward.'

He shook his head. 'No. You have suffered much pain along with the joy. I have become a labour. And we began in such tragedy – the death of your beloved husband.'

My breath caught at his acknowledgement of my suffering. I bowed my head, unable to think of a response.

'I pray that you remember me with love, no matter what may come.' I lifted my head to reassure him, but he continued before I could speak. 'I fear you shall face one more labour before you rest, but I pray it may prove unexpectedly happy.'

'What labour? What are you talking about, my love?' The apology in his eyes made my stomach ache.

He lifted my hands and kissed each in turn, then let them go and tapped the finger on which he wore the signet ring with which he sealed his letters to me. 'When you see that I am gone, remove this from my finger and keep it. Remember me by it, my beloved.'

I caught up the hand with the signet ring on it and kissed it. 'You are not dying yet, my love.' But it was a denial of what I felt to be true. We had little time left together.

'I have also arranged for an account in gold to be opened for you in France. In case of exile. I do not trust the commons to honour my pardon once I am dead. Joan and Jane, take them away. They must not be harmed.'

'Exile,' I whispered. Fleeing to France with our daughters. 'Oh, Edward!'

He drew me into his arms and held me, whispering of his love, but also words that were less comforting: 'What have I done? What have I done?'

I reassured him out of habit, though I shivered with fear. He foresaw exile, danger to our daughters. Would our son be safe?

I put all my hopes and prayers for John into the needlework on the robes for his knighting. At the Feast of St George, Prince Richard would be knighted and admitted into the Order of the Garter, and our son would be knighted. Princess Joan was helping with the work on her son's robes. I was comforted by her presence in the palace. She took charge of the household and of my few leisure hours, insisting that I rest, eat, and pour out my heart to her.

I did not tell her about Edward's fears for my exile, nor did I confide in her my worries regarding Lancaster. I could not tell how she herself felt about the Duke, her brother-in-law.

But I did enquire of the Duke himself when he arrived at Windsor as to the disposition of my jewels.

He leaned towards me, and in a conspiratorial whisper assured me that they were safe. 'They will be there for you when you have need of them. If you wish to add to them, you have only to ask.'

I found it difficult to warm myself after that until a long ride brought me out in a good sweat.

I worked on Edward's robes as well as John's. Despite its being his jubilee year there would be no extravagant headdress for Edward this time, for he was unlikely to remember to hold his head upright. It would besides only call attention to his tremors. I designed robes with gold and silver threads and the most dazzling whites we could find, to give him a beatific glow. We trimmed his long white hair and beard and used some of Princess Joan's lotions to brighten his hair. He enjoyed the fuss.

We had become like father and daughter these days, most fond of one another, sharing years of memories. Sometimes we were almost mother and child. It hurt my heart to see him so confused, so impatient with himself, so frightened. My vibrant, passionate Edward was gone. It was as if the glorious shell had cracked open and exposed an infant within. I played the fool with him to rouse a sparkle in his eyes and some weak laughter. I danced jigs, sang the silly songs with which I cheered my children. In the chapel or out riding, I wept. Wept for Edward and for myself. I was losing him. Every day brought subtle changes, a new weakness, another memory gone. His remaining time grew short.

Joan knew. Having recently stepped into her own grief, she understood when to speak and when to be still. I saw the fear in her eyes that her too-young son would soon be King.

His knighting ceremony came none too soon. It was a glorious celebration. Prince Richard had been well trained by Joan to look every inch the King-to-be, walking straight and tall, his head held high. He was Plantagenet in all but his stature, carrying his beauty on a smaller frame than Edward and his sons. It was said that he favoured his maternal grandfather, Joan's father Edmund, who had been of smaller stature than his half-brother, the former King.

I wept to see my own son knighted. How proud he looked, how straight he walked. Sir John Southery. His child-wife seemed impressed by the event, though I had heard her ask rather loudly why the King looked like a magician, not a ruler. Fortunately, Edward did not hear.

As soon as the last guests departed he and I took the barge to Sheen, hastening to have him out of sight of the gossiping court before he succumbed to exhaustion. We were there but two nights when he suffered another spell, this one robbing him of the use of his left arm and leg. In his immobility, he grew by turns irritable and filled with vague regrets.

On a particularly grey May morning, Edward was overcome with remorse over having handed over some of Richard Lyons's lands to his sons Edmund and Thomas when my friend had been in the Tower. Richard had, of course, been included in the general pardon. I thought it a pity that on the days on which his mind cleared and his memory sharpened, Edward should fall into such trivial obsessions.

'Richard will accrue more lands, my love.'

'He has been a good friend to you and a comfort to your family, Alice. I would do something for him. My sons do not need his properties. If I restore those to him, and pardon the several hundred pounds he owes the Exchequer, would that be of use to him? Would it be enough for him to begin again?'

I called it generous.

As with Lancaster's obvious knowledge of Edward's advice to me to hide some of my jewels, this private conversation became public knowledge and would later be used as proof that I told the King to give Richard Lyons money. I became the hunted, the prey.

Death, when at last he stepped forward to take my beloved Edward, chose an exquisite setting in which to claim his dance. Tempted from our reverences in the chapel by the balmy, fragrant air, Edward and I walked out into the May morning, marvelling at the explosion of colour in the gardens, the sensuous feel of the breeze.

'Let us dine out here today,' he exclaimed.

I had agreed and was about to call for a servant when Edward suddenly clutched my hand tightly. Seeing the paroxysm of pain in his face, I called out to the guards to help me return him to his chamber.

'Call for the King's physicians!' I shouted at the servants as we hurried past – Edward still had hold of my hand even as the guards carried him in their intertwined arms. I had never seen such torment on anyone's face.

'My head, my head,' he moaned as the guards laid him on his bed. Stury managed to release my hand from Edward's desperate grasp. Death now took my place, luring him away from me.

I sat on the bed beside Edward, begging him to look at me, to speak to me. His eyes did not seem able to fix on me. His words became garbled. Death laughed at my confusion.

I remember little of the days that followed. I stayed by his side as much as I was permitted, but the physicians often sent me away, to eat, to sleep, to walk or ride.

'He will need you,' Master Adam reminded me. 'You must not fall ill.'

Gwen took care of me as I had of Edward. I was at a loss now. I had no role but to care for the shadow of the man I had loved.

Gradually Edward recovered enough to speak a little and sit up for brief periods. Death toyed with him.

I sent for Wykeham. I did not care what Lancaster thought of that. Edward knew that he was dying and needed someone he trusted to shrive him, someone who loved him.

Edward lived as if in a dream for several weeks, so broken and depleted that in my prayers I asked that his soul be released from the prison of his unruly body. Though frightened what it would mean to me and my children to lose his protection, remembering all too well the terror with which Janyn and his mother had received the news of the death of their protector, I could not bear to see him thus diminished. Death was like a cat, playing with his prey. I prayed for Edward's release.

On the twenty-first of June he suddenly suffered another most grievous pain in his head, shouting for relief. The servant who had watched with me hurried away for the physicians. But within moments, clutching my hand so hard it was as if he shared the pain with me, Edward mercifully let go his mortal prison and was at peace.

I had followed so closely his every tortured breath that when it ceased, so did mine. I imagined Death spreading his light-swallowing robe over Edward, and felt a flutter of panic. I must follow them. Edward needed me. Death shook his head. *He is mine.* Pain gripped me and I doubled over, at last gasping for breath. All the agony of watching Edward's suffering flamed within me, all the emotion I had hidden from him.

I squeezed Edward's hand, the large, once beautiful, once warm and enticing hand, remembering how his mere touch could melt me. I felt the signet and, remembering Edward's request, forced myself to ease my hand out of his death grip and work the ring off his finger. I did it clumsily, chafing his finger, and wept as I hid the ring in my bodice. When the physicians arrived, and Lancaster and Thomas of Woodstock, they ordered me to leave the room. I threw myself across Edward's body, wanting no one else to touch him, for I knew that once they did his soul would leave. I was not ready. Master Adam peeled me away. In that uncoupling I felt a terrifying emptiness, a void of echoing nothingness. No purpose, no anchor. Looking round, I saw only anger and condemnation in these men's faces. Death laughed at my confusion. I stumbled out of the chamber, seeking solace in the chapel.

Princess Joan advised me then to leave, to seek sanctuary and peace at one of my manors. She herself trembled at the thought of her sweet ten-year-old son being crowned.

But there was much to do before I departed. Numbly I went about the palace for several days, managing the servants, advising on the locations of Edward's belongings. I could not leave him. Could not part from my life with him. I completed tasks I had promised to do for Edward, disposing of all signs of his illness, giving presents to his physicians.

Later I heard rumours that I had taken all his rings and hurried out of the palace with them. No one came forward to declare that I had lingered at Sheen for days. No one.

Edward was to be taken in grand procession to Westminster in early-July. I would not be in the funeral party. Nor did I stand with the crowds who came from near and far to line the way, straining to catch a glimpse of his hearse, draped in a red silk pall on which were displayed his arms.

I heard that his funeral effigy carried his death mask, revealing to all who saw it the droop of the right side of his face. Edward would have hated having his weakness so exposed.

Robert arrived to escort me to Gaynes. Apparently Stury had asked Richard Lyons to find him and bring him to Sheen. By the time he arrived I could not wait to leave the palace, my emotions all played out, all sense of Edward gone from these rooms, the corridors and gardens. Perhaps no one came forth to deny the rumours of my rushing from Edward's death bed because to all but the servants I had disappeared the moment the King died. All around his body the household, the family, the court, had rushed into activity, ignoring me. I had been played out and was now out of the game. I pressed myself back against walls as the courtiers and household and family hurried past. I kept to the shadows of the chapel. As Gwen and a few servants packed my belongings, I took my leave of the bedchamber in which Edward and I had spent so many loving days and nights, lost in our delight in one another. I wondered whether I would ever return.

This room had been decorated with gifts from Edward and everywhere were cherished memories. One cushion held his scent; another a bloodstain from the bouquet of roses Edward had cut himself on, forgetting to trim the thorns. Here was the nick from the mazer I'd dropped as Edward swept me up in his arms.

Memories of our love overwhelmed me on every side. I fell to my knees and wept, hugging the cushion that smelled of him.

I could not sleep in that place. I escaped as soon as Robert sent word a barge was arranged. As I left the Palace of Sheen for the final time I felt as if I had been stripped of past and purpose, walking naked and bewildered into an obscure future. I had loved Edward with my heart, body and soul.

Book IV

A Phoenix

Naked and bewildered, I had lost myself. I was yet spinning in the dance, dizzy, seeing but shreds of memories, spinning, spinning, and Edward's hand was not there to pull me out of the gyre. Death had interrupted our dance.

Edward, my beloved Edward, was gone, and with him my life, my purpose. With him died the intimate history of my role at court. The Dowager Queen Isabella, Dame Tommasa, Janyn, Queen Philippa and King Edward – they were now silent. Not even Edward's sons or Princess Joan knew all the story. How could they?

Voices whirled about me but none of them the voice I strained to hear – the voice of Edward, my beloved, calling for me, guiding me to his side. The voices accused me, threatened me, condemned me. I could say nothing, for I was a sinner, though my sins be not the ones they intoned. How might I find my way to absolution . . . salvation? Spinning, spinning, breathless and overwhelmed with grief and remorse. Where had I fallen off the path of righteousness? At what moment had I misstepped? When had I a choice to be other than I was?

IV-1

'It is neither fitting nor safe that all the keys should hang from the belt of one woman.'

– Bishop Thomas Brinton, referring to Alice Perrers, sermon delivered in Westminster Abbey, 18 May 1376

A hand reached out. Robert beckoned me. I heard his voice as if from a great distance, more memory than sound. I remembered. My daughters needed me. Joan and Jane were too young to be without their mother. I must not abandon my precious Bella. And John. My son would mourn his father, might need me in his grief.

I strained towards Robert's hand, spinning towards it and away, towards it and away, and at last the sickening movement slowed, I felt warm fingers curl round my wrist, and I was still. I was Alice, sitting in the barge, my hand in Robert's, warm, alive. I saw the riverbank sliding by. Gwen sat nearby.

'I must see my daughters. Are Joan and Jane at Gaynes?' My own voice startled me.

In his eyes I could see that Robert had been aware of my absence. 'Yes. Joan and Jane are safely awaiting you at Gaynes in the company of their aunt. But before we join them, would you care to rest at Barking Abbey? I thought you might find comfort in Bella's company.'

My heart swelled with the thought of my eldest child. 'Bella! Oh, yes, Robert, I would see her first.'

That he had suggested something so certain to comfort me helped me come to a decision. I drew out from my scrip Edward's signet. 'I entrust this to you,' I said, closing his hand over it.

He knew what it was when he saw the intaglio. 'Are you certain?'

'I am. I trust that you will keep it safe for my son John. When he is ready, I shall ask for it.'

Robert kissed my hand, then looked at me with his steady eyes, blue, but a softer shade than Edward's, greyer, as if he knew the world he looked on would not always be gladsome. 'I swear that I will prove worthy of the trust with which you honour me, Alice.'

His gaze steadied me.

'I have always believed you trustworthy, Robert.'

When we arrived at Barking I went at once to the chapel while a sister fetched Bella. Gwen offered to assist in arranging some light refreshment for us. She who had been with me so many years understood that I yearned to be alone with my grief.

The dimness of the nave after the golden morning sun at once seemed to quiet and cool my anxious, feverish mind. The smoky, spicy aroma of incense mingled with the delicate fragrance of roses and the ordinary scent of candle wax, all familiar smells calling me to prayer. I found myself kneeling before the Lady altar without having consciously chosen it. Ribbons, prayer beads, flowers and jewellery adorned the statue of the Mother of God. With a sob I remembered the woman holding out Janyn's paternoster beads in the church – could that truly be twenty years ago? I could see it so clearly, feel it so sharply, that it seemed it had been only a few weeks past. I took out my own beads and bowed my head.

This was no time for remembering Janyn. Today I wished to remember Edward. Edward, the King who had loved me. Edward, the man who had satisfied me and filled me with beautiful children. Edward, the friend who had delighted in my achievements. Edward, my companion in riding and hawking, my opponent in chess, the frightened, ill, aged man who had feared little when I held his hand. He had filled me and depleted me, over and over again.

There, in the chapel at Barking, I prayed for release from Edward, from the spell with which he had bound me, for release from the dance. I prayed to reawaken, to remember my family, my friends, my purpose. Work I might now be free to enjoy. At any moment I would hear Bella's voice. I would soon be with my precious Joan and Jane, my sister Mary and my brother John and their children, and my friends. Robert and Gwen would take me there. I could walk and work in the gardens at Gaynes, become reacquainted with my hawks and horses. I reminded myself of all this, of life's continuance, the possibility of joy.

A rustle of silk. The abbess of Barking was high-born and

elegant. She took my hand, cupped it in her warm palms, waited until I looked her in the eyes.

'I had not recognised you at first in your widow's garb, Dame Alice.'

'I was not permitted to wear it when my husband died years ago, Mother Abbess. Now I am free openly to mourn him and the King.'

She pressed her hands together and gave me a little bow. 'God grant you peace now, Dame Alice.'

'May God protect and guide me.'

'Your daughter suggested that you might be in need of her prayers and companionship in your mourning. Would it please you if she were to bide with you for a fortnight?'

I felt a warmth rush through me, the promise of a thaw. 'I can think of no greater comfort.' I bowed to kiss the hand of the abbess.

Later, Bella cried out with raw emotion to see me in mourning.

'For Father?' she asked.

'For Janyn, yes, and for Edward.'

'Both good men,' she said.

We talked for a while in the abbess's parlour, remembering. I warned her that there would be trouble ahead, at the least a trial.

'I fear that you will hear horrible things said of me. And I fear the outcome.' I told her of the possibilities – forfeiture of my lands, even imprisonment or exile.

She held me and assured me that her love for me was unwavering.

The following morning we continued on to Gaynes, Bella, Gwen, Robert and me. Joan, Jane, Mary and her small tribe, all came rushing from the hall to greet us, encircling me in love. I did my best to push aside my fear of the future and give myself up to the joy of homecoming.

I fell into bed exhausted that first evening at home and slept as one drugged, a blessedly dreamless night. In the pale hour of dawn I placed a statue of the Blessed Virgin and a reliquary containing a drop of her milk on a low table in the corner of my chamber. On a cushion I knelt and began a prayer vigil. For a week I prayed while memories assailed me, tears cleansed me, prostrations purged my soul. Sometime during the first day Bella joined me, and stayed by my side, a blessed companion, until week's end, when at last I slept for a day and a night.

On the eighth morning Gwen helped me dress in one of my simple country gowns, humming as she worked on the buttons, shaking her head a little at how loosely it fitted.

'At least I set aside the weeds,' I said. 'I promise to fill this out by summer's end.'

'I shall see to that,' she said with a little laugh.

When I descended to the hall the following morning, Joan and Jane timidly looked up from their milky bread with wary eyes.

'I am well again,' I said, kissing each of them on the forehead.

After breaking my fast with bread, cheese and watered wine, I went in search of Robert, and together we rode out to see the manor. It was a joy to be out in the air with someone I trusted completely. I was ready to see my land and talk of the mundane chores of managing it. Once back at the hall, Joan and Jane, curious to see the contents of the chests I had brought from Sheen, begged to help Gwen and me redecorate my bedchamber with the finery that Mary Percy, now Southery, had told them they must contain. She was still living in my household while John was serving as a page in Henry Percy's.

I did not like to dip into those chests, especially in the presence of my daughter-in-law, drawing forth memories still raw and painful, but my daughters were seven and five years of age, too young to understand this reticence.

By evening I was agitated by the memories released in my bedchamber and loath to return to it. I sat in the hall until even Bella reluctantly left me. Only Robert remained, sitting by the fire opposite me, working oil into the leather of a harness as he had done all evening while the women talked.

'Surely that is the groom's work?' I said, crossing over to him and settling on the edge of the bench.

He looked up at me, his blue-grey eyes warming me. 'I find it soothing.'

'You are troubled?'

'I am worried about you. Lyons is worried about you.'

'I am as well, Robert.'

We sat quietly for a time, occasionally commenting on the fire or some trivial event of the day. I began to calm. My daughter Jane's favourite cat, Willow, a battle-scarred calico with a notch in one ear and missing one eye, curled up on my lap. I stroked her to the rhythm of her loud purr and thanked her for gracing me with her warmth.

After a long silence Robert left the hall, promising to return in a few moments. I waited, gazing into the fire, stroking Willow, wishing that I might put all the past behind me and settle into a quiet life. Wishing again that I might be forgotten. Robert returned, standing before me, reaching out to me with clean hands. I could smell the soap he had used to remove the oil.

Willow jumped off my lap and curled up on a cushion near the fire.

'Come,' Robert said, 'I shall sit with you until you sleep.'

Up in the solar, Gwen was nowhere to be seen. She must have noticed us in the hall and guessed we might go up together.

Robert took a turn around the room, admiring the finery, the silken cushions, the tapestries, the great bed. I had thought he might be uneasy there, but he seemed quite relaxed, curious even, and when he returned to where I stood by the door, simply said, 'I have never been in a room this fine.'

I smiled at his words and gestured to a chair. 'Do sit with me a while. I do not want to be alone just yet with the memories furnishing this chamber.'

He drew me close and held me for a moment, then released me. 'Are you certain?' He studied my face, his smoky blue eyes crinkling as he read my expression.

'I am.'

We talked of crops and boundaries, tenants and livestock, until the chamber felt familiar to me once more.

It was a morning of billowy white clouds moving languorously across a deep blue sky. I had invited Bella, Joan and Jane for a long walk, leaving their cousins behind for the nonce. The air was warm but with a freshening breeze that lifted our skirts and tousled our hair. I had already decided with Bella that it was time to tell Joan and Jane of the death of their father.

Hand in hand, my sweet young daughters danced along the

garden paths, their simple, bright-coloured gowns blending with the blossoms. Their hats hung down their backs, secured by the ribbons that had been tied beneath their chins. I could see that they had worn their hats in such wise much of the summer, for the sun had worked its magic on their tresses, lightening them and bringing out the highlights – Joan's hair was almost white in the sun, Jane's a mixture of dark blonde and red.

Bella and I walked behind them, laughing as we were forced to move more briskly than we might have liked in order to keep up with the two girls.

'How much do you think they understand?' Bella asked.

'Edward remained rather vague to them. I doubt they will mourn him, particularly because they believe I shall not leave them again – the King can no longer summon me.' Even such a simple statement gave me pause, brought a tightness to my throat. I missed Edward so. 'They will be sorely disappointed when I am summoned by Parliament.'

'*If* you are.' Bella caught my hand, though she neither slowed down nor abandoned her watch over her half-sisters. She knew how frightened I was.

'Joan and Jane are two angels,' I said, forcing myself to look to my blessings, not my fears. 'As are you as well.' I pressed her hand, grateful for her loving companionship.

First we visited the mews, the falconer giving the girls an account of the latest feeding.

'Each hawk believes it is King or Queen of the fowls,' he concluded.

'Father was a king,' said Jane, looking very proud.

'God bless him, he was, and the best of them, Mistress Jane.'

It seemed a perfect introduction to the topic I wished to raise. From the dovecote and the stables we adjourned to a lovely spot beneath an oak, settling in a circle on spread blankets to enjoy pieces of cake that Cook had wrapped up for us. When the young ones seemed content, I took a deep breath and explained to Joan and Jane that their father had succumbed to the long illness that had made it difficult for him to be with them. I wondered a little why at this late date I still made excuses for Edward's indifference to our daughters. I could see from Bella's puzzled expression that she did as well.

Joan asked, 'He was not locked up in a dungeon and murdered like Grandfather?'

'Murdered like Grandfather?' For a moment I could think only of my father-in-law's suspicious death.

'Your Edward's father,' Bella whispered.

It was strange, but I had never thought about Edward and Isabella as my children's grandparents. They seemed so far removed.

'No, my loves. I was with your father when he died.'

Jane slipped her hand into her sister Bella's and would not look up at me but stuck her other fist in her mouth.

I was uncomfortable pursuing the question of their grandfather's murder, yet as Joan closely watched my face with eyes so like her father's that they made my heart ache, I sensed it was important for me, their mother, to do so. 'Who told you that your grandfather was murdered?' I asked her. I could not imagine either my sister or any of the household saying such a thing.

'Mary.'

'Ah.' Of course, the poisonous Percy in our midst. I quickly countered with a comment on the way gossip runs through the court; how Mary might have heard such a rumour. 'But your father was ill. He suffered from a problem in his head that gradually weakened him. I was with him. He was not frightened. We were walking in the garden and he was at peace when God called him.'

'Do you have a problem with your head, Mother?' Jane asked.

I gathered my youngest into my lap and hugged her. 'Sometimes I am quite silly, but other than that my head is healthy, my sweet.'

Joan laughed. The sound was a great relief, and I was delighted when Jane and then Bella joined in. I felt blessed to have such beautiful, loving, delightful daughters all with me. They had few questions about Edward's death and what it might mean to them.

'I do not think he made much impression on their lives,' Bella remarked as we watched them rush off to join their cousins back in the hall. 'Far less than my father made in mine.'

I put an arm round Bella and rested my head on her shoulder for a moment. 'You were blessed with the most loving of fathers,

Bella. Janyn adored you. He had waited so long for a child, and you more than fulfilled his dreams.'

I heard her breath catch.

Later on Robert came to me after everyone else had retired and we talked far into the night, so easy with one another that I felt free to broach more personal concerns than I had the previous night. I told him about Joan's revelation of Mary Percy's gossip; allowed him to soothe my fears about my daughter-in-law, and my regret that Joan and Jane had not known Edward well enough to miss him.

'There is no grace in regret, Alice,' Robert said. 'I might spend my life regretting all the petty arguments and slights in my brief marriage, but I do not believe God would bless such a life.'

I had not known his late wife, Helena. The few years they had been together I had been busy with Edward.

'Were you very much in love with her?'

Robert dropped his head to his chest for a moment and took a deep breath, as if gathering his energies to speak of her. 'We were more like brother and sister than husband and wife. A teasing affection that did not carry as far as our bed. I frightened her with my need, and eventually she closed her mind to me when evening fell. When she lay dying, she asked my forgiveness. "I was afraid," she said. "And I pushed you away. Now it is too late." I, too, was afraid, afraid to hold her as the life ebbed from her. But I did. I lay beside her and held her until her heart stopped.'

I crossed myself. 'Janyn died so far away. I would have held him so.'

On the third night that Robert came to my bedchamber I greeted him with a kiss, a long, searching kiss, for all the day I had watched him, desiring him. It was not like my desire for Janyn or Edward. There was no recklessness, no fear or helplessness in this. I simply wanted Robert, body and soul, and believed we might be happy.

He traced the lines of my brow, my cheek, my jawline, then gathered me in his arms and carried me to the bed.

Our lovemaking was tentative at first. I could not believe my flesh was once more pressed against the warm, muscled flesh of a man I desired, and who desired me. Perhaps he, too, could not quite believe this blessing. As we explored each other's body, our kisses and our touches grew more urgent, until the boundaries between us blurred.

I woke in the night to find the lamp still burning.

'You are so beautiful,' he whispered.

I did not answer at once, cradled in the warmth of his presence. For this moment I felt content, beloved, safe. His body delighted me. It was strong and supple, the body of a man active and temperate. He was like Edward in colouring, but more like Janyn in proportion.

I wondered if it was possible that I might be so blessed as to find happiness with Robert. That I might be forgotten by Parliament and left free to live out my days in peace and love. I prayed for that miracle.

To wake beside Robert in the dawn light was a sweet experience. He lay on his side, gently tracing the aureoles of my nipples and smiling a smile without guile, without secrets. I had no doubt that he loved me. How delicious it was to lie with a man I had chosen, a man my heart had chosen.

The days were warm and sun-filled. I felt blessed to be surrounded by young ones, being coaxed out to search for a wandering kitten, to see a strange-looking egg, to marvel at the water fowl. Joan and Jane truly seemed to have accepted the death of their father with little ado. Joan had enjoyed the pomp of the court, but Jane had been frightened by the elaborate clothing and loud voices, the confusion of so many adults hurrying about her. Edward's death meant that they would have me with them, and it was difficult for them to see that as anything but good.

They had no idea of the trouble that almost certainly lay ahead, and I was able to forget it for long, wonderful interludes while with them. Until someone appeared to remind me.

I had been at Gaynes almost a month when William Wyndsor arrived. I had walked out into the garden to gather flowers. My basket was filled with roses and the pale green blossoms of lady's mantle, sprigs of rosemary and lavender.

'You gathered no such garlands for me.' William slouched down on to a bench near where I knelt. The sun picked out the silver threads that had feathered his dark hair. He had aged since last we'd met. Ireland had aged him. Yet he was still a handsome man.

I felt a warning drumming along my bones when I looked him in the eyes, but could not control my tongue. 'How dare you show your face here? You told Edward we were betrothed. I cannot fathom what you thought to gain, but you have forfeited any shred of trust I had in you.' I offered him a handful of roses. 'Take these and leave me in peace with my family.' *And may the thorns prick your pride.*

He shrugged and looked towards the house. 'The King is dead. It is my time now.'

I sat back on my heels, dumbfounded. 'I wish you to go, William.'

A cold laugh. 'I have the jewels, the ones you entrusted to the Duke.'

I did not want to hear what he had said. I stared down at the ground, catching my breath. 'The jewels? You? What possessed the Duke to entrust them to you?'

William rose up so suddenly that I had no time to back away. He grabbed my arm, lifting me to my feet, flowers and all, and shook me. 'You are my betrothed!' he shouted, his face red, his eyes wild with rage. 'You dare not deny me!'

From the corner of my eye I saw a movement. 'We are observed, William. Be so kind as to unhand me.'

He let go, glancing around. Robert was now approaching from the house, two male servants right behind him. I sensed more than saw someone hurrying off in the other direction. My daughter-in-law had been lurking in the garden, gathering gossip, I had no doubt.

Though I was shivering with fear, I lifted a hand to stop Robert and the other men. I hoped to avoid a confrontation between him and William. Turning to the latter, who was now fussing with his clothes, I said as quietly as I might, 'Leave me now, William. When we are both calmer we shall discuss the jewels. But I tell you this: I will never consent to marry you. Never.'

'We shall see.' He managed to walk away with stiff dignity. I sank on to the bench he had vacated, praying for calm. But I shook so violently my teeth chattered. He had my jewels, my gifts from Edward, my daughters' dowries if my lands were taken from me. I cursed Lancaster.

'May I sit?'

I nodded to Robert. 'I was glad to see you there. You gave me strength.'

'How dare he lay hands on you?' His voice was taut with controlled anger. 'I have distrusted his intentions all along. I see that I was right.'

'Yes, you were.'

'Why did you stop me?'

'I feared that if you were even half as angry as I was, you might kill him.'

We were quiet a moment, both imagining what might have happened.

'His is not the manner of a lover,' Robert said after a while. 'It is your wealth that attracts him. Where was he when you were beset a year ago?'

'In Ireland.'

'But summoned here. He might have come at any time. He comes at last when you are no longer under the protection of the King.'

I sensed that Robert was speaking of a concern even more disturbing to him than what he had just witnessed. 'What have you heard?'

'He has requested a list of your manors . . . their incomes, the livestock . . . as if he considers himself master of your domain.'

And he had the jewels. My nerves thrummed with alarm. 'God help me.' I told Robert about the jewels.

'What will you do?'

'I do not know yet. I must think. I welcome your counsel — once you have calmed yourself.'

He nodded.

'I pray you, hold me for a moment.'

I wished Robert might hold me always, warming and reassuring me with his strength and affection. But the encounter with William had reminded me of the trouble yet to come. Parliament was not finished with me, and neither apparently was William. Robert and I needed to discuss the danger that still lay ahead.

'We can create a new life, Alice. I shall love your daughters and care for them as my own.'

He stroked my hair, then lifted my chin and kissed me.

'I believe you, Robert, and I do love you. But there is trouble ahead, and I know not what form it will take, I warn you.'

'I care not.'

I moved out of his embrace. Looking into his eyes, I saw the life I wanted. 'I have lived in a wonderful dream these past days, hiding from what lies ahead. Parliament threatened me, but in such vague terms I cannot predict what they might do – on what grounds they might judge me. Even here at Gaynes they might have spies . . . Mary Percy, William himself. I pray that nothing happens, Robert, that I am forgotten. That we can be together.'

He kissed both my hands. 'I pray for that as well. I pledge you my troth, Alice.'

My heart pounded. I wanted to complete that pledge, to bind us together. 'I am so afraid, Robert.'

'Say the words and it matters not, my love. We will be together.'

'I pledge you my troth, Robert.'

We held each other, our hearts beating, our breath mingling. It was all I wanted, Robert's arms round me and my children, and I prayed that God was now ready to grant me this quiet joy.

As I had suspected, it had been Mary Percy who had been hiding in the garden. She was adept at listening from the shadows and understood far more than I had anticipated. She was quick to tell Jane, Joan and Bella that William Wyndsor intended to be their new father. It might have been a more complicated tale had she waited to hear what Robert and I had discussed, or witnessed our embrace, our vows. So far only my sister and Gwen seemed aware of what had been unfolding between Robert and me.

Bella reassured her half-sisters and came to me with the tale.

'So young and such a shrew. Poor John,' she murmured. 'How will you rescue him? Surely you might think of something to cause her to annul the marriage?'

'It is not a good time to make an enemy of Henry Percy. I am too vulnerable.' I brought her back to what I thought was the more important issue. 'Tell me, Joan and Jane did not like the thought of William Wyndsor joining our family, I trust?'

I watched her pretty face, more beautiful than ever surrounded by the crisp wimple of her habit, as Bella struggled for the right words. I was relieved when she looked me in the eyes and said, 'No, they do not like him. Nor do I, Mother. In faith, I know it is not my part to criticise your choice of husband, but have you not suffered enough? Would it not be better to find someone quiet and steady? Like Robert.'

The wisdom of my child moved me to tears. 'I have no intention of wedding Wyndsor, my sweet. I have pledged myself to Robert. But I very much fear what Wyndsor is about.' For the second time that day I sank down on a bench, this time in the hall, and this time it was my daughter who joined me. She pulled me into her embrace and rocked me gently as I wept.

'God grant you peace,' she murmured. 'God grant you joy.' Over and over she wished me such blessings.

Peace and joy. I treasured what I had of both at that moment, for I did not believe I would enjoy either in the near future.

Gradually, over the summer and into the autumn, I became reacquainted with my family, my properties, and myself. It was a happy time, but not altogether peaceful. There were rumours I was to be brought before Parliament to answer for my 'crimes against the King and kingdom', rumblings from past holders of my properties, hoping to catch me at a vulnerable time and grab back their property without compensating me. Robert, Dom Hanneye and Richard Lyons were busy assisting me in keeping the wolves at bay.

Because of the unsettled situation, Robert was not so often at Gaynes, and I missed him sorely. Over the summer I had lived for our moments together during the day, our lovemaking at night. When he was away I often brought Joan and Jane to my chamber to sleep with me.

The rumours proved true. In the first Parliament of the reign of the young King Richard, I was brought to trial for my 'misdeeds'. This time the knives came out, well sharpened. The Duke of Lancaster and Princess Joan assured me that no matter what the commons and the court said, what they threatened, I would be safe. They recommended that I remain at Gaynes until actually summoned to appear. When I did arrive at Westminster, Lancaster forbade me to wear widow's garb.

'You are not my father's widow.'

'I am Janyn's widow. But in any case, these are not widow's weeds, my lord.' I wore a dark, simple gown and plain headdress, without decoration.

'You have never dressed so plainly. You are not to wear weeds.' His coldness sufficiently frightened me that I did not argue. I detected neither gentleness nor understanding in his eyes.

I had been assigned a large, beautiful bedchamber in the palace, one that I had never seen before, though I recognised several tapestries, cushions, and chests that had once been mine. Someone had perhaps meant that as a kindness. Gwen found some of my more elegant gowns in the chests, and with a little work we changed the bodices so that I would at the least appear less provocative. I wore no jewels. Those that I still had, I had hidden.

Two of the most serious charges against me were lies, but with enough truth behind them that it would be impossible for me to disprove them. I was accused of having used my influence over the King to prevent Nicholas Dagworth from going to Ireland to consider the charges against William Wyndsor, and I had persuaded the King to make reparation to Richard Lyons. Both William and Richard were referred to as my partners in business.

I was tried as a *femme sole*, a woman alone, solely responsible for my actions. Had I not been so terrified I might have enjoyed the irony, that I was solely responsible for obeying my King and his family.

As the trial wore on the charges against me multiplied. Folk came forward, invited by Parliament, to make their claims. The allegations were, for the most part, trivial, people petulantly claiming unpaid debts, kin claiming that I had coerced their relatives to enfeoff land to me that they were furious was now out of their reach – all the usual petty complaints made against wealthy persons. But they were threatening nevertheless, because *invited*. Parliament was searching for enough to condemn me, once and for all.

I heard beneath the trivial accusations that Richard Stury had been right. They needed someone to blame for the losses the realm had suffered in the last years of Edward's reign – so much sovereignty lost in western France after years of costly wars, so much taxation. Of course, no one believed that I had somehow caused the defeats, but they accused me of weakening the King with lovemaking.

We had succeeded too well in hiding his illness from the people, and no one in the royal family was coming forward to defend me. They could not afford to open the discussion to the subject of a flawed king – that had led to armed rebellion in the time of my Edward's father. Such talk would be dangerous with a boy now on the throne.

My very soul seemed to be on trial. In an attempt to prove that I had cast a spell over King Edward, they sought out and arrested the Dominican friar, Dom Clovis, whom I had consulted so long ago.

I heard Lancaster ascribe to me Edward's arguments about the inappropriateness of relying solely on Nicholas Dagworth's biased judgement regarding William's service in Ireland. Half a dozen of the men whom I'd counted, if not friends, certainly not my enemies in Edward's household, exaggerated my influence over the King.

How they could speak such lies in my presence, I could not understand. I had always treated Edward's household officers with respect. With each new condemnation I stood taller, refusing to hang my head in the face of such lies. But my courage left me at night. Then I was haunted by nightmares of being taken to the Tower, of being beheaded . . . such horrors every time I slept that I took to pacing my chamber rather than close my eyes.

All the while the trial dragged on I screamed within, *I am powerless! How can you fear me? Why do you need to encase me in walls six feet thick? I have never had a choice except to do what I could to protect my chicks.*

I had benefited from my liaison with the King, yes, of course I had. I did not deny that. But so had he benefited, and through him the realm. And what of his children? My children? I feared what would become of them if I were imprisoned or exiled.

After a great deal more, on which I was forbidden to speak out in my defence, Parliament's judgement was thus: the property I had accrued as gifts from the King *or through my own means* during my liaison with him were forfeit – they took care to state that only in my case were they waiving the laws that protected enfeoffments and other property transactions, fearful lest any of themselves might so forfeit their own property in due course. Apparently I was a uniquely undeserving landowner. All the jewels they could seize from me were also forfeit. The worst of this was my pearls – they confiscated what they believed to be all the pearls Edward had given me. Twenty thousand according to their count. That was the punishment that cut the deepest. Those gifts of love . . . even they were taken from me. Confiscated as well were the jewels entrusted to Lancaster – how Parliament had known of them I could not fathom except that either the Duke or William had been indiscreet. Though to what purpose, I could not understand. Even the gold Edward had intended for my support in exile had been discovered.

The crowning punishment was my exile. Exile! I was forbidden on English soil, on pain of imprisonment in the Tower . . . or worse. All I could think of was never seeing my son John again – or my sister and brother. And Bella! My faithfulness to Edward had cost me everything. I swore in my heart that I would at least take with me my precious younger daughters. I would not be parted from Joan and Jane.

I stood there before the hate-twisted faces in the ornately carved, painted and gilded hall of Westminster, feeling stripped of all honour.

And I was forbidden to speak a word in my own defence. Inwardly I demanded to be heard. *Listen to me! I obeyed the Dowager Queen Isabella, Queen Philippa, King Edward, Prince Edward, the Duke of Lancaster . . . I obeyed them in everything. What do you gain from destroying me?*

Ah, but that was the key, of course. They gained property; they gained a fortune in jewels. I wondered to whom the spoils would be presented. I cursed them all.

What of the promises Princess Joan and Lancaster had made? It was after my appearance before Parliament, after my fate had been determined, that I was escorted back to the Palace of Westminster to meet them. Unbeknownst to me, another guest had been invited: William Wyndsor. I had not spoken to him since that afternoon in the gardens at Gaynes when I had refuted him.

That evening I learned of a condition regarding their reassurances of my safety about which I had not been informed, plainly because I might not have co-operated in shielding Edward from the gossips had I done so. My beloved Edward, his sons the Prince and Lancaster, and William Wyndsor, had made a pact regarding how I was to be made docile after I was no longer needed to attend the King. My exile would not be enforced so long as I lived under William's rule as his wife. I might live peacefully with my children so long as I acknowledged that he was my husband.

I had stopped breathing while I listened to this. My mouth was so dry that even after I remembered to draw breath, I could not speak for several long moments while everyone waited for my humble submission.

'Might live with my children?' I managed at last. 'Do you threaten to take Joan and Jane from me if I do not agree?'

'They are the daughters of the late King,' said Lancaster. 'As his son, I am responsible for them.'

Bastard! Changeling! I hissed inwardly, cursing him. My worst nightmares had not touched this depth of betrayal. I would rather be beheaded than live with no hope of seeing my precious daughters. But I knew that nothing I said would matter to them. My fate had long since been decided. I was the scapegoat. I simply sat there, in a throne-like chair, a jewelled mazer before me, facing those three I had counted as friends from time to time – particularly Princess Joan. Lancaster I had long distrusted. But I had believed in her friendship.

How had I not foreseen this? William's persistence . . . his thick skin.

Edward had planned this. I remembered his words in the garden the day he told me to keep his signet ring. *I fear you shall face one more labour before you rest, but I pray it may prove unexpectedly happy.* How could he think so? What a pawn I had been! But, of course, he had not been in his right mind then. Lancaster had taken advantage of his father's confusion; had tricked him into agreeing to this travesty.

'A marriage is not valid unless both parties agree,' I declared.

Lancaster coughed, no doubt hiding a chuckle. 'Dame Alice, you have lain with Sir William many times. You would find it difficult to convince Archbishop Sudbury that you were not willing.'

'I have not! Never!' I looked to William, who stared at a spot to my left. I was nauseated. I loathed him.

'It is this or exile?' I asked.

Lancaster gave the subtlest of nods, as if not entirely approving of his own inhumanity.

'And my lands?'

'Those we cannot save for you. But, in time, Sir William might win them back.'

I cursed William then and there. Cursed him and vowed that he would never enjoy the wealth I had so carefully accrued for my daughters.

Joan reached out to me, gently covering my hand with hers. She explained that the people would forget me as soon as they knew I was safely under the control of a husband, and one with strong connections to the great ones of the land. William was known as a fierce guardian of the law. A man of martial skill, a respected knight of the realm.

I was aghast. 'It is you who have kept him adamant about our having pledged our troth?'

'Not me, my friend,' said Joan. 'I have only this past week learned of this agreement.'

But William had told Richard Lyons of it long before. And Edward had told me. I had wilfully ignored the writing on the wall. I cursed myself for having been so blind as to think it was passion that drove William when it was anger, his sense of being robbed of his due, that had always been the fiercest of his emotions.

'How can you trust him to keep me safe? He failed you in Ireland. Why William, of all men?'

Lancaster was unmoved. 'He is my man, Alice. He has always served me well.'

But not Edward, not his King. No, that was not true. William had earned him the money to fight in France. He had a thick skin. Perhaps he enjoyed playing antagonist. I must remember that.

'Is this your wish, William?' I asked. 'To wed a woman who does not want you?'

He had sat all this time with eyes trained on a spot on the table before him. While I had questioned his trustworthiness he had finally moved, clenching his jaw. He looked at me now, his eyes assessing me, as if he were sizing up a filly for purchase. 'Alice, my love, surely by now you should have no illusions about marriage.' He reached for my hand but I withdrew into myself. 'In time you will want me, Alice. You will.'

Never, I shouted inside. *Never. And I shall never forgive you, any of you.*

My public ordeal was not yet over. I was commanded to present myself at a public Mass in Westminster Abbey, so recently the scene of my son's wedding. To the Archbishop of Canterbury I was to confess my sins and humble myself, begging forgiveness. For this I stubbornly wore my widow's weeds. Simon Sudbury raised an eyebrow, but said nothing.

I did all that was demanded of me. I had no choice. I was ordered to accept responsibility for all that I had achieved as well as all that I had humbly done in obedience. It was not enough that I had lost Edward, that his family had robbed me of Janyn and my family for so long.

And to add to the insult, though I wanted neither William Wyndsor nor Mary Percy, I was shackled with both.

At least for the moment, until I could gather my wits about me. I had said nothing of my betrothal to Robert. At least I might protect him.

I could not sleep as long as I resided in the palace. I veered between anger and anguish over what Robert and Bella would say – I could see the sympathy in Gwen's eyes, and the disappointment.

The fetters, so lately slipped from my ankles, were back, but now without even the sweetness of my love for Edward to soothe their restraint.

I hated them all for the regret I now felt for loving him.

IV-2

'Hire face, lik of Paradys the ymage,
Was al ychaunged in another kynde.
The pleye, the laughter, men was wont to fynde
On hire, and ek hire joies everichone,
Ben fled; and thus lith now Criseyde allone.

Aboute hire eyen two a purpre ryng
Bytrent, in sothfast tokenyng of hire peyne,
That to biholde it was a dedly thyng . . .'

– Geoffrey Chaucer, *Troilus and Criseyde*, IV, ll. 864–71

January 1378

I was granted a few days' grace at Westminster, and made use of the time to send messages to Bella, Robert and Mary, who was at Gaynes with the children, warning them of the impending change in my status. That cold, practical phrase was more suitable for my situation than 'marriage'. The messenger was given a letter for each, the longest one going to Robert. I vowed my steadfast love for him, telling him that it was only so that I would not be parted from him or my children that I would acquiesce, and begged him not to interfere. I hated the fact I could not speak to the three of them in person, and prepare Joan and Jane.

But I was effectively a prisoner in Westminster Palace. Though preferable by far to the Tower, it was still a prison, and a cold one at that. Princess Joan and young King Richard were not in residence, nor was Lancaster.

When he had forbidden me to use the few days' grace I was granted to return to Gaynes and prepare my household, I had asked the Duke what he feared I might do if permitted to travel.

Elegant in a dark robe that accentuated his fair colouring but also the shadows beneath his eyes, a sign of ill health or at least poor sleep that I had rarely seen on him, Lancaster lightly touched my arm as we stood by a window looking out at the wintry Thames. 'I would protect you from taking some unwise action while your mind is in turmoil, Dame Alice, such as fleeing the country with my nieces. That would be regrettable, for it would render impossible our plan for your peaceful, comfortable withdrawal from the centre of controversy. You have had a great shock in the judgement brought against you. Such a disturbance while still in mourning would shake the most courageous knight to his core. I admire your strength throughout my father's illnesses, his death, the vindictive attacks of the commons.'

His expression of concern served only to nauseate me. In my mind I retorted, *Surely you would prefer that I escaped with my daughters? You would then be rid of me and have all my properties, jewels, money. Even Sir William to wed to another you seek to control.*

But I said none of that, nor did I tell him that I was already betrothed. He might look vulnerable, but he was the wealthiest, most powerful man in the realm, and I dared not antagonise him. I feared what he would do to Robert.

When he left I sent away the servants and paced the corridor, spewing all the venom inside me. My booted feet pounded the wooden planks while I hissed and shrieked the curses I had so long held within. I wept, I tore at my hair and pounded my breast until I was spent. Let the servants and the guards whisper and cross themselves, I did not care.

The palace these days felt like a mere shade of the Westminster I had known with Edward. To a person, the servants seeing to our needs behaved so indifferently towards Gwen and me, though many of them had been accustomed to seeking our advice when Edward was alive, that we avoided talking to them when we might, the contrast being too painful. And I had frightened them with my fury, I knew. They, in turn, were stingy with food, drink and fuel for the braziers. I yearned to go to one of my own homes, in truth to be almost anywhere but in one of the royal residences, fraught as they were with painful memories.

Gwen fretted over my cold hands and feet, my lack of appetite. 'I almost preferred your mad rage,' she said.

I assured her that I would thrive once I was able to ride and hawk, once I was home – for it seemed I would be permitted to keep Fair Meadow and the home in which Janyn and I had lived in London.

'Will Sir William agree to bide in one of your homes?' she asked me.

'Agree? I should think it is his most fervent wish. Why else would he co-operate in this farce but to acquire all that is mine? No one ever speaks of *his* residences, Gwen. No doubt they are merely adequate.'

Indeed, William was not in residence at Westminster, but reportedly occupied in readying his home just north of the city for our wedding night. He had sent a message inviting me for a walk in the palace gardens, but I had begged a headache and heard no more. Robert had been right – William did not behave like a man in love. I was simply his current mission for Lancaster. A page had brought a wedding gift, a gold fillet set with diamonds and emeralds, nominally from William though it, too, smelled of Lancaster.

Long ago Princess Joan had warned me: '. . . they will envy you. Envy is an ugly emotion. It inspires cruelty. Meanness . . . If aught goes wrong, you are one of the people who will be blamed. Because you have no connections. Because he loves you . . . keep your eyes open. At all times remember who you are, where you are . . . Find and nurture a few trustworthy friends. But do not blindly trust them. Nor should you blindly trust the King. He is a man, as William Wyndsor is a man. Your William is angry, I noticed that. He may yet be your salvation if aught goes wrong, but if you wed him, try to keep some of your property secret. Just in case.'

Joan had said that she had learned of the pact only the previous week. How then had she warned me so long ago?

I requested a meeting with her. She arrived with servants bearing gifts for me: jewelled mazers, several silver spoons, fat cushions covered in silk and velvet, a generous length of escarlatte in a rich gold hue, another in brunette, a soft, patterned wool in shades of red ranging from a pale rose to a deep wine colour, and a small casket filled with gold and silver buttons inlaid with mother of pearl. Wedding gifts.

'You must believe me, Alice, I knew nothing of this until shortly before you learned of the plan. I had intended these gifts to cheer you and the homes you were permitted to keep, or else your abode in exile if the worst happened. I had not known of this arrangement with Sir William, I swear.'

Whether or not I believed her did not matter to me at that moment. I was desperate for advice. 'I cannot wed him, Joan. I cannot love him.'

'You must try, Alice. For the sake of your family. Think, my friend – for once you shall be free to live with Joan and Jane, and be near Bella.'

My heart quickened at her mention of being near Bella. Gaynes was near Barking Abbey. 'Is Gaynes not forfeit?'

Joan shook her head. 'Gaynes is yours, so long as you wed Sir William. You once found him pleasing, Alice. Is not this far better than exile?'

It was a fair question. I considered telling her of Robert. She of all people would understand, having been forced into marriage with William Montague when she was secretly betrothed to Thomas Holland. But I no longer trusted her with information she might let slip.

'I shall be grateful to remain close to my son and my daughter Bella. But for them, I would have preferred making a new life with my two youngest children in France or the Low Countries. I might eventually have felt comfortable in my life there, at peace. I cannot imagine ever being so as an unwilling wife.'

'Neither John nor his brothers would have permitted you to take their nieces out of the country, Alice.'

'I find it strange that, though they were not recognised by their father, their uncles have acquired them. To what purpose? They will not suddenly give them the Plantagenet name or find noble husbands for my girls. The Duke does this only to tie me to William, so that he might reward him with my properties.'

I could see from her beautiful, expressive face that Joan had no counter to that. It had been of so little interest to her she had not wondered why the brothers were suddenly so keen to keep their bastard nieces close to them.

She held out her hand to me. 'You look so pale.'

So did she, I noticed, though her hair was once more brightened, the white that had been evident at her husband's death hidden with bleaches and oils. She also looked swollen, as if the weight she had gained in the last years in Bordeaux and then lost once back in England had returned. She seemed to eat when worried. I regretted having argued with her. A little.

'Let us walk in the garden,' she said. 'It is fair and mild for January, a gift we should not squander in chilly, dank, echoing chambers.'

The palace did echo, with so few in residence.

As Joan and I walked in the deserted gardens, she spoke not of my coming marriage but of her fears regarding her son, so young to be King, and her inability to sleep through the night since Prince Edward's death.

'It is not as if we had slept in the same bed every night. But somehow my sleeping self knows that he is gone, that our son is vulnerable, and I wake with my heart racing.'

I was relieved to be distracted from my own worries and anger for a while. Joan had lost far more than a husband. She had lost a most magnificent future and the time her son needed to grow into a young man suited to rule a kingdom.

But soon she turned the conversation to my distrust of the Duke.

'John is fighting to keep a delicate balance, Alice. My husband charged him with protecting the realm for our son while Richard was too young to rule on his own. John knows that there are those in commons and among the barons who suspect him of wishing to keep that power for himself. Such a rumour would only grow if he challenged it, and so he trusts that by acting impeccably on Richard's behalf, he will convince the people that to rule this realm is not his intent. Like you, he is condemned for taking a lover to whom he is not wed, and for having children with that lover. In his liaison with Katherine, he understands you better than anyone else in the family.'

I sighed with impatience.

Joan gave my arm a little shake. 'He means to save you, Alice! Marriage to Sir William is a way in which he might calm the temper of the crowd, safely settle you with a knight. John intended to *honour* you with such a noble connection.'

'I wish I might believe all that you say of him.' It would be so much easier to welcome this marriage. But I distrusted it. And I loved Robert, not William. I drew my squirrel-lined cloak up under my chin.

'Come, you are chilled. Let us withdraw to your chamber and some hot spiced wine.' As we hurried along the garden path Joan said, 'I pray that joy surprises you, Alice. You have done so much for this family, and I wish you happiness.'

When she had departed I spent a long while in the chapel, praying for the wisdom and grace to behave as if I accepted my lot. I also prayed that Joan was right about the Duke. But it was difficult to push aside panicky thoughts of flight.

William and I were wed in a simple ceremony in that same chapel in Westminster Palace in which I had prayed so earnestly for acceptance. Archbishop Sudbury, he to whom I had humbled myself days earlier, presided. I wore a dark gold brocade gown and blue-green undergown. Gwen had sprinkled the brocade with the buttons Princess Joan had given me. I wore over my coiled hair the diamond and emerald fillet from William. He wore a slim-fitting jacket of deep indigo embroidered with silver thread that swirled into the shape of a swan. A hat of lighter indigo sported a peacock feather. His leggings were dark brown. We were a handsome couple, so elegant we would not stoop to revealing any emotion. The guests were fortunate: were we to do so, I would scream, and William most likely laugh.

For the sake of my children, I vowed to do all in my power to find peace in this hateful situation. But I would never give William my heart. That was Robert's.

As we rode to William's home north of London I forced my thoughts to a neutral topic. I was now the wife of a man of more modest means than either Janyn or Edward, albeit a knight, and prepared myself for a small, plain dwelling. It turned out to be a sizeable house and quite new.

'In summer the huge oaks surrounding it must give pleasant shade,' I remarked. 'And is that a pond farther down?'

'A fish pond, well stocked when I am in residence.'

We had exchanged few words all day, swept along on the falsely cheerful chatter of our 'sponsors', as William referred to the Duke and the Princess. In a peculiar gesture, my father and his wife – whom I had not previously met, being such a danger to her soul when I was Edward's mistress – were invited to the ceremony. Knowing nothing of my feelings about the union,

Father wished me all happiness. When his wife would have added her simpering congratulations he drew her away, no doubt apprehensive of my response.

'You said little to your mother,' William remarked.

'My mother is long dead.'

My stomach clenched at the prospect of years of this empty civility.

His household greeted me warmly. The hall was modest and simply furnished, tidy and inviting, especially the fire in the centre fragrant with apple wood. I complimented William on the fine meal set before us and attempted to converse about safe topics, for the moment we had arrived at the house he had begun to quaff brandywine. By the end of the meal, which he hardly touched, he had consumed copious amounts and seemed hungry for an argument.

He began a litany of slights – my sending him away from Gaynes, my refusal to permit him to stay at Tibenham many summers past, my leaving his letters unanswered, and my insulting him in front of Lancaster and Joan. When he reached the end of his litany he began again. I said little. Neither Janyn nor Edward had ever behaved so, and I was unsure what would make him even angrier.

'I am here now, William,' I reminded him when we finally withdrew to our bedchamber. I sat down beside him on the bed. 'Might we not be courteous to one another?'

He grunted. 'That would suit you, would it? Coax me into forgetting all your insults and pretend we have just met?'

'What else are we to do? How do you propose we live?'

He lurched to his feet and stumbled towards the door. When he was almost there he turned. About to lose his balance, he flung up a hand and caught hold of a rafter to steady himself, took a deep breath and blinked, as if trying to clear his mind and vision. 'How can you not know that from the moment I first saw you, I vowed you would be my wife?'

So I had not been wrong in believing that long ago. I rose and approached him, reaching out to steady him. 'Come, William, come to bed.' I wanted any spies in the household to report that we had slept together.

He slipped one hand behind my head and pulled me close,

kissing me on the mouth. I managed to disengage myself and lead him to the bed, undress him while being partially undressed myself, ease him under a pile of blankets and coverlets, all before he proceeded to snore.

When I was certain that he was deeply asleep I called Gwen in to help me prepare for bed. I lay awake, imagining how I must behave in the next few days and weeks to win William's trust, wondering if that were possible. I prayed we might come to a mutually satisfactory agreement.

I woke to find him kissing me, and as he sensed me awaken he gently entered me. His breath smelled of anise and his skin of some exotic perfume. I realised that he had washed and prepared himself for me. He was considerate in his lovemaking, but I did not respond. Afterwards we lay side by side, eyes averted from one another, as if wondering whether we dared communicate further.

He turned back towards me and lifted my shift to gaze on my body. 'Well, my silent Alice, be assured you shall be so awakened as often as I can manage. I cannot think how I would wake beside this body and not be aroused.' His smile was lazy and sensual as he eased himself on top of me once more, this time to suck and tickle my nipples.

I did not pretend to do more than endure, and he did not seem to care. I prayed that he would soon tire of my unresponsiveness.

Later in the morning, after we broke our fast in front of the fragrant fire in the hall, William and I talked. It was clear that I was not the only one who had spent some time considering how to make the best of our marriage. He vowed that if I accepted his apology for our arranged match and gave him a chance to prove himself a loving husband, he would work through the courts to clear my name, revoke my exile, and reclaim the property I had purchased in my own name.

I agreed in principle. Silently I vowed to secure what I could of the properties I had purchased in partnerships by working once again with my old friends and business partners. I had not forgotten Robert's warning about William having demanded information about my properties, nor Joan's about keeping some property secret.

For several days we both made great efforts in courtesy, but it was plain that it would require constant vigilance and restraint on my part. William managed to forgo too much drink the first few evenings in his home, and I tolerated his sexual demands. It was strange to me, to be sickened by a man's touch. When we talked we chose safe topics such as the household, his other properties, what items he intended to take to Gaynes. But on the fourth day he drank too much at the midday meal, and by evening was alternately vicious about my nun-like demeanour and morosely silent. By the time we made our way to the barge at Westminster staithe, we were eyeing one another warily. I dreaded the homecoming ahead.

Though Princess Joan and the Duke of Lancaster were granting me safe passage home, there were inevitably those in their retinues and that of the young King who might seek praise and advancement by capturing me. After all, I had been exiled, which would not usually entitle me to a life spent in England, much less the use of a royal barge. William and I had been warned to dress simply and remain well covered.

As I watched the familiar riverscape slip past, I was overcome by memories of ferrying to and from my homes and Edward's palaces in the past. Then the royal bargemen and guards had treated me with respect; now all eyes were curious, and most cold. I tried to avoid the memory of a more recent journey home with Robert, when I had thought myself a free woman.

I hated the fact that I'd been unable to prepare him and my family for this latest development, and that Joan and Jane, and possibly my son, knew nothing of my marriage to William. My two youngest children had been happy to have me living in the same house with them, without a man insisting on my undivided attention most of the day and all of the night. I anticipated tears when they realised that from now on William would be sharing my bedchamber and my life. I tried to reassure myself that at least he was not a stranger to them. They had met him before, and he had tried to win their liking. He would do well to continue in that, for my children would always be first in my heart.

But Robert . . . my beloved, true husband! My letter to him had been clumsy for I'd found it most painful to write. The look on his face when he met the barge was one of betrayal and hope forsaken. But he quickly gained control of himself and welcomed

William. I, however, was shattered. I had thought I could make the best of it but I could not. I felt as if I might be sick.

Joan and Jane were confused, but William greeted them with such hilariously exaggerated courtesy that for days he had but to bow to them to reduce them both to giggles. For that I was grateful. I had not expected such sensitivity. Mary Percy ignored him, but that was her wont. I had recently agreed to her having her own lady's maid, and the two of them gossiped and simpered in a corner of the hall as they bent over their embroidery and other stitching most of the day. I counted it a godsend that she was thus occupied.

Gwen was very quiet. We had been through so many changes together, but this one seemed the most difficult for her to accept. As she tidied my bedchamber the first night at Gaynes, I asked for her thoughts. She seemed sad.

'I cannot bear to see you so unhappy when . . .' She pressed her fingers to her lips for a moment, her expression alarmed. 'Forgive me, Dame Alice. I forget my place.'

'You are one of my oldest and dearest companions, Gwen. You are welcome to speak freely whenever we are alone.'

'In Master Robert you have found a husband you love and respect and enjoy being with. I fear what will happen now. How long can you play the role of Sir William's wife? How will Master Robert bear it? How will you?'

'I do not know what will become of us, Gwen. Each time I believe I am free, I am shackled anew.'

She sighed and latched the chest she had filled, pressing her hands to her lower back as she rose. She would age someday, and I would lose her – if I did not go first. I could not imagine my life without her.

'Perhaps Sir William will surprise you,' she said, without conviction.

Nor could I imagine it. On his best behaviour, William drank moderately the first evening at Gaynes. We began it in pleasant conversation, and ended it in a rough coupling. But the following morning I woke to find him gone. The servants said that he had ridden out early.

I sought out Robert in the fields. His sun-bleached hair, the way his skin wrinkled about his eyes when he squinted against the light, the way he held himself, it was all so familiar and dear to me. But his greeting was too formal. I talked over it, told him freely of all that had transpired at Westminster. We walked along the hedgerow he had been inspecting while I talked. We paused in an old shed, sitting side by side on a wobbly bench.

'They have no right,' he said, staring at the mud floor.

I put my hand over his. 'It is I who have no rights, Robert. It seems I never had. My father arranged my marriage with Janyn, and Janyn bound me to the Queen's household.'

'If you might choose . . .?'

He had turned to look me in the eyes. As he did so my side of the bench gave way. He caught me in his arms, lifting us both to our feet.

'I *have* chosen you, Robert. Surely you can see that in my eyes? Surely I made that plain in our precious nights together, in pledging my troth?'

We kissed long and tenderly, pressing ourselves against one another.

'God may yet set this right,' he whispered.

'I do not dare to hope, but I pray William will quickly tire of the pretence and leave us in peace.'

'Until then, I shall watch over you, Alice.'

I did not like those words, *until then*. 'Robert, we shall be together when he is away. Surely we need not deny our love?'

He shook his head. 'I cannot share you with him, Alice.'

I felt panic rising. 'Robert, do not punish me! I am doing this for us. Protecting you, protecting my children—' I broke off, hearing Janyn telling me he had arranged for my summons to court for my safety, for Bella's. 'What have I done, Robert?'

He took my hands and stared at them, kissed each in turn then looked up at me. His love for me was writ on his face; also his pain. But he managed a crooked smile. 'You have done what had to be done. I could not love you as I do and remain ignorant of the fact that you would never be able to bear a separation from your children.'

'No, I could not.' I took a deep breath. 'What will you do now?'

'I will stay away from your presence as much as possible, travel to our distant properties, oversee them.'

'I cannot bear it . . .'

He kissed my forehead, my cheeks, my lips, with great tenderness, then backed away. 'This is how it must be, for now. I cannot stay, Alice. I would do him violence.'

We parted there. Later that day he rode off to a distant manor.

Gradually, after much prayer and thought, I calmed myself and strove continually to be grateful for all that I had, to push away the yearning for what I had not.

In the next few weeks we entertained a stream of guests: Richard Lyons, Dom Hanneye, Geoffrey, Pippa and their son Thomas, my brother John and his family. I had urged William to allow us some quiet in which to adjust, but he wished all to congratulate us. He wanted to know my family and friends. As I observed him greeting our guests, I realised how little we knew of each other.

On the first morning of Richard's visit I proposed we should all go hawking. It was a mild February day, and Joan and Jane had asked if we might. My daughters were utterly entranced by the hawks and all the ritual surrounding hunting with birds.

'A tedious pastime.' William was slumped on a bench near the fire circle in the hall, staring into it as if conjuring spirits. He did not even look up to pronounce his opinion. With a wave of his hand, he added, 'Be gone if you will. I shall find other occupation.'

Even Mary Percy showed more interest, though her participation began with much simpering about how the various birds should be assigned, according to the status of the hawker, with insulting references to Richard and myself being unworthy of our falcons.

'Your poor son,' Richard whispered in my ear, 'he will be wanting a gentle, sweet-natured mistress within days of setting up household with that shrew.'

The guest in whom William took most interest was Pippa Chaucer. I caught him hungrily eyeing her round breasts which were accentuated by the cut of her gown. At first she shamelessly flirted with him but thought better of it one evening when he asked too many questions about her sister Katherine, some of them crude. His thin veneer of courtesy was easily dissolved by brandywine, it seemed.

'Being Lancaster's man, I should think you see far more of my sister than I do,' she said curtly, and moved away to talk to Richard.

William chose that moment to launch a volley of insults my way. As he had referred to Katherine as Lancaster's concubine, he called me the King's. I'd 'not had the wit to find a real husband after Janyn's death, but fell into the aged King's bed with no thought to the future'.

I'd encountered drunks before, but none with the power so to sting me, to twist the knives that plainly protruded from my still-grieving heart.

I glanced at Geoffrey's face, livid with anger, and shook my head.

'My friend, do not engage him in argument. He is beyond reason when in his cups.'

The fissure between William and me yawned wider as our guests departed. He was not accustomed to life in a country manor. He had no patience for accounts, less interest in plans. He belittled me for gardening – 'peasants' work' – and I berated him for his increasing nastiness towards the children, not only Joan and Jane but my nieces and nephews, too. I thanked God that I had taken precautions not to become pregnant by him. Mary spoke of finding somewhere else to lodge, and I eventually agreed that she was better off in my home in London. Of course, then William too wished to remove to my home in London, to 'see to business'.

'But you have a home so near by, you've no need to stay in mine.'

'Ours,' he reminded me.

'Janyn's,' I countered.

He withdrew to his own home north of London for a few months. I rejoiced at the peace that settled over the house.

Even more wonderful was the afternoon Robert reappeared. I greeted him as my steward and friend when he arrived, and invited him to walk out to a far paddock to inspect a drainage problem. When we were safely out of sight of anyone who might report to William, I stopped and took his hands.

'Robert, does this mean . . .?'

I managed to say no more before he had silenced me with a

494

long, passionate kiss. When at last we stepped apart, we stood for awhile looking into each other's eyes, needing no words.

'You were right, my love,' he said as we walked on through the fields. 'When he is away, we shall be together. It is how it must be for now.'

We planned with care how we would manage our nights together, and agreed to speak of William as little as possible.

'It is not as I would wish it,' he said, 'but it is far better than being without you at all.'

Our mood was so light, our hearts so full, we found it difficult to return to the mundane topic of drainage, and somehow our discussion of the boggy ground provoked much laughter between us.

My husband returned in the summer to plague me, and Robert went away. William attempted a reconciliation, sleeping with me a few times, but our arguments began anew and he would have recourse to brandywine to sharpen his venom, afterwards sleeping where he fell. I ordered the servants to prepare a small chamber for him and told them to ensure he was there when they woke. I did not want my daughters to find him lying in the rushes when they came to the hall to break their fasts.

I learned to listen to William just long enough to know when to agree or disagree, to nod or shake my head.

In early-autumn we moved to the manor of Crofton in Wiltshire, ostensibly to meet William's family – they had property within a day's ride. His parents were both long dead, but cousins, siblings and the younger generation lived there-about. I found his nephew John Wyndsor, who had expected to be William's heir and still was in his will as it stood, an ignorant lout of a man, but William's sister was a lovely woman with whom I enjoyed talking about children.

The family had been scandalised by our wedding. I felt them covertly examining me, this infamous woman about whom they would love to hear more scandalous details. How perverse of such a well-favoured figure of a man, who had so valiantly and nobly served King Edward and the Duke of Lancaster, to settle for a merchant's daughter with three bastards, no matter that one was a knight wed to a Percy. In truth, they were all too careful to say such things in my presence, but my daughter-in-law Mary made certain to repeat all that she had gleaned by listening behind tapestries and at partially closed doors.

Mary was too self-centred, and perhaps too young, to realise that I prompted her to repeat to me what she regarded as hurtful comments. She was only too delighted, and I was grateful to learn the lie of the land. I must know as much as possible about William in order to protect myself from him. I maintained a courteous demeanour towards him in public, and, on those increasingly rare evenings when he had not overindulged in brandywine, tried to be civil in private.

My efforts in the latter eventuality were seldom completely successful, leading me to wonder whether he was as unhappy as I. One evening I dared ask him. I could not help but hope he had a mistress with whom he would prefer to bide.

'Unhappy with you, wife? What cause might I have? That you insulted me in front of the Duke of Lancaster and the mother of the King? That you refused my affections until you had no choice? That you still refer to *our* properties as yours – or, worse, your first husband's . . . that Lombard smuggler?'

And this on a night during which he had, I thought, drunk little.

'Why, then, do you stay?'

'To torment you.'

It was a kind of power, antagonising me, forcing me to submit. I realised with dismay that it might be true, and if so, there was little hope that he would walk away for good.

Despite the hostility between us, in October, before a new Parliament, William fulfilled his promise to begin working towards restoring my forfeited properties. He made the claim that I had been his wife when tried as a *femme sole* the previous year, and therefore my forfeited property was *his* forfeited property; as he had been accused of nothing, his property had been unlawfully taken. This would also render many of the private petitions enrolled against me null and void, for they named me and not my husband. It was legal sleight of hand that we hoped would work in our favour.

I dreaded any and all news of the proceedings, wanting to be quit of that life as much as I wanted to be quit of William himself.

I felt cursed. But it was important for me to know how things stood, and so I listened to my husband's and Geoffrey's accounts of proceedings.

My impression of the petitions in general was that people accused me of having accepted gifts proffered in exchange for my efforts to obtain a favour from the King, the Chancellor or the Chamberlain, and when they received no satisfaction, accused me of having made no effort on their behalf. I had seen such complaints made against all in Edward's household and on his council over the years, and knew full well that they were seldom credited. One might work diligently on behalf of another, but if the King or his officers refused to change their judgement, there was nothing more to be done. When I wondered aloud why few had made such complaints about me before, yet now so many came forth, William told me the petitioners had a common refrain: 'But I did not dare pursue my rights, for it was well known that no one could touch the King's mistress' – or words to that effect.

I felt a great fool. Far from the giddy glamour of the court life and the safety of Edward's love, I was angry with myself for my naïveté. Now that I was back in the circle of London merchants among whom I had been raised, once more influenced by their practical approach of luxury without prodigality, I did not understand my own hubris at court. I had known that what was legal for a man was rarely so for a woman; likewise a noble versus a commoner. Had I been more modest in my ambitions for my daughters, had I refused more of Edward's gifts, I might now be free to live openly as Robert's wife. Remorse ate at me.

William sensed it and goaded me by reciting petitions from memory when he was in the mood for attack. But when he found me weeping one afternoon in my bedchamber, he relented.

'I promise you I will speak no more of this, Alice. You have been cruelly used, and I would make it up to you.'

He often made such pretty speeches, but seldom kept his promises. This time he did. For a while we enjoyed a fragile peace.

His petition was taken under consideration, but no decisions regarding my lands came out of that Parliament. Because of William's argument that I was now a married woman, I was henceforth required to do business as such, which compounded my difficulties, for William's credit was poor. And despite letters from the Duke of Lancaster stating that I and all who traded with me were under his protection, merchants were wary of trading with me because my sentence of exile had not yet been officially revoked.

Once again I was fortunate in my friends. Richard Lyons and Robert smoothed out the ruffled feathers of those merchants I most needed to deal with.

Robert and I lived for the times when William would disappear for a fortnight or longer. Wrapped in Robert's arms, I dreamed of freedom.

My daughter Joan seemed to have fallen in love with Robert as well, becoming suddenly vain about her dress and following him about the estate, hoping to catch his eye, hanging on his every word. He was most gallant with her. Jane was obsessed with animals, her appearance the opposite of her sister's, feathers, hay, mud, and blood adorning her, her badges of honour. Caring for my daughters absorbed me, nurtured my ailing heart.

In the Parliament held a little over a year later William and I were issued pardons for my not going into exile and for William having sheltered me all that time. But I was not yet fully exonerated and nor were my forfeited lands returned.

William went to Lancaster for advice, and was encouraged to volunteer for a campaign that was to be undertaken in Brittany the following year under Thomas of Woodstock, Edward and Philippa's youngest son, now Earl of Buckingham. Lancaster suggested that if William not only took part in the campaign but agreed to bear some of the costs for the contingent, he would gain King Richard's favour, which could very well lead to the restoration of my forfeited lands. I exhorted Richard Lyons and my old merchant friends to finance William's part of the campaign – not one of his own kinsmen contributed. The plan worked. Within months, long before he departed for Brittany, the majority of my forfeited lands were restored – but to William, not to me.

When he informed me of this, I could not believe my ears. I had done everything Lancaster demanded of me. I had cared for his father when I might most reasonably have taken my leave of court. I had given up everything for the royal family, yet still I was punished. Now I had been used to provide William with a lordly living, just as I had suspected on that fateful evening at Westminster when he was presented as my betrothed.

I rushed out of the house, seeking shelter in the church. *What do You want of me, Lord?* I asked over and over. *What more do You require of me before You allow me peace?* I prayed for deliverance.

Life with my husband grew ever more intolerable. We spoke hardly a civil word to one another and rarely slept together – at least that was a blessing. He was adept at feeding my resentment by insisting not only that he was right, but demanding I admit to being wrong. Which I refused to do, though I also refused to argue unless it had to do with my children, which infuriated him. I saw how his unyielding insistence on being right, on never considering the possibility of being otherwise, had led to his downfall in Ireland and elsewhere. It was this tendency to excessive pride in him that caused problems with our tenants and the shopkeepers leasing my properties in London.

His nephew John was adept at feeding William's appetite for antagonism. During one visit he had been particularly busy. William returned from John's home in a quiet mood, the sort of quiet that alerted me to stormy days ahead. He was coldly polite if asked a question, vague about his time away, and his eyes wandered continually between his surroundings and me, as if he were reassessing our life together. As the days wore on he grew sullen and rude, treating me like an inconvenient guest whom he'd been irritated to find ensconced in his home on his return. The one night he came to my bed I refused him, calling loudly for Gwen, for he was drunk and had gripped my wrists as if he meant to rape me, not make love to me. I had already suffered this behaviour on a few darksome occasions, and had no intention of submitting to it again. The following morning, he at last confronted me.

'You lied to me about the King's rings.'

'Rumours, William. I kept only the signet he had told me to keep.'

'They've not found the rings.'

This was old news. 'I know, and you are well aware that I have told them all I know of it. Why are you bringing this up?'

'Where is the signet now?'

I fought to show no emotion. 'In a safe place. I shall bequeath it to my son John.' I was grateful I had given it to Robert for safekeeping. But I also worried that somehow William would find out that it was in his possession.

'What of Queen Philippa's jewels?'

I grew hot with the nerve of him. His greed knew no bounds.

'The Bishop of Winchester has vouched for me that I never possessed them, though I had worn them. You know all this, William. What is your intent?'

'Walsingham has told my nephew much about you and your whoring ways.'

So John Wyndsor had been to St Albans. It explained much. Thomas Walsingham, a monk at that troublesome abbey, wrote with a pen dipped in venom and spoke from a soul filled with hatred for the Duke of Lancaster and for me.

'Tell your nephew to have a care. If Lancaster should hear of his friendship with Walsingham, he might lose favour. Bereft of the Duke's patronage, your nephew might find life difficult.'

'Until he inherits from me,' William snarled.

I could hold my tongue no longer. 'You already have my lands and jewels . . . why stay if you despise me so?'

'You are my lawful wife, Alice. We are bound till death do us part.'

'We need not live together. Release me from this false marriage, William. Grant us both some rest.'

'It suits me to stay.'

I lived for midsummer when he would leave for the Brittany campaign. He did not expect to return until late-autumn. As the time drew near for him to leave he became more civil, however, and seemed to look upon the household with more affection.

One evening he had been most courteous, even charming, at dinner, entertaining our guests with stories of his previous time in Brittany and in Ireland, providing amusing imitations of both sides on the battlefield and in negotiations. I had never witnessed this talent of his. The last tale had been of a skirmish in Ireland that had been particularly bloody and was won by a clever ruse. Such talk had excited him, it was quite clear.

'You have a passion for soldiering,' I said after our guests departed.

'I do. I feel most truly alive in arms, riding to challenge the enemy. That is why I have advised your son to take up arms likewise in Lancaster's service.'

The pleasant glow I had been enjoying after a successful evening abruptly dimmed. 'What? You advised John? When did you see him?'

John had not stayed in my home since my marriage to William. I had not seen him in more than a year, and then but briefly at an inn near where he was biding for a few nights. Although I had never gleaned a clear reason from Percy as to why my son had not been at liberty to visit, I had assumed it had something to do with his dislike of William, who had antagonised so many of the nobles with properties in Ireland. To learn that William had seen John was therefore a cruel shock.

'I have met him often in the company of the Duke of Lancaster.'

I waited for more of an explanation, but William rose from his seat and moved toward the stairs with a yawn and a stretch, as if to retire for the night without explaining himself further.

I hurried to block his way. 'Why have you never mentioned this?'

His expression was one of slightly drunken indifference. 'I thought it best not to. I knew you would feel slighted. But these were official meetings, nothing to which you might reasonably have been invited.' He patted my forearm.

'Except as your wife.'

'You were not with me at the time.'

Life as a battle was pleasing to him. All I wished for was peace, and to be with my children.

'You know how I've ached to see John. Why does he not come here? Is it Mary, his wife? Does he avoid her?'

'Ask him yourself.'

'I do not like to quiz him in letters.'

He shrugged. 'I am weary of our arguments, Alice.'

'So am I. How might we mend the situation, William?'

He sniffed. 'What more do you want? What needs mending?' He pushed past me.

I grabbed his arm. 'William!'

He shook off my hand. 'If you want to talk, look to your beloved Robert Broun.' He stalked off to his chamber.

I lay awake long into the night so heavy of heart I could not even weep. So William knew about Robert. I wondered how long he had known, whether my unfaithfulness was why my lands had gone to him – whether he had informed Lancaster, and the Duke had informed the King. The lands I could somehow come to live without. I would find another way to provide for my daughters. But my son! I was furious that William had kept his meetings with my son from me, but even worse was John's silence on the matter. That defection was a terrible blow. I did not know how I might learn to live with it.

> 'N'y sey nat this al oonly for thise men,
> But moost for wommen that bitraised be
> Thorugh false folk – God yeve hem sorwe, amen! –
> That with hire grete wit and subtilte
> Bytraise yow. And this commeveth me
> To speke, and in effect yow alle I preye,
> Beth war of men, and herkneth what I seye!'

– Geoffrey Chaucer, *Troilus and Criseyde*, V, ll. 1779–1785

Spring 1380

William departed shortly after that night, refusing to enter into further discussion regarding either Robert or his visits with John. He behaved as if our conversation about them had never taken place. I held my breath while he remained with me, watching for any sign that he knew precisely how close Robert and I were, thinking he would surely enjoy destroying our happiness if he knew of our love. I tried to engage him in further conversation about my son. Asked again if he knew why John did not make more effort to visit, or why Percy did not permit it – for if it was not to avoid William, I worried that John meant to avoid me. William said that if my son wished for me to know aught, he would tell me himself. I could see no way through William's armour against me, polished to a sheen with painful resentment and reinforced by hatred. In my son he had found the surest weapon against me.

Even after he left, I worried. He was not departing for Brittany until midsummer, but said he had much to do on his own estates first. I imagined him whispering in Lancaster's ear, expecting the Duke's men to come for me at any time.

I decided to move the household to Gaynes, where I hoped to live peaceably at my favourite manor through the summer and into the autumn. I had much to think about, the sort of thought that required solitude. I had written to Henry Percy to inform him of the move, and requested that John might pay me a visit there. I prayed that my son would wish to be with me and that he would dispel my concerns by openly talking of his meetings with William.

The flurry of activity necessary before a move kept me blessedly distracted, but not so much that I missed an instance of uncharacteristic behaviour. My young daughter-in-law Mary was usually the most irritating member of the household at such times, insisting on more than her share of space in the carts. But this time, while Joan, Jane, Gwen and I rushed about, filling chests with clothing and household furnishings, Mary and her maid quietly saw to their own preparations and expressed indifference as to the household's plans. Always alert to her moods, I was troubled by her lack of interest. A few days before our departure, I received a messenger from Henry Percy who quickly explained my daughter-in-law's behaviour. She was not to accompany my household to Gaynes.

The message was delivered by one of Percy's retainers, who had been sent to escort Mary to a manor belonging to his lord. As he sipped wine in my hall, armed as if expecting his reception to be less than cordial, the man informed me that Mary had appealed to the Pope in Avignon for an annulment of her marriage with my son. Lord Henry felt it proper she should remove herself from my household during the papal investigation of her accusations.

My stomach clenched. 'What are these accusations?'

'I beg your patience, Dame Alice, but I was provided with no details.' The messenger fidgeted on a bench as he spoke. 'You will duly be receiving word from the cleric appointed by the Pope to examine the case.'

I was quite sure by his discomfiture that he had the information but preferred not to anger me by sharing it. He was wise to avoid antagonising me further, for I already fumed from the insult. Mary was but twelve, so I had no doubt she'd had assistance in arranging the request. I imagined Henry, Lord Percy wished to marry her off to someone of higher standing, someone who might help his own advance to power.

Mary had lived with me for three long years and in all that time had never once spoken of an annulment.

'What of my original request for my son's company?'

'Sir John Southery has been sent to study in the household of the Bishop of Exeter. My master has forwarded your request to the Bishop.'

I said as little as I might, wishing to provide Percy with no indication of my reaction to such evidence of meticulous planning. Indeed, the elegance of his moves left me shaken. The long period of preparation for the Brittany campaign had allowed Percy time to arrange this betrayal strategically so that William was not there to support me. Though he would not have done so for my sake alone. My husband would have seen it as an insult to our status, and that would have infuriated him.

When summoned, Mary entered the hall garbed in an elegant gown, her expression smug and sickening to me. She departed with little fanfare. I detected nary a tear among the servants or my little family. Jane, who had held my hand as we observed the procession of servants carrying Mary's possessions to the waiting cart, gave a sigh as the conveyance at last rolled away.

I looked down on her with concern. 'Are you unwell, my sweet?'

She met my worried gaze with merry eyes. 'I am very well. Joan and I can talk as loud as we please now.'

'Mary did not like you to speak loudly?'

'Oh, she liked it very well, Mother, but we did not like her telling our secrets to the servants, especially the grooms.'

Joan agreed. 'She bought special treatment with gossip.'

For the moment, I rejoiced in the gift of peace for all our household. It would be an immense relief to have the deceitful girl out of my house, out of my family.

But peace did not last long. I knew that no matter what he privately thought of Mary, my son John could not but feel the insult of her defection. I prayed it would not widen the wedge between us, the one that William had already begun to drive home with his talk of my being unwelcome at court.

Within days of our remove to Gaynes, I learned that Thomas Arundel, the current Bishop of Ely, had been assigned by Pope Clement to find the truth of Mary's case.

I was grateful that Robert arrived before the interview with Arundel's clerk. I felt stronger with him by my side.

'Mary Percy claims to have been held in your home against her will, Dame Alice. That is her argument.'

I fought down the anger that rose in me at such a bare-faced claim. 'Lord Percy and the late King Edward arranged the betrothal and marriage of Mary and the King's son, Sir John Southery,' I stated without emotion. 'What is the substance of her petition, other than this false claim?'

'That your son is not of noble birth, and she would have children with a man of noble blood.'

I did not respond at once, feeling pierced to the heart by the insult. This would wound John, it could not help but do so. I fought for calm.

'Granted, I am of common though respectable birth, but my son's father was the King of England. There is no more noble blood in the realm; not even Percy blood is so noble.'

The clerk coughed and coloured as he was forced at last to declare that John was a bastard.

'Yet knighted by his father, the King.'

'That is not for me to argue, Dame Alice.'

It was fait accompli, this interview a mere pretence of courtesy. Why they bothered I could not imagine, being only the harlot who had borne the bastard. Such ugly thoughts. I bowed my head and prayed.

'I pray you, forgive me, Dame Alice,' said the clerk. 'I would not cause you such pain.'

Robert showed him out. The clerk would bide with the parish priest while awaiting our formal response.

My consolation was that John came east to Westminster in the party of the Bishop of Exeter and then continued on to Gaynes. For his part, he had been grievously insulted by Mary's petition and was ready to protest to the Percy family, as I had expected. That did nothing to dampen my joy in seeing him – he was fifteen now, as tall as me and looking every inch Edward's son, from his piercingly blue eyes to his long-fingered hands and shapely legs. My heart swelled with pride and love. But we needed to talk at once. I invited him to accompany me to watch the training of a new falcon, a gift from one of Janyn's old friends.

As we walked through the spring garden, the beds tidy and hopeful with fresh shoots, I asked him how he liked the Bishop's household.

'It is pleasant enough, but I shall not be returning. I am now in the service of the Duke of Lancaster.'

I sought for a way to express surprise without appearing false. 'So you did not care for Exeter?'

John quickened his stride for a moment, then paused as I laughingly begged him to consider the limitations of my skirts. He turned a flushed face to me – it is the bane of the fair to wear their emotions so brightly.

'If Mary wins her annulment, and you know that Henry Percy will spare no expense to ensure that she does so, I must find a way to erase that dishonour, Mother. My skill in arms should do that. The Duke has promised that I shall take part in a major military expedition within the year.'

'John, you have a comfortable estate from your father.'

We had resumed our walk to the rookery, but at a more leisurely pace. My son, who had been remarking on how lovely everything looked at Gaynes, was now focusing on the path before him, looking neither up nor around, and had clasped his hands behind his back – both characteristic signs, as with his father, that he was ill at ease and choosing his words with care. I yearned to help him by letting him know what William had told me, but stopped myself before destroying my chance for reassurance. I needed John to tell me in his own time. I needed to know he meant to tell me.

'It is not my comfort but my honour at stake, Mother,' he said, frowning at the pebbled path. He cursed the Percy family for being so eager to own him before Parliament had ruled against me and now so ignobly rejecting him. 'I hate what they are doing to you. You have suffered enough.'

His loyalty to me gladdened my heart. 'I have found much peace in being here, John, away from the city and far from court.' I sought to reassure him a little.

'I mean to protest the petition.'

I was certain that would be a waste of time and money. Unless he was disappointed in love, something I had not considered. 'John, do you love Mary? Do you desire her?'

'Love her? No. Desire her? In faith, I have often wished to feel her breasts.' He grinned, a good sign that he was relaxing a little. 'But I'd as lief kiss a braying ass as kiss Mary Percy.'

We laughed together.

'Yet you would fight for her?'

'It is a matter of honour, Mother.'

'We shall find you someone much more to your liking, eh?'

'That is not what angers me. You have reached a settled state in your life. Sir William is a good husband, he is fighting to reinstate your properties and status.'

He, of course, did not know the truth of our loveless marriage.

'And now you have been grievously insulted – and I know you will worry about my losing the de Orby lands.'

Those extensive lands Edward had urged on me, Mary Percy's inheritance. I had invested a great sum in them to make up for years of poor management.

'They would have brought you considerable income,' I said, 'but you already have enough. Your father provided a goodly estate for you. Has Lancaster said aught about Mary's petition or your inheritance?'

'As far as I am aware, my half-brothers have no quarrel with my inheritance. Sir William assured me that the Duke of Lancaster is pleased with all he hears of me. As, of course, he must be to accept me in his service.'

The last statement was said in a rush as John tried to distract me from his comment about William. But it was precisely what I had been listening for.

'Sir William?'

John ducked his head, suddenly commenting on the state of the rookery, which we were approaching.

'John, when did you speak to William?'

His shrug made my heart race.

'John!'

He stopped and turned to me, his blue eyes imploring. 'I saw him at the Duke's residences when I was included in Lord Henry's party. Sir William counselled me to say nothing to you, fearing you might be jealous. He believed you were not welcome in court circles.'

Of course I was not. I was an embarrassment to them, the scapegoat who should be safely in exile where I might fade from their notice.

I gently touched his forearm, looking into his eyes. 'I am glad to be free from court, you know that, John. What troubles me is this secrecy. I would that you had spoken to me of it. We must have no secrets from one another.'

He pecked me on the forehead. 'No more. I am glad it does not trouble you.'

We resumed our walk.

'How often have you seen him?' I asked.

'Several times a year.'

I worked hard to hide my distress. 'What do you talk about?'

'Nothing that should worry you.'

'John, why are you so uncomfortable about this?'

'Because I was not to speak of it. I promised.'

I relented at that moment, too stunned and angry to pursue my son further. But over the next few days he grew more talkative, eventually confiding in me that the only complaint William made of me was my obsession with his will and dislike of his nephew.

'That seems an area of deep distrust between you,' he said.

'Is it any wonder, John? As my husband, William seeks to restore my properties to himself, not me, and has not rewritten his will to include Joan and Jane. The properties I accrued for the future comfort of your sisters will otherwise go to a lying, scheming nephew who despises me.'

John had begun to look sullen. 'He claims Joan and Jane are the daughters of Robert Broun, and that Robert should provide for them.'

For a moment I forgot how to breathe.

'Mother?' John touched my forearm. 'Are you unwell?'

I found a bench and sank down on to it. 'It is a lie! I never betrayed your father. Never. You've only to look at Joan to see that she — like you — is pure Plantagenet. Jane looks more like me, true, but they are both your full sisters. Both!'

John sank down beside me. 'I did not want to believe you had betrayed Father.'

'William tried hard to lure me into his bed while your father lived. He, of all people, should know how fiercely faithful I was to Edward.'

John put his arms around me and held me close. 'I will try to change his heart in this, Mother, I promise.'

It was a loving gesture, and I abandoned my ire as best I could so that I might enjoy this precious moment with my son, now so grown that I could rest my head on his shoulder. But I knew full well William would not relent.

'I beg you, John, do not let him poison our affections for one another.'

'No, Mother, never,' John said.

My years at court had trained me well in the art of hiding my feelings. For the remainder of my son's visit I struggled to keep my outrage to myself. I was too grateful to know now of the secret liaison, too relieved that John had relented and confided in me, and that he seemed to believe that I had been faithful to his father.

Though I held my tongue in an effort to keep the peace, a procession of family and friends tried to dissuade my son from military service, but he was adamant.

We had one additional, difficult conversation.

'I want you to know that I would never have believed what Sir William said about Robert had I not known of your love for him, and his for you,' John said one afternoon.

It was my turn to blush. 'It was Robert who comforted me when your father died. You are old enough now to know the truth, John.' I explained to him how I had come to wed William; that our marriage was a façade. But I did not tell him the whole truth about Robert and me. I did not dare let down my guard, even to my beloved son.

We had been reviewing items he might wish to take with him. At that moment we were in the stables looking at Janyn's fine saddle, one that male guests often used. As I had spoken about Lancaster's ultimatum and how it had dashed my hopes of happiness with Robert, John had run his hands over the leather again and again. He had neither looked at me nor spoken. When I had finished, the silence lengthened.

'Italian leather, very finely worked and tooled,' I remarked to ease the tension.

'Sir William said you were bitter towards him. That you would say cruel things to turn me against him.'

I gently touched my son's chin, drawing it up so that his eyes were level with mine. 'John, I've told you nothing but the truth.'

'He is a good man. But for him, I would be stuck with the Bishop of Exeter.'

'Oh, John, that is not true. The Duke is your half-brother. You'd but to ask him yourself for anything you wished.'

I saw a flicker of doubt in my son's eyes, but he was young and confused, and doubted himself most of all. He simply shrugged.

'How do you know about Robert? We tried to be so careful.'

John grunted. 'How could you hope to hide anything with Mary Percy living under your roof?'

That night in bed Robert held me until I fell asleep. He was a blessing to me, a loving and supportive partner, in all the most important ways my husband. My family and all the household loved him. I felt as much passion for him as I had for Janyn, but it was not as sharp or as desperate a love as that had been. I did not adore Robert, for ours was a love between equals. I loved him deeply, trusted him implicitly, and sought his opinion often to assist me in making my own decisions.

Without Robert's solid and loving presence, what I had learned from John might have inspired reckless behaviour – an attempt to annul my marriage to William on the grounds of my prior betrothal to Robert, or something equally risky to my family. But he steadied me. I would do nothing to provoke exile – though I held my breath when I considered what William was waiting for. If he truly believed Joan and Jane were Robert's daughters, why then had he not exposed us? I wished I might safely ask John how much he knew, but could not risk his reporting to William that I was anxious.

My longed for peace was shattered.

In late-winter of the following year John announced that he was to take up arms under the command of Edmund of Langley, my Edward's second youngest son, on a mission to Portugal. Lancaster still sought to recover the Castilian throne. The Portuguese were his greatest supporters in the region, but were now beset by the forces of the usurper, Henry of Trastamara. Remembering the catastrophic consequences of the late Prince Edward's campaign in the region, I feared for my son. But I knew his father would have been proud of him.

In the weeks before joining Langley, John begged me for tales of his father. Joan and Jane also loved it when I described my life with Edward, especially while we hawked or rode through the countryside, knowing these were some of the King's favourite activities. On those winter evenings we sat by the fire and I regaled them with descriptions of the glories of Edward's court, his prowess in arms and the hunt, his way with the falcons, the heady joy of dancing with him, his magnificent singing voice.

One evening, after the girls had gone to bed, I gave John his father's signet ring.

'It is time you had this, my son.'

He slipped it on his finger, wondered at how well it fitted him.

'A little wax will keep it secure,' I said.

His eyes shone with pride. 'I shall wear it with honour, Mother.'

'I know that you will.'

John's properties provided sufficient income for him to be smartly fitted for the expedition, and I was grateful that he welcomed and appreciated my advice and assistance in planning. We had become close again, though neither of us mentioned William.

But my husband would soon return, and he would be in an even fouler temper than usual for the Brittany expedition had proved an embarrassing failure. He erupted into our sweet household like a sudden squall on a quiet day. Robert departed, and Gwen gave instructions to Betys to keep Joan and Jane away from William as much as possible. He was furious to have thrown good money – albeit not his but mine and my friends' – after the incompetent Buckingham. This unfortunately rendered him ripe for a temper tantrum. When he discovered Mary Percy gone and learned that the marriage would very likely be annulled, he flew into a fury and swore that he would make it right. He would petition King Richard for his support.

Now quite happy at the prospect of finding a more suitable mate, John assured William he was content. I watched my son's puzzlement as his step-father ignored him and ranted and raved until drink silenced him.

When he returned from carrying William to his bedchamber, John asked me how to prevent such interference.

'The King has far too much on his mind to become involved in this case, John. William will find no remedy. Be at peace. Your father would have left such a petition to his trusted clerics. So will King Richard.' I had found that advice couched thus, in terms of how his father might have acted, carried much authority and usually reassured John.

Joan and Jane were fascinated by his accumulated gear: the armour, the horses, the weapons. But when the day came for his departure, they were dismayed to overhear a servant wishing him God's protection in battle.

'Battle?' Jane asked, her little hands fluttering as if she might fend off the possibility. 'No, John, you must not fight!'

Her elder sister took her aside, quietly explaining what it meant to be a knight. Jane was inconsolable for days afterwards. So was I.

My only comfort was that the day after John rode from the yard, William departed for his own home in London.

In spring all the countryside was alive with rumours of an uprising gathering in Essex. King Richard and the Parliament had so overwhelmed the people with the poll tax of the previous year, following close on one a year earlier, that the money had proved exceedingly difficult to collect. Thousands of taxpayers had evaded the collectors. Now, a year later, new commissioners were sent out into the shires, intent on finding the tax evaders and collecting from them by whatever means they saw fit. My old friend William Wykeham, Bishop of Winchester, sent a message advising me to move the household to a manor near Winchester.

I invited Mary's and John's families, but they chose to stay and protect their homes and businesses. Richard Lyons refused to be intimidated also. Geoffrey's family had already departed for Lincolnshire, leaving him, apparently happily, in the city, where he intended to stay. All of them relayed tales of William's drunkenness and whoring there, and assured me he showed no sign of wishing to flee the city.

The violence quickly spread from Essex through the southeast, moving towards London. As the number of rebels swelled, so did their anger. They blamed not only the commissioners but the Lord Chancellor and others on the King's council, particularly clerics, who to them represented the greed of the Church; but it seemed they blamed Lancaster most of all. The Duke was held responsible for all that had gone wrong with the French wars as well. Knowing from experience the danger he faced, having seen the damage the rabble had inflicted on his Palace of the Savoy a little over five years earlier, Lancaster fled to Scotland.

Had it not been for my fear for my friends and family in London, I might have felt relieved – Lancaster would hardly come after me now.

As the uprising spread through Kent, closer and closer to London, King Richard and his mother Joan, as well as many barons, withdrew into the Tower of London. The mob were committing vicious acts: beheadings, hangings, the desecration of churches and abbeys.

All my household listened in awe to a report of young King Richard's courage. He rode out to meet the rebels and calmly enquired what they sought. They demanded the heads of Lancaster and an assortment of others they had decided were to blame. He did not capitulate, and the rebels swarmed into London, freeing the inmates of the Marshalsea prison and this time not stopping at damaging Lancaster's Palace of the Savoy but razing it, and destroying much else in their path. Eventually they reached the Tower and accosted those within. When it was over, the Chancellor and one of the council had been dragged out and beheaded. Nothing like this had happened in Edward's time. But I remembered the hatred on the faces of the Londoners who had beheld me as the Lady of the Sun. I did not doubt that a crowd moved by such festering hatred might erupt into madness.

One morning Wykeham rode into the yard, and joined Robert and me as we walked towards the stables. He looked haggard and unshaven, his colour so chalky beneath the flush from his exertions that I feared he might be ill.

'My lady, I bring terrible tidings. Our friend Richard Lyons . . .' His voice broke.

Robert put his arm around me as I took the Bishop's hand. 'Dead?' I whispered.

'Executed. Three dozen Flemings have been brutally murdered. Richard – he was dragged from his home, beaten and beheaded.'

'May God grant him rest.' Robert bowed his head and crossed himself.

I pressed my head to Wykeham's ring, praying for Richard's soul. My good and loyal friend . . . I could not believe it.

'Why Richard?' I asked of no one in particular as we sat later over a flagon of brandywine. 'His fellow Flemings in the city looked to him for leadership. Why had he not fled?'

Wykeham did not answer at once, but stared long into his mazer. 'We all live with our own guilt, Dame Alice. We played a game of chance, profiting from the war in France. It does not matter that it has always been so, we knew we were taking a risk.'

'I cannot accept this was in any way just.'

'Pray God we learn from it,' Wykeham said. 'We have a choice how we live.'

Then he departed, slumped in the saddle, his spirit depleted, as was mine, Robert led me to my bedchamber and sat with me as I wept for my loyal and loving friend. He assured me that Geoffrey and my family would be safe.

'They have nothing to single them out to the crowd. But I will go to London to seek news.'

I clung to him, forbidding him to leave me and ride into danger. I could not bear it if I lost Robert.

When the King's troops had put down the rebellion and London was quiet, Robert and I left the children in Winchester and rode to the city to see to our families and friends. My siblings and their families were blessedly unscathed, although Mary's in-laws' home had been damaged. Geoffrey was subdued, leading us round the city to view the destruction. It was as if a mighty fist had come down on the Savoy and then swept its rubble into the Thames. Even a week later, debris floated in the water. Blood-stained pillars and posts were visible in the streets where Flemings and other foreigners, including Lombards, had lived.

Geoffrey joined Robert and me at the Requiem Mass for Richard Lyons.

The morning after the service, as I woke from a troubled sleep, Gwen greeted me with the unpleasant news that my husband William was in the hall. I had heard no news of him since returning to the city.

He was dressed more elegantly than he had been of late and wore a badge indicating he was in the King's household.

'What is this, William?'

'I wished to show you that I am still appreciated. That I have not come to ruin over our failed marriage.'

'I am glad, though I never thought you would come to ruin on my account. You have lived apart from me most of your life, with every appearance of success.' I hated the coldness of my own voice and words, but I felt nothing for William and would not pretend otherwise. I did invite him to share some wine and tell me his news.

He continued to find favour with King Richard, apparently, receiving modest gifts from the King, much as I had when first in Queen Philippa's household – some property, rents, a few wardships.

I thought perhaps he might now consider revising the provision of a trust for his nephew in his will, so that my former properties might go to my children, particularly my daughters.

'I do not ask this for me, but for them. You have a sufficient estate of your own to leave your nephew.'

He laughed. 'Always scheming! You get a pinched look when you scheme, Alice. It does not become you. Had you given me a son and heir, John Wyndsor would have been forgotten.'

'You should have told Lancaster to command me to conceive a son, William. But I do not recall that being a part of the arrangement explained to me at Westminster.'

He was still laughing as he departed. I did not see him again for more than a year.

Life had settled into a comfortable pattern. Joan and Jane attended school in the city in autumn and winter, making friends with the children of my childhood friends and many others. My daughters had a way about them that endeared them to their peers. Bella did as well, having recently been encouraged to assist the infirmarian because of her ability to calm those in distress. I felt my old guilt about leaving my children so often in the care of others begin to melt away. Except for John. Except for my son.

Memories of my notoriety seemed to fade from the London community. Any cross words spoken now concerned my absent husband's bad behaviour. For this I was grateful. Gwen and I enjoyed strolling through the markets, taking up the life we had lived before our days at court.

During the long winter nights Robert and I made most delicious, affectionate, passionate love, and in between bared our souls to one another. We grew to know each other as no one else ever had, perhaps even ourselves. We disproved my old belief that no person ever shared their entire being with another – though I understood that it was only through experience and pain that we had arrived at such a miracle.

In spring we retired to Fair Meadow and Gaynes. It was bliss to have Robert by my side. But ever I worried about John. I heard vague rumours that the expedition in Portugal was disappointing.

When he returned the following summer, John was quiet and withdrawn. Though delighted to have their big brother home, Joan and Jane tiptoed in his presence. At thirteen and eleven they were mature enough to discern his need for privacy and reflection.

Unfortunately, before John had recovered sufficiently to confide in me, William appeared. I silently cursed him for returning after over a year to ruin this time with my son, but I could not turn him away. He was legally my husband, and it was his right to bide in the house. His presence sent my mind and heart into shadowy places filled with hateful imaginings and robbed me of my anchor in Robert. Worst of all, I feared his influence on John.

On William's first morning in my home I was awakened by his shouts down in the hall. I hurriedly dressed and went to the top of the steps to listen and assess what to do. I was accustomed to mitigating the effects of his ill temper on the household.

'You ungrateful wretch!' William was shouting. 'I arranged your post and you disgrace me like this? I placed you in the service of the Duke of Lancaster and you rebel against his brother? You have ruined me, you graceless, arrogant bastard!'

I hurried down to them. Considering the hour, I felt anxious to discover my son sharing a tankard of ale with William, both looking as if they had been drinking through the night.

I pounded my fist on the table to prevent another round of cursing.

'I remind you, William, that you are speaking to the son of the former King, Lancaster's half-brother. You might have fooled him at fifteen into thinking he needed you to approach the Duke, but he knows better now. In his veins flows royal blood.'

John reached out to grab the tankard from William, but I intercepted, removing the temptation.

'What a sorry sight you both are, and so early in the morning. Get back to your rooms before Joan and Jane see you so.'

For a week John retreated into silence, taking long walks or lying on his bed staring up at the ceiling. William disappeared. I sought out Geoffrey to learn the truth of the matter.

'It seems John is in disfavour with Lancaster. A year ago he led a near mutiny in Portugal, against Edmund of Langley, his commander,' said Geoffrey. 'Word is just beginning to circulate on the streets now that the men have come home.'

'A mutiny? How did I not hear of this? Surely at court—'

'There you are seen as the mother of the mutineer – not a person in whom to confide.'

'I might have interceded.' I was frightened for John. Lancaster was a formidable enemy, as I knew to my cost.

Geoffrey put his hands on my shoulders and looked me in the eyes. 'I shall investigate the matter fully and come to you.'

On the day that my friend sent me word he now had the information, I requested that John be present for the report.

'You have made it plain since your return that you do not wish to explain your situation to me, and so I shall hear it from Geoffrey. But you must hear it also, learn what people are saying of you. You must know where you stand, John. The longer you hide, the harder everything will be.'

By some alchemy William appeared at the door at almost the same moment as Geoffrey.

We sat, an unhappy foursome, in my parlour, away from the servants' ears and the curiosity of John's young sisters.

Dressed in dark, quietly elegant clothing, his hair and beard freshly trimmed, Geoffrey served as stark contrast to William's fiercely bright garb but dishevelled self, and John's diminished flesh, huddled in clothes now too large for him.

Geoffrey began addressing me, describing the situation about which I had heard so little. How Edmund of Langley's troops had grown restive over his indifferent leadership and their lack of pay for almost a year. His knights accused him of keeping the money for himself and the King of Portugal of betraying them. Among themselves, they proposed bonding together into a brotherhood under the flag of St George, and becoming such nuisances that Langley would have to heed their grievances.

'John was chosen to be their leader, no doubt because he was half-brother to Langley.' Geoffrey nodded at my son.

John sighed, never lifting his gaze from the floor. And how could he resist such an 'honour', I thought, when his stated goal had been to win back the honour of which Mary Percy's insulting petition had robbed him.

The knights had set off under their flag, with the battle cry 'For Southery, the valiant bastard!', to make war on the King of Portugal. Oh, my son. I could not look at him while Geoffrey spoke of this. They were saved by the intervention of more experienced English knights who convinced them of the folly of battling the King thus. Instead, they urged John to present their grievances to his half-brother.

'John countered Langley's claim that the war was not his but the King of Portugal's with the proposal that, if it were so, the knights would simply take their wages by overrunning the country, each man taking what he might. Langley reminded John of the consequences of mutiny, and the dishonour he would thus bring on his cousin the King of England.'

I turned to John. 'I can imagine how proud you must have felt to be so trusted by your fellows, my son. I am not condemning you. I wish to know only what was in your mind. Hear your account of this.'

At last he looked me in the eye. 'I had come to my senses even before Langley reminded me of my duty . . . of the honour I owed you and the King. It was the heat, the thirst, the tedium, that had robbed me of my good sense. I made a fool of myself.'

'No, not a fool. You are but seventeen,' I said.

'The King is three years my junior and would never behave so.'

'John is courageous!' William cried, applauding him. 'Langley then sent knights to treat with King Ferdinand, and the men received their wages.'

'And Ferdinand then made a treaty with Castile, rendering the entire expedition pointless,' Geoffrey said. 'And now the King has assigned a commission to arrest the mutineers. Nineteen have been named.'

My heart ached at the pain in my son's expression. He bowed his head.

'I know,' he said. 'His Grace addressed me with much anger, but as I am family chose to believe that the others had put me forward to treat with my half-brother against my will. King Richard made me out to be but a child, easily led.'

'I hardly believe he could think that,' said Geoffrey. 'Froissart says that when Langley gathered the men together to pay them, you said, "Now see if this mutiny has not served its purpose! He who is feared fares well." '

I was dismayed to hear that the Fleming had included this incident in his chronicle. It would haunt John for life now.

'And still I am pardoned while my brothers-in-arms are punished,' he said.

Geoffrey met my gaze and shrugged.

'He proved himself a bit of his mother, a bit of his father, eh?' said William. 'Greedy for his money, brave as a fighting cock.'

'Be still, William, you embarrass yourself,' I said, rising. 'John, we shall discuss this more anon. Come out to see the tenements and shops I have built, Geoffrey.'

Better to leave William alone to drink himself into a stupor or disappear to a tavern where the women were more pleasing to him. I prayed he would soon depart. I yearned to have Robert beside me again.

But John did not recover from his shame. How I wished his father were still alive. Edward would have known how to turn this around, would have known how to save his son, and John would have listened. He needed his father. He had been deprived of him too young. Now I could find no way to reach him. Nor could his sisters, nor Robert, nor Geoffrey. He eventually took up drinking and I shuddered to think what else with William.

I tried to focus on Joan and Jane, on Robert, but a sense of dread that I had failed Edward's and my beloved son so weakened me that I fell sick with fever. I was so afraid for John. Bella came and cared for me for half the autumn. And in that time my son used the excuse of my illness to take up residence with William.

He returned at Christmas, William in tow.

'We are a family, Mother.'

John looked older than his seventeen years, his complexion poor, his eyes glassy, as if feverish. I went from being nursed to nursing, coaxing him to eat, to ride out into the fresh air.

That winter William obtained the keeping of the castle and town of Cherbourg in Normandy. He was to have all ransoms and gains of war by land and sea, and the King would provide his shipping, food, weapons, and an annual fee of £4,000. It was a more lucrative honour than William had expected.

'Will you go to Cherbourg?' I asked when he announced his boon at the dinner table.

'In time. But to begin I shall send a deputy.' He turned to smile at my son.

The expression on John's face, of delight and pride tempered with a hint of guilt, bespoke an agreement long kept secret from me.

My heart stopped. 'Why John?'

'It will be a fine opportunity for him.'

'If it is such a fine opportunity, why send a deputy? Are you not man enough to go yourself?'

'I want to go, Mother,' said John. 'I am grateful for the chance to prove myself to King Richard.'

'Why not send your beloved nephew and heir, William?' I asked. 'Why waste your benefices on my son?'

William smirked.

'Why do you risk my only son?' I demanded.

John came to sit beside me. Putting an arm round me, he said, 'You will see, Mother. You will be proud of me.'

'I *am* proud of you, John.'

On my knees before bed I prayed God's forgiveness for allowing my son to become a battlefield between William and me. I tried to accept that John was doing what he truly wanted. 'Grant him peace and joy,' I prayed. 'Even if it means he is far from me.'

In late-winter he departed for Cherbourg.

On his last evening at home he had talked of making a name for himself so that he might find a wife who respected him for his accomplishments and not for being the late King's bastard. As I had feared, it had been gnawing at his heart all this time.

'Your father was proud of you, John, so very proud of you. That you were a bastard diminished you in no way in his eyes. He insisted that you be knighted.' I did not mention his insistence also on the betrothal to Mary Percy, the seed of all this anguish.

John gave me back Edward's signet. 'Keep this for me until I have earned it.'

My heart bled for him. I had not fully appreciated until now that being Edward's son was both a gift and a curse.

And in my mind I raged at William.

'If he makes me proud, I shall change my will in his favour,' he had said during one of our more amicable meals together.

Damn William Wyndsor, the bane of my fine, noble son!

All through that spring and summer I felt as if I were treading on unsteady ground that might open up and swallow me at any moment. My sister thought perhaps I was praying too much and not spending enough time out in the sun and air. Bella understood that I was doing penance for my own part in John's unhappiness, and urged me to remember that all God's children were blessed, no matter what their parentage, and that my son's despair or imagined shame was his burden to bear or to shed.

'That is his path, Mother, his cross. You cannot take this burden from him.'

Nor could any of my loved ones lift my burden from me. And it only grew heavier. For in late-summer, the ship on which John was sailing home to meet William and the King in order to discuss the problems at Cherbourg vanished in a sudden storm. I waited and waited, praying for word that it had safely berthed elsewhere.

I thought I might go mad. Lost at sea . . . John might yet live. A boat might have plucked him from the waves. He might lie ill and bereft of memory somewhere. I had nightmares linking his disappearance to Janyn's. I shunned sleep. Robert held me through the night, praying, singing, talking of my other children, anything to pull me from my darkness.

William, pale and hollow-eyed, came to beg my forgiveness. 'It should have been me.'

'Would that it had been! Or your hateful nephew. Not one of

my precious children.' I could not be troubled to comfort him. 'Are you happy now? You have done your worst. You have torn out my heart.'

He replied that he had loved John as well, but I could not bear his presence.

'My son had such a good heart, but you poisoned him with your bitterness.'

'You *made* me bitter.'

'I take no responsibility for your crabbed heart, William. Go. Get out of my house!'

But I did blame myself for not better shielding John from him. I agonised over what else I might have done – whether I should have told him all the truth about my marriage to William from the beginning, not waiting until the damage had been done, or risked Edward's ire in refusing to betroth John to such a changeling as Mary Percy. There must have been something I could have done to save my son.

It was Gwen who tried to wake me up to the fact that I was neglecting Joan and Jane in my grief. 'You must accept that John is gone and see to your daughters, Mistress. They are inconsolable. John was their beloved brother, a handsome, gallant knight, a last reminder of their glorious father. They have lost him as well. They need you to hold them, to show them how they must accept their loss, pray for their brother's soul, and find peace.'

I saw the wisdom in her words. That very night I invited them into my bed, and the three of us wept until we had no more tears to shed.

Henry Percy came to the Requiem Mass that King Richard arranged at Westminster Abbey. He spoke of what an admirable young man John had been, and expressed his regret that Mary had annulled the marriage. He might easily say all that now he need no longer fear my son's contamination. Lancaster also attended, as my son's godfather, half-brother and lord, speaking of his martial skill, his honour. Princess Joan embraced me and wept with me for my beautiful son.

William swore that he would change his will, that John's death had shaken him to the core. 'I have been cruel and do repent,

Alice. All I ever wanted was to live with you as your husband, and I have poisoned my chances.'

I wanted nothing to do with him. He showed me a new will he had signed, leaving my properties to Joan and Jane. I thanked him for that but could not bring myself to forgive him. Though my son had been free to refuse William's suggestion that he be his deputy at Cherbourg, I blamed him for making the offer, and he knew it. We could not find a way to cross the chasm that divided us.

He stayed away for a long while. Robert helped me heal, pick up the pieces of my life and move on. Joan, Jane and I planted oaks at each of our homes to remind us of John, how tall and strong he had been. How he had blessed our lives.

In late-summer, almost a year to the day after John's disappearance, William came to me in London, deathly ill of a fever. All through the autumn Gwen and I nursed him; Robert saw to everything else. This time he did not need to leave. With illness in the house, I arranged for Joan and Jane to board at their school. William rarely spoke, never looked me in the eyes, ate and drank as little as possible. It was clear from the first that he did not intend to recover. He had come home to die.

At Gaynes I had begun to recreate Dame Tommasa's garden. I had commissioned a mason to build high walls around freshly dug ground, and it was my escape from the house of death to leave early in the morning for Gaynes to see how work progressed, then return the following day. I often took the girls from school to go with me, and coaxed Gwen into entrusting William to a servant so that she was free to accompany us. I felt she bore too much of the burden already. We would breathe more easily as the barge moved out of London waters, and at Gaynes we would walk in the fog-shrouded woods, talking of the future.

'This fever should not cling as it does,' said Gwen one morning.

'No. Perhaps he sincerely mourns John. What is clear is that William has lost his will to live. When chance brought on an illness, he surrendered.'

He died shortly after Michaelmas. We mourned the passing of a life, but all the household seemed to breathe a concerted sigh of relief at the possibility of moving forward. I prayed for the grace to forgive William, and allow him to rest in peace.

But I could never forgive his nephew John. Upon William's death, John Wyndsor produced a copy of the old will, favouring himself. I searched everywhere for the one William had shown me, but never found it. I swore I would fight John Wyndsor in the courts until I won back all that was rightfully mine. This was my poison, my purgatory, my inheritance from William, the last lingering resentment. It was the only thing that ever came between Robert and me. He could not understand why I allowed that one thorn to continue to infect my soul.

In the same month in which William died, I petitioned Parliament to withdraw the judgements against me. William had been clever, focusing his petitions on the reclamation of my properties in his name, refraining from any attempt to clear my name.

Eventually I did forgive him, and even mourned him. How strange that in his death, without the noise of our arguments, I remembered how he had initially charmed me. I mourned my brief dream of the handsome, exciting knight I thought had loved me. I mourned my dreams for my son John. I mourned all the dreams that had been destroyed by my tie to the House of Plantagenet. I had reaped little lasting reward for my loyalty to the Crown.

Now I abandoned the old dreams and reached for peace.

After William's death, Princess Joan invited me and my daughters to Kennington for a fortnight. Though my sentence of exile had been withdrawn, I had not been in a royal palace since my marriage in Westminster. At John's funeral I had kept to the abbey grounds, avoiding the palace. It was strange to be back in a royal household, strange to have occasion to wear my jewels and grandest gowns.

Until John's Requiem Mass at Windsor I had not seen Joan in several years, and had been dismayed by the change in her then. She had grown fat and walked with a cane – an exquisitely wrought cane with silver chasing and a mother-of-pearl handle. Her gown was resplendent with jewels, her hair still pale gold, though years of ensuring that had left it looking brittle. Her eyes were red-rimmed, which suited the occasion, but she had not looked so at other memorials at which I had seen her. Now I learned that she suffered from gout and seldom rode, never hawked.

'Let me inspire you to move about. You know that is the cure for what is ailing you,' I offered. There was a time when we had talked so, encouraging one another.

She declined. 'If gout were the sole cause of my decline, I would have fought it with all my will, Alice.'

One afternoon when we were alone, the children on an expedition with some of Joan's wards, she looked me in the eyes.

'You have been so good, listening to my woes. Now I must ask yet another favour. I must beg your forgiveness, my friend. It is time I confessed to you that it was I who betrayed you regarding William Wyndsor. I mentioned his passion for you to my husband Edward, never dreaming he would use the information. I am certain he told his brother John.'

I had blamed Henry Percy. Or sometimes Geoffrey – he did so love to gossip. Never Joan, though I had suspected she long knew of the agreement that I would wed William.

'You might have saved me a great deal of pain had you kept your counsel,' I said. Yet I saw how easily it might have happened.

'They used you, Alice. Edward and John protected you as long as they needed you as their father's caretaker, and then they sold you to William. I am sorry. I wish that there were something I might do. If you have need of me . . .'

I excused myself and went out to walk off my anger. She was aged, she was weak, and in her proud way she was apologetic. *I am sorry.* How easily that was said, how little it did to comfort me. *I will walk on burning coals in penance. I will tear out my hair.* Those words might begin to express how she should suffer for what she had done to me. But she had not intended me harm. As I tired, I abandoned my wish that she might suffer. She had not foreseen such use of her gossip. How could she? But I would use her in her turn.

I told her of my petition to Parliament, of the contested will.

'I shall speak to Richard,' she said. 'But do not expect too much. He does not hold the hearts of the barons as his grandfather did. Or Parliament.'

'When you speak to him, remember that I might yet have had

my son to hold to my heart, Edward's glorious son, had William and I not been forced together in unholy matrimony.'

'I did not know until the King's death what they planned,' Joan whispered, her eyes haunted.

As I departed from Kennington I sensed that I would not come that way again, that Joan, like William, would surrender soon to eternal rest. Sad, aching, disappointed.

Yet I felt a lifting of a curse from my shoulders, the curse of Isabella of France and her love child. At last I was free. I felt I owed Edward's family nothing, and they could do no more for me – or to me.

IV-4

1384

Widowed a third time – for in my heart I was Edward's widow – at forty-two years of age I prayed that I might at last order my own life. I had been with Janyn for almost four years, two of them happy; with Edward for roughly fifteen years, many of them happy, many unhappy; I had endured seven years of William, my time with him unrelievedly painful, but with Robert's love supporting me.

Not all of my unhappiness had been caused by others – I was only too aware of my own sins, of my passions, my weaknesses. I had misjudged the value of my security in worldly goods and neglected the importance of strong alliances. I had not stood up against my son's betrothal to a young woman I knew to be devoid of compassion and honour.

At last, however, I was free to choose how to conduct the rest of my life.

My first choice was to give my daughters a long winter of my undivided attention. Joan was now fifteen, Jane thirteen, and I wished to enjoy them, for in a little while they would be wanting husbands, and we would be caught up in the excitement of courtships and celebrations. Bella visited often. Her abbess was a woman with a kind heart. My daughters were my salvation, lifting me from my sorrow, my regrets. How could I regret having birthed these magnificent creatures? One of my favourite pastimes was turning the gorgeous fabrics of gowns I no longer wore into pretty clothes for Joan and Jane. To watch their delight rekindled in me an appreciation for the beauty all around me. Though I wore dark colours in memory of Janyn, Edward and William, my headdresses were of silk and my gowns fashionably cut and studded with pearls and gems. I played my part of grand lady of the manor and benefactress of the parish. My daughters loved to see me so, as did the friends who visited often. Robert and I remained discreet in our arrangement for a while.

I think we both most enjoyed one surprisingly regular house guest: Geoffrey. He came and stayed without Pippa – indeed, they were now seldom seen together. 'We are not so fond,' he said in response to my concern. 'It is as it is.'

I must have winced when he said that.

'Is it not the truth, Alice?'

'"It is as it is" was one of Edward's mottos.'

Geoffrey pressed hands to heart and made a little bow. 'Forgive me. I'd forgotten.'

'There is nothing to forgive. Your gift to me is your willingness to listen to me. I am grateful to have a friend in whom I can confide without fear of lectures or censure.' Each night after my daughters went to bed we would sit and talk – or rather I would talk. I revealed my heart to my old friend, my loves and hates, my dreams for my marriages and my children, my regrets.

Geoffrey claimed that being in my home inspired his poetic endeavours.

'And I am much admired by His Grace and the Queen, so I must provide them with fresh verse.'

He was often invited to read at court, a great compliment.

One afternoon as he made notes to himself on his ubiquitous wax tablets and bits of parchment, in between staring out of the open door to the courtyard garden, he suddenly paused and asked, 'Do you remember the story of Criseyde that so troubled you?'

'I have never forgotten,' I said.

'Your arguments have been much on my mind.'

'Are you writing of her?'

By the inward expression on his face I guessed that he was.

But he said only, 'Would it trouble you to know that your story inspired me to wonder how it might have been for Criseyde?'

'I am honoured, my good friend.'

'I understand now – they hated you for showing them that their King, he with the power to heal with his hands, he with the well-being of the realm in his care – was yet human.'

'More so at the end than they were ever permitted to see.'

'I would show how alone Criseyde was upon her father's defection, how vulnerable and without guidance. How her uncle used that to his own end. But I cannot make her so worthy of love and admiration as you, my friend. Nor so tragic. In that story, Troilus is the tragic player.'

Worthy of love and admiration? 'You do me great compliment, Geoffrey. But as for the tragic, not all has been tragedy for me. I have experienced much joy, and have much yet to live for.'

While in London I often spent the morning at St Antonin's, the beloved parish church of my youth and innocence, and I often paused without the house in which Dame Tommasa and Master John had lived, remembering all the joy I had known there.

When at last my little family returned to Gaynes in spring, Robert invited me to ride out with him. The freshly ploughed fields smelled rich and loamy. New leaves softened the hedgerows and the trees that followed the line of the river. We paused in a meadow where a fallen tree provided seating for two.

Robert took my hands in his and looked me in the eyes with such determination that I feared bad news.

'My love, I believe that at last it is our time. Would you be content to bide with me as my wife? Would you take me as your husband? For I would have you as my wife, if you will, to cherish and to love through the rest of my days, as long as God grants me.'

Relief flooded me with warmth. I looked into Robert's steady grey-blue eyes and saw love, comfort, laughter and companionship. Everything about him was dear to me: his crinkly smile, his broad shoulders that had supported me through so much sorrow, his scent, his deep voice and quiet laugh that was more movement than sound. I loved him for never forsaking me, never failing me. I loved who I was when I was with him.

'I take you as my husband, Robert, willingly, with all my heart and soul.'

His kiss warmed me to my core and set my heart strumming. When we paused for breath, I glanced round. Seeing that we were quite alone, I rose, taking his hand.

'Shall we seal the pact, my love?'

On the horse blankets we lay, our coupling slow and yet passionate as we made use of all we knew would give pleasure to the other. There was no need to hurry, no one who would have any cause to creep up on us. Afterwards we lay in each other's arms, drowsing, until the afternoon chill prompted us to continue our ride.

Joan and Jane observed us closely during the evening meal. Robert had a different air about him, comfortable, already settled. As if he had practised this in his imagination for a long while.

As the table was cleared, he leaned towards my daughters and asked, 'Would you permit me to wed your mother?'

Jane frowned a little, tilting her head to one side as if considering. Joan poked her in the ribs and with a dazzling smile asked, 'Could we call you Father?'

'I would be honoured.'

'I shall call you Robert,' said Jane, 'but I do give you my blessing.'

He reached for my hand beneath the table. 'And you, Joan?'

'I would rather you wed *me*. But if you have already lost your heart to Mother, you have my blessing.'

That evening, as Gwen brushed my hair, we spoke of our first weeks together at Dame Agnes's, preparing for my marriage to Janyn, the beginning of my liaison with Edward, how frightened we had been, and the frustration of my marriage to William.

'You deserve happiness, Mistress. I pray that God blesses you both. I am so happy for you. You have loved one another for so long. At last your hearts are one.'

Our old friend Dom Hanneye witnessed our vows in the church at Upminster. We invited only family to the wedding, and Geoffrey. I wore a patterned silk gown in deep, rich hues of blue and green, the feather pattern picked out in seed pearls on the bodice and sleeves. Robert wore a red velvet jacket that I had lovingly made him, with matching hat ablaze on his fair hair, and leggings of indigo. I so enjoyed dressing him, for he had never given much thought to his appearance and was startled to see himself in his new clothes. I imagine we were the most elegant couple ever to take their vows in the small church. But what I loved most was that it had not mattered whether or not we fussed with our clothing, we had no one to impress but one another, and our love transcended all that. Life away from court – I embraced it with all my heart.

Through the spring and summer Joan, Jane, Gwen and I continued our work at Gaynes, recreating what I could remember of Dame Tommasa's garden in London and the one that she had helped me plant at Janyn's and my London home when I carried Bella. Robert brought clippings of the most unusual plants from our other manors, and I brought clippings from the garden in London. By late summer, when I discovered that I was with child, the garden was truly taking shape. I had worried that I might not conceive after seven years of potions to prevent it, and considering my age, but Robert and I were blessed.

'I am the most fortunate man under heaven,' he whispered, one ear to my swelling stomach.

Joan, Jane and I all blossomed that summer. Joan met another Robert much to her liking, a young lawyer from Kingston-upon-Thames, Robert Skerne, whom we had retained for some property transactions. They were a handsome couple, and I found myself praying that he would return for her when he considered himself capable of supporting a household. Jane proved a passionate and creative gardener, and I left much of the planning of Tommasa's garden to her. I had never been happier. Walking, hawking, plunging my hands in the earth and creating a garden I expected to enjoy for years to come, strolling across the fields or along the streets of London on Robert's arm, spending an afternoon sewing with my daughters and Gwen . . . all these simple pleasures were a constant delight to me.

I wished I might forgo William's first year obit at Windsor, for though I was not very great with child yet I no longer enjoyed riding. Nor did I wish to be reminded of my unhappy marriage. But I could not forget William as he was at the end, so lost, so disappointed, and could not refuse to pay him that one last honour. Fortunately most of the journey would be by barge. My daughters and Gwen put much effort into designing a silk-velvet surcoat to hide my swelling stomach. Although Robert escorted me to Windsor, he did not attend the Mass. Geoffrey escorted me in his place.

Sir Robert Linton, the friend who had offered his home in Somerset as a haven for me and my children in my darkest hour, had come to pay his respects. He asked after me and the children.

'We are well. Thriving. I shall never forget your kindness in my time of need.'

I saw several old acquaintances from court – Richard Stury made a point of speaking to me. He was not so grim-visaged as in the past, his hair now snow-white and his smile more relaxed and sincere. He found he enjoyed retirement.

'Quietly stalking the wildfowl, deer and boar on my estates, becoming acquainted with my wife at last – I should think it about time I knew the woman who bore me five children!' He chuckled at his own words, something he had never done in my presence. 'And you, Dame Alice?'

'I feel blessed to be free at last to enjoy my daughters, my lands, and my memories, Sir Richard. God has been good to me.'

John Wyndsor I ignored, and he ignored me. We were locked in litigation, though it was no longer entirely by my choice – Joan and Jane wanted to see me vindicated in this.

This time I did enter the palace, with great trepidation, and walked about in the company of ghosts, my eyes finding it impossible to alight on anything in Windsor that did not conjure a memory, particularly of my dear Queen Philippa. I had not expected to feel my grief over her death still so poignant. For me she still ruled the castle. I could still hear her merry laughter and exclamations of delight; could smell her evening almond milk. And Edward – his striding steps sounded just ahead, his scent was in the air. Suddenly, as I was about to step into the pretty chamber to which I had been moved after the attack in Oxford all those years ago, I lost my courage. I rushed back to the hall and out into the yard, grateful to breathe air untainted by shades of the past. I prayed I need never return.

Nor did the gossip around us inspire regret in me that I was no longer at court. Indeed, as I listened I grew increasingly eager to withdraw again to my quiet life. Princess Joan was not in attendance, having retired to Kennington with a vague malady, some said a broken heart. Poor, beautiful Joan, who might have been Queen.

When Joan, Jane, Gwen and I stepped on to the river landing on our return to Gaynes, Robert, who had gone on ahead to alert the servants, awaited us with our horses. We rode home along lanes made colourful with falling leaves. We were all quiet from the solemnity of the occasion and travellers' weariness. As usual, within moments of arriving home Joan and Jane were off to the stables, the immediate lure the litters of puppies and kittens, anxious to see how much they had grown in a week.

'They will be out for a long while,' said Robert, taking my hand and leading me into the garden.

Now the flowers were mostly spent and going to seed, the saplings almost bare. But it held promise of more to come in another spring, and I found it beautiful.

We sat on a wooden bench, on a prettily embroidered cushion that Joan and Jane had presented me on my birthday. 'For your bench in the rose arbour,' Joan had said. 'Bella told us that Dame Tommasa always made cushions to fit the garden benches.'

'So she did.' The cushion they had given me was embroidered with the moon and stars, and reminded me of the surcoat I'd not thought my mother-in-law would dare to wear, silver and gold moons and stars on a dark background. 'Bless Bella. Bless you angels for this.'

In February I gave birth to a sweet, fair-haired daughter. Though her godmother was my brother John's wife Agnes, Robert and I chose to name her Agnes Joanna, and as she grew into a beauty like her namesake Princess Joan, we soon forgot her first given name. Joan had been as good a friend to me as she could, I had come to understand that.

A year later, her brother Geoffrey was born. My old friend Geoffrey Chaucer was of course his first godfather, and made much of the fair-haired boy.

After Geoffrey's birth I knew that I had passed my childbearing years and I did mourn for that. Though I loved my children above all else, even Robert, I had not forgotten how utterly my life had changed when I reached childbearing age. It was good to move beyond that. I had been most fortunate in my children. I had lost only two before birth, and only one who had lived and thrived. Four beautiful daughters and one adorable son survived.

It was then that I began to write this history of my life, or in truth dictate it to my dear Bella. I felt my years and worried that death might take me before Agnes Joanna and Geoffrey might have a chance to know me, to hear my story from my lips. I did not wish them to hear only the gossip about their mother, but to know all, and then be free to judge the truth of it.

Joan wed the lawyer Robert Skerne when she was seventeen. He *had* returned for her. Jane wed a wealthy merchant, Richard Northland, and made the journey to Italy with him that I had so yearned to make with Janyn. She saw Milan, and many Perrers, but learned nothing more of the fates of Janyn and Tommasa. She found the family unwilling to speak of that trouble.

Joanna was an imp of a girl, always courting laughter with her japes. She was a freer spirit than any of her sisters, always surrounded by family, especially her doting parents, and knew no fear. She adored her brother Geoffrey, who looked so like my long-dead brother Will that my sister Mary often forgot and called him that by mistake. He was a dreamer, a lover of animals like Jane, always nursing a wounded or sick wild creature. I worked to see him not as a replacement for my dear John but as his own wondrous person. Robert envisioned him as a conscientious landholder, reviving woodlands, enriching the fields. To our great sorrow, Geoffrey died of fever when he was but six years old.

On my last visit to Kennington, Princess Joan had said of the loss of my son John, 'Perhaps it is a blessing he did not live long enough to disappoint you as my sons have disappointed me.'

I would gladly have suffered any disappointment to watch my son Geoffrey grow to manhood. Though with a father like Robert guiding him, I do not believe he would ever have disappointed either of us.

My daughters and I continue to fight John Wyndsor in the courts. In my will I have stated that all my manors and advowsons other than Gaynes I leave to my daughters Joan and Jane, including all 'those which John Wyndsor, or others, have, by his consent, usurped, the which I desire my heirs and executors to recover and see them parted between my daughters, for that I say, on the pain of my soul, he hath no right there nor never had'. Sometimes I wish that William had never shown me the revised will. I pray that my daughters win. Gaynes I have bequeathed to Joanna. And I have no doubt that Robert shall be generous to all my daughters in his will.

We are all of us horrified by the overthrow of dear King Richard by Lancaster's son and heir, who calls himself Henry IV. Joan's fears for her son's reign have proved tragically prescient. Geoffrey does not care for Harry, as he calls him. Nor does Harry care for Geoffrey; censure is his favourite instrument of rule, and Geoffrey's poetry has been judged dangerous. It is Harry's loss, for Geoffrey's poem of Criseyde is a true rendering of a torn heart.

Sometimes I fall to brooding over the past. Should I have been more selfish, more stubborn, more rebellious? Have I been too compliant, too quick to give the men in my life what they thought they wanted? Am I a fallen woman or an obedient handmaiden? And ever I return to the puzzle: when had I a choice to be other than I was?

I count myself blessed, all in all. Loving Robert as I do, I no longer yearn for Janyn. But I have not forgotten the passion and the pain of our union, nor the heady honour and deep sorrow of my liaison with Edward.

In the early-morning, when Robert and I move out into the fields with our hawks, I often feel as if Edward is with us, as if I can hear his deep laughter just ahead. I always wear red when hawking. And pearls.

Author's Note

I wrote this book to satisfy my curiosity about Alice Perrers and to give her a voice, to allow her to speak through me, a feminine psyche. I have a dyspeptic monk to thank for my fascination with Alice. My first encounter with her was in Thomas Walsingham's *St Albans Chronicle*.*

> . . . there was a woman in England called Alice Perrers. She was a shameless, impudent harlot, and of low birth . . . She was not attractive or beautiful, but knew how to compensate for these defects by her seductive voice. Blind fortune elevated this woman to such heights and promoted her to a greater intimacy with the King than was proper, since she had been the maidservant and mistress of a man of Lombardy . . . Even while the queen was still alive, the King loved this woman more than he loved the queen. (p. 43)

Walsingham used his 'history' as a weapon for executing a vendetta primarily aimed at Alice Perrers and John of Gaunt, but in the process he grossly insulted the beloved King Edward III as well: 'O King, you deserve to be called not master, but a slave of the lowest order. For since slavery is the obedience of a broken and shameful spirit that lacks a will of its own, who will deny that all who are fickle-minded, all who are lustful, in short, all who are shameless are slaves?' (p. 59) This was rant, not reason.

And yet . . . Walsingham's description of Alice has long been considered only slightly exaggerated.

I never found plausible the underlying assumption that she had so grossly manipulated the King – that a commoner had been in any position to *choose* to be King Edward's mistress and that she had somehow bewitched him. Nor could I see the logic in condemning her for staying with him in his last illnesses – an opportunist would have taken the fabulous gifts and wealth she'd

*Taylor, John, Wendy R. Childs, and Leslie Watkiss, trans. and ed. *The St Albans Chronicle: The* Chronica maiora *of Thomas Walsingham, I, 1376–1394*. Oxford, Clarendon Press, 2003.

accrued and disappeared at the first signs of Edward's flagging power. Alice must have seen the handwriting on the wall, yet she stayed.

I am grateful to Walsingham for his outrageousness – it inspired me to delve further into the records.

I also owe him thanks for a small detail that began to work in my subconscious, his mention of a daughter named nowhere else: 'In the mean time the King grew weaker, and the doctors began to despair of him, though Alice and her daughter Isabella would spend the whole night with him.' (p. 63) It was this 'Isabella', a daughter unremarked in any of the histories I'd consulted, that inspired my connecting Janyn Perrers with Isabella, the Dowager Queen.

Regarding the tumultuous period following Isabella and Mortimer's rebellion the most famous rumour was that King Edward II had not actually been murdered as reported, but that the story had been concocted to allow the deposed King to withdraw into a continental monastery. But I was more intrigued by another rumour, that Isabella had been pregnant with Mortimer's child when her lover was accused of treason and taken into custody. She supposedly miscarried almost at once. I wanted to explore what might have happened had the child lived, had it been the child rather than the deposed King who was spirited away to a monastery. Janyn Perrers's death less than two years after Isabella's death, according to a claim against his estate naming Alice as his wife and executor, led me to wonder whether those who had protected all knowledge of the child would have lost their protection once Isabella was dead. And so the story began . . .

I've mentioned the source for Alice's daughter Isabella; most historians count her as having had two daughters, Joan and Jane. Whence came the fourth, Agnes Joanna? I thought it interesting that in her will Alice specifically left 'to Joane, my younger daughter', her manor of Gaynes, in Upminster, and then 'to Jane and Joane, my daughters', all other manors and advowsons. Of course this might have been simply an awkward repetition for legal purposes, but I like to think that Alice had at least another child by her third husband, a man I have a hunch existed – something about the picture of lady of the manor her will evinces suggested to me that she'd remarried after Wyndsor's death. Robert Broun is someone who appears in many of her land transactions, along with John Hanneye. His becoming Alice's third husband is my invention. Her will identified her as 'Alice, widow of William Wyndesor, Knight', and, of course, she *was*, whether or not she was also the wife of someone yet living. A woman did not always take her husband's surname.

Geoffrey Chaucer was Alice's contemporary, and of London merchant stock. Several disproved theories have attempted to connect them in various ways, but I've used none of them. I simply thought that as Londoners finding themselves in court circles they might very well have been friends. From my first reading of Chaucer's poem *Troilus and Criseyde* I have been moved by the psychological depth and emotional complexity he infused into the tale and have suspected he based his portrait of Criseyde on someone he knew well.

I shaped a life for Alice. I think she might be pleased with it.

For Further Reading

Bak, János M. 'Queens as Scapegoats in Medieval Hungary,' in *Queens and Queenship in Medieval Europe*, ed. Anne J. Duggan. Boydell Press, 1997, pp.223–233.

Beardwood, Alice. *Alien Merchants in England 1350 to 1377: Their Legal and Economic Position.* The Medieval Academy of America, 1931.

Bothwell, James. 'The Management of Position: Alice Perrers, Edward III, and the Creation of a Landed Estate, 1362–1377,' *Journal of Medieval History* 24 (1998), pp. 31–51.

Dodd, Gwilym. 'Crown, Magnates and Gentry: The English Parliament, 1369–1421', unpublished D.Phil. thesis, University of York, 1998.

Given-Wilson, Chris, and Alice Curteis. *The Royal Bastards of Medieval England.* Routledge and Kegan Paul, 1984, pp.136–142.

Given-Wilson, Chris. *The Royal Household and the King's Affinity: Service, Politics and Finance in England 1360–1413.* Yale University Press, 1986.

Harbison, S. 'William of Windsor, the Court Party and the Administration of Ireland,' in *England and Ireland in the Later Middle Ages*, ed. J Lydon. Dublin, 1981, pp.158–162.

Holmes, George. *The Good Parliament.* Oxford, Clarendon Press, 1975.

Lacey, Helen. 'The Politics of Mercy: The Use of the Royal Pardon in Fourteenth-Century England,' unpublished D. Phil. thesis, University of York, 2005.

Mieszkowski, Gretchen. 'The Reputation of Criseyde 1155–1500,' in *Transactions of the Connecticut Academy of Arts and Sciences* 43, Dec 71, pp.71–153.

Mortimer, Ian. *The Perfect King: The Life of Edward III, Father of the English Nation.* Jonathan Cape, 2006.

Myers, A. R. 'The Wealth of Richard Lyons,' in *Essays in Medieval History Presented to Bertie Wilkinson*, ed. T. A. Sandquist and M. R. Powicke. University of Toronto Press, 1969, pp. 301–329.

Ormrod, W. M. 'Alice Perrers and John Salisbury,' *English Historical Review* 123, 2008.

Ormrod, W. M. *Political Life in Medieval England, 1300–1450.* St Martin's Press, 1995.

Ormrod, W. M. *The Reign of Edward III.* Tempus, 2000.

Ormrod, W. M. 'The Trials of Alice Perrers,' *Speculum*, 83(2), 2008, pp. 366–396.

Ormrod, W. M. 'Who was Alice Perrers?', *Chaucer Review*, xl, 2006, pp.219–29.

Taylor, John. *English Historical Literature in the Fourteenth Century.* Oxford, Clarendon Press, 1987.

Taylor, John, Wendy R. Childs, and Leslie Watkiss, trans. and ed. *The St Albans Chronicle: The* Chronica maiora *of Thomas Walsingham, I, 1376–1394.* Oxford, Clarendon Press, 2003.

Vale, Juliet. *Edward III and Chivalry: Chivalric Society and Its Context 1270–1350.* Boydell Press, 1982.

Vale, Malcolm. *The Princely Court: Medieval Courts and Culture in North-West Europe 1270–1380.* Oxford University Press, 2001.

Innocent Traitor

Alison Weir

Lady Jane Grey was born into times of extreme danger. Child of a scheming father and a ruthless mother, for whom she was merely a pawn in a dynastic power game with the highest stakes, she lived a life in thrall to political machinations and lethal religious fervour.

Jane's astonishing and essentially tragic story was played out during one of the most momentous periods of English history. As a great-niece of Henry VIII, and the cousin of Edward VI, Mary I and Elizabeth I, she grew up to realise that she could never throw off the chains of her destiny. Her honesty, intelligence and strength of character carry the reader through all the vicious twists of Tudor power politics, to her nine-day reign and its unbearably poignant conclusion.

'Weir manages her heroine's voice brilliantly, respecting the past's distance while conjuring a dignified and fiercely modern spirit'
Daily Mail

'This is a novel that will grip readers and give great pleasure'
Scotsman

arrow books

THE POWER OF READING